AGATHA CHRIST

1920s

VOLUME THREE

BY THE SAME AUTHOR

The ABC Murders
The Adventure of the Christmas Pudding
After the Funeral
And Then There Were None
Appointment with Death
At Bertram's Hotel
The Big Four
The Body in the Library
By the Pricking of My Thumbs
Cards on the Table
A Caribbean Mystery
Cat Among the Pigeons
The Clocks
Crooked House
Curtain: Poirot's Last Case
Dead Man's Folly
Death Comes as the End
Death in the Clouds
Death on the Nile
Destination Unknown
Dumb Witness
Elephants Can Remember
Endless Night
Evil Under the Sun
Five Little Pigs
4.50 from Paddington
Hallowe'en Party
Hercule Poirot's Christmas
Hickory Dickory Dock
The Hollow
The Hound of Death
The Labours of Hercules
The Listerdale Mystery
Lord Edgware Dies
The Man in the Brown Suit
The Mirror Crack'd from Side to Side
Miss Marple's Final Cases
The Moving Finger
Mrs McGinty's Dead
The Murder at the Vicarage
Murder in Mesopotamia
Murder in the Mews
A Murder is Announced
Murder is Easy
The Murder of Roger Ackroyd
Murder on the Links
Murder on the Orient Express
The Mysterious Affair at Styles
The Mysterious Mr Quin

The Mystery of the Blue Train
Nemesis
N or M?
One, Two, Buckle My Shoe
Ordeal by Innocence
The Pale Horse
Parker Pyne Investigates
Partners in Crime
Passenger to Frankfurt
Peril at End House
A Pocket Full of Rye
Poirot's Early Cases
Poirot Investigates
Postern of Fate
Problem at Pollensa Bay
Sad Cypress
The Secret Adversary
The Secret of Chimneys
The Seven Dials Mystery
The Sittaford Mystery
Sleeping Murder
Sparkling Cyanide
Taken at the Flood
They Came to Baghdad
They Do It With Mirrors
Third Girl
The Thirteen Problems
Three-Act Tragedy
Towards Zero
Why Didn't They Ask Evans?

Novels under the Nom de Plume of 'Mary Westmacott'
Absent in the Spring
The Burden
A Daughter's A Daughter
Giant's Bread
The Rose and the Yew Tree
Unfinished Portrait

Books under the name of Agatha Christie Mallowan
Come Tell Me How You Live
Star over Bethlehem

Collections of Plays
The Mousetrap and Selected Plays
Witness for the Prosecution and Selected Plays

Autobiography
Agatha Christie: An Autobiography

AGATHA CHRISTIE

OMNIBUS

1920S

———◦———

VOLUME THREE

The Murder of Roger Ackroyd
The Big Four
The Mystery of the Blue Train

Background notes by Jacques Baudou

HarperCollins*Publishers*

HarperCollins*Publishers*
77–85 Fulham Palace Road,
Hammersmith, London w6 8jb

This paperback edition 1996
1 3 5 7 9 8 6 4 2

The Murder of Roger Ackroyd copyright Agatha Christie 1926
The Big Four copyright Agatha Christie 1927
The Mystery of the Blue Train copyright Agatha Christie 1928

isbn 0 00 649897 3

Set in Linotron Baskerville by
Rowland Phototypesetting Limited
Bury St Edmunds, Suffolk

Printed and bound in Great Britain by
Caledonian International Book Manufacturer, Glasgow

All rights reserved. No part of this publication may be
reproduced, stored in a retrieval system, or transmitted,
in any form or by any means, electronic, mechanical,
photocopying, recording or otherwise, without the prior
permission of the publishers.

This book is sold subject to the condition that it shall not,
by way of trade or otherwise, be lent, re-sold, hired out or
otherwise circulated without the publisher's prior consent
in any form of binding or cover other than that in which it
is published and without a similar condition including this
condition being imposed on the subsequent purchaser.

Contents

THE MURDER OF
ROGER ACKROYD

To Punkie
who likes an orthodox detective
story, murder, inquest, and
suspicion falling on everyone
in turn!

CHAPTER I

Dr Sheppard
at the Breakfast Table

Mrs Ferrars died on the night of the 16th–17th September – a Thursday. I was sent for at eight o'clock on the morning of Friday the 17th. There was nothing to be done. She had been dead some hours.

It was just a few minutes after nine when I reached home once more. I opened the front door with my latch-key, and purposely delayed a few moments in the hall, hanging up my hat and the light overcoat that I had deemed a wise precaution against the chill of an early autumn morning. To tell the truth, I was considerably upset and worried. I am not going to pretend that at that moment I foresaw the events of the next few weeks. I emphatically did not do so. But my instinct told me that there were stirring times ahead.

From the dining-room on my left there came the rattle of tea-cups and the short, dry cough of my sister Caroline.

'Is that you, James?' she called.

An unnecessary question, since who else could it be? To tell the truth, it was precisely my sister Caroline who was the cause of my few minutes' delay. The motto of the mongoose family, so Mr Kipling tells us, is: 'Go and find out.' If Caroline ever adopts a crest, I should certainly suggest a mongoose rampant. One might omit the first part of the motto. Caroline can do any amount of finding out by sitting placidly at home. I don't know how she manages it, but there it is. I suspect that the servants and the tradesmen constitute her Intelligence Corps. When she goes out, it is not to gather in information, but to spread it. At that, too, she is amazingly expert.

It was really this last named trait of hers which was causing me these pangs of indecision. Whatever I told Caroline now concerning the demise of Mrs Ferrars would be common knowledge all over the village within the space of an hour and a half. As a professional man, I naturally aim at discretion. Therefore I have got into the habit of continually withholding all information possible from my sister. She usually finds out just the same, but I have the moral satisfaction of knowing that I am in no way to blame.

Mrs Ferrars' husband died just over a year ago, and Caroline has constantly asserted, without the least foundation for the assertion, that his wife poisoned him.

She scorns my invariable rejoinder that Mr Ferrars died of acute gastritis, helped on by habitual overindulgence in alcoholic beverages. The symptoms of gastritis and arsenical poisoning are not, I agree, unlike, but Caroline bases her accusation on quite different lines.

'You've only got to look at her,' I have heard her say.

Mrs Ferrars, though not in her first youth, was a very attractive woman, and her clothes, though simple, always seemed to fit her very well, but all the same, lots of women buy their clothes in Paris, and have not, on that account, necessarily poisoned their husbands.

As I stood hesitating in the hall, with all this passing through my mind, Caroline's voice came again, with a sharper note in it.

'What on earth are you doing out there, James? Why don't you come and get your breakfast?'

'Just coming, my dear,' I said hastily. 'I've been hanging up my overcoat.'

'You could have hung up half a dozen overcoats in this time.'

She was quite right. I could have.

I walked into the dining-room, gave Caroline the accustomed peck on the cheek, and sat down to eggs and bacon. The bacon was rather cold.

'You've had an early call,' remarked Caroline.

'Yes,' I said. 'King's Paddock. Mrs Ferrars.'

'I know,' said my sister.

'How did you know?'

'Annie told me.'

Annie is the house parlourmaid. A nice girl, but an inveterate talker.

There was a pause. I continued to eat eggs and bacon. My sister's nose, which is long and thin, quivered a little at the tip, as it always does when she is interested or excited over anything.

'Well?' she demanded.

'A sad business. Nothing to be done. Must have died in her sleep.'

'I know,' said my sister again.

This time I was annoyed.

'You can't know,' I snapped. 'I didn't know myself until I got there, and haven't mentioned it to a soul yet. If that girl Annie knows, she must be a clairvoyant.'

'It wasn't Annie who told me. It was the milkman. He had it from the Ferrarses' cook.'

As I say, there is no need for Caroline to go out to get information. She sits at home and it comes to her.

My sister continued:

'What did she die of? Heart failure?'

'Didn't the milkman tell you that?' I inquired sarcastically.

Sarcasm is wasted on Caroline. She takes it seriously and answers accordingly.

'He didn't know,' she explained.

After all, Caroline was bound to hear sooner or later. She might as well hear from me.

'She died of an overdose of veronal. She's been taking it lately for sleeplessness. Must have taken too much.'

'Nonsense,' said Caroline immediately. 'She took it on purpose. Don't tell me!'

It is odd, when you have a secret belief of your own which you do not wish to acknowledge, the voicing of it by someone else will rouse you to a fury of denial. I burst immediately into indignant speech.

'There you go again,' I said. 'Rushing along without rhyme

or reason. Why on earth should Mrs Ferrars wish to commit suicide? A widow, fairly young still, very well off, good health, and nothing to do but enjoy life. It's absurd.'

'Not at all. Even you must have noticed how different she has been looking lately. It's been coming on for the last six months. She's looked positively hag-ridden. And you have just admitted that she hasn't been able to sleep.'

'What is your diagnosis?' I demanded coldly. 'An unfortunate love affair, I suppose?'

My sister shook her head.

'*Remorse,*' she said, with a great gusto.

'Remorse?'

'Yes. You never would believe me when I told you she poisoned her husband. I'm more than ever convinced of it now.'

'I don't think you're very logical,' I objected. 'Surely if a woman committed a crime like murder, she'd be sufficiently cold-blooded to enjoy the fruits of it without any weak-minded sentimentality such as repentance.'

Caroline shook her head.

'There probably are women like that – but Mrs Ferrars wasn't one of them. She was a mass of nerves. An overmastering impulse drove her on to get rid of her husband because she was the sort of person who simply can't endure suffering of any kind, and there's no doubt that the wife of a man like Ashley Ferrars must have had to suffer a good deal –'

I nodded.

'And ever since she's been haunted by what she did. I can't help feeling sorry for her.'

I don't think Caroline ever felt sorry for Mrs Ferrars whilst she was alive. Now that she has gone where (presumably) Paris frocks can no longer be worn, Caroline is prepared to indulge in the softer emotions of pity and comprehension.

I told her firmly that her whole idea was nonsense. I was all the more firm because I secretly agreed with some part, at least, of what she had said. But it is all wrong that Caroline should arrive at the truth simply by a kind of inspired guesswork. I wasn't going to encourage that sort of thing. She will go round the village airing her views, and everyone will think that she is doing so on medical data supplied by me. Life is very trying.

'Nonsense,' said Caroline, in reply to my strictures. 'You'll see. Ten to one she's left a letter confessing everything.'

'She didn't leave a letter of any kind,' I said sharply, and not seeing where the admission was going to land me.

'Oh!' said Caroline. 'So you *did* inquire about that, did you? I believe, James, that in your heart of hearts, you think very much as I do. You're a precious old humbug.'

'One always has to take the possibility of suicide into consideration,' I said impressively.

'Will there be an inquest?'

'There may be. It all depends. If I am able to declare myself absolutely satisfied that the overdose was taken accidentally, an inquest might be dispensed with.'

'And are you absolutely satisfied?' asked my sister shrewdly.

I did not answer, but got up from the table.

CHAPTER II

Who's Who in King's Abbot

Before I proceed further with what I said to Caroline and what Caroline said to me, it might be as well to give some idea of what I should describe as our local geography. Our village, King's Abbot, is, I imagine, very much like any other village. Our big town is Cranchester, nine miles away. We have a large railway station, a small post office, and two rival 'General Stores'. Able-bodied men are apt to leave the place early in life, but we are rich in unmarried ladies and retired military officers. Our hobbies and recreations can be summed up in the one word, 'gossip'.

There are only two houses of any importance in King's Abbot. One is King's Paddock, left to Mrs Ferrars by her late husband. The other, Fernly Park, is owned by Roger Ackroyd. Ackroyd has always interested me by being a man more impossibly like a country squire than any country squire could really be. He reminds me of the red-faced sportsmen who always appeared early in the first act on an old-fashioned musical comedy, the setting being the village green. They usually sang a song about going up to London. Nowadays we have revues, and the country squire has died out of musical fashion.

Of course, Ackroyd is not really a country squire. He is an immensely successful manufacturer of (I think) wagon wheels. He is a man of nearly fifty years of age, rubicund of face and genial of manner. He is hand and glove with the vicar, subscribes liberally to parish funds (though rumour has it that he is extremely mean in personal expenditure), encourages cricket matches, Lads' Clubs, and Disabled Soldiers' Institutes. He is, in fact, the life and soul of our peaceful village of King's Abbot.

Now when Roger Ackroyd was a lad of twenty-one, he fell in

love with, and married, a beautiful woman some five or six years his senior. Her name was Paton, and she was a widow with one child. The history of the marriage was short and painful. To put it bluntly, Mrs Ackroyd was a dipsomaniac. She succeeded in drinking herself into her grave four years after her marriage.

In the years that followed, Ackroyd showed no disposition to make a second matrimonial adventure. His wife's child by her first marriage was only seven years old when his mother died. He is now twenty-five. Ackroyd has always regarded him as his own son, and has brought him up accordingly, and he has been a wild lad and a continual source of worry and trouble to his stepfather. Nevertheless we are all very fond of Ralph Paton in King's Abbot. He is such a good-looking youngster for one thing.

As I said before, we are ready enough to gossip in our village. Everybody noticed from the first that Ackroyd and Mrs Ferrars got on very well together. After her husband's death, the intimacy became more marked. They were always seen about together, and it was freely conjectured that at the end of her period of mourning, Mrs Ferrars would become Mrs Roger Ackroyd. It was felt, indeed, that there was a certain fitness in the thing. Roger Ackroyd's wife had admittedly died of drink. Ashley Ferrars had been a drunkard for many years before his death. It was only fitting that these two victims of alcoholic excess should make up to each other for all that they had previously endured at the hands of their former spouses.

The Ferrars only came to live here just over a year ago, but a halo of gossip has surrounded Ackroyd for many years past. All the time that Ralph Paton was growing up to manhood a series of lady housekeepers presided over Ackroyd's establishment, and each in turn was regarded with lively suspicion by Caroline and her cronies. It is not too much to say that for at least fifteen years the whole village has confidently expected Ackroyd to marry one of his housekeepers. The last of them, a redoubtable lady called Miss Russell, has reigned undisputed for five years, twice as long as any of her predecessors. It is felt that, but for the advent of Mrs Ferrars, Ackroyd could hardly have escaped. That – and one other factor – the unexpected arrival of a widowed sister-in-law with her daughter from Canada. Mrs Cecil Ackroyd, widow of Ackroyd's ne'er-do-well younger brother, has taken up her residence at Fernly Park, and has succeeded, according to Caroline, in putting Miss Russell in her proper place.

I don't know exactly what a 'proper place' constitutes – it sounds chilly and unpleasant – but I know that Miss Russell goes about with pinched lips, and what I can only describe as an acid smile, and that she professes the utmost sympathy for 'poor Mrs Ackroyd – dependent on the charity of her husband's brother. The bread of charity is so bitter, is it not? *I* should be quite miserable if I did not work for my living.'

I don't know what Mrs Cecil Ackroyd thought of the Ferrars affair when it came on the tapis. It was clearly to her advantage that Ackroyd should remain unmarried. She was always very charming – not to say gushing – to Mrs Ferrars when they met. Caroline says that proves less than nothing.

Such have been our preoccupations in King's Abbot for the last few years. We have discussed Ackroyd and his affairs from every standpoint. Mrs Ferrars has fitted into her place in the scheme.

Now there has been a rearrangement of the kaleidoscope. From a mild discussion of probable wedding presents, we had been jerked into the midst of tragedy.

Revolving these and sundry other matters in my mind, I went mechanically on my round. I had no cases of special interest to attend, which was, perhaps, as well, for my thoughts returned again and again to the mystery of Mrs Ferrars's death. Had she taken her own life? Surely, if she had done so, she would have left some word behind to say what she contemplated doing? Women, in my experience, if they once reach the determination to commit suicide, usually wish to reveal the state of mind that led to the fatal action. They covet the limelight.

When had I last seen her? Not for over a week. Her manner then had been normal enough considering – well – considering everything.

Then I suddenly remembered that I had seen her, though not to speak to, only yesterday. She had been walking with Ralph Paton, and I had been surprised because I had had no idea that he was likely to be in King's Abbot. I thought, indeed, that he had quarrelled finally with his stepfather. Nothing had been seen of him down here for nearly six months. They had been walking along, side by side, their heads close together, and she had been talking very earnestly.

I think I can safely say that it was at this moment that a foreboding of the future first swept over me. Nothing tangible as yet – but a vague premonition of the way things were setting. That earnest *tête-à-tête* between Ralph Paton and Mrs Ferrars the day before struck me disagreeably.

I was still thinking of it when I came face to face with Roger Ackroyd.

'Sheppard!' he exclaimed. 'Just the man I wanted to get hold of. This is a terrible business.'

'You've heard then?'

He nodded. He had felt the blow keenly, I could see. His big red cheeks seemed to have fallen in, and he looked a positive wreck of his usual joy, healthy self.

'It's worse than you know,' he said quietly. 'Look here, Sheppard, I've got to talk to you. Can you come back with me now?'

'Hardly. I've got three patients to see still, and I must be back by twelve to see my surgery patients.'

'Then this afternoon – no, better still, dine tonight. At 7.30. Will that suit you?'

'Yes, I can manage that all right. What's wrong? Is it Ralph?'

I hardly knew why I said that – except, perhaps, that it had so often been Ralph.

Ackroyd stared blankly at me as though he hardly understood. I began to realize that there must be something very wrong indeed somewhere. I had never seen Ackroyd so upset before.

'Ralph?' he said vaguely. 'Oh! no, it's not Ralph. Ralph's in London – Damn! Here's old Miss Gannett coming. I don't want to have to talk to her about this ghastly business. See you tonight, Sheppard. Seven-thirty.'

I nodded, and he hurried away, leaving me wondering. Ralph in London? But he had certainly been in King's Abbot the preceding afternoon. He must have gone back to town last night or early this morning, and yet Ackroyd's manner had conveyed quite a different impression. He had spoken as though Ralph had not been near the place for months.

I had no time to puzzle the matter out further. Miss Gannett was upon me, thirsting for information. Miss Gannett has all the characteristics of my sister Caroline, but she lacks that unerring aim in jumping to conclusions which lends a touch of greatness to Caroline's manoeuvres. Miss Gannett was breathless and interrogatory.

Wasn't it sad about poor dear Mrs Ferrars? A lot of people were saying she had been a confirmed drug-taker for years. So wicked the way people went about saying things. And yet, the worst of it was, there was usually a grain of truth somewhere in these wild statements. No smoke without fire! They were saying too that Mr Ackroyd had found out about it, and had broken off the engagement – because there *was* an engagement. She, Miss Gannett, had proof positive of that. Of course *I* must know all about it – doctors always did – but they never tell?

And all this with a sharp beady eye on me to see how I reacted to these suggestions. Fortunately, long association with Caroline has led me to preserve an impassive countenance, and to be ready with small non-committal remarks.

On this occasion I congratulated Miss Gannett on not joining in ill-natured gossip. Rather a neat counter-attack, I thought. It left her in difficulties, and before she could pull herself together, I had passed on.

I went home thoughtful, to find several patients waiting for me in the surgery.

I had dismissed the last of them, as I thought, and was just contemplating a few minutes in the garden before lunch when I perceived one more patient waiting for me. She rose and came towards me as I stood somewhat surprised.

I don't know why I should have been, except that there is a

suggestion of cast iron about Miss Russell, a something that is above the ills of the flesh.

Ackroyd's housekeeper is a tall woman, handsome but forbidding in appearance. She has a stern eye, and lips that shut tightly, and I feel that if I were an under housemaid or a kitchenmaid I should run for my life whenever I heard her coming.

'Good morning, Dr Sheppard,' said Miss Russell. 'I should be much obliged if you would take a look at my knee.'

I took a look, but, truth to tell, I was very little wiser when I had done so. Miss Russell's account of vague pains was so unconvincing that with a woman of less integrity of character I should have suspected a trumped-up tale. It did cross my mind for one moment that Miss Russell might have deliberately invented this affection of the knee in order to pump me on the subject of Mrs Ferrars's death, but I soon saw that there, at least, I had misjudged her. She made a brief reference to the tragedy, nothing more. Yet she certainly seemed disposed to linger and chat.

'Well, thank you very much for this bottle of liniment, doctor,' she said at last. 'Not that I believe it will do the least good.'

I didn't think it would either, but I protested in duty bound. After all, it couldn't do any harm, and one must stick up for the tools of one's trade.

'I don't believe in all these drugs,' said Miss Russell, her eyes sweeping over my array of bottles disparagingly. 'Drugs do a lot of harm. Look at the cocaine habit.'

'Well, as far as that goes –'

'It's very prevalent in high society.'

I'm sure Miss Russell knows far more about high society than I do. I didn't attempt to argue with her.

'Just tell me this, doctor, said Miss Russell. 'Suppose you are really a slave of the drug habit, is there any cure?'

One cannot answer a question like that off-hand. I gave her a short lecture on the subject, and she listened with close attention. I still suspected her of seeking information about Mrs Ferrars.

'Now, veronal, for instance –' I proceeded.

But, strangely enough, she didn't seem interested in veronal. Instead she changed the subject, and asked me if it was true that there were certain poisons so rare as to baffle detection.

'Ah!' I said. 'You've been reading detective stories.'

She admitted that she had.

'The essence of a detective story,' I said, 'is to have a rare poison – if possible something from South America, that nobody has ever heard of – something that one obscure tribe of savages use to poison their arrows with. Death is instantaneous, and Western science is powerless to detect it. Is that the kind of thing you mean?'

'Yes. Is there really such a thing?'

I shook my head regretfully.

'I'm afraid there isn't. There's *curare*, of course.'

I told her a good deal about curare, but she seemed to have lost interest once more. She asked me if I had any in my poison cupboard, and when I replied in the negative I fancy I fell in her estimation.

She said she must be getting back, and I saw her out at the surgery door just as the luncheon gong went.

I should never have suspected Miss Russell of a fondness for detective stories. It pleases me very much to think of her stepping out of the housekeeper's room to rebuke a delinquent housemaid, and then returning to a comfortable perusal of *The Mystery of the Seventh Death*, or something of the kind.

CHAPTER III

The Man Who Grew
Vegetable Marrows

I told Caroline at lunch that I should be dining at Fernly. She expressed no objection – on the contrary.

'Excellent,' she said. 'You'll hear all about it. By the way, what is the trouble with Ralph?'

'With Ralph?' I said, surprised; 'there isn't any.'

'Then why is he staying at the Three Boars instead of at Fernly Park?'

I did not for a minute question Caroline's statement that Ralph Paton was staying at the local inn. That Caroline said so was enough for me.

'Ackroyd told me he was in London,' I said. In the surprise of the moment I departed from my valuable rule of never parting with information.

'Oh!' said Caroline. I could see her nose twitching as she worked on this.

'He arrived at the Three Boars yesterday morning,' she said. 'And he's still there. Last night he was out with a girl.'

That did not surprise me in the least. Ralph, I should say, is out with a girl most nights of his life. But I did rather wonder that he chose to indulge in the pastime in King's Abbot instead of in the gay Metropolis.

'One of the barmaids?' I asked.

'No. That's just it. He went out to meet her. I don't know who she is.'

(Bitter for Caroline to have to admit such a thing.)

'But I can guess,' continued my indefatigable sister.

I waited patiently.

'His cousin.'

'Flora Ackroyd?' I exclaimed in surprise.

Flora Ackroyd is, of course, no relation whatever really to Ralph Paton but Ralph has been looked upon for so long as practically Ackroyd's own son, that cousinship is taken for granted.

'Flora Ackroyd,' said my sister.

'But why not go to Fernly if he wanted to see her?'

'Secretly engaged,' said Caroline, with immense enjoyment. 'Old Ackroyd won't hear of it, and they have to meet this way.'

I saw a good many flaws in Caroline's theory, but I forbore to point them out to her. An innocent remark about our new neighbour created a diversion.

The house next door, The Larches, has recently been taken by a stranger. To Caroline's extreme annoyance, she has not been able to find out anything about him, except that he is a foreigner. The Intelligence Corps has proved a broken reed. Presumably the man has milk and vegetables and joints of meat and occasional whitings just like everybody else, but none of the people who make it their business to supply these things seem to have acquired any information. His name, apparently, is Mr Porrott – a name which conveys an odd feeling of unreality. The one thing we do know about him is that he is interested in the growing of vegetable marrows.

But that is certainly not the sort of information that Caroline is after. She wants to know where he comes from, what he does, whether he is married, what his wife was, or is, like, whether he has children, what his mother's maiden name was – and so on. Somebody very like Caroline must have invented the questions on passports, I think.

'My dear Caroline,' I said. 'There's no doubt at all about what the man's profession has been. He's a retired hairdresser. Look at that moustache of his.'

Caroline dissented. She said that if the man was a hair-dresser, he would have wavy hair – not straight. All hairdressers did.

I cited several hairdressers personally known to me who had straight hair, but Caroline refused to be convinced.

'I can't make him out at all,' she said in an aggrieved voice. 'I borrowed some garden tools the other day, and he was most polite, but I couldn't get anything out of him. I asked him point blank at last whether he was a Frenchman, and he said he wasn't – and, somehow, I didn't like to ask him any more.'

I began to be more interested in our mysterious neighbour. A man who is capable of shutting up Caroline and sending her, like the Queen of Sheba, empty away, must be something of a personality.

'I believe,' said Caroline, 'that he's got one of those new vacuum cleaners –'

I saw a meditated loan and the opportunity of further questioning gleaming from her eye. I saw the chance to escape into the garden. I am rather fond of gardening. I was busily exterminating dandelion roots when a shout of warning sounded from close by and a heavy body whizzed by my ears and fell at my feet with a repellent squelch. It was a vegetable marrow!

I looked up angrily. Over the wall, to my left, there appeared a face. An egg-shaped head, partially covered with suspiciously black hair, two immense moustaches, and a pair of watchful eyes. It was our mysterious neighbour, Mr Porrott.

He broke at once into fluent apologies.

'I demand of you a thousand pardons, monsieur. I am without defence. For some months now I cultivate the marrows. This morning suddenly I enrage myself with these marrows. I send them to promenade themselves – alas! not only mentally but physically. I seize the biggest. I hurl him over the wall. Monsieur, I am ashamed. I prostrate myself.'

Before such profuse apologies, my anger was forced to melt. After all, the wretched vegetable hadn't hit me. But I sincerely hoped that throwing large vegetables over walls was not our new friend's hobby. Such a habit could hardly endear him to us as a neighbour.

The strange little man seemed to read my thoughts.

'Ah! no,' he exclaimed. 'Do not disquiet yourself. It is not with me a habit. But you can figure to yourself, monsieur, that a man may work towards a certain object, may labour and toil to attain a certain kind of leisure and occupation, and then find that, after all, he yearns for the old busy days, and the old occupations that he thought himself so glad to leave?'

'Yes,' I said slowly. 'I fancy that that is a common enough occurrence. I myself am perhaps an instance. A year ago I came into a legacy – enough to enable me to realize a dream. I have always wanted to travel, to see the world. Well, that was a year ago, as I said, and – I am still here.'

My little neighbour nodded.

'The chains of habit. We work to attain an object, and the object gained, we find that what we miss is the daily toil. And mark you, monsieur, my work was interesting work. The most interesting work there is in the world.'

'Yes?' I said encouragingly. For the moment the spirit of Caroline was strong within me.

'The study of human nature, monsieur!'

'Just so,' I said kindly.

Clearly a retired hairdresser. Who knows the secrets of human nature better than a hairdresser?

'Also, I had a friend – a friend who for many years never left my side. Occasionally of an imbecility to make one afraid, nevertheless he was very dear to me. Figure to yourself that I miss even his stupidity. His *naïveté*, his honest outlook, the pleasure of delighting and surprising him by my superior gifts – all these I miss more than I can tell you.'

'He died?' I asked sympathetically.

'Not so. He lives and flourishes – but on the other side of the world. He is now in the Argentine.'

'In the Argentine,' I said enviously.

I have always wanted to go to South America. I sighed, and then looked up to find Mr Porrott eyeing me sympathetically. He seemed an understanding little man.

'Will you go there, yes?' he asked.

I shook my head with a sigh.

'I could have gone,' I said. 'A year ago. But I was foolish – greedy. I risked the substance for the shadow.'

'I comprehend,' said Mr Porrott. 'You speculated?'

I nodded mournfully, but in spite of myself I felt secretly entertained. This ridiculous little man was so portentously solemn.

'Not the Porcupine Oilfields?' he asked suddenly.

I stared.

'I thought of them, as a matter of fact, but in the end I plumped for a gold mine in Western Australia.'

My neighbour was regarding me with a strange expression which I could not fathom.

'It is Fate,' he said at last.

'What is Fate?' I asked irritably.

'That I should live next to a man who seriously considers Porcupine Oilfields, and also West Australian Gold Mines. Tell me, have you also a penchant for auburn hair?'

I stared at him open-mouthed, and he burst out laughing.

'No, no, it is not the insanity that I suffer from. Make your mind easy. It was a foolish question that I put to you there, for, you see, my friend of whom I spoke was a young man, a man who thought all women good, and most of them beautiful. But you are a man of middle age, a doctor, a man who knows the folly and the vanity of most things in this life of ours. Well, well, we are neighbours. I beg of you to accept and present to your excellent sister my best marrow.'

He stooped, and with a flourish produced an immense specimen of the tribe, which I duly accepted in the spirit in which it was offered.

'Indeed,' said the little man cheerfully, 'this has not been a wasted morning. I have made the acquaintance of a man who in some ways resembles my far-off friend. By the way, I should like to ask you a question. You doubtless know everyone in this tiny village. Who is the young man with the very dark hair and eyes, and the handsome face? He walks with his head flung back, and an easy smile on his lips.'

The description left me in no doubt.

'That must be Captain Ralph Paton,' I said slowly.

'I have not seen him about here before?'

'No, he has not been here for some time. But he is the son – adopted son, rather – of Mr Ackroyd of Fernly Park.'

My neighbour made a slight gesture of impatience.

'Of course, I should have guessed. Mr Ackroyd spoke of him many times.'

'You know Mr Ackroyd?' I said, slightly surprised.

'Mr Ackroyd knew me in London – when I was at work there. I have asked him to say nothing of my profession down here.'

'I see,' I said, rather amused by this patent snobbery, as I thought it.

But the little man went on with an almost grandiloquent smirk.

'One prefers to remain incognito. I am not anxious for notoriety. I have not even troubled to correct the local version of my name.'

'Indeed,' I said, not knowing quite what to say.

'Captain Ralph Paton,' mused Mr Porrott. 'And so he is engaged to Mr Ackroyd's niece, the charming Miss Flora.'

'Who told you so?' I asked, very much surprised.

'Mr Ackroyd. About a week ago. He is very pleased about it – has long desired that such a thing should come to pass, or so I understood from him. I even believe that he brought some pressure to bear upon the young man. That is never wise. A young man should marry to please himself – not to please a stepfather from whom he has expectations.'

My ideas were completely upset. I could not see Ackroyd taking a hairdresser into his confidence, and discussing the marriage of his niece and stepson with him. Ackroyd extends a genial patronage to the lower orders, but he has a very great sense of his own dignity. I began to think that Porrott couldn't be a hairdresser after all.

To hide my confusion, I said the first thing that came into my head.

'What made you notice Ralph Paton? His good looks?'

'No, not that alone – though he is unusually good-looking for an Englishman – what your lady novelists would call a Greek God. No, there was something about that young man that I did not understand.'

He said the last sentence in a musing tone of voice which made an indefinable impression upon me. It was as though he was summing up the boy by the light of some inner knowledge that I did not share. It was that impression that was left with me, for at that moment my sister's voice called me from the house.

I went in. Caroline had her hat on, and had evidently just come in from the village. She began without preamble.

'I met Mr Ackroyd.'

'Yes?' I said.

'I stopped him, of course, but he seemed in a great hurry, and anxious to get away.'

I have no doubt but that that was the case. He would feel towards Caroline much as he had felt towards Miss Gannett earlier in the day – perhaps more so. Caroline is less easy to shake off.

'I asked him at once about Ralph. He was absolutely astonished. Had no idea the boy was down here. He actually said he thought I must have made a mistake. I! A mistake!'

'Ridiculous,' I said. 'He ought to have known you better.'

'Then he went on to tell me that Ralph and Flora are engaged.'

'I knew that, too,' I interrupted, with modest pride.

'Who told you?'

'Our new neighbour.'

Caroline visibly wavered for a second or two, much as a roulette ball might coyly hover between two numbers. Then she declined the tempting red herring.

'I told Mr Ackroyd that Ralph was staying at the Three Boars.'

'Caroline,' I said, 'do you never reflect that you might do a lot of harm with this habit of yours of repeating everything indiscriminately?'

'Nonsense,' said my sister. 'People ought to know things. I

consider it my duty to tell them. Mr Ackroyd was very grateful to me.'

'Well,' I said, for there was clearly more to come.

'I think he went straight off to the Three Boars, but if so he didn't find Ralph there.'

'No?'

'No. Because I was coming back through the wood –'

'Coming back through the wood?' I interrupted.

Caroline had the grace to blush.

'It was such a lovely day,' she exclaimed. 'I thought I would make a little round. The woods with their autumnal tints are so perfect at this time of year.'

Caroline does not care a hang for woods at any time of year. Normally she regards them as places where you get your feet damp, and where all kinds of unpleasant things may drop on your head. No, it was good sound mongoose instinct which took her to our local wood. It is the only place adjacent to the village of King's Abbot where you can talk with a young woman unseen by the whole of the village. It adjoins the Park of Fernly.

'Well,' I said, 'go on.'

'As I say, I was just coming back through the wood when I heard voices.'

Caroline paused.

'Yes?'

'One was Ralph Paton's – I knew it at once. The other was a girl's. Of course I didn't mean to listen –'

'Of course not,' I interjected, with patent sarcasm – which was, however, wasted on Caroline.

'But I simply couldn't help overhearing. The girl said something – I didn't quite catch what it was, and Ralph answered. He sounded very angry. "My dear girl," he said. "Don't you realize that it is quite on the cards the old man will cut me off with a shilling? He's been pretty fed up with me for the last few years. A little more would do it. And we need the dibs, my dear. I shall be a very rich man when the old fellow pops off. He's mean as they make 'em, but he's rolling in money really. I don't want him to go altering his will. You leave it to me, and don't worry." Those were his exact words. I remember them perfectly. Unfortunately, just then I stepped on a dry twig or something, and they lowered their voices and moved away. I couldn't, of course, go rushing after them, so wasn't able to see who the girl was.'

'That must have been most vexing,' I said. 'I suppose, though, you hurried on to the Three Boars, felt faint, and went into the bar for a glass of brandy, and so were able to see if both the barmaids were on duty?'

'It wasn't a barmaid,' said Caroline unhesitatingly. 'In fact, I'm almost sure that it was Flora Ackroyd, only –'

'Only it doesn't seem to make sense,' I agreed.

'But if it wasn't Flora, who could it have been?'

Rapidly my sister ran over a list of maidens living in the neighbourhood, with profuse reasons for and against.

When she paused for breath, I murmured something about a patient, and slipped out.

I proposed to make my way to the Three Boars. It seemed likely that Ralph Paton would have returned there by now.

I knew Ralph very well – better, perhaps, than anyone else in King's Abbot, for I had known his mother before him, and therefore I understood much in him that puzzled others. He was, to a certain extent, the victim of heredity. He had not inherited his mother's fatal propensity for drink, but nevertheless he had in him a strain of weakness. As my new friend of this morning had declared, he was extraordinarily handsome. Just on six feet, perfectly proportioned, with the easy grace of an athlete, he was dark, like his mother, with a handsome, sunburnt face always ready to break into a smile. Ralph Paton was of those born to charm easily and without effort. He was self-indulgent and extravagant, with no veneration for anything on earth, but he was lovable nevertheless, and his friends were all devoted to him.

Could I do anything with the boy? I thought I could.

On inquiry at the Three Boars I found that Captain Paton had just come in. I went up to his room and entered unannounced.

For a moment, remembering what I had heard and seen, I was

doubtful of my reception, but I need have had no misgivings.

'Why, it's Sheppard! Glad to see you.'

He came forward to meet me, hand outstretched, a sunny smile lighting up his face.

'The one person I am glad to see in this infernal place.'

I raised my eyebrows.

'What's the place been doing?'

He gave a vexed laugh.

'It's a long story. Things haven't been going well with me, doctor. But have a drink, won't you?'

'Thanks,' I said, 'I will.'

He pressed the bell, then coming back threw himself into a chair.

'Not to mince matters,' he said gloomily, 'I'm in the devil of a mess. In fact, I haven't the least idea what to do next.'

'What's the matter?' I asked sympathetically.

'It's my confounded stepfather.'

'What has he done?'

'It isn't what he's done yet, but what he's likely to do.'

The bell was answered, and Ralph ordered the drinks. When the man had gone again, he sat hunched in the armchair, frowning to himself.

'Is it really – serious?' I asked.

He nodded.

'I'm fairly up against it this time,' he said soberly.

The unusual ring of gravity in his voice told me that he spoke the truth. It took a good deal to make Ralph grave.

'In fact,' he continued, 'I can't see my way ahead … I'm damned if I can.'

'If I could help –' I suggested diffidently.

But he shook his head very decidedly.

'Good of you, doctor. But I can't let you in on this. I've got to play a lone hand.'

He was silent a minute and then repeated in a slightly different tone of voice:

'Yes – I've got to play a lone hand …'

CHAPTER IV

Dinner at Fernly

It was just a few minutes before half-past seven when I rang the front-door bell of Fernly Park. The door was opened with admirable promptitude by Parker, the butler.

The night was such a fine one that I had preferred to come on foot. I stepped into the big square hall and Parker relieved me of my overcoat. Just then Ackroyd's secretary, a pleasant young fellow by the name of Raymond, passed through the hall on his way to Ackroyd's study, his hands full of papers.

'Good evening, doctor. Coming to dine? Or is this a professional call?'

The last was in allusion to my black bag which I had laid down on the oak chest.

I explained that I expected a summons to a confinement case at any moment, and so had come out prepared for an emergency call. Raymond nodded, and went on his way, calling over his shoulder:

'Go into the drawing-room. You know the way. The ladies will be down in a minute. I must take these papers to Mr Ackroyd, and I'll tell him you're here.'

On Raymond's appearance Parker had withdrawn, so I was alone in the hall. I settled my tie, glanced in a large mirror which hung there, and crossed to the door directly facing me, which was, as I knew, the door of the drawing-room.

I noticed, just as I was turning the handle, a sound from within – the shutting down of a window, I took it to be. I noticed it, I may say, quite mechanically, without attaching any importance to it at the time.

I opened the door and walked in. As I did so I almost collided with Miss Russell who was just coming out. We both apologized.

For the first time I found myself appraising the housekeeper and thinking what a handsome woman she must once have been – indeed, as far as that goes, still was. Her dark hair was unstreaked with grey, and when she had a colour, as she had at this minute, the stern quality of her looks was not so apparent.

Quite subconsciously I wondered whether she had been out, for she was breathing hard, as though she had been running.

'I'm afraid I'm a few minutes early,' I said.

'Oh! I don't think so. It's gone half-past seven, Dr Sheppard.' She paused a minute before saying, 'I – didn't know you were expected to dinner tonight. Mr Ackroyd didn't mention it.'

I received a vague impression that my dining there displeased her in some way, but I couldn't imagine why.

'How's the knee?' I inquired.

'Much the same, thank you, doctor. I must be going now. Mrs Ackroyd will be down in a moment. I – I only came in here to see if the flowers were all right.'

She passed quickly out of the room. I strolled to the window, wondering at her evident desire to justify her presence in the room. As I did so, I saw what, of course, I might have known all the time had I troubled to give my mind to it, namely, that the windows were long french ones opening on the terrace. The sound I had heard, therefore, could not have been that of a window being shut down.

Quite idly, and more to distract my mind from painful thoughts than for any other reason, I amused myself by trying to guess what could have caused the sound in question.

Coals on the fire? No, that was not the kind of noise at all. A drawer of a bureau pushed in? No, not that.

Then my eye was caught by what, I believe, is called a silver table, the lid of which lifts, and through the glass of which you can see the contents. I crossed over to it, studying the contents. There were one or two pieces of old silver, a baby shoe belonging to King Charles I, some Chinese jade figures, and quite a number of African implements and curios. Wanting to examine one of the jade figures more closely, I lifted the lid. It slipped through my fingers and fell.

At once I recognized the sound I had heard. It was this same table lid being shut down gently and carefully. I repeated the action once or twice for my own satisfaction. Then I lifted the lid to scrutinize the contents more closely.

I was still bending over the open silver table when Flora Ackroyd came into the room.

Quite a lot of people do not like Flora Ackroyd, but nobody can help admiring her. And to her friends she can be very charming. The first thing that strikes you about her is her extraordinary fairness. She has the real Scandinavian pale gold hair. Her eyes are blue – blue as the waters of a Norwegian fiord, and her skin is cream and roses. She has square, boyish shoulders and slight hips. And to a jaded medical man it is very refreshing to come across such perfect health.

A simple straightforward English girl – I may be old-fashioned, but I think the genuine article takes a lot of beating.

Flora joined me by the silver table, and expressed heretical doubts as to King Charles I ever having worn the baby shoe.

'And anyway,' continued Miss Flora, 'all this making a fuss about things because someone wore or used them seems to me all nonsense. They're not wearing or using them now. That pen that George Eliot wrote *The Mill on the Floss* with – that sort of thing – well, it's only just a pen after all. If you're really keen on George Eliot, why not get *The Mill on the Floss* in a cheap edition and read it.'

'I suppose you never read such old out-of-date stuff, Miss Flora?'

'You're wrong, Dr Sheppard. I love *The Mill on the Floss*.'

I was rather pleased to hear it. The things young women read nowadays and profess to enjoy positively frighten me.

'You haven't congratulated me yet, Dr Sheppard,' said Flora. 'Haven't you heard?'

She held out her left hand. On the third finger of it was an exquisitely set single pearl.

'I'm going to marry Ralph, you know,' she went on. 'Uncle is very pleased. It keeps me in the family, you see.'

I took both her hands in mine.

'My dear,' I said, 'I hope you'll be very happy.'

'We've been engaged for about a month,' continued Flora
in her cool voice, 'but it was only announced yesterday. Uncle
is going to do up Cross-stones, and give it to us to live in, and
we're going to pretend to farm. Really, we shall hunt all the
winter, town for the season, and then go yachting. I love the
sea. And, of course, I shall take a great interest in the parish
affairs, and attend all the Mothers' Meetings.'

Just then Mrs Ackroyd rustled in, full of apologies for being
late.

I am sorry to say I detest Mrs Ackroyd. She is all chains and
teeth and bones. A most unpleasant woman. She has small pale
flinty blue eyes, and however gushing her words may be, those
eyes of hers always remain coldly speculative.

I went across to her, leaving Flora by the window. She gave
me a handful of assorted knuckles and rings to squeeze, and
began talking volubly.

Had I heard about Flora's engagement? So suitable in every
way. The dear young things had fallen in love at first sight. Such
a perfect pair, he so dark and she so fair.

'I can't tell you, my dear Dr Sheppard, the relief to a mother's
heart.'

Mrs Ackroyd sighed – a tribute to her mother's heart, whilst
her eyes remained shrewdly observant of me.

'I was wondering. You are such an old friend of dear Roger's.
We know how much he trusts to your judgment. So difficult for
me – in my position as poor Cecil's widow. But there are so
many tiresome things – settlements, you know – all that. I fully
believe that Roger intends to make settlements upon dear Flora,
but, as you know, he is just a *leetle* peculiar about money. Very
usual, I've heard, amongst men who are captains of industry. I
wondered, you know, if you could just *sound* him on the subject?
Flora is so fond of you. We feel you are quite an old friend,
although we have only really known you just over two years.'

Mrs Ackroyd's eloquence was cut short as the drawing-room
door opened once more. I was pleased at the interruption. I
hate interfering in other people's affairs, and I had not the

least intention of tackling Ackroyd on the subject of Flora's settlements. In another moment I should have been forced to tell Mrs Ackroyd as much.

'You know Major Blunt, don't you, doctor?'

'Yes, indeed,' I said.

A lot of people knew Hector Blunt – at least by repute. He has shot more wild animals in unlikely places than any man living, I suppose. When you mention him, people say: 'Blunt – you don't mean the big-game man, do you?'

His friendship with Ackroyd has always puzzled me a little. The two men are so totally dissimilar. Hector Blunt is perhaps five years Ackroyd's junior. They made friends early in life, and though their ways have diverged, the friendship still holds. About once in two years Blunt spends a fortnight at Fernly, and an immense animal's head, with an amazing number of horns which fixes you with a glazed stare as soon as you come inside the front door, is a permanent reminder of the friendship.

Blunt had entered the room now with his own peculiar, deliberate, yet soft-footed tread. He is a man of medium height, sturdily and rather stockily built. His face is almost mahogany coloured, and is peculiarly expressionless. He has grey eyes that give the impression of always watching something that is happening very far away. He talks little, and what he does say is said jerkily, as though the words were forced out of him unwillingly.

He said now: 'How are you, Sheppard?' in his usual abrupt fashion, and then stood squarely in front of the fireplace looking over our heads as though he saw something very interesting happening in Timbuctoo.

'Major Blunt,' said Flora, 'I wish you'd tell me about these African things. I'm sure you know what they all are.'

I have heard Hector Blunt described as a woman-hater, but I noticed that he joined Flora at the silver table with what might be described as alacrity. They bent over it together.

I was afraid Mrs Ackroyd would begin talking about settlements again, so I made a few hurried remarks about the new sweet pea. I knew there was a new sweet pea because the *Daily*

Mail had told me so that morning. Mrs Ackroyd knows nothing about horticulture, but she is the kind of woman who likes to appear well-informed about the topics of the day, and she, too, reads the *Daily Mail.* We were able to converse quite intelligently until Ackroyd and his secretary joined us, and immediately afterwards Parker announced dinner.

My place at table was between Mrs Ackroyd and Flora. Blunt was on Mrs Ackroyd's other side, and Geoffrey Raymond next to him.

Dinner was not a cheerful affair. Ackroyd was visibly preoccupied. He looked wretched, and ate next to nothing. Mrs Ackroyd, Raymond, and I kept the conversation going. Flora seemed affected by her uncle's depression, and Blunt relapsed into his usual taciturnity.

Immediately after dinner Ackroyd slipped his arm through mine and led me off to his study.

'Once we've had coffee, we shan't be disturbed again,' he explained. 'I told Raymond to see to it that we shouldn't be interrupted.'

I studied him quietly without appearing to do so. He was clearly under the influence of some strong excitement. For a minute or two he paced up and down the room, then, as Parker entered with the coffee tray, he sank into an armchair in front of the fire.

The study was a comfortable apartment. Bookshelves lined one wall of it. The chairs were big and covered in dark blue leather. A large desk stood by the window and was covered with papers neatly docketed and filed. On a round table were various magazines and sporting papers.

'I've had a return of that pain after food lately,' remarked Ackroyd calmly, as he helped himself to coffee. 'You must give me some more of those tablets of yours.'

It struck me that he was anxious to convey the impression that our conference was a medical one. I played up accordingly.

'I thought as much. I brought some up with me.'

'Good man. Hand them over now.'

'They're in my bag in the hall. I'll get them.'

Ackroyd arrested me.

'Don't you trouble. Parker will get them. Bring in the doctor's bag, will you, Parker?'

'Very good, sir.'

Parker withdrew. As I was about to speak, Ackroyd threw up his hand.

'Not yet. Wait. Don't you see I'm in such a state of nerves that I can hardly contain myself?'

I saw that plainly enough. And I was very uneasy. All sorts of forebodings assailed me.

Ackroyd spoke again almost immediately.

'Make certain that window's closed, will you,' he asked.

Somewhat surprised, I got up and went to it. It was not a french window, but one of the ordinary sash type. The heavy blue velvet curtains were drawn in front of it, but the window itself was open at the top.

Parker re-entered the room with my bag while I was still at the window.

'That's all right,' I said, emerging again into the room.

'You've put the latch across?'

'Yes, yes. What's the matter with you, Ackroyd?'

The door had just closed behind Parker, or I would not have put the question.

Ackroyd waited just a minute before replying.

'I'm in hell,' he said slowly, after a minute. 'No, don't bother with those damn tablets. I only said that for Parker. Servants are so curious. Come here and sit down. The door's closed too, isn't it?'

'Yes. Nobody can overhear; don't be uneasy.'

'Sheppard, nobody knows what I've gone through in the last twenty-four hours. If a man's house ever fell in ruin about him, mine has about me. This business of Ralph's is the last straw. But we won't talk about that now. It's the other – the other! – I don't know what to do about it. And I've got to make up my mind soon.'

'What's the trouble?'

Ackroyd remained silent for a minute or two. He seemed curiously averse to beginning. When he did speak, the question he asked came as a complete surprise. It was the last thing I expected.

'Sheppard, you attended Ashley Ferrars in his last illness, didn't you?'

'Yes, I did.'

He seemed to find even greater difficulty in framing his next question.

'Did you ever suspect – did it ever enter your head – that – well, that he might have been poisoned?'

I was silent for a minute or two. Then I made up my mind what to say. Roger Ackroyd was not Caroline.

'I'll tell you the truth,' I said. 'At the time I had no suspicion whatever, but since – well, it was mere idle talk on my sister's part that first put the idea into my head. Since then I haven't been able to get it out again. But, mind you, I've no foundation whatever for that suspicion.'

'He *was* poisoned,' said Ackroyd.

He spoke in a dull heavy voice.

'Who by?' I asked sharply.

'His wife.'

'How do you know that?'

'She told me so herself.'

'When?'

'Yesterday! My God! yesterday! It seems ten years ago.'

I waited a minute, then he went on.

'You understand, Sheppard, I'm telling you this in confidence. It's to go no further. I want your advice – I can't carry the whole weight by myself. As I said just now, I don't know what to do.'

'Can you tell me the whole story?' I said. 'I'm still in the dark. How did Mrs Ferrars come to make this confession to you?'

'It's like this. Three months ago I asked Mrs Ferrars to marry me. She refused. I asked her again and she consented, but she refused to allow me to make the engagement public until her year of mourning was up. Yesterday I called upon her, pointed out that a year and three weeks had now elapsed since her husband's death, and that there could be no further objection to making the engagement public property. I had noticed that she had been very strange in her manner for some days. Now, suddenly, without the least warning, she broke down completely. She – she told me everything. Her hatred of her brute of a husband, her growing love for me, and the – the dreadful means she had taken. Poison! My God! It was murder in cold blood.'

I saw the repulsion, the horror, in Ackroyd's face. So Mrs Ferrars must have seen it. Ackroyd's is not the type of the great lover who can forgive all for love's sake. He is fundamentally a good citizen. All that was sound and wholesome and law-abiding in him must have turned from her utterly in that moment of revelation.

'Yes,' he went on, in a low, monotonous voice, 'she confessed everything. It seems that there is one person who has known all along – who has been blackmailing her for huge sums. It was the strain of that that drove her nearly mad.'

'Who was the man?'

Suddenly before my eyes there arose the picture of Ralph Paton and Mrs Ferrars side by side. Their heads so close together. I felt a momentary throb of anxiety. Supposing – oh! but surely that was impossible. I remembered the frankness of Ralph's greeting that very afternoon. Absurd!

'She wouldn't tell me his name,' said Ackroyd slowly. 'As a matter of fact, she didn't actually say that it was a man. But of course –'

'Of course,' I agreed. 'It must have been a man. And you've no suspicion at all?'

For answer Ackroyd groaned and dropped his head into his hands.

'It can't be,' he said. 'I'm mad even to think of such a thing. No, I won't even admit to you the wild suspicion that crossed my mind. I'll tell you this much, though. Something she said made me think that the person in question might be actually among my household – but that can't be so. I must have misunderstood her.'

'What did you say to her?' I asked.

'What could I say? She saw, of course, the awful shock it had been to me. And then there was the question, what was my duty in the matter? She had made me, you see, an accessory after the fact. She saw all that, I think, quicker than I did. I was stunned, you know. She asked me for twenty-four hours – made me promise to do nothing till the end of that time. And she steadfastly refused to give me the name of the scoundrel who had been blackmailing her. I suppose she was afraid that I might go straight off and hammer him, and then the fat would have been in the fire as far as she was concerned. She told me that I should hear from her before twenty-four hours had passed. My God! I swear to you, Sheppard, that it never entered my head what she meant to do. Suicide! And I drove her to it.'

'No, no,' I said. 'Don't take an exaggerated view of things. The responsibility for her death doesn't lie at your door.'

'The question is, what am I to do now? The poor lady is dead. Why rake up past trouble?'

'I rather agree with you,' I said.

'But there's another point. How am I to get hold of that scoundrel who drove her to death as surely as if he'd killed her? He knew of the first crime, and he fastened on to it like some obscene vulture. She's paid the penalty. Is he to go scot free?'

'I see,' I said slowly. 'You want to hunt him down? It will mean a lot of publicity, you know.'

'Yes, I've thought of that. I've zigzagged to and fro in my mind.'

'I agree with you that the villain ought to be punished, but the cost has got to be reckoned.'

Ackroyd rose and walked up and down. Presently he sank into the chair again.

'Look here, Sheppard, suppose we leave it like this. If no word comes from her, we'll let the dead things lie.'

'What do you mean by word coming from her?' I asked curiously.

'I have the strongest impression that somewhere or somehow she must have left a message for me – before she went. I can't argue about it, but there it is.'

I shook my head.

'She left no letter or word of any kind?' I asked.

'Sheppard, I'm convinced that she did. And more, I've a feeling that by deliberately choosing death, she wanted the whole thing to come out, if only to be revenged on the man who drove her to desperation. I believe that if I could have seen her then, she would have told me his name and bid me go for him for all I was worth.'

He looked at me.

'You don't believe in impressions?'

'Oh, yes, I do, in a sense. If, as you put it, word should come from her –'

I broke off. The door opened noiselessly and Parker entered with a salver on which were some letters.

'The evening post, sir,' he said, handing the salver to Ackroyd. Then he collected the coffee cups and withdrew.

My attention, diverted for a moment, came back to Ackroyd. He was staring like a man turned to stone at a long blue envelope. The other letters he had let drop to the ground.

'*Her writing*,' he said in a whisper. 'She must have gone out and posted it last night, just before – before –'

He ripped open the envelope and drew out a thick enclosure. Then he looked up sharply.

'You're sure you shut the window?' he said.

'Quite sure,' I said, surprised. 'Why?'

'All this evening I've had a queer feeling of being watched, spied upon. What's that –'

He turned sharply. So did I. We both had the impression of hearing the latch of the door give ever so slightly. I went across to it and opened it. There was no one there.

'Nerves,' murmured Ackroyd to himself.

He unfolded the thick sheets of paper, and read aloud in a low voice.

'My dear, my very dear Roger, – A life calls for a life. I
see that – I saw it in your face this afternoon. So I am
taking the only road open to me. I leave to you the
punishment of the person who has made my life a hell
upon earth for the last year. I would not tell you the
name, this afternoon, but I propose to write it to you
now. I have no children or near relations to be spared,
so do not fear publicity. If you can, Roger, my very dear
Roger, forgive me the wrong I meant to do you, since
when the time came, I could not do it after all . . .'

Ackroyd, his finger on the sheet to turn it over, paused.

'Sheppard, forgive me, but I must read this alone,' he said
unsteadily. 'It was meant for my eyes, and my eyes only.'

He put the letter in the envelope and laid it on the table.

'Later, when I am alone.'

'No,' I cried impulsively, 'read it now.'

Ackroyd stared at me in some surprise.

'I beg your pardon,' I said, reddening. 'I do not mean read
it aloud to me. But read it through whilst I am still here.'

Ackroyd shook his head.

'No, I'd rather wait.'

But for some reason, obscure to myself, I continued to urge
him.

'At least, read the name of the man,' I said.

Now Ackroyd is essentially pig-headed. The more you urge
him to do a thing, the more determined he is not to do it. All
my arguments were in vain.

The letter had been brought in at twenty minutes to nine. It
was just on ten minutes to nine when I left him, the letter still
unread. I hesitated with my hand on the door handle, looking
back and wondering if there was anything I had left undone. I
could think of nothing. With a shake of the head I passed out
and closed the door behind me.

I was startled by seeing the figure of Parker close at hand.
He looked embarrassed, and it occurred to me that he might
have been listening at the door.

What a fat, smug, oily face the man had, and surely there was something decidedly shifty in his eye.

'Mr Ackroyd particularly does not want to be disturbed,' I said coldly. 'He told me to tell you so.'

'Quite so, sir. I – I fancied I heard the bell ring.'

This was such a palpable untruth that I did not trouble to reply. Preceding me to the hall, Parker helped me on with my overcoat, and I stepped out into the night. The moon was overcast, and everything seemed very dark and still.

The village church clock chimed nine o'clock as I passed through the lodge gates. I turned to the left towards the village, and almost cannoned into a man coming in the opposite direction.

'This the way to Fernly Park, mister?' asked the stranger in a hoarse voice.

I looked at him. He was wearing a hat pulled down over his eyes, and his coat collar turned up. I could see little or nothing of his face, but he seemed a young fellow. The voice was rough and uneducated.

'These are the lodge gates here,' I said.

'Thank you, mister.' He paused, and then added, quite unnecessarily, 'I'm a stranger in these parts, you see.'

He went on, passing through the gates as I turned to look after him.

The odd thing was that his voice reminded me of someone's voice that I knew, but whose it was I could not think.

Ten minutes later I was at home once more. Caroline was full of curiosity to know why I had returned so early. I had to make up a slightly fictitious account of the evening in order to satisfy her, and I had an uneasy feeling that she saw through the transparent device.

At ten o'clock I rose, yawned, and suggested bed. Caroline acquiesced.

It was Friday night, and on Friday night I wind the clocks. I did it as usual, whilst Caroline satisfied herself that the servants had locked up the kitchen properly.

It was a quarter past ten as we went up the stairs. I had just reached the top when the telephone rang in the hall below.

'Mrs Bates,' said Caroline immediately.

'I'm afraid so,' I said ruefully.

I ran down the stairs and took up the receiver.

'What?' I said. '*What?* Certainly, I'll come at once.'

I ran upstairs, caught up my bag, and stuffed a few extra dressings into it.

'Parker telephoning,' I shouted to Caroline, 'from Fernly. They've just found Roger Ackroyd murdered.'

CHAPTER V

Murder

I got out the car in next to no time, and drove rapidly to Fernly. Jumping out, I pulled the bell impatiently. There was some delay in answering, and I rang again.

Then I heard the rattle of the chain and Parker, his impassivity of countenance quite unmoved, stood in the open doorway.

I pushed past him into the hall.

'Where is he?' I demanded sharply.

'I beg your pardon, sir?'

'Your master. Mr Ackroyd. Don't stand there staring at me, man. Have you notified the police?'

'The police, sir? Did you say the police?' Parker stared at me as though I were a ghost.

'What's the matter with you, Parker? If, as you say, your master has been murdered –'

A gasp broke from Parker.

'The master? Murdered? Impossible, sir!'

It was my turn to stare.

'Didn't you telephone to me, not five minutes ago, and tell me that Mr Ackroyd had been found murdered?'

'Me, sir? Oh! no indeed, sir. I wouldn't dream of doing such a thing.'

'Do you mean to say it's all a hoax? That there's nothing the matter with Mr Ackroyd?'

'Excuse me, sir, did the person telephoning use my name?'

'I'll give you the exact words I heard. *"Is that Dr Sheppard? Parker, the butler at Fernly, speaking. Will you please come at once, sir. Mr Ackroyd has been murdered."* '

Parker and I stared at each other blankly.

'A very wicked joke to play, sir,' he said at last, in a shocked tone. 'Fancy saying a thing like that.'

'Where is Mr Ackroyd?' I asked suddenly.

'Still in the study, I fancy, sir. The ladies have gone to bed, and Major Blunt and Mr Raymond are in the billiard room.'

'I think I'll just look in and see him for a minute,' I said. 'I know he didn't want to be disturbed again, but this odd practical joke has made me uneasy. I'd just like to satisfy myself that he's all right.'

'Quite so, sir. It makes me feel quite uneasy myself. If you don't object to my accompanying you as far as the door, sir –?'

'Not at all,' I said. 'Come along.'

I passed through the door on the right, Parker on my heels, traversed the little lobby where a small flight of stairs led upstairs to Ackroyd's bedroom, and tapped on the study door.

There was no answer. I turned the handle, but the door was locked.

'Allow me, sir,' said Parker.

Very nimbly, for a man of his build, he dropped on one knee and applied his eye to the keyhole.

'Key is in the lock all right, sir,' he said, rising. 'On the inside. Mr Ackroyd must have locked himself in and possibly just dropped off to sleep.'

I bent down and verified Parker's statement.

'It seems all right,' I said, 'but, all the same, Parker, I'm going to wake your master up. I shouldn't be satisfied to go home without hearing from his own lips that he's quite all right.'

So saying, I rattled the handle and called out, 'Ackroyd, Ackroyd, just a minute.'

But still there was no answer. I glanced over my shoulder.

'I don't want to alarm the household,' I said hesitatingly.

Parker went across and shut the door from the big hall through which we had come.

'I think that will be all right now, sir. The billiard room is at the other side of the house, and so are the kitchen quarters and the ladies' bedrooms.'

I nodded comprehendingly. Then I banged once more frantically on the door, and stooping down, fairly bawled through the keyhole:

'Ackroyd, Ackroyd! It's Sheppard. Let me in.'

And still – silence. Not a sign of life from within the locked room. Parker and I glanced at each other.

'Look here, Parker,' I said, 'I'm going to break this door in – or rather, we are. I'll take the responsibility.'

'If you say so, sir,' said Parker, rather doubtfully.

'I do say so. I'm seriously alarmed about Mr Ackroyd.'

I looked round the small lobby and picked up a heavy oak chair. Parker and I held it between us and advanced to the assault. Once, twice, and three times we hurled it against the lock. At the third blow it gave, and we staggered into the room.

Ackroyd was sitting as I had left him in the arm-chair before the fire. His head had fallen sideways, and clearly visible, just below the collar of his coat, was a shining piece of twisted metalwork.

Parker and I advanced till we stood over the recumbent figure. I heard the butler draw in his breath with a sharp hiss.

'Stabbed from be'ind,' he murmured. ''Orrible!'

He wiped his moist brow with his handkerchief, then stretched out a gingerly hand towards the hilt of the dagger.

'You mustn't touch that,' I said sharply. 'Go at once to the telephone and ring up the police station. Inform them of what has happened. Then tell Mr Raymond and Major Blunt.'

'Very good, sir.'

Parker hurried away, still wiping his perspiring brow.

I did what little had to be done. I was careful not to disturb the position of the body, and not to handle the dagger at all. No object was to be attained by moving it. Ackroyd had clearly been dead some little time.

Then I heard young Raymond's voice, horror-stricken and incredulous, outside.

'What do you say? Oh! impossible! Where's the doctor?'

He appeared impetuously in the doorway, then stopped dead, his face very white. A hand put him aside, and Hector Blunt came past him into the room.

'My God!' said Raymond from behind him; 'it's true, then.'

Blunt came straight on till he reached the chair. He bent over the body, and I thought that, like Parker, he was going to lay hold of the dagger hilt. I drew him back with one hand.

'Nothing must be moved,' I explained. 'The police must see him exactly as he is now.'

Blunt nodded in instant comprehension. His face was expressionless as ever, but I thought I detected signs of emotion beneath the stolid mask. Geoffrey Raymond had joined us now, and stood peering over Blunt's shoulder at the body.

'This is terrible,' he said in a low voice.

He had regained his composure, but as he took off the pince-nez he habitually wore and polished them I observed that his hand was shaking.

'Robbery, I suppose,' he said. 'How did the fellow get in? Through the window? Has anything been taken?'

He went towards the desk.

'You think it's burglary?' I said slowly.

'What else could it be? There's no question of suicide, I suppose?'

'No man could stab himself in such a way,' I said confidently. 'It's murder right enough. But with what motive?'

'Roger hadn't an enemy in the world,' said Blunt quietly. 'Must have been burglars. But what was the thief after? Nothing seems to be disarranged?'

He looked round the room. Raymond was still sorting the papers on the desk.

'There seems nothing missing, and none of the drawers show signs of having been tampered with,' the secretary observed at last. 'It's very mysterious.'

Blunt made a slight motion with his head.

'There are some letters on the floor here,' he said.

I looked down. Three or four letters still lay where Ackroyd had dropped them earlier in the evening.

But the blue envelope containing Mrs Ferrars's letter had disappeared. I half opened my mouth to speak, but at that moment the sound of a bell pealed through the house. There was a confused murmur of voices in the hall, and then Parker appeared with our local inspector and a police constable.

'Good evening, gentlemen,' said the inspector. 'I'm terribly sorry for this! A good kind gentleman like Mr Ackroyd. The butler says it's murder. No possibility of accident or suicide, doctor?'

'None whatever,' I said.

'Ah! A bad business.'

He came and stood over the body.

'Been moved at all?' he asked sharply.

'Beyond making certain that life was extinct – an easy matter – I have not disturbed the body in any way.'

'Ah! And everything points to the murderer having got clear away – for the moment, that is. Now then, let me hear all about it. Who found the body?'

I explained the circumstances carefully.

'A telephone message, you say? From the butler?'

'A message that I never sent,' declared Parker earnestly. 'I've not been near the telephone the whole evening. The others can bear me out that I haven't.'

'Very odd, that. Did it sound like Parker's voice, doctor?'

'Well – I can't say I noticed. I took it for granted, you see.'

'Naturally. Well, you got up here, broke in the door, and found poor Mr Ackroyd like this. How long should you say he had been dead, doctor?'

'Half an hour at least – perhaps longer,' I said.

'The door was locked on the inside, you say? What about the window?'

'I myself closed and bolted it earlier in the evening at Mr Ackroyd's request.'

The inspector strode across to it and threw back the curtains.

'Well, it's open now, anyway,' he remarked.

True enough, the window was open, the lower sash being raised to its fullest extent.

The inspector produced a pocket torch and flashed it along the sill outside.

'This is the way he went all right,' he remarked, '*and* got in. See here.'

In the light of the powerful torch, several clearly defined footmarks could be seen. They seemed to be those of shoes with rubber studs in the soles. One particularly clear one pointed inwards, another, slightly overlapping it, pointed outwards.

'Plain as a pikestaff,' said the inspector. 'Any valuables missing?'

Geoffrey Raymond shook his head.

'Not so far that we can discover. Mr Ackroyd never kept anything of particular value in this room.'

'H'm,' said the inspector. 'Man found an open window. Climbed in, saw Mr Ackroyd sitting there – maybe he'd fallen asleep. Man stabbed him from behind, then lost his nerve and made off. But he's left his tracks pretty clearly. We ought to get hold of *him* without much difficulty. No suspicious strangers been hanging about anywhere?'

'Oh!' I said suddenly.

'What is it, doctor?'

'I met a man this evening – just as I was turning out of the gate. He asked me the way to Fernly Park.'

'What time would that be?'

'Just nine o'clock. I heard it chime the hour as I was turning out of the gate.'

'Can you describe him?'

I did so to the best of my ability.

The inspector turned to the butler.

'Anyone answering that description come to the front door?'

'No, sir. No one has been to the house at all this evening.'

'What about the back?'

'I don't think so, sir, but I'll make inquiries.'

He moved towards the door, but the inspector held up a large hand.

'No, thanks. I'll do my own inquiring. But first of all I want to fix the times a little more clearly. When was Mr Ackroyd last seen alive?'

'Probably by me,' I said, 'when I left at – let me see – about ten minutes to nine. He told me that he didn't wish to be disturbed, and I repeated the order to Parker.'

'Just so, sir,' said Parker respectfully.

'Mr Ackroyd was certainly alive at half-past nine,' put in Raymond, 'for I heard his voice in here talking.'

'Who was he talking to?'

'That I don't know. Of course, at the time I took it for granted that it was Dr Sheppard who was with him. I wanted to ask him a question about some papers I was engaged upon, but when I heard the voices I remembered that he had said he wanted to talk to Dr Sheppard without being disturbed, and I went away again. But now it seems that the doctor had already left?'

I nodded.

'I was at home by a quarter past nine,' I said. 'I didn't go out again until I received the telephone call.'

'Who could have been with him at half-past nine?' queried the inspector. 'It wasn't you, Mr – er –'

'Major Blunt,' I said.

'Major Hector Blunt?' asked the inspector, a respectful tone creeping into his voice.

Blunt merely jerked his head affirmatively.

'I think we've seen you down here before, sir,' said the inspector. 'I didn't recognize you for the moment, but you were staying with Mr Ackroyd a year ago last May.'

'June,' corrected Blunt.

'Just so, June it was. Now, as I was saying, it wasn't you with Mr Ackroyd at nine-thirty this evening?'

Blunt shook his head.

'Never saw him after dinner,' he volunteered.

The inspector turned once more to Raymond.

'You didn't overhear any of the conversation going on, did you, sir?'

'I did catch just a fragment of it,' said the secretary, 'and, supposing as I did that it was Dr Sheppard who was with Mr Ackroyd, that fragment struck me as distinctly odd. As far as I can remember, the exact words were these. Mr Ackroyd was speaking. "The calls on my purse have been so frequent of late" – that is what he was saying – "of late, that I fear it is impossible for me to accede to your request..." I went away again at once, of course, so I did not hear any more. But I rather wondered because Dr Sheppard –'

'– Does not ask for loans for himself or subscriptions for others,' I finished.

'A demand for money,' said the inspector musingly. 'It may be that here we have a very important clue.' He turned to the butler. 'You say, Parker, that nobody was admitted by the front door this evening?'

'That's what I say, sir.'

'Then it seems almost certain that Mr Ackroyd himself must have admitted this stranger. But I don't quite see –'

The inspector went into a kind of day-dream for some minutes.

'One thing's clear,' he said at length, rousing himself from his absorption, 'Mr Ackroyd was alive and well at nine-thirty. That is the last moment at which he is known to have been alive.'

Parker gave vent to an apologetic cough which brought the inspector's eyes on him at once.

'Well?' he said sharply.

'If you'll excuse me, sir, Miss Flora saw him after that.'

'Miss Flora?'

'Yes, sir. About a quarter to ten that would be. It was after that that she told me Mr Ackroyd wasn't to be disturbed again tonight.'

'Did he send her to you with that message?'

'Not exactly, sir. I was bringing a tray with soda and whisky when Miss Flora, who was just coming out of this room, stopped me and said her uncle didn't want to be disturbed.'

The inspector looked at the butler with rather closer attention than he had bestowed on him up to now.

'You'd already been told that Mr Ackroyd didn't want to be disturbed, hadn't you?'

Parker began to stammer. His hands shook.

'Yes, sir. Yes, sir. Quite so, sir.'

'And yet you were proposing to do so?'

'I'd forgotten, sir. At least I mean, I always bring the whisky and soda about that time, sir, and ask if there's anything more, and I thought – well, I was doing as usual without thinking.'

It was at this moment that it began to dawn upon me that Parker was most suspiciously flustered. The man was shaking and twitching all over.

'H'm,' said the inspector. 'I must see Miss Ackroyd at once. For the moment we'll leave this room exactly as it is. I can return here after I've heard what Miss Ackroyd has to tell me. I shall just take the precaution of shutting and bolting the window.'

This precaution accomplished, he led the way into the hall and we followed him. He paused a moment, as he glanced up at the little staircase, then spoke over his shoulder to the constable.

'Jones, you'd better stay here. Don't let anyone go into that room.'

Parker interposed deferentially.

'If you'll excuse me, sir. If you were to lock the door into the main hall, nobody could gain access to this part. That staircase leads only to Mr Ackroyd's bedroom and bathroom. There is no communication with the other part of the house. There once was a door through, but Mr Ackroyd had it blocked up. He liked to feel that his suite was entirely private.'

To make things clear and explain the position, I have appended a rough sketch of the right-hand wing of the house. The small staircase leads, as Parker explained, to a big bedroom made by two being knocked into one, and an adjoining bathroom and lavatory.

The inspector took in the position at a glance. We went through into the large hall and he locked the door behind him, slipping the key into his pocket. Then he gave the constable some low-voiced instructions, and the latter prepared to depart.

'We must get busy on those shoe tracks,' explained the inspector. 'But first of all, I must have a word with Miss Ackroyd. She

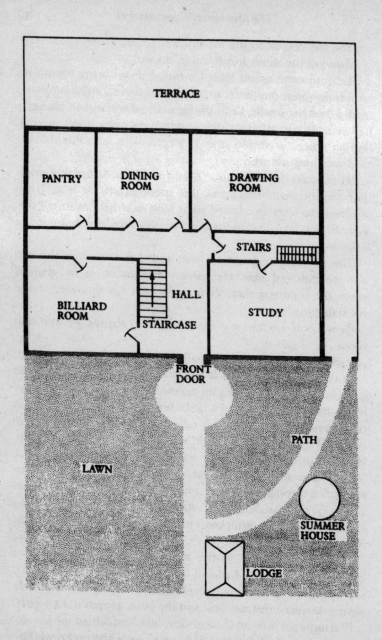

TERRACE

PANTRY

DINING ROOM

DRAWING ROOM

STAIRS

BILLIARD ROOM

HALL

STAIRCASE

STUDY

FRONT DOOR

PATH

LAWN

SUMMER HOUSE

LODGE

was the last person to see her uncle alive. Does she know yet?'

Raymond shook his head.

'Well, no need to tell her for another five minutes. She can answer my questions better without being upset by knowing the truth about her uncle. Tell her there's been a burglary, and ask her if she would mind dressing and coming down to answer a few questions.'

It was Raymond who went upstairs on this errand.

'Miss Ackroyd will be down in a minute,' he said, when he returned. 'I told her just what you suggested.'

In less than five minutes Flora descended the staircase. She was wrapped in a pale pink silk kimono. She looked anxious and excited.

The inspector stepped forward.

'Good evening, Miss Ackroyd,' he said civilly. 'We're afraid there's been an attempt at robbery, and we want you to help us. What's this room – the billiard room? Come in here and sit down.'

Flora sat down composedly on the wide divan which ran the length of the wall, and looked up at the inspector.

'I don't quite understand. What has been stolen? What do you want me to tell you?'

'It's just this, Miss Ackroyd. Parker here says you came out of your uncle's study at about a quarter to ten. Is that right?'

'Quite right. I had been to say goodnight to him.'

'And the time is correct?'

'Well, it must have been about then. I can't say exactly. It might have been later.'

'Was your uncle alone, or was there anyone with him?'

'He was alone. Dr Sheppard had gone.'

'Did you happen to notice whether the window was open or shut?'

Flora shook her head.

'I can't say. The curtains were drawn.'

'Exactly. And your uncle seemed quite as usual?'

'I think so.'

'Do you mind telling us exactly what passed between you?'

Flora paused a minute, as though to collect her recollections.

'I went in and said, "Goodnight, Uncle, I'm going to bed now. I'm tired tonight." He gave a sort of grunt, and – I went over and kissed him, and he said something about my looking nice in the frock I had on, and then he told me to run away as he was busy. So I went.'

'Did he ask specially not to be disturbed?'

'Oh! yes, I forgot. He said: "Tell Parker I don't want anything more tonight, and that he's not to disturb me." I met Parker just outside the door and gave him Uncle's message.'

'Just so,' said the inspector.

'Won't you tell me what it is that has been stolen?'

'We're not quite – certain,' said the inspector hesitatingly.

A wide look of alarm came into the girl's eyes. She started up.

'What is it? You're hiding something from me?'

Moving in his usual unobtrusive manner, Hector Blunt came between her and the inspector. She half stretched out her hand, and he took it in both of his, patting it as though she were a very small child, and she turned to him as though something in his stolid, rocklike demeanour promised comfort and safety.

'It's bad news, Flora,' he said quietly. 'Bad news for all of us. Your Uncle Roger –'

'Yes?'

'It will be a shock to you. Bound to be. Poor Roger's dead.'

Flora drew away from him, his eyes dilating with horror.

'When?' she whispered. 'When?'

'Very soon after you left him, I'm afraid,' said Blunt gravely.

Flora raised her hand to her throat, gave a little cry, and I hurried to catch her as she fell. She had fainted, and Blunt and I carried her upstairs and laid her on her bed. Then I got him to wake Mrs Ackroyd and tell her the news. Flora soon revived, and I brought her mother to her, telling her what to do for the girl. Then I hurried downstairs again.

CHAPTER VI

The Tunisian Dagger

I met the inspector just coming from the door which led into the kitchen quarters.

'How's the young lady, doctor?'

'Coming round nicely. Her mother's with her.'

'That's good. I've been questioning the servants. They all declare that no one has been to the back door tonight. Your description of that stranger was rather vague. Can't you give us something more definite to go upon?'

'I'm afraid not,' I said regretfully. 'It was a dark night, you see, and the fellow had his coat collar well pulled up and his hat squashed down over his eyes.'

'H'm,' said the inspector. 'Looked as though he wanted to conceal his face. Sure it was no one you know?'

I replied in the negative, but not as decidedly as I might have done. I remembered my impression that the stranger's voice was not unfamiliar to me. I explained this rather haltingly to the inspector.

'It was a rough, uneducated voice, you say?'

I agreed, but it occurred to me that the roughness had been of an almost exaggerated quality. If, as the inspector thought, the man had wished to hide his face, he might equally well have tried to disguise his voice.

'Do you mind coming into the study with me again, doctor? There are one or two things I want to ask you.'

I acquiesced. Inspector Davis unlocked the door of the lobby, we passed through, and he locked the door again behind him.

'We don't want to be disturbed,' he said grimly. 'And we don't want any eavesdropping either. What's all this about blackmail?'

'Blackmail!' I exclaimed, very much startled.

'Is it an effort of Parker's imagination? Or is there something in it?'

'If Parker heard anything about blackmail,' I said slowly, 'he must have been listening outside this door with his ear glued against the keyhole.'

Davis nodded.

'Nothing more likely. You see, I've been instituting a few inquiries as to what Parker has been doing with himself this evening. To tell the truth, I didn't like his manner. The man knows something. When I began to question him, he got the wind up, and plumped out some garbled story of blackmail.'

I took an instant decision.

'I'm rather glad you've brought the matter up,' I said. 'I've been trying to decide whether to make a clean breast of things or not. I'd already practically decided to tell you everything, but I was going to wait for a favourable opportunity. You might as well have it now.'

And then and there I narrated the whole events of the evening as I have set them down here. The inspector listened keenly, occasionally interjecting a question.

'Most extraordinary story I ever heard,' he said, when I had finished. 'And you say that letter has completely disappeared? It looks bad – it looks very bad indeed. It gives us what we've been looking for – a motive for the murder.'

I nodded.

'I realize that.'

'You say that Mr Ackroyd hinted at a suspicion he had that some member of his household was involved? Household's rather an elastic term.'

'You don't think that Parker himself might be the man we're after?' I suggested.

'It looks very like it. He was obviously listening at the door when you came out. Then Miss Ackroyd came across him later bent on entering the study. Say he tried again when she was safely out of the way. He stabbed Ackroyd, locked the door on the inside, opened the window, and got out that way, and went round to a side door which he had previously left open. How's that?'

'There's only one thing against it,' I said slowly. 'If Ackroyd went on reading that letter as soon as I left, as he intended to do, I don't see him continuing to sit on here and turn things over in his mind for another hour. He'd have had Parker in at once, accused him then and there, and there would have been a fine old uproar. Remember, Ackroyd was a man of choleric temper.'

'Mightn't have had time to go on with the letter just then,' suggested the inspector. 'We know someone was with him at half-past nine. If that visitor turned up as soon as you left, and after he went, Miss Ackroyd came in to say goodnight – well, he wouldn't be able to go on with the letter until close upon ten o'clock.'

'And the telephone call?'

'Parker sent that all right – perhaps before he thought of the locked door and open window. Then he changed his mind – or got in a panic – and decided to deny all knowledge of it. That was it, depend upon it.'

'Ye – es,' I said rather doubtfully.

'Anyway, we can find out the truth about the telephone call from the exchange. If it was put through from here, I don't see how anyone else but Parker could have sent it. Depend upon it, he's our man. But keep it dark – we don't want to alarm him just yet, till we've got all the evidence. I'll see to it he doesn't give us the slip. To all appearances we'll be concentrating on your mysterious stranger.'

He rose from where he had been sitting astride the chair belonging to the desk, and crossed over to the still form in the arm-chair.

'The weapon ought to give us a clue,' he remarked, looking up. 'It's something quite unique – a curio, I should think, by the look of it.'

He bent down, surveying the handle attentively, and I heard him give a grunt of satisfaction. Then, very gingerly, he pressed his hands down below the hilt and drew the blade out from the wound. Still carrying it so as not to touch the handle, he placed it in a wide china mug which adorned the mantelpiece.

'Yes,' he said, nodding at it. 'Quite a work of art. There can't be many of them about.'

It was indeed a beautiful object. A narrow, tapering blade, and a hilt of elaborately intertwined metals of curious and careful workmanship. He touched the blade gingerly with his finger, testing its sharpness, and made an appreciative grimace.

'Lord, what an edge,' he exclaimed. 'A child could drive that into a man – as easy as cutting butter. A dangerous sort of toy to have about.'

'May I examine the body properly now?' I asked.

He nodded.

'Go ahead.'

I made a thorough examination.

'Well?' said the inspector, when I had finished.

'I'll spare you the technical language,' I said. 'We'll keep that for the inquest. The blow was delivered by a right-handed man standing behind him, and death must have been instantaneous. By the expression on the dead man's face, I should say that the blow was quite unexpected. He may have died without knowing who his assailant was.'

'Butlers can creep about as soft-footed as cats,' said Inspector Davis. 'There's not going to be much mystery about this crime. Take a look at the hilt of that dagger.'

I took the look.

'I dare say they're not apparent to you, but *I* can see them clearly enough.' He lowered his voice. *'Fingerprints!'*

He stood off a few steps to judge of his effect.

'Yes,' I said mildly. 'I guessed that.'

I do not see why I should be supposed to be totally devoid of intelligence. After all, I read detective stories, and the newspapers, and am a man of quite average ability. If there had been toe marks on the dagger handle, now, that would have been quite a different thing. I would then have registered any amount of surprise and awe.

I think the inspector was annoyed with me for declining to

get thrilled. He picked up the china mug and invited me to accompany him to the billiard room.

'I want to see if Mr Raymond can tell us anything about this dagger,' he explained.

Locking the outer door behind us again, we made our way to the billiard room, where we found Geoffrey Raymond. The inspector held up his exhibit.

'Ever seen this before, Mr Raymond?'

'Why – I believe – I'm almost sure that is a curio given to Mr Ackroyd by Major Blunt. It comes from Morocco – no, Tunis. So the crime was committed with that? What an extraordinary thing. It seems almost impossible, and yet there could hardly be two daggers the same. May I fetch Major Blunt?'

Without waiting for an answer, he hurried off.

'Nice young fellow that,' said the inspector. 'Something honest and ingenuous about him.'

I agreed. In the two years that Geoffrey Raymond has been secretary to Ackroyd, I have never seen him ruffled or out of temper. And he has been, I know, a most efficient secretary.

In a minute or two Raymond returned, accompanied by Blunt.

'I was right,' said Raymond excitedly. 'It *is* the Tunisian dagger.'

'Major Blunt hasn't looked at it yet,' objected the inspector.

'Saw it the moment I came into the study,' said the quiet man.

'You recognized it, then?'

Blunt nodded.

'You said nothing about it,' said the inspector suspiciously.

'Wrong moment,' said Blunt. 'Lot of harm done by blurting out things at the wrong time.'

He returned the inspector's stare placidly enough.

The latter grunted at last and turned away. He brought the dagger over to Blunt.

'You're quite sure about it, sir. You identify it positively?'

'Absolutely. No doubt whatever.'

'Where was this – er – curio usually kept? Can you tell me that, sir?'

It was the secretary who answered.

'In the silver table in the drawing-room.'

'What?' I exclaimed.

The others looked at me.

'Yes, doctor?' said the inspector encouragingly.

'It's nothing,' said the inspector again, still encouragingly.

'It's so trivial,' I explained apologetically. 'Only that when I arrived last night for dinner I heard the lid of the silver table being shut down in the drawing-room.'

I saw profound scepticism and a trace of suspicion on the inspector's countenance.

'How did you know it was the silver table lid?'

I was forced to explain in detail – a long, tedious explanation which I would infinitely rather not have had to make.

The inspector heard me to the end.

'Was the dagger in its place when you were looking over the contents?' he asked.

'I don't know,' I said. 'I can't say I remember noticing it – but, of course, it may have been there all the time.'

'We'd better get hold of the housekeeper,' remarked the inspector, and pulled the bell.

A few minutes later Miss Russell, summoned by Parker, entered the room.

'I don't think I went near the silver table,' she said, when the inspector had posed his question. 'I was looking to see that all the flowers were fresh. Oh! yes, I remember now. The silver table was open – which it had no business to be, and I shut the lid down as I passed.'

She looked at him aggressively.

'I see,' said the inspector. 'Can you tell me if this dagger was in its place then?'

Miss Russell looked at the weapon composedly.

'I can't say I'm sure,' she replied. 'I didn't stop to look. I knew the family would be down any minute, and I wanted to get away.'

'Thank you,' said the inspector.

There was just a trace of hesitation in his manner, as though he would have liked to question her further, but Miss Russell clearly accepted the words as a dismissal, and glided from the room.

'Rather a Tartar, I should fancy, eh?' said the inspector, looking after her. 'Let me see. This silver table is in front of one of the windows, I think you said, doctor?'

Raymond answered for me.

'Yes, the left-hand window.'

'And the window was open?'

'They were both ajar.'

'Well, I don't think we need go into the question much further. Somebody – I'll just say somebody – could get that dagger any time he liked, and exactly when he got it doesn't matter in the least. I'll be coming up in the morning with the chief constable, Mr Raymond. Until then, I'll keep the key of that door. I want Colonel Melrose to see everything exactly as it is. I happen to know that he's dining out the other side of the county, and, I believe, staying the night . . .'

We watched the inspector take up the jar.

'I shall have to pack this carefully,' he observed. 'It's going to be an important piece of evidence in more ways than one.'

A few minutes later as I came out of the billiard room with Raymond, the latter gave a low chuckle of amusement.

I felt the pressure of his hand on my arm, and followed the direction of his eyes. Inspector Davis seemed to be inviting Parker's opinion of a small pocket diary.

'A little obvious,' murmured my companion. 'So Parker is the suspect, is he? Shall we oblige Inspector Davis with a set of our fingerprints also?'

He took two cards from the card tray, wiped them with his silk handkerchief, then handed one to me and took the other himself. Then, with a grin, he handed them to the police inspector.

'Souvenirs,' he said. 'No. 1. Dr Sheppard; No. 2, my humble self. One from Major Blunt will be forthcoming in the morning.'

Youth is very buoyant. Even the brutal murder of his friend and employer could not dim Geoffrey Raymond's spirits for long. Perhaps that is as it should be. I do not know. I have lost the quality of resilience long since myself.

It was very late when I got back, and I hoped that Caroline would have gone to bed. I might have known better.

She had hot cocoa waiting for me, and whilst I drank it, she extracted the whole history of the evening from me. I said nothing of the blackmailing business, but contented myself with giving her the facts of the murder.

'The police suspect Parker,' I said, as I rose to my feet and prepared to ascend to bed. 'There seems a fairly clear case against him.'

'Parker!' said my sister. 'Fiddlesticks! That inspector must be a perfect fool. Parker indeed! Don't tell me.'

With which obscure pronouncement we went up to bed.

CHAPTER VII

I Learn My Neighbour's Profession

On the following morning I hurried unforgivably over my round. My excuse can be that I had no very serious cases to attend. On my return Caroline came into the hall to greet me.

'Flora Ackroyd is here,' she announced in an excited whisper.

'What?'

I concealed my surprise as best as I could.

'She's very anxious to see you. She's been here half an hour.'

Caroline led the way into our small sitting-room, and I followed.

Flora was sitting on the sofa by the window. She was in black and she sat nervously twisting her hands together. I was shocked by the sight of her face. All the colour had faded away from it. But when she spoke her manner was as composed and resolute as possible.

'Dr Sheppard, I have come to ask you to help me?'

'Of course he'll help you, my dear,' said Caroline.

I don't think Flora wished Caroline to be present at the interview. She would, I am sure, have infinitely preferred to speak to me privately. But she also wanted to waste no time, so she made the best of it.

'I want you to come to The Larches with me.'

'The Larches?' I queried, surprised.

'To see that funny little man?' exclaimed Caroline.

'Yes. You know who he is, don't you?'

'We fancied,' I said, 'that he might be a retired hairdresser.'

Flora's blue eyes opened very wide.

'Why, he's Hercule Poirot! You know who I mean – the private detective. They say he's done the most wonderful things – just like detectives do in books. A year ago he retired and came to live down here. Uncle knew who he was, but he promised not to tell anyone, because M. Poirot wanted to live quietly without being bothered by people.'

'So that's who he is,' I said slowly.

'You've heard of him, of course?'

'I'm rather an old fogey, as Caroline tells me,' I said, 'but I *have* just heard of him.'

'Extraordinary!' commented Caroline.

I don't know what she was referring to – possibly her own failure to discover the truth.

'You want to go and see him?' I asked slowly. 'Now why?'

'To get him to investigate this murder, of course,' said Caroline sharply. 'Don't be so stupid, James.'

I was not really being stupid. Caroline does not always understand what I am driving at.

'You haven't got confidence in Inspector Davis?' I went on.

'Of course she hasn't,' said Caroline. 'I haven't either.'

Anyone would have thought it was Caroline's uncle who had been murdered.

'And how do you know he would take up the case?' I asked. 'Remember he has retired from active work.'

'That's just it,' said Flora simply. 'I've got to persuade him.'

'You are sure you are doing wisely?' I asked gravely.

'Of course she is,' said Caroline. 'I'll go with her myself if she likes.'

'I'd rather the doctor came with me, if you don't mind, Miss Sheppard,' said Flora.

She knows the value of being direct on certain occasions. Any hints would certainly have been wasted on Caroline.

'You see,' she explained, following directness with tact, 'Dr Sheppard being the doctor, and having found the body, he would be able to give all the details to M. Poirot.'

'Yes,' said Caroline grudgingly, 'I see that.'

I took a turn or two up and down the room.

'Flora,' I said gravely, 'be guided by me. I advise you not to drag this detective into the case.'

Flora sprang to her feet. The colour rushed into her cheeks.

'I know why you say that,' she cried. 'But it's exactly for that reason I'm so anxious to go. You're afraid! But I'm not. I know Ralph better than you do.'

'Ralph!' said Caroline. 'What has Ralph got to do with it?'

Neither of us heeded her.

'Ralph may be weak,' continued Flora. 'He may have done foolish things in the past – wicked things even – but he wouldn't murder anyone.'

'No, no,' I exclaimed. 'I never thought it of him.'

'Then why did you go to the Three Boars last night?' demanded Flora, 'on your way home – after Uncle's body was found?'

I was momentarily silenced. I had hoped that that visit of mine would remain unnoticed.

'How did you know about that?' I countered.

'I went there this morning,' said Flora. 'I heard from the servants that Ralph was staying there –'

I interrupted her.

'You had no idea that he was in King's Abbot?'

'No. I was astounded. I couldn't understand it. I went there and asked for him. They told me, what I suppose they told you last night, that he went out at about nine o'clock yesterday evening – and – and never came back.'

Her eyes met mine defiantly, and as though answering something in my look, she burst out:

'Well, why shouldn't he? He might have gone – anywhere. He may even have gone back to London.'

'Leaving his luggage behind?' I asked gently.

Flora stamped her foot.

'I don't care. There must be a simple explanation.'

'And that's why you want to go to Hercule Poirot? Isn't it better to leave things as they are? The police don't suspect Ralph in the least, remember. They're working on quite another tack.'

'But that's just *it*,' cried the girl. 'They *do* suspect him. A man from Cranchester turned up this morning – Inspector Raglan, a horrid, weaselly little man. I found he had been to the Three Boars this morning before me. They told me all about his having been there, and the questions he had asked. He must think Ralph did it.'

'That's a change of mind from last night, if so,' I said slowly. 'He doesn't believe in Davis's theory that it was Parker then?'

'Parker indeed,' said my sister, and snorted.

Flora came forward and laid her hand on my arm.

'Oh! Dr Sheppard, let us go at once to this M. Poirot. He will find out the truth.'

'My dear Flora,' I said gently, laying my hand on hers. 'Are you quite sure it is the truth we want?'

She looked at me, nodding her head gravely.

'You're not sure,' she said. 'I am. I know Ralph better than you do.'

'Of course he didn't do it,' said Caroline, who had been keeping silent with great difficulty. 'Ralph may be extravagant, but he's a dear boy, and has the nicest manners.'

I wanted to tell Caroline that large numbers of murderers have had nice manners, but the presence of Flora restrained me. Since the girl was determined, I was forced to give in to her and we started at once, getting away before my sister was able to fire off any more pronouncements beginning with her favourite words, 'Of course.'

An old woman with an immense Breton cap opened the door of The Larches to us. M. Poirot was at home, it seemed.

We were ushered into a little sitting-room arranged with formal precision, and there, after a lapse of a minute or so, my friend of yesterday came to us.

'Monsieur le docteur,' he said, smiling. 'Mademoiselle.'

He bowed to Flora.

'Perhaps,' I began, 'you have heard of the tragedy which occurred last night.'

His face grew grave.

'But certainly I have heard. It is horrible. I offer mademoiselle all my sympathy. In what way can I serve you?'

'Miss Ackroyd,' I said, 'wants you to – to –'

'To find the murderer,' said Flora in a clear voice.

'I see,' said the little man. 'But the police will do that, will they not?'

'They might make a mistake,' said Flora. 'They are on their way to make a mistake now, I think. Please, M. Poirot, won't you help us? If – if it is a question of money –'

Poirot held up his hand.

'Not that, I beg of you, mademoiselle. Not that I do not care for money.' His eyes showed a momentary twinkle. 'Money, it means much to me and always has done. No, if I go into this, you must understand one thing clearly. *I shall go through with it to the end.* The good dog, he does not leave the scent, remember! You may wish that, after all, you had left it to the local police.'

'I want the truth,' said Flora, looking him straight in the eyes.

'All the truth?'

'All the truth.'

'Then I accept,' said the little man quietly. 'And I hope you will not regret those words. Now, tell me all the circumstances.'

'Dr Sheppard had better tell you,' said Flora. 'He knows more than I do.'

Thus enjoined, I plunged into a careful narrative, embodying all the facts I have previously set down. Poirot listened carefully, inserting a question here and there, but for the most part sitting in silence, his eyes on the ceiling.

I brought my story to a close with the departure of the inspector and myself from Fernly Park the previous night.

'And now,' said Flora, as I finished, 'tell him all about Ralph.'

I hesitated, but her imperious glance drove me on.

'You went to this inn – this Three Boars – last night on your way home?' asked Poirot, as I brought my tale to a close. 'Now exactly why was that?'

I paused a moment to choose my words carefully.

'I thought someone ought to inform the young man of his uncle's death. It occurred to me after I had left Fernly that possibly no one but myself and Mr Ackroyd were aware that he was staying in the village.'

Poirot nodded.

'Quite so. That was your only motive in going there, eh?'

'That was my only motive,' I said stiffly.

'It was not to – shall we say – reassure yourself about *ce jeune homme?*'

'Reassure myself?'

'I think, M. le docteur, that you know very well what I mean, though you pretend not to do so. I suggest that it would have been a relief to you if you had found that Captain Paton had been at home all the evening.'

'Not at all,' I said sharply.

The little detective shook his head at me gravely.

'You have not the trust in me of Miss Flora,' he said. 'But no matter. What we have to look at is this – Captain Paton is missing, under circumstances which call for an explanation. I will not hide from you that the matter looks grave. Still, it may admit of a perfectly simple explanation.'

'That's just what I keep saying,' cried Flora eagerly.

Poirot touched no more upon that theme. Instead he suggested an immediate visit to the local police. He thought it better for Flora to return home, and for me to be the one to accompany him there and introduce him to the officer in charge of the case.

We carried out this plan forthwith. We found Inspector Davis outside the police station looking very glum indeed. With him was Colonel Melrose, the Chief Constable, and another man whom, from Flora's description of 'weaselly', I had no difficulty in recognizing as Inspector Raglan from Cranchester.

I know Melrose fairly well, and I introduced Poirot to him and explained the situation. The chief constable was clearly vexed, and Inspector Raglan looked as black as thunder. Davis, however, seemed slightly exhilarated by the sight of his superior officer's annoyance.

'The case is going to be plain as a pikestaff,' said Raglan. 'Not the least need for amateurs to come butting in. You'd think any fool would have seen the way things were last night, and then we shouldn't have lost twelve hours.'

He directed a vengeful glance at poor Davis, who received it with perfect stolidity.

'Mr Ackroyd's family must, of course, do what they see fit,' said Colonel Melrose. 'But we cannot have the official investigation hampered in any way. I know M. Poirot's great reputation, of course,' he added courteously.

'The police can't advertise themselves, worse luck,' said Raglan.

It was Poirot who saved the situation.

'It is true that I have retired from the world,' he said. 'I never intended to take up a case again. Above all things, I have a horror of publicity. I must beg, that in the case of my being able to contribute something to the solution of the mystery, my name may not be mentioned.'

Inspector Raglan's face lightened a little.

'I've heard of some very remarkable successes of yours,' observed the colonel, thawing.

'I have had much experience,' said Poirot quietly. 'But most of my successes have been obtained by the aid of the police. I admire enormously your English police. If Inspector Raglan permits me to assist him, I shall be both honoured and flattered.'

The inspector's countenance became still more gracious.

Colonel Melrose drew me aside.

'From all I hear, this little fellow's done some really remarkable things,' he murmured. 'We're naturally anxious not to have to call in Scotland Yard. Raglan seems very sure of himself, but I'm not quite certain that I agree with him. You see, I – er – know the parties concerned better than he does. This fellow doesn't seem out after kudos, does he? Would work in with us unobtrusively, eh?'

'To the greater glory of Inspector Raglan,' I said solemnly.

'Well, well,' said Colonel Melrose breezily in a louder voice, 'we must put you wise to the latest developments, M. Poirot.'

'I thank you,' said Poirot. 'My friend, Dr Sheppard, said something of the butler being suspected?'

'That's all bunkum,' said Raglan instantly. 'These high-class servants get in such a funk that they act suspiciously for nothing at all.'

'The fingerprints?' I hinted.

'Nothing like Parker's.' He gave a faint smile, and added: 'And yours and Mr Raymond's don't fit either, doctor.'

'What about those of Captain Ralph Paton?' asked Poirot quietly.

I felt a secret admiration of the way he took the bull by the horns. I saw a look of respect creep into the inspector's eye.

'I see you don't let the grass grow under your feet, Mr Poirot. It will be a pleasure to work with you, I'm sure. We're going to take that young gentleman's fingerprints as soon as we can lay hands upon him.'

'I can't help thinking you're mistaken, Inspector,' said Colonel Melrose warmly. 'I've known Ralph Paton from a boy upward. He'd never stoop to murder.'

'Maybe not,' said the inspector tonelessly.

'What have you got against him?' I asked.

'Went out just on nine o'clock last night. Was seen in the neighbourhood of Fernly Park somewhere about nine-thirty. Not been seen since. Believed to be in serious money difficulties. I've got a pair of his shoes here – shoes with rubber studs in them. He had two pairs, almost exactly alike. I'm going up now to compare them with those footmarks. The constable is up there seeing that no one tampers with them.'

'We'll go at once,' said Colonel Melrose. 'You and M. Poirot will accompany us, will you not?'

We assented, and all drove up in the colonel's car. The inspector was anxious to get at once to the footmarks, and asked to be put down at the lodge. About half-way up the drive, on the right, a path branched off which led round to the terrace and the window of Ackroyd's study.

'Would you like to go with the inspector, M. Poirot?' asked the chief constable, 'or would you prefer to examine the study?'

Poirot chose the latter alternative. Parker opened the door to us. His manner was smug and deferential, and he seemed to have recovered from his panic of the night before.

Colonel Melrose took a key from his pocket, and unlocking the door which let into the lobby, he ushered us through into the study.

'Except for the removal of the body, M. Poirot, this room is exactly as it was last night.'

'And the body was found – where?'

As precisely as possible, I described Ackroyd's position. The arm-chair still stood in front of the fire.

Poirot went and sat down in it.

'The blue letter you speak of, where was it when you left the room?'

'Mr Ackroyd had laid it down on this little table at his right hand.'

Poirot nodded.

'Except for that, everything was in its place?'

'Yes, I think so.'

'Colonel Melrose, would you be so extremely obliging as to sit down in this chair a minute. I thank you. Now, M. le docteur, will you kindly indicate to me the exact position of the dagger?'

I did so, whilst the little man stood in the doorway.

'The hilt of the dagger was plainly visible from the door then. Both you and Parker could see it at once?'

'Yes.'

Poirot went next to the window.

'The electric light was on, of course, when you discovered the body?' he asked over his shoulder.

I assented, and joined him where he was studying the marks on the window-sill.

'The rubber studs are the same pattern as those in Captain Paton's shoes,' he said quietly.

Then he came back once more to the middle of the room. His eye travelled round, searching everything in the room with a quick, trained glance.

'Are you a man of good observation, Dr Sheppard?' he asked at last.

'I think so,' I said, surprised.

'There was a fire in the grate, I see. When you broke the door down and found Mr Ackroyd dead, how was the fire? Was it low?'

I gave a vexed laugh.

'I – I really can't say. I didn't notice. Perhaps Mr Raymond or Major Blunt –'

The little man opposite me shook his head with a faint smile.

'One must always proceed with method. I made an error of judgment in asking you that question. To each man his own knowledge. You could tell me the details of the patient's appearance – nothing there would escape you. If I wanted information about the papers on that desk, Mr Raymond would have noticed anything there was to see. To find out about the fire, I must ask the man whose business it is to observe such things. You permit –'

He moved swiftly to the fireplace and rang the bell.

After a lapse of a minute or two Parker appeared.

'The bell rang, sir,' he said hesitatingly.

'Come in, Parker,' said Colonel Melrose. 'This gentleman wants to ask you something.'

Parker transferred a respectful attention to Poirot.

'Parker,' said the little man, 'when you broke down the door with Dr Sheppard last night, and found your master dead, what was the state of the fire?'

Parker replied without a pause.

'It had burned very low, sir. It was almost out.'

'Ah!' said Poirot. The exclamation sounded almost triumphant. He went on:

'Look round you, my good Parker. Is this room exactly as it was then?'

The butler's eye swept round. It came to rest on the windows.

'The curtains were drawn, sir, and the electric light was on.'

Poirot nodded approval.

'Anything else?'

'Yes, sir, this chair was drawn out a little more.'

He indicated a big grandfather chair to the left of the door between it and the window. I append a plan of the room with the chair in question marked with an 'X'.

'Just show me,' said Poirot.

The butler drew the chair in question out a good two feet from the wall, turning it so that the seat faced the door.

'*Voilà ce qui est curieux*,' murmured Poirot. 'No one would want to sit in a chair in such a position, I fancy. Now who pushed it back into place again, I wonder? Did you, my friend?'

'No, sir,' said Parker. 'I was too upset with seeing the master and all.'

Poirot looked across at me.

'Did you, doctor?'

I shook my head.

'It was back in position when I arrived with the police, sir,' put in Parker. 'I'm sure of that.'

'Curious,' said Poirot again.

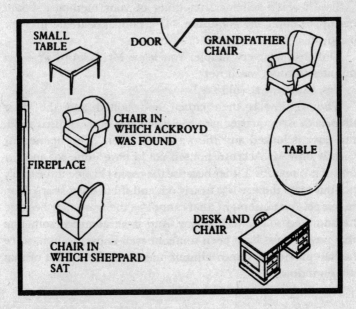

'Raymond or Blunt must have pushed it back,' I suggested. 'Surely it isn't important?'

'It is completely unimportant,' said Poirot. 'That is why it is so interesting,' he added softly.

'Excuse me a minute,' said Colonel Melrose. He left the room with Parker.

'Do you think Parker is speaking the truth?' I asked.

'About the chair, yes. Otherwise I do not know. You will find, M. le docteur, if you have much to do with cases of this kind, that they all resemble each other in one thing.'

'What is that?' I asked curiously.

'Everyone concerned in them has something to hide.'

'Have I?' I asked, smiling.

Poirot looked at me attentively.

'I think you have,' he said quietly.

'But –'

'Have you told me everything known to you about this young man Paton?' He smiled as I grew red. 'Oh! do not fear. I will not press you. I shall learn it in good time.'

'I wish you'd tell me something of your methods,' I said hastily, to cover my confusion. 'The point about the fire, for instance?'

'Oh! that was very simple. You leave Mr Ackroyd at – ten minutes to nine, was it not?'

'Yes, exactly, I should say.'

'The window is then closed and bolted and the door unlocked. At a quarter past ten when the body is discovered, the door is locked and the window is open. Who opened it? Clearly only Mr Ackroyd himself could have done so, and for one of two reasons. Either because the room became unbearably hot but since the fire was nearly out and there was a sharp drop in temperature last night, that cannot be the reason, or because he admitted someone that way. And if he admitted someone that way, it must have been someone well known to him, since he had previously shown himself uneasy on the subject of that same window.'

'It sounds very simple,' I said.

'Everything is simple, if you arrange the facts methodically. We are concerned now with the personality of the person who was with him at nine-thirty last night. Everything goes to show that that was the individual admitted by the window, and though Mr Ackroyd was seen alive later by Miss Flora, we cannot approach a solution of the mystery until we know who that visitor was. The window may have been left open after his departure and so afforded entrance to the murderer, or the same person may have returned a second time. Ah! here is the colonel who returns.'

Colonel Melrose entered with an animated manner.

'That telephone call has been traced at last,' he said. 'It did not come from here. It was put through to Dr Sheppard at 10.15 last night from a public call office at King's Abbot station. And at 10.23 the night mail leaves for Liverpool.'

CHAPTER VIII

Inspector Raglan is Confident

We looked at each other.

'You'll have inquiries made at the station, of course?' I said.

'Naturally, but I'm not over sanguine as to the result. You know what that station is like.'

I did. King's Abbot is a mere village, but its station happens to be an important junction. Most of the big expresses stop there, and trains are shunted, re-sorted, and made up. It has two or three public telephone boxes. At that time of night, three local trains come in close upon each other, to catch the connection with the express for the north which comes in at 10.19 and leaves at 10.23. The whole place is in a bustle, and the chances of one particular person being noticed telephoning or getting into the express are very small indeed.

'But why telephone at all?' demanded Melrose. 'That is what I find so extraordinary. There seems no rhyme or reason in the thing.'

Poirot carefully straightened a china ornament on one of the bookcases.

'Be sure there was a reason,' he said over his shoulder.

'But what reason could it be?'

'When we know that, we shall know everything. This case is very curious and very interesting.'

There was something almost indescribable in the way he said those last words. I felt that he was looking at the case from some peculiar angle of his own, and what he saw I could not tell.

He went to the window and stood there, looking out.

'You say it was nine o'clock, Dr Sheppard, when you met this stranger outside the gate?'

He asked the question without turning round.

'Yes,' I replied. 'I heard the church clock chime the hour.'

'How long would it take him to reach the house – to reach this window, for instance?'

'Five minutes at the outside. Two or three minutes only if he took the path at the right of the drive and came straight here.'

'But to do that he would have to know the way. How can I explain myself? – it would mean that he had been here before – that he knew his surroundings.'

'That is true,' replied Colonel Melrose.

'We could find out, doubtless, if Mr Ackroyd had received any strangers during the past week?'

'Young Raymond could tell us that,' I said.

'Or Parker,' suggested Colonel Melrose.

'*Ou tous les deux,*' suggested Poirot, smiling.

Colonel Melrose went in search of Raymond, and I rang the bell once more for Parker.

Colonel Melrose returned almost immediately, accompanied by the young secretary, whom he introduced to Poirot. Geoffrey Raymond was fresh and debonair as ever. He seemed surprised and delighted to make Poirot's acquaintance.

'No idea you'd been living among us incognito, M. Poirot,' he said. 'It will be a great privilege to watch you at work – Hallo, what's this?'

Poirot had been standing just to the left of the door. Now he moved aside suddenly, and I saw that while my back was turned he must have swiftly drawn out the arm-chair till it stood in the position Parker had indicated.

'Want me to sit in the chair whilst you take a blood test?' asked Raymond good-humouredly. 'What's the idea?'

'M. Raymond, this chair was pulled out – so – last night when Mr Ackroyd was found killed. Someone moved it back again into place. Did you do so?'

The secretary's reply came without a second's hesitation.

'No, indeed I didn't. I don't even remember that it was in that position, but it must have been if you say so. Anyway, somebody else must have moved it back to its proper place. Have they destroyed a clue in doing so? Too bad!'

'It is of no consequence,' said the detective. 'Of no consequence whatever. What I really want to ask you is this, M. Raymond: Did any stranger come to see Mr Ackroyd during this past week?'

The secretary reflected for a minute or two, knitting his brows, and during the pause Parker appeared in answer to the bell.

'No,' said Raymond at last. 'I can't remember anyone. Can you, Parker?'

'I beg your pardon, sir?'

'Any stranger coming to see Mr Ackroyd this week?'

The butler reflected for a minute or two.

'There was the young man who came on Wednesday, sir,' he said at last. 'From Curtis and Troute, I understand he was.'

Raymond moved this aside with an impatient hand.

'Oh! yes, I remember, but that is not the kind of stranger this gentleman means.' He turned to Poirot. 'Mr Ackroyd had some idea of purchasing a dictaphone,' he explained. 'It would have enabled us to get through a lot more work in a limited time. The firm in question sent down their representative, but nothing came of it. Mr Ackroyd did not make up his mind to purchase.'

Poirot turned to the butler.

'Can you describe this young man to me, my good Parker?'

'He was fair-haired, sir, and short. Very neatly dressed in a blue serge suit. A very presentable young man, sir, for his station in life.'

Poirot turned to me.

'The man you met outside the gate, doctor, was tall, was he not?'

'Yes,' I said. 'Somewhere about six feet, I should say.'

'There is nothing in that, then,' declared the Belgian. 'I thank you, Parker.'

The butler spoke to Raymond.

'Mr Hammond has just arrived, sir,' he said. 'He is anxious

to know if he can be of any service, and he would be glad to have a word with you.'

'I'll come at once,' said the young man. He hurried out. Poirot looked inquiringly at the chief constable.

'The family solicitor, M. Poirot,' said the latter.

'It is a busy time for this young M. Raymond,' murmured M. Poirot. 'He has the air efficient, that one.'

'I believe Mr Ackroyd considered him a most able secretary.'

'He has been here – how long?'

'Just on two years, I fancy.'

'His duties he fulfils punctiliously. Of that I am sure. In what manner does he amuse himself? Does he go in for *le sport*?'

'Private secretaries haven't much time for that sort of thing,' said Colonel Melrose, smiling. 'Raymond plays golf, I believe. And tennis in the summer time.'

'He does not attend the courses – I should say the running of the horses?'

'Race meetings? No, I don't think he's interested in racing.'

Poirot nodded and seemed to lose interest. He glanced slowly round the study.

'I have seen, I think, all that there is to be seen here.'

I, too, looked round.

'If those walls could speak,' I murmured.

Poirot shook his head.

'A tongue is not enough,' he said. 'They would have to have also eyes and ears. But do not be too sure that these dead things' – he touched the top of the bookcase as he spoke – 'are always dumb. To me they speak sometimes – chairs, tables – they have their message!'

He turned away towards the door.

'What message?' I cried. 'What have they said to you today?'

He looked over his shoulder and raised one eyebrow quizzically.

'An opened window,' he said. 'A locked door. A chair that apparently moved itself. To all three I say "Why?" and I find no answer.'

He shook his head, puffed out his chest, and stood blinking

at us. He looked ridiculously full of his own importance. It crossed my mind to wonder whether he was really any good as a detective. Had his big reputation been built up on a series of lucky chances?

I think the same thought must have occurred to Colonel Melrose, for he frowned.

'Anything more you want to see, M. Poirot?' he inquired brusquely.

'You would perhaps be so kind as to show me the silver table from which the weapon was taken? After that, I will trespass on your kindness no longer.'

We went to the drawing-room, but on the way the constable waylaid the colonel, and after a muttered conversation the latter excused himself and left us together. I showed Poirot the silver table, and after raising the lid once or twice and letting it fall, he pushed open the window and stepped out on the terrace. I followed him.

Inspector Raglan had just turned the corner of the house, and was coming towards us. His face looked grim and satisfied.

'So there you are, M. Poirot,' he said. 'Well, this isn't going to be much of a case. I'm sorry, too. A nice enough young fellow gone wrong.'

Poirot's face fell, and he spoke very mildly.

'I'm afraid I shall not be able to be of much aid to you, then?'

'Next time, perhaps,' said the inspector soothingly. 'Though we don't have murders every day in this quiet little corner of the world.'

Poirot's gaze took on an admiring quality.

'You have been of a marvellous promptness,' he observed. 'How exactly did you go to work, if I may ask?'

'Certainly,' said the inspector. 'To begin with – method. That's what I always say – method!'

'Ah!' cried the other. 'That, too, is my watchword. Method, order, and the little grey cells.'

'The cells?' said the inspector, staring.

'The little grey cells of the brain,' explained the Belgian.

'Oh, of course; well, we all use them, I suppose.'

'In a greater or lesser degree,' murmured Poirot. 'And there are, too, differences in quality. Then there is the psychology of a crime. One must study that.'

'Ah!' said the inspector, 'you've been bitten with all this psycho-analysis stuff? Now, I'm a plain man –'

'Mrs Raglan would not agree, I am sure, to that,' said Poirot, making him a little bow.

Inspector Raglan, a little taken aback, bowed.

'You don't understand,' he said, grinning broadly. 'Lord, what a lot of difference language makes. I'm telling you how I set to work. First of all, method. Mr Ackroyd was last seen alive at a quarter to ten by his niece, Miss Flora Ackroyd. That's fact number one, isn't it?'

'If you say so.'

'Well, it is. At half-past ten, the doctor here says that Mr Ackroyd had been dead at least half an hour. You stick to that, doctor?'

'Certainly,' I said. 'Half an hour or longer.'

'Very good. That gives us exactly a quarter of an hour in which the crime must have been committed. I make a list of everyone in the house, and work through it, setting down opposite their names where they were and what they were doing between the hour of 9.45 and 10 p.m.'

He handed a sheet of paper to Poirot. I read it over his shoulder. It ran as follows, written in a neat script:

Major Blunt. – In billiard room with Mr Raymond. (Latter confirms.)

Mr Raymond. – Billiard room. (See above.)

Mrs Ackroyd. – 9.45 watching billiard match. Went up to bed 9.55. (Raymond and Blunt watched her up staircase.)

Miss Ackroyd. – Went straight from her uncle's room upstairs. (Confirmed by Parker, also housemaid, Elsie Dale.)

Servants:

Parker. – Went straight to butler's pantry. (Confirmed by housekeeper, Miss Russell, who came down to speak to him about something at 9.47, and remained at least ten minutes.)

> *Miss Russell. – As above. Spoke to housemaid, Elsie Dale, upstairs at 9.45.*
>
> *Ursula Bourne (parlourmaid). – In her own room until 9.55. Then in Servants' Hall.*
>
> *Mrs Cooper (cook). – In Servants' Hall.*
>
> *Gladys Jones (second housemaid). – In Servants' Hall.*
>
> *Elsie Dale. – Upstairs in bedroom. Seen there by Miss Russell and Miss Flora Ackroyd.*
>
> *Mary Thripp (kitchenmaid). – Servants' Hall.*

'The cook has been here seven years, the parlourmaid eighteen months, and Parker just over a year. The others are new. Except for something fishy about Parker, they all seem quite all right.'

'A very complete list,' said Poirot, handing it back to him. 'I am quite sure that Parker did not do the murder,' he added gravely.

'So is my sister,' I struck in. 'And she's usually right.' Nobody paid any attention to my interpolation.

'That disposes pretty effectually of the household,' continued the inspector. 'Now we come to a very grave point. The woman at the lodge – Mary Black – was pulling the curtains last night when she saw Ralph Paton turn in at the gate and go up towards the house.'

'She is sure of that?' I asked sharply.

'Quite sure. She knows him well by sight. He went past very quickly and turned off by the path to the right, which is a short cut to the terrace.'

'And what time was that?' asked Poirot, who had sat with an immovable face.

'Exactly twenty-five minutes past nine,' said the inspector gravely.

There was a silence. Then the inspector spoke again.

'It's all clear enough. It fits in without a flaw. At twenty-five minutes past nine, Captain Paton is seen passing the lodge; at nine-thirty or thereabouts, Mr Geoffrey Raymond hears someone in here asking for money and Mr Ackroyd refusing. What happens next? Captain Paton leaves the same way – through the window. He walks along the terrace, angry and baffled. He comes to the open drawing-room window. Say it's now a quarter to ten. Miss Flora Ackroyd is saying goodnight to her uncle. Major Blunt, Mr Raymond, and Mrs Ackroyd are in the billiard room. The drawing-room is empty. He steals in, takes the dagger from the silver table, and returns to the study window. He slips off his shoes, climbs in, and – well, I don't need to go into details. Then he slips out again and goes off. Hadn't the nerve to go back to the inn. He makes for the station, rings up from there –'

'Why?' said Poirot softly.

I jumped at the interruption. The little man was leaning forward. His eyes shone with a queer green light.

For a moment Inspector Raglan was taken aback by the question.

'It's difficult to say exactly why he did that,' he said at last. 'But murderers do funny things. You'd know that if you were in the police force. The cleverest of them make stupid mistakes sometimes. But come along and I'll show you those footprints.'

We followed him round the corner of the terrace to the study window. At a word from Raglan a police constable produced the shoes which had been obtained from the local inn.

The inspector laid them over the marks.

'They're the same,' he said confidently. 'That is to say, they're not the same pair that actually made these prints. He went away in those. This is a pair just like them, but older – see how the studs are worn down?'

'Surely a great many people wear shoes with rubber studs in them?' asked Poirot.

'That's so, of course,' said the inspector. 'I shouldn't put so much stress on the footmarks if it wasn't for everything else.'

'A very foolish young man, Captain Ralph Paton,' said Poirot thoughtfully. 'To leave so much evidence of his presence.'

'Ah! well,' said the inspector, 'it was a dry, fine night, you know. He left no prints on the terrace or on the gravelled path. But, unluckily for him, a spring must have welled up just lately at the end of the path from the drive. See here.'

A small gravelled path joined the terrace a few feet away. In one spot, a few yards from its termination, the ground was wet and boggy. Crossing this wet place there were again the marks of footsteps, and amongst them the shoes with rubber studs.

Poirot followed the path on a little way, the inspector by his side.

'You noticed the women's footprints?' he said suddenly.

The inspector laughed.

'Naturally. But several different women have walked this way – and men as well. It's a regular short cut to the house, you see. It would be impossible to sort out all the footsteps. After all, it's the ones on the window-sill that are really important.'

Poirot nodded.

'It's no good going farther,' said the inspector, as we came in view of the drive. 'It's all gravelled again here, and hard as it can be.'

Again Poirot nodded, but his eyes were fixed on a small garden house – a kind of superior summer-house. It was a little to the left of the path ahead of us, and a gravelled walk ran up to it.

Poirot lingered about until the inspector had gone back towards the house. Then he looked at me.

'You must have indeed been sent from the good God to replace my friend Hastings,' he said, with a twinkle. 'I observe that you do not quit my side. How say you, Dr Sheppard, shall we investigate that summer-house? It interests me.'

He went up to the door and opened it. Inside, the place was almost dark. There were one or two rustic seats, a croquet set, and some folded deck-chairs.

I was startled to observe my new friend. He had dropped to his hands and knees and was crawling about the floor. Every now and then he shook his head as though not satisfied. Finally, he sat back on his heels.

'Nothing,' he murmured. 'Well, perhaps it was not to be expected. But it would have meant so much –'

He broke off, stiffening all over. Then he stretched out his hand to one of the rustic chairs. He detached something from one side of it.

'What is it?' I cried. 'What have you found?'

He smiled, unclosing his hand so that I should see what lay in the palm of it. A scrap of stiff white cambric.

I took it from him, looked at it curiously, and then handed it back.

'What do you make of it, eh, my friend?' he asked, eyeing me keenly.

'A scrap torn from a handkerchief,' I suggested, shrugging my shoulders.

He made another dart and picked up a small quill – a goose quill by the look of it.

'And that?' he cried triumphantly. 'What do you make of that?'

I only stared.

He slipped the quill into his pocket, and looked again at the scrap of white stuff.

'A fragment of a handkerchief?' he mused. 'Perhaps you are right. But remember this – *a good laundry does not starch a handkerchief.*'

He nodded at me triumphantly, then he put away the scrap carefully in his pocket-book.

CHAPTER IX

The Goldfish Pond

We walked back to the house together. There was no sign of the inspector. Poirot paused on the terrace and stood with his back to the house, slowly turning his head from side to side.

'*Une belle propriété*,' he said at last appreciatively. 'Who inherits it?'

His words gave me almost a shock. It is an odd thing, but until that moment the question of inheritance had never come into my head. Poirot watched me keenly.

'It is a new idea to you, that,' he said at last. 'You had not thought of it before – eh?'

'No,' I said truthfully. 'I wish I had.'

He looked at me again curiously.

'I wonder just what you mean by that,' he said thoughtfully. 'Oh! no,' as I was about to speak. '*Inutile!* You would not tell me your real thought.'

'Everyone has something to hide,' I quoted, smiling.

'Exactly.'

'You still believe that?'

'More than ever, my friend. But it is not easy to hide things from Hercule Poirot. He has a knack of finding out.'

He descended the steps of the Dutch garden as he spoke.

'Let us walk a little,' he said over his shoulder. 'The air is pleasant today.'

I followed him. He led me down a path to the left enclosed in yew hedges. A walk led down the middle, bordered each side with formal flower beds, and at the end was a round paved recess with a seat and a pond of goldfish. Instead of pursuing the path to the end, Poirot took another which wound up the side of a wooded slope. In one spot the trees had been cleared away, and a seat had been put. Sitting there one had a splendid view over the countryside, and one looked right down on the paved recess and the goldfish pond.

'England is very beautiful,' said Poirot, his eyes straying over the prospect. Then he smiled. 'And so are English girls,' he said in a lower voice. 'Hush, my friend, and look at the pretty picture below us.'

It was then that I saw Flora. She was moving along the path we had just left and she was humming a little snatch of song. Her step was more dancing than walking, and, in spite of her black dress, there was nothing but joy in her whole attitude. She gave a sudden pirouette on her toes, and her black draperies swung out. At the same time she flung her head back and laughed outright.

As she did so a man stepped out from the trees. It was Hector Blunt.

The girl started. Her expression changed a little.

'How you startled me – I didn't see you.'

Blunt said nothing, but stood looking at her for a minute or two in silence.

'What I like about you,' said Flora, with a touch of malice, 'is your cheery conversation.'

I fancy that at that Blunt reddened under his tan. His voice, when he spoke, sounded different – it had a curious sort of humility in it.

'Never was much of a fellow for talking. Not even when I was young.'

'That was a very long time ago, I suppose,' said Flora gravely.

I caught the undercurrent of laughter in her voice, but I don't think Blunt did.

'Yes,' he said simply, 'it was.'

'How does it feel to be Methuselah?' asked Flora.

This time the laughter was more apparent, but Blunt was following out an idea of his own.

'Remember the johnny who sold his soul to the devil? In return for being made young again? There's an opera about it.'

'Faust, you mean?'

'That's the beggar. Rum story. Some of us would do it if we could.'

'Anyone would think you were creaking at the joints to hear you talk,' cried Flora, half vexed, half amused.

Blunt said nothing for a minute or two. Then he looked away from Flora into the middle distance and observed to an adjacent tree trunk that it was about time he got back to Africa.

'Are you going on another expedition – shooting things?'

'Expect so. Usually do, you know – shoot things, I mean.'

'You shot that head in the hall, didn't you?'

Blunt nodded. Then he jerked out, going rather red as he did so:

'Care for some decent skins any time? If so, I could get 'em for you.'

'Oh! please do,' cried Flora. 'Will you really? You won't forget?'

'I shan't forget,' said Hector Blunt.

He added, in a sudden burst of communicativeness:

'Time I went. I'm no good in this sort of life. Haven't got the manners for it. I'm a rough fellow, no use in society. Never remember the things one's expected to say. Yes, time I went.'

'But you're not going at once,' cried Flora. 'No – not while we're in all this trouble. Oh! please. If you go –'

She turned away a little.

'You want me to stay?' asked Blunt.

He spoke deliberately but quite simply.

'We all –'

'I meant you personally,' said Blunt, with directness.

Flora turned slowly back again and met his eyes.

'I want you to stay,' she said, 'if – if that makes any difference.'

'It makes all the difference,' said Blunt.

There was a moment's silence. They sat down on the stone seat by the goldfish pond. It seemed as though neither of them knew quite what to say next.

'It – it's such a lovely morning,' said Flora at last. 'You know,

I can't help feeling happy, in spite – in spite of everything. That's awful, I suppose?'

'Quite natural,' said Blunt. 'Never saw your uncle until two years ago, did you? Can't be expected to grieve very much. Much better to have no humbug about it.'

'There's something awfully consoling about you,' said Flora. 'You make things so simple.'

'Things are simple as a rule,' said the big-game hunter.

'Not always,' said Flora.

Her voice had lowered itself, and I saw Blunt turn and look at her, bringing his eyes back from (apparently) the coast of Africa to do so. He evidently put his own construction on her change of tone, for he said, after a minute or two, in rather an abrupt manner:

'I say, you know, you mustn't worry. About that young chap, I mean. Inspector's an ass. Everybody knows – utterly absurd to think he could have done it. Man from outside. Burglar chap. That's the only possible solution.'

Flora turned to look at him.

'You really think so?'

'Don't you?' said Blunt quickly.

'I – oh, yes, of course.'

Another silence, and then Flora burst out:

'I'm – I'll tell you why I felt so happy this morning. However heartless you think me, I'd rather tell you. It's because the lawyer has been – Mr Hammond. He told us about the will. Uncle Roger has left me twenty thousand pounds. Think of it – twenty thousand beautiful pounds.'

Blunt looked surprised.

'Does it mean so much to you?'

'Mean much to me? Why, it's everything. Freedom – life – no more scheming and scraping and lying –'

'Lying?' said Blunt, sharply interrupting.

Flora seemed taken aback for a minute.

'You know what I mean,' she said uncertainly. 'Pretending to be thankful for all the nasty cast-off things rich relations give you. Last year's coat and skirts and hats.'

'Don't know much about ladies' clothes; should have said you were always very well turned out.'

'It cost me something, though,' said Flora in a low voice. 'Don't let's talk of horrid things. I'm so happy. I'm free. Free to do what I like. Free not to –'

She stopped suddenly.

'Not to what?' asked Blunt quickly.

'I forget now. Nothing important.'

Blunt had a stick in his hand, and he thrust it into the pond, poking at something.

'What are you doing, Major Blunt?'

'There's something bright down there. Wondered what it was – looks like a gold brooch. Now I've stirred up the mud and it's gone.'

'Perhaps it's a crown,' suggested Flora. 'Like the one Mélisande saw in the water.'

'Mélisande,' said Blunt reflectively – 'she's in an opera, isn't she?'

'Yes, you seem to know a lot about operas.'

'People take me sometimes,' said Blunt sadly. 'Funny idea of pleasure – worse racket than the natives make with their tom-toms.'

Flora laughed.

'I remember Mélisande,' continued Blunt, 'married an old chap old enough to be her father.'

He threw a small piece of flint into the goldfish pond. Then, with a change of manner, he turned to Flora.

'Miss Ackroyd, can I do anything? About Paton, I mean. I know how dreadfully anxious you must be.'

'Thank you,' said Flora in a cold voice. 'There is really nothing to be done. Ralph will be all right. I've got hold of the most wonderful detective in the world, and he's going to find out all about it.'

For some time I had felt uneasy as to our position. We were not exactly eavesdropping, since the two in the garden below had only to lift their heads to see us. Nevertheless, I should have drawn attention to our presence before now, had not my companion put a warning pressure on my arm. Clearly he wished me to remain silent. Now, however, he acted briskly.

He rose quickly to his feet, clearing his throat.

'I demand pardon,' he cried. 'I cannot allow mademoiselle thus extravagantly to compliment me, and not draw attention to my presence. They say the listener hears no good of himself, but that is not the case this time. To spare my blushes, I must join you and apologize.'

He hurried down the path with me close behind him, and joined the others by the pond.

'This is M. Hercule Poirot,' said Flora. 'I expect you've heard of him.'

Poirot bowed.

'I know Major Blunt by reputation,' he said politely. 'I am glad to have encountered you, monsieur. I am in need of some information that you can give me.'

Blunt looked at him inquiringly.

'When did you last see M. Ackroyd alive?'

'At dinner.'

'And you neither saw nor heard anything of him after that?'

'Didn't see him. Heard his voice.'

'How was that?'

'I strolled out on the terrace –'

'Pardon me, what time was that?'

'About half-past nine. I was walking up and down smoking in front of the drawing-room window. I heard Ackroyd talking in his study –'

Poirot stopped and removed a microscopic weed.

'Surely you couldn't hear voices in the study from that part of the terrace,' he murmured.

He was not looking at Blunt, but I was, and to my intense surprise, I saw the latter flush.

'Went as far as the corner,' he explained unwillingly.

'Ah! indeed?' said Poirot.

In the mildest manner he conveyed an impression that more was wanted.

'Thought I saw – a woman disappearing into the bushes. Just

a gleam of white, you know. Must have been mistaken. It was while I was standing at the corner of the terrace that I heard Ackroyd's voice speaking to that secretary of his.'

'Speaking to Mr Geoffrey Raymond?'

'Yes – that's what I supposed at the time. Seems I was wrong.'

'Mr Ackroyd didn't address him by name?'

'Oh, no.'

'Then, if I may ask, why did you think –?'

Blunt explained laboriously.

'Took it for granted that it *would* be Raymond, because he had said just before I came out that he was taking some papers to Ackroyd. Never thought of it being anybody else.'

'Can you remember what the words you heard were?'

'Afraid I can't. Something quite ordinary and unimportant. Only caught a scrap of it. I was thinking of something else at the time.'

'It is of no importance,' murmured Poirot. 'Did you move a chair back against the wall when you went into the study after the body was discovered?'

'Chair? No, why should I?'

Poirot shrugged his shoulders but did not answer. He turned to Flora.

'There is one thing I should like to know from you, mademoiselle. When you were examining the things in the silver table with Dr Sheppard, was the dagger in its place, or was it not?'

Flora's chin shot up.

'Inspector Raglan has been asking me that,' she said resentfully. 'I've told him, and I'll tell you. I'm perfectly certain the dagger was *not* there. He thinks it was and that Ralph sneaked it later in the evening. And – and he doesn't believe me. He thinks I'm saying it so – to shield Ralph.'

'And aren't you?' I asked gravely.

Flora stamped her foot.

'You, too, Dr Sheppard! Oh! it's too bad.'

Poirot tactfully made a diversion.

'It is true what I heard you say, Major Blunt. There is something that glitters in this pond. Let us see if I can reach it.'

He knelt down by the pond, baring his arm to the elbow, and lowered it in very slowly, so as not to disturb the bottom of the pond. But in spite of all his precautions the mud eddied and swirled, and he was forced to draw his arm out again empty-handed.

He gazed ruefully at the mud upon his arm. I offered him my handkerchief, which he accepted with fervent protestations of thanks. Blunt looked at his watch.

'Nearly lunch time,' he said. 'We'd better be getting back to the house.'

'You will lunch with us, M. Poirot?' asked Flora. 'I should like you to meet my mother. She is – very fond of Ralph.'

The little man bowed.

'I shall be delighted, mademoiselle.'

'And you will stay, too, won't you, Dr Sheppard?'

I hesitated.

'Oh, do!'

I wanted to, so I accepted the invitation without further ceremony.

We set out towards the house, Flora and Blunt walking ahead.

'What hair,' said Poirot to me in a low tone, nodding towards Flora. 'The real gold! They will make a pretty couple. She and the dark, handsome Captain Paton. Will they not?'

I looked at him inquiringly, but he began to fuss about a few microscopic drops of water on his coat sleeve. The man reminded me in some ways of a cat. His green eyes and his finicking habits.

'And all for nothing, too,' I said sympathetically. 'I wonder what it was in the pond?'

'Would you like to see?' asked Poirot.

I stared at him. He nodded.

'My good friend,' he said gently and reproachfully, 'Hercule Poirot does not run the risk of disarranging his costume without being sure of attaining his object. To do so would be ridiculous and absurd. I am never ridiculous.'

'But you brought your hand out empty,' I objected.

'There are times when it is necessary to have discretion. Do

you tell your patients everything – but everything, doctor? I
think not. Nor do you tell your excellent sister everything either,
is it not so? Before showing my empty hand, I dropped what it
contained into my other hand. You shall see what that was.'

He held out his left hand, palm open. On it lay a little circlet
of gold. A woman's wedding ring.

I took it from him.

'Look inside,' commanded Poirot.

I did so. Inside was an inscription in fine writing:

From R., March 13th.

I looked at Poirot, but he was busy inspecting his appearance
in a tiny pocket glass. He paid particular attention to his moustaches, and none at all to me. I saw that he did not intend to
be communicative.

CHAPTER X

The Parlourmaid

We found Mrs Ackroyd in the hall. With her was a small dried-up little man, with an aggressive chin and sharp grey eyes, and 'lawyer' written all over him.

'Mr Hammond is staying to lunch with us,' said Mrs Ackroyd. 'You know Major Blunt, Mr Hammond? And dear Dr Sheppard – also a close friend of poor Roger's. And, let me see –'

She paused, surveying Hercule Poirot in some perplexity.

'This is M. Poirot, Mother,' said Flora. 'I told you about him this morning.'

'Oh! yes,' said Mrs Ackroyd vaguely. 'Of course, my dear, of course. He is to find Ralph, is he not?'

'He is to find out who killed Uncle,' said Flora.

'Oh! my dear,' cried her mother. 'Please! My poor nerves. I am a wreck this morning, a positive wreck. Such a dreadful thing to happen. I can't help feeling that it must have been an accident of some kind. Roger was so fond of handling queer curios. His hand must have slipped, or something.'

This theory was received in polite silence. I saw Poirot edge up to the lawyer, and speak to him in a confidential undertone. They moved aside into the embrasure of the window. I joined them – then hesitated.

'Perhaps I'm intruding,' I said.

'Not at all,' cried Poirot heartily. 'You and I, M. le docteur, we investigate this affair side by side. Without you I should be lost. I desire a little information from the good Mr Hammond.'

'You are acting on behalf of Captain Ralph Paton, I understand,' said the lawyer cautiously.

Poirot shook his head.

'Not so. I am acting in the interests of justice. Miss Ackroyd has asked me to investigate the death of her uncle.'

Mr Hammond seemed slightly taken aback.

'I cannot seriously believe that Captain Paton can be concerned in this crime,' he said, 'however strong the circumstantial evidence against him may be. The mere fact that he was hard pressed for money – '

'Was he hard pressed for money?' interpolated Poirot quickly.

The lawyer shrugged his shoulders.

'It was a chronic condition with Ralph Paton,' he said drily. 'Money went through his hands like water. He was always applying to his stepfather.'

'Had he done so of late? During the last year, for instance?'

'I cannot say. Mr Ackroyd did not mention the fact to me.'

'I comprehend. Mr Hammond, I take it that you are acquainted with the provisions of Mr Ackroyd's will?'

'Certainly. That is my principal business here today.'

'Then, seeing that I am acting for Miss Ackroyd, you will not object to telling me the terms of that will?'

'They are quite simple. Shorn of legal phraseology, and after paying certain legacies and bequests – '

'Such as – ?' interrupted Poirot.

Mr Hammond seemed a little surprised.

'A thousand pounds to his housekeeper, Miss Russell; fifty pounds to the cook, Emma Cooper; five hundred pounds to his secretary, Mr Geoffrey Raymond. Then to various hospitals – '

Poirot held up his hand.

'Ah! the charitable bequests, they interest me not.'

'Quite so. The income on ten thousand pounds' worth of shares to be paid to Mrs Cecil Ackroyd during her lifetime. Miss Flora Ackroyd inherits twenty thousand pounds outright. The residue – including this property, and the shares in Ackroyd and Son – to his adopted son, Ralph Paton.'

'Mr Ackroyd possessed a large fortune?'

'A very large fortune. Captain Paton will be an exceedingly wealthy young man.'

There was a silence. Poirot and the lawyer looked at each other.

'Mr Hammond,' came Mrs Ackroyd's voice plaintively from the fireplace.

The lawyer answered the summons. Poirot took my arm and drew me right into the window.

'Regard the irises,' he remarked in a rather loud voice. 'Magnificent, are they not? A straight and pleasing effect.'

At the same time I felt the pressure of his hand on my arm, and he added in a low tone:

'Do you really wish to aid me? To take part in this investigation?'

'Yes, indeed,' I said eagerly. 'There's nothing I should like better. You don't know what a dull old fogey's life I lead. Never anything out of the ordinary.'

'Good, we will be colleagues then. In a minute or two I fancy Major Blunt will join us. He is not happy with the good mamma. Now there are some things I want to know – but I do not wish to seem to want to know them. You comprehend? So it will be your part to ask the questions.'

'What questions do you want me to ask?' I asked apprehensively.

'I want you to introduce the name of Mrs Ferrars.'

'Yes?'

'Speak of her in a natural fashion. Ask him if he was down here when her husband died. You understand the kind of thing I mean. And while he replies, watch his face without seeming to watch it. *C'est compris?*'

There was no time for more, for at that minute, as Poirot had prophesied, Blunt left the others in his abrupt fashion and came over to us.

I suggested strolling on the terrace, and he acquiesced. Poirot stayed behind.

I stopped to examine a late rose.

'How things change in the course of a day or two,' I observed. 'I was up here last Wednesday, I remember, walking up and down this same terrace. Ackroyd was with me – full of spirits.

And now – three days later – Ackroyd's dead, poor fellow. Mrs Ferrars dead – you knew her, didn't you? But of course you did.'

Blunt nodded his head.

'Had you seen her since you'd been down this time?'

'Went with Ackroyd to call. Last Tuesday, think it was. Fascinating woman – but something queer about her. Deep – one would never know what she was up to.'

I looked into his steady grey eyes. Nothing there surely. I went on:

'I suppose you'd met her before?'

'Last time I was here – she and her husband had just come here to live.' He paused a minute and then added: 'Rum thing, she had changed a lot between then and now.'

'How – changed?' I asked.

'Looked ten years older.'

'Were you down here when her husband died?' I asked, trying to make the question sound as casual as possible.

'No. From all I heard it would be good riddance. Uncharitable, perhaps, but the truth.'

I agreed.

'Ashley Ferrars was by no means a pattern husband,' I said cautiously.

'Blackguard, I thought,' said Blunt.

'No,' I said, 'only a man with more money than was good for him.'

'Oh! money! All the troubles in the world can be put down to money – or the lack of it.'

'Which has been your particular trouble?' I asked.

'Enough for what I want. I'm one of the lucky ones.'

'Indeed.'

'I'm not too flush just now, as a matter of fact. Came into a legacy a year ago, and like a fool let myself be persuaded into putting it into some wild-cat scheme.'

I sympathized, and narrated my own similar trouble.

Then the gong pealed out, and we all went in to lunch. Poirot drew me back a little.

'*Eh bien?*'

'He's all right,' I said. 'I'm sure of it.'

'Nothing – disturbing?'

'He had a legacy just a year ago,' I said. 'But why not? Why shouldn't he? I'll swear the man is perfectly square and above board.'

'Without doubt, without doubt,' said Poirot soothingly. 'Do not upset yourself.'

He spoke as though to a fractious child.

We all trooped into the dining-room. It seemed incredible that less than twenty-four hours had passed since I last sat at that table.

Afterwards, Mrs Ackroyd took me aside and sat down with me on a sofa.

'I can't help feeling a little hurt,' she murmured, producing a handkerchief of the kind obviously not meant to be cried into. 'Hurt, I mean, by Roger's lack of confidence in me. That twenty thousand pounds ought to have been left to *me* – not to Flora. A mother could be trusted to safeguard the interests of her child. A lack of trust, I call it.'

'You forget, Mrs Ackroyd,' I said, 'Flora was Ackroyd's own niece, a blood relation. It would have been different had you been his sister instead of his sister-in-law.'

'As poor Cecil's widow, I think my feelings ought to have been considered,' said the lady, touching her eyelashes gingerly with the handkerchief. 'But Roger was always most peculiar – not to say *mean* – about money matters. It has been a most difficult position for both Flora and myself. He did not even give the poor child an allowance. He would pay her bills, you know, and even that with a good deal of reluctance and asking what she wanted all those fallals for – so like a man – but – now I've forgotten what it was I was going to say! Oh, yes, not a penny we could call our own, you know. Flora resented it – yes, I must say she resented it – very strongly. Though devoted to her uncle, of course. But any girl would have resented it. Yes, I must say Roger had very strange ideas about money. He wouldn't even buy new face towels, though I told him the old ones were in holes. And then,' proceeded Mrs Ackroyd, with a sudden leap highly characteristic of her conversation, 'to leave all that money – a thousand pounds, fancy, a thousand pounds! – to that woman.'

'What woman?'

'That Russell woman. Something very queer about her, and so I've always said. But Roger wouldn't hear a word against her. Said she was a woman of great force of character, and that he admired and respected her. He was always going on about her rectitude and independence and moral worth. *I* think there's something fishy about her. She was certainly doing her best to marry Roger. But I soon put a stop to that. She always hated me. Naturally. *I* saw through her.'

I began to wonder if there was any chance of stemming Mrs Ackroyd's eloquence, and getting away.

Mr Hammond provided the necessary diversion by coming up to say goodbye. I seized my chance and rose also.

'About the inquest,' I said. 'Where would you prefer it to be held? Here, or at the Three Boars?'

Mrs Ackroyd stared at me with a dropped jaw.

'The inquest?' she asked, the picture of consternation. 'But surely there won't have to be an inquest?'

Mr Hammond gave a dry little cough and murmured, 'Inevitable. Under the circumstances,' in two short little barks.

'But surely Dr Sheppard can arrange –'

'There are limits to my powers of arrangement,' I said drily.

'If his death was an accident –'

'He was murdered, Mrs Ackroyd,' I said brutally.

She gave a little cry.

'No theory of accident will hold water for a minute.'

Mrs Ackroyd looked at me in distress. I had no patience with what I thought was her silly fear of unpleasantness.

'If there's an inquest, I – I shan't have to answer questions and all that, shall I?' she asked.

'I don't know what will be necessary,' I answered. 'I imagine Mr Raymond will take the brunt of it off you. He knows all the circumstances, and can give formal evidence of identification.'

The lawyer assented with a little bow.

'I really don't think there is anything to dread, Mrs Ackroyd,' he said. 'You will be spared all the unpleasantness. Now, as to the question of money, have you all you need for the present? I mean,' he added, as she looked at him inquiringly, 'ready money. Cash, you know. If not, I can arrange to let you have whatever you require.'

'That ought to be all right,' said Raymond, who was standing by. 'Mr Ackroyd cashed a cheque for a hundred pounds yesterday.'

'A hundred pounds?'

'Yes. For wages and other expenses due today. At the moment it is still intact.'

'Where is this money? In his desk?'

'No, he always kept his cash in his bedroom. In an old collar-box, to be accurate. Funny idea, wasn't it?'

'I think,' said the lawyer, 'we ought to make sure the money is there before I leave.'

'Certainly,' agreed the secretary. 'I'll take you up now ... Oh! I forgot. The door's locked.'

Inquiry from Parker elicited the information that Inspector Raglan was in the housekeeper's room asking a few supplementary questions. A few minutes later the inspector joined the party in the hall, bringing the key with him. He unlocked the door and we passed into the lobby and up the small staircase. At the top of the stairs the door into Ackroyd's bedroom stood open. Inside the room it was dark, the curtains were drawn, and the bed was turned down just as it had been last night. The inspector drew the curtains, letting in the sunlight, and Geoffrey Raymond went to the top drawer of a rosewood bureau.

'He kept his money like that, in an unlocked drawer. Just fancy,' commented the inspector.

The secretary flushed a little.

'Mr Ackroyd had perfect faith in the honesty of all the servants,' he said hotly.

'Oh! quite so,' said the inspector hastily.

Raymond opened the drawer, took out a round leather collar-box from the back of it, and opening it, drew out a thick wallet.

'Here is the money,' he said, taking out a fat roll of notes. 'You will find the hundred intact, I know, for Mr Ackroyd put it in the collar-box in my presence last night when he was dressing for dinner, and of course it has not been touched since.'

Mr Hammond took the roll from him and counted it. He looked up sharply.

'A hundred pounds, you said. But there is only sixty here.'

Raymond stared at him.

'Impossible,' he cried, springing forward. Taking the notes from the other's hand, he counted them aloud.

Mr Hammond had been right. The total amounted to sixty pounds.

'But – I can't understand it,' cried the secretary, bewildered.

Poirot asked a question.

'You saw Mr Ackroyd put this money away last night when he was dressing for dinner? You are sure he had not paid away any of it already?'

'I'm sure he hadn't. He even said, "I don't want to take a hundred pounds down to dinner with me. Too bulgy."'

'Then the affair is very simple,' remarked Poirot. 'Either he paid out that forty pounds some time last evening, or else it has been stolen.'

'That's the matter in a nutshell,' agreed the inspector. He turned to Mrs Ackroyd. 'Which of the servants would come in here yesterday evening?'

'I suppose the housemaid would turn down the bed.'

'Who is she? What do you know about her?'

'She's not been here very long,' said Mrs Ackroyd. 'But she's a nice ordinary country girl.'

'I think we ought to clear this matter up,' said the inspector. 'If Mr Ackroyd paid that money away himself, it may have a bearing on the mystery of the crime. The other servants all right, as far as you know?'

'Oh, I think so.'

'Not missed anything before?'

'No.'

'None of them leaving, or anything like that?'

'The parlourmaid is leaving.'

'When?'

'She gave notice yesterday, I believe.'

'To you?'

'Oh, no. *I* have nothing to do with servants. Miss Russell attends to the household matters.'

The inspector remained lost in thought for a minute or two. Then he nodded his head and remarked, 'I think I'd better have a word with Miss Russell, and I'll see the girl Dale as well.'

Poirot and I accompanied him to the housekeeper's room. Miss Russell received us with her usual sang-froid.

Elsie Dale had been at Fernly five months. A nice girl, quick at her duties, and most respectable. Good references. The last girl in the world to take anything not belonging to her.

What about the parlourmaid?

'She, too, was a most superior girl. Very quiet and ladylike. An excellent worker.'

'Then why is she leaving?' asked the inspector.

Miss Russell pursed up her lips.

'It was none of my doing. I understand Mr Ackroyd found fault with her yesterday afternoon. It was her duty to do the study, and she disarranged some of the papers on his desk, I believe. He was very annoyed about it, and she gave notice. At least, that is what I understand from her, but perhaps you'd like to see her yourselves?'

The inspector assented. I had already noticed the girl when she was waiting on us at lunch. A tall girl, with a lot of brown hair rolled tightly away at the back of her neck, and very steady grey eyes. She came in answer to the housekeeper's summons, and stood very straight with those same grey eyes fixed on us.

'You are Ursula Bourne?' asked the inspector.

'Yes, sir.'

'I understand you are leaving?'

'Yes, sir.'

'Why is that?'

'I disarranged some papers on Mr Ackroyd's desk. He was

very angry about it, and I said I had better leave. He told me to go as soon as possible.'

'Were you in Mr Ackroyd's bedroom at all last night? Tidying up or anything?'

'No, sir. That is Elsie's work. I never went near that part of the house.'

'I must tell you, my girl, that a large sum of money is missing from Mr Ackroyd's room.'

At last I saw her roused. A wave of colour swept over her face.

'I know nothing about any money. If you think I took it, and that that is why Mr Ackroyd dismissed me, you are wrong.'

'I'm not accusing you of taking it, my girl,' said the inspector. 'Don't flare up so.'

The girl looked at him coldly.

'You can search my things if you like,' she said disdainfully. 'But you won't find anything.'

Poirot suddenly interposed.

'It was yesterday afternoon that Mr Ackroyd dismissed you – or you dismissed yourself – was it not?' he asked.

The girl nodded.

'How long did the interview last?'

'The interview?'

'Yes, the interview between you and Mr Ackroyd in the study?'

'I – I don't know.'

'Twenty minutes? Half an hour?'

'Something like that.'

'Not longer?'

'Not longer than half an hour, certainly.'

'Thank you, mademoiselle.'

I looked curiously at him. He was rearranging a few objects on the table, setting them straight with precise fingers. His eyes were shining.

'That'll do,' said the inspector.

Ursula Bourne disappeared. The inspector turned to Miss Russell.

'How long has she been here? Have you got a copy of the reference you had with her?'

Without answering the first question, Miss Russell moved to an adjacent bureau, opened one of the drawers, and took out a handful of letters clipped together with a patent fastener. She selected one and handed it to the inspector.

'H'm,' said he. 'Reads all right. Mrs Richard Folliott, Marby Grange, Marby. Who's this woman?'

'Quite good country people,' said Miss Russell.

'Well,' said the inspector, handing it back, 'let's have a look at the other one, Elsie Dale.'

Elsie Dale was a big fair girl, with a pleasant but slightly stupid face. She answered our questions readily enough, and showed much distress and concern at the loss of the money.

'I don't think there's anything wrong with her,' observed the inspector, after he had dismissed her. 'What about Parker?'

Miss Russell pursed her lips together and made no reply.

'I've a feeling there's something wrong about that man,' the inspector continued thoughtfully. 'The trouble is that I don't quite see when he got his opportunity. He'd be busy with his duties immediately after dinner, and he'd got a pretty good alibi all through the evening. I know, for I've been devoting particular attention to it. Well, thank you very much, Miss Russell. We'll leave things as they are for the present. It's highly probable Mr Ackroyd paid that money away himself.'

The housekeeper bade us a dry good afternoon, and we took our leave.

I left the house with Poirot.

'I wonder,' I said, breaking the silence, 'what the papers the girl disarranged could have been for Ackroyd to have got into such a state about them? I wonder if there is any clue there to the mystery.'

'The secretary said there were no papers of particular importance on the desk,' said Poirot quietly.

'Yes, but –' I paused.

'It strikes you as odd that Ackroyd should have flown into a rage about so trivial a matter?'

'Yes, it does rather.'

'But was it a trivial matter?'

'Of course,' I admitted, 'we don't know what those papers may have been. But Raymond certainly said –'

'Leave M. Raymond out of it for a minute. What did you think of that girl?'

'Which girl? The parlourmaid?'

'Yes, the parlourmaid. Ursula Bourne.'

'She seemed a nice girl,' I said hesitatingly.

Poirot repeated my words, but whereas I had laid a slight stress on the fourth word, he put it on the second.

'She *seemed* a nice girl – yes.'

Then, after a minute's silence, he took something from his pocket and handed it to me.

'See, my friend, I will show you something. Look there.'

The paper he had handed me was that compiled by the inspector and given by him to Poirot that morning. Following the pointing finger, I saw a small cross marked in pencil opposite the name Ursula Bourne.

'You may not have noticed it at the time, my good friend, but there was one person on this list whose alibi had no kind of confirmation. Ursula Bourne.'

'You don't think –?'

'Dr Sheppard, I dare to think anything. Ursula Bourne may have killed Mr Ackroyd, but I confess I can see no motive for her doing so. Can you?'

He looked at me very hard – so hard that I felt uncomfortable.

'Can you?' he repeated.

'No motive whatsoever,' I said firmly.

His gaze relaxed. He frowned and murmured to himself:

'Since the blackmailer was a man, it follows that she cannot be the blackmailer, then –'

I coughed.

'As far as that goes –' I began doubtfully.

He spun round on me.

'What? What are you going to say?'

'Nothing, nothing. Only that, strictly speaking, Mrs Ferrars in her letter mentioned a *person* – she didn't actually specify a man. But we took it for granted, Ackroyd and I, that it *was* a man.'

Poirot did not seem to be listening to me. He was muttering to himself again.

'But then it is possible after all – yes, certainly it is possible – but then – ah! I must rearrange my ideas. Method, order, never have I needed them more. Everything must fit in – in its appointed place – otherwise I am on the wrong track.'

He broke off, and whirled round upon me again.

'Where is Marby?'

'It's on the other side of Cranchester.'

'How far away?'

'Oh! – fourteen miles, perhaps.'

'Would it be possible for you to go there? Tomorrow, say?'

'Tomorrow? Let me see, that's Sunday. Yes, I could arrange it. What do you want me to do there?'

'See this Mrs Folliott. Find out all you can about Ursula Bourne.'

'Very well. But – I don't much care for the job.'

'It is not the time to make difficulties. A man's life may hang on this.'

'Poor Ralph,' I said with a sigh. 'You believe him to be innocent, though?'

Poirot looked at me very gravely.

'Do you want to know the truth?'

'Of course.'

'Then you shall have it. My friend, everything points to the assumption that he is guilty.'

'What!' I exclaimed.

Poirot nodded.

'Yes, that stupid inspector – for he is stupid – has everything pointing his way. I seek for the truth – and the truth leads me every time to Ralph Paton. Motive, opportunity, means. But I will leave no stone unturned. I promised Mademoiselle Flora. And she was very sure, that little one. But very sure indeed.'

CHAPTER XI

Poirot Pays a Call

I was slightly nervous when I rang the bell at Marby Grange the following afternoon. I wondered very much what Poirot expected to find out. He had entrusted the job to me. Why? Was it because, as in the case of questioning Major Blunt, he wished to remain in the background? The wish, intelligible in the first case, seemed to me quite meaningless here.

My meditations were interrupted by the advent of a smart parlourmaid.

Yes, Mrs Folliott was at home. I was ushered into a big drawing-room, and looked round me curiously as I waited for the mistress of the house. A large bare room, some good bits of old china, and some beautiful etchings, shabby covers and curtains. A lady's room in every sense of the term.

I turned from the inspection of a Bartolozzi on the wall as Mrs Folliott came into the room. She was a tall woman, with untidy brown hair, and a very winning smile.

'Dr Sheppard,' she said hesitatingly.

'That is my name,' I replied. 'I must apologize for calling upon you like this, but I wanted some information about a parlourmaid previously employed by you, Ursula Bourne.'

With the utterance of the name the smile vanished from her face, and all the cordiality froze out of her manner. She looked uncomfortable and ill at ease.

'Ursula Bourne?' she said hesitatingly.

'Yes,' I said. 'Perhaps you don't remember the name?'

'Oh, yes, of course. I – I remember perfectly.'

'She left you just over a year ago, I understand?'

'Yes. Yes, she did. That is quite right.'

'And you were satisfied with her whilst she was with you? How long was she with you, by the way?'

'Oh! a year or two – I can't remember exactly how long. She – she is very capable. I'm sure you will find her quite satisfactory. I didn't know she was leaving Fernly. I hadn't the least idea of it.'

'Can you tell me anything about her?' I asked.

'Anything about her?'

'Yes, where she comes from, who her people are – that sort of thing?'

Mrs Folliott's face wore more than ever its frozen look.

'I don't know at all.'

'Who was she with before she came to you?'

'I'm afraid I don't remember.'

There was a spark of anger now underlying her nervousness. She flung up her head in a gesture that was vaguely familiar.

'Is it really necessary to ask all these questions?'

'Not at all,' I said, with an air of surprise and a tinge of apology in my manner. 'I had no idea you would mind answering them. I am very sorry.'

Her anger left her and she became confused again.

'Oh! I don't mind answering them. I assure you I don't. Why should I? It – it just seemed a little odd, you know. That's all. A little odd.'

One advantage of being a medical practitioner is that you can usually tell when people are lying to you. I should have known from Mrs Folliott's manner, if from nothing else, that she did mind answering my questions – minded intensely. She was thoroughly uncomfortable and upset, and there was plainly some mystery in the background. I judged her to be a woman quite unused to deception of any kind, and consequently rendered acutely uneasy when forced to practise it. A child could have seen through her.

But it was also clear that she had no intention of telling me anything further. Whatever the mystery centring round Ursula Bourne might be, I was not going to learn it through Mrs Folliott.

Defeated, I apologized once more for disturbing her, took my hat and departed.

I went to see a couple of patients and arrived home about six o'clock. Caroline was sitting beside the wreck of tea things. She had that look of suppressed exultation on her face which I know only too well. It is a sure sign with her of either the getting or the giving of information. I wondered which it had been.

'I've had a very interesting afternoon,' began Caroline, as I dropped into my own particular easy-chair and stretched out my feet to the inviting blaze in the fireplace.

'Have you?' I said. 'Miss Gannett drop in to tea?'

Mrs Gannett is one of the chief of our newsmongers.

'Guess again,' said Caroline, with intense complacency.

I guessed several times, working slowly through all the members of Caroline's Intelligence Corps. My sister received each guess with a triumphant shake of the head. In the end she volunteered the information herself.

'M. Poirot!' she said. 'Now, what do you think of that?'

I thought a good many things of it, but I was careful not to say them to Caroline.

'Why did he come?' I asked.

'To see me, of course. He said that, knowing my brother so well, he hoped he might be permitted to make the acquaintance of his charming sister – your charming sister, I've got mixed up – but you know what I mean.'

'What did he talk about?' I asked.

'He told me a lot about himself and his cases. You know that Prince Paul of Mauretania – the one who's just married a dancer?'

'Yes?'

'I saw the most intriguing paragraph about her in *Society Snippets* the other day, hinting that she was really a Russian Grand Duchess – one of the Czar's daughters who managed to escape from the Bolsheviks. Well, it seems that M. Poirot solved a baffling murder mystery that threatened to involve them both. Prince Paul was beside himself with gratitude.'

'Did he give him an emerald tie pin the size of a plover's egg?' I inquired sarcastically.

'He didn't mention it. Why?'

'Nothing,' I said. 'I thought it was always done. It is in detective fiction anyway. The super-detective always has his rooms littered with rubies and pearls and emeralds from grateful Royal clients.'

'It's very interesting to hear about these things from the inside,' said my sister complacently.

It would be – to Caroline. I could not but admire the ingenuity of M. Hercule Poirot, who had selected unerringly the case of all others that would most appeal to an elderly lady living in a small village.

'Did he tell you if the dancer was really a Grand Duchess?' I inquired.

'He was not at liberty to speak,' said Caroline importantly.

I wondered how far Poirot had strained the truth in talking to Caroline – probably not at all. He had conveyed his innuendoes by means of his eyebrows and his shoulders.

'And after all this,' I remarked, 'I suppose you were ready to eat out of his hand?'

'Don't be coarse, James. I don't know where you get these vulgar expressions from.'

'Probably from my only link with the outside world – my patients. Unfortunately, my practice does not lie amongst Royal princes and interesting Russian *émigrés*.'

Caroline pushed her spectacles up and looked at me.

'You seem very grumpy, James. It must be your liver. A blue pill, I think, tonight.'

To see me in my own home, you would never imagine that I was a doctor of medicine. Caroline does the home prescribing both for herself and me.

'Damn my liver,' I said irritably. 'Did you talk about the murder at all?'

'Well, naturally, James. What else is there to talk about locally? I was able to set M. Poirot straight upon several points. He was very grateful to me. He said I had the makings of a born detective in me – and a wonderful psychological insight into human nature.'

Caroline was exactly like a cat that is full to overflowing with rich cream. She was positively purring.

'He talked a lot about the little grey cells of the brain, and of their functions. His own, he says, are of the first quality.'

'He would say so,' I remarked bitterly. 'Modesty is certainly not his middle name.'

'I wish you wouldn't be so horribly American, James. He thought it very important that Ralph should be found as soon as possible, and induced to come forward and give an account of himself. He says that his disappearance will produce a very unfortunate impression at the inquest.'

'And what did you say to that?'

'I agreed with him,' said Caroline importantly. 'And I was able to tell him the way people were talking already about it.'

'Caroline,' I said sharply, 'did you tell M. Poirot what you overheard in the wood that day?'

'I did,' said Caroline complacently.

I got up and began to walk about.

'You realize what you're doing, I hope,' I jerked out. 'You're putting a halter round Ralph Paton's neck as surely as you're sitting in that chair.'

'Not at all,' said Caroline, quite unruffled. 'I was surprised *you* hadn't told him.'

'I took very good care not to,' I said. 'I'm fond of that boy.'

'So am I. That's why I say you're talking nonsense. I don't believe Ralph did it, and so the truth can't hurt him, and we ought to give M. Poirot all the help we can. Why, think, it's very likely Ralph was out with that identical girl on the night of the murder, and if so, he's got a perfect alibi.'

'If he's got a perfect alibi,' I retorted, 'why doesn't he come forward and say so?'

'Might get the girl into trouble,' said Caroline sapiently. 'But if M. Poirot gets hold of her, and puts it to her as her duty, she'll come forward of her own accord and clear Ralph.'

'You seem to have invented a romantic fairy story of your own,' I said. 'You read too many trashy novels, Caroline. I've always told you so.'

I dropped into my chair again.

'Did Poirot ask you any more questions?' I inquired.

'Only about the patients you had that morning.'

'The patients?' I demanded, unbelievingly.

'Yes, your surgery patients. How many and who they were.'

'Do you mean to say you were able to tell him that?' I demanded.

Caroline is really amazing.

'Why not?' asked my sister triumphantly. 'I can see the path up to the surgery door perfectly from this window. And I've got an excellent memory, James. Much better than yours, let me tell you.'

'I'm sure you have,' I murmured mechanically.

My sister went on, checking the names on her fingers.

'There was old Mrs Bennett, and that boy from the farm with the bad finger, Dolly Grice to have a needle out of her finger; that American steward off the liner. Let me see – that's four. Yes, and old George Evans with his ulcer. And lastly –'

She paused significantly.

'Well?'

Caroline brought out her climax triumphantly. She hissed it in the most approved style – aided by the fortunate number of 's's at her disposal.

'*Miss Russell!*'

She sat back in her chair and looked at me meaningly, and when Caroline looks at you meaningly, it is impossible to miss it.

'I don't know what you mean,' I said, quite untruthfully. 'Why shouldn't Miss Russell consult me about her bad knee?'

'Bad knee,' said Caroline. 'Fiddlesticks! No more bad knee than you and I. She was after something else.'

'What?' I asked.

Caroline had to admit that she didn't know.

'But depend upon it, that was what he was trying to get at –

M. Poirot, I mean. There's something fishy about that woman, and he knows it.'

'Precisely the remark Mrs Ackroyd made to me yesterday,' I said. 'That there was something fishy about Miss Russell.'

'Ah!' said Caroline darkly, 'Mrs Ackroyd! There's another!'

'Another what?'

Caroline refused to explain her remarks. She merely nodded her head several times, rolling up her knitting, and went upstairs to don the high mauve silk blouse and the gold locket which she calls dressing for dinner.

I stayed there staring into the fire and thinking over Caroline's words. Had Poirot really come to gain information about Miss Russell, or was it only Caroline's tortuous mind that interpreted everything according to her own ideas?

There had certainly been nothing in Miss Russell's manner that morning to arouse suspicion. At least –

I remembered her persistent conversation on the subject of drug-taking – and from that she had led the conversation to poisons and poisoning. But there was nothing in that. Ackroyd had not been poisoned. Still, it was odd . . .

I heard Caroline's voice, rather acid in tone, calling from the top of the stairs.

'James, you will be late for dinner.'

I put some coal on the fire and went upstairs obediently.

It is well at any price to have peace in the home.

CHAPTER XII

Round the Table

A joint inquest was held on Monday.

I do not propose to give the proceedings in detail. To do so would only be to go over the same ground again and again. By arrangement with the police, very little was allowed to come out. I gave evidence as to the cause of Ackroyd's death and the probable time. The absence of Ralph Paton was commented on by the coroner, but not unduly stressed.

Afterwards, Poirot and I had a few words with Inspector Raglan. The inspector was very grave.

'It looks bad, M. Poirot,' he said. 'I'm trying to judge the thing fair and square. I'm a local man, and I've seen Captain Paton many times in Cranchester. I'm not wanting him to be the guilty one – but it's bad whichever way you look at it. If he's innocent, why doesn't he come forward? We've got evidence against him, but it's just possible that the evidence could be explained away. Then why doesn't he give an explanation?'

A lot more lay behind the inspector's words than I knew at the time. Ralph's description had been wired to every port and railway station in England. The police everywhere were on the alert. His rooms in town were watched, and any houses he had been known to be in the habit of frequenting. With such a cordon it seemed impossible that Ralph should be able to evade detection. He had no luggage, and, as far as anyone knew, no money.

'I can't find anyone who saw him at the station that night,' continued the inspector. 'And yet he's well known down here, and you'd think somebody would have noticed him. There's no news from Liverpool either.'

'You think he went to Liverpool?' queried Poirot.

'Well, it's on the cards. That telephone message from the station, just three minutes before the Liverpool express left – there ought to be something in that.'

'Unless it was deliberately intended to throw you off the scent. That might just possibly be the point of the telephone message.'

'That's an idea,' said the inspector eagerly. 'Do you really think that's the explanation of the telephone call?'

'My friend,' said Poirot gravely, 'I do not know. But I will tell you this: I believe that when we find the explanation of that telephone call we shall find the explanation of the murder.'

'You said something like that before, I remember,' I observed, looking at him curiously.

Poirot nodded.

'I always come back to it,' he said seriously.

'It seems to me utterly irrelevant,' I declared.

'I wouldn't say that,' demurred the inspector. 'But I must confess I think Mr Poirot here harps on it a little too much. We've better clues than that. The fingerprints on the dagger, for instance.'

Poirot became suddenly very foreign in manner, as he often did when excited over anything.

'M. l'Inspecteur,' he said, 'beware of the blind – the blind – *comment dire?* – the little street that has no end to it.'

Inspector Raglan stared, but I was quicker.

'You mean a blind alley?' I said.

'That is it – the blind street that leads nowhere. So it may be with those fingerprints – they may lead you nowhere.'

'I don't see how that can well be,' said the police officer. 'I suppose you're hinting that they're faked? I've read of such things being done, though I can't say I've ever come across it in my experience. But fake or true – they're bound to lead *somewhere.*'

Poirot merely shrugged his shoulders, flinging out his arms wide.

The inspector then showed us various enlarged photographs of the fingerprints, and proceeded to become technical on the subject of loops and whorls.

'Come now,' he said at last, annoyed by Poirot's detached manner, 'you've got to admit that those prints were made by someone who was in the house that night?'

'*Bien entendu*,' said Poirot, nodding his head.

'Well, I've taken the prints of every member of the household, everyone, mind you, from the old lady down to the kitchenmaid.'

I don't think Mrs Ackroyd would enjoy being referred to as the old lady. She must spend a considerable amount on cosmetics.

'Everyone's,' repeated the inspector fussily.

'Including mine,' I said drily.

'Very well. None of them correspond. That leaves us two alternatives. Ralph Paton, or the mysterious stranger the doctor here tells us about. When we get hold of those two –'

'Much valuable time may have been lost,' broke in Poirot.

'I don't quite get you, Mr Poirot.'

'You have taken the prints of everyone in the house, you say,' murmured Poirot. 'Is that the exact truth you are telling me there, M. l'Inspecteur?'

'Certainly.'

'Without overlooking anyone?'

'Without overlooking anyone.'

'The quick or the dead?'

For a moment the inspector looked bewildered at what he took to be a religious observation. Then he reacted slowly.

'You mean –?'

'The dead, M. l'Inspecteur.'

The inspector still took a minute or two to understand.

'I am suggesting,' said Poirot placidly, 'that the fingerprints on the dagger handle are those of Mr Ackroyd himself. It is an easy matter to verify. His body is still available.'

'But why? What would be the point of it? You're surely not suggesting suicide, Mr Poirot?'

'Ah! no. My theory is that the murderer wore gloves or wrapped something round his hand. After the blow was struck, he picked up the victim's hand and closed it round the dagger handle.'

'But why?'

Poirot shrugged his shoulders again.

'To make a confusing case even more confusing.'

'Well,' said the inspector. 'I'll look into it. What gave you the idea in the first place?'

'When you were so kind as to show me the dagger and draw attention to the fingerprints. I know very little of loops and whorls – see, I confess my ignorance frankly. But it did occur to me that the position of the prints was somewhat awkward. Not so would I have held a dagger in order to strike. Naturally, with the right hand brought up over the shoulder backwards, it would have been difficult to put it in exactly the right position.'

Inspector Raglan stared at the little man. Poirot, with an air of great unconcern, flecked a speck of dust from his coat sleeve.

'Well,' said the inspector. 'It's an idea. I'll look into it all right, but don't you be disappointed if nothing comes of it.'

He endeavoured to make his tone kindly and patronizing. Poirot watched him go off. Then he turned to me with twinkling eyes.

'Another time,' he observed, 'I must be more careful of his *amour propre*. And now that we are left to our own devices, what do you think, my good friend, of a little reunion of the family?'

The 'little reunion,' as Poirot called it, took place about half an hour later. We sat round the table in the dining-room at Fernly, Poirot at the head of the table, like the chairman of some ghastly board meeting. The servants were not present, so we were six in all. Mrs Ackroyd, Flora, Major Blunt, young Raymond, Poirot, and myself.

When everyone was assembled, Poirot rose and bowed.

'Messieurs, mesdames, I have called you together for a certain purpose.' He paused. 'To begin with, I want to make a very special plea to mademoiselle.'

'To me?' said Flora.

'Mademoiselle, you are engaged to Captain Ralph Paton. If anyone is in his confidence, you are. I beg you, most earnestly, if you know of his whereabouts, to persuade him to come forward. One little minute' – as Flora raised her head to speak – 'say nothing till you have well reflected. Mademoiselle, his position grows daily more dangerous. If he had come forward at once, no matter how damning the facts, he might have had a chance of explaining them away. But this silence – this flight – what can it mean? Surely only one thing, knowledge of guilt. Mademoiselle, if you really believe in his innocence, persuade him to come forward before it is too late.'

Flora's face had gone very white.

'Too late!' she repeated, very low.

Poirot leant forward, looking at her.

'See now, mademoiselle,' he said very gently, 'it is Papa Poirot who asks you this. The old Papa Poirot who has much knowledge and much experience. I would not seek to entrap you, mademoiselle. Will you not trust me – and tell me where Ralph Paton is hiding?'

The girl rose and stood facing him.

'M. Poirot,' she said in a clear voice, 'I swear to you – swear solemnly – that I have no idea where Ralph is, and that I have neither seen him nor heard from him either on the day of – of the murder, or since.'

She sat down again. Poirot gazed at her in silence for a minute or two, then he brought his hand down on the table with a sharp rap.

'*Bien!* That is that,' he said. His face hardened. 'Now I appeal to these others who sit round this table, Mrs Ackroyd, Major Blunt, Dr Sheppard, Mr Raymond. You are all friends and intimates of the missing man. If you know where Ralph Paton is hiding, speak out.'

There was a long silence. Poirot looked to each in turn.

'I beg of you,' he said in a low voice, 'speak out.'

But still there was silence, broken at last by Mrs Ackroyd.

'I must say,' she observed in a plaintive voice, 'that Ralph's absence is most peculiar – most peculiar indeed. Not to come forward at such a time. It looks, you know, as though there were something *behind* it. I can't help thinking, Flora dear, that it was a very fortunate thing your engagement was never formally announced.'

'Mother!' cried Flora angrily.

'Providence,' declared Mrs Ackroyd. 'I have a devout belief in Providence – a divinity that shapes our ends, as Shakespeare's beautiful line runs.'

'Surely you don't make the Almighty directly responsible for thick ankles, Mrs Ackroyd, do you?' asked Geoffrey Raymond, his irresponsible laugh ringing out.

His idea was, I think, to loosen the tension, but Mrs Ackroyd threw him a glance of reproach and took out her handkerchief.

'Flora has been saved a terrible amount of notoriety and unpleasantness. Not for a moment that I think dear Ralph had anything to do with poor Roger's death. I *don't* think so. But then I have a trusting heart – I always have had, ever since a child. I am loath to believe the worst of anyone. But, of course, one must remember that Ralph was in several air raids as a young boy. The results are apparent long after, sometimes, they say. People are not responsible for their actions in the least. They lose control, you know, without being able to help it.'

'Mother,' cried Flora, 'you don't think Ralph did it?'

'Come, Mrs Ackroyd,' said Blunt.

'I don't know what to think,' said Mrs Ackroyd tearfully. 'It's all very upsetting. What would happen to the estate, I wonder, if Ralph were found guilty?'

Raymond pushed his chair away from the table violently. Major Blunt remained very quiet, looking thoughtfully at her.

'Like shell-shock, you know,' said Mrs Ackroyd obstinately, 'and I dare say Roger kept him very short of money – with the best intentions, of course. I can see you are all against me, but I do think it is very odd that Ralph has not come forward, and I must say I am thankful Flora's engagement was never announced formally.'

'It will be tomorrow,' said Flora in a clear voice.

'Flora!' cried her mother, aghast.

Flora had turned to the secretary.

'Will you send the announcement to the *Morning Post*. And *The Times*, please, Mr Raymond.'

'If you are sure that it is wise, Miss Ackroyd,' he replied gravely.

She turned impulsively to Blunt.

'You understand,' she said. 'What else can I do? As things are, I must stand by Ralph. Don't you see that I must?'

She looked very searchingly at him, and after a long pause he nodded abruptly.

Mrs Ackroyd burst out into shrill protests. Flora remained unmoved. Then Raymond spoke.

'I appreciate your motives, Miss Ackroyd. But don't you think you're being rather precipitate? Wait a day or two.'

'Tomorrow,' said Flora in a clear voice. 'It's no good, Mother, going on like this. Whatever else I am, I'm not disloyal to my friends.'

'M. Poirot,' Mrs Ackroyd appealed tearfully. 'Can't you say anything at all?'

'Nothing to be said,' interpolated Blunt. 'She's doing the right thing. I'll stand by her through thick and thin.'

Flora held out her hand to him.

'Thank you, Major Blunt,' she said.

'Mademoiselle,' said Poirot, 'will you let an old man congratulate you on your courage and your loyalty? And will you not misunderstand me if I ask you – ask you most solemnly – to postpone the announcement you speak of for at least two days more?'

Flora hesitated.

'I ask it in Ralph Paton's interests as much as in yours, mademoiselle. You frown. You do not see how that can be. But I assure you that it is so. *Pas de blagues.* You put the case into my hands – you must not hamper me now.'

Flora paused a few minutes before replying.

'I do not like it,' she said at last, 'but I will do what you say.'

She sat down again at the table.

'And now, messieurs et mesdames,' said Poirot rapidly, 'I will continue with what I was about to say. Understand this, I mean to arrive at the truth. The truth, however ugly in itself, is always curious and beautiful to the seeker after it. I am much aged, my powers may not be what they were.' Here he clearly expected a contradiction. 'In all probability this is the last case I shall ever investigate. But Hercule Poirot does not end with a failure. Messieurs et mesdames, I tell you, I mean to *know*. And I shall know – in spite of you all.'

He brought out the last words provocatively, hurling them in our face as it were. I think we all flinched back a little, excepting Geoffrey Raymond, who remained good-humoured and imperturbable as usual.

'How do you mean – in spite of us all?' he asked, with slightly raised eyebrows.

'But – just that, monsieur. Every one of you in this room is concealing something from me.' He raised his hand as a faint murmur of protest arose. 'Yes, yes, I know what I am saying. It may be something unimportant – trivial – which is supposed to have no bearing on the case, but there it is. *Each one of you has something to hide.* Come now, am I right?'

His glance, challenging and accusing, swept round the table. And every pair of eyes dropped before his. Yes, mine as well.

'I am answered,' said Poirot, with a curious laugh. He got up from his seat. 'I appeal to you all. Tell me the truth – the whole truth.' There was a silence. 'Will no one speak?'

He gave the same short laugh again.

'*C'est dommage*,' he said, and went out.

CHAPTER XIII

The Goose Quill

That evening, at Poirot's request, I went over to his house after dinner. Caroline saw me depart with visible reluctance. I think she would have liked to have accompanied me.

Poirot greeted me hospitably. He had placed a bottle of Irish whiskey (which I detest) on a small table, with a soda water siphon and a glass. He himself was engaged in brewing hot chocolate. It was a favourite beverage of his, I discovered later.

He inquired politely after my sister, whom he declared to be a most interesting woman.

'I'm afraid you've been giving her a swelled head,' I said drily. 'What about Sunday afternoon?'

He laughed and twinkled.

'I always like to employ the expert,' he remarked obscurely, but he refused to explain the remark.

'You got all the local gossip anyway,' I remarked. 'True, and untrue.'

'And a great deal of valuable information,' he added quietly.

'Such as –'

He shook his head.

'Why not have told me the truth?' he countered. 'In a place like this, all Ralph Paton's doings were bound to be known. If your sister had not happened to pass through the wood that day somebody else would have done so.'

'I suppose they would,' I said grumpily. 'What about this interest of yours in my patients?'

Again he twinkled.

'Only one of them, doctor. Only one of them.'

'The last?' I hazarded.

'I find Miss Russell a study of the most interesting,' he said evasively.

'Do you agree with my sister and Mrs Ackroyd that there is something fishy about her?' I asked.

'Eh? What do you say – fishy?'

I explained to the best of my ability.

'And they say that, do they?'

'Didn't my sister convey as much to you yesterday afternoon?'

'*C'est possible.*'

'For no reason whatever,' I declared.

'*Les femmes,*' generalized Poirot. 'They are marvellous! They invent haphazard – and by miracle they are right. Not that it is that, really. Women observe subconsciously a thousand little details, without knowing that they are doing so. Their subconscious mind adds these little things together – and they call the result intuition. Me, I am very skilled in psychology. I know these things.'

He swelled his chest out importantly, looking so ridiculous, that I found it difficult not to burst out laughing. Then he took a small sip of his chocolate, and carefully wiped his moustache.

'I wish you'd tell me,' I burst out, 'what you really think of it all?'

He put down his cup.

'You wish that?'

'I do.'

'You have seen what I have seen. Should not our ideas be the same?'

'I'm afraid you're laughing at me,' I said stiffly. 'Of course, I've no experience of matters of this kind.'

Poirot smiled at me indulgently.

'You are like the little child who wants to know the way the engine works. You wish to see the affair, not as the family doctor sees it, but with the eye of a detective who knows and cares for no one – to whom they are all strangers and all equally liable to suspicion.'

'You put it very well,' I said.

'So I give you, then, a little lecture. The first thing is to get a clear history of what happened that evening – always bearing in mind that the person who speaks may be lying.'

I raised my eyebrows.

'Rather a suspicious attitude.'

'But necessary – I assure you, necessary. Now first – Dr Sheppard leaves the house at ten minutes to nine. How do I know that?'

'Because I told you so.'

'But you might not be speaking the truth – or the watch you went by might be wrong. But Parker also says that you left the house at ten minutes to nine. So we accept that statement and pass on. At nine o'clock you run into a man – and here we come to what we will call the Romance of the Mysterious Stranger – just outside the Park gates. How do I know that that is so?'

'I told you so,' I began again, but Poirot interrupted me with a gesture of impatience.

'Ah! but it is that you are a little stupid tonight, my friend. *You* know that it is so – but how am *I* to know? *Eh bien*, I am able to tell you that the Mysterious Stranger was not a hallucination on your part, because the maid of a Miss Gannett met him a few minutes before you did, and of her too he inquired the way to Fernly Park. We accept his presence, therefore, and we can be fairly sure of two things about him – that he was a stranger to the neighbourhood, and that whatever his object in going to Fernly, there was no great secrecy about it, since he twice asked the way there.'

'Yes,' I said, 'I see that.'

'Now I have made it my business to find out more about this man. He had a drink at the Three Boars, I learn, and the barmaid there says that he spoke with an American accent and mentioned having just come over from the States. Did it strike you that he had an American accent?'

'Yes, I think he had,' I said, after a minute or two, during which I cast my mind back; 'but a very slight one.'

'*Précisément*. There is also this, which, you will remember, I picked up in the summer-house.'

He held out to me the little quill. I looked at it curiously. Then a memory of something I had read stirred in me.

Poirot, who had been watching my face, nodded.

'Yes, heroin, "snow." Drug-takers carry it like this, and sniff it up the nose.'

'Diamorphine hydrochloride,' I murmured mechanically.

'This method of taking the drug is very common on the other side. Another proof, if we wanted one, that the man came from Canada or the States.'

'What first attracted your attention to that summer-house?' I asked curiously.

'My friend the inspector took it for granted that anyone using that path did so as a short cut to the house, but as soon as I saw the summer-house, I realized that the same path would be taken by anyone using the summer-house as a rendezvous. Now it seems fairly certain that the stranger came neither to the front nor to the back door. Then did someone from the house go out and meet him? If so, what could be a more convenient place than that little summer-house? I searched it with the hope that I might find some clue inside. I found two, the scrap of cambric and the quill.'

'And the scrap of cambric?' I asked curiously. 'What about that?'

Poirot raised his eyebrows.

'You do not use your little grey cells,' he remarked drily. 'The scrap of starched cambric should be obvious.'

'Not very obvious to me.' I changed the subject. 'Anyway,' I said, 'this man went to the summer-house to meet somebody. Who was that somebody?'

'Exactly the question,' said Poirot. 'You will remember that Mrs Ackroyd and her daughter came over from Canada to live here?'

'Is that what you meant today when you accused them of hiding the truth?'

'Perhaps. Now another point. What did you think of the parlourmaid's story?'

'What story?'

'The story of her dismissal. Does it take half an hour to dismiss a servant? Was the story of those important papers a likely one? And remember, though she says she was in her bedroom from nine-thirty until ten o'clock, there is no one to confirm her statement.'

'You bewilder me,' I said.

'To me it grows clearer. But tell me now your own ideas and theories.'

I drew a piece of paper from my pocket.

'I just scribbled down a few suggestions,' I said apologetically.

'But excellent – you have method. Let us hear them.'

I read out in a somewhat embarrassed voice.

'To begin with, one must look at the thing logically –'

'Just what my poor Hastings used to say,' interrupted Poirot, 'but alas! he never did so.'

'*Point No. 1.* – Mr Ackroyd was heard talking to someone at half-past nine.

'*Point No. 2.* – At some time during the evening Ralph Paton must have come in through the window, as evidenced by the prints of his shoes.

'*Point No. 3.* – Mr Ackroyd was nervous that evening, and would only have admitted someone he knew.

'*Point No. 4.* – The person with Mr Ackroyd at nine-thirty was asking for money. We know Ralph Paton was in a scrape.

'*These four points go to show that the person with Mr Ackroyd at nine-thirty was Ralph Paton. But we know that Mr Ackroyd was alive at a quarter to ten, therefore it was not Ralph who killed him. Ralph left the window open. Afterwards the murderer came in that way.*'

'And who was the murderer?' inquired Poirot.

'The American stranger. He may have been in league with Parker, and possibly in Parker we have the man who blackmailed Mrs Ferrars. If so, Parker may have heard enough to realize the game was up, have told his accomplice so, and the latter did the crime with the dagger which Parker gave him.'

'It is a theory that,' admitted Poirot. 'Decidedly you have cells of a kind. But it leaves a good deal unaccounted for.'

'Such as –'

'The telephone call, the pushed-out chair –'

'Do you really think that latter important?' I interrupted.

'Perhaps not,' admitted my friend. 'It may have been pulled out by accident, and Raymond or Blunt may have shoved it into place unconsciously under the stress of emotion. Then there is the missing forty pounds.'

'Given by Ackroyd to Ralph,' I suggested. 'He may have reconsidered his first refusal.'

'That still leaves one thing unexplained.'

'What?'

'Why was Blunt so certain in his own mind that it was Raymond with Mr Ackroyd at nine-thirty?'

'He explained that,' I said.

'You think so? I will not press the point. Tell me, instead, what were Ralph Paton's reasons for disappearing?'

'That's rather more difficult,' I said slowly. 'I shall have to speak as a medical man. Ralph's nerves must have gone phut! If he suddenly found out that his uncle had been murdered within a few minutes of his leaving him – after, perhaps, a rather stormy interview – well, he might get the wind up and clear right out. Men have been known to do that – act guiltily when they're perfectly innocent.'

'Yes, that is true,' said Poirot. 'But we must not lose sight of one thing.'

'I know what you're going to say,' I remarked: 'motive. Ralph Paton inherits a great fortune by his uncle's death.'

'That is one motive,' agreed Poirot.

'One?'

'*Mais oui.* Do you realize that there are three separate motives staring us in the face. Somebody certainly stole the blue envelope and its contents. That is one motive. Blackmail! Ralph Paton may have been the man who blackmailed Mrs Ferrars. Remember, as far as Hammond knew, Ralph Paton had not applied to his uncle for help of late. That looks as though he were being supplied with money elsewhere. Then there is the fact that he was in some – how do you say – scrape? – which he feared might get to his uncle's ears. And finally there is the one you have just mentioned.'

'Dear me,' I said, rather taken aback. 'The case does seem black against him.'

'Does it?' said Poirot. 'That is where we disagree, you and I. Three motives – it is almost too much. I am inclined to believe that, after all, Ralph Paton is innocent.'

CHAPTER XIV

Mrs Ackroyd

After the evening talk I have just chronicled, the affair seemed to me to enter on a different phase. The whole thing can be divided into two parts, each clear and distinct from the other. Part I ranges from Ackroyd's death on the Friday evening to the following Monday night. It is the straightforward narrative of what occurred, as presented to Hercule Poirot. I was at Poirot's elbow the whole time. I saw what he saw. I tried my best to read his mind. As I know now, I failed in this latter task. Though Poirot showed me all his discoveries – as, for instance, the gold wedding ring – he held back the vital and yet logical impressions that he formed. As I came to know later, this secrecy was characteristic of him. He would throw out hints and suggestions, but beyond that he would not go.

As I say, up till the Monday evening, my narrative might have been that of Poirot himself. I played Watson to his Sherlock. But after Monday our ways diverged. Poirot was busy on his own account. I got to hear of what he was doing, because in King's Abbot, you get to hear of everything, but he did not take me into his confidence beforehand. And I, too, had my own preoccupations.

On looking back, the thing that strikes me most is the piece-meal character of this period. Everyone had a hand in the elucidation of the mystery. It was rather like a jig-saw puzzle to which everyone contributed their own little piece of knowledge or discovery. But their task ended there. To Poirot alone belongs the renown of fitting those pieces into their correct place.

Some of the incidents seemed at the time irrelevant and unmeaning. There was, for instance, the question of the black boots. But that comes later . . . To take things strictly in chronological order, I must begin with the summons from Mrs Ackroyd.

She sent for me early on Tuesday morning, and since the summons sounded an urgent one, I hastened there, expecting to find her *in extremis.*

The lady was in bed. So much did she concede to the etiquette of the situation. She gave me her bony hand, and indicated a chair drawn up to the bedside.

'Well, Mrs Ackroyd,' I said, 'and what's the matter with you?'

I spoke with that kind of spurious geniality which seems to be expected of general practitioners.

'I'm prostrated,' said Mrs Ackroyd in a faint voice. 'Absolutely prostrated. It's the shock of poor Roger's death. They say these things often aren't felt at the *time*, you know. It's the reaction afterwards.'

It is a pity that a doctor is precluded by his profession from being able sometimes to say what he really thinks.

I would have given anything to be able to answer, 'Bunkum!'

Instead, I suggested a tonic. Mrs Ackroyd accepted the tonic. One move in the game seemed now to be concluded. Not for a moment did I imagine that I had been sent for because of the shock occasioned by Ackroyd's death. But Mrs Ackroyd is totally incapable of pursuing a straightforward course on any subject. She always approaches her object by tortuous means. I wondered very much why it was she had sent for me.

'And then that scene – yesterday,' continued my patient.

She paused as though expecting me to take up a cue.

'What scene?'

'Doctor, how can you? Have you forgotten? That dreadful little Frenchman – or Belgian – or whatever he is. Bullying us all like he did. It has quite upset me. Coming on the top of Roger's death.'

'I'm very sorry, Mrs Ackroyd,' I said.

'I don't know what he meant – shouting at us like he did. I should hope I know my duty too well to *dream* of concealing anything. I have given the police *every* assistance in my power.'

Mrs Ackroyd paused, and I said, 'Quite so.' I was beginning to have a glimmering of what all the trouble was about.

'No one can say that I have failed in my duty,' continued Mrs Ackroyd. 'I am sure Inspector Raglan is perfectly satisfied. Why should this little upstart of a foreigner make a fuss? A most ridiculous-looking creature he is too – just like a comic Frenchman in a revue. I can't think why Flora insisted on bringing him into the case. She never said a word to me about it. Just went off and did it on her own. Flora is too independent. I am a woman of the world and her mother. She should have come to me for advice first.'

I listened to all this in silence.

'What does he think? That's what I want to know. Does he actually imagine I'm hiding something? He – he – positively *accused* me yesterday.'

I shrugged my shoulders.

'It is surely of no consequence, Mrs Ackroyd,' I said. 'Since you are not concealing anything, any remarks he may have made do not apply to you.'

Mrs Ackroyd went off at a tangent, after her usual fashion.

'Servants are so tiresome,' she said. 'They gossip, and talk amongst themselves. And then it gets round – and all the time there's probably nothing in it at all.'

'Have the servants been talking?' I asked. 'What about?'

Mrs Ackroyd cast a very shrewd glance at me. It quite threw me off my balance.

'I was sure *you'd* know, doctor, if anyone did. You were with M. Poirot all the time, weren't you?'

'I was.'

'Then of course you know. It was that girl, Ursula Bourne, wasn't it? Naturally – she's leaving. She *would* want to make all the trouble she could. Spiteful, that's what they are. They're all alike. Now, you being there, doctor, you must know exactly what she did say? I'm most anxious that no wrong impression should get about. After all, you don't repeat every little detail to the police, do you? There are family matters sometimes – nothing to do with the question of the murder. But if the girl was spiteful, she may have made out all sorts of things.'

I was shrewd enough to see that a very real anxiety lay behind these outpourings. Poirot had been justified in his premises. Of the six people round the table yesterday, Mrs Ackroyd at least had had something to hide. It was for me to discover what that something might be.

'If I were you, Mrs Ackroyd,' I said brusquely, 'I should make a clean breast of things.'

She gave a little scream.

'Oh! doctor, how can you be so abrupt. It sounds as though – as though – And I can explain everything so simply.'

'Then why not do so?' I suggested.

Mrs Ackroyd took out a frilled handkerchief, and became tearful.

'I thought, doctor, that you might put it to M. Poirot – explain it, you know – because it's so difficult for a foreigner to see our point of view. And you don't know – nobody could know – what I've had to contend with. A martyrdom – a long martyrdom. That's what my life has been. I don't like to speak ill of the dead – but there it is. Not the smallest bill but it had all to be gone over – just as though Roger had had a few miserly hundreds a year instead of being (as Mr Hammond told me yesterday) one of the wealthiest men in these parts.'

Mrs Ackroyd paused to dab her eyes with the frilled handkerchief.

'Yes,' I said encouragingly. 'You were talking about bills?'

'Those dreadful bills. And some I didn't like to show Roger at all. They were things a man wouldn't understand. He would have said the things weren't necessary. And of course they mounted up, you know, and they kept coming in –'

She looked at me appealingly, as though asking me to condole with her on this striking peculiarity.

'It's a habit they have,' I agreed.

And the tone altered – became quite abusive. 'I assure you, doctor, I was becoming a nervous wreck. I couldn't sleep at nights. And a dreadful fluttering round the heart. And then I got a letter from a Scotch gentleman – as a matter of fact there were two letters – both Scotch gentlemen. Mr Bruce

MacPherson was one, and the other was Colin MacDonald. Quite a coincidence.'

'Hardly that,' I said drily. 'They are usually Scotch gentlemen, but I suspect a Semitic strain in their ancestry.'

'Ten pounds to ten thousand on note of hand alone,' murmured Mrs Ackroyd reminiscently. 'I wrote to one of them, but it seemed there were difficulties.'

She paused.

I gathered that we were just coming to delicate ground. I have never known anyone more difficult to bring to the point.

'You see,' murmured Mrs Ackroyd, 'it's all a question of expectations, isn't it? Testamentary expectations. And though, of course, I expected that Roger would provide for me, I didn't *know.* I thought that if only I could glance over a copy of his will – not in any sense of vulgar prying – but just so that I could make my own arrangements.'

She glanced sideways at me. The position was now very delicate indeed. Fortunately words, ingeniously used, will serve to mask the ugliness of naked facts.

'I could only tell this to you, dear Dr Sheppard,' said Mrs Ackroyd rapidly. 'I can trust you not to misjudge me, and to represent the matter in the right light to M. Poirot. It was on Friday afternoon –'

She came to a stop and swallowed uncertainly.

'Yes,' I repeated encouragingly. 'On Friday afternoon. Well?'

'Everyone was out, or so I thought. And I went into Roger's study – I had some real reason for going there – I mean, there was nothing underhand about it. And as I saw all the papers heaped on the desk, it just came to me, like a flash: "I wonder if Roger keeps his will in one of the drawers of the desk." I'm so impulsive, always was, from a child. I do things on the spur of the moment. He'd left his keys – very careless of him – in the lock of the top drawer.'

'I see,' I said helpfully. 'So you searched the desk. Did you find the will?'

Mrs Ackroyd gave a little scream, and I realized that I had not been sufficiently diplomatic.

'How dreadful it sounds. But it wasn't at all like that really.'

'Of course it wasn't,' I said hastily. 'You must forgive my unfortunate way of putting things.'

'Of course, men are so peculiar. In dear Roger's place, I should have not objected to revealing the provisions of my will. But men are so secretive. One is forced to adopt little subterfuges in self-defence.'

'And the result of the little subterfuge?' I asked.

'That's just what I'm telling you. As I got to the bottom drawer, Bourne came in. Most awkward. Of course I shut the drawer and stood up, and I called her attention to a few specks of dust on the surface. But I didn't like the way she looked – quite respectful in manner, but a very nasty light in her eyes. Almost contemptuous, if you know what I mean. I never have liked that girl very much. She's a good servant, and she says Ma'am, and doesn't object to wearing caps and aprons (which I declare to you a lot of them do nowadays), and she can say "Not at home" without scruples if she has to answer the door instead of Parker, and she doesn't have those peculiar gurgling noises inside which so many parlourmaids seem to have when they wait at table – Let me see, where was I?'

'You were saying, that in spite of several valuable qualities, you never liked Bourne.'

'No more I do. She's – odd. There's something different about her from the others. Too well educated, that's my opinion. You can't tell who are ladies and who aren't nowadays.'

'And what happened next?' I asked.

'Nothing. At last, Roger came in. And I thought he was out for a walk. And he said: "What's all this?" and I said, "Nothing. I just came in to fetch *Punch*." And I took *Punch* and went out with it. Bourne stayed behind. I heard her asking Roger if she could speak to him for a minute. I went straight up to my room, to lie down. I was very upset.'

There was a pause.

'You will explain to M. Poirot, won't you? You can see for yourself what a trivial matter the whole thing was. But, of course, when he was so stern about concealing things, I thought of this

at once. Bourne may have made some extraordinary story out
of it, but you can explain, can't you?'

'That is all?' I said. 'You have told me everything?'

'Ye-es,' said Mrs Ackroyd. 'Oh! yes,' she added firmly.

But I had noted the momentary hesitation, and I knew that
there was still something she was keeping back. It was nothing
less than a flash of sheer genius that prompted me to ask the
question I did.

'Mrs Ackroyd,' I said, 'was it you who left the silver table
open?'

I had my answer in the blush of guilt that even rouge and
powder could not conceal.

'How did you know?' she whispered.

'It was you, then?'

'Yes – I – you see – there were one or two pieces of old silver
– very interesting. I had been reading up the subject and there
was an illustration of quite a small piece which had fetched an
immense sum at Christie's. It looked to be just the same as the
one in the silver table. I thought I would take it up to London
with me when I went – and – and have it valued. Then if it
really was a valuable piece, just think what a charming surprise
it would have been for Roger.'

I refrained from comments, accepting Mrs Ackroyd's story
on its merits. I even forbore to ask her why it was necessary to
abstract what she wanted in such a surreptitious manner.

'Why did you leave the lid open?' I asked. 'Did you forget?'

'I was startled,' said Mrs Ackroyd. 'I heard footsteps coming
along the terrace outside. I hastened out of the room and just
got up the stairs before Parker opened the front door to you.'

'That must have been Miss Russell,' I said thoughtfully. Mrs
Ackroyd had revealed to me one fact that was extremely interesting. Whether her designs upon Ackroyd's silver had been strictly
honourable I neither knew nor cared. What did interest me was
the fact that Miss Russell must have entered the drawing-room
by the window, and that I had not been wrong when I judged
her to be out of breath with running. Where had she been? I
thought of the summer-house and the scrap of cambric.

'I wonder if Miss Russell has had her handkerchiefs starched!' I exclaimed on the spur of the moment.

Mrs Ackroyd's start recalled me to myself, and I rose.

'You think you can explain to M. Poirot?' she asked anxiously.

'Oh, certainly. Absolutely.'

I got away at last, after being forced to listen to more justifications of her conduct.

The parlourmaid was in the hall, and it was she who helped me on with my overcoat. I observed her more closely than I had done heretofore. It was clear that she had been crying.

'How is it,' I asked, 'that you told us that Mr Ackroyd sent for you on Friday to his study? I hear now that it was *you* who asked to speak to *him*.'

For a minute the girl's eyes dropped before mine.

Then she spoke.

'I meant to leave in any case,' she said uncertainly.

I said no more. She opened the front door for me. Just as I was passing out, she said suddenly in a low voice:

'Excuse me, sir, is there any news of Captain Paton?'

I shook my head, looking at her inquiringly.

'He ought to come back,' she said. 'Indeed – indeed he ought to come back.'

She was looking at me with appealing eyes.

'Does no one know where he is?' she asked.

'Do you?' I said sharply.

She shook her head.

'No, indeed. I know nothing. But anyone who was a friend to him would tell him this: he ought to come back.'

I lingered, thinking that perhaps the girl would say more. Her next question surprised me.

'When do they think the murder was done? Just before ten o'clock?'

'That is the idea,' I said. 'Between a quarter to ten and the hour.'

'Not earlier? Not before a quarter to ten?'

I looked at her attentively. She was so clearly eager for a reply in the affirmative.

'That's out of the question,' I said. 'Miss Ackroyd saw her uncle alive at a quarter to ten.'

She turned away, and her whole figure seemed to droop.

'A handsome girl,' I said to myself as I drove off. 'An exceedingly handsome girl.'

Caroline was at home. She had had a visit from Poirot and was very pleased and important about it.

'I am helping him with the case,' she explained.

I felt rather uneasy. Caroline is bad enough as it is. What will she be like with her detective instincts encouraged?

'Are you going round the neighbourhood looking for Ralph Paton's mysterious girl?' I inquired.

'I might do that on my own account,' said Caroline. 'No, this is a special thing M. Poirot wants me to find out for him.'

'What is it?' I asked.

'He wants to know whether Ralph Paton's boots were black or brown,' said Caroline with tremendous solemnity.

I stared at her. I see now that I was unbelievably stupid about these boots. I failed altogether to grasp the point.

'They were brown shoes,' I said. 'I saw them.'

'Not shoes, James, boots. M. Poirot wants to know whether a pair of boots Ralph had with him at the hotel were brown or black. A lot hangs on it.'

Call me dense if you like. I didn't see.

'And how are you going to find out?' I asked.

Caroline said there would be no difficulty about that. Our Annie's dearest friend was Miss Gannett's maid, Clara. And Clara was walking out with the Boots at the Three Boars. The whole thing was simplicity itself, and by the aid of Miss Gannett, who co-operated loyally, at once giving Clara leave of absence, the matter was rushed through at express speed.

It was when we were sitting down to lunch that Caroline remarked, with would-be unconcern:

'About those boots of Ralph Paton's.'

'Well,' I said, 'what about them?'

'M. Poirot thought they were probably brown. He was wrong. They're black.'

And Caroline nodded her head several times. She evidently felt that she had scored a point over Poirot.

I did not answer. I was puzzling over what the colour of a pair of Ralph Paton's boots had to do with the case.

CHAPTER XV

Geoffrey Raymond

I was to have a further proof that day of the success of Poirot's tactics. That challenge of his had been a subtle touch born of his knowledge of human nature. A mixture of fear and guilt had wrung the truth from Mrs Ackroyd. She was the first to react.

That afternoon when I returned from seeing my patients, Caroline told me that Geoffrey Raymond had just left.

'Did he want to see me?' I asked, as I hung up my coat in the hall.

Caroline was hovering by my elbow.

'It was M. Poirot he wanted to see,' she said. 'He'd just come from The Larches. M. Poirot was out. Mr Raymond thought that he might be here, or that you might know where he was.'

'I haven't the least idea.'

'I tried to make him wait,' said Caroline, 'but he said he would call back at The Larches in half an hour, and went away down the village. A great pity, because M. Poirot came in practically the minute after he left.'

'Came in here?'

'No, to his own house.'

'How do you know?'

'The side window,' said Caroline briefly.

It seemed to me that we had now exhausted the topic. Caroline thought otherwise.

'Aren't you going across?'

'Across where?'

'To The Larches, of course.'

'My dear Caroline,' I said, 'what for?'

'Mr Raymond wanted to see him very particularly,' said Caroline. 'You might hear what it's all about.'

I raised my eyebrows.

'Curiosity is not my besetting sin,' I remarked coldly. 'I can exist comfortably without knowing exactly what my neighbours are doing and thinking.'

'Stuff and nonsense, James,' said my sister. 'You want to know just as much as I do. You're not so honest, that's all. You always have to pretend.'

'Really, Caroline,' I said, and retired into my surgery.

Ten minutes later Caroline tapped at the door and entered. In her hand she held what seemed to be a pot of jam.

'I wonder, James,' she said, 'if you would mind taking this pot of medlar jelly across to M. Poirot? I promised it to him. He has never tasted any home-made medlar jelly.'

'Why can't Annie go?' I asked coldly.

'She's doing some mending. I can't spare her.'

Caroline and I looked at each other.

'Very well,' I said, rising. 'But if I take the beastly thing, I shall just leave it at the door. You understand that?'

My sister raised her eyebrows.

'Naturally,' she said. 'Who suggested you should do anything else?'

The honours were with Caroline.

'If you *do* happen to see M. Poirot,' she said, as I opened the front door, 'you might tell him about the boots.'

It was a most subtle parting shot. I wanted dreadfully to understand the enigma of the boots. When the old lady with the Breton cap opened the door to me, I found myself asking if M. Poirot was in, quite automatically.

Poirot sprang up to meet me, with every appearance of pleasure.

'Sit down, my good friend,' he said. 'The big chair? This small one? The room is not too hot, no?'

I thought it was stifling, but refrained from saying so. The windows were closed, and a large fire burned in the grate.

'The English people, they have a mania for the fresh air,'

declared Poirot. 'The big air, it is all very well outside, where it belongs. Why admit it to the house? But let us not discuss such banalities. You have something for me, yes?'

'Two things,' I said. 'First – this – from my sister.'

I handed over the pot of medlar jelly.

'How kind of Mademoiselle Caroline. She has remembered her promise. And the second thing?'

'Information – of a kind.'

And I told him of my interview with Mrs Ackroyd. He listened with interest, but not much excitement.

'It clears the ground,' he said thoughtfully. 'And it has a certain value as confirming the evidence of the housekeeper. She said, you remember, that she found the silver table lid open and closed it down in passing.'

'What about her statement that she went into the drawing-room to see if the flowers were fresh?'

'Ah! we never took that very seriously, did we, my friend? It was patently an excuse, trumped up in a hurry, by a woman who felt it urgent to explain her presence – which, by the way, you would probably never have thought of questioning. I considered it possible that her agitation might arise from the fact that she had been tampering with the silver table, but I think now that we must look for another cause.'

'Yes,' I said. 'Whom did she go out to meet? And why?'

'You think she went to meet someone?'

'I do.'

Poirot nodded.

'So do I,' he said thoughtfully.

There was a pause.

'By the way,' I said, 'I've got a message for you from my sister. Ralph Paton's boots were black, not brown.'

I was watching him closely as I gave the message, and I fancied that I saw a momentary flicker of discomposure. If so, it passed almost immediately.

'She is absolutely positive they are not brown?'

'Absolutely.'

'Ah!' said Poirot regretfully. 'That is a pity.'

And he seemed quite crestfallen.

He entered into no explanations, but at once started a new subject of conversation.

'The housekeeper, Miss Russell, who came to consult you on that Friday morning – is it indiscreet to ask what passed at the interview – apart from the medical details, I mean?'

'Not at all,' I said. 'When the professional part of the conversation was over, we talked for a few minutes about poisons, and the ease or difficulty of detecting them, and about drug-taking and drug-takers.'

'With special reference to cocaine?' asked Poirot.

'How did you know?' I asked, somewhat surprised.

For answer, the little man rose and crossed the room to where newspapers were filed. He brought me a copy of the *Daily Budget*, dated Friday, 16th September, and showed me an article dealing with the smuggling of cocaine. It was a somewhat lurid article, written with an eye to picturesque effect.

'That is what put cocaine into her head, my friend,' he said.

I would have catechized him further, for I did not quite understand his meaning, but at that moment the door opened and Geoffrey Raymond was announced.

He came in fresh and debonair as ever, and greeted us both.

'How are you, doctor? M. Poirot, this is the second time I've been here this morning. I was anxious to catch you.'

'Perhaps I'd better be off,' I suggested rather awkwardly.

'Not on my account, doctor. No, it's just this,' he went on, seating himself at a wave of invitation from Poirot, 'I've got a confession to make.'

'*En vérité?*' said Poirot, with an air of polite interest.

'Oh, it's of no consequence, really. But, as a matter of fact, my conscience has been pricking me ever since yesterday afternoon. You accused us all of keeping back something, M. Poirot. I plead guilty. I've had something up my sleeve.'

'And what is that, M. Raymond?'

'As I say, it's nothing of consequence – just this. I was in debt – badly, and that legacy came in the nick of time. Five hundred pounds puts me on my feet again with a little to spare.'

He smiled at us both with that engaging frankness that made him such a likeable youngster.

'You know how it is. Suspicious-looking policemen – don't like to admit you were hard up for money – think it will look bad to them. But I was a fool, really, because Blunt and I were in the billiard room from a quarter to ten onwards, so I've got a watertight alibi and nothing to fear. Still, when you thundered out that stuff about concealing things, I felt a nasty prick of conscience, and I thought I'd like to get it off my mind.'

He got up again and stood smiling at us.

'You are a very wise young man,' said Poirot, nodding at him with approval. 'See you, when I know that anyone is hiding things from me, I suspect that the thing hidden may be something very bad indeed. You have done well.'

'I'm glad I'm cleared from suspicion,' laughed Raymond. 'I'll be off now.'

'So that is that,' I remarked, as the door closed behind the young secretary.

'Yes,' agreed Poirot. 'A mere bagatelle – but if he had not been in the billiard room – who knows? After all, many crimes have been committed for the sake of less than five hundred pounds. It all depends on what sum is sufficient to break a man. A question of relativity, is it not so? Have you reflected, my friend, that many people in that house stood to benefit by Mr Ackroyd's death? Mrs Ackroyd, Miss Flora, young Mr Raymond, the housekeeper, Miss Russell. Only one, in fact, does not. Major Blunt.'

His tone in uttering that name was so peculiar that I looked up, puzzled.

'I don't understand you,' I said.

'Two of the people I accused have given me the truth.'

'You think Major Blunt has something to conceal also?'

'As for that,' remarked Poirot nonchalantly, 'there is a saying, is there not, that Englishmen conceal only one thing – their love? And Major Blunt, I should say, is not good at concealments.'

'Sometimes,' I said, 'I wonder if we haven't rather jumped to conclusions on one point.'

'What is that?'

'We've assumed that the blackmailer of Mrs Ferrars is necessarily the murderer of Mr Ackroyd. Mightn't we be mistaken?'

Poirot nodded energetically.

'Very good. Very good indeed. I wondered if that idea would come to you. Of course it is possible. But we must remember one point. The letter disappeared. Still, that, as you say, may not necessarily mean that the murderer took it. When you first found the body, Parker may have abstracted the letter unnoticed by you.'

'Parker?'

'Yes, Parker. I always come back to Parker – not as the murderer – no, he did not commit the murder; but who is more suitable than he as the mysterious scoundrel who terrorized Mrs Ferrars? He may have got his information about Mr Ferrars's death from one of the King's Paddock servants. At any rate, he is more likely to have come upon it than a casual guest such as Blunt, for instance.'

'Parker might have taken the letter,' I admitted. 'It wasn't till later that I noticed it was gone.'

'How much later? After Blunt and Raymond were in the room, or before?'

'I can't remember,' I said slowly. 'I think it was before – no, afterwards. Yes, I'm almost sure it was afterwards.'

'That widens the field to three,' said Poirot thoughtfully. 'But Parker is the most likely. It is in my mind to try a little experiment with Parker. How say you, my friend, will you accompany me to Fernly?'

I acquiesced, and we set out at once. Poirot asked to see Miss Ackroyd, and presently Flora came to us.

'Mademoiselle Flora,' said Poirot, 'I have to confide in you a little secret. I am not yet satisfied of the innocence of Parker. I propose to make a little experiment with your assistance. I want to reconstruct some of his actions on that night. But we must think of something to tell him – ah! I have it. I wish to satisfy myself as to whether voices in the little lobby could have been heard outside on the terrace. Now, ring for Parker, if you will be so good.'

I did so, and presently the butler appeared, suave as ever.

'You rang, sir?'

'Yes, my good Parker. I have in mind a little experiment. I have placed Major Blunt on the terrace outside the study window. I want to see if anyone there could have heard the voices of Miss Ackroyd and yourself in the lobby that night. I want to enact that little scene over again. Perhaps you would fetch the tray or whatever it was you were carrying?'

Parker vanished, and we repaired to the lobby outside the study door. Presently we heard a chink in the outer hall, and Parker appeared in the doorway carrying a tray with a siphon, a decanter of whisky, and two glasses on it.

'One moment,' cried Poirot, raising his hand and seemingly very excited. 'We must have everything in order. Just as it occurred. It is a little method of mine.'

'A foreign custom, sir,' said Parker. 'Reconstruction of the crime they call it, do they not?'

He was quite imperturbable as he stood there politely waiting on Poirot's orders.

'Ah! he knows something, the good Parker,' cried Poirot. 'He has read of these things. Now, I beg you, let us have everything of the most exact. You came from the outer hall – so. Mademoiselle was – where?'

'Here,' said Flora, taking up her stand just outside the study door.

'Quite right, sir,' said Parker.

'I had just closed the door,' continued Flora.

'Yes, miss,' agreed Parker. 'Your hand was still on the handle as it is now.'

'Then *allez*,' said Poirot. 'Play me the little comedy.'

Flora stood with her hand on the door handle, and Parker came stepping through the door from the hall, bearing the tray.

He stopped just inside the door. Flora spoke.

'Oh! Parker. Mr Ackroyd doesn't want to be disturbed again tonight.'

'Is that right?' she added in an undertone.

'To the best of my recollection, Miss Flora,' said Parker, 'but I fancy you used the word "evening" instead of "night".' Then, raising his voice in a somewhat theatrical fashion: 'Very good, miss. Shall I lock up as usual?'

'Yes, please.'

Parker retired through the door, Flora followed him, and started to ascend the main staircase.

'Is that enough?' she asked over her shoulder.

'Admirable,' declared the little man, rubbing his hands. 'By the way, Parker, are you sure there were two glasses on the tray that evening? Who was the second one for?'

'I always bring two glasses, sir,' said Parker. 'Is there anything further?'

'Nothing. I thank you.'

Parker withdrew, dignified to the last.

Poirot stood in the middle of the hall frowning. Flora came down and joined us.

'Has your experiment been successful?' she asked. 'I don't quite understand, you know –'

Poirot smiled admiringly at her.

'It is not necessary that you should,' he said. 'But tell me, were there indeed two glasses on Parker's tray that night?'

Flora wrinkled her brows a minute.

'I really can't remember,' she said. 'I think there were. Is – is that the object of your experiment?'

Poirot took her hand and patted it.

'Put it this way,' he said. 'I am always interested to see if people will speak the truth.'

'And did Parker speak the truth?'

'I rather think he did,' said Poirot thoughtfully.

A few minutes later saw us retracing our steps to the village.

'What was the point of that question about the glasses?' I asked curiously.

Poirot shrugged his shoulders.

'One must say something,' he remarked. 'That particular question did as well as any other.'

I stared at him.

'At any rate, my friend,' he said seriously, 'I know now something I wanted to know. Let us leave it at that.'

CHAPTER XVI

An Evening at Mah Jong

That night we had a little Mah Jong party. This kind of simple entertainment is very popular in King's Abbot. The guests arrive in galoshes and waterproofs after dinner. They partake of coffee and later of cake, sandwiches and tea.

On this particular night our guests were Miss Gannett and Colonel Carter, who lives near the church. A good deal of gossip is handed round at these evenings, sometimes seriously interfering with the game in progress. We used to play bridge – chatty bridge of the worst description. We find Mah Jong much more peaceful. The irritated demand as to why on earth your partner did not lead a certain card is entirely done away with, and though we still express criticisms frankly, there is not the same acrimonious spirit.

'Very cold evening, eh, Sheppard?' said Colonel Carter, standing with his back to the fire. Caroline had taken Miss Gannett to her own room, and was there assisting her to disentangle herself from her many wraps. 'Reminds me of the Afghan passes.'

'Indeed?' I said politely.

'Very mysterious business this about poor Ackroyd,' continued the colonel, accepting a cup of coffee. 'A deuce of a lot behind it – that's what I say. Between you and me, Sheppard, I've heard the word 'blackmail' mentioned!'

The colonel gave me the look which might be tabulated 'one man of the world to another.'

'A woman in it, no doubt,' he said. 'Depend upon it, a woman in it.'

Caroline and Miss Gannett joined us at this minute. Miss

Gannett drank coffee whilst Caroline got out the Mah Jong box and poured out the tiles upon the table.

'Washing the tiles,' said the colonel facetiously. 'That's right – washing the tiles, as we used to say in the Shanghai Club.'

It is the private opinion of both Caroline and myself that Colonel Carter has never been in the Shanghai Club in his life. More, that he has never been farther east than India, where he juggled with tins of bully beef and plum and apple jam during the Great War. But the colonel is determinedly military, and in King's Abbot we permit people to indulge their little idiosyncrasies freely.

'Shall we begin?' said Caroline.

We sat round the table. For some five minutes there was complete silence, owing to the fact that there is tremendous secret competition amongst us as to who can build their wall quickest.

'Go on, James,' said Caroline at last. 'You're East Wind.'

I discarded a tile. A round or two proceeded, broken by the monotonous remarks of 'Three Bamboos', 'Two Circles', 'Pung', and frequently from Miss Gannett 'Unpung', owing to that lady's habit of too hastily claiming tiles to which she had no right.

'I saw Flora Ackroyd this morning,' said Miss Gannett. 'Pung – no – Unpung. I made a mistake.'

'Four Circles,' said Caroline. 'Where did you see her?'

'She didn't see *me*,' said Miss Gannett, with that tremendous significance only to be met with in small villages.

'Ah!' said Caroline interestedly. 'Chow.'

'I believe,' said Miss Gannett, temporarily diverted, 'that it's the right thing nowadays to say "Chee" not "Chow".'

'Nonsense,' said Caroline. 'I have always said "*Chow*".'

'In the Shanghai Club,' said Colonel Carter, 'they say "*Chow*."'

Miss Gannett retired, crushed.

'What were you saying about Flora Ackroyd?' asked Caroline, after a moment or two devoted to the game. 'Was she with anyone?'

'Very much so,' said Miss Gannett.

The eyes of the two ladies met, and seemed to exchange information.

'Really,' said Caroline interestedly. 'Is that it? Well, it doesn't surprise me in the least.'

'We're waiting for you to discard, Miss Caroline,' said the colonel. He sometimes affects the pose of the bluff male, intent on the game and indifferent to gossip. But nobody is deceived.

'If you ask me,' said Miss Gannett. '(Was that a Bamboo you discarded, dear? Oh! no, I see now – it was a Circle.) As I was saying, if you ask me, Flora's been exceedingly lucky. Exceedingly lucky she's been.'

'How's that, Miss Gannett?' asked the colonel. 'I'll Pung that Green Dragon. How do you make out that Miss Flora's been lucky? Very charming girl and all that, I know.'

'I mayn't know very much about crime,' said Miss Gannett, with the air of one who knows everything there is to know, 'but I can tell you one thing. The first question that's always asked is "Who last saw the deceased alive?" And the person who did is regarded with suspicion. Now, Flora Ackroyd last saw her uncle alive. It might have looked very nasty for her – very nasty indeed. It's my opinion – and I give it for what it's worth, that Ralph Paton is staying away on her account, to draw suspicion away from her.'

'Come, now,' I protested mildly, 'you surely can't suggest that a young girl like Flora Ackroyd is capable of stabbing her uncle in cold blood?'

'Well, I don't know,' said Miss Gannett. 'I've just been reading a book from the library about the underworld of Paris, and it says that some of the worst women criminals are young girls with the faces of angels.'

'That's in France,' said Caroline instantly.

'Just so,' said the colonel. 'Now, I'll tell you a very curious thing – a story that was going round the Bazaars in India . . .'

The colonel's story was one of interminable length, and of curiously little interest. A thing that happened in India many years ago cannot compare for a moment with an event that took place in King's Abbot the day before yesterday.

It was Caroline who brought the colonel's story to a close by fortunately going Mah Jong. After the slight unpleasantness always caused by my corrections of Caroline's somewhat faulty arithmetic, we started a new hand.

'East Wind passes,' said Caroline. 'I've got an idea of my own about Ralph Paton. Three Characters. But I'm keeping it to myself for the present.'

'Are you, dear?' said Miss Gannett. 'Chow – I mean Pung.'

'Yes,' said Caroline firmly.

'Was it all right about the boots?' asked Miss Gannett. 'Their being black, I mean?'

'Quite all right,' said Caroline.

'What was the point, do you think?' asked Miss Gannett.

Caroline pursed up her lips, and shook her head with an air of knowing all about it.

'Pung,' said Miss Gannett. 'No – Unpung. I suppose that now the doctor's in with M. Poirot he knows all the secrets?'

'Far from it,' I said.

'James is so modest,' said Caroline. 'Ah! A concealed Kong.'

The colonel gave vent to a whistle. For the moment gossip was forgotten.

'Your own wind, too,' he said. '*And* you've got two Pungs of Dragons. We must be careful. Miss Caroline's out for a big hand.'

We played for some minutes with no irrelevant conversation.

'This M. Poirot now,' said Colonel Carter, 'is he really such a great detective?'

'The greatest the world has ever known,' said Caroline solemnly. 'He has to come here incognito to avoid publicity.'

'Chow,' said Miss Gannett. 'Quite wonderful for our little village, I'm sure. By the way, Clara – my maid, you know – is great friends with Elsie, the housemaid at Fernly, and what do you think Elsie told her? That there's been a lot of money stolen, and it's her opinion – Elsie's – I mean, that the parlourmaid had something to do with it. She's leaving at the end of the month, and she's crying a good deal at night. If you ask me, the girl is very likely in league with a *gang*. She's always been a queer girl – she's not friends with any of the girls round here. She goes off by herself on her days out – very unnatural, I call it, and most suspicious. I asked her once to come to our Friendly Girls' Evenings, but she refused, and then I asked her a few questions about her home and her family – all that sort of thing, and I'm bound to say I considered her manner most impertinent. Outwardly very respectful – but she shut me up in the most barefaced way.'

Miss Gannett stopped for breath, and the colonel, who was totally uninterested in the servant question, remarked that in the Shanghai Club brisk play was the invariable rule.

We had a round of brisk play.

'That Miss Russell,' said Caroline. 'She came here pretending to consult James on Friday morning. It's my opinion she wanted to see where the poisons were kept. Five Characters.'

'Chow,' said Miss Gannett. 'What an extraordinary idea! I wonder if you can be right.'

'Talking of poisons,' said the colonel. 'Eh – what? Haven't I discarded? Oh! Eight Bamboos.'

'Mah Jong!' said Miss Gannett.

Caroline was very much annoyed.

'One Red Dragon,' she said regretfully, 'and I should have had a hand of three doubles.'

'I've had two Red Dragons all the time,' I mentioned.

'So exactly like you, James,' said Caroline reproachfully. 'You've no conception of the spirit of the game.'

I myself thought I had played rather cleverly. I should have had to pay Caroline an enormous amount if she had gone Mah Jong. Miss Gannett's Mah Jong was of the poorest variety possible, as Caroline did not fail to point out to her.

East Wind passed, and we started a new hand in silence.

'What I was going to tell you just now was this,' said Caroline.

'Yes?' said Miss Gannett encouragingly.

'My idea about Ralph Paton, I mean.'

'Yes, dear,' said Miss Gannett, still more encouragingly. 'Chow!'

'It's a sign of weakness to Chow so early,' said Caroline severely. 'You should go for a big hand.'

'I know,' said Miss Gannett. 'You were saying – about Ralph Paton, you know?'

'Yes. Well, I've a pretty shrewd idea where he is.'

We all stopped to stare at her.

'This is very interesting, Miss Caroline,' said Colonel Carter. 'All your own idea, eh?'

'Well, not exactly. I'll tell you about it. You know that big map of the county we have in the hall?'

We all said Yes.

'As M. Poirot was going out the other day, he stopped and looked at it, and he made some remark – I can't remember exactly what it was. Something about Cranchester being the only big town anywhere near us – which is true, of course. But after he had gone – it came to me suddenly.'

'What came to you?'

'His meaning. Of course Ralph is in Cranchester.'

It was at that moment that I knocked down the rack that held my pieces. My sister immediately reproved me for clumsiness, but half-heartedly. She was intent on her theory.

'Cranchester, Miss Caroline?' said Colonel Carter. 'Surely not Cranchester! It's so near.'

'That's exactly it,' cried Caroline triumphantly. 'It seems quite clear by now that he didn't get away from here by train. He must simply have walked into Cranchester. And I believe he's there still. No one would dream of his being so near at hand.'

I pointed out several objections to the theory, but when once Caroline has got something firmly into her head, nothing dislodges it.

'And you think M. Poirot has the same idea,' said Miss Gannett thoughtfully. 'It's a curious coincidence, but I was out for a walk this afternoon on the Cranchester road, and he passed me in a car coming from that direction.'

We all looked at each other.

'Why, dear me,' said Miss Gannett suddenly, 'I'm Mah Jong all the time, and I never noticed it.'

Caroline's attention was distracted from her own inventive exercises. She pointed out to Miss Gannett that a hand consisting of mixed suits and too many Chows was hardly worth going Mah Jong on. Miss Gannett listened imperturbably and collected her counters.

'Yes, dear, I know what you mean,' she said. 'But it rather depends on what kind of a hand you have to start with, doesn't it?'

'You'll never get the big hands if you don't go for them,' urged Caroline.

'Well, we must all play our own way, mustn't we?' said Miss Gannett. She looked down at her counters. 'After all, I'm up, so far.'

Caroline, who was considerably down, said nothing.

East Wind passed, and we set to once more. Annie brought in the tea things. Caroline and Miss Gannett were both slightly ruffled as is often the case during one of these festive evenings.

'If you would only play a leetle quicker, dear,' said Caroline, as Miss Gannett hesitated over her discard. 'The Chinese put down the tiles so quickly it sounds like little birds pattering.'

For some minutes we played like the Chinese.

'You haven't contributed much to the sum of information, Sheppard,' said Colonel Carter genially. 'You're a sly dog. Hand in glove with the great detective, and not a hint as to the way things are going.'

'James is an extraordinary creature,' said Caroline. 'He can *not* bring himself to part with information.'

She looked at me with some disfavour.

'I assure you,' I said, 'that I don't know anything. Poirot keeps his own counsel.'

'Wise man,' said the colonel with a chuckle. 'He doesn't give himself away. But they're wonderful fellows, these foreign detectives. Up to all sorts of dodges, I believe.'

'Pung,' said Miss Gannett, in a tone of quiet triumph. 'And Mah Jong.'

The situation became more strained. It was annoyance at Miss Gannett's going Mah Jong for the third time running which prompted Caroline to say to me as we built a fresh wall:

'You are too tiresome, James. You sit there like a deadhead, and say nothing at all!'

'But, my dear,' I protested, 'I have really nothing to say – that is, of the kind you mean.'

'Nonsense,' said Caroline, as she sorted her hand. 'You *must* know something interesting.'

I did not answer for a moment. I was overwhelmed and intoxicated. I had read of there being such a thing as the Perfect Winning – going Mah Jong on one's original hand. I had never hoped to hold the hand myself.

With suppressed triumph I laid my hand face upwards on the table.

'As they say in the Shanghai Club,' I remarked – 'Tin-ho – the Perfect Winning!'

The colonel's eyes nearly bulged out of his head.

'Upon my soul,' he said, 'what an extraordinary thing. I never saw that happen before!'

It was then that I went on, goaded by Caroline's gibes, and rendered reckless by my triumph.

'And as to anything interesting,' I said. 'What about a gold wedding ring with a date and "From R." inside.'

I pass over the scene that followed. I was made to say exactly where this treasure was found. I was made to reveal the date.

'March 13th,' said Caroline. 'Just six months ago. Ah!'

Out of a babel of excited suggestions and suppositions three theories were evolved:

1. That of Colonel Carter: that Ralph was secretly married to Flora. The first or most simple solution.

2. That of Miss Gannett: that Roger Ackroyd had been secretly married to Mrs Ferrars.

3. That of my sister: that Roger Ackroyd had married his housekeeper, Miss Russell.

A fourth or super-theory was propounded by Caroline later as we went up to bed.

'Mark my words,' she said suddenly, 'I shouldn't be at all surprised if Geoffrey Raymond and Flora weren't married.'

'Surely it would be "From G.," not "From R." then,' I suggested.

'You never know. Some girls call men by their surnames. And you heard what Miss Gannett said this evening – about Flora's carryings on.'

Strictly speaking, I had not heard Miss Gannett say anything of the kind, but I respected Caroline's knowledge of innuendoes.

'How about Hector Blunt?' I hinted. 'If it's anybody –'

'Nonsense,' said Caroline. 'I dare say he admires her – may even be in love with her. But depend upon it a girl isn't going to fall in love with a man old enough to be her father when there's a good-looking secretary about. She may encourage Major Blunt just as a blind. Girls are very artful. But there's one thing I *do* tell you, James Sheppard. Flora Ackroyd does not care a penny piece for Ralph Paton, and never has. You can take it from me.'

I took it from her meekly.

CHAPTER XVII

Parker

It occurred to me the next morning that under the exhilaration produced by Tin-ho or the Perfect Winning, I might have been slightly indiscreet. True, Poirot had not asked me to keep the discovery of the ring to myself. On the other hand, he had said nothing about it whilst at Fernly, and as far as I knew, I was the only person aware that it had been found. I felt distinctly guilty. The fact was by now spreading through King's Abbot like wildfire. I was expecting wholesale reproaches from Poirot any minute.

The joint funeral of Mrs Ferrars and Roger Ackroyd was fixed for eleven o'clock. It was a melancholy and impressive ceremony. All the party from Fernly were there.

After it was over, Poirot, who had also been present, took me by the arm, and invited me to accompany him back to The Larches. He was looking very grave, and I feared that my indiscretion of the night before had got round to his ears. But it soon transpired that his thoughts were occupied by something of a totally different nature.

'See you,' he said. 'We must act. With your help I propose to examine a witness. We will question him, we will put such fear into him that the truth is bound to come out.'

'What witness are you talking about?' I asked, very much surprised.

'Parker!' said Poirot. 'I asked him to be at my house this morning at twelve o'clock. He should await us there at this very minute.'

'What do you think?' I ventured, glancing sideways at his face.

'I know this – that I am not satisfied.'

'You think that it was he who blackmailed Mrs Ferrars?'

'Either that, or –'

'Well?' I said, after waiting a minute or two.

'My friend, I will say this to you – I hope it was he.'

The gravity of his manner, and something indefinable that tinged it, reduced me to silence.

On arrival at The Larches, we were informed that Parker was already there awaiting our return. As we entered the room, the butler rose respectfully.

'Good morning, Parker,' said Poirot pleasantly. 'One instant, I pray of you.'

He removed his overcoat and gloves.

'Allow me, sir,' said Parker, and sprang forward to assist him. He deposited the articles neatly on a chair by the door. Poirot watched him with approval.

'Thank you, my good Parker,' he said. 'Take a seat, will you not? What I have to say may take some time.'

Parker seated himself with an apologetic bend of the head.

'Now what do you think I asked you to come here for this morning – eh?'

Parker coughed.

'I understood, sir, that you wished to ask me a few questions about my late master – private like.'

'*Précisément*,' said Poirot, beaming. 'Have you made many experiments in blackmail?'

'Sir!'

The butler sprang to his feet.

'Do not excite yourself,' said Poirot placidly. 'Do not play the farce of the honest, injured man. You know all there is to know about the blackmail, is it not so?'

'Sir, I – I've never – never been –'

'Insulted,' suggested Poirot, 'in such a way before. Then why, my excellent Parker, were you so anxious to overhear the conversation in Mr Ackroyd's study the other evening, after you had caught the word "blackmail"?'

'I wasn't – I –'

'Who was your last master?' rapped out Poirot suddenly.

'My last master?'

'Yes, the master you were with before you came to Mr Ackroyd.'

'A Major Ellerby, sir –'

Poirot took the words out of his mouth.

'Just so, Major Ellerby. Major Ellerby was addicted to drugs, was he not? You travelled about with him. When he was in Bermuda there was some trouble – a man was killed. Major Ellerby was partly responsible. It was hushed up. But you knew about it. How much did Major Ellerby pay you to keep your mouth shut?'

Parker was staring at him open-mouthed. The man had gone to pieces, his cheeks shook flabbily.

'You see, me, I have made inquiries,' said Poirot pleasantly. 'It is as I say. You got a good sum then as blackmail, and Major Ellerby went on paying you until he died. Now I want to hear about your latest experiment.'

Parker still stared.

'It is useless to deny. Hercule Poirot *knows*. It is so, what I have said about Major Ellerby, is it not?'

As though almost against his will, Parker nodded reluctantly once. His face was ashen pale.

'But I never hurt a hair of Mr Ackroyd's head,' he moaned. 'Honest to God, sir, I didn't. I've been afraid of this coming all the time. And I tell you I didn't – I didn't kill him.'

His voice rose almost to a scream.

'I am inclined to believe you, my friend,' said Poirot. 'You have not the nerve – the courage. But I must have the truth.'

'I'll tell you anything, sir, anything you want to know. It's true that I tried to listen that night. A word or two I heard made me curious. And Mr Ackroyd's wanting not to be disturbed, and shutting himself up with the doctor the way he did. It's God's own truth what I told the police. I heard the word "blackmail", sir, and well –'

He paused.

'You thought there might be something in it for you?' suggested Poirot smoothly.

'Well – well, yes, I did, sir. I thought that if Mr Ackroyd

was being blackmailed, why shouldn't I have a share of the pickings?'

A very curious expression passed over Poirot's face. He leaned forward.

'Had you any reason to suppose before that night that Mr Ackroyd was being blackmailed?'

'No, indeed, sir. It was a great surprise to me. Such a regular gentleman in all his habits.'

'How much did you overhear?'

'Not very much, sir. There seemed what I might call a spite against me. Of course I had to attend to my duties in the pantry. And when I did creep along once or twice to the study it was no use. The first time Dr Sheppard came out and almost caught me in the act, and another time Mr Raymond passed me in the big hall and went that way, so I knew it was no use; and when I went with the tray, Miss Flora headed me off.'

Poirot stared for a long time at the man, as if to test his sincerity. Parker returned his gaze earnestly.

'I hope you believe me, sir. I've been afraid all along the police would rake up that old business with Major Ellerby and be suspicious of me in consequence.'

'*Eh bien,*' said Poirot at last. 'I am disposed to believe you. But there is one thing I must request of you – to show me your bank-book. You have a bank-book, I presume?'

'Yes, sir, as a matter of fact, I have it with me now.'

With no sign of confusion, he produced it from his pocket. Poirot took the slim, green-covered book and perused the entries.

'Ah! I perceive you have purchased £500 worth of National Savings Certificates this year?'

'Yes, sir. I have already over a thousand pounds saved – the result of my connection with – er – my late master, Major Ellerby. And I have had quite a little flutter on some horses this year – very successful. If you remember, sir, a rank outsider won the Jubilee. I was fortunate enough to back it – £20.'

Poirot handed him back the book.

'I will wish you good morning. I believe that you have told

me the truth. If you have not – so much the worse for you, my friend.'

When Parker had departed, Poirot picked up his overcoat once more.

'Going out again?' I asked.

'Yes, we will pay a little visit to the good M. Hammond.'

'You believe Parker's story?'

'It is credible enough on the face of it. It seems clear that – unless he is a very good actor indeed – he genuinely believes it was Ackroyd himself who was the victim of blackmail. If so, he knows nothing at all about the Mrs Ferrars business.'

'Then in that case – who –?'

'*Précisément!* Who? But our visit to M. Hammond will accomplish one purpose. It will either clear Parker completely or else –'

'Well?'

'I fall into the bad habit of leaving my sentences unfinished this morning,' said Poirot apologetically. 'You must bear with me.'

'By the way,' I said, rather sheepishly, 'I've got a confession to make. I'm afraid I have inadvertently let out something about that ring.'

'What ring?'

'The ring you found in the goldfish pond.'

'Ah! yes,' said Poirot, smiling broadly.

'I hope you're not annoyed? It was very careless of me.'

'But not at all, my good friend, not at all. I laid no commands upon you. You were at liberty to speak of it if you so wished. She was interested, your sister?'

'She was indeed. It created a sensation. All sorts of theories are flying about.'

'Ah! And yet it is so simple. The true explanation leapt to the eye, did it not?'

'Did it?' I said drily.

Poirot laughed.

'The wise man does not commit himself,' he observed. 'Is not that so? But here we are at Mr Hammond's.'

The lawyer was in his office, and we were ushered in without any delay. He rose and greeted us in his dry, precise manner.

Poirot came at once to the point.

'Monsieur, I desire from you certain information, that is, if you will be so good as to give it to me. You acted, I understand, for the late Mrs Ferrars of King's Paddock?'

I noticed the swift gleam of surprise which showed in the lawyer's eyes, before his professional reserve came down once more like a mask over his face.

'Certainly. All her affairs passed through our hands.'

'Very good. Now, before I ask you to tell me anything, I should like you to listen to the story Dr Sheppard will relate to you. You have no objection, have you, my friend, to repeating the conversation you had with Mr Ackroyd last Friday night?'

'Not in the least,' I said, and straightway began the recital of that strange evening.

Hammond listened with close attention.

'That is all,' I said, when I had finished.

'Blackmail,' said the lawyer thoughtfully.

'You are surprised?' asked Poirot.

The lawyer took off his pince-nez and polished them with his handkerchief.

'No,' he replied, 'I can hardly say that I am surprised. I have suspected something of the kind for some time.'

'That brings us,' said Poirot, 'to the information for which I am asking. If anyone can give us an idea of the actual sums paid, you are the man, monsieur.'

'I see no object in withholding the information,' said Hammond, after a moment or two. 'During the past year, Mrs Ferrars has sold out certain securities, and the money for them was paid into her account and not re-invested. As her income was a large one, and she lived very quietly after her husband's death, it seems certain that these sums of money were paid away for some special purpose. I once sounded her on the subject, and she said that she was obliged to support several of her husband's poor relations. I let the matter drop, of course. Until now, I have always imagined that the money was paid to some woman who had had a claim on Ashley Ferrars. I never dreamed that Mrs Ferrars herself was involved.'

'And the amount?' asked Poirot.

'In all, I should say the various sums totalled at least twenty thousand pounds.'

'Twenty thousand pounds!' I exclaimed. 'In one year!'

'Mrs Ferrars was a very wealthy woman,' said Poirot drily. 'And the penalty for murder is not a pleasant one.'

'Is there anything else that I can tell you?' inquired Mr Hammond.

'I thank you, no,' said Poirot, rising. 'All my excuses for having deranged you.'

'Not at all, not at all.'

'The word "derange",' I remarked, when we were outside again, 'is applicable to mental disorder only.'

'Ah!' cried Poirot, 'never will my English be quite perfect. A curious language. I should then have said disarranged, *n'est-ce pas?*'

'Disturbed is the word you had in mind.'

'I thank you, my friend. The word "exact", you are zealous for it. *Eh bien,* what about our friend Parker now? With twenty-thousand pounds in hand, would he have continued being a butler? *Je ne pense pas.* It is, of course, possible that he banked the money under another name, but I am disposed to believe he spoke the truth to us. If he is a scoundrel, he is a scoundrel on a mean scale. He has not the big ideas. That leaves us as a possibility, Raymond, or – well – Major Blunt.'

'Surely not Raymond,' I objected. 'Since we know that he was desperately hard up for a matter of five hundred pounds.'

'That is what he says, yes.'

'And as to Hector Blunt –'

'I will tell you something as to the good Major Blunt,' interrupted Poirot. 'It is my business to make inquiries. I make them. *Eh bien* – that legacy of which he speaks, I have discovered that the amount of it was close upon twenty thousand pounds. What do you think of that?'

I was so taken aback that I could hardly speak.

'It's impossible,' I said at last. 'A well-known man like Hector Blunt.'

Poirot shrugged his shoulders.

'Who knows? At least he is a man with big ideas. I confess that I hardly see him as a blackmailer, but there is another possibility that you have not even considered.'

'What is that?'

'The fire, my friend. Ackroyd himself may have destroyed that letter, blue envelope and all, after you left him.'

'I hardly think that likely,' I said slowly. 'And yet – of course, it may be so. He might have changed his mind.'

We had just arrived at my house, and on the spur of the moment I invited Poirot to come in and take pot luck.

I thought Caroline would be pleased with me, but it is hard to satisfy one's womenfolk. It appears that we were eating chops for lunch – the kitchen staff being regaled on tripe and onions. And two chops set before three people are productive of embarrassment.

But Caroline is seldom daunted for long. With magnificent mendacity, she explained to Poirot that although James laughed at her for doing so, she adhered strictly to a vegetarian diet. She descanted ecstatically on the delights of nut cutlets (which I am quite sure she has never tasted) and ate a Welsh rarebit with gusto and frequent cutting remarks as to the dangers of 'flesh' foods.

Afterwards, when we were sitting in front of the fire and smoking, Caroline attacked Poirot directly.

'Not found Ralph Paton yet?' she asked.

'Where should I find him, mademoiselle?'

'I thought, perhaps, you'd found him in Cranchester,' said Caroline, with intense meaning in her tone.

Poirot looked merely bewildered.

'In Cranchester? But why in Cranchester?'

I enlightened him with a touch of malice.

'One of our ample staff of private detectives happened to see you in a car on the Cranchester road yesterday,' I explained.

Poirot's bewilderment vanished. He laughed heartily.

'Ah, that! A simple visit to the dentist, *c'est tout*. My tooth, it aches. I go there. My tooth, it is at once better. I think to return quickly. The dentist, he says No. Better to have it out. I argue. He insists. He has his way! That particular tooth, it will never ache again.'

Caroline collapsed rather like a pricked balloon.

We fell to discussing Ralph Paton.

'A weak nature,' I insisted. 'But not a vicious one.'

'Ah!' said Poirot. 'But weakness, where does it end?'

'Exactly,' said Caroline. 'Take James here – weak as water, if I weren't about to look after him.'

'My dear Caroline,' I said irritably, 'can't you talk without dragging in personalities?'

'You *are* weak, James,' said Caroline, quite unmoved. 'I'm eight years older than you are – oh! I don't mind M. Poirot knowing that –'

'I should never have guessed it, mademoiselle,' said Poirot, with a gallant little bow.

'Eight years older. And I've always considered it my duty to look after you. With a bad bringing up, Heaven knows what mischief you might have got into by now.'

'I might have married a beautiful adventuress,' I murmured, gazing at the ceiling, and blowing smoke rings.

'Adventuress!' said Caroline, with a snort. 'If we're talking of adventuresses –'

She left the sentence unfinished.

'Well?' I said, with some curiosity.

'Nothing. But I can think of someone not a hundred miles away.'

Then she turned to Poirot suddenly.

'James sticks to it that you believe someone in the house committed the murder. All I can say is, you're wrong.'

'I should not like to be wrong,' said Poirot. 'It is not – how do you say – my *métier*?'

'I've got the facts pretty clearly,' continued Caroline, taking no notice of Poirot's remark, 'from James and others. As far as

I can see, of the people in the house, only two *could* have had the chance of doing it. Ralph Paton and Flora Ackroyd.'

'My dear Caroline –'

'Now, James, don't interrupt me. I know what I'm talking about. Parker met her *outside* the door, didn't he? He didn't hear her uncle saying goodnight to her. She could have killed him then and there.'

'Caroline!'

'I'm not saying she *did*, James. I'm saying she *could* have done. As a matter of fact, though Flora is like all these young girls nowadays, with no veneration for their betters and thinking they know best on every subject under the sun, I don't for a minute believe she'd kill even a chicken. But there it is. Mr Raymond and Major Blunt have alibis. Mrs Ackroyd's got an alibi. Even that Russell woman seems to have one – and a good job for her it is she has. Who is left? Only Ralph and Flora! And say what you will, I don't believe Ralph Paton is a murderer. A boy we've known all our lives.'

Poirot was silent for a minute, watching the curling smoke rise from his cigarette. When at last he spoke, it was in a gentle far-away voice that produced a curious impression. It was totally unlike his usual manner.

'Let us take a man – a very ordinary man. A man with no idea of murder in his heart. There is in him somewhere a strain of weakness – deep down. It has so far never been called into play. Perhaps it never will be – and if so he will go to his grave honoured and respected by everyone. But let us suppose that something occurs. He is in difficulties – or perhaps not that even. He may stumble by accident on a secret – a secret involving life or death to someone. And his first impulse will be to speak out – to do his duty as an honest citizen. And then the strain of weakness tells. Here is a chance of money – a great amount of money. He wants money – he desires it – and it is so easy. He has to do nothing for it – just keep silence. That is the beginning. The desire for money grows. He must have more and more! He is intoxicated by the gold mine which has opened at his feet. He becomes greedy. And in his greed he overreaches himself. One can press a man as far as one likes – but with a woman one must not press too far. For a woman has at heart a great desire to speak the truth. How many husbands who have deceived their wives go comfortably to their graves, carrying their secret with them! How many wives who have deceived their husbands wreck their lives by throwing the fact in those same husbands' teeth! They have been pressed too far. In a reckless moment (which they will afterwards regret, *bien entendu*) they fling safety to the winds and turn at bay, proclaiming the truth with great momentary satisfaction to themselves. So it was, I think, in this case. The strain was too great. And so there came your proverb, the death of the goose that laid the golden eggs. But that is not the end. Exposure faced the man of whom we are speaking. And he is not the same man he was – say, a year ago. His moral fibre is blunted. He is desperate. He is fighting a losing battle, and he is prepared to take any means that come to his hand, for exposure means ruins to him. And so – the dagger strikes!'

He was silent for a moment. It was as though he had laid a spell upon the room. I cannot try to describe the impression his words produced. There was something in the merciless analysis, and the ruthless power of vision which struck fear into both of us.

'Afterwards,' he went on softly, 'the dagger removed, he will be himself again, normal, kindly. But if the need again arises, then once more he will strike.'

Caroline roused herself at last.

'You are speaking of Ralph Paton,' she said. 'You may be right, you may not, but you have no business to condemn a man unheard.'

The telephone bell rang sharply. I went out into the hall, and took off the receiver.

'What?' I said. 'Yes. Dr Sheppard speaking.'

I listened for a minute or two, then replied briefly. Replacing the receiver, I went back into the drawing-room.

'Poirot,' I said, 'they have detained a man at Liverpool. His

name is Charles Kent, and he is believed to be the stranger who
visited Fernly that night. They want me to go to Liverpool at
once and identify him.'

CHAPTER XVIII

Charles Kent

Half an hour later saw Poirot, myself, and Inspector Raglan in the train on the way to Liverpool. The inspector was clearly very excited.

'We may get a line on the blackmailing part of the business, if on nothing else,' he declared jubilantly. 'He's a rough customer, this fellow, by what I heard over the phone. Takes dope, too. We ought to find it easy to get what we want out of him. If there was the shadow of a motive, nothing's more likely than that he killed Mr Ackroyd. But in that case, why is young Paton keeping out of the way. The whole thing's a muddle – that's what it is. By the way, M. Poirot, you were quite right about those fingerprints. They were Mr Ackroyd's own. I had rather the same idea myself, but I dismissed it as hardly feasible.'

I smiled to myself. Inspector Raglan was so very plainly saving his face.

'As regard this man,' said Poirot, 'he is not yet arrested, eh?'

'No, detained under suspicion.'

'And what account does he give of himself?'

'Precious little,' said the inspector, with a grin. 'He's a wary bird, I gather. A lot of abuse, but very little more.'

On arrival at Liverpool I was surprised to find that Poirot was welcomed with acclamation. Superintendent Hayes, who met us, had worked with Poirot over some case long ago, and had evidently an exaggerated opinion of his powers.

'Now we've got M. Poirot here we shan't be long,' he said cheerfully. 'I thought you'd retired, moosior?'

'So I had, my good Hayes, so I had. But how tedious is retirement! You cannot imagine to yourself the monotony with which day comes after day.'

'Very likely. So you've come to have a look at our own particular find? Is this Dr Sheppard? Think you'll be able to identify him, sir?'

'I'm not very sure,' I said doubtfully.

'How did you get hold of him?' inquired Poirot.

'Description was circulated, as you know. In the press and privately. Not much to go on, I admit. This fellow has an American accent all right, and he doesn't deny that he was near King's Abbot that night. Just asks what the hell it is to do with us, and that he'll see us in – before he answers any questions.'

'Is it permitted that I, too, see him?' asked Poirot.

The superintendent closed one eye knowingly.

'Very glad to have you, sir. You've got permission to do anything you please. Inspector Japp of Scotland Yard was asking after you the other day. Said he'd heard you were connected unofficially with this case. Where's Captain Paton hiding, sir, can you tell me that?'

'I doubt if it would be wise at the present juncture,' said Poirot primly, and I bit my lips to prevent a smile.

The little man really did it very well.

After some further parley, we were taken to interview the prisoner.

He was a young fellow, I should say not more than twenty-two or three. Tall, thin, with slightly shaking hands, and the evidences of considerable physical strength somewhat run to seed. His hair was dark, but his eyes were blue and shifty, seldom meeting a glance squarely. I had all along cherished the illusion that there was something familiar about the figure I had met that night, but if this were indeed he, I was completely mistaken. He did not remind me in the least of anyone I knew.

'Now then, Kent,' said the superintendent. 'Stand up. Here are some visitors come to see you. Recognize any of them?'

Kent glared at us sullenly, but did not reply. I saw his glance waver over the three of us, and come back to rest on me.

'Well, sir,' said the superintendent to me, 'what do you say?'

'The height's the same,' I said, 'and as far as general

appearance goes it might well be the man in question. Beyond that, I couldn't go.'

'What the hell's the meaning of all this?' asked Kent. 'What have you got against me? Come on, out with it? What am I supposed to have done?'

I nodded my head.

'It's the man,' I said. 'I recognize the voice.'

'Recognize my voice, do you? Where do you think you heard it before?'

'On Friday evening last, outside the gates of Fernly Park. You asked me the way there.'

'I did, did I?'

'Do you admit it?' asked the inspector.

'I don't admit anything. Not till I know what you've got on me.'

'Have you not read the papers in the last few days?' asked Poirot, speaking for the first time.

The man's eyes narrowed.

'So that's it, is it? I saw an old gent had been croaked at Fernly. Trying to make out I did the job, are you?'

'You were there that night,' said Poirot quietly.

'How do you know, mister?'

'By this.' Poirot took something from his pocket and held it out.

It was the goose quill we had found in the summer-house.

At the sight of it the man's face changed. He half held out his hand.

'Snow,' said Poirot thoughtfully. 'No, my friend, it is empty. It lay where you dropped it in the summer-house that night.'

Charles Kent looked at him uncertainly.

'You seem to know a hell of a lot about everything, you little foreign cock duck. Perhaps you remember this: the papers say that the old gent was croaked between a quarter to ten and ten o'clock?'

'That is so,' agreed Poirot.

'Yes, but is it really so? That's what I'm getting at.'

'This gentleman will tell you,' said Poirot.

He indicated Inspector Raglan. The latter hesitated, glanced at Superintendent Hayes, then at Poirot, and finally, as though receiving sanction, he said:

'That's right. Between a quarter to ten and ten o'clock.'

'Then you've nothing to keep me here for,' said Kent. 'I was away from Fernly Park by twenty-five minutes past nine. You can ask at the Dog and Whistle. That's a saloon about a mile out of Fernly on the road to Cranchester. I kicked up a bit of a row there, I remember. As near as nothing to quarter to ten, it was. How about that?'

Inspector Raglan wrote down something in his notebook.

'Well?' demanded Kent.

'Inquiries will be made,' said the inspector. 'If you've spoken the truth, you won't have anything to complain about. What were you doing at Fernly Park anyway?'

'Went there to meet someone.'

'Who?'

'That's none of your business.'

'You'd better keep a civil tongue in your head, my man,' the superintendent warned him.

'To hell with a civil tongue. I went there on my own business, and that's all there is to it. If I was clear away before the murder was done, that's all that concerns the cops.'

'Your name, it is Charles Kent,' said Poirot. 'Where were you born?'

The man stared at him, then he grinned.

'I'm a full-blown Britisher all right,' he said.

'Yes,' said Poirot meditatively. 'I think you are. I fancy you were born in Kent.'

The man stared.

'Why's that? Because of my name? What's that to do with it? Is a man whose name is Kent bound to be born in that particular county?'

'Under certain circumstances, I can imagine he might be,' said Poirot very deliberately. 'Under certain circumstances, you comprehend.'

There was so much meaning in his voice as to surprise the

two police officers. As for Charles Kent, he flushed a brick red, and for a moment I thought he was going to spring at Poirot. He thought better of it, however, and turned away with a kind of laugh.

Poirot nodded as though satisfied, and made his way out through the door. He was joined presently by the two officers.

'We'll verify that statement,' remarked Raglan. 'I don't think he's lying, though. But he's got to come clean with a statement as to what he was doing at Fernly. It looks to me as though we'd got our blackmailer all right. On the other hand, granted his story's correct, he couldn't have had anything to do with the actual murder. He'd got ten pounds on him when he was arrested – rather a large sum. I fancy that forty pounds went to him – the numbers of the notes didn't correspond, but of course he'd have changed them first thing. Mr Ackroyd must have given him the money, and he made off with it as fast as possible. What was that about Kent being his birthplace? What's that got to do with it?'

'Nothing whatever,' said Poirot mildly. 'A little idea of mine, that was all. Me, I am famous for my little ideas.'

'Are you really?' said Raglan, studying him with a puzzled expression.

The superintendent went into a roar of laughter.

'Many's the time I've heard Inspector Japp say that. M. Poirot and his little ideas! Too fanciful for me, he'd say, but always something in them.'

'You mock yourself at me,' said Poirot, smiling; 'but never mind. The old ones they laugh last sometimes, when the young, clever ones do not laugh at all.'

And nodding his head at them in a sage manner he walked out into the street.

He and I lunched together at an hotel. I know now that the whole thing lay clearly unravelled before him. He had got the last thread he needed to lead him to the truth.

But at the time I had no suspicion of the fact. I overestimated his general self-confidence, and I took it for granted that the things which puzzled me must be equally puzzling to him.

My chief puzzle was what the man Charles Kent could have been doing at Fernly. Again and again I put the question to myself and could get no satisfactory reply. At last I ventured a tentative query to Poirot. His reply was immediate.

'*Mon ami, I* do not think, I know.'

'Really?' I said incredulously.

'Yes, indeed. I suppose now that to you it would not make sense if I said that he went to Fernly that night because he was born in Kent?'

I stared at him.

'It certainly doesn't seem to make sense to me,' I said drily.

'Ah!' said Poirot pityingly. 'Well, no matter. I have still my little idea.'

CHAPTER XIX

Flora Ackroyd

As I was returning from my round the following morning, I was hailed by Inspector Raglan. I pulled up, and the inspector mounted on the step.

'Good morning, Dr Sheppard,' he said. 'Well, that alibi is all right enough.'

'Charles Kent's?'

'Charles Kent's. The barmaid at the Dog and Whistle, Sally Jones, she remembers him perfectly. Picked out his photograph from among five others. It was just a quarter to ten when he came into the bar, and the Dog and Whistle is well over a mile from Fernly Park. The girl mentions that he had a lot of money on him – she saw him take a handful of notes out of his pocket. Rather surprised her, it did, seeing the class of fellow he was, with a pair of boots clean dropping off him. That's where that forty pounds went right enough.'

'The man still refuses to give an account of his visit to Fernly?'

'Obstinate as a mule he is. I had a chat with Hayes at Liverpool over the wire this morning.'

'Hercule Poirot says he knows the reason the man went there that night,' I observed.

'Does he?' cried the inspector eagerly.

'Yes,' I said maliciously. 'He says he went there because he was born in Kent.'

I felt a distinct pleasure in passing on my own discomfiture.

Raglan stared at me for a moment or two uncomprehending. Then a grin overspread his weasely countenance and he tapped his forehead significantly.

'But gone here,' he said. 'I've thought so for some time. Poor old chap, so that's why he had to give up and come down here.

In the family, very likely. He's got a nephew who's quite off his crumpet.'

'Poirot has?' I said, very surprised.

'Yes. Hasn't he ever mentioned him to you? Quite docile, I believe, and all that, but mad as a hatter, poor lad.'

'Who told you that?'

Again a grin showed itself on Inspector Raglan's face.

'Your sister, Miss Sheppard, she told me all about it.'

Really, Caroline is amazing. She never rests until she knows the last details of everybody's family secrets. Unfortunately, I have never been able to instil into her the decency of keeping them to herself.

'Jump in, Inspector,' I said, opening the door of the car. 'We'll go up to The Larches together, and acquaint our Belgian friend with the latest news.'

'Might as well, I suppose. After all, even if he is a bit balmy, it was a useful tip he gave me about those fingerprints. He's got a bee in his bonnet about the man Kent, but who knows – there may be something useful behind it.'

Poirot received us with his usual smiling courtesy.

He listened to the information we had brought him, nodding his head now and then.

'Seems quite OK, doesn't it?' said the inspector rather gloomily. 'A chap can't be murdering someone in one place when he's drinking in the bar in another place a mile away.'

'Are you going to release him?'

'Don't see what else we can do. We can't very well hold him for obtaining money on false pretences. Can't prove a ruddy thing.'

The inspector tossed a match into the grate in a disgruntled fashion. Poirot retrieved it and put it neatly in a little receptacle designed for the purpose. His action was purely mechanical. I could see that his thoughts were on something very different.

'If I were you,' he said at last, 'I should not release the man Charles Kent yet.'

'What do you mean?'

Raglan stared at him.

'What I say. I should not release him yet.'

'You don't think he can have had anything to do with the murder, do you?'

'I think probably not – but one cannot be certain yet.'

'But haven't I just told you –?'

Poirot raised a hand protestingly.

'*Mais oui, mais oui.* I heard. I am not deaf – or stupid, thank the good God! But you see, you approach the matter from the wrong – the wrong – premises, is not that the word?'

The inspector stared at him heavily.

'I don't see how you make that out. Look here, we know Mr Ackroyd was alive at a quarter to ten. You admit that, don't you?'

Poirot looked at him for a moment, then shook his head with a quick smile.

'I admit nothing that is not – *proved*!'

'Well, we've got proof enough of that. We've got Miss Flora Ackroyd's evidence.'

'That she said goodnight to her uncle? But me – I do not always believe what a young lady tells me – no, not even when she is charming and beautiful.'

'But hang it all, man, Parker saw her coming out of the door.'

'No.' Poirot's voice rang out with sudden sharpness. 'That is just what he did not see. I satisfied myself of that by a little experiment the other day – you remember, doctor? Parker saw her *outside* the door, with her hand on the handle. He did not see her come out of the room.'

'But – where else could she have been?'

'Perhaps on the stairs.'

'The stairs?'

'That is my little idea – yes.'

'But those stairs only lead to Mr Ackroyd's bedroom.'

'Precisely.'

And still the inspector stared.

'You think she'd been up to her uncle's bedroom? Well, why not? Why should she lie about it?'

'Ah! that is just the question. It depends on what she was doing there, does it not?'

'You mean – the money? Hang it all, you don't suggest that it was Miss Ackroyd who took that forty pounds?'

'I suggest nothing,' said Poirot. 'But I will remind you of this. Life was not very easy for that mother and daughter. There were bills – there was constant trouble over small sums of money. Roger Ackroyd was a peculiar man over money matters. The girl might be at her wits' end for a comparatively small sum. Figure to yourself then what happens. She has taken the money, she descends the little staircase. When she is half-way down she hears the chink of glass from the hall. She has not a doubt of what it is – Parker coming to the study. At all costs she must not be found on the stairs – Parker will not forget it, he will think it odd. If the money is missed, Parker is sure to remember having seen her come down those stairs. She has just time to rush down to the study door – with her hand on the handle to show that she has just come out, when Parker appears in the doorway. She says the first thing that comes into her head, a repetition of Roger Ackroyd's orders earlier in the evening, and then goes upstairs to her own room.'

'Yes, but later,' persisted the inspector, 'she must have realized the vital importance of speaking the truth? Why, the whole case hinges on it!'

'Afterwards,' said Poirot drily, 'it was a little difficult for Mademoiselle Flora. She is told simply that the police are here and that there has been a robbery. Naturally she jumps to the conclusion that the theft of the money has been discovered. Her one idea is to stick to her story. When she learns that her uncle is dead she is panic-stricken. Young women do not faint nowadays, monsieur, without considerable provocation. *Eh bien!* there it is. She is bound to stick to her story, or else confess everything. And a young and pretty girl does not like to admit that she is a thief – especially before those whose esteem she is anxious to retain.'

Raglan brought his fist down with a thump on the table.

'I'll not believe it,' he said. 'It's – it's not credible. And you – you've known this all along?'

'The possibility has been in my mind from the first,' admitted Poirot. 'I was always convinced that Mademoiselle Flora was hiding something from us. To satisfy myself, I made the little experiment I told you of. Dr Sheppard accompanied me.'

'A test for Parker, you said it was,' I remarked bitterly.

'*Mon ami*,' said Poirot apologetically, 'as I told you at the time, one must say something.'

The inspector rose.

'There's only one thing for it,' he declared. 'We must tackle the young lady right away. You'll come up to Fernly with me, M. Poirot?'

'Certainly. Dr Sheppard will drive us up in his car.'

I acquiesced willingly.

On inquiry for Miss Ackroyd, we were shown into the billiard room. Flora and Major Hector Blunt were sitting on the long window seat.

'Good morning, Miss Ackroyd,' said the inspector. 'Can we have a word or two alone with you?'

Blunt got up at once and moved to the door.

'What is it?' asked Flora nervously. 'Don't go, Major Blunt. He can stay, can't he?' she asked, turning to the inspector.

'That's as you like,' said the inspector drily. 'There's a question or two it's my duty to put to you, miss, but I'd prefer to do so privately, and I dare say you'd prefer it also.'

Flora looked keenly at him. I saw her face grow whiter. Then she turned and spoke to Blunt.

'I want you to stay – please – yes, I mean it. Whatever the inspector has to say to me, I'd rather you heard it.'

Raglan shrugged his shoulders.

'Well, if you will have it so, that's all there is to it. Now, Miss Ackroyd, M. Poirot here has made a certain suggestion to me. He suggests that you weren't in the study at all last Friday night, that you never saw Mr Ackroyd to say goodnight to him, that instead of being in the study you were on the stairs leading down from your uncle's bedroom when you heard Parker coming across the hall.'

Flora's gaze shifted to Poirot. He nodded back at her.

'Mademoiselle, the other day, when we sat round the table, I implored you to be frank with me. What one does not tell to Papa Poirot he finds out. It was that, was it not? See, I will make it easy for you. You took the money, did you not?'

'The money?' said Blunt sharply.

There was a silence which lasted for at least a minute.

Then Flora drew herself up and spoke.

'M. Poirot is right. I took that money. I stole. I am a thief – yes, a common, vulgar little thief. Now you know! I am glad it has come out. It's been a nightmare, these last few days!' She sat down suddenly and buried her face in her hands. She spoke huskily through her fingers. 'You don't know what my life has been since I came here. Wanting things, scheming for them, lying, cheating, running up bills, promising to pay – oh! I hate myself when I think of it all! That's what brought us together, Ralph and I. We were both weak! I understand him, and I was sorry – because I'm the same underneath. We're not strong enough to stand alone, either of us. We're weak, miserable, despicable things.'

She looked at Blunt and suddenly stamped her foot.

'Why do you look at me like that – as though you couldn't believe? I may be a thief – but at any rate I'm real now. I'm not lying any more. I'm not pretending to be the kind of girl you like, young and innocent and simple. I don't care if you never want to see me again. I hate myself, despise myself – but you've got to believe one thing, if speaking the truth would have made things better for Ralph, I would have spoken out. But I've seen all along that it wouldn't be better for Ralph – it makes the case against him blacker than ever. I was not doing him any harm by sticking to my lie.'

'Ralph,' said Blunt. 'I see – always Ralph.'

'You don't understand,' said Flora hopelessly. 'You never will.'

She turned to the inspector.

'I admit everything; I was at my wits' end for money. I never saw my uncle that evening after he left the dinner-table. As to the money, you can take what steps you please. Nothing could be worse than it is now!'

Suddenly she broke down again, hid her face in her hands, and rushed from the room.

'Well,' said the inspector in a flat tone, 'so that's that.'

He seemed rather at a loss what to do next.

Blunt came forward.

'Inspector Raglan,' he said quietly, 'that money was given to me by Mr Ackroyd for a special purpose. Miss Ackroyd never touched it. When she says she did, she is lying with the idea of shielding Captain Paton. The truth is as I said, and I am prepared to go into the witness-box and swear to it.'

He made a kind of jerky bow, then turning abruptly he left the room.

Poirot was after him in a flash. He caught the other up in the hall.

'Monsieur – a moment, I beg of you, if you will be so good.'

'Well, sir?'

Blunt was obviously impatient. He stood frowning down on Poirot.

'It is this,' said Poirot rapidly: 'I am not deceived by your little fantasy. No, indeed. It was truly Miss Flora who took the money. All the same it is well imagined what you say – it pleases me. It is very good what you have done there. You are a man quick to think and to act.'

'I'm not in the least anxious for your opinion, thank you,' said Blunt coldly.

He made once more as though to pass on, but Poirot, not at all offended, laid a detaining hand on his arm.

'Ah! but you are to listen to me. I have more to say. The other day I spoke of concealments. Very well, all along I have seen what you are concealing. Mademoiselle Flora, you love her with all your heart. From the first moment you saw her, is it not so? Oh! let us not mind saying these things – why must one in England think it necessary to mention love as though it were some disgraceful secret? You love Mademoiselle Flora. You seek to conceal that fact from all the world. That is very good – that is as it should be. But take the advice of Hercule Poirot – do not conceal it from mademoiselle herself.'

Blunt has shown several signs of restlessness whilst Poirot was speaking, but the closing words seemed to rivet his attention.

'What d'you mean by that?' he said sharply.

'You think that she loves the Capitaine Ralph Paton – but I, Hercule Poirot, tell you that that is not so. Mademoiselle Flora accepted Captain Paton to please her uncle, and because she saw in the marriage a way of escape from her life here which was becoming frankly insupportable to her. She liked him, and there was much sympathy and understanding between them. But love – no! It is not Captain Paton Mademoiselle Flora loves.'

'What the devil do you mean?' asked Blunt.

I saw the dark flush under his tan.

'You have been blind, monsieur. Blind! She is loyal, the little one. Ralph Paton is under a cloud, she is bound in honour to stick by him.'

I felt it was time I put in a word to help on the good work.

'My sister told me the other night,' I said encouragingly, 'that Flora had never cared a penny piece for Ralph Paton, and never would. My sister is always right about these things.'

Blunt ignored my well-meant offers. He spoke to Poirot.

'D'you really think –' he began, and stopped.

He is one of those inarticulate men who find it hard to put things into words.

Poirot knows no such disability.

'If you doubt me, ask her yourself, monsieur. But perhaps you no longer care to – the affair of the money –'

Blunt gave a sound like an angry laugh.

'Think I'd hold that against her? Roger was always a queer chap about money. She got in a mess and didn't dare tell him. Poor kid. Poor lonely kid.'

Poirot looked thoughtfully at the side door.

'Mademoiselle Flora went into the garden, I think,' he murmured.

'I've been every kind of a fool,' said Blunt abruptly. 'Rum

conversation we've been having. Like one of those Danish plays. But you're a sound fellow, M. Poirot. Thank you.'

He took Poirot's hand and gave it a grip which caused the other to wince in anguish. Then he strode to the side door and passed out into the garden.

'Not every kind of a fool,' murmured Poirot, tenderly nursing the injured member. 'Only one kind – the fool in love.'

CHAPTER XX

Miss Russell

Inspector Raglan had received a bad jolt. He was not deceived by Blunt's valiant lie any more than we had been. Our way back to the village was punctuated by his complaints.

'This alters everything, this does. I don't know whether you've realized it, Monsieur Poirot?'

'I think so, yes, I think so,' said Poirot. 'You see, me, I have been familiar with the idea for some time.'

Inspector Raglan, who had only had the idea presented to him a short half-hour ago, looked at Poirot unhappily, and went on with his discoveries.

'Those alibis now. Worthless! Absolutely worthless. Got to start again. Find out what everyone was doing from nine-thirty onwards. Nine-thirty – that's the time we've got to hang on to. You were quite right about the man Kent – we don't release *him* yet awhile. Let me see now – nine forty-five at the Dog and Whistle. He might have got there in a quarter of an hour if he ran. It's just possible that it was *his* voice Mr Raymond heard talking to Mr Ackroyd – asking for money which Mr Ackroyd refused. But one thing's clear – it wasn't he who sent the telephone message. The station is half a mile in the other direction – over a mile and a half from the Dog and Whistle, and he was at the Dog and Whistle until about ten minutes past ten. Dang that telephone call! We always come up against it.'

'We do indeed,' agreed Poirot. 'It is curious.'

'It's just possible that if Captain Paton climbed into his uncle's room and found him there murdered, *he* may have sent it. Got the wind up, thought he'd be accused, and cleared out. That's possible, isn't it?'

'Why should he have telephoned?'

'May have had doubts if the old man was really dead. Thought he'd get the doctor up there as soon as possible, but didn't want to give himself away. Yes, I say now, how's that for a theory? Something in that, I should say.'

The inspector swelled his chest out importantly. He was so plainly delighted with himself that any words of ours would have been quite superfluous.

We arrived back at my house at this minute, and I hurried in to my surgery patients, who had all been waiting a considerable time, leaving Poirot to walk to the police station with the inspector.

Having dismissed the last patient, I strolled into the little room at the back of the house which I call my workshop – I am rather proud of the home-made wireless set I turned out. Caroline hates my workroom. I have kept my tools there, and Annie is not allowed to wreak havoc with a dustpan and brush. I was just adjusting the interior of an alarm clock which had been denounced as wholly unreliable by the household, when the door opened and Caroline put her head in.

'Oh! there you are, James,' she said, with deep disapproval. 'M. Poirot wants to see you.'

'Well,' I said, rather irritably, for her sudden entrance had startled me and I had let go of a piece of delicate mechanism. 'If he wants to see me, he can come in here.'

'In here?' said Caroline.

'That's what I said – in here.'

Caroline gave a sniff of disapproval and retired. She returned in a moment or two, ushering in Poirot, and then retired again, shutting the door with a bang.

'Aha! my friend,' said Poirot, coming forward and rubbing his hands. 'You have not got rid of me so easily, you see!'

'Finished with the inspector?' I asked.

'For the moment, yes. And you, you have seen all the patients?'

'Yes.'

Poirot sat down and looked at me, tilting his egg-shaped head on one side, with the air of one who savours a very delicious joke.

'You are in error,' he said at last. 'You have still one patient to see.'

'Not you?' I exclaimed in surprise.

'Ah, not me, *bien entendu*. Me, I have the health magnificent. No, to tell you the truth, it is a little *complot* of mine. There is someone I wish to see, you understand – and at the same time it is not necessary that the whole village should intrigue itself about the matter – which is what would happen if the lady were seen to come to my house – for it is a lady. But to you she has already come as a patient before.'

'Miss Russell!' I exclaimed.

'*Précisément.* I wish much to speak with her, so I send her the little note and make the appointment in your surgery. You are not annoyed with me?'

'On the contrary,' I said. 'That is, presuming I am allowed to be present at the interview?'

'But naturally! In your own surgery!'

'You know,' I said, throwing down the pincers I was holding, 'it's extraordinarily intriguing, the whole thing. Every new development that arises is like the shake you give to a kaleidoscope – the thing changes entirely in aspect. Now, why are you so anxious to see Miss Russell?'

Poirot raised his eyebrows.

'Surely it is obvious?' he murmured.

'There you go again,' I grumbled. 'According to you everything is obvious. But you leave me walking about in a fog.'

Poirot shook his head genially to me.

'You mock yourself at me. Take the matter of Mademoiselle Flora. The inspector was surprised – but you – you were not.'

'I never dreamed of her being the thief,' I expostulated.

'That – perhaps no. But I was watching your face and you were not – like Inspector Raglan – startled and incredulous.'

I thought for a minute or two.

'Perhaps you are right,' I said at last. 'All along I've felt that Flora was keeping back something – so the truth, when it came, was subconsciously expected. It upset Inspector Raglan very much indeed, poor man.'

'Ah! *pour ça oui!* The poor man must rearrange all his ideas. I profited by his state of mental chaos to induce him to grant me a little favour.'

'What was that?'

Poirot took a sheet of notepaper from his pocket. Some words were written on it, and he read them aloud.

'The police have, for some days, been seeking for Captain Ralph Paton, the nephew of Mr Ackroyd of Fernly Park, whose death occurred under such tragic circumstances last Friday. Captain Paton has been found at Liverpool, where he was on the point of embarking for America.'

He folded up the piece of paper again.

'That, my friend, will be in the newspapers tomorrow morning.'

I stared at him, dumbfounded.

'But – but it isn't true! He's not at Liverpool!'

Poirot beamed on me.

'You have the intelligence so quick! No, he has not been found at Liverpool. Inspector Raglan was very loath to let me send this paragraph to the press, especially as I could not take him into my confidence. But I assured him most solemnly that very interesting results would follow its appearance in print, so he gave in, after stipulating that he was, on no account, to bear the responsibility.'

I stared at Poirot. He smiled back at me.

'It beats me,' I said at last, 'what you expect to get out of that.'

'You should employ your little grey cells,' said Poirot gravely.

He rose and came across to the bench.

'It is that you have really the love of the machinery,' he said, after inspecting the débris of my labours.

Every man has his hobby. I immediately drew Poirot's attention to my home-made wireless. Finding him sympathetic, I showed him one or two little inventions of my own – trifling things, but useful in the house.

'Decidedly,' said Poirot, 'you should be an inventor by trade, not a doctor. But I hear the bell – that is your patient. Let us go into the surgery.'

Once before I had been struck by the remnants of beauty in the housekeeper's face. This morning I was struck anew. Very simply dressed in black, tall, upright and independent as ever, with her big dark eyes and an unwonted flush of colour in her usually pale cheeks, I realized that as a girl she must have been startlingly handsome.

'Good morning, mademoiselle,' said Poirot. 'Will you be seated? Dr Sheppard is so kind as to permit me the use of his surgery for a little conversation I am anxious to have with you.'

Miss Russell sat down with her usual composure. If she felt any inward agitation, it did not display itself in any outward manifestation.

'It seems a queer way of doing things, if you'll allow me to say so,' she remarked.

'Miss Russell – I have news to give you.'

'Indeed!'

'Charles Kent has been arrested at Liverpool.'

Not a muscle of her face moved. She merely opened her eyes a trifle wider, and asked, with a tinge of defiance:

'Well, what of it?'

But at that moment it came to me – the resemblance that had haunted me all along, something familiar in the defiance of Charles Kent's manner. The two voices, one rough and coarse, the other painfully ladylike – were strangely the same in timbre. It was of Miss Russell that I had been reminded that night outside the gates of Fernly Park.

I looked at Poirot, full of my discovery, and he gave me an imperceptible nod.

In answer to Miss Russell's question, he threw out his hands in a thoroughly French gesture.

'I thought you might be interested, that is all,' he said mildly.

'Well I'm not particularly,' said Miss Russell. 'Who is this Charles Kent anyway?'

'He is a man, mademoiselle, who was at Fernly on the night of the murder.'

'Really?'

'Fortunately for him, he has an alibi. At a quarter to ten he was at a public-house a mile from here.'

'Lucky for him,' commented Miss Russell.

'But we still do not know what he was doing at Fernly – who it was he went to meet, for instance.'

'I'm afraid I can't help you at all,' said the housekeeper politely. 'Nothing came to *my* ears. If that is all –'

She made a tentative movement as though to rise. Poirot stopped her.

'It is not quite all,' he said smoothly. 'This morning fresh developments have arisen. It seems now that Mr Ackroyd was murdered, not at a quarter to ten, but *before*. Between ten minutes to nine, when Dr Sheppard left, and a quarter to ten.'

I saw the colour drain from the housekeeper's face, leaving it dead white. She leaned forward, her figure swaying.

'But Miss Ackroyd said – Miss Ackroyd said –'

'Miss Ackroyd has admitted that she was lying. She was never in the study at all that evening.'

'Then –'

'Then it would seem that in this Charles Kent we have the man we are looking for. He came to Fernly, can give no account of what he was doing there –'

'I can tell you what he was doing there. He never touched a hair of old Ackroyd's head – he never went near the study. He didn't do it, I tell you.'

She was leaning forward. That iron self-control was broken through at last. Terror and desperation was in her face.

'M. Poirot! M. Poirot! Oh, do believe me.'

Poirot got up and came to her. He patted her reassuringly on the shoulder.

'But yes – but yes, I will believe. I had to make you speak, you know.'

For an instant suspicion flared up in her.

'Is what you said true?'

'That Charles Kent is suspected of the crime? Yes, that is true. You alone can save him, by telling the reason for his being at Fernly.'

'He came to see me.' She spoke in a low, hurried voice. 'I went out to meet him –'

'In the summer-house, yes, I know.'

'How do you know?'

'Mademoiselle, it is the business of Hercule Poirot to know things. I know that you went out earlier in the evening, that you left a message in the summer-house to say what time you would be there.'

'Yes, I did. I had heard from him – saying he was coming. I dared not let him come to the house. I wrote to the address he gave me and said I would meet him in the summer-house, and described it to him so that he would be able to find it. Then I was afraid he might not wait there patiently, and I ran out and left a piece of paper to say I would be there about ten minutes past nine. I didn't want the servants to see me, so I slipped out through the drawing-room window. As I came back, I met Dr Sheppard, and I fancied that he would think it queer. I was out of breath, for I had been running. I had no idea that he was expected to dinner that night.'

She paused.

'Go on,' said Poirot. 'You went out to meet him at ten minutes past nine. What did you say to each other?'

'It's difficult. You see –'

'Mademoiselle,' said Poirot, interrupting her, 'in this matter I must have the whole truth. What you tell us need never go beyond these four walls. Dr Sheppard will be discreet, and so shall I. See, I will help you. This Charles Kent, he is your son, is he not?'

She nodded. The colour had flamed into her cheeks.

'No one has ever known. It was long ago – long ago – down in Kent. I was not married . . .'

'So you took the name of the county as a surname for him. I understand.'

'I got work. I managed to pay for his board and lodging. I

never told him that I was his mother. But he turned out badly, he drank, then took to drugs. I managed to pay his passage out to Canada. I didn't hear of him for a year or two. Then, somehow or other, he found out that I was his mother. He wrote asking me for money. Finally, I heard from him back in this country again. He was coming to see me at Fernly, he said. I dared not let him come to the house. I have always been considered so – so very respectable. If anyone got an inkling – it would have been all up with my post as housekeeper. So I wrote to him in the way I have just told you.'

'And in the morning you came to see Dr Sheppard?'

'Yes. I wondered if something could be done. He was not a bad boy – before he took to drugs.'

'I see,' said Poirot. 'Now let us go on with the story. He came that night to the summer-house?'

'Yes, he was waiting for me when I got there. He was very rough and abusive. I had brought with me all the money I had, and I gave it to him. We talked a little, and then he went away.'

'What time was that?'

'It must have been between twenty and twenty-five minutes past nine. It was not yet half-past when I got back to the house.'

'Which way did he go?'

'Straight out the same way he came, by the path that joined the drive just inside the lodge gates.'

Poirot nodded.

'And you, what did you do?'

'I went back to the house. Major Blunt was walking up and down the terrace smoking, so I made a detour to get round to the side door. It was just then on half-past nine, as I tell you.'

Poirot nodded again. He made a note or two in a microscopic pocket-book.

'I think that is all,' he said thoughtfully.

'Ought I –?' she hesitated. 'Ought I to tell all this to Inspector Raglan?'

'It may come to that. But let us not be in a hurry. Let us proceed slowly, with due order and method. Charles Kent is not yet formally charged with murder. Circumstances may arise which will render your story unnecessary.'

Miss Russell rose.

'Thank you very much, M. Poirot,' she said. 'You have been very kind – very kind indeed. You – you do believe me, don't you? That Charles had nothing to do with this wicked murder!'

'There seems no doubt that the man who was talking to Mr Ackroyd in the library at nine-thirty could not possibly have been your son. Be of good courage, mademoiselle. All will yet be well.'

Miss Russell departed. Poirot and I were left together.

'So that's that,' I said. 'Every time we come back to Ralph Paton. How did you manage to spot Miss Russell as the person Charles Kent came to meet? Did you notice the resemblance?'

'I had connected her with the unknown man long before we actually came face to face with him. As soon as we found that quill. The quill suggested dope, and I remembered your account of Miss Russell's visit to you. Then I found the article on cocaine in that morning's paper. It all seemed very clear. She had heard from someone that morning – someone addicted to drugs, she read the article in the paper, and she came to ask you a few tentative questions. She mentioned cocaine, since the article in question was on cocaine. Then, when you seemed too interested, she switched hurriedly to the subject of detective stories and untraceable poisons. I suspected a son or a brother, or some other undesirable male relation. Ah! but I must go. It is the time of the lunch.'

'Stay and lunch with us,' I suggested.

Poirot shook his head. A faint twinkle came into his eye.

'Not again today. I should not like to force Mademoiselle Caroline to adopt a vegetarian diet two days in succession.'

It occurred to me that there was not much which escaped Hercule Poirot.

CHAPTER XXI

The Paragraph in the Paper

Caroline, of course, had not failed to see Miss Russell come to the surgery door. I had anticipated this, and had ready an elaborate account of the lady's bad knee. But Caroline was not in a cross-questioning mood. Her point of view was that she knew what Miss Russell had really come for and that *I* didn't.

'Pumping you, James,' said Caroline. 'Pumping you in the most shameless manner, I've no doubt. It's no good interrupting. I dare say you hadn't the least idea she was doing it even. Men *are* so simple. She knows that you are in M. Poirot's confidence, and she wants to find out things. Do you know what I think, James?'

'I couldn't begin to imagine. You think so many extraordinary things.'

'It's no good being sarcastic. I think Miss Russell knows more about Mr Ackroyd's death than she is prepared to admit.'

Caroline leaned back triumphantly in her chair.

'Do you really think so?' I said absently.

'You are very dull today, James. No animation about you. It's that liver of yours.'

Our conversation then dealt with purely personal matters.

The paragraph inspired by Poirot duly appeared in our daily paper the next morning. I was in the dark as to its purpose, but its effect on Caroline was immense.

She began by stating, most untruly, that she had said as much all along. I raised my eyebrows, but did not argue. Caroline, however, must have felt a prick of conscience, for she went on:

'I mayn't have actually mentioned Liverpool, but I knew he'd try to get away to America. That's what Crippen did.'

'Without much success,' I reminded her.

'Poor boy, and so they've caught him. I consider, James, that it's your duty to see that he isn't hung.'

'What do you expect me to do?'

'Why, you're a medical man, aren't you? You've known him from a boy upwards. Not mentally responsible. That's the line to take, clearly. I read only the other day that they're very happy in Broadmoor – it's quite like a high-class club.'

But Caroline's words had reminded me of something.

'I never knew that Poirot had an imbecile nephew?' I said curiously.

'Didn't you? Oh, he told me all about it. Poor lad. It's a great grief to all the family. They've kept him at home so far, but it's getting to such a pitch that they're afraid he'll have to go into some kind of institution.'

'I suppose you know pretty well everything there is to know about Poirot's family by this time,' I said, exasperated.

'Pretty well,' said Caroline complacently. 'It's a great relief to people to be able to tell all their troubles to someone.'

'It might be,' I said, 'if they were ever allowed to do so spontaneously. Whether they enjoy having confidences screwed out of them by force is another matter.'

Caroline merely looked at me with an air of a Christian martyr enjoying martyrdom.

'You are so self-contained, James,' she said. 'You hate speaking out, or parting with any information yourself, and you think everybody else must be just like you. I should hope that I never screw confidences out of anybody. For instance, if M. Poirot comes in this afternoon, as he said he might do, I shall not dream of asking him who it was arrived at his house early this morning.'

'Early this morning?' I queried.

'Very early,' said Caroline. 'Before the milk came. I just happened to be looking out of the window – the blind was flapping. It was a man. He came in a closed car, and he was all muffled up. I couldn't get a glimpse of his face. But I will tell you *my* idea, and you'll see that I'm right.'

'What's your idea?'

Caroline dropped her voice mysteriously.

'A Home Office expert,' she breathed.

'A Home Office expert,' I said, amazed. 'My dear Caroline!'

'Mark my words, James, you'll see that I'm right. That Russell woman was here that morning after your poisons. Roger Ackroyd might easily have been poisoned in his food that night.'

I laughed out loud.

'Nonsense,' I cried. 'He was stabbed in the neck. You know that as well as I do.'

'After death, James,' said Caroline; 'to make a false clue.'

'My good woman,' I said, 'I examined the body, and I know what I'm talking about. That wound wasn't inflicted after death – it was the cause of death, and you need make no mistake about it.'

Caroline merely continued to look omniscient, which so annoyed me that I went on:

'Perhaps you will tell me, Caroline, if I have a medical degree or if I have not?'

'You have the medical degree, I dare say, James – at least, I mean I know you have. But you've no imagination whatever.'

'Having endowed you with a treble portion, there was none left over for me,' I said drily.

I was amused to see Caroline's manoeuvres that afternoon when Poirot duly arrived. My sister, without asking a direct question, skirted the subject of the mysterious guest in every way imaginable. By the twinkle in Poirot's eyes, I saw that he realized her object. He remained blandly impervious, and blocked her bowling so successfully that she herself was at a loss how to proceed.

Having, I suspect, enjoyed the little game, he rose to his feet and suggested a walk.

'It is that I need to reduce the figure a little,' he explained. 'You will come with me, doctor? And perhaps later, Miss Caroline will give us some tea.'

'Delighted,' said Caroline. 'Won't your – er – guest come in also?'

'You are too kind,' said Poirot. 'But no, my friend reposes himself. Soon you must make his acquaintance.'

'Quite an old friend of yours, so somebody told me,' said Caroline, making one last valiant effort.

'Did they?' murmured Poirot. 'Well, we must start.'

Our tramp took us in the direction of Fernly. I had guessed beforehand that it might do so. I was beginning to understand Poirot's methods. Every little irrelevancy had a bearing upon the whole.

'I have a commission for you, my friend,' he said at last. 'Tonight, at my house. I desire to have a little conference. You will attend, will you not?'

'Certainly,' I said.

'Good. I need also those in the house – that is to say: Mrs Ackroyd, Mademoiselle Flora, Major Blunt, Mr Raymond. I want you to be my ambassador. This little reunion is fixed for nine o'clock. You will ask them – yes?'

'With pleasure; but why not ask them yourself?'

'Because they will then put the questions: Why? What for? They will demand what my idea is. And, as you know, my friend, I much dislike to have to explain my little ideas until the time comes.'

I smiled a little.

'My friend Hastings, he of whom I told you, used to say of me that I was the human oyster. But he was unjust. Of facts, I keep nothing to myself. But to everyone his own interpretation of them.'

'When do you want me to do this?'

'Now, if you will. We are close to the house.'

'Aren't you coming in?'

'No, me, I will promenade myself in the grounds. I will rejoin you by the lodge gates in a quarter of an hour's time.'

I nodded, and set off on my task. The only member of the family at home proved to be Mrs Ackroyd, who was sipping an early cup of tea. She received me very graciously.

'So grateful to you, doctor,' she murmured, 'for clearing up that little matter with M. Poirot. But life is one trouble after another. You have heard about Flora, of course?'

'What exactly?' I asked cautiously.

'This new engagement. Flora and Hector Blunt. Of course not such a good match as Ralph would have been. But after all, happiness comes first. What dear Flora needs is an older man – someone steady and reliable, and then Hector is really a very distinguished man in his way. You saw the news of Ralph's arrest in the paper this morning?'

'Yes,' I said, 'I did.'

'Horrible.' Mrs Ackroyd closed her eyes and shuddered. 'Geoffrey Raymond was in a terrible way. Rang up Liverpool. But they wouldn't tell him anything at the police station there. In fact, they said they hadn't arrested Ralph at all. Mr Raymond insists that it's all a mistake – a – what do they call it? – *canard* of the newspaper's. I've forbidden it to be mentioned before the servants. Such a terrible disgrace. Fancy if Flora had actually been married to him.'

Mrs Ackroyd shut her eyes in anguish. I began to wonder how soon I should be able to deliver Poirot's invitation.

Before I had time to speak, Mrs Ackroyd was off again.

'You were here yesterday, weren't you, with that dreadful Inspector Raglan? Brute of a man – he terrified Flora into saying she took that money from poor Roger's room. And the matter was so simple, really. The dear child wanted to borrow a few pounds, didn't like to disturb her uncle since he'd given strict orders against it. But knowing where he kept his notes she went there and took what she needed.'

'Is that Flora's account of the matter?' I asked.

'My dear doctor, you know what girls are nowadays. So easily acted on by suggestion. You, of course, know all about hypnosis and that sort of thing. The inspector shouts at her, says the word "steal" over and over again, until the poor child gets an inhibition – or is it a complex? – I always mix up those two words – and actually thinks herself that she has stolen the money. I saw at once how it was. But I can't be too thankful for the whole misunderstanding in one way – it seems to have brought those two together – Hector and Flora, I mean. And I assure you that I have been very much worried about Flora in the past: why, at one time I actually thought there was going to be some kind of understanding between her and young Raymond. Just think of it!' Mrs Ackroyd's voice rose in shrill horror. 'A private secretary – with practically no means of his own.'

'It would have been a severe blow to you,' I said. 'Now, Mrs Ackroyd, I've got a message for you from M. Hercule Poirot.'

'For me?'

Mrs Ackroyd looked quite alarmed.

I hastened to reassure her, and I explained what Poirot wanted.

'Certainly,' said Mrs Ackroyd rather doubtfully. 'I suppose we must come if M. Poirot says so. But what is it all about? I like to know beforehand.'

I assured the lady truthfully that I myself did not know any more than she did.

'Very well,' said Mrs Ackroyd at last, rather grudgingly, 'I will tell the others, and we will be there at nine o'clock.'

Thereupon I took my leave, and joined Poirot at the agreed meeting-place.

'I've been longer than a quarter of an hour, I'm afraid,' I remarked. 'But once that good lady starts talking it's a matter of the utmost difficulty to get a word in edgeways.'

'It is of no matter,' said Poirot. 'Me, I have been well amused. This park is magnificent.'

We set off homewards. When we arrived, to our great surprise Caroline, who had evidently been watching for us, herself opened the door.

She put her finger to her lips. Her face was full of importance and excitement.

'Ursula Bourne,' she said, 'the parlourmaid from Fernly. She's here! I've put her in the dining-room. She's in a terrible way, poor thing. Says she must see M. Poirot at once. I've done all I could. Taken her a cup of hot tea. It really goes to one's heart to see anyone in such a state.'

'In the dining-room?' asked Poirot.

'This way,' I said, and flung open the door.

Ursula Bourne was sitting by the table. Her arms were spread out in front of her, and she had evidently just lifted her head from where it had been buried. Her eyes were red with weeping.

'Ursula Bourne,' I murmured.

But Poirot went past me with outstretched hands.

'No,' he said, 'that is not quite right, I think. It is not Ursula Bourne, is it, my child – but Ursula Paton? Mrs Ralph Paton.'

CHAPTER XXII

Ursula's Story

For a moment or two the girl looked mutely at Poirot. Then, her reserve breaking down completely, she nodded her head once, and burst into an outburst of sobs.

Caroline pushed past me, and putting her arm round the girl, patted her on the shoulder.

'There, there, my dear,' she said soothingly, 'it will be all right. You'll see – everything will be all right.'

Buried under curiosity and scandal-mongering there is a lot of kindness in Caroline. For the moment, even the interest of Poirot's revelation was lost in the sight of the girl's distress.

Presently Ursula sat up and wiped her eyes.

'This is very weak and silly of me,' she said.

'No, no, my child,' said Poirot kindly. 'We can all realize the strain of this last week.'

'It must have been a terrible ordeal,' I said.

'And then to find that you knew,' continued Ursula. 'How did you know? Was it Ralph who told you?'

Poirot shook his head.

'You know what brought me to you tonight,' went on the girl. '*This* –'

She held out a crumpled piece of newspaper, and I recognized the paragraph that Poirot had had inserted.

'It says that Ralph has been arrested. So everything is useless. I need not pretend any longer.'

'Newspaper paragraphs are not always true, mademoiselle,' murmured Poirot, having the grace to look ashamed of himself. 'All the same, I think you will do well to make a clean breast of things. The truth is what we need now.'

The girl hesitated, looking at him doubtfully.

'You do not trust me,' said Poirot gently. 'Yet all the same you came here to find me, did you not? Why was that?'

'Because I don't believe that Ralph did it,' said the girl in a very low voice. 'And I think that you are clever, and will find out the truth. And also –'

'Yes?'

'I think you are kind.'

Poirot nodded his head several times.

'It is very good that – yes, it is very good. Listen, I do in verity believe that this husband of yours is innocent – but the affair marches badly. If I am to save him, I must know all there is to know – even if it should seem to make the case against him blacker than before.'

'How well you understand,' said Ursula.

'So you will tell me the whole story, will you not? From the beginning.'

'You're not going to send *me* away, I hope,' said Caroline, settling herself comfortably in an arm-chair. 'What I want to know,' she continued, 'is why this child was masquerading as a parlourmaid?'

'Masquerading?' I queried.

'That's what I said. Why did you do it, child? For a wager?'

'For a living,' said Ursula drily.

And encouraged, she began the story which I reproduce here in my own words.

Ursula Bourne, it seemed, was one of a family of seven – impoverished Irish gentlefolk. On the death of her father, most of the girls were cast out into the world to earn their own living. Ursula's eldest sister was married to Captain Folliott. It was she whom I had seen that Sunday, and the cause of her embarrassment was clear enough now. Determined to earn her living and not attracted to the idea of being a nursery governess – the one profession open to an untrained girl, Ursula preferred the job of parlourmaid. She scorned to label herself a 'lady parlourmaid.' She would be the real thing, her reference being supplied by her sister. At Fernly, despite an aloofness which, as has been seen, caused some comment, she was a success at her job – quick, competent, and thorough.

'I enjoyed the work,' she explained. 'And I had plenty of time to myself.'

And then came her meeting with Ralph Paton, and the love affair which culminated in a secret marriage. Ralph had persuaded her into that, somewhat against her will. He had declared that his stepfather would not hear of his marrying a penniless girl. Better to be married secretly, and break the news to him at some later and more favourable minute.

And so the deed was done, and Ursula Bourne became Ursula Paton. Ralph had declared that he meant to pay off his debts, find a job, and then, when he was in a position to support her, and independent of his adopted father, they would break the news to him.

But to people like Ralph Paton, turning over a new leaf is easier in theory than in practice. He hoped that his stepfather, whilst still in ignorance of the marriage, might be persuaded to pay his debts and put him on his feet again. But the revelation of the amount of Ralph's liabilities merely enraged Roger Ackroyd, and he refused to do anything at all. Some months passed, and then Ralph was bidden once more to Fernly. Roger Ackroyd did not beat about the bush. It was the desire of his heart that Ralph should marry Flora, and he put the matter plainly before the young man.

And here it was that the innate weakness of Ralph Paton showed itself. As always, he grasped at the easy, the immediate solution. As far as I could make out, neither Flora nor Ralph made any pretence of love. It was, on both sides, a business arrangement. Roger Ackroyd dictated his wishes – they agreed to them. Flora accepted a chance of liberty, money, and an enlarged horizon, Ralph, of course, was playing a different game. But he was in a very awkward hole financially. He seized at the chance. His debts would be paid. He could start again with a clean sheet. His was not a nature to envisage the future, but I gather that he saw vaguely the engagement with Flora being broken off after a decent interval had elapsed. Both Flora and he stipulated that it should be kept a secret for the present. He was anxious to conceal it from Ursula. He felt instinctively that her nature, strong and resolute, with an inherent distaste for duplicity, was not one to welcome such a course.

Then came the crucial moment when Roger Ackroyd, always high-handed, decided to announce the engagement. He said no word of his intention to Ralph – only to Flora, and Flora, apathetic, raised no objection. On Ursula, the news fell like a bombshell. Summoned by her, Ralph came hurriedly down from town. They met in the wood, where part of their conversation was overheard by my sister. Ralph implored her to keep silent for a little while longer, Ursula was equally determined to have done with concealments. She would tell Mr Ackroyd the truth without any further delay. Husband and wife parted acrimoniously.

Ursula, steadfast in her purpose, sought an interview with Roger Ackroyd that very afternoon, and revealed the truth to him. Their interview was a stormy one – it might have been even more stormy had not Roger Ackroyd been already obsessed with his own troubles. It was bad enough, however. Ackroyd was not the kind of man to forgive the deceit that had been practised upon him. His rancour was mainly directed to Ralph, but Ursula came in for her share, since he regarded her as a girl who had deliberately tried to 'entrap' the adopted son of a very wealthy man. Unforgivable things were said on both sides.

That same evening Ursula met Ralph by appointment in the small summer-house, stealing out from the house by the side door in order to do so. Their interview was made up of reproaches on both sides. Ralph charged Ursula with having irretrievably ruined his prospects by her ill-timed revelation. Ursula reproached Ralph with his duplicity.

They parted at last. A little over half an hour later came the discovery of Roger Ackroyd's body. Since that night Ursula had neither seen nor heard from Ralph.

As the story unfolded itself, I realized more and more what a damning series of facts it was. Alive, Ackroyd could hardly have failed to alter his will – I knew him well enough to realize that to do so would be his first thought. His death came in the nick of time for Ralph and Ursula Paton. Small wonder the girl had held her tongue, and played her part so consistently.

My meditations were interrupted. It was Poirot's voice speaking, and I knew from the gravity of his tone that he, too, was fully alive to the implications of the position.

'Mademoiselle, I must ask you one question, and you must answer it truthfully, for on it everything may hang: What time was it when you parted from Captain Ralph Paton in the summer-house? Now, take a little minute so that your answer may be very exact.'

The girl gave a half laugh, bitter enough in all conscience.

'Do you think I haven't gone over that again and again in my own mind? It was just half-past nine when I went out to meet him. Major Blunt was walking up and down the terrace, so I had to go round through the bushes to avoid him. It must have been about twenty-seven minutes to ten when I reached the summer-house. Ralph was waiting for me. I was with him ten minutes – not longer, for it was just a quarter to ten when I got back to the house.'

I saw now the insistence of her question the other day. If only Ackroyd could have been proved to have been killed before a quarter to ten, and not after.

I saw the reflection of that thought in Poirot's next question.

'Who left the summer-house first?'

'I did.'

'Leaving Ralph Paton in the summer-house?'

'Yes – but you don't think – '

'Mademoiselle, it is of no importance what I think. What did you do when you got back to the house?'

'I went up to my room.'

'And stayed there until when?'

'Until about ten o'clock.'

'Is there anyone who can prove that?'

'Prove? That I was in my room, you mean? Oh! no. But surely – oh! I see, they might think – they might think – '

I saw the dawning horror in her eyes.

Poirot finished the sentence for her.

'That it was *you* who entered by the window and stabbed Mr Ackroyd as he sat in his chair? Yes, they might think just that.'

'Nobody but a fool would think any such thing,' said Caroline indignantly.

She patted Ursula on the shoulder.

The girl had her face hidden in her hands.

'Horrible,' she was murmuring. 'Horrible.'

Caroline gave her a friendly shake.

'Don't worry, my dear,' she said. 'M. Poirot doesn't think that really. As for that husband of yours, I don't think much of him, and I tell you so candidly. Running away and leaving you to face the music.'

But Ursula shook her head energetically.

'Oh, no,' she cried. 'It wasn't like that at all. Ralph would not run away on his own account. I see now. If he heard of his stepfather's murder, he might think himself that I had done it.'

'He wouldn't think any such thing,' said Caroline.

'I was so cruel to him that night – so hard and bitter. I wouldn't listen to what he was trying to say – wouldn't believe that he really cared. I just stood there telling him what I thought of him, and saying the coldest, cruellest things that came into my mind – trying my best to hurt him.'

'Do him no harm,' said Caroline. 'Never worry about what you say to a man. They're so conceited that they never believe you mean it if it's unflattering.'

Ursula went on nervously twisting and untwisting her hands.

'When the murder was discovered and he didn't come forward, I was terribly upset. Just for a moment I wondered – but then I knew he couldn't – he couldn't . . . But I wished he would come forward and say openly that he'd had nothing to do with it. I knew that he was fond of Dr Sheppard, and I fancied that perhaps Dr Sheppard might know where he was hiding.'

She turned to me.

'That's why I said what I did to you that day. I thought, if you knew where he was, you might pass on the message to him.'

'I?' I exclaimed.

'Why should James know where he was?' demanded Caroline sharply.

'It was very unlikely, I know,' admitted Ursula, 'but Ralph had often spoken of Dr Sheppard, and I knew that he would be likely to consider him as his best friend in King's Abbot.'

'My dear child,' I said, 'I have not the least idea where Ralph Paton is at the present moment.'

'That is true enough,' said Poirot.

'But –' Ursula held out the newspaper cutting in a puzzled fashion.

'Ah! that,' said Poirot, slightly embarrassed; 'a *bagatelle*, mademoiselle. A *rien du tout*. Not for a moment do I believe that Ralph Paton has been arrested.'

'But then –' began the girl slowly.

Poirot went on quickly:

'There is one thing I should like to know – did Captain Paton wear shoes or boots that night?'

Ursula shook her head.

'I can't remember.'

'A pity! But how should you? Now, madame,' he smiled at her, his head on one side, his forefinger wagging eloquently, 'no questions. And do not torment yourself. Be of good courage, and place your faith in Hercule Poirot.'

CHAPTER XXIII

Poirot's Little Reunion

'And now,' said Caroline, rising, 'that child is coming upstairs to lie down. Don't you worry, my dear. M. Poirot will do everything he can for you – be sure of that.'

'I ought to go back to Fernly,' said Ursula uncertainly.

But Caroline silenced her protests with a firm hand.

'Nonsense. You're in my hands for the time being. You'll stay here for the present, anyway – eh, M. Poirot?'

'It will be the best plan,' agreed the little Belgian. 'This evening I shall want mademoiselle – I beg her pardon, madame – to attend my little reunion. Nine o'clock at my house. It is most necessary that she should be there.'

Caroline nodded, and went with Ursula out of the room. The door shut behind them. Poirot dropped down into a chair again.

'So far, so good,' he said. 'Things are straightening themselves out.'

'They're getting to look blacker and blacker against Ralph Paton,' I observed gloomily.

Poirot nodded.

'Yes, that is so. But it was to be expected, was it not?'

I looked at him, slightly puzzled by the remark. He was leaning back in the chair, his eyes half closed, the tips of his fingers just touching each other. Suddenly he sighed and shook his head.

'What is it?' I asked.

'It is that there are moments when a great longing for my friend Hastings comes over me. That is the friend of whom I spoke to you – the one who resides now in the Argentine. Always, when I have had a big case, he has been by my side. And he has helped me – yes, often he has helped me. For he had a knack, that one, of stumbling over the truth unawares – without noticing it himself, *bien entendu*. At times, he has said something particularly foolish, and behold that foolish remark has revealed the truth to me! And then, too, it was his practice to keep a written record of the cases that proved interesting.'

I gave a slightly embarrassed cough.

'As far as that goes,' I began, and then stopped.

Poirot sat upright in his chair. His eyes sparkled.

'But yes? What is it that you would say?'

'Well, as a matter of fact, I've read some of Captain Hastings's narratives, and I thought, why not try my hand at something of the same kind. Seemed a pity not to – unique opportunity – probably the only time I'll be mixed up with anything of this kind.'

I felt myself getting hotter and hotter, and more and more incoherent, as I floundered through the above speech.

Poirot sprang from his chair. I had a moment's terror that he was going to embrace me French fashion, but mercifully he refrained.

'But this is magnificent – you have then written down your impressions of the case as you went along?'

I nodded.

'*Épatant!*' cried Poirot. 'Let me see them – this instant.'

I was not quite prepared for such a sudden demand. I racked my brains to remember certain details.

'I hope you won't mind,' I stammered. 'I may have been a little – er – *personal* now and then.'

'Oh! I comprehend perfectly; you have referred to me as comic – as, perhaps, ridiculous now and then? It matters not at all. Hastings, he also was not always polite. Me, I have the mind above such trivialities.'

Still somewhat doubtful, I rummaged in the drawers of my desk and produced an untidy pile of manuscript which I handed over to him. With an eye on possible publication in the future, I had divided the work into chapters, and the night before I had brought it up to date with an account of Miss Russell's visit. Poirot had therefore twenty chapters.

I left him with them.

I was obliged to go out to a case at some distance away, and it was past eight o'clock when I got back, to be greeted with a plate of hot dinner on a tray, and the announcement that Poirot and my sister had supped together at half-past seven, and that the former had then gone to my workshop to finish his reading of the manuscript.

'I hope, James,' said my sister, 'that you've been careful in what you say about me in it?'

My jaw dropped. I had not been careful at all.

'Not that it matters very much,' said Caroline, reading my expression correctly. 'M. Poirot will know what to think. He understands me much better than you do.'

I went into the workshop. Poirot was sitting by the window. The manuscript lay neatly piled on a chair beside him. He laid his hand on it and spoke.

'*Eh bien,*' he said, 'I congratulate you – on your modesty!'

'Oh!' I said, rather taken aback.

'And on your reticence,' he added.

I said, 'Oh!' again.

'Not so did Hastings write,' continued my friend. 'On every page, many, many times was the word "I". What *he* thought – what *he* did. But you – you have kept your personality in the background; only once or twice does it obtrude – in scenes of home life, shall we say?'

I blushed a little before the twinkle of his eye.

'What do you really think of the stuff?' I asked nervously.

'You want my candid opinion?'

'Yes.'

Poirot laid his jesting manner aside.

'A very meticulous and accurate account,' he said kindly. 'You have recorded all the facts faithfully and exactly – though you have shown yourself becomingly reticent as to your own share in them.'

'And it has helped you?'

'Yes. I may say that it has helped me considerably. Come, we must go over to my house and set the stage for my little performance.'

Caroline was in the hall. I think she hoped that she might be invited to accompany us. Poirot dealt with the situation tactfully.

'I should much like to have had you present, mademoiselle,' he said regretfully, 'but at this juncture it would not be wise. See you, all these people tonight are suspects. Amongst them, I shall find the person who killed Mr Ackroyd.'

'You really believe that?' I said incredulously.

'I see that you do not,' said Poirot drily. 'Not yet do you appreciate Hercule Poirot at his true worth.'

At that minute Ursula came down the staircase.

'You are ready, my child?' said Poirot. 'That is good. We will go to my house together. Mademoiselle Caroline, believe me, I do everything possible to render you service. Good evening.'

We went off, leaving Caroline rather like a dog who has been refused a walk, standing on the front doorstep gazing after us.

The sitting-room at The Larches had been got ready. On the table were various *sirops* and glasses. Also a plate of biscuits. Several chairs had been brought in from the other room.

Poirot ran to and fro rearranging things. Pulling out a chair here, altering the position of a lamp there, occasionally stooping to straighten one of the mats that covered the floor. He was specially fussing over the lighting. The lamps were arranged in such a way as to throw a clear light on the side of the room where the chairs were grouped, at the same time leaving the other end of the room, where I presumed Poirot himself would sit, in a dim twilight.

Ursula and I watched him. Presently a bell was heard.

'They arrive,' said Poirot. 'Good, all is in readiness.'

The door opened and the party from Fernly filed in. Poirot went forward and greeted Mrs Ackroyd and Flora.

'It is most good of you to come,' he said. 'And Major Blunt and Mr Raymond.'

The secretary was debonair as ever.

'What's the great idea?' he said, laughing. 'Some scientific machine? Do we have bands round our wrists which register guilty heart-beats? There is such an invention isn't there?'

'I have read of it, yes,' admitted Poirot. 'But me, I am

old-fashioned. I used the old methods. I work only with the little grey cells. Now let us begin – but first I have an announcement to make to you all.'

He took Ursula's hand and drew her forward.

'This lady is Mrs Ralph Paton. She was married to Captain Paton last March.'

A little shriek burst from Mrs Ackroyd.

'Ralph! Married! Last March! Oh! but it's absurd. How could he be?'

She stared at Ursula as though she had never seen her before.

'Married to Bourne?' she said. 'Really, M. Poirot, I don't believe you.'

Ursula flushed and began to speak, but Flora forestalled her.

Going quickly to the other girl's side, she passed her hand through her arm.

'You must not mind our being surprised,' she said. 'You see, we had no idea of such a thing. You and Ralph have kept your secret very well. I am – very glad about it.'

'You are very kind, Miss Ackroyd,' said Ursula in a low voice, 'and you have every right to be exceedingly angry. Ralph behaved very badly – especially to you.'

'You needn't worry about that,' said Flora, giving her arm a consoling little pat. 'Ralph was in a corner and took the only way out. I should probably have done the same in his place. I do think he might have trusted me with the secret, though. I wouldn't have let him down.'

Poirot rapped gently on a table and cleared his throat significantly.

'The board meeting's going to begin,' said Flora. 'M. Poirot hints that we mustn't talk. But just tell me one thing. Where is Ralph? You must know if anyone does.'

'But I don't,' cried Ursula, almost in a wail. 'That's just it, I don't.'

'Isn't he detained at Liverpool?' asked Raymond. 'It said so in the paper.'

'He is not at Liverpool,' said Poirot shortly.

'In fact,' I remarked, 'no one knows where he is.'

'Except Hercule Poirot, eh?' said Raymond.

Poirot replied seriously to the other's banter.

'Me, I know everything. Remember that.'

Geoffrey Raymond lifted his eyebrows.

'Everything?' He whistled. 'Whew! that's a tall order.'

'Do you mean to say you can really guess where Ralph Paton is hiding?' I asked incredulously.

'You call it guessing. I call it knowing, my friend.'

'In Cranchester?' I hazarded.

'No,' replied Poirot gravely, 'not in Cranchester.'

He said no more, but at a gesture from him the assembled party took their seats. As they did so, the door opened once more and two other people came in and sat down near the door. They were Parker and the housekeeper.

'The number is complete,' said Poirot. 'Everyone is here.'

There was a ring of satisfaction in his tone. And with the sound of it I saw a ripple of something like uneasiness pass over all those faces grouped at the other end of the room. There was a suggestion in all this as of a trap – a trap that had closed.

Poirot read from a list in an important manner.

'Mrs Ackroyd, Miss Flora Ackroyd, Major Blunt, Mr Geoffrey Raymond, Mrs Ralph Paton, John Parker, Elizabeth Russell.'

He laid the paper down on the table.

'What's the meaning of all this?' began Raymond.

'The list I have just read,' said Poirot, 'is a list of suspected persons. Every one of you present had the opportunity to kill Mr Ackroyd –'

With a cry Mrs Ackroyd sprang up, her throat working.

'I don't like it,' she wailed. 'I don't like it. I would much prefer to go home.'

'You cannot go home, madame,' said Poirot sternly, 'until you have heard what I have to say.'

He paused a moment, then cleared his throat.

'I will start at the beginning. When Miss Ackroyd asked me to investigate the case, I went up to Fernly Park with the good Dr Sheppard. I walked with him along the terrace, where I was shown the footprints on the window-sill. From there Inspector

Raglan took me along the path which leads to the drive. My
eye was caught by a little summer-house, and I searched it
thoroughly. I found two things – a scrap of starched cambric
and an empty goose quill. The scrap of cambric immediately
suggested to me a maid's apron. When Inspector Raglan showed
me his list of the people in the house, I noticed at once that
one of the maids – Ursula Bourne, the parlourmaid – had no
real alibi. According to her own story, she was in her bedroom
from nine-thirty until ten. But supposing that instead she was
in the summer-house? If so, she must have gone there to meet
someone. Now we know from Dr Sheppard that someone from
outside *did* come to the house that night – the stranger whom
he met just by the gate. At first glance it would seem that our
problem was solved, and that the stranger went to the summer-
house to meet Ursula Bourne. It was fairly certain that he *did*
go to the summer-house because of the goose quill. That suggested at once to my mind a taker of drugs – and one who had
acquired the habit on the other side of the Atlantic where
sniffing "snow" is more common than in this country. The man
whom Dr Sheppard met had an American accent, which fitted
in with that supposition.

'But I was held up by one point. *The times did not fit.* Ursula
Bourne could certainly not have gone to the summer-house
before nine-thirty, whereas the man must have got there by a
few minutes past nine. I could, of course, assume that he waited
there for half an hour. The only alternative supposition was
that there had been two separate meetings in the summer-house
that night. *Eh bien*, as soon as I went into that alternative I
found several significant facts. I discovered that Miss Russell,
the housekeeper, had visited Dr Sheppard that morning, and
had displayed a good deal of interest in cures for victims of the
drug habit. Taking that in conjunction with the goose quill, I
assumed that the man in question came to Fernly to meet the
housekeeper, and not Ursula Bourne. Who, then, did Ursula
Bourne come to the rendezvous to meet? I was not long in
doubt. First I found a ring – a wedding ring – with "From R."
and a date inside it. Then I learnt that Ralph Paton had been

seen coming up the path which led to the summer-house at twenty-five minutes past nine, and I also heard of a certain conversation which had taken place in the wood near the village that very afternoon – a conversation between Ralph Paton and some unknown girl. So I had my facts succeeding each other in a neat and orderly manner. A secret marriage, an engagement announced on the day of the tragedy, the stormy interview in the wood, and the meeting arranged for the summer-house that night.

'Incidentally this proved to me one thing, that both Ralph Paton and Ursula Bourne (or Paton) had the strongest motives for wishing Mr Ackroyd out of the way. And it also made one other point unexpectedly clear. It could not have been Ralph Paton who was with Mr Ackroyd in the study at nine-thirty.

'So we come to another and most interesting aspect of the crime. Who was it in the room with Mr Ackroyd at nine-thirty? Not Ralph Paton, who was in the summer-house with his wife. Not Charles Kent, who had already left. Who, then? I posed my cleverest – my most audacious question: *Was anyone with him?*'

Poirot leaned forward and shot the last words triumphantly at us, drawing back afterwards with the air of one who has made a decided hit.

Raymond, however, did not seem impressed, and lodged a mild protest.

'I don't know if you're trying to make me out a liar, M. Poirot, but the matter does not rest on my evidence alone – except perhaps as to the exact words used. Remember, Major Blunt also heard Mr Ackroyd talking to someone. He was on the terrace outside, and couldn't catch the words clearly, but he distinctly heard the voices.'

Poirot nodded.

'I have not forgotten,' he said quietly. 'But Major Blunt was under the impression that it was *you* to whom Mr Ackroyd was speaking.'

For a moment Raymond seemed taken aback. Then he recovered himself.

'Blunt knows now that he was mistaken,' he said.

'Exactly,' agreed the other man.

'Yet there must have been some reason for his thinking so,' mused Poirot. 'Oh! no,' he held up his hand in protest, 'I know the reason you will give – but it is not enough. We must seek elsewhere. I will put it this way. From the beginning of the case I have been struck by one thing – the nature of those words which Mr Raymond overheard. It has been amazing to me that no one has commented on them – has seen anything odd about them.'

He paused a minute, and then quoted softly:

'. . . *the calls on my purse have been so frequent of late that I fear it is impossible for me to accede to your request.* Does nothing strike you as odd about that?'

'I don't think so,' said Raymond. 'He has frequently dictated letters to me, using almost exactly those same words.'

'Exactly,' cried Poirot. 'That is what I seek to arrive at. Would any man use such a phrase in *talking* to another? Impossible that that should be part of a real conversation. Now, if he had been dictating a letter –'

'You mean he was reading a letter aloud,' said Raymond slowly. 'Even so, he must have been reading to someone.'

'But why? We have no evidence that there was anyone else in the room. No other voice but Mr Ackroyd's was heard, remember.'

'Surely a man wouldn't read letters of that type aloud to himself – not unless he was – well – going balmy.'

'You have all forgotten one thing,' said Poirot softly: 'the stranger who called at the house the preceding Wednesday.'

They all stared at him.

'But yes,' said Poirot, nodding encouragingly, 'on Wednesday. The young man was not of himself important. But the firm he represented interested me very much.'

'The Dictaphone Company,' gasped Raymond. 'I see it now. A dictaphone. That's what you think?'

Poirot nodded.

'Mr Ackroyd had promised to invest in a dictaphone, you

remember. Me, I had the curiosity to inquire of the company in question. Their reply is that Mr Ackroyd *did* purchase a dictaphone from their representative. Why he concealed the matter from you, I do not know.'

'He must have meant to surprise me with it,' murmured Raymond. 'He had quite a childish love of surprising people. Meant to keep it up his sleeve for a day or so. Probably was playing with it like a new toy. Yes, it fits in. You're quite right – no one would use quite those words in casual conversation.'

'It explains, too,' said Poirot, 'why Major Blunt thought it was you who were in the study. Such scraps as came to him were fragments of dictation, and so his subconscious mind deduced that you were with him. His conscious mind was occupied with something quite different – the white figure he had caught a glimpse of. He fancied it was Miss Ackroyd. Really, of course, it was Ursula Bourne's white apron he saw as she was stealing down to the summer-house.'

Raymond had recovered from his first surprise.

'All the same,' he remarked, 'this discovery of yours, brilliant though it is (I'm quite sure I should never have thought of it), leaves the essential position unchanged. Mr Ackroyd was alive at nine-thirty, since he was speaking into the dictaphone. It seems clear that the man Charles Kent was really off the premises by then. As to Ralph Paton –?'

He hesitated, glancing at Ursula.

Her colour flared up, but she answered steadily enough.

'Ralph and I parted just before a quarter to ten. He never went near the house, I am sure of that. He had no intention of doing so. The last thing on earth he wanted was to face his stepfather. He would have funked it badly.'

'It isn't that I doubt your story for a moment,' explained Raymond. 'I've always been quite sure Captain Paton was innocent. But one has to think of a court of law – and the questions that would be asked. He is in a most unfortunate position, but if he were to come forward –'

Poirot interrupted.

'That is your advice, yes? That he should come forward?'

'Certainly. If you know where he is –'

'I perceive that you do not believe that I do know. And yet I have told you just now that I know everything. The truth of the telephone call, of the footprints on the window-sill, of the hiding-place of Ralph Paton –'

'Where is he?' said Blunt sharply.

'Not very far away,' said Poirot, smiling.

'In Cranchester?' I asked.

Poirot turned towards me.

'Always you ask me that. The idea of Cranchester, it is with you an *idée fixe*. No, he is not in Cranchester. He is – *there!*'

He pointed a dramatic forefinger. Everyone's head turned.

Ralph Paton was standing in the doorway.

CHAPTER XXIV

Ralph Paton's Story

It was a very uncomfortable minute for *me*. I hardly took in what happened next, but there were exclamations and cries of surprise! When I was sufficiently master of myself to be able to realize what was going on, Ralph Paton was standing by his wife, her hand in his, and he was smiling across the room at me.

Poirot, too, was smiling, and at the same time shaking an eloquent finger at me.

'Have I not told you at least thirty-six times that it is useless to conceal things from Hercule Poirot?' he demanded. 'That in such a case he finds out?'

He turned to the others.

'One day, you remember, we held a little séance about a table – just the six of us. I accused the other five persons present of concealing something from me. Four of them gave up their secret. Dr Sheppard did not give up his. But all along I have had my suspicions. Dr Sheppard went to the Three Boars that night hoping to find Ralph. He did not find him there; but supposing, I said to myself, that he met him in the street on his way home? Dr Sheppard was a friend of Captain Paton's, and he had come straight from the scene of the crime. He must know that things looked very black against him. Perhaps he knew more than the general public did –'

'I did,' I said ruefully. 'I suppose I might as well make a clean breast of things now. I went to see Ralph that afternoon. At first he refused to take me into his confidence, but later he told me about his marriage, and the hole he was in. As soon as the murder was discovered, I realized that once the facts were known, suspicion could not fail to attach to Ralph – or, if not to him, to the girl he loved. That night I put the facts plainly before him. The thought of having possibly to give evidence which might incriminate his wife made him resolve at all costs to – to –'

I hesitated, and Ralph filled up the gap.

'To do a bunk,' he said graphically. 'You see, Ursula left me to go back to the house. I thought it possible that she might have attempted to have another interview with my stepfather. He had already been very rude to her that afternoon. It occurred to me that he might have so insulted her – in such an unforgivable manner – that without knowing what she was doing –'

He stopped. Ursula released her hand from his, and stepped back.

'You thought that, Ralph! You actually thought that I might have done it?'

'Let us get back to the culpable conduct of Dr Sheppard,' said Poirot drily. 'Dr Sheppard consented to do what he could to help him. He was successful in hiding Captain Paton from the police.'

'Where?' asked Raymond. 'In his own house?'

'Ah, no, indeed,' said Poirot. 'You should ask yourself the question that I did. If the good doctor is concealing the young man, what place would he choose? It must necessarily be somewhere near at hand. I think of Cranchester. A hotel? No. Lodgings? Even more emphatically, no. Where, then? Ah! I have it. A nursing home. A home for the mentally unfit. I test my theory. I invent a nephew with mental trouble. I consult Mademoiselle Sheppard as to suitable homes. She gives me the names of two near Cranchester to which her brother has sent patients. I make inquiries. Yes, at one of them a patient was brought there by the doctor himself early on Saturday morning. That patient, though known by another name, I had no difficulty in identifying as Captain Paton. After certain necessary formalities, I was allowed to bring him away. He arrived at my house in the early hours of yesterday morning.'

I looked at him ruefully.

'Caroline's Home Office expert,' I murmured. 'And to think I never guessed!'

'You see now why I drew attention to the reticence of your manuscript,' murmured Poirot. 'It was strictly truthful as far as it went – but it did not go very far, eh, my friend?'

I was too abashed to argue.

'Dr Sheppard has been very loyal,' said Ralph. 'He has stood by me through thick and thin. He did what he thought was best. I see now, from what M. Poirot has told me, that it was not really the best. I should have come forward and faced the music. You see, in the home, we never saw a newspaper. I knew nothing of what was going on.'

'Dr Sheppard has been a model of discretion,' said Poirot drily. 'But me, I discover all the little secrets. It is my business.'

'Now we can have your story of what happened that night,' said Raymond impatiently.

'You know it already,' said Ralph. 'There's very little for me to tell. I left the summer-house about nine forty-five, and tramped about the lanes, trying to make up my mind as to what to do next – what line to take. I'm bound to admit that I've not the shadow of an alibi, but I give you my solemn word that I never went to the study, that I never saw my stepfather alive – or dead. Whatever the world thinks, I'd like all of you to believe me.'

'No alibi,' murmured Raymond. 'That's bad. I believe you, of course, but – it's a bad business.'

'It makes things very simple, though,' said Poirot, in a cheerful voice. 'Very simple indeed.'

We all stared at him.

'You see what I mean? No? Just this – to save Captain Paton the real criminal must confess.'

He beamed round at us all.

'But yes – I mean what I say. See now, I did not invite Inspector Raglan to be present. That was for a reason. I did not want to tell him all that I knew – at least I did not want to tell him tonight.'

He leaned forward, and suddenly his voice and his whole personality changed. He suddenly became dangerous.

'I who speak to you – I know the murderer of Mr Ackroyd is

in this room now. It is to the murderer I speak. *Tomorrow the truth goes to Inspector Raglan.* You understand?'

There was a tense silence. Into the midst of it came the old Breton woman with a telegram on a salver. Poirot tore it open.

Blunt's voice rose abrupt and resonant.

'The murderer is amongst us, you say? You know – which?'

Poirot had read the message. He crumpled it up in his hand.

'I know – now.'

He tapped the crumpled ball of paper.

'What is that?' said Raymond sharply.

'A wireless message – from a steamer now on her way to the United States.'

There was a dead silence. Poirot rose to his feet bowing.

'Messieurs et Mesdames, this reunion of mine is at an end. Remember – *the truth goes to Inspector Raglan in the morning.*'

CHAPTER XXV

The Whole Truth

A slight gesture from Poirot enjoined me to stay behind the rest. I obeyed, going over to the fire and thoughtfully stirring the big logs on it with the toe of my boot.

I was puzzled. For the first time I was absolutely at sea as to Poirot's meaning. For a moment I was inclined to think that the scene I had just witnessed was a gigantic piece of bombast – that he had been what he called 'playing the comedy' with a view to making himself interesting and important. But, in spite of myself, I was forced to believe in an underlying reality. There had been real menace in his words – a certain indisputable sincerity. But I still believed him to be on entirely the wrong tack.

When the door shut behind the last of the party he came over to the fire.

'Well, my friend,' he said quietly, 'and what do you think of it all?'

'I don't know what to think,' I said frankly. 'What was the point? Why not go straight to Inspector Raglan with the truth instead of giving the guilty person this elaborate warning?'

Poirot sat down and drew out his case of tiny Russian cigarettes. He smoked for a minute or two in silence. Then:

'Use your little grey cells,' he said. 'There is always a reason behind my actions.'

I hesitated for a moment, and then I said slowly:

'The first one that occurs to me is that you yourself do not know who the guilty person is, but that you are sure that he is to be found amongst the people here tonight. Therefore your words were intended to force a confession from the unknown murderer?'

Poirot nodded approvingly.

'A clever idea, but not the truth.'

'I thought, perhaps, that by making him believe you knew, you might force him out into the open – not necessarily by confession. He might try to silence you as he formerly silenced Mr Ackroyd – before you could act tomorrow morning.'

'A trap with myself as the bait! *Merci, mon ami,* but I am not sufficiently heroic for that.'

'Then I fail to understand you. Surely you are running the risk of letting the murderer escape by thus putting him on his guard?'

Poirot shook his head.

'He cannot escape,' he said gravely. 'There is only one way out – and that way does not lead to freedom.'

'You really believe that one of those people here tonight committed the murder?' I asked incredulously.

'Yes, my friend.'

'Which one?'

There was a silence for some minutes. Then Poirot tossed the stump of his cigarette into the grate and began to speak in a quiet, reflective tone.

'I will take you the way that I have travelled myself. Step by step you shall accompany me, and see for yourself that all the facts point indisputably to one person. Now, to begin with, there were two facts and a little discrepancy in time which especially attracted my attention. The first fact was the telephone call. If Ralph Paton were indeed the murderer, the telephone call became meaningless and absurd. Therefore, I said to myself, Ralph Paton is not the murderer.

'I satisfied myself that the call could not have been sent by anyone in the house, yet I was convinced that it was amongst those present on the fatal evening that I had to look for my criminal. Therefore I concluded that the telephone call must have been sent by an accomplice. I was not quite pleased with that deduction, but I let it stand for the minute.

'I next examined the *motive* for the call. That was difficult. I could only get at it by judging its *result*. Which was – that the murder was discovered that night instead of – in all probability – the following morning. You agree with that?'

'Ye-es,' I admitted. 'Yes. As you say, Mr Ackroyd having given orders that he was not to be disturbed, nobody would have been likely to go to the study that night.'

'*Très bien.* The affair marches, does it not? But matters were still obscure. What was the advantage of having the crime discovered that night in preference to the following morning? The only idea I could get hold of was that the murderer, knowing the crime was to be discovered at a certain time, could make sure of being present when the door was broken in – or at any rate immediately afterwards. And now we come to the second fact – the chair pulled out from the wall. Inspector Raglan dismissed that as of no importance. I, on the contrary, have always regarded it as of supreme importance.

'In your manuscript you have drawn a neat little plan of the study. If you had it with you this minute you would see that – the chair being drawn out in the position indicated by Parker – it would stand in a direct line between the door and the window.'

'The window!' I said quickly.

'You, too, have my first idea. I imagined that the chair was drawn out so that something connected with the window should not be seen by anyone entering through the door. But I soon abandoned that supposition, for though the chair was a grand-father with a high back, it obscured very little of the window – only the part between the sash and the ground. No, *mon ami* – but remember that just in front of the window there stood a table with books and magazines upon it. Now that table *was* completely hidden by the drawn-out chair – and immediately I had my first shadowy suspicion of the truth.

'Supposing that there had been something on that table not intended to be seen? Something placed there by the murderer? As yet I had no inkling of what that something might be. But I knew certain very interesting facts about it. For instance, it was something that the murderer had not been able to take away with him at the time that he committed the crime. At the same time it was vital that it should be removed as soon as possible after the crime had been discovered. And so – the telephone message, and the opportunity for the murderer to be on the spot when the body was discovered.

'Now four people were on the scene before the police arrived. Yourself, Parker, Major Blunt, and Mr Raymond. Parker I eliminated at once, since at whatever time the crime was discovered, he was the one person certain to be on the spot. Also it was he who told me of the pulled-out chair. Parker, then, was cleared (of the murder, that is. I still thought it possible that he had been blackmailing Mrs Ferrars). Raymond and Blunt, however, remained under suspicion since, if the crime had been discovered in the early hours of the morning, it was quite possible that they might have arrived on the scene too late to prevent the object on the round table being discovered.

'Now what was that object? You heard my arguments tonight in reference to the scrap of conversation overheard? As soon as I learned that a representative of a dictaphone company had called, the idea of a dictaphone took root in my mind. You heard what I said in this room not half an hour ago? They all agreed with my theory – but one vital fact seems to have escaped them. Granted that a dictaphone was being used by Mr Ackroyd that night – why was no dictaphone found?'

'I never thought of that,' I said.

'We know that a dictaphone was supplied to Mr Ackroyd. But no dictaphone has been found amongst his effects. So, if something was taken from the table – why should not that something be the dictaphone? But there were certain difficulties in the way. The attention of everyone was, of course, focused on the murdered man. I think anyone could have gone to the table unnoticed by the other people in the room. But a dictaphone has a certain bulk – it cannot be slipped casually into a pocket. There must have been a receptacle of some kind capable of holding it.

'You see where I am arriving? The figure of the murderer is taking shape. A person who was on the scene straightaway, but who might not have been if the crime had been discovered the following morning. A person carrying a receptacle into which the dictaphone might be fitted –'

I interrupted.

'By why remove the dictaphone? What was the point?'

'You are like Mr Raymond. You take it for granted that what was heard at nine-thirty was Mr Ackroyd's voice speaking into a dictaphone. But consider this useful invention for a little minute. You dictate into it, do you not? And at some later time a secretary or a typist turns it on, and the voice speaks again.'

'You mean –?' I gasped.

Poirot nodded.

'Yes, I meant that. *At nine-thirty Mr Ackroyd was already dead.* It was the dictaphone speaking – not the man.'

'And the murderer switched it on. Then he must have been in the room at that minute?'

'Possibly. But we must not exclude the likelihood of some mechanical device having been applied – something after the nature of a time lock, or even of a simple alarm clock. But in that case we must add two qualifications to our imaginary portrait of the murderer. It must be someone who knew of Mr Ackroyd's purchase of the dictaphone and also someone with the necessary mechanical knowledge.

'I had got thus far in my own mind when we came to the footprints on the window ledge. Here there were three conclusions open to me. (1) They might really have been made by Ralph Paton. He had been at Fernly that night, and might have climbed into the study and found his uncle dead there. That was one hypothesis. (2) There was the possibility that the footmarks might have been made by somebody else who happened to have the same kind of studs in his shoes. But the inmates of the house had shoes soled with crêpe rubber, and I declined to believe in the coincidence of someone from outside having the same kind of shoes as Ralph Paton wore. Charles Kent, as we know from the barmaid of the Dog and Whistle, had on a pair of boots "clean dropping off him". (3) Those prints were made by someone deliberately trying to throw suspicion on Ralph Paton. To test this last conclusion, it was necessary to ascertain

certain facts. One pair of Ralph's shoes had been obtained from the Three Boars by the police. Neither Ralph nor anyone else could have worn them that evening, since they were downstairs being cleaned. According to the police theory, Ralph was wearing another pair of the same kind, and I found out that it was true that he had two pairs. Now for my theory to be proved correct it was necessary for the murderer to have worn Ralph's shoes that evening – in which case Ralph must have been wearing yet a *third* pair of footwear of some kind. I could hardly suppose that he would bring three pairs of shoes all alike – the third pair of footwear were more likely to be boots. I got your sister to make inquiries on this point – laying some stress on the colour, in order – I admit it frankly – to obscure the real reason for my asking.

'You know the result of her investigations. Ralph Paton *had* had a pair of boots with him. The first question I asked him when he came to my house yesterday morning was what he was wearing on his feet on the fatal night. He replied at once that he had worn *boots* – he was still wearing them, in fact – having nothing else to put on.

'So we get a step further in our description of the murderer – a person who had the opportunity to take these shoes of Ralph Paton's from the Three Boars that day.'

He paused, and then said, with a slightly raised voice:

'There is one further point. The murderer must have been a person who had the opportunity to purloin that dagger from the silver table. You might argue that anyone in the house might have done so, but I will recall to you that Flora Ackroyd was very positive that the dagger was not there when she examined the silver table.'

He paused again.

'Let us recapitulate – now that all is clear. A person who was at the Three Boars earlier that day, a person who knew Ackroyd well enough to know that he had purchased a dictaphone, a person who was of a mechanical turn of mind, who had the opportunity to take the dagger from the silver table before Miss Flora arrived, who had with him a receptacle suitable for hiding the dictaphone – such as a black bag, and who had the study to himself for a few minutes after the crime was discovered while Parker was telephoning for the police. In fact – *Dr Sheppard!*'

CHAPTER XXVI

And Nothing But The Truth

There was a dead silence for a minute and a half.

Then I laughed.

'You're mad,' I said.

'No,' said Poirot placidly. 'I am not mad. It was the little discrepancy in time that first drew my attention to you – right at the beginning.'

'Discrepancy in time?' I queried, puzzled.

'But yes. You will remember that everyone agreed – you yourself included – that it took five minutes to walk from the lodge to the house – less if you took the short cut to the terrace. But you left the house at ten minutes to nine – both by your own statement and that of Parker, and yet it was nine o'clock when you passed through the lodge gates. It was a chilly night – not an evening a man would be inclined to dawdle; why had you taken ten minutes to do a five minutes' walk? All along I realized that we had only your statement for it that the study window was ever fastened. Ackroyd asked you if you had done so – he never looked to see. Supposing, then, that the study window was unfastened? Would there be time in that ten minutes for you to run round the outside of the house, change your shoes, climb in through the window, kill Ackroyd, and get to the gate by nine o'clock? I decided against that theory since in all probability a man as nervous as Ackroyd was that night would hear you climbing in, and then there would have been a struggle. But supposing that you killed Ackroyd *before* you left – as you were standing beside his chair? Then you go out of the front door, run round to the summer-house, take Ralph Paton's shoes out of the bag you brought up with you that night, slip them on, walk through the mud in them, and leave prints on the window ledge, you climb in, lock the study door on the inside, run back to the summer-house, change back into your own shoes, and race down to the gate. (I went through similar actions the other day, when you were with Mrs Ackroyd – it took ten minutes exactly.) Then home – and an alibi – since you had timed the dictaphone for half-past nine.'

'My dear Poirot,' I said in a voice that sounded strange and forced to my own ears, 'you've been brooding over this case too long. What on earth had I to gain by murdering Ackroyd?'

'Safety. It was you who blackmailed Mrs Ferrars. Who could have had a better knowledge of what killed Mr Ferrars than the doctor who was attending him? When you spoke to me that first day in the garden, you mentioned a legacy received about a year ago. I have been unable to discover any trace of a legacy. You had to invent some way of accounting for Mrs Ferrars's twenty thousand pounds. It has not done you much good. You lost most of it in speculation – then you put the screw on too hard, and Mrs Ferrars took a way out that you had not expected. If Ackroyd had learnt the truth he would have had no mercy on you – you were ruined for ever.'

'And the telephone call?' I asked, trying to rally. 'You have a plausible explanation of that also, I suppose?'

'I will confess to you that it was my greatest stumbling block when I found that a call had actually been put through to you from King's Abbot station. I at first believed that you had simply invented the story. It was a very clever touch, that. You must have some excuse for arriving at Fernly, finding the body, and so getting the chance to remove the dictaphone on which your alibi depended. I had a very vague notion of how it was worked when I came to see your sister that first day and inquired as to what patients you had seen on Friday morning. I had no thought of Miss Russell in my mind at that time. Her visit was a lucky coincidence, since it distracted your mind from the real object of my questions. I found what I was looking for. Among your patients that morning was the steward of an American liner. Who more suitable than he to be leaving for Liverpool by the train that evening? And afterwards he would be on the high seas, well out of the way. I noted that the *Orion* sailed on Saturday, and having obtained the name of the steward I sent him a wireless message asking a certain question. This is his reply you saw me receive just now.'

He held out the message to me. It ran as follows:

'Quite correct. Dr Sheppard asked me to leave a note at a patient's house. I was to ring him up from the station with the reply. Reply was "No answer."'

'It was a clever idea,' said Poirot. 'The call was genuine. Your sister saw you take it. But there was only one man's word as to what was actually said – your own!'

I yawned.

'All this,' I said, 'is very interesting – but hardly in the sphere of practical politics.'

'You think not? Remember what I said – the truth goes to Inspector Raglan in the morning. But, for the sake of your good sister, I am willing to give you the chance of another way out. There might be, for instance, an overdose of a sleeping draught. You comprehend me? But Captain Ralph Paton must be cleared – *ça va sans dire*. I should suggest that you finish that very interesting manuscript of yours – but abandoning your former reticence.'

'You seem to be very prolific of suggestions,' I remarked. 'Are you sure you've quite finished?'

'Now that you remind me of the fact, it is true that there is one thing more. It would be most unwise on your part to attempt to silence me as you silenced M. Ackroyd. That kind of business does not succeed against Hercule Poirot, you understand.'

'My dear Poirot,' I said, smiling a little, 'whatever else I may be, I am not a fool.'

I rose to my feet.

'Well, well,' I said, with a slight yawn, 'I must be off home. Thank you for a most interesting and instructive evening.'

Poirot also rose and bowed with his accustomed politeness as I passed out of the room.

CHAPTER XXVII

Apologia

Five A.M. I am very tired – but I have finished my task. My arm aches from writing.

A strange end to my manuscript. I meant it to be published some day as the history of one of Poirot's failures! Odd, how things pan out.

All along I've had a premonition of disaster, from the moment I saw Ralph Paton and Mrs Ferrars with their heads together. I thought then that she was confiding in him; as it happened I was quite wrong there, but the idea persisted even after I went into the study with Ackroyd that night, until he told me the truth.

Poor old Ackroyd. I'm always glad that I gave him a chance. I urged him to read that letter before it was too late. Or let me be honest – didn't I subconsciously realize that with a pig-headed chap like him, it was my best chance of getting him *not* to read it? His nervousness that night was interesting psychologically. He knew danger was close at hand. And yet he never suspected *me*.

The dagger was an afterthought. I'd brought up a very handy little weapon of my own, but when I saw the dagger lying in the silver table, it occurred to me at once how much better it would be to use a weapon that couldn't be traced to me.

I suppose I must have meant to murder him all along. As soon as I heard of Mrs Ferrars's death, I felt convinced that she would have told him everything before she died. When I met him and he seemed so agitated, I thought that perhaps he knew the truth, but that he couldn't bring himself to believe it, and was going to give me the chance of refuting it.

So I went home and took my precautions. If the trouble were

after all only something to do with Ralph – well, no harm would have been done. The dictaphone he had given me two days ago to adjust. Something had gone a little wrong with it, and I persuaded him to let me have a go at it, instead of sending it back. I did what I wanted to, and took it up with me in my bag that evening.

I am rather pleased with myself as a writer. What could be neater, for instance, than the following:

'The letters were brought in at twenty minutes to nine. It was just on ten minutes to nine when I left him, the letter still unread. I hesitated with my hand on the door handle, looking back and wondering if there was anything I had left undone.'

All true, you see. But suppose I had put a row of stars after the first sentence! Would somebody then have wondered what exactly happened in that blank ten minutes?

When I looked round the room from the door, I was quite satisfied. Nothing had been left undone. The dictaphone was on the table by the window, timed to go off at nine-thirty (the mechanism of that little device was rather clever – based on the principle of an alarm clock), and the armchair was pulled out so as to hide it from the door.

I must admit that it gave me rather a shock to run into Parker just outside the door. I have faithfully recorded that fact.

Then later, when the body was discovered, and I sent Parker to telephone for the police, what a judicious use of words: *'I did what little had to be done!'* It was quite little – just to shove the dictaphone into my bag and push back the chair against the wall in its proper place. I never dreamed that Parker would have noticed that chair. Logically, he ought to have been so agog over the body as to be blind to everything else. But I hadn't reckoned with the trained servant complex.

I wish I could have known beforehand that Flora was going to say she'd seen her uncle alive at a quarter to ten. That puzzled me more than I can say. In fact, all through the case there have been things that puzzled me hopelessly. Everyone seems to have taken a hand.

My greatest fear all through has been Caroline. I have fancied she might guess. Curious the way she spoke that day of my 'strain of weakness.'

Well, she will never know the truth. There is, as Poirot said, one way out . . .

I can trust him. He and Inspector Raglan will manage it between them. I should not like Caroline to know. She is fond of me, and then, too, she is proud . . . My death will be a grief to her, but grief passes . . .

When I have finished writing, I shall enclose this whole manuscript in an envelope and address it to Poirot.

And then – what shall it be? Veronal? There would be a kind of poetic justice. Not that I take any responsibility for Mrs Ferrars's death. It was the direct consequence of her own actions. I feel no pity for her.

I have no pity for myself either.

So let it be veronal.

But I wish Hercule Poirot had never retired from work and come here to grow vegetable marrows.

Postscript

The Murder of Roger Ackroyd, *at its time Agatha Christie's first big success (indeed, 'far and away my most successful to date,' as she later wrote in her autobiography), is considered today, without any contest, one of her true works of art. It deserves this status for its outstanding and original plot, its genuine* tour de force *and its phenomenal twist in the tail. Two different people suggested the idea of it to her. The first was her brother-in-law, James Watts, the husband of her sister Madge, who had declared to her, 'Almost everybody turns out to be a criminal nowadays in detective stories – even the detective. What I would like to see is a Watson who turned out to be the criminal.' Agatha Christie thought this idea original and mulled over it, but she met with some misgivings when faced with transforming Hastings, the gallant and honest Hastings, into a murderer. Then, a very similar suggestion was made to her by Lord Louis Mountbatten, who wrote a letter to her (forwarded by* The Sketch *magazine) on 28 March 1924, in which he envisaged a story told in the first person where the culprit would be the narrator himself.*

The intervention of Lord Louis Mountbatten in the genesis of The Murder of Roger Ackroyd *was only disclosed in the course of the 1970s, when Agatha Christie's first biographer (Gwen Robyns), questioning Lord Mountbatten about a photo in which he was shown in the company of the author, learnt the anecdote and the existence of one of Agatha Christie's letters in which she admitted her debt to Mountbatten and James Watts.*

But however clever this idea was, it was also necessary to have the talent of executing it and getting a story of the highest quality out of it. In fact, all the credit comes back to Agatha Christie, who has written here one of the most original stories in detective literature.

In January 1924, her literary agent Edmund Cork had negotiated a profitable contract for her – £200 per book and good royalties for three titles in preparation – with a new publisher, Collins, who was starting at that time to build up a strong list of crime authors. The Murder of Roger Ackroyd *was the first novel published out of this new stable.*

Dedicated ironically to Punkie – the nickname of Madge Watts, Agatha Christie's sister – 'who likes an orthodox detective story, murder, inquest, and suspicion falling on everyone in turn!', The Murder of Roger Ackroyd *was received by the critics and public alike with a welcome that was split between enthusiasm and indignation. Some appreciated the manner in which the author's narrative misled the reader, others called it trickery – one reader even wrote to* The Times *to say how much the dénouement of the novel had shocked him and how he proposed to boycott all of Agatha Christie's works! He criticized her for not respecting the tacit rules which governed both the mystery story and the relationship between author and reader.*

Agatha Christie always defended herself from having cheated. In an interview with Francis Wyndham, she affirmed there were sometimes omissions in her writing but never lies. She stated in An Autobiography *: 'Of course, a lot of people say that* The Murder of Roger Ackroyd *is cheating; but if they read it carefully they will see that they are wrong. Such little lapses of time as there have to be are nicely concealed in an ambiguous sentence, and Dr Sheppard, in writing it down, took great pleasure in writing nothing but the truth, though not the whole truth.'*

When it was published, she received noticeable support from one of her most eminent colleagues, Dorothy L. Sayers, who proclaimed strongly that the reader should have the frame of mind to suspect everyone.

In 1928, The Murder of Roger Ackroyd *was adapted for the theatre by Michael Morton. Agatha Christie did not like the first version of the play at all, where Poirot's name was changed to Beau instead of Hercule, and he regained about twenty years of youth and found himself surrounded by a bevy of beautiful women. With the support of the producer, Gerald du Maurier, Agatha Christie got the playwright to bring Poirot closer to the person she had created. On 15 May 1928 the play, entitled* Alibi, *opened at the Prince of Wales Theatre in London* with Charles Laughton in the role of Hercule Poirot, J. H. Roberts as Dr Sheppard, and Basil Loder, Henry Daniell, James Welsh and others. It was a great success and ran for some 250 performances.

THE BIG FOUR

CHAPTER I

The Unexpected Guest

I have met people who enjoy a channel crossing; men who can sit calmly in their deckchairs and, on arrival, wait until the boat is moored, then gather their belongings together without fuss and disembark. Personally, I can never manage this. From the moment I get on board I feel that the time is too short to settle down to anything. I move my suitcases from one spot to another, and if I go down to the saloon for a meal, I bolt my food with an uneasy feeling that the boat may arrive unexpectedly whilst I am below. Perhaps all this is merely a legacy from one's short leaves in the War, when it seemed a matter of such importance to secure a place near the gangway, and to be amongst the first to disembark lest one should waste precious minutes of one's three or five days' leave.

On this particular July morning, as I stood by the rail and watched the white cliffs of Dover drawing nearer, I marvelled at the passengers who could sit calmly in their chairs and never even raise their eyes for the first sight of their native land. Yet perhaps their case was different from mine. Doubtless many of them had only crossed to Paris for the weekend, whereas I had spent the last year and a half on a ranch in the Argentine. I had prospered there, and my wife and I had both enjoyed the free and easy life of the South American continent, nevertheless it was with a lump in my throat that I watched the familiar shore draw nearer and nearer.

I had landed in France two days before, transacted some necessary business, and was now en route for London. I should be there some months – time enough to look up old friends, and one old friend in particular. A little man with an egg-shaped head and green eyes – Hercule Poirot! I proposed to take him completely by surprise. My last letter from the Argentine had given no hint of my intended voyage – indeed, that had been decided upon hurriedly as a result of certain business complications – and I spent many amused moments picturing to myself his delight and stupefaction on beholding me.

He, I knew, was not likely to be far from his headquarters. The time when his cases had drawn him from one end of England to the other was past. His fame had spread, and no longer would he allow one case to absorb all his time. He aimed more and more, as time went on, at being considered a 'consulting detective' – as much a specialist as a Harley Street physician. He had always scoffed at the popular idea of the human bloodhound who assumed wonderful disguises to track criminals, and who paused at every footprint to measure it.

'No, my friend Hastings,' he would say, 'we leave that to Giraud and his friends. Hercule Poirot's methods are his own. Order and method, and "the little grey cells". Sitting at ease in our own armchairs we see the things that these others overlook, and we do not jump to the conclusion like the worthy Japp.'

No; there was little fear of finding Hercule Poirot far afield. On arrival in London, I deposited my luggage at an hotel and drove straight on to the old address. What poignant memories it brought back to me! I hardly waited to greet my old landlady, but hurried up the stairs two at a time and rapped on Poirot's door.

'Enter, then,' cried a familiar voice from within.

I strode in. Poirot stood facing me. In his arms he carried a small valise, which he dropped with a crash on beholding me.

'*Mon ami*, Hastings!' he cried. '*Mon ami*, Hastings!'

And, rushing forward, he enveloped me in a capacious embrace. Our conversation was incoherent and inconsequent. Ejaculations, eager questions, incomplete answers, messages from my wife, explanations as to my journey, were all jumbled up together.

'I suppose there's someone in my old rooms?' I asked at last, when we had calmed down somewhat. 'I'd love to put up here again with you.'

Poirot's face changed with startling suddenness.

'*Mon Dieu!* but what a *chance épouvantable*. Regard around you, my friend.'

For the first time I took note of my surroundings. Against the wall stood a vast ark of a trunk of prehistoric design. Near to it were placed a number of suitcases, ranged neatly in order of size from large to small. The inference was unmistakable.

'You are going away?'

'Yes.'

'Where to?'

'South America.'

'*What?*'

'Yes, it is a droll farce, is it not? It is to Rio I go, and every day I say to myself, I will write nothing in my letters – but oh! the surprise of the good Hastings when he beholds me!'

'But when are you going?'

Poirot looked at his watch.

'In an hour's time.'

'I thought you always said nothing would induce you to make a long sea voyage?'

Poirot closed his eyes and shuddered.

'Speak not of it to me, my friend. My doctor, he assures me that one dies not of it – and it is for the one time only; you understand, that never – never shall I return.'

He pushed me into a chair.

'Come, I will tell you how it all came about. Do you know who is the richest man in the world? Richer even than Rockefeller? Abe Ryland.'

'The American Soap King?'

'Precisely. One of his secretaries approached me. There is some very considerable, as you would call it, hocus-pocus going on in connection with a big company in Rio. He wished me to investigate matters on the spot. I refused. I told him that if the facts were laid before me, I would give him my expert opinion.

But that he professed himself unable to do. I was to be put in possession of the facts only on my arrival out there. Normally, that would have closed the matter. To dictate to Hercule Poirot is sheer impertinence. But the sum offered was so stupendous that for the first time in my life I was tempted by mere money. It was a competence – a fortune! And there was a second attraction – *you*, my friend. For this last year and a half I have been a very lonely old man. I thought to myself, Why not? I am beginning to weary of this unending solving of foolish problems. I have achieved sufficient fame. Let me take this money and settle down somewhere near my old friend.'

I was quite affected by this token of Poirot's regard.

'So I accepted,' he continued, 'and in an hour's time I must leave to catch the boat train. One of the life's little ironies, is it not? But I will admit to you, Hastings, that had not the money offered been so big, I might have hesitated, for just lately I have begun a little investigation of my own. Tell me, what is commonly meant by the phrase, "The Big Four"?'

'I suppose it had its origin at the Versailles Conference, and then there's the famous "Big Four" in the film world, and the term is used by hosts of smaller fry.'

'I see,' said Poirot thoughtfully. 'I have come across the phrase, you understand, under certain circumstances where none of those explanations would apply. It seems to refer to a gang of international criminals or something of that kind; only –'

'Only what?' I asked, as he hesitated.

'Only that I fancy that it is something on a large scale. Just a little idea of mine, nothing more. Ah, but I must complete my packing. The time advances.'

'Don't go,' I urged. 'Cancel your package and come out on the same boat with me.'

Poirot drew himself up and glanced at me reproachfully.

'Ah, is it that you don't understand! I have passed my word, you comprehend – the word of Hercule Poirot. Nothing but a matter of life or death could detain me now.'

'And that's not likely to occur,' I murmured ruefully. 'Unless at the eleventh hour "the door opens and the unexpected guest comes in".'

I quoted the old saw with a slight laugh, and then, in the pause that succeeded it, we both started as a sound came from the inner room.

'What's that?' I cried.

'*Ma foi!*' retorted Poirot. 'It sounds very like your "unexpected guest" in my bedroom.'

'But how can anyone be in there? There's no door except into this room.'

'Your memory is excellent, Hastings. Now for the deductions.'

'The window! But it's a burglar, then? He must have had a stiff climb of it – I should say it was almost impossible.'

I had risen to my feet and was striding in the direction of the door when the sound of fumbling at the handle from the other side arrested me.

The door swung slowly open. Framed in the doorway stood a man. He was coated from head to foot with dust and mud; his face was thin and emaciated. He stared at us for a moment, and then swayed and fell. Poirot hurried to his side, then he looked up and spoke to me.

'Brandy – quickly.'

I dashed some brandy into a glass and brought it. Poirot managed to administer a little, and together we raised him and carried him to the couch. In a few minutes he opened his eyes and looked round him with an almost vacant stare.

'What is it you want, monsieur?' asked Poirot.

The man opened his lips and spoke in a queer mechanical voice.

'M. Hercule Poirot, 14 Farraway Street.'

'Yes, yes; I am he.'

The man did not seem to understand, and merely repeated in exactly the same tone:

'M. Hercule Poirot, 14 Farraway Street.'

Poirot tried him with several questions. Sometimes the man did not answer at all; sometimes he repeated the same phrase. Poirot made a sign to me to ring up on the telephone.

'Get Dr Ridgeway to come round.'

The doctor was in, luckily; and as his house was only just round the corner, few minutes elapsed before he came bustling in.

'What's all this, eh?'

Poirot gave him a brief explanation, and the doctor started examining our strange visitor, who seemed quite unconscious of his presence or ours.

'H'm!' said Dr Ridgeway, when he had finished. 'Curious case.'

'Brain fever?' I suggested.

The doctor immediately snorted with contempt.

'Brain fever! Brain fever! No such thing as brain fever. An invention of novelists. No; the man's had a shock of some kind. He's come here under the force of a persistent idea – to find M. Hercule Poirot, 14 Farraway Street – and he repeats those words mechanically without in the least knowing what they mean.'

'Aphasia?' I said eagerly.

This suggestion did not cause the doctor to snort quite as violently as my last one had done. He made no answer, but handed the man a sheet of paper and a pencil.

'Let's see what he'll do with that,' he remarked.

The man did nothing with it for some moments, then he suddenly began to write feverishly. With equal suddenness he stopped and let both paper and pencil fall to the ground. The doctor picked it up, and shook his head.

'Nothing here. Only the figure 4 scrawled a dozen times, each one bigger than the last. Wants to write 14 Farraway Street, I expect. It's an interesting case – very interesting. Can you possibly keep him here until this afternoon? I'm due at the hospital now, but I'll come back this afternoon and make all arrangements about him. It's too interesting a case to be lost sight of.'

I explained Poirot's departure and the fact that I proposed to accompany him to Southampton.

'That's all right. Leave the man here. He won't get into mischief. He's suffering from complete exhaustion. Will probably sleep for eight hours on end. I'll have a word with that excellent Mrs Funnyface of yours, and tell her to keep an eye on him.'

And Dr Ridgeway bustled out with his usual celerity. Poirot himself completed his packing, with one eye on the clock.

'The time, it marches with a rapidity unbelievable. Come now, Hastings, you cannot say that I have left you with nothing to do. A most sensational problem. The man from the unknown. Who is he? What is he? Ah, *sapristi*, but I would give two years of my life to have this boat go tomorrow instead of today. There is something here very curious – very interesting. But one must have time – *time*. It may be days – or even months – before he will be able to tell us what he came to tell.'

'I'll do my best, Poirot,' I assured him. 'I'll try to be an efficient substitute.'

'Ye-es.'

His rejoinder struck me as being a shade doubtful. I picked up the sheet of paper.

'If I were writing a story,' I said lightly, 'I should weave this in with your latest idiosyncrasy and call it *The Mystery of the Big Four.*' I tapped the pencilled figures as I spoke.

And then I started, for our invalid, roused suddenly from his stupor, sat up in his chair and said clearly and distinctly:

'Li Chang Yen.'

He had the look of a man suddenly awakened from sleep. Poirot made a sign to me not to speak. The man went on. He spoke in a clear, high voice, and something in his enunciation made me feel that he was quoting from some written report or lecture.

'Li Chang Yen may be regarded as representing the brains of the Big Four. He is the controlling and motive force. I have designated him, therefore, as Number One. Number Two is seldom mentioned by name. He is represented by an "S" with two lines through it – the sign for a dollar; also by two stripes and a star. It may be conjectured, therefore, that he is an American subject, and that he represents the power of wealth. There seems no doubt that Number Three is a woman, and her nationality is French. It is possible that she may be one of the sirens of the *demi-monde*, but nothing is known definitely. Number Four –'

His voice faltered and broke. Poirot leant forward.

'Yes,' he prompted eagerly, 'Number Four?'

His eyes were fastened on the man's face. Some overmastering terror seemed to be gaining the day; the features were distorted and twisted.

'The *Destroyer*,' gasped the man. Then, with a final convulsed movement, he fell back in a dead faint.

'*Mon Dieu!*' whispered Poirot, 'I was right then. I was right.'

'You think –?'

He interrupted me.

'Carry him on to the bed in my room. I have not a minute to lose if I would catch my train. Not that I want to catch it. Oh, that I could miss it with a clear conscience! But I gave my word. Come, Hastings!'

Leaving our mysterious visitor in the charge of Mrs Pearson, we drove away, and duly caught the train by the skin of our teeth. Poirot was alternately silent and loquacious. He would sit staring out of the window like a man lost in a dream, apparently not hearing a word that I said to him. Then, reverting to animation suddenly, he would shower injunctions and commands upon me, and urge the necessity of constant marconigrams.

We had a long fit of silence just after we passed Woking. The train, of course, did not stop anywhere until Southampton; but just here it happened to be held by a signal.

'Ah! *Sacré mille tonnerres!*' cried Poirot suddenly. 'But I have been an imbecile. I see clearly at last. It is undoubtedly the blessed saints who stopped the train. Jump, Hastings, but jump, I tell you.'

In an instant he had unfastened the carriage door, and jumped out on the line.

'Throw out the suitcases and jump yourself.'

I obeyed him. Just in time. As I alighted beside him, the train moved on.

'And now, Poirot,' I said, in some exasperation, 'perhaps you will tell me what all this is about.'

'It is, my friend, that I have seen the light.'

'That,' I said, 'is very illuminating to me.'

'It should be,' said Poirot, 'but I fear – I very much fear that it is not. If you can carry two of these valises, I think I can manage the rest.'

CHAPTER II

The Man from the Asylum

Fortunately the train had stopped near a station. A short walk brought us to a garage where we were able to obtain a car, and half an hour later we were spinning rapidly back to London. Then, and not till then, did Poirot deign to satisfy my curiosity.

'You do not see? No more did I. But I see now. Hastings, *I was being got out of the way.*'

'What!'

'Yes. Very cleverly. Both the place and the method were chosen with great knowledge and acumen. They were afraid of me.'

'Who were?'

'Those four geniuses who have banded themselves together to work outside the law. A Chinaman, an American, a Frenchman, and – another. Pray the good God we arrive back in time, Hastings.'

'You think there is danger to our visitor?'

'I am sure of it.'

Mrs Pearson greeted us on arrival. Brushing aside her ecstasies of astonishment on beholding Poirot, we asked for information. It was reassuring. No one had called, and our guest had not made any sign.

With a sigh of relief we went up to the rooms. Poirot crossed the outer one and went through to the inner one. Then he called me, his voice strangely agitated.

'Hastings, he's dead.'

I came running to join him. The man was lying as we had left him, but he was dead, and had been dead some time. I rushed out for a doctor. Ridgeway, I knew, would not have returned yet. I found one almost immediately, and brought him back with me.

'He's dead right enough, poor chap. Tramp you've been befriending, eh?'

'Something of the kind,' said Poirot evasively. 'What was the cause of death, doctor?'

'Hard to say. Might have been some kind of fit. There are signs of asphyxiation. No gas laid on, is there?'

'No, electric light – nothing else.'

'And both windows wide open, too. Been dead about two hours, I should say. You'll notify the proper people, won't you?'

He took his departure. Poirot did some necessary telephoning. Finally, somewhat to my surprise, he rang up our old friend Inspector Japp, and asked him if he could possibly come round.

No sooner were these proceedings completed than Mrs Pearson appeared, her eyes as round as saucers.

'There's a man here from 'Anwell – from the 'Sylum. Did you ever? Shall I show him up?'

We signified assent, and a big burly man in uniform was ushered in.

''Morning, gentlemen,' he said cheerfully. 'I've got reason to believe you've got one of my birds here. Escaped last night, he did.'

'He *was* here,' said Poirot quietly.

'Not got away again, has he?' asked the keeper, with some concern.

'He is dead.'

The man looked more relieved than otherwise.

'You don't say so. Well, I dare say it's best for all parties.'

'Was he – dangerous?'

''Omicidal, d'you mean? Oh, no. 'Armless enough. Persecution mania very acute. Full of secret societies from China that had got him shut up. They're all the same.'

I shuddered.

'How long has he been shut up?' asked Poirot.

'A matter of two years now.'

'I see,' said Poirot quietly. 'It never occurred to anybody that he might – be sane?'

The keeper permitted himself to laugh.

'If he was sane, what would he be doing in a lunatic asylum? They all *say* they're sane, you know.'

Poirot said no more. He took the man in to see the body. The identification came immediately.

'That's him – right enough,' said the keeper callously: 'funny sort of bloke, ain't he? Well, gentlemen, I had best go off now and make arrangements under the circumstances. We won't trouble you with the corpse much longer. If there's a hinquest, you will have to appear at it, I dare say. Good morning, sir.'

With a rather uncouth bow he shambled out of the room.

A few minutes later Japp arrived. The Scotland Yard inspector was jaunty and dapper as usual.

'Here I am, Moosior Poirot. What can I do for you? Thought you were off to the coral strands of somewhere or other today?'

'My good Japp, I want to know if you have ever seen this man before.'

He led Japp into the bedroom. The inspector stared down at the figure on the bed with a puzzled face.

'Let me see now – he seems sort of familiar – and I pride myself on my memory, too. Why, God bless my soul, it's Mayerling!

'Secret Service chap – not one of our people. Went to Russia five years ago. Never heard of again. Always thought the Bolshies had done him in.'

'It all fits in,' said Poirot, when Japp had taken his leave, 'except for the fact that he seems to have died a natural death.'

He stood looking down on the motionless figure with a dissatisfied frown. A puff of wind set the window-curtains flying out, and he looked up sharply.

'I suppose you opened the windows when you laid him down on the bed, Hastings?'

'No, I didn't,' I replied. 'As far as I remember, they were shut.'

Poirot lifted his head suddenly.

'Shut – and now they are open. What can that mean?'

'Somebody came in that way,' I suggested.

'Possibly,' agreed Poirot, but he spoke absently and without conviction. After a minute or two he said:

'That is not exactly the point I had in mind, Hastings. If only one window was open it would not intrigue me so much. It is both windows being open that strikes me as curious.'

He hurried into the other room.

'The sitting-room window is open, too. That also we left shut. Ah!'

He bent over the dead man, examining the corners of the mouth minutely. Then he looked up suddenly.

'He has been gagged, Hastings. Gagged and then poisoned.'

'Good heavens!' I exclaimed, shocked. 'I suppose we shall find out all about it from the post-mortem.'

'We shall find out nothing. He was killed by inhaling strong prussic acid. It was jammed right under his nose. Then the murderer went away again, first opening all the windows. Hydrocyanic acid is exceedingly volatile, but it has a pronounced smell of bitter almonds. With no trace of the smell to guide them, and no suspicion of foul play, death would be put down to some natural cause by the doctors. So this man was in the Secret Service, Hastings. And five years ago he disappeared in Russia.'

'The last two years he's been in the asylum,' I said. 'But what of the three years before that?'

Poirot shook his head, and then caught my arm.

'The clock, Hastings, look at the clock.'

I followed his gaze to the mantelpiece. The clock had stopped at four o'clock.

'*Mon ami*, someone has tampered with it. It had still three days to run. It is an eight-day clock, you comprehend?'

'But what should they want to do that for? Some idea of a false scent by making the crime appear to have taken place at four o'clock?'

'No, no; rearrange your ideas, *mon ami*. Exercise your little grey cells. You are Mayerling. You hear something perhaps – and you know well enough that your doom is sealed. You have just time to leave a sign. *Four* o'clock, Hastings. Number Four, the *destroyer*. Ah! an idea!'

Hé rushed into the other room and seized the telephone. He asked for Hanwell.

'You are the asylum, yes? I understand there has been an escape today? What is that you say? A little moment, if you please. Will you repeat that? Ah! *parfaitement.*'

He hung up the receiver, and turned to me.

'You heard, Hastings? *There has been no escape.*'

'But the man who came – the keeper?' I said.

'I wonder – I very much wonder.'

'You mean –?'

'Number Four – the Destroyer.'

I gazed at Poirot dumbfounded. A minute or two after, on recovering my voice, I said:

'We shall know him again, anywhere, that's one thing. He was a man of very pronounced personality.'

'Was he, *mon ami?* I think not. He was burly and bluff and red-faced, with a thick moustache and a hoarse voice. He will be none of those things by this time, and for the rest, he has nondescript eyes, nondescript ears, and a perfect set of false teeth. Identification is not such an easy matter as you seem to think. Next time –'

'You think there will be a next time?' I interrupted.

Poirot's face grew very grave.

'It is a duel to the death, *mon ami.* You and I on the one side, the Big Four on the other. They have won the first trick; but they have failed in their plan to get me out of the way, and in the future they have to reckon with Hercule Poirot!'

CHAPTER III

We Hear More About
Li Chang Yen

For a day or two after our visit from the fake asylum attendant I was in some hopes that he might return, and I refused to leave the flat even for a moment. As far as I could see, he had no reason to suspect that we had penetrated his disguise. He might, I thought, return and try to remove the body, but Poirot scoffed at my reasoning.

'*Mon ami,*' he said, 'if you wish you may wait in to put salt on the little bird's tail, but for me I do not waste my time so.'

'Well, then, Poirot,' I argued, 'why did he run the risk of coming at all? If he intended to return later for the body, I can see some point in his visit. He would at least be removing the evidence against himself; as it is, he does not seem to have gained anything.'

Poirot shrugged his most Gallic shrug. 'But you do not see with the eyes of Number Four, Hastings,' he said. 'You talk of evidence, but what evidence have we against him? True, we have a body, but we have no proof even that the man was murdered – prussic acid, when inhaled, leaves no trace. Again, we can find no one who saw anyone enter the flat during our absence, and we have found out nothing about the movements of our late friend, Mayerling ...

'No, Hastings, Number Four has left no trace, and he knows it. His visit we may call a reconnaissance. Perhaps he wanted to make quite sure that Mayerling was dead, but more likely, I think, he came to see Hercule Poirot, and to have speech with the adversary whom alone he must fear.'

Poirot's reasoning appeared to be typically egotistical, but I forbore to argue.

'And what about the inquest?' I asked. 'I suppose you will explain things clearly there, and let the police have a full description of Number Four.'

'And to what end? Can we produce anything to impress a coroner's jury of your solid Britishers? Is our description of Number Four of any value? No; we shall allow them to call it "Accidental Death", and maybe, although I have not much hope, our clever murderer will pat himself on the back that he deceived Hercule Poirot in the first round.'

Poirot was right as usual. We saw no more of the man from the asylum, and the inquest, at which I gave evidence, but which Poirot did not even attend, aroused no public interest.

As, in view of his intended trip to South America, Poirot had wound up his affairs before my arrival, he had at this time no cases in hand, but although he spent most of his time in the flat I could get little out of him. He remained buried in an armchair, and discouraged my attempts at conversation.

And then one morning, about a week after the murder, he asked me if I would care to accompany him on a visit he wished to make. I was pleased, for I felt he was making a mistake in trying to work things out so entirely on his own, and I wished to discuss the case with him. But I found he was not communicative. Even when I asked where we were going, he would not answer.

Poirot loves being mysterious. He will never part with a piece of information until the last possible moment. In this instance, having taken successively a bus and two trains, and arrived in the neighbourhood of one of London's most depressing southern suburbs, he consented at last to explain matters.

'We go, Hastings, to see the one man in England who knows most of the underground life of China.'

'Indeed! Who is he?'

'A man you have never heard of – a Mr John Ingles. To all intents and purposes, he is a retired Civil Servant of mediocre intellect, with a house full of Chinese curios with which he bores his friends and acquaintances. Nevertheless, I am assured by those who should know that the only man capable of giving me the information I seek is this same John Ingles.'

A few moments more saw us ascending the steps of The Laurels, as Mr Ingles's residence was called. Personally, I did not notice a laurel bush of any kind, so deduced that it had been named according to the usual obscure nomenclature of the suburbs.

We were admitted by an impassive-faced Chinese servant and ushered into the presence of his master. Mr Ingles was a squarely-built man, somewhat yellow of countenance, with deep-set eyes that were oddly reflective in character. He rose to greet us, setting aside an open letter which he had held in his hand. He referred to it after his greeting.

'Sit down, won't you? Hasley tells me that you want some information and that I may be useful to you in the matter.'

'That is so, monsieur. I ask of you if you have any knowledge of a man named Li Chang Yen?'

'That's rum – very rum indeed. How did you come to hear about the man?'

'You know him, then?'

'I've met him once. And I know something of him – not quite as much as I should like to. But it surprises me that anyone else in England should even have heard of him. He's a great man in his way – mandarin class and all that, you know – but that's not the crux of the matter. There's good reason to suppose that he's the man behind it all.'

'Behind what?'

'Everything. The world-wide unrest, the labour troubles that beset every nation, and the revolutions that break out in some. There are people, not scaremongers, who know what they are talking about, and they say that there is a force behind the scenes which aims at nothing less than the disintegration of civilization. In Russia, you know, there were many signs that Lenin and Trotsky were mere puppets whose every action was dictated by another's brain. I have no definite proof that would count with you, but I am quite convinced that this brain was Li Chang Yen's.'

'Oh, come,' I protested, 'isn't that a bit far-fetched? How would a Chinaman cut any ice in Russia?'

Poirot frowned at me irritably.

'For you, Hastings,' he said, 'everything is far-fetched that comes not from your own imagination; for me, I agree with this gentleman. But continue, I pray, monsieur.'

'What exactly he hopes to get out of it all I cannot pretend to say for certain,' went on Mr Ingles; 'but I assume his disease is one that has attacked great brains from the time of Akbar and Alexander to Napoleon – a lust for power and personal supremacy. Up to modern times armed force was necessary for conquest, but in this century of unrest a man like Li Chang Yen can use other means. I have evidence that he has unlimited money behind him for bribery and propaganda, and there are signs that he controls some scientific force more powerful than the world has dreamed of.'

Poirot was following Mr Ingles's words with the closest attention.

'And in China?' he asked. 'He moves there too?'

The other nodded in emphatic assent.

'There,' he said, 'although I can produce no proof that would count in a court of law, I speak from my own knowledge. I know personally every man who counts for anything in China today, and this I can tell you: the men who loom most largely in the public eye are men of little or no personality. They are marionettes who dance to the wires pulled by a master hand, and that hand is Li Chang Yen's. His is the controlling brain of the East today. We don't understand the East – we never shall; but Li Chang Yen is its moving spirit. Not that he comes out into the limelight – oh, not at all; he never moves from his palace in Peking. But he pulls strings – that's it, pulls strings – and things happen far away.'

'And there is no one to oppose him?' asked Poirot.

Mr Ingles leant forward in his chair.

'Four men have tried in the last four years,' he said slowly; 'men of character, and honesty, and brain power. Any one of them might in time have interfered with his plans.' He paused.

'Well?' I queried.

'Well, they are dead. One wrote an article, and mentioned Li Chang Yen's name in connection with the riots in Peking, and within two days he was stabbed in the street. His murderer was never caught. The offences of the other two were similar. In a speech or an article, or in conversation, each linked Li Chang Yen's name with rioting or revolution, and within a week of his indiscretion each was dead. One was poisoned; one died of cholera, an isolated case – not part of an epidemic; and one was found dead in his bed. The cause of the last death was never determined, but I was told by a doctor who saw the corpse that it was burnt and shrivelled as though a wave of electrical energy of incredible power had passed through it.'

'And Li Chang Yen?' inquired Poirot. 'Naturally nothing is traced to him, but there are signs, eh?'

Mr Ingles shrugged.

'Oh, signs – yes, certainly. And once I found a man who would talk, a brilliant young Chinese chemist who was a protégé of Li Chang Yen's. He came to me one day, this chemist, and I could see that he was on the verge of a nervous breakdown. He hinted to me of experiments on which he'd been engaged in Li Chang Yen's palace under the mandarin's direction – experiments on coolies in which the most revolting disregard for human life and suffering had been shown. His nerve had completely broken, and he was in the most pitiable state of terror. I put him to bed in a top room of my own house, intending to question him the next day – and that, of course, was stupid of me.'

'How did they get him?' demanded Poirot.

'That I shall never know. I woke that night to find my house in flames, and was lucky to escape with my life. Investigation showed that a fire of amazing intensity had broken out on the top floor, and the remains of my young chemist friend were charred to a cinder.'

I could see from the earnestness with which he had been speaking that Mr Ingles was a man mounted on his hobby horse, and evidently he, too, realized that he had been carried away, for he laughed apologetically.

'But, of course,' he said, 'I have no proofs, and you, like the others, will merely tell me that I have a bee in my bonnet.'

'On the contrary,' said Poirot quietly, 'we have every reason
to believe your story. We ourselves are more than a little interested in Li Chang Yen.'

'Very odd your knowing about him. Didn't fancy a soul in
England had ever heard of him. I'd rather like to know how
you did come to hear of him – if it's not indiscreet.'

'Not in the least, monsieur. A man took refuge in my rooms.
He was suffering badly from shock, but he managed to tell us
enough to interest us in this Li Chang Yen. He described four
people – the Big Four – an organization hitherto undreamed
of. Number One is Li Chang Yen, Number Two is an unknown
American, Number Three an equally unknown Frenchwoman,
Number Four may be called the executive of the organization
– the *Destroyer*. My informant died. Tell me, monsieur, is that
phrase known to you at all? The Big Four.'

'Not in connection with Li Chang Yen. No, I can't say it is.
But I've heard it, or read it, just lately – and in some unusual
connection too. Ah, I've got it.'

He rose and went across to an inlaid lacquer cabinet – an
exquisite thing, as even I could see. He returned with a letter
in his hand.

'Here you are. Note from an old sea-faring man I ran against
once in Shanghai. Hoary old reprobate – maudlin with
drink by now, I should say. I took this to be the ravings of
alcoholism.'

He read it aloud:

'Dear Sir – You may not remember me, but you did me
a good turn once in Shanghai. Do me another now. I
must have money to get out of the country. I'm well hid
here, I hope, but any day they may get me. The Big Four,
I mean. It's life or death. I've plenty of money, but I
daren't get at it, for fear of putting them wise. Send me
a couple of hundred in notes. I'll repay it faithful – I
swear to that. – Your servant, sir,

Jonathan Whalley

'Dated from Granite Bungalow, Hoppaton, Dartmoor. I'm afraid I regarded it as rather a crude method of relieving me of a couple of hundred which I can ill spare. If it's any use to you –' He held it out.

'*Je vous remercie,* monsieur. I start for Hoppaton *à l'heure même.*'

'Dear me, this is very interesting. Supposing I came along too? Any objection?'

'I should be charmed to have your company, but we must start at once. We shall not reach Dartmoor until close on nightfall, as it is.'

John Ingles did not delay us more than a couple of minutes, and soon we were in the train moving out of Paddington bound for the West Country. Hoppaton was a small village clustering in a hollow right on the fringe of the moorland. It was reached by a nine-mile drive from Moretonhampstead. It was about eight o'clock when we arrived; but as the month was July, the daylight was still abundant.

We drove into the narrow street of the village and then stopped to ask our way of an old rustic.

'Granite Bungalow,' said the old man reflectively, 'it be Granite Bungalow you do want? Eh?'

We assured him that this was what we did want.

The old man pointed to a small grey cottage at the end of the street.

'There be t'Bungalow. Do yee want to see t'Inspector?'

'What Inspector?' asked Poirot sharply; 'what do you mean?'

'Haven't yee heard about t'murder, then? A shocking business t'was seemingly. Pools of blood, they do say.'

'*Mon Dieu!*' murmured Poirot. 'This Inspector of yours, I must see him at once.'

Five minutes later we were closeted with Inspector Meadows. The Inspector was inclined to be stiff at first, but at the magic name of Inspector Japp of Scotland Yard he unbent.

'Yes, sir; murdered this morning. A shocking business. They phoned to Moreton, and I came out at once. Looked a mysterious thing to begin with. The old man – he was about seventy, you know, and fond of his glass, from all I hear – was lying on the floor of the living-room. There was a bruise on his head and his throat was cut from ear to ear. Blood all over the place, as you can understand. The woman who cooks for him, Betsy Andrews, she told us that her master had several little Chinese jade figures, that he'd told her were very valuable, and these had disappeared. That, of course, looked like assault and robbery; but there were all sorts of difficulties in the way of that solution. The old fellow had two people in the house; Betsy Andrews, who is a Hoppaton woman, and a rough kind of man-servant, Robert Grant. Grant had gone to the farm to fetch the milk, which he does every day, and Betsy had stepped out to have a chat with a neighbour. She was only away twenty minutes – between ten and half-past – and the crime must have been done then. Grant returned to the house first. He went in by the back door, which was open – no one locks up doors round here – not in broad daylight, at all events – put the milk in the larder, and went into his own room to read the paper and have a smoke. He had no idea anything unusual had occurred – at least, that's what he says. Then Betsy comes in, goes into the living-room, sees what's happened, and lets out a screech to wake the dead. That's all fair and square. Someone got in whilst those two were out, and did the poor old man in. But it struck me at once that he must be a pretty cool customer. He'd have to come right up the village street, or creep through someone's back yard. Granite Bungalow has got houses all round it, as you can see. How was it that no one had seen him?'

The Inspector paused with a flourish.

'Aha, I perceive your point,' said Poirot. 'To continue?'

'Well, sir, fishy, I said to myself – fishy. And I began to look about me. Those jade figures, now. Would a common tramp ever suspect that they were valuable? Anyway, it was madness to try such a thing in broad daylight. Suppose the old man had yelled for help?'

'I suppose, Inspector,' said Mr Ingles, 'that the bruise on the head was inflicted before death?'

'Quite right, sir. First knocked him silly, the murderer did, and then cut his throat. That's clear enough. But how the dickens did he come or go? They notice strangers quick enough in a little place like this. It came to me all at once – nobody did come. I took a good look round. It had rained the night before, and there were footprints clear enough going in and out of the kitchen. In the living-room there were two sets of footprints only (Betsy Andrews's stopped at the door) – Mr Whalley's (he was wearing carpet slippers) and another man's. The other man had stepped in the bloodstains, and I traced his bloody footprints – I beg your pardon, sir.'

'Not at all,' said Mr Ingles, with a faint smile; 'the adjective is perfectly understood.'

'I traced them to the kitchen – but not beyond. Point Number One. On the lintel of Robert Grant's door was a faint smear – a smear of blood. That's point Number Two. Point Number Three was when I got hold of Grant's boots – which he had taken off – and fitted them to the marks. That settled it. It was an inside job. I warned Grant and took him into custody; and what do you think I found packed away in his port-manteau? The little jade figures and a ticket-of-leave. Robert Grant was also Abraham Biggs, convicted for felony and housebreaking five years ago.'

The Inspector paused triumphantly.

'What do you think of that, gentlemen?'

'I think,' said Poirot, 'that it appears a very clear case – of a surprising clearness, in fact. This Biggs, or Grant, he must be a man very foolish and uneducated, eh?'

'Oh, he is that – a rough, common sort of fellow. No idea of what a footprint may mean.'

'Clearly he reads not the detective fiction! Well, Inspector, I congratulate you. We may look at the scene of the crime. Yes?'

'I'll take you there myself this minute. I'd like you to see those footprints.'

'I, too, should like to see them. Yes, yes, very interesting, very ingenious.'

We set out forthwith. Mr Ingles and the Inspector forged ahead. I drew Poirot back a little so as to be able to speak to him out of the Inspector's hearing.

'What do you really think, Poirot? Is there more in this than meets the eye?'

'That is just the question, *mon ami*. Whalley says plainly enough in his letter that the Big Four are on his track, and we know, you and I, that the Big Four is no bogey for the children. Yet everything seems to say that this man Grant committed the crime. Why did he do so? For the sake of the little jade figures? Or is he an agent of the Big Four? I confess that this last seems more likely. However valuable the jade, a man of that class was not likely to realize the fact – at any rate, not to the point of committing murder for them. (That, *par exemple*, ought to have struck the Inspector.) He could have stolen the jade and made off with it instead of committing a brutal murder. Ah, yes; I fear our Devonshire friend has not used his little grey cells. He has measured footprints, and has omitted to reflect and arrange his ideas with the necessary order and method.'

CHAPTER IV

The Importance of
a Leg of Mutton

The Inspector drew a key from his pocket and unlocked the door of Granite Bungalow. The day had been fine and dry, so our feet were not likely to leave any prints; nevertheless, we wiped them carefully on the mat before entering.

A woman came up out of the gloom and spoke to the Inspector, and he turned aside. Then he spoke over his shoulder.

'Have a good look round, Mr Poirot, and see all there is to be seen. I'll be back in about ten minutes. By the way, here's Grant's boot. I brought it along with me for you to compare the impressions.'

We went into the living-room, and the sound of the Inspector's footsteps died away outside. Ingles was attracted immediately by some Chinese curios on a table in the corner, and went over to examine them. He seemed to take no interest in Poirot's doings. I, on the other hand, watched him with breathless interest. The floor was covered with a dark-green linoleum which was ideal for showing up footprints. A door at the farther end led into the small kitchen. From there another door led into the scullery (where the back door was situated), and another into the bedroom which had been occupied by Robert Grant. Having explored the ground, Poirot commented upon it in a low running monologue.

'Here is where the body lay; that big dark stain and the splashes all around mark the spot. Traces of carpet slippers and "number nine" boots, you observe, but all very confused. Then two sets of tracks leading to and from the kitchen; whoever the murderer was, he came in that way. You have the boot, Hastings?

Give it to me.' He compared it carefully with the prints. 'Yes, both made by the same man, Robert Grant. He came in that way, killed the old man, and went back to the kitchen. He had stepped in the blood; see the stains he left as he went out? Nothing to be seen in the kitchen – all the village has been walking about in it. He went into his own room – no, first he went back again to the scene of the crime – was that to get the little jade figures? Or had he forgotten something that might incriminate him?'

'Perhaps he killed the old man the second time he went in?' I suggested.

'*Mais non,* you do not observe. On one of the outgoing foot-marks stained with blood there is superimposed an ingoing one. I wonder what he went back for – the little jade figures as an afterthought? It is all ridiculous – stupid.'

'Well, he's given himself away pretty hopelessly.'

'*N'est-ce pas?* I tell you, Hastings, it goes against reason. It offends my little grey cells. Let us go into his bedroom – ah, yes; there is the smear of blood on the lintel and just a trace of footmarks – bloodstained. Robert Grant's footmarks, and his only, near the body – Robert Grant the only man who went near the house. Yes, it must be so.'

'What about the old woman?' I said suddenly. 'She was in the house alone after Grant had gone for the milk. She might have killed him and then gone out. Her feet would leave no prints if she hadn't been outside.'

'Very good, Hastings. I wondered whether that hypothesis would occur to you. I had already thought of it and rejected it. Betsy Andrews is a local woman, well known hereabouts. She can have no connection with the Big Four; and, besides, old Whalley was a powerful fellow, by all accounts. This is a man's work – not a woman's.'

'I suppose the Big Four couldn't have had some diabolical contrivance concealed in the ceiling – something which descended automatically and cut the old man's throat and was afterwards drawn up again?'

'Like Jacob's ladder? I know, Hastings, that you have an

imagination of the most fertile – but I implore of you to keep it within bounds.'

I subsided, abashed. Poirot continued to wander about, poking into rooms and cupboards with a profoundly dissatisfied expression on his face. Suddenly he uttered an excited yelp, reminiscent of a Pomeranian dog. I rushed to join him. He was standing in the larder in a dramatic attitude. In his hand he was brandishing a leg of mutton!

'My dear Poirot!' I cried. 'What is the matter? Have you suddenly gone mad?'

'Regard, I pray you, this mutton. But regard it closely!'

I regarded it as closely as I could, but could see nothing unusual about it. It seemed to me a very ordinary leg of mutton. I said as much. Poirot threw me a withering glance.

'But do you not see this – and this – and this –'

He illustrated each 'this' with a jab at the unoffending joint, dislodging small icicles as he did so.

Poirot had just accused me of being imaginative, but I now felt that he was far more wildly so than I had ever been. Did he seriously think these slivers of ice were crystals of a deadly poison? That was the only construction I could put upon his extraordinary agitation.

'It's frozen meat,' I explained gently. 'Imported, you know. New Zealand.'

He stared at me for a moment or two and then broke into a strange laugh.

'How marvellous is my friend Hastings! He knows everything – but everything! How do they say – Inquire Within Upon Everything. That is my friend Hastings.'

He flung down the leg of mutton on to its dish again and left the larder. Then he looked through the window.

'Here comes our friend the Inspector. It is well. I have seen all I want to see here.' He drummed on the table absent-mindedly, as though absorbed in calculation, and then asked suddenly, 'What is the day of the week, *mon ami*?'

'Monday,' I said, rather astonished. 'What –?'

'Ah! Monday, is it? A bad day of the week. To commit a murder on a Monday is a mistake.'

Passing back to the living-room, he tapped the glass on the wall and glanced at the thermometer.

'Set fair, and seventy degrees Fahrenheit. An orthodox English summer's day.'

Ingles was still examining various pieces of Chinese pottery.

'You do not take much interest in this inquiry, monsieur?' said Poirot.

The other gave a slow smile.

'It's not my job, you see. I'm a connoisseur of some things, but not of this. So I just stand back and keep out of the way. I've learnt patience in the East.'

The Inspector came bustling in, apologizing for having been so long away. He insisted on taking us over most of the ground again, but finally we got away.

'I must appreciate your thousand politenesses, Inspector,' said Poirot, as we were walking down the village street again. 'There is just one more request I should like to put to you.'

'You want to see the body, perhaps, sir?'

'Oh, dear me, no! I have not the least interest in the body. I want to see Robert Grant.'

'You'll have to drive back with me to Moreton to see him, sir.'

'Very well, I will do so. But I must see him and be able to speak to him alone.'

The Inspector caressed his upper lip.

'Well, I don't know about that, sir.'

'I assure you that if you can get through to Scotland Yard you will receive full authority.'

'I've heard of you, of course, sir and I know you've done us a good turn now and again. But it's very irregular.'

'Nevertheless, it is necessary,' said Poirot calmly. 'It is necessary for this reason – Grant is not the murderer.'

'What? Who is, then?'

'The murderer was, I should fancy, a youngish man. He drove up to Granite Bungalow in a trap, which he left outside. He went in, committed the murder, came out, and drove away again. He was bareheaded, and his clothing was slightly bloodstained.'

'But – but the whole village would have seen him!'

'Not under certain circumstances.'

'Not if it was dark, perhaps; but the crime was committed in broad daylight.'

Poirot merely smiled.

'And the horse and trap, sir – how could you tell that? Any amount of wheeled vehicles have passed along outside. There's no mark of one in particular to be seen.'

'Not with the eyes of the body, perhaps; but with the eyes of the mind, yes.'

The Inspector touched his forehead significantly with a grin at me. I was utterly bewildered, but I had faith in Poirot. Further discussion ended in our all driving back to Moreton with the Inspector. Poirot and I were taken to Grant, but a constable was to be present during the interview. Poirot went straight to the point.

'Grant, I know you to be innocent of this crime. Relate to me in your own words exactly what happened.'

The prisoner was a man of medium height, with a somewhat unpleasing cast of features. He looked a jailbird if ever a man did.

'Honest to God, I never did it,' he whined. 'Someone put those little glass figures amongst my traps. It was a frame-up, that's what it was. I went straight to my rooms when I came in, like I said. I never knew a thing till Betsy screeched out. S'welp me, God, I didn't.'

Poirot rose.

'If you can't tell me the truth, that is the end of it.'

'But, guv'nor –'

'You *did* go into the room – you *did* know your master was dead; and you were just preparing to make a bolt of it when the good Betsy made her terrible discovery.'

The man stared at Poirot with a dropped jaw.

'Come now, is it not so? I tell you solemnly – on my word of honour – that to be frank now is your only chance.'

'I'll risk it,' said the man suddenly. 'It was just as you say. I came in, and went straight to the master – and there he was, dead on the floor and blood all round. Then I got the wind up proper. They'd ferret out my record, and for a certainty they'd say it was me as had done him in. My only thought was to get away – at once – before he was found –'

'And the jade figures?'

The man hesitated.

'You see –'

'You took them by a kind of reversion to instinct, as it were? You had heard your master say that they were valuable, and you felt you might as well go the whole hog. That, I understand. Now, answer me this. Was it the second time that you went into the room that you took the figures?'

'I didn't go in a second time. Once was enough for me.'

'You are sure of that?'

'Absolutely certain.'

'Good. Now, when did you come out of prison?'

'Two months ago.'

'How did you obtain this job?'

'Through one of them Prisoners' Help Societies. Bloke met me when I came out.'

'What was he like?'

'Not exactly a parson, but looked like one. Soft black hat and mincing way of walking. Got a broken front tooth. Spectacled chap. Saunders his name was. Said he hoped I was repentant, and that he'd find me a good post. I went to old Whalley on his recommendation.'

Poirot rose once more.

'I thank you. I know all now. Have patience.' He paused in the doorway and added: 'Saunders gave you a pair of boots, didn't he?'

Grant looked very astonished.

'Why, yes, he did. But how did you know?'

'It is my business to know things,' said Poirot gravely.

After a word or two to the Inspector, the three of us went to the White Hart and discussed eggs and bacon and Devonshire cider.

'Any elucidations yet?' asked Ingles, with a smile.

'Yes, the case is clear enough now; but, see you, I shall have a good deal of difficulty in proving it. Whalley was killed by order of the Big Four – but not by Grant. A very clever man got Grant the post and deliberately planned to make him the scapegoat – an easy matter with Grant's prison record. He gave him a pair of boots, one of two duplicate pairs. The other he kept himself. It was all so simple. When Grant is out of the house, and Betsy is chatting in the village (which she probably did every day of her life), he drives up wearing the duplicate boots, enters the kitchen, goes through into the living-room, fells the old man with a blow, and then cuts his throat. Then he returns to the kitchen, removes the boots, puts on another pair, and, carrying the first pair, goes out to his trap and drives off again.'

Ingles looked steadily at Poirot.

'There's a catch in it still. Why did nobody see him?'

'Ah! That is where the cleverness of Number Four, I am convinced, comes in. Everybody saw him – and yet nobody saw him. You see, he drove up in a butcher's cart!'

I uttered an exclamation.

'The leg of mutton?'

'Exactly, Hastings, the leg of mutton. Everybody swore that no one had been to Granite Bungalow that morning, but, nevertheless, I found in the larder a leg of mutton, still frozen. It was Monday, so the meat must have been delivered that morning; for if on Saturday, in this hot weather, it would not have remained frozen over Sunday. So someone *had* been to the Bungalow, and a man on whom a trace of blood here and there would attract no attention.'

'Damned ingenious!' cried Ingles approvingly.

'Yes, he is clever, Number Four.'

'As clever as Hercule Poirot?' I murmured.

My friend threw me a glance of dignified reproach.

'There are some jests that you should not permit yourself, Hastings,' he said sententiously. 'Have I not saved an innocent man from being sent to the gallows? That is enough for one day.'

CHAPTER V

Disappearance of a Scientist

Personally, I don't think that, even when a jury had acquitted Robert Grant, alias Biggs, of the murder of Jonathan Whalley, Inspector Meadows was entirely convinced of his innocence. The case which he had built up against Grant – the man's record, the jade which he had stolen, the boots which fitted the footprints so exactly – was to his matter-of-fact mind too complete to be easily upset; but Poirot, compelled much against his inclination to give evidence, convinced the jury. Two witnesses were produced who had seen the butcher's cart drive up to the bungalow on that Monday morning, and the local butcher testified that his cart only called there on Wednesdays and Fridays.

A woman was actually found who, when questioned, remembered seeing the butcher's man leaving the bungalow, but she could furnish no useful description of him. The only impression he seemed to have left on her mind was that he was clean-shaven, of medium height, and looked exactly like a butcher's man. At this description Poirot shrugged his shoulders philosophically.

'It is as I tell you, Hastings,' he said to me, after the trial. 'He is an artist, this one. He disguises himself not with the false beard and the blue spectacles. He alters his features, yes; but that is the least part. For the time being he *is* the man he would be. He lives in his part.'

Certainly I was compelled to admit that the man who had visited us from Hanwell had fitted in exactly with my idea of what an asylum attendant should look like. I should never for a moment have dreamt of doubting that he was genuine.

It was all a little discouraging, and our experience on Dartmoor did not seem to have helped us at all. I said as much to Poirot, but he would not admit that we had gained nothing.

'We progress,' he said; 'we progress. At every contact with this man we learn a little of his mind and his methods. Of us and our plans he knows nothing.'

'And there, Poirot,' I protested, 'he and I seem to be in the same boat. You don't seem to me to have any plans, you seem to sit and wait for him to do something.'

Poirot smiled.

'*Mon ami*, you do not change. Always the same Hastings, who would be up and at their throats. Perhaps,' he added, as a knock sounded on the door, 'you have here your chance; it may be our friend who enters.' And he laughed at my disappointment when Inspector Japp and another man entered the room.

'Good evening, moosior,' said the Inspector. 'Allow me to introduce Captain Kent of the United States Secret Service.'

Captain Kent was a tall, lean American, with a singularly impassive face which looked as though it had been carved out of wood.

'Pleased to meet you, gentlemen,' he murmured, as he shook hands jerkily.

Poirot threw an extra log on the fire, and brought forward more easy chairs. I brought out glasses and the whisky and soda. The captain took a deep draught, and expressed appreciation.

'Legislation in your country is still sound,' he observed.

'And now to business,' said Japp. 'Moosior Poirot here made a certain request to me. He was interested in some concern that went by the name of the Big Four, and he asked me to let him know at any time if I came across a mention of it in my official line of business. I didn't take much stock in the matter, but I remembered what he said, and when the captain here came over with rather a curious story, I said at once, "We'll go round to Moosior Poirot's."'

Poirot looked across at Captain Kent, and the American took up the tale.

'You may remember reading, M. Poirot, that a number of torpedo boats and destroyers were sunk by being dashed upon

the rocks off the American coast. It was just after the Japanese
earthquake, and the explanation given was that the disaster was
the result of a tidal wave. Now, a short time ago, a roundup
was made of certain crooks and gunmen, and with them were
captured some papers which put an entirely new face upon the
matter. They appeared to refer to some organization called
the "Big Four", and gave an incomplete description of some
powerful wireless installation – a concentration of wireless
energy far beyond anything so far attempted, and capable of
focusing a beam of great intensity upon some given spot. The
claims made for this invention seemed manifestly absurd, but
I turned them in to headquarters for what they were worth, and
one of our highbrow professors got busy on them. Now it
appears that one of your British scientists read a paper upon
the subject before the British Association. His colleagues didn't
think great shakes of it, by all accounts, thought it far-fetched
and fanciful, but your scientist stuck to his guns, and declared
that he himself was on the eve of success in his experiments.'

'*Eh bien?*' demanded Poirot, with interest.

'It was suggested that I should come over here and get an
interview with this gentleman. Quite a young fellow, he is, Halliday by name. He is the leading authority on the subject, and I
was to get from him whether the thing suggested was anyway
possible.'

'And was it?' I asked eagerly.

'That's just what I don't know. I haven't seen Mr Halliday –
and I'm not likely to, by all accounts.'

'The truth of the matter is,' said Japp shortly, 'Halliday's
disappeared.'

'When?'

'Two months ago.'

'Was his disappearance reported?'

'Of course it was. His wife came to us in a great state. We did
what we could, but I knew all along it would be no good.'

'Why not?'

'Never is – when a man disappears that way.' Japp winked.

'What way?'

'Paris.'

'So Halliday disappeared in Paris?'

'Yes. Went over there on scientific work – so he said. Of course, he'd have to say something like that. But you know what it means when a man disappears over there. Either it's Apache work, and that's the end of it – or else it's voluntary disappearance – and that's a great deal the commoner of the two, I can tell you. Gay Paree and all that, you know. Sick of home life. Halliday and his wife had had a tiff before he started, which all helps to make it a pretty clear case.'

'I wonder,' said Poirot thoughtfully.

The American was looking at him curiously.

'Say, mister,' he drawled, 'what's this Big Four idea?'

'The Big Four,' said Poirot, 'is an international organization which has at its head a Chinaman. He is known as Number One. Number Two is an American. Number Three is a Frenchwoman, Number Four, "the Destroyer", is an Englishman.'

'A Frenchwoman, eh?' The American whistled. 'And Halliday disappeared in France. Maybe there's something in this. What's her name?'

'I don't know. I know nothing about her.'

'But it's a mighty big proposition, eh?' suggested the other.

Poirot nodded, as he arranged the glasses in a neat row on the tray. His love of order was as great as ever.

'What was the idea in sinking those boats? Are the Big Four a German stunt?'

'The Big Four are for themselves – and for themselves only, M. le Capitaine. Their aim is world domination.'

The American burst out laughing, but broke off at the sight of Poirot's serious face.

'You laugh, monsieur,' said Poirot, shaking a finger at him. 'You reflect not – you use not the little grey cells of the brain. Who are these men who send a portion of your navy to destruction simply as a trial of their power? For that was all it was, monsieur, a test of this new force of magnetical attraction which they hold.'

'Go on with you, moosior,' said Japp good-humouredly. 'I've

read of super criminals many a time, but I've never come across them. Well, you've heard Captain Kent's story. Anything further I can do for you?'

'Yes, my good friend. You can give me the address of Mrs Halliday – and also a few words of introduction to her if you will be so kind.'

Thus it was that the following day saw us bound for Chetwynd Lodge, near the village of Chobham in Surrey.

Mrs Halliday received us at once, a tall, fair woman, nervous and eager in manner. With her was her little girl, a beautiful child of five.

Poirot explained the purpose of our visit.

'Oh! M. Poirot, I am so glad, so thankful. I have heard of you, of course. You will not be like these Scotland Yard people, who will not listen or try to understand. And the French police are just as bad – worse, I think. They're all convinced that my husband has gone off with some other woman. But he wasn't like that! All he thought of in life was his work. Half our quarrels came from that. He cared for it more than he did for me.'

'Englishmen, they are like that,' said Poirot soothingly. 'And if it is not work, it is the games, the sport. All those things they take *au grand sérieux*. Now, madame, recount to me exactly, in detail, and as methodically as you can, the exact circumstances of your husband's disappearance.'

'My husband went to Paris on Thursday, the 20th of July. He was to meet and visit various people there connected with his work, amongst them Madame Olivier.'

Poirot nodded at the mention of the famous French woman chemist, who had eclipsed even Madame Curie in the brilliance of her achievements. She had been decorated by the French Government, and was one of the most prominent personalities of the day.

'He arrived there in the evening and went at once to the Hotel Castiglione in the rue de Castiglione. On the following morning he had an appointment with Professor Bourgoneau, which he kept. His manner was normal and pleasant. The two men had a most interesting conversation, and it was arranged that he should witness some experiments in the professor's laboratory on the following day. He lunched alone at the Café Royal, went for a walk in the Bois, and then visited Madame Olivier at her house at Passy. There, also, his manner was perfectly normal. He left about six. Where he dined is not known, probably alone at some restaurant. He returned to the hotel about eleven o'clock and went straight up to his room, after inquiring if any letters had come for him. On the following morning, he walked out of the hotel, and has not been seen again.'

'At what time did he leave the hotel? At the hour when he would normally leave it to keep his appointment at Professor Bourgoneau's laboratory?'

'We do not know. He was not remarked leaving the hotel. But no *petit déjeuner* was served to him, which seems to indicate that he went out early.'

'Or he might, in fact, have gone out again after he came in the night before?'

'I do not think so. His bed had been slept in, and the night porter would have remembered anyone going out at that hour.'

'A very just observation, madame. We may take it, then, that he left early on the following morning – and that is reassuring from one point of view. He is not likely to have fallen a victim to any apache assault at that hour. His baggage, now, was it all left behind?'

Mrs Halliday seemed rather reluctant to answer, but at last she said:

'No – he must have taken one small suitcase with him.'

'H'm,' said Poirot thoughtfully, 'I wonder where he was that evening. If we knew that, we should know a great deal. Whom did he meet? – there lies the mystery. Madame, myself, I do not of necessity accept the view of the police; with them it is always *"Cherchez la femme."* Yet it is clear that something occurred that night to alter your husband's plans. You say he asked for letters on returning to the hotel. Did he receive any?'

'One only, and that must have been the one I wrote to him on the day he left England.'

Poirot remained sunk in thought for a full minute, then he rose briskly to his feet.

'Well, madame, the solution of the mystery lies in Paris, and to find it I myself journey to Paris on the instant.'

'It is all a long time ago, monsieur.'

'Yes, yes. Nevertheless, it is there that we must seek.'

He turned to leave the room, but paused with his hand on the door.

'Tell me, madame, do you ever remember your husband mentioning the phrase, "The Big Four"?'

'The Big Four,' she repeated thoughtfully. 'No, I can't say I do.'

CHAPTER VI

The Woman on the Stairs

That was all that could be elicited from Mrs Halliday. We hurried back to London, and the following day saw us en route for the Continent. With rather a rueful smile, Poirot observed:

'This Big Four, they make me to bestir myself, *mon ami*. I run up and down, all over the ground, like our old friend "the human foxhound".'

'Perhaps you'll meet him in Paris,' I said, knowing that he referred to a certain Giraud, one of the most trusted detectives of the Sûreté, whom he had met on a previous occasion.

Poirot made a grimace. 'I devoutly hope not. He loved me not, that one.'

'Won't it be a very difficult task?' I asked. 'To find out what an unknown Englishman did on an evening two months ago?'

'Very difficult, *mon ami*. But as you know well, difficulties rejoice the heart of Hercule Poirot.'

'You think the Big Four kidnapped him?'

Poirot nodded.

Our inquiries necessarily went over old ground, and we learnt little to add to what Mrs Halliday had already told us. Poirot had a lengthy interview with Professor Bourgoneau, during which he sought to elicit whether Halliday had mentioned any plan of his own for the evening, but we drew a complete blank.

Our next source of information was the famous Madame Olivier. I was quite excited as we mounted the steps of her villa at Passy. It has always seemed to me extraordinary that a woman should go so far in the scientific world. I should have thought a purely masculine brain was needed for such work.

The door was opened by a young lad of seventeen or thereabouts, who reminded me vaguely of an acolyte, so ritualistic was his manner. Poirot had taken the trouble to arrange our interview beforehand, as he knew Madame Olivier never received anyone without an appointment, being immersed in research work most of the day.

We were shown into a small salon, and presently the mistress of the house came to us there. Madame Olivier was a very tall woman, her tallness accentuated by the long white overall she wore, and a coif like a nun's that shrouded her head. She had a long pale face, and wonderful dark eyes that burnt with a light almost fanatical. She looked more like a priestess of old than a modern Frenchwoman. One cheek was disfigured by a scar, and I remembered that her husband and co-worker had been killed in an explosion in the laboratory three years before, and that she herself had been terribly burned. Ever since then she had shut herself away from the world, and plunged with fiery energy into the work of scientific research. She received us with cold politeness.

'I have been interviewed by the police many times, messieurs. I think it hardly likely that I can help you, since I have not been able to help them.'

'Madame, it is possible that I shall not ask you quite the same questions. To begin with, of what did you talk together, you and M. Halliday?'

She looked a trifle surprised.

'But of his work! His work – and also mine.'

'Did he mention to you the theories he had embodied recently in his paper read before the British Association?'

'Certainly he did. It was chiefly of those we spoke.'

'His ideas were somewhat fantastic, were they not?' asked Poirot carelessly.

'Some people have thought so. I do not agree.'

'You consider them practicable?'

'Perfectly practicable. My own line of research has been somewhat similar, though not undertaken with the same end in view. I have been investigating the gamma rays emitted by the substance usually know as Radium C, a product of Radium emanation, and in doing so I have come across some very interesting magnetical phenomena. Indeed, I have a theory as to the actual nature of the force we all call magnetism, but it is not yet time for my discoveries to be given to the world. Mr Halliday's experiments and views were exceedingly interesting to me.'

Poirot nodded. Then he asked a question which surprised me.

'Madame, where did you converse on these topics. In here?'

'No, monsieur. In the laboratory.'

'May I see it?'

'Certainly.'

She led the way to the door from which she had entered. It opened on a small passage. We passed through two doors and found ourselves in the big laboratory, with its array of beakers and crucibles and a hundred appliances of which I did not even know the names. There were two occupants, both busy with some experiment. Madame Olivier introduced them.

'Mademoiselle Claude, one of my assistants.' A tall, serious-faced young girl bowed to us. 'Monsieur Henri, an old and trusted friend.'

The young man, short and dark, bowed jerkily.

Poirot looked round him. There were two other doors besides the one by which we had entered. One, madame explained, led into the garden, the other into a smaller chamber also devoted to research. Poirot took all this in, then declared himself ready to return to the salon.

'Madame, were you alone with M. Halliday during your interview?'

'Yes, monsieur. My two assistants were in the smaller room next door.'

'Could your conversation be overheard – by them or anyone else?'

Madame reflected, then shook her head.

'I do not think so. I am almost sure it could not. The doors were all shut.'

'Could anyone have been concealed in the room?'

'There is a big cupboard in the corner – but the idea is absurd.'

'*Pas tout à fait,* madame. One thing more: did M. Halliday make any mention of his plans for the evening?'

'He said nothing whatever, monsieur.'

'I thank you, madame, and I apologize for disturbing you. Pray do not trouble – we can find our way out.'

We stepped out into the hall. A lady was just entering the front door as we did so. She ran quickly up the stairs, and I was left with an impression of the heavy mourning that denotes a French widow.

'A most unusual type of woman, that,' remarked Poirot, as we walked away.

'Madame Olivier? Yes, she –'

'*Mais non,* not Madame Olivier. *Cela va sans dire!* There are not many geniuses of her stamp in the world. No, I referred to the other lady – the lady on the stairs.'

'I didn't see her face,' I said, staring. 'And I hardly see how you could have done. She never looked at us.'

'That is why I said she was an unusual type,' said Poirot placidly. 'A woman who enters her home – for I presume that it is her home since she enters with a key – and runs straight upstairs without even looking at two strange visitors in the hall to see who they are, is a *very* unusual type of woman – quite unnatural, in fact. *Mille tonnerres!* what is that?'

He dragged me back – just in time. A tree had crashed down on to the sidewalk, just missing us. Poirot stared at it, pale and upset.

'It was a near thing that! But clumsy, all the same – for I had no suspicion – at least hardly any suspicion. Yes, but for my quick eyes, the eyes of a cat, Hercule Poirot might now be crushed out of existence – a terrible calamity for the world. And you, too, *mon ami* – though that would not be such a national catastrophe.'

'Thank you,' I said coldly. 'And what are we going to do now?'

'Do?' cried Poirot. 'We are going to think. Yes, here and now, we are going to exercise our little grey cells. This M. Halliday now, was he really in Paris? Yes, for Professor Bourgoneau, who knows him, saw and spoke to him.'

'What on earth are you driving at?' I cried.

'That was Friday morning. He was last seen at eleven, Friday night – but *was* he seen then?'

'The porter –'

'A night porter – who had not previously seen Halliday. A man comes in, sufficiently like Halliday – we may trust Number Four for that – asks for letters, goes upstairs, packs a small suitcase, and slips out the next morning. Nobody saw Halliday all that evening – no, because he was already in the hands of his enemies. Was it Halliday whom Madame Olivier received? Yes, for though she did not know him by sight, an impostor could hardly deceive her on her own special subject. He came here, he had his interview, he left. What happened next?'

Seizing me by the arm, Poirot was fairly dragging me back to the villa.

'Now, *mon ami*, imagine that it is the day after the disappearance, and that we are tracking footprints. You love footprints, do you not? See – here they go, a man's, M. Halliday's . . . He turns to the right as we did, he walks briskly – ah! other footsteps following behind – very quickly – small footsteps, a woman's. See, she catches him up – a slim young woman, in a widow's veil. "Pardon, monsieur, Madame Olivier desires that I recall you." He stops, he turns. Now where would the young woman take him? Is it coincidence that she catches up with him just where a narrow alleyway opens, dividing two gardens? She leads him down it. "It is shorter this way, monsieur." On the right is the garden of Madame Olivier's villa, on the left the garden of another villa – and from that garden, mark you, the tree fell – so nearly on us. Garden doors from both open on the alley. The ambush is there. Men pour out, overpower him, and carry him into the strange villa.'

'Good gracious, Poirot,' I cried, 'are you pretending to see all this?'

'I see it with the eyes of the mind, *mon ami*. So, and only so, could it have happened. Come, let us go back to the house.'

'You want to see Madame Olivier again?'

Poirot gave a curious smile.

'No, Hastings, I want to see the face of the lady on the stairs.'

'Who do you think she is, a relation of Madame Olivier's?'

'More probably a secretary – and a secretary engaged not very long ago.'

The same gentle acolyte opened the door to us.

'Can you tell me,' said Poirot, 'the name of the lady, the widow lady, who came in just now?'

'Madame Veroneau? Madame's secretary?'

'That is the lady. Would you be so kind as to ask her to speak to us for a moment.'

The youth disappeared. He soon reappeared.

'I am sorry. Madame Veroneau must have gone out again.'

'I think not,' said Poirot quietly. 'Will you give her my name, M. Hercule Poirot, and say that it is important I should see her at once, as I am just going to the Préfecture.'

Again our messenger departed. This time the lady descended. She walked into the salon. We followed her. She turned and raised her veil. To my astonishment I recognized our old antagonist, the Countess Rossakoff, a Russian countess, who had engineered a particularly smart jewel robbery in London.

'As soon as I caught sight of you in the hall, I feared the worst,' she observed plaintively.

'My dear Countess Rossakoff –'

She shook her head.

'Inez Veroneau now,' she murmured. 'A Spaniard, married to a Frenchman. What do you want of me, M. Poirot? You are a terrible man. You hunted me from London. Now, I suppose, you will tell our wonderful Madame Olivier about me, and hunt me from Paris? We poor Russians, we must live, you know.'

'It is more serious than that, madame,' said Poirot, watching her. 'I propose to enter the villa next door, and release M. Halliday, if he is still alive. I know everything, you see.'

I saw her sudden pallor. She bit her lip. Then she spoke with her usual decision.

'He is still alive – but he is not at the villa. Come, monsieur,

I will make a bargain with you. Freedom for me – and M. Halliday, alive and well, for you.'

'I accept,' said Poirot. 'I was about to propose the same bargain myself. By the way, are the Big Four your employers, madame?'

Again I saw that deathly pallor creep over her face, but she left his question unanswered.

Instead, 'You permit me to telephone?' she asked, and crossing to the instrument she rang up a number. 'The number of the villa,' she explained, 'where our friend is now imprisoned. You may give it to the police – the nest will be empty when they arrive. Ah! I am through. Is that you, André? It is I, Inez. The little Belgian knows all. Send Halliday to the hotel, and clear out.'

She replaced the receiver, and came towards us, smiling.

'You will accompany us to the hotel, madame.'

'Naturally. I expected that.'

I got a taxi, and we drove off together. I could see by Poirot's face that he was perplexed. The thing was almost too easy. We arrived at the hotel. The porter came up to us.

'A gentleman has arrived. He is in your rooms. He seems very ill. A nurse came with him, but she has left.'

'That is all right,' said Poirot, 'he is a friend of mine.'

We went upstairs together. Sitting in a chair by the window was a haggard young fellow who looked in the last stages of exhaustion. Poirot went over to him.

'Are you John Halliday?' The man nodded. 'Show me your left arm. John Halliday has a mole just below the left elbow.'

The man stretched out his arm. The mole was there. Poirot bowed to the countess. She turned and left the room.

A glass of brandy revived Halliday somewhat.

'My God!' he muttered. 'I have been through hell – hell . . . Those fiends are devils incarnate. My wife, where is she? What does she think? They told me that she would believe – would believe –'

'She does not,' said Poirot firmly. 'Her faith in you has never wavered. She is waiting for you – she and the child.'

'Thank God for that. I can hardly believe that I am free once more.'

'Now that you are a little recovered, monsieur, I should like to hear the whole story from the beginning.'

Halliday looked at him with an indescribable expression.

'I remember – nothing,' he said.

'What?'

'Have you ever heard of the Big Four?'

'Something of them,' said Poirot drily.

'You do not know what I know. They have unlimited power. If I remain silent, I shall be safe – if I say one word – not only I, but my nearest and dearest will suffer unspeakable things. It is no good arguing with me. *I know* . . . I remember – nothing.'

And, getting up, he walked from the room.

Poirot's face wore a baffled expression.

'So it is like that, is it?' he muttered. 'The Big Four win again. What is that you are holding in your hand, Hastings?'

I handed it to him.

'The countess scribbled it before she left,' I explained.

He read it.

'Au revoir. – I.V.'

'Signed with her initials – I.V. Just a coincidence, perhaps, that they also stand for *Four*. I wonder, Hastings, I wonder.'

CHAPTER VII

The Radium Thieves

On the night of his release, Halliday slept in the room next to ours at the hotel, and all night long I heard him moaning and protesting in his sleep. Undoubtedly his experience in the villa had broken his nerve, and in the morning we failed completely to extract any information from him. He would only repeat his statement about the unlimited power at the disposal of the Big Four, and his assurance of the vengeance which would follow if he talked.

After lunch he departed to rejoin his wife in England, but Poirot and I remained behind in Paris. I was all for energetic proceedings of some kind or other, and Poirot's quiescence annoyed me.

'For heaven's sake, Poirot,' I urged, 'let us be up and at them.'

'Admirable, *mon ami*, admirable! Up where, and at whom? Be precise, I beg of you.'

'At the Big Four, of course.'

'*Cela va sans dire.* But how would you set about it?'

'The police,' I hazarded doubtfully.

Poirot smiled.

'They would accuse us of romancing. We have nothing to go upon – nothing whatever. We must wait.'

'Wait for what?'

'Wait for them to make a move. See now, in England you all comprehend and adore *la boxe*. If one man does not make a move, the other must, and by permitting the adversary to make the attack one learns something about him. That is our part – to let the other side make the attack.'

'You think they will?' I said doubtfully.

'I have no doubt whatever of it. To begin with, see, they try to get me out of England. That fails. Then, in the Dartmoor affair, we step in and save their victim from the gallows. And yesterday, once again, we interfere with their plans. Assuredly, they will not leave the matter there.'

As I reflected on this, there was a knock on the door. Without waiting for a reply, a man stepped into the room and closed the door behind him. He was a tall, thin man, with a slightly hooked nose and a sallow complexion. He wore an overcoat buttoned up to his chin, and a soft hat well pulled down over his eyes.

'Excuse me, gentlemen, for my somewhat unceremonious entry,' he said in a soft voice, 'but my business is of a rather unorthodox nature.'

Smiling, he advanced to the table and sat down by it. I was about to spring up, but Poirot restrained me with a gesture.

'As you say, monsieur, your entry is somewhat unceremonious. Will you kindly state your business?'

'My dear M. Poirot, it is very simple. You have been annoying my friends.'

'In what way?'

'Come, come, M. Poirot. You do not seriously ask me that? You know as well as I do.'

'It depends, monsieur, upon who these friends of yours are.'

Without a word, the man drew from his pocket a cigarette case, and, opening it, took out four cigarettes and tossed them on the table. Then he picked them up and returned them to his case, which he replaced in his pocket.

'Aha!' said Poirot, 'so it is like that, is it? And what do your friends suggest?'

'They suggest, monsieur, that you should employ your talents – your very considerable talents – in the detection of legitimate crime – return to your former avocations, and solve the problems of London society ladies.'

'A peaceful programme,' said Poirot. 'And supposing I do not agree?'

The man made an eloquent gesture.

'We should regret it, of course, exceedingly,' he said. 'So would all the friends and admirers of the great M. Hercule Poirot. But regrets, however poignant, do not bring a man to life again.'

'Put very delicately,' said Poirot, nodding his head. 'And supposing I – accept?'

'In that case I am empowered to offer you – compensation.'

He drew out a pocket-book, and threw ten notes on the table. They were for ten thousand francs each.

'That is merely a guarantee of our good faith,' he said. 'Ten times that amount will be paid you.'

'Good God,' I cried, springing up, 'you dare to think –'

'Sit down, Hastings.' said Poirot autocratically. 'Subdue your so beautiful and honest nature and sit down. To you, monsieur, I will say this. What is to prevent me ringing up the police and giving you into their custody, whilst my friend here prevents you from escaping?'

'By all means do so if you think it advisable,' said our visitor calmly.

'Oh! look here, Poirot,' I cried. 'I can't stand this. Ring up the police and have done with it.'

Rising swiftly, I strode to the door and stood with my back against it.

'It seems the obvious course,' murmured Poirot, as though debating with himself.

'But you distrust the obvious, eh?' said our visitor, smiling.

'Go on, Poirot,' I urged.

'It will be your responsibility, *mon ami.*'

As he lifted the receiver, the man made a sudden cat-like jump at me. I was ready for him. In another minute we were locked together, staggering round the room. Suddenly I felt him slip and falter. I pressed my advantage. He went down before me. And then, in the very flush of victory, an extraordinary thing happened. I felt myself flying forwards. Head first, I crashed into the wall in a complicated heap. I was up in a minute, but the door was already closing behind my late adversary. I rushed to it and shook it, it was locked on the outside. I seized the telephone from Poirot.

'Is that the bureau? Stop a man who is coming out. A tall man, with a buttoned-up overcoat and a soft hat. He is wanted by the police.'

Very few minutes elapsed before we heard a noise in the corridor outside. The key was turned and the door flung open. The manager himself stood in the doorway.

'The man – you have got him?' I cried.

'No, monsieur. No one has descended.'

'You must have passed him.'

'We have passed no one, monsieur. It is incredible that he can have escaped.'

'You have passed someone, I think,' said Poirot, in his gentle voice. 'One of the hotel staff, perhaps?'

'Only a waiter carrying a tray, monsieur.'

'Ah!' said Poirot, in a tone that spoke infinities.

'So that was why he wore his overcoat buttoned up to his chin,' mused Poirot, when we had finally got rid of the excited hotel officials.

'I'm awfully sorry, Poirot,' I murmured, rather crestfallen. 'I thought I'd downed him all right.'

'Yes, that was a Japanese trick, I fancy. Do not distress yourself, *mon ami*. All went according to plan – his plan. That is what I wanted.'

'What's this?' I cried, pouncing on a brown object that lay on the floor.

It was a slim pocket-book of brown leather, and had evidently fallen from our visitor's pocket during his struggle with me. It contained two receipted bills in the name of M. Felix Laon, and a folded-up piece of paper which made my heart beat faster. It was a half sheet of notepaper on which a few words were scrawled in pencil, but they were words of supreme importance.

'The next meeting of the council will be on Friday at 34 rue de Echelles at 11 A.M.'

It was signed with a big figure 4.

And today was Friday, and the clock on the mantelpiece showed the hour to be 10.30.

'My God, what a chance!' I cried. 'Fate is playing into our hands. We must start at once, though. What stupendous luck.'

'So that was why he came,' murmured Poirot. 'I see it all now.'

'See what? Come on, Poirot, don't stay day-dreaming there.'

Poirot looked at me, and slowly shook his head, smiling as he did so.

'"Will you walk into my parlour, said the spider to the fly?" That is your little English nursery rhyme, is it not? No, no – they are subtle – but not so subtle as Hercule Poirot.'

'What on earth are you driving at, Poirot?'

'My friend, I have been asking myself the reason of this morning's visit. Did our visitor really hope to succeed in bribing me? Or, alternatively, in frightening me into abandoning my task? It seemed hardly credible. Why, then, did he come? And now I see the whole plan – very neat – very pretty – the ostensible reason to bribe or frighten me – the necessary struggle which he took no pains to avoid, and which should make the dropped pocket-book natural and reasonable – and finally – the pitfall! Rue des Echelles, 11 A.M.? I think not, *mon ami*! One does not catch Hercule Poirot as easily as that.'

'Good heavens,' I gasped.

Poirot was frowning to himself.

'There is still one thing I do not understand.'

'What is that?'

'The time, Hastings – the time. If they wanted to decoy me away, surely night time would be better? Why this early hour? Is it possible that something is about to happen this morning? Something which they are anxious Hercule Poirot should not know about?'

He shook his head.

'We shall see. Here I sit, *mon ami*. We do not stir out this morning. We await events here.'

It was at half-past eleven exactly that the summons came. A *petit bleu*. Poirot tore it open, then handed it to me. It was from Madame Olivier, the world-famous scientist, whom we had visited yesterday in connection with the Halliday case. It asked us to come out to Passy at once.

We obeyed the summons without an instant's delay. Madame Olivier received us in the same small salon. I was struck anew with the wonderful power of this woman, with her long nun's face and burning eyes – this brilliant successor of Becquerel and the Curies. She came to the point at once.

'Messieurs, you interviewed me yesterday about the disappearance of M. Halliday. I now learn that you returned to the house a second time, and asked to see my secretary, Inez Veroneau. She left the house with you, and has not returned here since.'

'Is that all, madame?'

'No, monsieur, it is not. Last night the laboratory was broken into, and several valuable papers and memoranda were stolen. The thieves had a try for something more precious still, but luckily they failed to open the big safe.'

'Madame, these are the facts of the case. Your late secretary, Madame Veroneau, was really the Countess Rossakoff, an expert thief, and it was she who was responsible for the disappearance of M. Halliday. How long had she been with you?'

'Five months, monsieur. What you say amazes me.'

'It is true, nevertheless. These papers, were they easy to find? Or do you think an inside knowledge was shown?'

'It is rather curious that the thieves knew exactly where to look. You think Inez –'

'Yes, I have no doubt that it was upon her information that they acted. But what is this precious thing that the thieves failed to find? Jewels?'

Madame Olivier shook her head with a faint smile.

'Something much more precious than that, monsieur.' She looked round her, then bent forward, lowering her voice. 'Radium, monsieur.'

'Radium?'

'Yes, monsieur. I am now at the crux of my experiments. I possess a small portion of radium myself – more has been lent to me for the process I am at work upon. Small though the actual quantity is, it comprises a large amount of the world's stock and represents a value of millions of francs.'

'And where is it?'

'In its leaden case in the big safe – the safe purposely appears to be of an old and worn-out pattern, but it is really a triumph of the safe-maker's art. That is probably why the thieves were unable to open it.'

'How long are you keeping this radium in your possession?'

'Only for two days more, monsieur. Then my experiments will be concluded.'

Poirot's eyes brightened.

'And Inez Veroneau is aware of the fact? Good – then our friends will come back. Not a word of me to anyone, madame. But rest assured, I will save your radium for you. You have a key of the door leading from the laboratory to the garden?'

'Yes, monsieur. Here it is. I have a duplicate for myself. And here is the key of the garden door leading out into the alleyway between this villa and the next one.'

'I thank you, madame. Tonight, go to bed as usual, have no fears, and leave all to me. But not a word to anyone – not to your two assistants – Mademoiselle Claude and Monsieur Henri, is it not? – particularly not a word to them.'

Poirot left the villa rubbing his hands in great satisfaction.

'What are we going to do now?' I asked.

'Now, Hastings, we are about to leave Paris – for England.'

'What?'

'We will pack our effects, have lunch, and drive to the Gare du Nord.'

'But the radium?'

'I said we were going to leave for England – I did not say we were going to arrive there. Reflect a moment, Hastings. It is quite certain that we are being watched and followed. Our enemies must believe that we are going back to England, and they certainly will not believe that unless they see us get on board the train and start.'

'Do you mean we are to slip off again at the last minute?'

'No, Hastings. Our enemies will be satisfied with nothing less than a *bona fide* departure.'

'But the train doesn't stop until Calais?'

'It will stop if it is paid to do so.'

'Oh, come now, Poirot – surely you can't pay an express to stop – they'd refuse.'

'My dear friend, have you never remarked the little handle – the *signal d'arrêt* – penalty for improper use, 100 francs, I think?'

'Oh! you are going to pull that?'

'Or rather a friend of mine, Pierre Combeau, will do so. Then, while he is arguing with the guard, and making a big scene, and all the train is agog with interest, you and I will fade quietly away.'

We duly carried out Poirot's plan. Pierre Combeau, an old crony of Poirot's, and who evidently knew my little friend's methods pretty well, fell in with the arrangements. The communication cord was pulled just as we got to the outskirts of Paris. Combeau 'made a scene' in the most approved French fashion, and Poirot and I were able to leave the train without anyone being interested in our departure. Our first proceeding was to make a considerable change in our appearance. Poirot had brought the materials for this with him in a small case. Two loafers in dirty blue blouses were the result. We had dinner in an obscure hostelry, and started back to Paris afterwards.

It was close on eleven o'clock when we found ourselves once more in the neighbourhood of Madame Olivier's villa. We looked up and down the road before slipping into the alleyway. The whole place appeared to be perfectly deserted. One thing we could be quite certain of, no one was following us.

'I do not expect them to be here yet,' whispered Poirot to me. 'Possibly they may not come until tomorrow night, but they know perfectly well that there are only two nights on which the radium will be there.'

Very cautiously we turned the key in the garden door. It opened noiselessly and we stepped into the garden.

And then, with complete unexpectedness, the blow fell. In a

minute we were surrounded, gagged, and bound. At least ten men must have been waiting for us. Resistance was useless. Like two helpless bundles we were lifted up and carried along. To my intense astonishment, they took us *towards* the house and not away from it. With a key they opened the door into the laboratory and carried us into it. One of the men stooped down before a big safe. The door of it swung open. I felt an unpleasant sensation down my spine. Were they going to bundle us into it, and leave us there to asphyxiate slowly?

However, to my amazement, I saw that from the inside of the safe steps led down beneath the floor. We were thrust down this narrow way and eventually came out into a big subterranean chamber. A woman stood there, tall and imposing, with a black velvet mask covering her face. She was clearly in command of the situation by her gestures of authority. The men slung us down on the floor and left us – alone with the mysterious creature in the mask. I had no doubt who she was. This was the unknown Frenchwoman – Number Three of the Big Four.

She knelt down beside us and removed the gags, but left us bound, then rising and facing us, with a sudden swift gesture she removed her mask.

It was Madame Olivier!

'M. Poirot,' she said, in a low mocking tone. 'The great, the wonderful, the unique, M. Poirot. I sent a warning to you yesterday morning. You chose to disregard it – you thought you could pit your wits against US. And now, you are here!'

There was a cold malignity about her that froze me to the marrow. It was so at variance with the burning fire of her eyes. She was mad – mad – with the madness of genius!

Poirot said nothing. His jaw had dropped, and he was staring at her.

'Well,' she said softly, 'this is the end. We cannot permit our plans to be interfered with. Have you any last request to make?'

Never before, or since, have I felt so near death. Poirot was magnificent. He neither flinched nor paled, just stared at her with unabated interest.

'Your psychology interests me enormously, madame,' he said

quietly. 'It is a pity that I have so short a time to devote to studying it. Yes, I have a request to make. A condemned man is always allowed a last smoke, I believe. I have my cigarette case on me. If you would permit –' He looked down at his bonds.

'Oh, yes!' she laughed. 'You would like me to untie your hands, would you not? You are clever, M. Hercule Poirot, I know that. I shall not untie your hands – but I will find you a cigarette.'

She knelt down by him, extracted his cigarette case, took out a cigarette, and placed it between his lips.

'And now a match,' she said, rising.

'It is not necessary, madame.' Something in his voice startled me. She, too, was arrested.

'Do not move, I pray of you, madame. You will regret it if you do. Are you acquainted at all with the properties of curare? The South American Indians use it as an arrow poison. A scratch with it means death. Some tribes use a little blow-pipe – I, too, have a little blow-pipe constructed so as to look exactly like a cigarette. I have only to blow ... Ah! you start. Do not move, madame. The mechanism of this cigarette is most ingenious. One blows – and a tiny dart resembling a fishbone flies through the air – to find its mark. You do not wish to die, madame. Therefore, I beg of you to release my friend Hastings from his bonds. I cannot use my hands, but I can turn my head – so – you are still covered, madame. Make no mistake, I beg of you.'

Slowly, with shaking hands, and rage and hate convulsing her face, she bent down and did his bidding. I was free. Poirot's voice gave me instructions.

'Your bonds will now do for the lady, Hastings. That is right. Is she securely fastened? Then release me, I pray of you. It is a fortunate circumstance she sent away her henchmen. With a little luck we may hope to find the way out unobstructed.'

In another minute, Poirot stood by my side. He bowed to the lady.

'Hercule Poirot is not killed so easily, madame. I wish you goodnight.'

The gag prevented her from replying, but the murderous

gleam in her eyes frightened me. I hoped devoutly that we should never fall into her power again.

Three minutes later we were outside the villa, and hurriedly traversing the garden., The road outside was deserted, and we were soon clear of the neighbourhood.

Then Poirot broke out.

'I deserve all that that woman said to me. I am a triple imbecile, a miserable animal, thirty-six times an idiot. I was proud of myself for not falling into their trap. And it was not even meant as a trap – except exactly in the way in which I fell into it. They knew I would see through it – they counted on my seeing through it. This explains all – the ease with which they surrendered. Halliday – everything. Madame Olivier was the ruling spirit – Vera Rossakoff only her lieutenant. Madame needs Halliday's ideas – she herself had the necessary genius to supply the gaps that perplexed him. Yes, Hastings, we know now who Number Three is – the woman who is probably the greatest scientist in the world! Think of it. The brain of the East, the science of the West – and two others whose identities we do not yet know. But we must find out. Tomorrow we will return to London and set about it.'

'You are not going to denounce Madame Olivier to the police?'

'I should not be believed. The woman is one of the idols of France. And we can prove nothing. We are lucky if she does not denounce *us*.'

'What?'

'Think of it. We are found at night upon the premises with keys in our possession which she will swear she never gave us. She surprises us at the safe, and we gag and bind her and make away. Have no illusions, Hastings. The boot is not upon the right leg – is that how you say it?'

CHAPTER VIII

In the House of the Enemy

After our adventure in the villa at Passy, we returned post-haste to London. Several letters were awaiting Poirot. He read one of them with a curious smile, and then handed it to me.

'Read this, *mon ami*.'

I turned first to the signature, 'Abe Ryland', and recalled Poirot's words: 'the richest man in the world'. Mr Ryland's letter was curt and incisive. He expressed himself as profoundly dissatisfied with the reason Poirot had given for withdrawing from the South American proposition at the last moment.

'This gives one furiously to think, does it not?' said Poirot.

'I suppose it's only natural he should be a bit ratty.'

'No, no, you comprehend not. Remember the words of Mayerling, the man who took refuge here – only to die by the hands of his enemies. "Number Two is represented by an 'S' with two lines through it – the sign of a dollar; also by two stripes and a star. It may be conjectured therefore that he is an American subject, and that he represents the power of wealth." Add to those words the fact that Ryland offered me a huge sum to tempt me out of England – and – and what about it, Hastings?'

'You mean,' I said, staring, 'that you suspect Abe Ryland, the multi-millionaire, of being Number Two of the Big Four.'

'Your bright intellect has grasped the idea, Hastings. Yes, I do. The tone in which you said multi-millionaire was eloquent but let me impress upon you one fact – this thing is being run by men at the top – and Mr Ryland has the reputation of being no beauty in his business dealings. An able, unscrupulous man, a man who has all the wealth that he needs, and is out for unlimited power.'

There was undoubtedly something to be said for Poirot's view.

I asked him when he had made up his mind definitely upon the point.

'That is just it. I am not sure. I cannot be sure. *Mon ami*, I would give anything to *know*. Let me but place Number Two definitely as Abe Ryland, and we draw nearer to our goal.'

'He has just arrived in London, I see by this,' I said, tapping the letter. 'Shall you call upon him, and make your apologies in person?'

'I might do so.'

Two days later, Poirot returned to our rooms in a state of boundless excitement. He grasped me by both hands in his most impulsive manner.

'My friend, an occasion stupendous, unprecedented, never to be repeated, has presented itself! But there is danger, grave danger. I should not even ask you to attempt it.'

If Poirot was trying to frighten me, he was going the wrong way to work, and so I told him. Becoming less incoherent, he unfolded his plan.

It seemed that Ryland was looking for an English secretary, one with a good social manner and presence. It was Poirot's suggestion that I should apply for the post.

'I would do it myself, *mon ami*,' he explained apologetically. 'But, see you, it is almost impossible for me to disguise myself in the needful manner. I speak the English very well – except when I am excited – but hardly so as to deceive the ear; and even though I were to sacrifice my moustaches, I doubt not but that I should still be recognizable as Hercule Poirot.'

I doubted it not also, and declared myself ready and willing to take up the part and penetrate into Ryland's household.

'Ten to one he won't engage me anyway,' I remarked.

'Oh, yes, he will. I will arrange for you such testimonials as shall make him lick his lips. The Home Secretary himself shall recommend you.'

This seemed to be carrying things a bit far, but Poirot waved aside my remonstrances.

'Oh, yes, he will do it. I investigated for him a little matter which might have caused a grave scandal. All was solved with discretion and delicacy, and now, as you would say, he perches upon my hand like the little bird and pecks the crumbs.'

Our first step was to engage the services of an artist in 'make up'. He was a little man, with a quaint bird-like turn of the head, not unlike Poirot's own. He considered me some time in silence, and then fell to work. When I looked at myself in the glass half an hour afterwards, I was amazed. Special shoes caused me to stand at least two inches taller, and the coat I wore was arranged so as to give me a long, lank, weedy look. My eyebrows had been cunningly altered, giving a totally different expression to my face, I wore pads in my cheeks, and the deep tan of my face was a thing of the past. My moustache had gone, and a gold tooth was prominent on one side of my mouth.

'Your name,' said Poirot, 'is Arthur Neville. God guard you, my friend – for I fear that you go into perilous places.'

It was with a beating heart that I presented myself at the Savoy, at an hour named by Mr Ryland, and asked to see the great man.

After being kept waiting a minute or two, I was shown upstairs to his suite.

Ryland was sitting at a table. Spread out in front of him was a letter which I could see out of the tail of my eye was in the Home Secretary's handwriting. It was my first sight of the American millionaire, and, in spite of myself, I was impressed. He was tall and lean, with a jutting out chin and slightly hooked nose. His eyes glittered cold and grey behind penthouse brows. He had thick grizzled hair, and a long black cigar (without which, I learned later, he was never seen) protruded rakishly from the corner of his mouth.

'Siddown,' he grunted.

I sat. He tapped the letter in front of him.

'According to this piece here, you're the goods all right, and I don't need to look further. Say, are you well up in the social matters?'

I said that I thought I could satisfy him in that respect.

'I mean to say, if I have a lot of dooks and earls and viscounts and suchlike down to the country place I've gotten, you'll be able to sort them out all right and put them where they should be round the dining-table?'

'Oh! quite easily,' I replied, smiling.

We exchanged a few more preliminaries, and then I found myself engaged. What Mr Ryland wanted was a secretary conversant with English society, as he already had an American secretary and a stenographer with him.

Two days later I went down to Hatton Chase, the seat of the Duke of Loamshire, which the American millionaire had rented for a period of six months.

My duties gave me no difficulty whatever. At one period of my life I had been private secretary to a busy member of Parliament, so I was not called upon to assume a role unfamiliar to me. Mr Ryland usually entertained a large party over the weekend, but the middle of the week was comparatively quiet. I saw very little of Mr Appleby, the American secretary, but he seemed a pleasant, normal young American, very efficient in his work. Of Miss Martin, the stenographer, I saw rather more. She was a pretty girl of about twenty-three or four, with auburn hair and brown eyes that could look mischievous enough upon occasion, though they were usually cast demurely down. I had an idea that she both disliked and distrusted her employer, though, of course, she was careful never to hint at anything of the kind, but the time came when I was unexpectedly taken into her confidence.

I had, of course, carefully scrutinized all the members of the household. One or two of the servants had been newly engaged, one of the footmen, I think, and some of the housemaids. The butler, the housekeeper, and the chef were the duke's own staff, who had consented to remain on in the establishment. The housemaids I dismissed as unimportant; I scrutinized James, the second footman, very carefully; but it was clear that he was an under-footman and an under-footman only. He had, indeed, been engaged by the butler. A person of whom I was far more suspicious was Deaves, Ryland's valet, whom he had brought over from New York with him. An Englishman by birth, with an irreproachable manner, I yet harboured vague suspicions about him.

I had been at Hatton Chase three weeks and not an incident of any kind had arisen which I could lay my finger on in support of our theory. There was no trace of the activities of the Big Four. Mr Ryland was a man of overpowering force and personality, but I was coming to believe that Poirot had made a mistake when he associated him with that dread organization. I even heard him mention Poirot in a casual way at dinner one night.

'Wonderful little man, they say. But he's a quitter. How do I know? I put him on a deal, and he turned me down the last minute. I'm not taking any more of your Monsieur Hercule Poirot.'

It was at moments such as these that I felt my cheek pads most wearisome!

And then Miss Martin told me a rather curious story. Ryland had gone to London for the day, taking Appleby with him. Miss Martin and I were strolling together in the garden after tea. I liked the girl very much, she was so unaffected and so natural. I could see that there was something on her mind, and at last out it came.

'Do you know, Major Neville,' she said, 'I am really thinking of resigning my post here.'

I looked somewhat astonished, and she went on hurriedly.

'Oh! I know it's a wonderful job to have got, in a way. I suppose most people would think me a fool to throw it up. But I can't stand abuse, Major Neville. To be sworn at like a trooper is more than I can bear. No gentleman would do such a thing.'

'Has Ryland been swearing at you?'

She nodded.

'Of course, he's always rather irritable and short-tempered. That one expects. It's all in the day's work. But to fly into such an absolute fury – over nothing at all. He really looked as though he could have murdered me! And, as I say, over nothing at all!'

'Tell me about it?' I said, keenly interested.

'As you know, I open all Mr Ryland's letters. Some I hand on to Mr Appleby, others I deal with myself, but I do all the preliminary sorting. Now there are certain letters that come, written on blue paper, and with a tiny 4 marked on the corner – I beg your pardon, did you speak?'

I had been unable to repress a stifled exclamation, but I hurriedly shook my head, and begged her to continue.

'Well, as I was saying, these letters come, and there are strict orders that they are never to be opened, but to be handed over to Mr Ryland intact. And, of course, I always do so. But there was an unusually heavy mail yesterday morning, and I was opening these letters in a terrific hurry. By mistake I opened one of these letters. As soon as I saw what I had done, I took it to Mr Ryland and explained. To my utter amazement he flew into the most awful rage. As I tell you, I was quite frightened.'

'What was there in the letter, I wonder, to upset him so?'

'Absolutely nothing – that's just the curious part of it. I had read it before I discovered my mistake. It was quite short. I can still remember it word for word, and there was nothing in it that could possibly upset anyone.'

'You can repeat it, you say?' I encouraged her.

'Yes.' She paused a minute and then repeated slowly, whilst I noted down the words unobtrusively, the following:

'Dear Sir – The essential thing now, I should say, is to see the property. If you insist on the quarry being included, then seventeen thousand seems reasonable. 11% commission too much, 4% is ample.

Yours truly

Arthur Leversham'

Miss Martin went on:

'Evidently about some property Mr Ryland was thinking of buying. But really, I do feel that a man who can get into a rage over such a trifle is, well, dangerous. What do you think I ought to do, Major Neville? You've more experience of the world than I have.'

I soothed the girl down, pointed out to her that Mr Ryland had probably been suffering from the enemy of his race – dyspepsia. In the end I sent her away quite comforted. But I was not so easily satisfied myself. When the girl had gone, and I was alone, I took out my notebook, and ran over the letter which I had jotted down. What did it mean – this apparently innocent-sounding missive? Did it concern some business deal which Ryland was undertaking, and was he anxious that no details about it should leak out until it was carried through? That was a possible explanation. But I remembered the small figure 4 with which the envelopes were marked, and I felt that, at last, I was on the track of the thing we were seeking.

I puzzled over the letter all that evening, and most of the next day – and then suddenly the solution came to me. It was so simple, too. The figure 4 was the clue. Read every fourth word in the letter, and an entirely different message appeared. 'Essential should see you quarry seventeen eleven four.'

The solution of the figures was easy. Seventeen stood for the seventeenth of October – which was tomorrow, eleven was the time, and four was the signature – either referring to the mysterious Number Four himself – or else it was the 'trademark', so to speak, of the Big Four. The quarry was also intelligible. There was a big disused quarry on the estate about half a mile from the house – a lonely spot, ideal for a secret meeting.

For a moment or two I was tempted to run the show myself. It would be such a feather in my cap, for once, to have the pleasure of crowing over Poirot.

But in the end I overcame the temptation. This was a big business – I had no right to play a lone hand, and perhaps jeopardize our chances of success. For the first time, we had stolen a march upon our enemies. We must make good this time – and, disguise the fact as I might, Poirot had the better brain of the two.

I wrote off post-haste to him, laying the facts before him, and explaining how urgent it was that we should overhear what went on at the interview. If he liked to leave it to me, well and good, but I gave him detailed instructions how to reach the quarry from the station in case he should deem it wise to be present himself.

I took the letter down to the village and posted it myself. I had been able to communicate with Poirot throughout my stay, but we agreed that he should not attempt to communicate with me in case my letters should be tampered with.

I was in a glow of excitement the following evening. No guests were staying in the house, and I was busy with Mr Ryland in his study all the evening. I had foreseen that this would be the case, which was why I had no hope of being able to meet Poirot at the station. I was, however, confident that I would be dismissed well before eleven o'clock.

Sure enough, just after ten-thirty, Mr Ryland glanced at the clock, and announced that he was 'through'. I took the hint and retired discreetly. I went upstairs as though going to bed, but slipped quietly down a side staircase and let myself out into the garden, having taken the precaution to don a dark overcoat to hide my white shirt-front.

I had gone some way down the garden when I chanced to look over my shoulder. Mr Ryland was just stepping out from his study window into the garden. He was starting to keep the appointment. I redoubled my pace, so as to get a clear start. I arrived at the quarry somewhat out of breath. There seemed no one about, and I crawled into a thick tangle of bushes and awaited developments.

Ten minutes later, just on the stroke of eleven, Ryland stalked up, his hat over his eyes and the inevitable cigar in his mouth. He gave a quick look round, and then plunged into the hollows of the quarry below. Presently I heard a low murmur of voices come up to me. Evidently the other man – or men – whoever they were, had arrived first at the rendezvous. I crawled cautiously out of the bushes, and inch by inch, using the utmost precaution against noise, I wormed myself down the steep path. Only a boulder now separated me from the talking men. Secure in the blackness, I peeped round the edge of it and found myself facing the muzzle of a black, murderous-looking automatic!

'Hands up!' said Mr Ryland succinctly. 'I've been waiting for you.'

He was seated in the shadow of the rock, so that I could not see his face, but the menace in his voice was unpleasant. Then

I felt a ring of cold steel on the back of my neck, and Ryland lowered his own automatic.

'That's right, George,' he drawled. 'March him around here.'

Raging inwardly, I was conducted to a spot in the shadows, where the unseen George (whom I suspected of being the impeccable Deaves) gagged and bound me securely.

Ryland spoke again in a tone which I had difficulty in recognizing, so cold and menacing was it.

'This is going to be the end of you two. You've got in the way of the Big Four once too often. Ever heard of landslides? There was one about here two years ago. There's going to be another tonight. I've fixed that good and square. Say, that friend of yours doesn't keep his dates very punctually.'

A wave of horror swept over me. Poirot! In another minute he would walk straight into the trap. And I was powerless to warn him. I could only pray that he had elected to leave the matter in my hands, and had remained in London. Surely, if he had been coming, he would have been here by now.

With every minute that passed, my hopes rose.

Suddenly they were dashed to pieces. I heard footsteps – cautious footsteps, but footsteps nevertheless. I writhed in impotent agony. They came down the path, paused and then Poirot himself appeared, his head a little on one side, peering into the shadows.

I heard the growl of satisfaction Ryland gave as he raised the big automatic and shouted, 'Hands up.' Deaves sprang forward as he did so, and took Poirot in the rear. The ambush was complete.

'Pleased to meet you, Mr Hercule Poirot,' said the American grimly.

Poirot's self-possession was marvellous. He did not turn a hair. But I saw his eyes searching in the shadows.

'My friend? He is here?'

'Yes, you are both in the trap – the trap of the Big Four.'

He laughed.

'A trap?' queried Poirot.

'Say, haven't you tumbled to it yet?'

'I comprehend that there is a trap – yes,' said Poirot gently. 'But you are in error, monsieur. It is *you* who are in it – not I and my friend.'

'What?' Ryland raised the big automatic, but I saw his gaze falter.

'If you fire, you commit murder watched by ten pairs of eyes, and you will be hanged for it. This place is surrounded – has been for the last hour – by Scotland Yard men. It is checkmate, Mr Abe Ryland.'

He uttered a curious whistle, and, as though by magic, the place was alive with men. They seized Ryland and the valet and disarmed them. After speaking a few words to the officer in charge, Poirot took me by the arm, and led me away.

Once clear of the quarry he embraced me with vigour.

'You are alive – you are unhurt. It is magnificent. Often have I blamed myself for letting you go.'

'I'm perfectly all right,' I said, disengaging myself. 'But I'm just a bit fogged. You tumbled to their little scheme, did you?'

'But I was waiting for it! For what else did I permit you to go there? Your false name, your disguise, not for a moment was it intended to deceive!'

'What?' I cried. 'You never told me.'

'As I have frequently told you, Hastings, you have a nature so beautiful and so honest that unless you are yourself deceived, it is impossible for you to deceive others. Good, then, you are spotted from the first, and they do what I had counted on their doing – a mathematical certainty to anyone who uses his grey cells properly – use you as a decoy. They set the girl on – By the way, *mon ami*, as an interesting fact psychologically, had she got red hair?'

'If you mean Miss Martin,' I said coldly. 'Her hair is a delicate shade of auburn, but –'

'They are *épatants* – these people! They have even studied your psychology. Oh! yes, my friend, Miss Martin was in the plot – very much so. She repeats the letter to you, together with her tale of Mr Ryland's wrath, you write it down, you puzzle your brains – the cipher is nicely arranged, difficult, but not too difficult – you solve it, and you send for me.

'But what they do not know is that I am waiting for just this very thing to happen. I go post-haste to Japp and arrange things. And so, as you see, all is triumph!'

I was not particularly pleased with Poirot, and I told him so. We went back to London on a milk train in the early hours of the morning, and a most uncomfortable journey it was.

I was just out of my bath and indulging in pleasurable thoughts of breakfast when I heard Japp's voice in the sitting-room. I threw on a bathrobe and hurried in.

'A pretty mare's nest you've got us into this time,' Japp was saying. 'It's too bad of you, M. Poirot. First time I've ever known you take a toss.'

Poirot's face was a study. Japp went on:

'There were we, taking all this Black Hand stuff seriously – and all the time it was the footman.'

'The footman?' I gasped.

'Yes, James, or whatever his name is. Seems he laid 'em a wager in the servants' hall that he could get taken for the old man by his nibs – that's you, Captain Hastings – and would hand him out a lot of spy stuff about a Big Four gang.'

'Impossible!' I cried.

'Don't you believe it. I marched our gentleman straight to Hatton Chase, and there was the real Ryland in bed and asleep, and the butler and the cook and God knows how many of them to swear to the wager. Just a silly hoax – that's all it was – and the valet is with him.'

'So that was why he kept in the shadow,' murmured Poirot.

After Japp had gone we looked at each other.

'We *know*, Hastings,' said Poirot at last. 'Number Two of the Big Four is Abe Ryland. The masquerading on the part of the footman was to ensure a way of retreat in case of emergencies. And the footman –'

'Yes,' I breathed.

'*Number Four,*' said Poirot gravely.

CHAPTER IX

The Yellow Jasmine Mystery

It was all very well for Poirot to say that we were acquiring information all the time and gaining an insight into our adversaries' minds – I felt myself that I required some more tangible success than this.

Since we had come into contact with the Big Four, they had committed two murders, abducted Halliday, and had been within an ace of killing Poirot and myself; whereas so far we had hardly scored a point in the game.

Poirot treated my complaints lightly.

'So far, Hastings,' he said, 'they laugh. That is true, but you have a proverb, have you not: "He laughs best who laughs at the end"? And at the end, *mon ami*, you shall see.

'You must remember, too,' he added, 'that we deal with no ordinary criminal, but with the second greatest brain in the world.'

I forbore to pander to his conceit by asking the obvious question. I knew the answer, at least I knew what Poirot's answer would be, and instead I tried without success to elicit some information as to what steps he was taking to track down the enemy. As usual he had kept me completely in the dark as to his movements, but I gathered that he was in touch with Secret Service agents in India, China, and Russia, and, from his occasional bursts of self-glorification, that he was at least progressing in his favourite game of gauging his enemy's mind.

He had abandoned his private practice almost entirely, and I know that at this time he refused some remarkably handsome fees. True, he would sometimes investigate cases which intrigued him, but he usually dropped them the moment he was convinced that they had no connection with the activities of the Big Four.

This attitude of his was remarkably profitable to our friend, Inspector Japp. Undeniably he gained much kudos for solving several problems in which his success was really due to a half-contemptuous hint from Poirot.

In return for such service Japp supplied full details of any case which he thought might interest the little Belgian, and when he was put in charge of what the newspapers called 'The Yellow Jasmine Mystery', he wired Poirot, asking him whether he would care to come down and look into the case.

It was in response to this wire that, about a month after my adventure in Abe Ryland's house, we found ourselves alone in a railway compartment whirling away from the smoke and dust of London, bound for the little town of Market Handford in Worcestershire, the seat of the mystery.

Poirot leant back in his corner.

'And what exactly is your opinion of the affair, Hastings?'

I did not at once reply to his question; I felt the need of going warily.

'It all seems so complicated,' I said cautiously.

'Does it not?' said Poirot delightedly.

'I suppose our rushing off like this is a pretty clear signal that you consider Mr Paynter's death to be murder – not suicide or the result of an accident?'

'No, no; you misunderstand me, Hastings. Granting that Mr Paynter died as a result of a particularly terrible accident, there are still a number of mysterious circumstances to be explained.'

'That was what I meant when I said it was all so complicated.'

'Let us go over all the main facts quietly and methodically. Recount them to me, Hastings, in an orderly and lucid fashion.'

I started forthwith, endeavouring to be as orderly and lucid as I could.

'We start,' I said, 'with Mr Paynter. A man of fifty-five, rich, cultured, and somewhat of a globe-trotter. For the last twelve years he has been little in England, but, suddenly tiring of incessant travelling, he bought a small place in Worcestershire, near Market Handford, and prepared to settle down. His first action was to write to his only relative, a nephew, Gerald Paynter, the son of his youngest brother, and to suggest to him that he should come and make his home at Croftlands (as the place is called) with his uncle. Gerald Paynter, who is an impecunious young artist, was glad enough to fall in with the arrangement, and had been living with his uncle for about seven months when the tragedy occurred.'

'Your narrative style is masterly,' murmured Poirot. 'I say to myself, it is a book that talks, not my friend Hastings.'

Paying no attention to Poirot, I went on, warming to the story.

'Mr Paynter kept up a fair staff at Croftlands – six servants as well as his own Chinese body servant – Ah Ling.'

'His Chinese servant, Ah Ling,' murmured Poirot.

'On Tuesday last, Mr Paynter complained of feeling unwell after dinner, and one of the servants was despatched to fetch the doctor. Mr Paynter received the doctor in his study, having refused to go to bed. What passed between them was not then known, but before Dr Quentin left, he asked to see the house-keeper, and mentioned that he had given Mr Paynter a hypoder-mic injection as his heart was in a very weak state, recommended that he should not be disturbed, and then proceeded to ask some rather curious questions about the servants, how long they had been there, from whom they had come, etc.

'The housekeeper answered these questions as best she could, but was rather puzzled as to their purport. A terrible discovery was made on the following morning. One of the housemaids, on descending, was met by a sickening odour of burned flesh which seemed to come from her master's study. She tried the door, but it was locked on the inside. With the assistance of Gerald Paynter and the Chinaman, that was soon broken in, but a terrible sight greeted them. Mr Paynter had fallen forward into the gas fire, and his face and head were charred beyond recognition.

'Of course, at the moment, no suspicion was aroused as to its being anything but a ghastly accident. If blame attached to anyone, it was to Dr Quentin for giving his patient a narcotic and leaving him in such a dangerous position. And then a rather curious discovery was made.

'There was a newspaper on the floor, lying where it had slipped from the old man's knees. On turning it over, words were found to be scrawled across it, feebly traced in ink. A writing-table stood close to the chair in which Mr Paynter had been sitting, and the forefinger of the victim's right hand was ink-stained up to the second joint. It was clear that, too weak to hold a pen, Mr Paynter had dipped his finger in the ink-pot and managed to scrawl these two words across the surface of the newspaper he held – but the words themselves seemed utterly fantastic: *Yellow Jasmine* – just that and nothing more.

'Croftlands has a large quantity of yellow jasmine growing up its walls, and it was thought that this dying message had some reference to them, showing that the poor old man's mind was wandering. Of course the newspapers, agog for anything out of the common, took up the story hotly, calling it the Mystery of the Yellow Jasmine – though in all probability the words are completely unimportant.'

'They are unimportant, you say?' said Poirot. 'Well, doubtless, since you say so, it must be so.'

I regarded him dubiously, but I could detect no mockery in his eye.

'And then,' I continued, 'there came the excitements of the inquest.'

'This is where you lick your lips, I perceive.'

'There was a certain amount of feeling evidenced against Dr Quentin. To begin with, he was not the regular doctor, only a locum, putting in a month's work, whilst Dr Bolitho was away on a well-earned holiday. Then it was felt that his carelessness was the direct cause of the accident. But his evidence was little short of sensational. Mr Paynter had been ailing in health since his arrival at Croftlands. Dr Bolitho had attended him for some time, but when Dr Quentin first saw his patient, he was mystified by some of the symptoms. He had only attended him once before the night when he was sent for after dinner. As soon as he was alone with Mr Paynter, the latter had unfolded a surprising tale. To begin with, he was not feeling ill at all, he explained, but the taste of some curry that he had been eating at dinner had struck him as peculiar. Making an excuse to get rid of Ah Ling for a few minutes, he had turned the contents of his plate into a bowl, and he now handed it over to the doctor with injunctions to find out if there were really anything wrong with it.

'In spite of his statement that he was not feeling ill, the doctor noted that the shock of his suspicions had evidently affected him, and that his heart was feeling it. Accordingly he administered an injection – not of a narcotic, but of strychnine.

'That, I think, completes the case – except for *the* crux of the whole thing – the fact that the uneaten curry, duly analysed, was found to contain enough powdered opium to have killed two men!'

I paused.

'And your conclusions, Hastings?' asked Poirot quietly.

'It's difficult to say. It *might* be an accident – the fact that someone attempted to poison him the same night might be merely a coincidence.'

'But you don't think so? You prefer to believe it – murder!'

'Don't you?'

'*Mon ami,* you and I do not reason in the same way. I am not trying to make up my mind between two opposite solutions – murder or accident – that will come when we have solved the other problem – the mystery of the "Yellow Jasmine". By the way, you have left out something there.'

'You mean the two lines at right angles to each other faintly indicated under the words? I did not think they could be of any possible importance.'

'What you think is always so important to yourself, Hastings. But let us pass from the Mystery of the Yellow Jasmine to the Mystery of the Curry.'

'I know. Who poisoned it? Why? There are a hundred questions one can ask. Ah Ling, of course, prepared it. But why should he wish to kill his master? Is he a member of a *tong*, or something like that? One reads of such things. The *tong* of the Yellow Jasmine, perhaps. Then there is Gerald Paynter.'

I came to an abrupt pause.

'Yes,' said Poirot, nodding his head. 'There is Gerald Paynter, as you say. He is his uncle's heir. He was dining out that night, though.'

'He might have got at some of the ingredients of the curry,' I suggested. 'And he would take care to be out, so as not to have to partake of the dish.'

I think my reasoning rather impressed Poirot. He looked at me with a more respectful attention than he had given me so far.

'He returns late,' I mused, pursuing a hypothetical case. 'Sees the light in his uncle's study, enters, and, finding his plan has failed, thrusts the old man down into the fire.'

'Mr Paynter, who was a fairly hearty man of fifty-five, would not permit himself to be burnt to death without a struggle, Hastings. Such a reconstruction is not feasible.'

'Well, Poirot,' I cried, 'we're nearly there, I fancy. Let us hear what you think?'

Poirot threw me a smile, swelled out his chest, and began in a pompous manner.

'Assuming murder, the question at once arises, why choose that particular method? I can think of only one reason – to confuse identity, the face being charred beyond recognition.'

'What?' I cried. 'You think –'

'A moment's patience, Hastings. I was going on to say that I examine that theory. Is there any ground for believing that the body is not that of Mr Paynter? Is there anyone else whose body it possibly could be? I examine these two questions and finally I answer them both in the negative.'

'Oh!' I said, rather disappointed. 'And then?'

Poirot's eyes twinkled a little.

'And then I say to myself, "since there is here something that I do not understand, it would be well that I should investigate the matter. I must not permit myself to be wholly engrossed by the Big Four." Ah! We are just arriving. My little clothes brush, where does it hide itself? Here it is – brush me down, I pray you, my friend, and then I will perform the same service for you.

'Yes,' said Poirot thoughtfully, as he put away the brush, 'one must not permit oneself to be obsessed by one idea. I have been in danger of that. Figure to yourself, my friend, that even here, in this case, I am in danger of it. Those two lines you mentioned, a downstroke and a line at right angles to it, what are they but the beginning of a 4?'

'Good gracious, Poirot,' I cried, laughing.

'Is it not absurd? I see the hand of the Big Four everywhere, it is well to employ one's wits in a totally different *milieu*. Ah! There is Japp come to meet us.'

CHAPTER X

We Investigate at Croftlands

The Scotland Yard Inspector was, indeed, waiting on the platform, and greeted us warmly.

'Well, Moosior Poirot, this is good. Thought you'd like to be let in on this. Tip-top mystery, isn't it?'

I read this aright as showing Japp to be completely puzzled and hoping to pick up a pointer from Poirot.

Japp had a car waiting, and we drove up in it to Croftlands. It was a square, white house, quite unpretentious, and covered with creepers, including the starry yellow jasmine. Japp looked up at it as we did.

'Must have been balmy to go writing that, poor old cove,' he remarked. 'Hallucinations, perhaps, and thought he was outside.'

Poirot was smiling at him.

'Which was it, my good Japp?' he asked; 'accident or murder?'

The Inspector seemed a little embarrassed by the question.

'Well, if it weren't for that curry business, I'd be for accident every time. There's no sense in holding a live man's head in the fire – why, he'd scream the house down.'

'Ah!' said Poirot in a low voice. 'Fool that I have been. Triple imbecile! You are a cleverer man than I am, Japp.'

Japp was rather taken aback by the compliment – Poirot being usually given to exclusive self-praise. He reddened and muttered something about there being a lot of doubt about that.

He led the way through the house to the room where the tragedy had occurred – Mr Paynter's study. It was a wide, low room, with book-lined walls and big leather armchairs.

Poirot looked across at once to the window which gave upon a gravelled terrace.

'The window, was it unlatched?' he asked.

'That's the whole point, of course. When the doctor left this room, he merely closed the door behind him. The next morning it was found locked. Who locked it? Mr Paynter? Ah Ling declares that the window was closed and bolted. Dr Quentin, on the other hand, has an impression that it was closed, but not fastened, but he won't swear either way. If he could, it would make a great difference. If the man *was* murdered, someone entered the room either through the door or the window – if through the door, it was an inside job; if through the window, it might have been anyone. First thing when they had broken the door down, they flung the window open, and the housemaid who did it thinks that it wasn't fastened, but she's a precious bad witness – will remember anything you ask her to!'

'What about the key?'

'There you are again. It was on the floor among the wreckage of the door. Might have fallen from the keyhole, might have been dropped there by one of the people who entered, might have been slipped underneath the door from the outside.'

'In fact everything is "might have been"?'

'You've hit it, Moosior Poirot. That's just what it is.'

Poirot was looking around him, frowning unhappily.

'I cannot see light,' he murmured. 'Just now – yes, I got a gleam, but now all is darkness once more. I have not the clue – the motive.'

'Young Gerald Paynter had a pretty good motive,' remarked Japp grimly. 'He's been wild enough in his time, I can tell you. *And* extravagant. You know what artists are, too – no morals at all.'

Poirot did not pay much attention to Japp's sweeping strictures on the artistic temperament. Instead he smiled knowingly.

'My good Japp, is it possible that you throw me the mud in my eyes? I know well enough that it is the Chinaman you suspect. But you are so artful. You want me to help you – and yet you drag the red kipper across the trail.'

Japp burst out laughing.

'That's you all over, Mr Poirot. Yes, I'd bet on the Chink, I'll admit it now. It stands to reason that it was he who doctored the curry, and if he'd try once in an evening to get his master out of the way, he'd try twice.'

'I wonder if he would,' said Poirot softly.

'But it's the motive that beats me. Some heathen revenge or other, I suppose.'

'I wonder,' said Poirot again. 'There has been no robbery? Nothing has disappeared? No jewellery, or money, or papers?'

'No – that is, not exactly.'

I pricked up my ears; so did Poirot.

'There's been no robbery, I mean,' explained Japp. 'But the old boy was writing a book of some sort. We only knew about it this morning when there was a letter from the publishers asking about the manuscript. It was just completed, it seems. Young Paynter and I have searched high and low, but can't find a trace of it – he must have hidden it away somewhere.'

Poirot's eyes were shining with the green light I knew so well.

'How was it called, this book?' he asked.

'The Hidden Hand in China, I think it was called.'

'Aha!' said Poirot, with almost a gasp. Then he said quickly, 'Let me see the Chinaman, Ah Ling.'

The Chinaman was sent for and appeared, shuffling along, with his eyes cast down, and his pigtail swinging. His impassive face showed no trace of any kind of emotion.

'Ah Ling,' said Poirot, 'are you sorry your master is dead?'

'I welly sorry. He good master.'

'You know who kill him?'

'I not know. I tell pleeceman if I know.'

The questions and answers went on. With the same impassive face, Ah Ling described how he had made the curry. The cook had had nothing to do with it, he declared, no hand had touched it but his own. I wondered if he saw where his admission was leading him. He stuck to it too, that the window to the garden was bolted that evening. If it was open in the morning, his master must have opened it himself. At last Poirot dismissed him.

'That will do, Ah Ling.' Just as the Chinaman had got to the door, Poirot recalled him. 'And you know nothing, you say, of the Yellow Jasmine?'

'No, what should I know?'

'Nor yet of the sign that was written underneath it?'

Poirot leaned forward as he spoke, and quickly traced something on the dust of a little table. I was near enough to see it before he rubbed it out. A down stroke, a line at right angles, and then a second line down which completed a big 4. The effect on the Chinaman was electrical. For one moment his face was a mask of terror. Then, as suddenly, it was impassive again, and repeating his grave disclaimer, he withdrew.

Japp departed in search of young Paynter, and Poirot and I were left alone together.

'The Big Four, Hastings,' cried Poirot. 'Once again, the Big Four. Paynter was a great traveller. In his book there was doubtless some vital information concerning the doings of Number One, Li Chang Yen, the head and brains of the Big Four.'

'But who – how –'

'Hush, here they come.'

Gerald Paynter was an amiable, rather weak-looking young man. He had a soft brown beard, and a peculiar flowing tie. He answered Poirot's questions readily enough.

'I dined out with some neighbours of ours, the Wycherleys,' he explained. 'What time did I get home? Oh, about eleven. I had a latchkey, you know. All the servants had gone to bed, and I naturally thought my uncle had done the same. As a matter of fact, I did think I caught sight of that soft-footed Chinese beggar, Ah Ling, just whisking round the corner of the hall, but I fancy I was mistaken.'

'When did you last see your uncle, Mr Paynter? I mean before you came to live with him?'

'Oh! not since I was a kid of ten. He and his brother (my father) quarrelled, you know.'

'But he found you again with very little trouble, did he not? In spite of all the years that had passed?'

'Yes, it was quite a bit of luck my seeing the lawyer's advertisement.'

Poirot asked no more questions.

Our next move was to visit Dr Quentin. His story was substantially the same as he had told at the inquest, and he had little to add to it. He received us in his surgery, having just come to the end of his consulting patients. He seemed an intelligent man. A certain primness of manner went well with his pince-nez, but I fancied that he would be thoroughly modern in his methods.

'I wish I could remember about the window,' he said frankly. 'But it's dangerous to think back, one becomes quite positive about something that never existed. That's psychology, isn't it, M. Poirot? You see, I've read all about your methods, and I may say I'm an enormous admirer of yours. No, I suppose it's pretty certain that the Chinaman put the powdered opium in the curry, but he'll never admit it, and we shall never know why. But holding a man down in a fire – that's not in keeping with our Chinese friend's character, it seems to me.'

I commented on this last point to Poirot as we walked down the main street of Market Handford.

'Do you think he let a confederate in?' I asked. 'By the way, I suppose Japp can be trusted to keep an eye on him?' (The Inspector had passed into the police station on some business or other.) 'The emissaries of the Big Four are pretty spry.'

'Japp is keeping an eye on both of them,' said Poirot grimly. 'They have been closely shadowed ever since the body was discovered.'

'Well, at any rate *we* know that Gerald Paynter had nothing to do with it.'

'You always know so much more than I do, Hastings, that it becomes quite fatiguing.'

'You old fox,' I laughed. 'You never will commit yourself.'

'To be honest, Hastings, the case is now quite clear to me – all but the words, *Yellow Jasmine* – and I am coming to agree with you that they have no bearing on the crime. In a case of this kind, you have got to make up your mind who is lying. I have done that. And yet –'

He suddenly darted from my side and entered an adjacent

bookshop. He emerged a few minutes later, hugging a parcel. Then Japp rejoined us, and we all sought quarters at the inn.

I slept late the next morning. When I descended to the sitting-room reserved for us, I found Poirot already there, pacing up and down, his face contorted with agony.

'Do not converse with me,' he cried, waving an agitated hand. 'Not until I know that all is well – that the arrest is made. Ah! but my psychology has been weak. Hastings, if a man writes a dying message, it is because it is important. Everyone has said – "Yellow Jasmine? There is yellow jasmine growing up the house – it means nothing."'

'Well, what does it mean? Just what it says. Listen.' He held up a little book he was holding.

'My friend, it struck me that it would be well to inquire into the subject. What exactly is yellow jasmine? This little book has told me. Listen.'

He read.

'"*Gelsemini Radix*. Yellow Jasmine. Composition: Alkaloids *gelseminine* $C_{22}H_{26}N_2O_3$, a potent poison acting like coniine; *gelsemine* $C_{12}H_{14}NO_2$, acting like strychnine; *gelsemic acid,* etc. Gelsemium is a powerful depressant to the central nervous system. At a late stage in its action it paralyses the motor nerve endings, and in large doses causes giddiness and loss of muscular power. Death is due to paralysis of the respiratory centre."'

'You see, Hastings? At the beginning I had an inkling of the truth when Japp made his remark about a live man being forced into the fire. I realized then that it was a dead man who was burned.'

'But why? What was the point?'

'My friend, if you were to shoot a man, or stab a man after he were dead, or even knock him on the head, it would be apparent that the injuries were inflicted after death. But with his head charred to a cinder, no one is going to hunt about for obscure causes of death, and a man who has apparently just escaped being poisoned at dinner is not likely to be poisoned just afterwards. *Who* is lying, that is always the question? I decided to believe Ah Ling –'

'What!' I exclaimed.

'You are surprised, Hastings? Ah Ling knew of the existence of the Big Four, that was evident – so evident that it was clear he knew nothing of their association with the crime until that moment. Had he been the murderer, he would have been able to retain his impassive face perfectly. So I decided, then, to believe Ah Ling, and I fixed my suspicions on Gerald Paynter. It seemed to me that Number Four would have found an impersonation of a long-lost nephew very easy.'

'What!' I cried. 'Number Four?'

'No, Hastings, *not* Number Four. As soon as I had read up the subject of yellow jasmine, I saw the truth. In fact, it leapt to the eye.'

'As always,' I said coldly, 'it doesn't leap to mine.'

'Because you will not use your little grey cells. Who had a chance to tamper with the curry?'

'Ah Ling. No one else.'

'No one else? *What about the doctor?*'

'But that was *afterwards.*'

'Of course it was afterwards. There was no trace of powdered opium in the curry served to Mr Paynter, but acting in obedience to the suspicions Dr Quentin had aroused, the old man eats none of it, and preserves it to give to his medical attendant, whom he summons according to plan. Dr Quentin arrives, takes charge of the curry, *and gives Mr Paynter an injection* – of strychnine, he says, but really of yellow jasmine – a poisonous dose. When the drug begins to take effect, he departs, after unlatching the window. Then, in the night, he returns by the window, finds the manuscript, and shoves Mr Paynter into the fire. He does not heed the newspaper that drops to the floor and is covered by the old man's body. Paynter knew what drug he had been given, and strove to accuse the Big Four of his murder. It is easy for Quentin to mix powdered opium with the curry before handing it over to be analysed. He gives his version of the conversation with the old man, and mentions the strychnine injection casually, in case the mark of the hypodermic needle is noticed. Suspicion at once is divided between accident and the guilt of Ah Ling owing to the poisoning of the curry.'

'But Dr Quentin cannot be Number Four?'

'I fancy he can. There is undoubtedly a real Dr Quentin who is probably abroad somewhere. Number Four has simply masqueraded as him for a short time. The arrangements with Dr Bolitho were all carried out by correspondence, the man who was to do locum originally having been taken ill at the last minute.'

At that minute, Japp burst in, very red in the face.

'Have you got him?' cried Poirot anxiously.

Japp shook his head, very out of breath.

'Bolitho came back from his holiday this morning – recalled by telegram. No one knows who sent it. The other man left last night. We'll catch him yet, though.'

Poirot shook his head quietly.

'I think not,' he said, and absentmindedly he drew a big 4 on the table with a fork.

CHAPTER XI

A Chess Problem

Poirot and I often dined at a small restaurant in Soho. We were there one evening, when we observed a friend at an adjacent table. It was Inspector Japp, and as there was room at our table, he came and joined us. It was some time since either of us had seen him.

'Never do you drop in to see us nowadays,' declared Poirot reproachfully. 'Not since the affair of the Yellow Jasmine have we met, and that is nearly a month ago.'

'I've been up north – that's why. How are things with you? Big Four still going strong – eh?'

Poirot shook a finger at him reproachfully.

'Ah! You mock yourself at me – but the Big Four – they exist.'

'Oh! I don't doubt that – but they're not the hub of the universe, as you make out.'

'My friend, you are very much mistaken. The greatest power for evil in the world today is this "Big Four". To what end they are tending, no one knows, but there has never been another such criminal organization. The finest brain in China at the head of it, an American millionaire and a French woman scientist as members, and for the fourth –'

Japp interrupted.

'I know – I know. Regular bee in your bonnet over it all. It's becoming your little mania, Moosior Poirot. Let's talk of something else for a change. Take any interest in chess?'

'I have played it, yes.'

'Did you see that curious business yesterday? Match between two players of world-wide reputation, and one died during the game?'

'I saw mention of it. Dr Savaronoff, the Russian champion,

was one of the players, and the other, who succumbed to heart failure, was the brilliant young American, Gilmour Wilson.'

'Quite right. Savaronoff beat Rubinstein and became Russian champion some years ago. Wilson was said to be a second Capablanca.'

'A very curious occurrence,' mused Poirot. 'If I mistake not, you have a particular interest in the matter?'

Japp gave a rather embarrassed laugh.

'You've hit it, Moosior Poirot. I'm puzzled. Wilson was sound as a bell – no trace of heart trouble. His death is quite inexplicable.'

'You suspect Dr Savaronoff of putting him out of the way?' I cried.

'Hardly that,' said Japp drily. 'I don't think even a Russian would murder another man in order not to be beaten at chess – and anyway, from all I can make out, the boot was likely to be on the other leg. The doctor is supposed to be very hot stuff – second to Lasker they say he is.'

Poirot nodded thoughtfully.

'Then what exactly is your little idea?' he asked. 'Why should Wilson be poisoned? For, I assume, of course, that it is poison you suspect.'

'Naturally. Heart failure means your heart stops beating – that's all there is to that. That's what a doctor says officially at the moment, but privately he tips us the wink that he's not satisfied.'

'When is the autopsy to take place?'

'Tonight. Wilson's death was extraordinarily sudden. He seemed quite as usual and was actually moving one of the pieces when he suddenly fell forward – dead!'

'There are very few poisons would act in such a fashion,' objected Poirot.

'I know. The autopsy will help us, I expect. But why should anyone want Gilmour Wilson out of the way – that's what I'd like to know? Harmless, unassuming young fellow. Just come over here from the States, and apparently hadn't an enemy in the world.'

'It seems incredible,' I mused.

'Not at all,' said Poirot, smiling. 'Japp has his theory, I can see.'

'I have, Moosior Poirot. I don't believe the poison was meant for Wilson – it was meant for the other man.'

'Savaronoff?'

'Yes. Savaronoff fell foul of the Bolsheviks at the outbreak of the Revolution. He was even reported killed. In reality he escaped, and for three years endured incredible hardships in the wilds of Siberia. His sufferings were so great that he is now a changed man. His friends and acquaintances declare they would hardly have recognized him. His hair is white, and his whole aspect that of a man terribly aged. He is a semi-invalid, and seldom goes out, living alone with a niece, Sonia Daviloff, and a Russian manservant in a flat down Westminster way. It is possible that he still considers himself a marked man. Certainly he was very unwilling to agree to this chess contest. He refused several times point blank, and it was only when the newspapers took it up and began making a fuss about the "unsportsmanlike refusal" that he gave in. Gilmour Wilson had gone on challenging him with real Yankee pertinacity, and in the end he got his way. Now I ask you, Moosior Poirot, why wasn't he willing? Because he didn't want attention drawn to him. Didn't want somebody or other to get on his track. That's my solution – Gilmour Wilson got pipped by mistake.'

'There is no one who has any private reason to gain by Savaronoff's death?'

'Well, his niece, I suppose. He's recently come into an immense fortune. Left him by Madame Gospoja whose husband was a sugar profiteer under the old regime. They had an affair together once, I believe, and she refused steadfastly to credit the reports of his death.'

'Where did the match take place?'

'In Savaronoff's own flat. He's an invalid, as I told you.'

'Many people there to watch it?'

'At least a dozen – probably more.'

Poirot made an expressive grimace.

'My poor Japp, your task is not an easy one.'

'Once I know definitely that Wilson was poisoned, I can get on.'

'Has it occurred to you that, in the meantime, supposing your assumption that Savaronoff was the intended victim to be correct, the murderer may try again?'

'Of course it has. Two men are watching Savaronoff's flat.'

'That will be very useful if anyone should call with a bomb under his arm,' said Poirot drily.

'You're getting interested, Moosior Poirot,' said Japp, with a twinkle. 'Care to come round to the mortuary and see Wilson's body before the doctors start on it? Who knows, his tie pin may be askew, and that may give you a valuable clue that will solve the mystery.'

'My dear Japp, all through dinner my fingers have been itching to rearrange your own tie pin. You permit, yes? Ah! that is much more pleasing to the eye. Yes, by all means, let us go to the mortuary.'

I could see that Poirot's attention was completely captivated by this new problem. It was so long since he had shown any interest over any outside case that I was quite rejoiced to see him back in his old form.

For my own part, I felt a deep pity as I looked down upon the motionless form and convulsed face of the hapless young American who had come by his death in such a strange way. Poirot examined the body attentively. There was no mark on it anywhere, except a small scar on the left hand.

'And the doctor says that's a burn, not a cut,' explained Japp.

Poirot's attention shifted to the contents of the dead man's pockets which a constable spread out for our inspection. There was nothing much – a handkerchief, keys, notecase filled with notes, and some unimportant letters. But one object standing by itself filled Poirot with interest.

'A chessman!' he exclaimed. 'A white bishop. Was that in his pocket?'

'No, clasped in his hand. We had quite a difficulty to get it out of his fingers. It must be returned to Dr Savaronoff some time. It's part of a very beautiful set of carved ivory chessmen.'

'Permit me to return it to him. It will make an excuse for my going there.'

'Aha!' cried Japp. 'So you want to come in on this case?'

'I admit it. So skilfully have you aroused my interest.'

'That's fine. Got you away from your brooding. Captain Hastings is pleased, too, I can see.'

'Quite right,' I said, laughing.

Poirot turned back towards the body.

'No other little detail you can tell me about – him?' he asked.

'I don't think so.'

'Not even – that he was left-handed?'

'You're a wizard, Moosior Poirot. How did you know that? He *was* left-handed. Not that it's anything to do with the case.'

'Nothing whatever,' agreed Poirot hastily, seeing that Japp was slightly ruffled. 'My little joke – that was all. I like to play you the trick, see you.'

We went out upon an amicable understanding.

The following morning saw us wending our way to Dr Savaronoff's flat in Westminster.

'Sonia Daviloff,' I mused. 'It's a pretty name.'

Poirot stopped, and threw me a look of despair.

'Always looking for romance! You are incorrigible. It would serve you right if Sonia Daviloff turned out to be our friend and enemy the Countess Vera Rossakoff.'

At the mention of the countess, my face clouded over.

'Surely, Poirot, you don't suspect –'

'But, no, no. It was a joke! I have not the Big Four on the brain to that extent, whatever Japp may say.'

The door of the flat was opened to us by a manservant with a peculiarly wooden face. It seemed impossible to believe that that impassive countenance could ever display emotion.

Poirot presented a card on which Japp had scribbled a few words of introduction, and we were shown into a low, long room furnished with rich hangings and curios. One or two wonderful ikons hung upon the walls, and exquisite Persian rugs lay upon the floor. A samovar stood upon a table.

I was examining one of the ikons which I judged to be of considerable value, and turned to see Poirot prone upon the floor. Beautiful as the rug was, it hardly seemed to me to necessitate such close attention.

'Is it such a very wonderful specimen?' I asked.

'Eh? Oh! the rug? But no, it was not the rug I was remarking. But it *is* a beautiful specimen, far too beautiful to have a large nail wantonly driven through the middle of it. No, Hastings,' as I came forward, 'the nail is not there now. But the hole remains.'

A sudden sound behind us made me spin round, and Poirot sprang nimbly to his feet. A girl was standing in the doorway. Her eyes, full upon us, were dark with suspicion. She was of medium height, with a beautiful, rather sullen face, dark blue eyes, and very black hair which was cut short. Her voice, when she spoke, was rich and sonorous, and completely un-English.

'I fear my uncle will be unable to see you. He is a great invalid.'

'That is a pity, but perhaps you will kindly help me instead. You are Mademoiselle Daviloff, are you not?'

'Yes, I am Sonia Daviloff. What is it you want to know?'

'I am making some inquiries about that sad affair the night before last – the death of M. Gilmour Wilson. What can you tell me about it?'

The girl's eyes opened wide.

'He died of heart failure – as he was playing chess.'

'The police are not so sure that it was – heart failure, mademoiselle.'

The girl gave a terrified gesture.

'It was true then,' she cried. 'Ivan was right.'

'Who is Ivan, and why do you say he was right?'

'It was Ivan who opened the door to you – and he has already said to me that in his opinion Gilmour Wilson did not die a natural death – that he was poisoned by mistake.'

'By mistake.'

'Yes, the poison was meant for my uncle.'

She had quite forgotten her first distrust now, and was speaking eagerly.

'Why do you say that, mademoiselle? Who should wish to poison Dr Savaronoff?'

She shook her head.

'I do not know. I am in the dark. And my uncle, he will not trust me. It is natural, perhaps. You see, he hardly knows me. He saw me as a child, and not since till I came to live with him here in London. But this much I do know, he is in fear of something. We have many secret societies in Russia, and one day I overheard something which made me think it was of just such a society he went in fear. Tell me, monsieur' – she came a step nearer, and dropped her voice – 'have you ever heard of a society called the "Big Four"?'

Poirot jumped nearly out of his skin. His eyes positively bulged with astonishment.

'Why do you – what do you know of the Big Four, mademoiselle?'

'There is such an association, then! I overheard a reference to them, and asked my uncle about it afterwards. Never have I seen a man so afraid. He turned all white and shaking. He was in fear of them, monsieur, in great fear, I am sure of it. And, by mistake, they killed the American Wilson.'

'The Big Four,' murmured Poirot. 'Always the Big Four! An astonishing coincidence, mademoiselle, your uncle is still in danger. I must save him. Now recount to me exactly the events of that fatal evening. Show me the chessboard, the table, how the two men sat – everything.'

She went to the side of the room and brought out a small table. The top of it was exquisite, inlaid with squares of silver and black to represent a chessboard.

'This was sent to my uncle a few weeks ago as a present, with the request that he would use it in the next match he played. It was in the middle of the room – so.'

Poirot examined the table with what seemed to me quite unnecessary attention. He was not conducting the inquiry at all as I would have done. Many of the questions seemed to me pointless, and upon really vital matters he seemed to have no questions to ask. I concluded that the unexpected mention of the Big Four had thrown him completely off his balance.

After a minute examination of the table and the exact position it had occupied, he asked to see the chessmen. Sonia Daviloff brought them to him in a box. He examined one or two of them in a perfunctory manner.

'An exquisite set,' he murmured absentmindedly.

Still not a question as to what refreshments there had been, or what people had been present.

I cleared my throat significantly.

'Don't you think, Poirot, that –'

He interrupted me peremptorily.

'Do not think, my friend. Leave all to me. Mademoiselle, is it quite impossible that I should see your uncle?'

A faint smile showed itself on her face.

'He will see you, yes. You understand, it is my part to interview all strangers first.'

She disappeared. I heard a murmur of voices in the next room, and a minute later she came back and motioned us to pass into the adjoining room.

The man who lay there on a couch was an imposing figure. Tall, gaunt, with huge bushy eyebrows and white beard, and a face haggard as the result of starvation and hardships, Dr Savaronoff was a distinct personality. I noted the peculiar formation of his head, its unusual height. A great chess player must have a great brain, I knew. I could easily understand Dr Savaronoff being the second greatest player in the world.

Poirot bowed.

'M. le Docteur, may I speak to you alone?'

Savaronoff turned to his niece.

'Leave us, Sonia.'

She disappeared obediently.

'Now, sir, what is it?'

'Dr Savaronoff, you have recently come into an enormous fortune. If you should – die unexpectedly, who inherits it?'

'I have made a will leaving everything to my niece, Sonia Daviloff. You do not suggest –'

'I suggest nothing, but you have not seen your niece since she was a child. It would have been easy for anyone to impersonate her.'

Savaronoff seemed thunderstruck by the suggestion. Poirot went on easily.

'Enough as to that: I give you the word of warning, that is all. What I want you to do now is to describe to me the game of chess the other evening.'

'How do you mean – describe it?'

'Well, I do not play the chess myself, but I understand that there are various regular ways of beginning – the gambit, do they not call it?'

Dr Savaronoff smiled a little.

'Ah! I comprehend you now. Wilson opened Ruy Lopez – one of the soundest openings there is, and one frequently adopted in tournaments and matches.'

'And how long had you been playing when the tragedy happened?'

'It must have been about the third or fourth move when Wilson suddenly fell forward over the table, stone dead.'

Poirot rose to depart. He flung out his last question as though it was of absolutely no importance, but I knew better.

'Had he anything to eat or drink?'

'A whisky and soda, I think.'

'Thank you, Dr Savaronoff. I will disturb you no longer.'

Ivan was in the hall to show us out. Poirot lingered on the threshold.

'The flat below this, do you know who lives there?'

'Sir Charles Kingwell, a member of Parliament, sir. It has been let furnished lately, though.'

'Thank you.'

We went out into the bright winter sunlight.

'Well, really, Poirot,' I burst out. 'I don't think you've distinguished yourself this time. Surely your questions were very inadequate.'

'You think so, Hastings?' Poirot looked at me appealingly. 'I was *bouleversé*, yes. What would you have asked?'

I considered the question carefully, and then outlined my scheme to Poirot. He listened with what seemed to be close interest. My monologue lasted until we had nearly reached home.

'Very excellent, very searching, Hastings,' said Poirot, as he inserted his key in the door and preceded me up the stairs. 'But quite unnecessary.'

'Unnecessary!' I cried, amazed. 'If the man was poisoned –'

'Aha,' cried Poirot, pouncing upon a note which lay on the table. 'From Japp. Just as I thought.' He flung it over to me. It was brief and to the point. No traces of poison had been found, and there was nothing to show how the man came by his death.

'You see,' said Poirot, 'our questions would have been quite unnecessary.'

'You guessed this beforehand?'

' "Forecast the probable result of the deal," ' quoted Poirot from a recent Bridge problem on which I had spent much time. '*Mon ami,* when you do that successfully, you do not call it guessing.'

'Don't let's split hairs,' I said impatiently. 'You foresaw this?'

'I did.'

'Why?'

Poirot put his hand into his pocket and pulled out – a white bishop.

'Why,' I cried, 'you forgot to give it back to Dr Savaronoff.'

'You are in error, my friend. That bishop still reposes in my left-hand pocket. I took its fellow from the box of chessmen Mademoiselle Daviloff kindly permitted me to examine. The plural of one bishop is two bishops.'

He sounded the final 's' with a great hiss. I was completely mystified.

'But why did you take it?'

'*Parbleu,* I wanted to see if they were exactly alike.'

Poirot looked at them with his head on one side.

'They seem so, I admit. But one should take no fact for

granted until it is proved. Bring me, I pray you, my little scales.'

With infinite care he weighed the two chessmen, then turned to me with a face alight with triumph.

'I was right. See you, I was right. Impossible to deceive Hercule Poirot!'

He rushed to the telephone – waited impatiently.

'Is that Japp? Ah! Japp, it is you. Hercule Poirot speaks. Watch the manservant. Ivan. On no account let him slip through your fingers. Yes, yes, it is as I say.'

He dashed down the receiver and turned to me.

'You see it not, Hastings? I will explain. Wilson was not poisoned, he was electrocuted. A thin metal rod passes up the middle of one of those chessmen. The table was prepared beforehand and set upon a certain spot on the floor. When the bishop was placed upon one of the silver squares, the current passed through Wilson's body, killing him instantly. The only mark was the electric burn upon his hand – his left hand, because he was left-handed. The "special table" was an extremely cunning piece of mechanism. The table I examined was a duplicate, perfectly innocent. It was substituted for the other immediately after the murder. The thing was worked from the flat below, which, if you remember, was let furnished. But one accomplice at least was in Savaronoff's flat. The girl is an agent of the Big Four, working to inherit Savaronoff's money.'

'And Ivan?'

'I strongly suspect that Ivan is none other than the famous Number Four.'

'*What?*'

'Yes. The man is a marvellous character actor. He can assume any part he pleases.'

I thought back over past adventures, the lunatic asylum keeper, the butcher's young man, the suave doctor, all the same man, and all totally unlike each other.

'It's amazing,' I said at last. 'Everything fits in. Savaronoff had an inkling of the plot, and that's why he was so averse to playing the match.'

Poirot looked at me without speaking. Then he turned abruptly away, and began pacing up and down.

'Have you a book on chess by any chance, *mon ami*?' he asked suddenly.

'I believe I have somewhere.'

It took me some time to ferret it out, but I found it at last, and brought it to Poirot, who sank down in a chair and started reading it with the greatest attention.

In about a quarter of an hour the telephone rang. I answered it. It was Japp. Ivan had left the flat, carrying a large bundle. He had sprung into a waiting taxi, and the chase had begun. He was evidently trying to lose his pursuers. In the end he seemed to fancy that he had done so, and had then driven to a big empty house at Hampstead. The house was surrounded.

I recounted all this to Poirot. He merely stared at me as though he scarcely took in what I was saying. He held out the chess book.

'Listen to this, my friend. This is the Ruy Lopez opening. 1 P-K4, P-K4; 2 Kt-KB3, K-QB3; 3 B-Kt5. Then there comes a question as to Black's best third move. He has the choice of various defences. It was White's third move that killed Gilmour Wilson, 3 B-Kt5. Only the third move – does that say nothing to you?'

I hadn't the least idea what he meant, and told him so.

'Suppose, Hastings, that, while you were sitting in this chair, you heard the front door being opened and shut, what would you think?'

'I should think someone had gone out, I suppose.'

'Yes – but there are always two ways of looking at things. Someone gone out – someone come *in* – two totally different things, Hastings. But if you assumed the wrong one, presently some little discrepancy would creep in and show you that you were on the wrong track.'

'What does all this mean, Poirot?'

Poirot sprang to his feet with sudden energy.

'It means that I have been a triple imbecile. Quick, quick, to the flat in Westminster. We may yet be in time.'

We tore off in a taxi. Poirot returned no answer to my excited questions. We raced up the stairs. Repeated rings and knocks brought no reply, but listening closely I could distinguish a hollow groan coming from within.

The hall porter proved to have a master key, and after a few difficulties he consented to use it.

Poirot went straight to the inner room. A whiff of chloroform met us. On the floor was Sonia Daviloff, gagged and bound, with a great wad of saturated cotton-wool over her nose and mouth. Poirot tore it off and began to take measures to restore her. Presently a doctor arrived, and Poirot handed her over to his charge and drew aside with me. There was no sign of Dr Savaronoff.

'What does it all mean?' I asked, bewildered.

'It means that before two equal deductions I chose the wrong one. You heard me say that it would be easy for anyone to impersonate Sonia Daviloff because her uncle had not seen her for so many years?'

'Yes?'

'Well, precisely the opposite held good also. It was equally easy for anyone to impersonate the uncle.'

'What?'

'Savaronoff *did* die at the outbreak of the Revolution. The man who pretended to have escaped with such terrible hardships, the man so changed "that his own friends could hardly recognize him", the man who successfully laid claim to an enormous fortune –'

'Yes. Who was he?'

'*Number Four.* No wonder he was frightened when Sonia let him know she had overheard one of his private conversations about the "Big Four". Again he has slipped through my fingers. He guessed I should get on the right track in the end, so he sent off the honest Ivan on a tortuous wild goose chase, chloroformed the girl, and got out, having by now doubtless realized most of the securities left by Madame Gospoja.'

'But – but who tried to kill him then?'

'Nobody tried to kill *him*. Wilson was the intended victim all along.'

'But why?'

'My friend, Savaronoff was the second greatest chess player in the world. In all probability Number Four did not even know the rudiments of the game. Certainly he could not sustain the fiction of a match. He tried all he knew to avoid the contest. When that failed, Wilson's doom was sealed. At all costs he must be prevented from discovering that the great Savaronoff did not even know how to play chess. Wilson was fond of the Ruy Lopez opening, and was certain to use it. Number Four arranged for death to come with the third move, before any complications of defence set in.'

'But, my dear Poirot,' I persisted, 'are we dealing with a lunatic? I quite follow your reasoning, and admit that you must be right, but to kill a man just to sustain his role! Surely there were simpler ways out of the difficulty than that? He could have said that his doctor forbade the strain of a match.'

Poirot wrinkled his forehead.

'*Certainement*, Hastings,' he said, 'there were other ways, but none so convincing. Besides, you are assuming that to kill a man is a thing to avoid, are you not? Number Four's mind, it does not act that way. I put myself in his place, a thing impossible for you. I picture his thoughts. He enjoys himself as the professor at that match, I doubt not he has visited the chess tourneys to study his part. He sits and frowns in thought; he gives the impression that he is thinking great plans, and all the time he laughs in himself. He is aware that two moves are all that he knows – and all that he *need know*. Again, it would appeal to his mind to foresee the time that suits Number Four ... Oh, yes, Hastings, I begin to understand our friend and his psychology.'

I shrugged.

'Well, I suppose you're right, but I can't understand anyone running a risk he could so easily avoid.'

'Risk!' Poirot snorted. 'Where then lay the risk? Would Japp have solved the problem? No; if Number Four had not made one small mistake he would have run no risk.'

'And his mistake?' I asked, although I suspected the answer.

'*Mon ami,* he overlooked the little grey cells of Hercule Poirot.'

Poirot has his virtues, but modesty is not one of them.

CHAPTER XII

The Baited Trap

It was mid-January – a typical English winter day in London, damp and dirty. Poirot and I were sitting in two chairs well drawn up to the fire. I was aware of my friend looking at me with a quizzical smile, the meaning of which I could not fathom.

'A penny for your thoughts,' I said lightly.

'I was thinking, my friend, that at midsummer, when you first arrived, you told me that you proposed to be in this country for a couple of months only.'

'Did I say that?' I asked, rather awkwardly. 'I don't remember.'

Poirot's smile broadened.

'You did, *mon ami.* Since then, you have changed your plan, is it not so?'

'Er – yes, I have.'

'And why is that?'

'Dash it all, Poirot, you don't think I'm going to leave you all alone when you're up against a thing like the "Big Four", do you?'

Poirot nodded gently.

'Just as I thought. You are a staunch friend, Hastings. It is to serve me that you remain on here. And your wife – little Cinderella as you call her, what does she say?'

'I haven't gone into details, of course, but she understands. She'd be the last one to wish me to turn my back on a pal.'

'Yes, yes, she, too, is a loyal friend. But it is going to be a long business, perhaps.'

I nodded, rather discouraged.

'Six months already,' I mused, 'and where are we? You know, Poirot, I can't help thinking that we ought to – well, to do something.'

'Always so energetic, Hastings! And what precisely would you have me do?'

This was somewhat of a poser, but I was not going to withdraw from my position.

'We ought to take the offensive,' I urged. 'What have we done all this time?'

'More than you think, my friend. After all, we have established the identity of Number Two and Number Three, and we have learnt more than a little about the ways and methods of Number Four.'

I brightened up a little. As Poirot put it, things didn't sound so bad.

'Oh! Yes, Hastings, we have done a great deal. It is true that I am not in a position to accuse either Ryland or Madame Olivier – who would believe me? You remember I thought once I had Ryland successfully cornered? Nevertheless I have made my suspicions known in certain quarters – the highest – Lord Aldington, who enlisted my help in the matter of the stolen submarine plans, is fully cognizant of all my information respecting the Big Four – and while others may doubt, he believes. Ryland and Madame Olivier, and Li Ching Yen himself may go their ways, but there is a searchlight turned on all their movements.'

'And Number Four?' I asked.

'As I said just now – I am beginning to know and understand his methods. You may smile, Hastings – but to penetrate a man's personality, to know exactly what he will do under any given circumstances – that is the beginning of success. It is a duel between us, and whilst he is constantly giving away his mentality to me, I endeavour to let him know little or nothing of mine. He is in the light, I in the shade. I tell you, Hastings, that every day they fear me the more for my chosen inactivity.'

'They've let us alone, anyway,' I observed. 'There have been no more attempts on your life, and no ambushes of any kind.'

'No,' said Poirot thoughtfully. 'On the whole, that rather surprises me. Especially as there are one or two fairly obvious ways of getting at us which I should have thought certain to have occurred to them. You catch my meaning, perhaps?'

'An infernal machine of some kind?' I hazarded.

Poirot made a sharp click with his tongue expressive of impatience.

'But no! I appeal to your imagination, and you can suggest nothing more subtle than bombs in the fireplace. Well, well, I have need of some matches, I will promenade myself despite the weather. Pardon, my friend, but is it possible that you read *The Future of the Argentine, Mirror of Society, Cattle Breeding, The Clue of Crimson* and *Sport in the Rockies* at one and the same time?'

I laughed, and admitted that *The Clue of Crimson* was at present engaging my sole attention. Poirot shook his head sadly.

'But replace then the others on the bookshelf! Never, never shall I see you embrace the order and the method. *Mon Dieu,* what then is a bookshelf for?'

I apologized humbly, and Poirot, after replacing the offending volumes, each in its appointed place, went out and left me to uninterrupted enjoyment of my selected book.

I must admit, however, that I was half asleep when Mrs Pearson's knock at the door aroused me.

'A telegram for you, captain.'

I tore the orange envelope open without much interest.

Then I sat as though turned to stone.

It was a cable from Bronsen, my manager out at the South American ranch, and it ran as follows:

> Mrs Hastings disappeared yesterday, feared been kidnapped by some gang calling itself big four cable instructions have notified police but no clue as yet Bronsen.

I waved Mrs Pearson out of the room, and sat as though stunned, reading the words over and over again. Cinderella – kidnapped! In the hands of the infamous Big Four! God, what could I do?

Poirot! I must have Poirot. He would advise me. He would checkmate them somehow. In a few minutes now, he would be back. I must wait patiently until then. But Cinderella – in the hands of the Big Four!

Another knock. Mrs Pearson put her head in once more.

'A note for you, captain – brought by a heathen Chinaman. He's a-waiting downstairs.'

I seized it from her. It was brief and to the point.

'If you ever wish to see your wife again, go with the bearer of this note immediately. Leave no message for your friend or she will suffer.'

It was signed with a big 4.

What ought I to have done? What would you who read have done in my place?

I had no time to think. I saw only one thing – Cinderella in the power of those devils. I must obey – I dare not risk a hair of her head. I must go with this Chinaman and follow whither he led. It was a trap, yes, and it meant certain capture and possible death, but it was baited with the person dearest to me in the whole world, and I dared not hesitate.

What irked me most was to leave no word for Poirot. Once set him on my track, and all might yet be well! Dare I risk it? Apparently I was under no supervision, but yet I hesitated. It would have been so easy for the Chinaman to come up and assure himself that I was keeping to the letter of the command. Why didn't he? His very abstention made me more suspicious. I had seen so much of the omnipotence of the Big Four that I credited them with almost superhuman powers. For all I know, even the little bedraggled servant girl might be one of their agents.

No, I dared not risk it. But one thing I could do, leave the telegram. He would know then that Cinderella had disappeared, and who was responsible for her disappearance.

All this passed through my head in less time than it takes to tell, and I had clapped my hat on my head and was descending the stairs to where my guide waited, in a little over a minute.

The bearer of the message was a tall impassive Chinaman, neatly but rather shabbily dressed. He bowed and spoke to me. His English was perfect, but he spoke with a slight sing-song intonation.

'You Captain Hastings?'

'Yes,' I said.

'You give me note, please.'

I had foreseen the request, and handed him over the scrap of paper without a word. But that was not all.

'You have a telegram today, yes? Come along just now? From South America, yes?'

I realized anew the excellence of their espionage system – or it might have been a shrewd guess. Bronsen was bound to cable me. They would wait until the cable was delivered and would strike hard upon it.

No good could come of denying what was palpably true.

'Yes,' I said. 'I did get a telegram.'

'You fetch him, yes? Fetch him now.'

I ground my teeth, but what could I do? I ran upstairs again. As I did so, I thought of confiding in Mrs Pearson, at any rate as far as Cinderella's disappearance went. She was on the landing, but close behind her was the little maidservant, and I hesitated. If she *was* a spy – the words of the note danced before my eyes, '. . . she will suffer . . .' I passed into the sitting-room without speaking.

I took up the telegram and was about to pass out again when an idea struck me. Could I not leave some sign which would mean nothing to my enemies but which Poirot himself would find significant. I hurried across to the bookcase and tumbled out four books on to the floor. No fear of Poirot's not seeing them. They would outrage his eyes immediately – and coming on top of his little lecture, surely he would find them unusual. Next I put a shovelful of coal on the fire and managed to spill four knobs into the grate. I had done all I could – pray heaven Poirot would read the sign aright.

I hurried down again. The Chinaman took the telegram from me, read it, then placed it in his pocket and with a nod beckoned me to follow him.

It was a long weary march that he led me. Once we took a bus and once we went for some considerable way in a tram, and always our route led us steadily eastward. We went through strange districts, whose existence I had never dreamed of. We were down by the docks now, I knew, and I realized that I was being taken into the heart of Chinatown.

In spite of myself I shivered. Still my guide plodded on, turning and twisting through mean streets and byways, until at last he stopped at a dilapidated house and rapped four times upon the door.

It was opened immediately by another Chinaman who stood aside to let us pass in. The clanging to of the door behind me was the knell of my last hopes. I was indeed in the hands of the enemy.

I was now handed over to the second Chinaman. He led me down some rickety stairs and into a cellar which was filled with bales and casks and which exhaled a pungent odour, as of eastern spices. I felt wrapped all round with the atmosphere of the East, tortuous, cunning, sinister –

Suddenly my guide rolled aside two of the casks, and I saw a low tunnel-like opening in the wall. He motioned me to go ahead. The tunnel was of some length, and it was too low for me to stand upright. At last, however, it broadened out into a passage, and a few minutes later we stood in another cellar.

My Chinaman went forward, and rapped four times on one of the walls. A whole section of the wall swung out, leaving a narrow doorway. I passed through, and to my utter astonishment found myself in a kind of Arabian Nights' palace. A low long subterranean chamber hung with rich oriental silks, brilliantly lighted and fragrant with perfumes and spices. There were five or six silk-covered divans, and exquisite carpets of Chinese workmanship covered the ground. At the end of the room was a curtained recess. From behind these curtains came a voice.

'You have brought our honoured guest?'

'Excellency, he is here,' replied my guide.

'Let our guest enter,' was the answer.

At the same moment, the curtains were drawn aside by an unseen hand, and I was facing an immense cushioned divan on which sat a tall thin Oriental dressed in wonderfully embroidered robes, and clearly, by the length of his fingernails, a great man.

'Be seated, I pray you, Captain Hastings,' he said, with a wave of his hand. 'You acceded to my request to come immediately, I am glad to see.'

'Who are you?' I asked. 'Li Chang Yen?'

'Indeed no, I am but the humblest of the master's servants. I carry out his behests, that is all – as do other of his servants in other countries – in South America, for instance.'

I advanced a step.

'Where is she? What have you done with her out there?'

'She is in a place of safety – where none will find her. As yet, she is unharmed. You observe that I say – *as yet*!'

Cold shivers ran down my spine as I confronted this smiling devil.

'What do you want?' I cried. 'Money?'

'My dear Captain Hastings. We have no designs on your small savings, I can assure you. Not – pardon me – a very intelligent suggestion on your part. Your colleague would not have made it, I fancy.'

'I suppose,' I said heavily, 'you wanted to get me into your toils. Well, you have succeeded. I have come here with my eyes open. Do what you like with me, and let her go. She knows nothing, and she can be of no possible use to you. You've used her to get hold of me – you've got me all right, and that settles it.'

The smiling Oriental caressed his smooth cheek, watching me obliquely out of his narrow eyes.

'You go too fast,' he said purringly. 'That does not quite – settle it. In fact, to "get hold of you" as you express it, is not really our objective. But through you, we hope to get hold of your friend, M. Hercule Poirot.'

'I'm afraid you won't do that,' I said, with a short laugh.

'What I suggest is this,' continued the other, his words running on as though he had not heard me. 'You will write M. Hercule Poirot a letter, such a letter as will induce him to hasten thither and join you.'

'I shall do no such thing,' I said angrily.

'The consequences of refusal will be disagreeable.'

'Damn your consequences.'

'The alternative might be death!'

A nasty shiver ran down my spine, but I endeavoured to put a bold face upon it.

'It's no good threatening me, and bullying me. Keep your threats for Chinese cowards.'

'My threats are very real ones, Captain Hastings. I ask you again, will you write this letter?'

'I will not, and what's more, you daren't kill me. You'd have the police on your tracks in no time.'

My interlocutor clapped his hands swiftly. Two Chinese attendants appeared as it were out of the blue, and pinioned me by both arms. Their master said something rapidly to them in Chinese, and they dragged me across the floor to a spot in one corner of the big chamber. One of them stooped, and suddenly, without the least warning, the flooring gave beneath my feet. But for the restraining hand of the other man I should have gone down the yawning gap beneath me. It was inky black, and I could hear the rushing of water.

'The river,' said my questioner from his place on the divan. 'Think well, Captain Hastings. If you refuse again, you go headlong to eternity, to meet your death in the dark waters below. For the last time, will you write that letter?'

I'm not braver than most men. I admit frankly that I was scared to death, and in a blue funk. That Chinese devil meant business, I was sure of that. It was goodbye to the good old world. In spite of myself, my voice wobbled a little as I answered.

'For the last time, no! To hell with your letter!'

Then involuntarily I closed my eyes and breathed a short prayer.

CHAPTER XIII

The Mouse Walks In

Not often in a lifetime does a man stand on the edge of eternity, but when I spoke those words in that East End cellar I was perfectly certain that they were my last words on earth. I braced myself for the shock of those black, rushing waters beneath, and experienced in advance the horror of that breath-choking fall.

But to my surprise a low laugh fell on my ears. I opened my eyes. Obeying a sign from the man on the divan, my two jailers brought me back to my old seat facing him.

'You are a brave man, Captain Hastings,' he said. 'We of the East appreciate bravery. I may say that I expected you to act as you have done. That brings us to the appointed second act of your little drama. Death for yourself you have faced – will you face death for another?'

'What do you mean?' I asked hoarsely, a horrible fear creeping over me.

'Surely you have not forgotten the lady who is in our power – the Rose of the Garden.'

I stared at him in dumb agony.

'I think, Captain Hastings, that you will write that letter. See, I have a cable form here. The message I shall write on it depends on you, and means life or death for your wife.'

The sweat broke out on my brow. My tormentor continued, smiling amiably, and speaking with perfect sangfroid:

'There, captain, the pen is ready to your hand. You have only to write. If not –'

'If not?' I echoed.

'If not, that lady that you love dies – and dies slowly. My master, Li Chang Yen, amuses himself in his spare hours by devising new and ingenious methods of torture –'

'My God' I cried. 'You fiend! Not that – you wouldn't do that –'

'Shall I recount to you some of his devices?'

Without heeding my cry of protest, his speech flowed on – evenly, serenely – till with a cry of horror I clapped my hands to my ears.

'It is enough, I see. Take up the pen and write.'

'You would not dare –'

'Your speech is foolishness, and you know it. Take up the pen and write.'

'If I do?'

'Your wife goes free. The cable shall be despatched immediately.'

'How do I know that you will keep faith with me?'

'I swear it to you on the sacred tombs of my ancestors. Moreover, judge for yourself – why should I wish to do her harm? Her detention will have answered its purpose.'

'And – and Poirot?'

'We will keep him in safe custody until we have concluded our operations. Then we will let him go.'

'Will you swear that also on the tombs of your ancestors?'

'I have sworn one oath to you. That should be sufficient.'

My heart sank. I was betraying my friend – to what? For a moment I hesitated – then the terrible alternative rose like a nightmare before my eyes. Cinderella – in the hands of these Chinese devils, dying by slow torture –

A groan rose to my lips. I seized the pen. Perhaps by careful wording of the letter I could convey a warning, and Poirot would be enabled to avoid the trap. It was the only hope.

But even that hope was not to remain. The Chinaman's voice rose, suave and courteous.

'Permit me to dictate to you.'

He paused, consulted a sheaf of notes that lay by his side, and then dictated as follows:

'Dear Poirot, I think I'm on the track of Number Four. A Chinaman came this afternoon and lured me down here with a bogus message. Luckily I saw through his little game in time, and gave him the slip. Then I turned the tables on him, and managed to do a bit of shadowing on my own account – rather neatly too, I flatter myself. I'm getting a bright young lad to carry this to you. Give him half a crown, will you? That's what I promised him if it was delivered safely. I'm watching the house, and daren't leave. I shall wait for you until six o'clock, and if you haven't come then, I'll have a try at getting into the house on my own. It's too good a chance to miss, and, of course, the boy mightn't find you. But if he does, get him to bring you down here right away. And cover up those precious moustaches of yours in case anyone's watching out from the house and might recognize you.

Yours in haste,

A.H.'

Every word that I wrote plunged me deeper in despair. The thing was diabolically clever. I realized how closely every detail of our life must be known. It was just such an epistle as I might have penned myself. The acknowledgment that the Chinaman who had called that afternoon had endeavoured to 'lure me away' discounted any good I might have done by leaving my 'sign' of four books. It *had* been a trap, and I had seen through it, that was what Poirot would think. The time, too, was cleverly planned. Poirot, on receiving the note, would have just time to rush off with his innocent-looking guide, and that he would do so I knew. My determination to make my way into the house would bring him post-haste. He always displayed a ridiculous distrust of my capacities. He would be convinced that I was running into danger without being equal to the situation, and would rush down to take command of the situation.

But there was nothing to be done. I wrote as bidden. My captor took the note from me, read it, then nodded his head approvingly and handed it to one of the silent attendants who disappeared with it behind one of the silken hangings on the wall which masked a doorway.

With a smile the man opposite me picked up a cable form and wrote. He handed it to me.

It read: 'Release the white bird with all despatch.'

I gave a sigh of relief.

'You will send it at once?' I urged.

He smiled, and shook his head.

'When M. Hercule Poirot is in my hands it shall be sent. Not until then.'

'But you promised –'

'If this device fails, I may have need of our white bird – to persuade you to further efforts.'

I grew white with anger.

'My God! If you–'

He waved a long, slim yellow hand.

'Be reassured, I do not think it will fail. And the moment M. Poirot is in our hands, I will keep my oath.'

'If you play me false –'

'I have sworn it by my honoured ancestors. Have no fear. Rest here awhile. My servants will see to your needs whilst I am absent.'

I was left alone in this strange underground nest of luxury. The second Chinese attendant had reappeared. One of them brought food and drink and offered it to me, but I waved them aside. I was sick – sick – at heart –

And then suddenly the master reappeared, tall and stately in his silken robes. He directed operations. By his orders I was hustled back through the cellar and tunnel into the original house I had entered. There they took me into a ground-floor room. The windows were shuttered, but one could see through the cracks into the street. An old ragged man was shuffling along the opposite side of the road, and when I saw him make a sign to the window, I understood that he was one of the gang on watch.

'It is well,' said my Chinese friend. 'Hercule Poirot has fallen into the trap. He approaches now – and alone except for the boy who guides him. Now, Captain Hastings, you have still one more part to play. Unless you show yourself he will not enter the house. When he arrives opposite, you must go out on the step and beckon him in.'

'What?' I cried, revolted.

'You play that part alone. Remember the price of failure. If Hercule Poirot suspects anything is amiss and does not enter the house, your wife dies by the Seventy lingering Deaths! Ah! Here he is.'

With a beating heart, and a feeling of deathly sickness, I looked through the crack in the shutters. In the figure walking along the opposite side of the street I recognized my friend at once, though his coat collar was turned up and an immense yellow muffler hid the bottom part of his face. But there was no mistaking that walk, and the pose of that egg-shaped head.

It was Poirot coming to my aid in all good faith, suspecting nothing amiss. By his side ran a typical London urchin, grimy of face and ragged of apparel.

Poirot paused, looking across at the house, whilst the boy spoke to him eagerly and pointed. It was the time for me to act. I went out into the hall. At a sign from the tall Chinaman, one of the servants unlatched the door.

'Remember the price of failure,' said my enemy in a low voice.

I was outside on the steps. I beckoned to Poirot. He hastened across.

'Aha! So all is well with you, my friend. I was beginning to be anxious. You managed to get inside? Is the house empty, then?'

'Yes,' I said, in a low voice I strove to make natural. 'There must be a secret way out of it somewhere. Come in and let us look for it.'

I stepped back across the threshold. In all innocence Poirot prepared to follow me.

And then something seemed to snap in my head. I saw only too clearly the part I was playing – the part of Judas.

'Back, Poirot!' I cried. 'Back for your life. It's a trap. Never mind me. Get away at once.'

Even as I spoke – or rather shouted – my warning, hands

gripped me like a vice. One of the Chinese servants sprang past me to grab Poirot.

I saw the latter spring back, his arm raised, then suddenly a dense volume of smoke was rising round me, choking me – killing me –

I felt myself falling – suffocating – this was death –

I came to myself slowly and painfully – all my senses dazed. The first thing I saw was Poirot's face. He was sitting opposite me watching me with an anxious face. He gave a cry of joy when he saw me looking at him.

'Ah, you revive – you return to yourself. All is well! My friend – my poor friend!'

'Where am I?' I said painfully.

'Where? But *chez vous*!'

I looked round me. True enough, I was in the old familiar surroundings. And in the grate were the identical four knobs of coal I had carefully spilt there.

Poirot had followed my glance.

'But yes, that was a famous idea of yours – that and the books. See you, if they should say to me any time, "That friend of yours, that Hastings, he has not the great brain, is it not so?" I shall reply to them: "You are in error." It was an idea magnificent and superb that occurred to you there.'

'You understood their meaning then?'

'Am I an imbecile? Of course I understood. It gave me just the warning I needed, and the time to mature my plans. Somehow or other the Big Four had carried you off. With what object? Clearly not for your *beaux yeux* – equally clearly not because they feared you and wanted to get you out of the way. No, their object was plain. You would be used as a decoy to get the great Hercule Poirot into their clutches. I have long been prepared for something of the kind. I make my little preparations, and presently, sure enough, the messenger arrives – such an innocent little street urchin. Me, I swallow everything, and hasten away with him, and, very fortunately, they permit you to come out on the doorstep. That was my one fear, that I should have to dispose of them before I had reached the place where you were concealed, and that I should have to search for you – perhaps in vain – afterwards.'

'Dispose of them, did you say?' I asked feebly. 'Singlehanded.'

'Oh, there is nothing very clever about that. If one is prepared in advance, all is simple – the motto of the Boy Scout, is it not? And a very fine one. Me, I was prepared. Not so long ago, I rendered a service to a very famous chemist, who did a lot of work in connection with poison gas during the war. He devised for me a little bomb – simple and easy to carry about – one has but to throw it and poof, the smoke – and then the unconsciousness. Immediately I blow a little whistle and straightaway some of Japp's clever fellows who were watching the house here long before the boy arrived, and who managed to follow us all the way to Limehouse, came flying up and took charge of the situation.'

'But how was it you weren't unconscious too?'

'Another piece of luck. Our friend Number Four (who certainly composed that ingenious letter) permitted himself a little jest at my moustaches, which rendered it extremely easy for me to adjust my respirator under the guise of a yellow muffler.'

'I remember,' I cried eagerly, and then with the word 'remember' all the ghastly horror that I had temporarily forgotten came back to me. *Cinderella* –

I fell back with a groan.

I must have lost consciousness again for a minute or two. I awoke to find Poirot forcing some brandy between my lips.

'What is it, *mon ami*? But what is it – then? Tell me.' Word by word, I got the thing told, shuddering as I did so. Poirot uttered a cry.

'My friend! My friend! But what you must have suffered! And I who knew nothing of all this! But reassure yourself! All is well!'

'You will find her, you mean? But she is in South America. And by the time we get there – long before, she will be dead – and God knows how and in what horrible way she will have died.'

'No, no, you do not understand. She is safe and well. She has never been in their hands for one instant.'

'But I got a cable from Bronsen?'

'No, no, you did not. You may have got a cable from South America signed Bronsen – that is a very different matter. Tell me, has it never occurred to you that an organization of this kind, with ramifications all over the world, might easily strike at us through the little girl, Cinderella, whom you love so well?'

'No, never,' I replied.

'Well, it did to me. I said nothing to you because I did not want to upset you unnecessarily – but I took measures of my own. Your wife's letters all seem to have been written from the ranch, but in reality she has been in a place of safety devised by me for over three months.'

I looked at him for a long time.

'You are sure of that?'

'*Parbleu!* I know it. They tortured you with a lie!'

I turned my head aside. Poirot put his hand on my shoulder. There was something in his voice that I had never heard there before.

'You like not that I should embrace you or display the emotion, I know well. I will be very British. I will say nothing – but nothing at all. Only this – that in this last adventure of ours, the honours are all with you, and happy is the man who has such a friend as I have!'

CHAPTER XIV

The Peroxide Blonde

I was very disappointed with the results of Poirot's bomb attack on the premises in Chinatown. To begin with, the leader of the gang had escaped. When Japp's men rushed up in response to Poirot's whistle they found four Chinamen unconscious in the hall, but the man who had threatened me with death was not among them. I remembered afterwards that when I was forced out on to the doorstep, to decoy Poirot into the house, this man had kept well in the background. Presumably he was out of the danger zone of the gas bomb, and made good his escape by one of the many exits which we afterwards discovered.

From the four who remained in our hands we learnt nothing. The fullest investigation by the police failed to bring to light anything to connect them with the Big Four. They were ordinary low-class residents of the district, and they professed bland ignorance of the name Li Chang Yen. A Chinese gentleman had hired them for service in the house by the waterside, and they knew nothing whatever of his private affairs.

By the next day I had, except for a slight headache, completely recovered from the effects of Poirot's gas bomb. We went down together to Chinatown and searched the house from which I had been rescued. The premises consisted of two ramshackle houses joined together by an underground passage. The ground floors and the upper storeys of each were unfurnished and deserted, the broken windows covered by decaying shutters. Japp had already been prying about in the cellars, and had discovered the secret of the entrance to the subterranean chamber where I had spent such an unpleasant half-hour. Closer investigation confirmed the impression that it had made on me the night before. The silks on the walls and divans and the carpets on the floor were of exquisite workmanship. Although I know very little about Chinese art, I could appreciate that every article in the room was perfect of its kind.

With the aid of Japp and some of his men we conducted a most thorough search of the apartment. I had cherished high hopes that we would find documents of importance. A list, perhaps, of some of the more important agents of the Big Four, or cipher notes of some of their plans, but we discovered nothing of the kind. The only papers we found in the whole place were the notes which the Chinaman had consulted whilst he was dictating the letter to Poirot. These consisted of a very complete record of each of our careers, and an estimate of our characters, and suggestions about the weaknesses through which we might best be attacked.

Poirot was most childishly delighted with this discovery. Personally I could not see that it was of any value whatever, especially as whoever compiled the notes was ludicrously mistaken in some of his opinions. I pointed this out to my friend when we were back in our rooms.

'My dear Poirot,' I said, 'you know now what the enemy thinks of us. He appears to have a grossly exaggerated idea of your brain power, and to have absurdly underrated mine, but I do not see how we are better off for knowing this.'

Poirot chuckled in rather an offensive way.

'You do not see, Hastings, no? But surely now we can prepare ourselves for some of their methods of attack now that we are warned of some of our faults. For instance, my friend, we know that you should think before you act. Again, if you meet a red-haired young woman in trouble you should eye her – what you say – askance, is it not?'

Their notes had contained some absurd references to my supposed impulsiveness, and had suggested that I was susceptible to the charms of young women with hair of a certain shade. I thought Poirot's reference to be in the worst of taste, but fortunately I was able to counter him.

'And what about you?' I demanded. 'Are you going to try to cure your "overweening vanity"? Your "finicky tidiness"?'

I was quoting, and I could see that he was not pleased with my retort.

'Oh, without doubt, Hastings, in some things they deceive themselves – *tant mieux*! They will learn in due time. Meanwhile we have learnt something, and to know is to be prepared.'

This last was a favourite axiom of his lately; so much so that I had begun to hate the sound of it.

'We know something, Hastings,' he continued. 'Yes, we know something – and that is to the good – but we do not know nearly enough. We must know more.'

'In what way?'

Poirot settled himself back in his chair, straightened a box of matches which I had thrown carelessly down on the table, and assumed an attitude that I knew only too well. I saw that he was prepared to hold forth at some length.

'See you, Hastings, we have to contend against four adversaries, that is against four different personalities. With Number One we have never come into personal contact – we know him, as it were, only by the impress of his mind – and in passing, Hastings, I will tell you that I begin to understand that mind very well – a mind most subtle and Oriental – every scheme and plot that we have encountered has emanated from the brain of Li Chang Yen. Number Two and Number Three are so powerful, so high up, that they are for the present immune from our attacks. Nevertheless what is their safeguard is, by a perverse chance, our safeguard also. They are so much in the limelight that their movements must be carefully ordered. And so we come to the last member of the gang – we come to the man known as Number Four.'

Poirot's voice altered a little, as it always did when speaking of this particular individual.

'Number Two and Number Three are able to succeed, to go on their way unscathed, owing to their notoriety and their assured position. Number Four succeeds for the opposite reason – he succeeds by the way of obscurity. Who is he? Nobody knows. What does he look like? Again nobody knows. How many times have we seen him, you and I? Five times, is it not? And could either of us say truthfully that we could be sure of recognizing him again?'

I was forced to shake my head, as I ran back in my mind over those five different people who, incredible as it seemed, were one and the same man. The burly lunatic asylum keeper, the man in the buttoned-up overcoat in Paris, James, the footman, the quiet young medical man in the Yellow Jasmine case, and the Russian professor. In no way did any two of these people resemble each other.

'No,' I said hopelessly. 'We've nothing to go by whatsoever.'

Poirot smiled.

'Do not, I pray of you, give way to such enthusiastic despair. We know one or two things.'

'What kind of things?' I asked sceptically.

'We know that he is a man of medium height, and of medium or fair colouring. If he were a tall man of swarthy complexion he could never have passed himself off as the fair, stocky doctor. It is child's play, of course, to put on an additional inch or so for the part of James, or the Professor. In the same way he must have a short, straight nose. Additions can be built on to a nose by skilful make-up, but a large nose cannot be successfully reduced at a moment's notice. Then again, he must be a fairly young man, certainly not over thirty-five. You see, we are getting somewhere. A man between thirty and thirty-five, of medium height and colouring, an adept in the art of make-up, and with very few or any teeth of his own.'

'What?'

'Surely, Hastings. As the keeper, his teeth were broken and discoloured, in Paris they were even and white, as a doctor they protruded slightly, and as Savaronoff they had unusually long canines. Nothing alters the face so completely as a different set of teeth. You see where all this is leading us?'

'Not exactly,' I said cautiously.

'A man carries his profession written in his face, they say.'

'He's a criminal,' I cried.

'He is an adept in the art of making-up.'

'It's the same thing.'

'Rather a sweeping statement, Hastings, and one which would hardly be appreciated by the theatrical world. Do you not see that the man is, or has been, at one time or another, an actor?'

'An actor?'

'But certainly. He has the whole technique at his fingertips. Now there are two classes of actors, the one who sinks himself in his part, and the one who manages to impress his personality upon it. It is from the latter class that actor-managers usually spring. They seize a part and mould it to their own personality. The former class is quite likely to spend its days doing Mr Lloyd George at different music halls, or impersonating old men with beards in repertory plays. It is among the former class that we must look for our Number Four. He is a supreme artist in the way he sinks himself in each part he plays.'

I was growing interested.

'So you fancy you may be able to trace his identity through his connection with the stage?'

'Your reasoning is always brilliant, Hastings.'

'It might have been better,' I said coldly, 'if the idea had come to you sooner. We have wasted a lot of time.'

'You are in error, *mon ami*. No more time has been wasted than was unavoidable. For some months now my agents have been engaged on the task. Joseph Aarons is one of them. You remember him? They have compiled a list for me of men fulfilling the necessary qualifications – young men round about the age of thirty, of more or less nondescript appearance, and with a gift for playing character parts – men, moreover, who have definitely left the stage within the last three years.'

'Well?' I said, deeply interested.

'The list was, necessarily, rather a long one. For some time now, we have been engaged on the task of elimination. And finally we have boiled the whole thing down to four names. Here they are, my friend.'

He tossed me over a sheet of paper. I read its contents aloud.

'"Ernest Luttrell. Sons of a North Country parson. Always had a kink of some kind in his moral make-up. Was expelled from his public school. Went on the stage at the age of twenty-three. (Then followed a list of parts he had played, with dates and places.) Addicted to drugs. Supposed to have gone to Australia four years ago. Cannot be traced after leaving England. Age 32, height 5ft. 10½in., clean-shaven, hair brown, nose straight, complexion fair, eyes grey.

' "John St Maur. Assumed name. Real name not known. Believed to be of cockney extraction. On stage since quite a child. Did music hall impersonations. Not been heard of for three years. Age, about 33, height 5ft. 10in., slim build, blue eyes, fair colouring

' "Austen Lee. Assumed name. Real name Austen Foly. Good family. Always had taste for acting and distinguished himself in that way at Oxford. Brilliant war record. Acted in – (The usual list followed. It included many repertory plays.) An enthusiast on criminology. Had bad nervous breakdown as the result of a motor accident three and half years ago, and has not appeared on the stage since. No clue to his present whereabouts. Age 35, height 5ft. 9½in., complexion fair, eyes blue, hair brown.

' "Claud Darrell. Supposed to be real name. Some mystery about his origin. Played at music halls, and also in repertory plays. Seems to have had no intimate friends. Was in China in 1919. Returned by way of America. Played a few parts in New York. Did not appear on stage one night, and has never been heard of since. New York police say most mysterious disappearance. Age about 33, hair brown, fair complexion, grey eyes. Height 5ft. 10½in."

'Most interesting,' I said, as I laid down the paper. 'And so this is the result of the investigation of months? These four names. Which of them are you inclined to suspect?'

Poirot made an eloquent gesture.

'*Mon ami,* for the moment it is an open question. I would just point out to you that Claud Darrell has been in China and America – a fact not without significance, perhaps, but we must not allow ourselves to be unduly biased by that point. It may be a mere coincidence.'

'And the next step?' I asked eagerly.

'Affairs are already in train. Every day cautiously worded

advertisements will appear. Friends and relatives of one or other will be asked to communicate with my solicitor at his office. Even today we might – Aha, the telephone! Probably it is, as usual, the wrong number, and they will regret to have troubled us, but it may be – yes, it may be – that something has arisen.'

I crossed the room and picked up the receiver.

'Yes, yes. M. Poirot's rooms. Yes, Captain Hastings speaking. Oh, it's you, Mr McNeil! (McNeil and Hodgson were Poirot's solicitors.) I'll tell him. Yes, we'll come round at once.'

I replaced the receiver and turned to Poirot, my eyes dancing with excitement.

'I say, Poirot, there's a woman there. Friend of Claud Darrell's. Miss Flossie Monro. McNeil wants you to come round.'

'At the instant!' cried Poirot, disappearing into his bedroom, and reappearing with a hat.

A taxi soon took us to our destination, and we were ushered into Mr McNeil's private office. Sitting in the armchair facing the solicitor was a somewhat lurid-looking lady no longer in her first youth. Her hair was of an impossible yellow, and was prolific in curls over each ear, her eyelids were heavily blackened, and she had by no means forgotten the rouge and the lip salve.

'Ah, here is M. Poirot!' said Mr McNeil. 'M. Poirot, this is Miss – er – Monro, who has very kindly called to give us some information.'

'Ah, but that is most kind!' cried Poirot.

He came forward with great empressement, and shook the lady warmly by the hand.

'Mademoiselle blooms like a flower in this dry-as-dust old office,' he added, careless of the feelings of Mr McNeil.

This outrageous flattery was not without effect. Miss Monro blushed and simpered.

'Oh, go on now, Mr Poirot!' she exclaimed. 'I know what you Frenchmen are like.'

'Mademoiselle, we are not mute like Englishmen before beauty. Not that I am a Frenchman – I am a Belgian, you see.'

'I've been to Ostend myself,' said Miss Monro.

The whole affair, as Poirot would have said, was marching splendidly.

'And so you can tell us something about Mr Claud Darrell?' continued Poirot.

'I knew Mr Darrell very well at one time,' explained the lady. 'And I saw your advertisement, being out of a shop for the moment, and, my time being my own, I said to myself: There, they want to know about poor old Claudie – lawyers, too – maybe it's fortune looking for the rightful heir. I'd better go round at once.'

Mr McNeil rose.

'Well, Monsieur Poirot, shall I leave you for a little conversation with Miss Monro?'

'You are too amiable. But stay – a little idea presents itself to me. The hour of the *déjeuner* approaches. Mademoiselle will perhaps honour me by coming out to luncheon with me?'

Miss Monro's eyes glistened. It struck me that she was in exceedingly low water, and that the chance of a square meal was not to be despised.

A few minutes later saw us all in a taxi, bound for one of London's most expensive restaurants. Once arrived there, Poirot ordered a most delectable lunch, and then turned to his guest.

'And for wine, mademoiselle? What do you say to champagne?'

Miss Monro said nothing – or everything.

The meal started pleasantly. Poirot replenished the lady's glass with thoughtful assiduity, and gradually slid on to the topic nearest his heart.

'The poor Mr Darrell. What a pity he is not with us.'

'Yes, indeed,' sighed Miss Monro. 'Poor boy, I do wonder what's become of him.'

'Is it a long time since you have seen him, yes?'

'Oh, simply ages – not since the war. He was a funny boy, Claudie, very close about things, never told you a word about himself. But, of course, that all fits in if he's a missing heir. Is it a title, Mr Poirot?'

'Alas, a mere heritage,' said Poirot unblushingly. 'But you see, it may be a question of identification. That is why it is necessary for us to find someone who knew him very well indeed. You knew him very well, did you not, mademoiselle?'

'I don't mind telling you, Mr Poirot. You're a gentleman. You know how to order a lunch for a lady – which is more than some of these young whippersnappers do nowadays. Downright mean, I call it. As I was saying, you being a Frenchman won't be shocked. Ah, you Frenchmen! Naughty, naughty!' She wagged her finger at him in an excess of archness. 'Well, there it was, me and Claudie, two young things – what else could you expect? And I've still a kindly feeling for him. Though, mind you, he didn't treat me well – no, he didn't – he didn't treat me well at all. Not as a lady should be treated. They're all the same when it comes to a question of money.'

'No, no, mademoiselle, do not say that,' protested Poirot, filling up her glass once more. 'Could you now describe this Mr Darrell to me?'

'He wasn't anything so very much to look at,' said Flossie Monro dreamily. 'Neither tall nor short, you know, but quite well set up. Spruce looking. Eyes a sort of blue-grey. And more or less fair-haired, I suppose. But oh, what an artist! *I* never saw anyone to touch him in the profession! He'd have made his name before now if it hadn't been for jealousy. Ah, Mr Poirot, jealousy – you wouldn't believe it, you really wouldn't, what we artists have to suffer through jealousy. Why, I remember once at Manchester –'

We displayed what patience we could in listening to a long complicated story about a pantomime, and the infamous conduct of the principal boy. Then Poirot led her gently back to the subject of Claud Darrell.

'It is very interesting, all this that you are able to tell us, mademoiselle, about Mr Darrell. Women are such wonderful observers – they see everything, they notice the little detail that escapes the mere man. I have seen a woman identify one man out of a dozen others – and why, do you think? She had observed that he had a trick of stroking his nose when he was agitated.

Now would a man ever have thought of noticing a thing like that?'

'Did you ever!' cried Miss Monro. 'I suppose we do notice things. I remember Claudie, now I come to think of it, always fiddling with his bread at table. He'd get a little piece between his fingers and then dab it round to pick up crumbs. I've seen him do it a hundred times. Why, I'd know him anywhere by that one trick of his.'

'Is not that just what I say? The marvellous observation of a woman. And did you ever speak to him about this little habit of his, mademoiselle?'

'No, I didn't, Mr Poirot. You know what men are! They don't like you to notice things – especially if it should seem you were telling them off about it. I never said a word – but many's the time I smiled to myself. Bless you, he never knew he was doing it even.'

Poirot nodded gently. I noticed that his own hand was shaking a little as he stretched it out to his glass.

'Then there is always handwriting as a means of establishing identity,' he remarked. 'Without doubt you have preserved a letter written by Mr Darrell?'

Flossie Monro shook her head regretfully.

'He was never one for writing. Never wrote me a line in his life.'

'That is a pity,' said Poirot.

'I tell you what, though,' said Miss Monro suddenly. 'I've got a photograph if that would be any good?'

'You have a photograph?'

Poirot almost sprang from his seat with excitement.

'It's quite an old one – eight years old at least.'

'*Ça ne fait rien!* No matter how old and faded! Ah, *ma foi*, but what stupendous luck! You will permit me to inspect that photograph, mademoiselle?'

'Why, of course.'

'Perhaps you will even permit me to have a copy made? It would not take long.'

'Certainly if you like.'

Miss Monro rose.

'Well, I must run away,' she declared archly. 'Very glad to have met you and your friend, Mr Poirot.'

'And the photograph? When may I have it?'

'I'll look it out tonight. I think I know where to lay my hands upon it. And I'll send it to you right away.'

'A thousand thanks, mademoiselle. You are all that is of the most amiable. I hope that we shall soon be able to arrange another little lunch together.'

'As soon as you like,' said Miss Monro. 'I'm willing.'

'Let me see, I do not think that I have your address?'

With a grand air, Miss Monro drew a card from her handbag, and handed it to him. It was a somewhat dirty card, and the original address had been scratched out and another substituted in pencil.

Then, with a good many bows and gesticulations on Poirot's part, we bade farewell to the lady and got away.

'Do you really think this photograph so important?' I asked Poirot.

'Yes, *mon ami*. The camera does not lie. One can magnify a photograph, seize salient points that otherwise would remain unnoticed. And then there are a thousand details – such as the structure of the ears, which no one could ever describe to you in words. Oh, yes, it is a great chance, this, which has come our way! That is why I propose to take precautions.'

He went across to the telephone as he finished speaking, and gave a number which I knew to be that of a private detective agency which he sometimes employed. His instructions were clear and definite. Two men were to go to the address he gave, and, in general terms, were to watch over the safety of Miss Monro. They were to follow her wherever she went.

Poirot hung up the receiver and came back to me.

'Do you really think that necessary, Poirot?' I asked.

'It may be. There is no doubt that we are watched, you and I, and since that is so, they will soon know with whom we were lunching today. And it is possible that Number Four will scent danger.'

About twenty minutes later the telephone bell rang. I answered it. A curt voice spoke into the phone.

'Is that Mr Poirot? St James's Hospital speaking. A young woman was brought in ten minutes ago. Street accident. Miss Flossie Monro. She is asking very urgently for Mr Poirot. But he must come at once. She can't possibly last long.'

I repeated the words to Poirot. His face went white.

'Quick, Hastings. We must go like the wind.'

A taxi took us to the hospital in less than ten minutes. We asked for Miss Monro, and were taken immediately to the Accident Ward. But a white-capped sister met us in the doorway.

Poirot read the news in her face.

'It is over, eh?'

'She died six minutes ago.'

Poirot stood as though stunned.

The nurse, mistaking his emotion, began speaking gently.

'She did not suffer, and she was unconscious towards the last. She was run over by a motor, you know – and the driver of the car did not even stop. Wicked, isn't it? I hope someone took the number.'

'The stars fight against us,' said Poirot, in a low voice.

'You would like to see her?'

The nurse led the way, and we followed.

Poor Flossie Monro, with her rouge and her dyed hair. She lay there very peacefully, with a little smile on her lips.

'Yes,' murmured Poirot. 'The stars fight against us – but is it the stars?' He lifted his head as though struck by a sudden idea. 'Is it the stars, Hastings? If it is not – if it is not . . . Oh, I swear to you, my friend, standing here by this poor woman's body, that I will have no mercy when the time comes!'

'What do you mean?' I asked.

But Poirot had turned to the nurse and was eagerly demanding information. A list of the articles found in her handbag was finally obtained. Poirot gave a suppressed cry as he read it over.

'You see, Hastings, you see?'

'See what?'

'There is no mention of a latch-key. But she must have had a latch-key with her. No, she was run down in cold blood, and the first person who bent over her took the key from her bag. But we may yet be in time. He may not have been able to find at once what he sought.'

Another taxi took us to the address Flossie Monro had given us, a squalid block of Mansions in an unsavoury neighbourhood. It was some time before we could gain admission to Miss Monro's flat, but we had at least the satisfaction of knowing that no one could leave it whilst we were on guard outside.

Eventually we got in. It was plain that someone had been before us. The contents of drawers and cupboards were strewn all over the floor. Locks had been forced, and small tables had even been overthrown, so violent had been the searcher's haste.

Poirot began to hunt through the débris. Suddenly he stood erect with a cry, holding out something. It was an old-fashioned photograph frame – empty.

He turned it slowly over. Affixed to the back was a small round label – a price label.

'It cost four shillings,' I commented.

'*Mon Dieu!* Hastings, use your eyes. That is a new clean label. It was stuck there by the man who took out the photograph, the man who was here before us, but knew that we should come, and so left this for us – Claud Darrell – alias Number Four.'

CHAPTER XV

The Terrible Catastrophe

It was after the tragic death of Miss Flossie Monro that I began to be aware of a change in Poirot. Up to now, his invincible confidence in himself had stood the test. But it seemed as though, at last, the long strain was beginning to tell. His manner was grave and brooding, and his nerves were on edge. In these days he was as jumpy as a cat. He avoided all discussion of the Big Four as far as possible, and seemed to throw himself into his ordinary work with almost his old ardour. Nevertheless, I knew that he was secretly active in the big matter. Extraordinary-looking Slavs were constantly calling to see him, and though he vouchsafed no explanation as to these mysterious activities, I realized that he was building some new defence or weapon of opposition with the help of these somewhat repulsive-looking foreigners. Once, purely by chance, I happened to see the entries in his passbook – he had asked me to verify some small item – and I noticed the paying out of a huge sum – a huge sum even for Poirot who was coining money nowadays – to some Russian with apparently every letter of the alphabet in his name.

But he gave no clue as to the line on which he proposed to operate. Only over and over again he gave utterance to one phrase. 'It is a mistake to underestimate your adversary. Remember that, *mon ami*.' And I realized that that was the pitfall he was striving at all costs to avoid.

So matters went on until the end of March, and then one morning Poirot made a remark which startled me considerably.

'This morning, my friend, I should recommend the best suit. We go to call upon the Home Secretary.'

'Indeed? That is very exciting. He has called you in to take up a case?'

'Not exactly. The interview is of my seeking. You may remember my saying that I once did him some small service? He is inclined to be foolishly enthusiastic over my capabilities in consequence, and I am about to trade on this attitude of his. As you know, the French Premier, M. Desjardeaux, is over in London, and at my request the Home Secretary has arranged for him to be present at our little conference this morning.'

The Right Honourable Sydney Crowther, His Majesty's Secretary of State for Home Affairs, was a well-known and popular figure. A man of some fifty years of age, with a quizzical expression and shrewd grey eyes, he received us with that delightful bonhomie of manner which was well-known to be one of his principal assets.

Standing with his back to the fireplace was a tall thin man with a pointed black beard and a sensitive face.

'M. Desjardeaux,' said Crowther. 'Allow me to introduce to you M. Hercule Poirot of whom you may, perhaps, already have heard.'

The Frenchman bowed and shook hands.

'I have indeed heard of M. Hercule Poirot,' he said pleasantly. 'Who has not?'

'You are too amiable, monsieur,' said Poirot, bowing, but his face flushed with pleasure.

'Any word for an old friend?' asked a quiet voice, and a man came forward from a corner by a tall bookcase.

It was our old acquaintance, Mr Ingles.

Poirot shook him warmly by the hand.

'And now, M. Poirot,' said Crowther. 'We are at your service. I understand you to say that you had a communication of the utmost importance to make to us.'

'That is so, monsieur. There is in the world today a vast organization – an organization of crime. It is controlled by four individuals, who are known and spoken of as the Big Four. Number One is a Chinaman, Li Chang Yen; Number Two is the American multi-millionaire, Abe Ryland; Number Three is a Frenchwoman; Number Four I have every reason to believe is an obscure English actor called Claud Darrell. These four are banded together to destroy the existing social order, and to replace it with an anarchy in which they would reign as dictators.'

'Incredible,' muttered the Frenchman. 'Ryland, mixed up with a thing of that kind? Surely the idea is too fantastic.'

'Listen, monsieur, whilst I recount to you some of the doings of this Big Four.'

It was an enthralling narrative which Poirot unfolded. Familiar as I was with all the details, they thrilled me anew as I heard the bald recital of our adventures and escapes.

M. Desjardeaux looked mutely at Mr Crowther as Poirot finished. The other answered the look.

'Yes, M. Desjardeaux, I think we must admit the existence of a "Big Four". Scotland Yard was inclined to jeer at first, but they have been forced to admit that M. Poirot was right in many of his claims. I cannot but feel that M. Poirot – er – exaggerates a little.'

For answer Poirot set forth ten salient points. I have been asked not to give them to the public even now, and so I refrain from doing so, but they included the extraordinary disasters to submarines which occurred in a certain month, and also a series of aeroplane accidents and forced landings. According to Poirot, these were all the work of the Big Four, and bore witness to the fact that they were in possession of various scientific secrets unknown to the world at large.

This brought us straight to the question which I had been waiting for the French Premier to ask.

'You say that the third member of this organization is a Frenchwoman. Have you any idea of her name?'

'It is a well-known name, monsieur. An honoured name. Number Three is no less than the famous Madame Olivier.'

At the mention of the world-famous scientist, successor to the Curies, M. Desjardeaux positively bounded from his chair, his face purple with emotion.

'Madame Olivier! Impossible! Absurd! It is an insult what you say there!'

Poirot shook his head gently, but made no answer.

Desjardeaux looked at him in stupefaction for some moments. Then his face cleared, and he glanced at the Home Secretary and tapped his forehead significantly.

'M. Poirot is a great man,' he observed. 'But even the great man – sometimes he has his little mania, does he not? And seeks in high places for fancied conspiracies. It is well-known. You agree with me, do you not, Mr Crowther?'

The Home Secretary did not answer for some minutes. Then he spoke slowly and heavily.

'Upon my soul, I don't know,' he said at last. 'I have always had and still have the utmost belief in M. Poirot, but – well, this takes a bit of believing.'

'This Li Chang Yen, too,' continued M. Desjardeaux. 'Who has ever heard of him?'

'I have,' said the unexpected voice of Mr Ingles.

The Frenchman stared at him, and he stared placidly back again, looking more like a Chinese idol than ever. 'Mr Ingles,' explained the Home Secretary, 'is the greatest authority we have on the interior of China.'

'And you have heard of this Li Chang Yen?'

'Until M. Poirot here came to me, I imagined that I was the only man in England who had. Make no mistake, M. Desjardeaux, there is only one man in China who counts today – Li Chang Yen. He has, perhaps, I only say perhaps, the finest brain in the world at the present time.'

M. Desjardeaux sat as though stunned. Presently, however, he rallied.

'There may be something in what you say, M. Poirot.' he said coldly. 'But as regards Madame Olivier, you are most certainly mistaken. She is a true daughter of France, and devoted solely to the cause of science.'

Poirot shrugged his shoulders and did not answer.

There was a minute or two's pause, and then my little friend rose to his feet, with an air of dignity that sat rather oddly upon his quaint personality.

'That is all I have to say, messieurs – to warn you. I thought it likely that I should not be believed. But at least you will be on your guard. My words will sink in, and each fresh event that comes along will confirm your wavering faith. It was necessary for me to speak now – later I might not have been able to do so.'

'You mean –?' asked Crowther, impressed in spite of himself by the gravity of Poirot's tone.

'I mean, monsieur, that since I have penetrated the identity of Number Four, my life is not worth an hour's purchase. He will seek to destroy me at all costs – and not for nothing is he named "the Destroyer". Messieurs, I salute you. To you, M. Crowther, I deliver this key, and this sealed envelope. I have got together all my notes on the case, and my ideas as to how best to meet the menace that any day may break upon the world, and have placed them in a certain safe deposit. In the event of my death, M. Crowther, I authorize you to take charge of those papers and make what use you can of them. And now, messieurs, I wish you good day.'

Desjardeaux merely bowed coldly, but Crowther sprang up and held out his hand.

'You have converted me, M. Poirot. Fantastic as the whole thing seems, I believe utterly in the truth of what you have told us.'

Ingles left at the same time as we did.

'I am not disappointed with the interview,' said Poirot, as we walked along. 'I did not expect to convince Desjardeaux, but I have at least ensured that, if I die, my knowledge does not die with me. And I have made one or two converts. *Pas si mal!*'

'I'm with you, as you know,' said Ingles. 'By the way, I'm going out to China as soon as I can get off.'

'Is that wise?'

'No,' said Ingles drily. 'But it's necessary. One must do what one can.'

'Ah, you are a brave man!' cried Poirot with emotion. 'If we were not in the street, I would embrace you.'

I fancied that Ingles looked rather relieved.

'I don't suppose that I shall be in any more danger in China than you are in London,' he growled.

'That is possibly true enough,' admitted Poirot. 'I hope that they will not succeed in massacring Hastings also, that is all. That would annoy me greatly.'

I interrupted this cheerful conversation to remark that I had no intention of letting myself be massacred, and shortly afterwards Ingles parted from us.

For some time we went along in silence, which Poirot at length broke by uttering a totally unexpected remark.

'I think – I really think – that I shall have to bring my brother into this.'

'Your brother,' I cried, astonished. 'I never knew you had a brother?'

'You surprise me, Hastings. Do you not know that all celebrated detectives have brothers who would be even more celebrated than they are were it not for constitutional indolence?'

Poirot employs a peculiar manner sometimes which makes it well nigh impossible to know whether he is jesting or in earnest. That manner was very evident at the moment.

'What is your brother's name?' I asked, trying to adjust myself to this new idea.

'Achille Poirot,' replied Poirot gravely. 'He lives near Spa in Belgium.'

'What does he do?' I asked with some curiosity, putting aside a half-formed wonder as to the character and disposition of the late Madame Poirot, and her classical taste in Christian names.

'He does nothing. He is, as I tell, of a singularly indolent disposition. But his abilities are hardly less than my own – which is saying a great deal.'

'Is he like you to look at?'

'Not unlike. But not nearly so handsome. And he wears no moustaches.'

'Is he older than you, or younger?'

'He happens to have been born on the same day.'

'A twin,' I cried.

'Exactly, Hastings. You jump to the right conclusion with unfailing accuracy. But here we are at home again. Let us at once get to work on that little affair of the Duchess's necklace.'

But the Duchess's necklace was doomed to wait awhile. A case of quite another description was waiting for us.

Our landlady, Mrs Pearson, at once informed us that a hospital nurse had called and was waiting to see Poirot.

We found her sitting in the big armchair facing the window, a pleasant-faced woman of middle age, in a dark blue uniform. She was a little reluctant to come to the point, but Poirot soon put her at her ease, and she embarked upon her story.

'You see, M. Poirot, I've never come across anything of the kind before. I was sent for, from the Lark Sisterhood, to go down to a case in Hertfordshire. An old gentleman, it is, Mr Templeton. Quite a pleasant house, and quite pleasant people. The wife, Mrs Templeton, is much younger than the husband, and he has a son by his first marriage who lives there. I don't know that the young man and the stepmother always get on together. He's not quite what you'd call normal – not "wanting" exactly, but decidedly dull in the intellect. Well, this illness of Mr Templeton's seemed to me from the first to be mysterious. At times there seemed really nothing the matter with him, and then he suddenly has one of these gastric attacks with pain and vomiting. But the doctor seemed quite satisfied, and it wasn't for me to say anything. But I couldn't help thinking about it. And then –' She paused, and became rather red.

'Something happened which aroused your suspicions?' suggested Poirot.

'Yes.'

But she still seemed to find it difficult to go on.

'I found the servants were passing remarks too.'

'About Mr Templeton's illness?'

'Oh, no! About – about this other thing –'

'Mrs Templeton?'

'Yes.'

'Mrs Templeton and the doctor, perhaps?'

Poirot had an uncanny flair in these things. The nurse threw him a grateful glance and went on.

'They *were* passing remarks. And then one day I happened to see them together myself – in the garden –'

It was left at that. Our client was in such an agony of outraged propriety that no one could feel it necessary to ask exactly what she had seen in the garden. She had evidently seen quite enough to make up her own mind on the situation.

'The attacks got worse and worse. Dr Treves said it was all perfectly natural and to be expected, and that Mr Templeton could not possibly live long, but I've never seen anything like it before myself – not in all my long experience of nursing. It seemed to me much more like some form of –'

She paused, hesitating.

'Arsenical poisoning?' said Poirot helpfully.

She nodded.

'And then, too, he, the patient, I mean, said something queer. "They'll do for me, the four of them. They'll do for me yet." '

'Eh?' said Poirot quickly.

'Those were his very words, M. Poirot. He was in great pain at the time, of course, and hardly knew what he was saying.'

' "They'll do for me, the four of them," ' repeated Poirot thoughtfully. 'What did he mean by "the four of them", do you think?'

'That I can't say, M. Poirot. I thought perhaps he meant his wife and son, and the doctor, and perhaps Miss Clark, Mrs Templeton's companion. That would make four, wouldn't it? He might think they were all in league against him.'

'Quite so, quite so,' said Poirot, in a preoccupied voice. 'What about food? Could you take no precautions about that?'

'I'm always doing what I can. But, of course, sometimes Mrs Templeton insists on bringing him his food herself, and then there are the times when I am off duty.'

'Exactly. And you are not sure enough of your ground to go to the police?'

The nurse's face showed her horror at the mere idea.

'What I have done, M. Poirot, is this. Mr Templeton had a very bad attack after partaking of a bowl of soup. I took a little from the bottom of the bowl afterwards, and have brought it up with me. I have been spared for the day to visit a sick mother, as Mr Templeton was well enough to be left.'

She drew out a little bottle of dark fluid and handed it to Poirot.

'Excellent, mademoiselle. We will have this analysed immediately. If you will return here in, say, an hour's time I think that we shall be able to dispose of your suspicions one way or another.'

First extracting from our visitor her name and qualifications, he ushered her out. Then he wrote a note and sent it off together with the bottle of soup. Whilst we waited to hear the result, Poirot amused himself by verifying the nurse's credentials, somewhat to my surprise.

'No, no, my friend,' he declared. 'I do well to be careful. Do not forget the Big Four are on our track.'

However, he soon elicited the information that a nurse of the name of Mabel Palmer was a member of the Lark Institute and had been sent to the case in question.

'So far, so good,' he said, with a twinkle. 'And now here comes Nurse Palmer back again, and here also is our analyst's report.'

'Is there arsenic in it?' she asked breathlessly.

Poirot shook his head, refolding the paper.

'No.'

We were both immeasurably surprised.

'There is no arsenic in it,' continued Poirot. 'But there is antimony, and that being the case, we will start immediately for Hertfordshire. Pray Heaven that we are not too late.'

It was decided that the simplest plan was for Poirot to represent himself truly as a detective, but that the ostensible reason of his visit should be to question Mrs Templeton about a servant formerly in her employment whose name he obtained from Nurse Palmer, and whom he could represent as being concerned in a jewel robbery.

It was late when we arrived at Elmstead, as the house was called. We had allowed Nurse Palmer to precede us by about twenty minutes, so that there should be no question of our all arriving together.

Mrs Templeton, a tall dark woman, with sinuous movements

and uneasy eyes, received us. I noticed that as Poirot announced his profession, she drew in her breath with a sudden hiss, as though badly startled, but she answered his question about the maidservant readily enough. And then, to test her, Poirot embarked upon a long history of a poisoning case in which a guilty wife had figured. His eyes never left her face as he talked, and try as she would, she could hardly conceal her rising agitation. Suddenly, with an incoherent word of excuse, she hurried from the room.

We were not long left alone. A squarely-built man with a small red moustache and pince-nez came in.

'Dr Treves,' he introduced himself. 'Mrs Templeton asked me to make her excuses to you. She's in a very bad state, you know. Nervous strain. Worry over her husband and all that. I've prescribed bed and bromide. But she hopes you'll stay and take pot luck, and I'm to do host. We've heard of you down here, M. Poirot, and we mean to make the most of you. Ah, here's Micky!'

A shambling young man entered the room. He had a very round face, and foolish-looking eyebrows raised as though in perpetual surprise. He grinned awkwardly as he shook hands. This was clearly the 'wanting' son.

Presently we all went into dinner. Dr Treves left the room – to open some wine, I think – and suddenly the boy's physiognomy underwent a startling change. He leant forward, staring at Poirot.

'You've come about Father,' he said, nodding his head. '*I* know. I know lots of things – but nobody thinks I do. Mother will be glad when Father's dead and she can marry Dr Treves. She isn't my own mother, you know. I don't like her. She wants Father to die.'

It was all rather horrible. Luckily, before Poirot had time to reply, the doctor came back, and we had to carry on a forced conversation.

And then suddenly Poirot lay back in his chair with a hollow groan. His face was contorted with pain.

'My dear sir, what's the matter?' cried the doctor.

'A sudden spasm. I am used to them. No, no, I require no assistance from you, doctor. If I might lie down upstairs.'

His request was instantly acceded to, and I accompanied him upstairs, where he collapsed on the bed, groaning heavily.

For the first minute or two I had been taken in, but I had quickly realized that Poirot was – as he would have put it – playing the comedy, and that his object was to be left alone upstairs near the patient's room.

Hence I was quite prepared when, the instant we were alone, he sprang up.

'Quick, Hastings, the window. There is ivy outside. We can climb down before they begin to suspect.'

'Climb down?'

'Yes, we must get out of this house at once. You saw him at dinner?'

'The doctor?'

'No, young Templeton. His trick with his bread. Do you remember what Flossie Monro told us before she died? That Claud Darrell had a habit of dabbing his bread on the table to pick up crumbs. Hastings, this is a vast plot, and that vacant-looking young man is our arch enemy – Number Four! Hurry.'

I did not wait to argue. Incredible as the whole thing seemed it was wiser not to delay. We scrambled down the ivy as quietly as we could and made a beeline for the small town and the railway station. We were just able to catch the last train, the 8.34 which would land us in town about eleven o'clock.

'A plot,' said Poirot thoughtfully. 'How many of them were in it, I wonder? I suspect that the whole Templeton family are just so many agents of the Big Four. Did they simply want to decoy us down there? Or was it more subtle than that? Did they intend to play the comedy down there and keep me interested until they had had time to do – what? I wonder now.'

He remained very thoughtful.

Arrived at our lodgings, he restrained me at the door of the sitting-room.

'Attention, Hastings. I have my suspicions. Let me enter first.'

He did so, and, to my slight amusement, took the precaution

to press on the electric switch with an old galosh. Then he went round the room like a strange cat, cautiously, delicately, on the alert for danger. I watched him for some time, remaining obediently where I had been put by the wall.

'It seems all right, Poirot,' I said impatiently.

'It seems so, *mon ami*, it seems so. But let us make sure.'

'Rot,' I said. 'I shall light the fire, anyway, and have a pipe. I've caught you out for once. You had the matches last and you didn't put them back in the holder as usual – the very thing you're always cursing me for doing.'

I stretched out my hand. I heard Poirot's warning cry – saw him leaping towards me – my hand touched the matchbox.

Then – a flash of blue flame – an ear-rending crash – and darkness –

I came to myself to find the familiar face of our old friend Dr Ridgeway bending over me. An expression of relief passed over his features.

'Keep still,' he said soothingly. 'You're all right. There's been an accident, you know.'

'Poirot?' I murmured.

'You're in my digs. Everything's quite all right.'

A cold fear clutched at my heart. His evasion woke a horrible fear.

'Poirot?' I reiterated. 'What of Poirot?'

He saw that I had to know and that further evasions were useless.

'By a miracle you escaped – Poirot – did not!'

A cry burst from my lips.

'Not dead? Not dead?'

Ridgeway bowed his head, his features working with emotion. With desperate energy I pulled myself to a sitting position.

'Poirot may be dead,' I said weakly. 'But his spirit lives on. I will carry on his work! Death to the Big Four!'

Then I fell back, fainting.

CHAPTER XVI

The Dying Chinaman

Even now I can hardly bear to write of those days in March.

Poirot – the unique, the inimitable Hercule Poirot – dead! There was a particularly diabolical touch in the disarranged matchbox, which was certain to catch his eye, and which he would hasten to rearrange – and thereby touch off the explosion. That, as a matter of fact, it was I who actually precipitated the catastrophe never ceased to fill me with unavailing remorse. It was, Dr Ridgeway said, a perfect miracle that I had not been killed, but had escaped with a slight concussion.

Although it had seemed to me as though I regained consciousness almost immediately, it was in reality over twenty-four hours before I came back to life. It was not until the evening of the day following that I was able to stagger feebly into an adjoining room, and view with deep emotion the plain elm coffin which held the remains of one of the most marvellous men this world has ever known.

From the very first moment of regaining consciousness I had had only one purpose in mind – to avenge Poirot's death, and to hunt down the Big Four remorselessly.

I had thought that Ridgeway would have been of one mind with me about this, but to my surprise the good doctor seemed unaccountably lukewarm.

'Get back to South America,' was his advice, tendered on every occasion. Why attempt the impossible? Put as delicately as possible, his opinion amounted to this: If Poirot, the unique Poirot, had failed, was it likely that I should succeed?

But I was obstinate. Putting aside any question as to whether I had the necessary qualifications for the task (and I may say in passing that I did not entirely agree with his views on this point) I had worked so long with Poirot that I knew his methods by heart, and felt fully capable of taking up the work where he had laid it down; it was, with me, a question of feeling. My friend had been foully murdered. Was I to go tamely back to South America without an effort to bring his murderers to justice?

I said all this and more to Ridgeway, who listened attentively enough.

'All the same,' he said when I had finished, 'my advice does not vary. I am earnestly convinced that Poirot himself, if he were here, would urge you to return. In his name, I beg of you, Hastings, abandon these wild ideas and go back to your ranch.'

To that only one answer was possible, and, shaking his head sadly, he said no more.

It was a month before I was fully restored to health. Towards the end of April, I sought, and obtained, an interview with the Home Secretary.

Mr Crowther's manner was reminiscent of that of Dr Ridgeway. It was soothing and negative. Whilst appreciating the offer of my services, he gently and considerately declined them. The papers referred to by Poirot had passed into his keeping, and he assured me that all possible steps were being taken to deal with the approaching menace.

With that cold comfort I was forced to be satisfied. Mr Crowther ended the interview by urging me to return to South America. I found the whole thing profoundly unsatisfactory.

I should, I suppose, in its proper place, have described Poirot's funeral. It was a solemn and moving ceremony, and the extraordinary number of floral tributes passed belief. They came from high and low alike, and bore striking testimony to the place my friend had made for himself in the country of his adoption. For myself, I was frankly overcome by emotion as I stood by the graveside and thought of all our varied experiences and the happy days we had passed together.

By the beginning of May I had mapped out a plan of campaign. I felt that I could not do better than keep to Poirot's scheme of advertising for any information respecting Claud

Darrell. I had an advertisement to this effect inserted in a number of morning newspapers, and I was sitting in a small restaurant in Soho, and judging of the effect of the advertisement, when a small paragraph in another part of the paper gave me a nasty shock.

Very briefly, it reported the mysterious disappearance of Mr John Ingles from the *SS Shanghai*, shortly after the latter had left Marseilles. Although the weather was perfectly smooth, it was feared that the unfortunate gentleman must have fallen overboard. The paragraph ended with a brief reference to Mr Ingles's long and distinguished service in China.

The news was unpleasant. I read into Ingles's death a sinister motive. Not for one moment did I believe the theory of an accident. Ingles had been murdered, and his death was only too clearly the handiwork of that accursed Big Four.

As I sat there, stunned by the blow, and turning the whole matter over in my mind, I was startled by the remarkable behaviour of the man sitting opposite me. So far I had not paid much attention to him. He was a thin, dark man of middle age, sallow of complexion, with a small pointed beard. He had sat down opposite me so quietly that I had hardly noticed his arrival.

But his actions now were decidedly peculiar, to say the least of them. Leaning forward, he deliberately helped me to salt, putting it in four little heaps round the edge of my plate.

'You will excuse me,' he said, in a melancholy voice. 'To help a stranger to salt is to help them to sorrow, they say. That may be an unavoidable necessity. I hope not, though. I hope that you will be reasonable.'

Then, with a certain significance, he repeated his operations with the salt on his own plate. The symbol 4 was too plain to be missed. I looked at him searchingly. In no way that I could see did he resemble the young Templeton, or James the footman, or any other of the various personalities we had come across. Nevertheless, I was convinced that I had to do with no less than the redoubtable Number Four himself. In his voice there was certainly a faint resemblance to the buttoned-up stranger who had called upon us in Paris.

I looked round, undecided as to my course of action. Reading my thoughts, he smiled and gently shook his head.

'I should not advise it,' he remarked. 'Remember what came of your hasty action in Paris. Let me assure you that my way of retreat is well assured. Your ideas are inclined to be a little crude, Captain Hastings, if I may say so.'

'You devil,' I said, choking with rage, 'you incarnate devil!'

'Heated – just a trifle heated. Your late lamented friend would have told you that a man who keeps calm has always a great advantage.'

'You dare to speak of him,' I cried. 'The man you murdered so foully. And you come here – '

He interrupted me.

'I came here for an excellent and peaceful purpose. To advise you to return at once to South America. If you do so, that is the end of the matter as far as the Big Four are concerned. You and yours will not be molested in any way. I give you my word as to that.'

I laughed scornfully.

'And if I refuse to obey your autocratic command?'

'It is hardly a command. Shall we say that it is – a warning?'

There was a cold menace in his tone.

'The first warning,' he said softly. 'You will be well advised not to disregard it.'

Then, before I had any hint of his intention, he rose and slipped quickly away towards the door. I sprang to my feet and was after him in a second, but by bad luck I cannoned straight into an enormously fat man who blocked the way between me and the next table. By the time I had disentangled myself, my quarry was just passing through the doorway, and the next delay was from a waiter carrying a huge pile of plates who crashed into me without the least warning. By the time I got to the door there was no sign of the thin man with the dark beard.

The waiter was fulsome in apologies, the fat man was sitting placidly at a table ordering his lunch. There was nothing to show that both occurrences had not been a pure accident. Nevertheless, I had my own opinion as to that. I knew well enough that the agents of the Big Four were everywhere.

Needless to say, I paid no heed to the warning given me. I would do or die in the good cause. I received in all only two answers to the advertisements. Neither of them gave me any information of value. They were both from actors who had played with Claud Darrell at one time or another. Neither of them knew him at all intimately, and no new light was thrown upon the problem of his identity and present whereabouts.

No further sign came from the Big Four until about ten days later. I was crossing Hyde Park, lost in thought, when a voice, rich with a persuasive foreign inflection, hailed me.

'Captain Hastings, is it not?'

A big limousine had just drawn up by the pavement. A woman was leaning out. Exquisitely dressed in black, with wonderful pearls, I recognized the lady first known to us as Countess Vera Rossakoff, and afterwards under a different alias as an agent of the Big Four. Poirot, for some reason or other, had always had a sneaking fondness for the countess. Something in her very flamboyance attracted the little man. She was, he was wont to declare in moments of enthusiasm, a woman in a thousand. That she was arrayed against us, on the side of our bitterest enemies, never seemed to weigh in his judgment.

'Ah, do not pass on!' said the countess. 'I have something most important to say to you. And do not try to have me arrested either, for that would be stupid. You were always a little stupid – yes, yes, it is so. You are stupid now, when you persist in disregarding the warning we sent you. It is the second warning I bring you. Leave England at once. You can do no good here – I tell you that frankly. You will never accomplish anything.'

'In that case,' I said stiffly, 'it seems rather extraordinary that you are all so anxious to get me out of the country.'

The countess shrugged her shoulders – magnificent shoulders, and a magnificent gesture.

'For my part, I think that, too, stupid. I would leave you here to play about happily. But the chiefs, you see, are fearful that some word of yours may give great help to those more intelligent than yourself. Hence – you are to be banished.'

The countess appeared to have a flattering idea of my abilities. I concealed my annoyance. Doubtless this attitude of hers was assumed expressly to annoy me and to give me the idea that I was unimportant.

'It would, of course, be quite easy to – remove you,' she continued, 'but I am quite sentimental sometimes. I pleaded for you. You have a nice little wife somewhere, have you not? And it would please the poor little man who is dead to know that you were not to be killed. I always liked him, you know. He was clever – but clever! Had it not been a case of four against one I honestly believe he might have been too much for us. I confess it frankly – he was my master! I sent a wreath to the funeral as a token of my admiration – an enormous one of crimson roses. Crimson roses express my temperament.'

I listened in silence and a growing distaste.

'You have the look of a mule when it puts its ears back and kicks. Well, I have delivered my warning. Remember this, the third warning will come by the hand of the Destroyer –'

She made a sign, and the car whirled away rapidly. I noted the number mechanically, but without the hope that it would lead to anything. The Big Four were not apt to be careless in details.

I went home a little sobered. One fact had emerged from the countess's flood of volubility. I was in real danger of my life. Though I had no intention of abandoning the struggle, I saw that it behoved me to walk warily and adopt every possible precaution.

Whilst I was reviewing all these facts and seeking for the best line of action, the telephone bell rang. I crossed the room and picked up the receiver.

'Yes. Hallo. Who's speaking?'

A crisp voice answered me.

'This is St Giles's Hospital. We have a Chinaman here, knifed in the street and brought in. He can't last long. We rang you up because we found in his pockets a piece of paper with your name and address on it.'

I was very much astonished. Nevertheless, after a moment's

reflection I said that I would come down at once. St Giles's Hospital, was, I knew, down by the docks, and it occurred to me that the Chinaman might have just come off some ship.

It was on my way down there that a sudden suspicion shot into my mind. Was the whole thing a trap? Wherever a Chinaman was, there might be the hand of Li Chang Yen. I remembered the adventure of the Baited Trap. Was the whole thing a ruse on the part of my enemies?

A little reflection convinced me that at any rate a visit to the hospital would do no harm. It was probable that the thing was not so much a plot as what is vulgarly know as a 'plant'. The dying Chinaman would make some revelation to me upon which I should act, and which would have the result of leading me into the hands of the Big Four. The thing to do was to preserve an open mind, and whilst feigning credulity be secretly on my guard.

On arriving at St Giles's Hospital, and making my business known, I was taken at once to the accident ward, to the bedside of the man in question. He lay absolutely still, his eyelids closed, and only a very faint movement of the chest showed that he still breathed. A doctor stood by the bed, his fingers on the Chinaman's pulse.

'He's almost gone,' he whispered to me. 'You know him, eh?'

I shook my head.

'I've never seen him before.'

'Then what was he doing with your name and address in his pocket? You are Captain Hastings, aren't you?'

'Yes, but I can't explain it any more than you can.'

'Curious thing. From his papers he seems to have been the servant of a man called Ingles – a retired Civil Servant. Ah, you know him, do you?' he added quickly, as I started at the name.

Ingles's servant! Then I *had* seen him before. Not that I had ever succeeded in being able to distinguish one Chinaman from another. He must have been with Ingles on his way to China, and after the catastrophe he had returned to England with a message, possibly, for me. It was vital, imperative that I should hear that message.

'Is he conscious?' I asked. 'Can he speak? Mr Ingles was an old friend of mine, and I think it possible that this poor fellow has brought me a message from him. Mr Ingles is believed to have gone overboard about ten days ago.'

'He's just conscious, but I doubt if he has the force to speak. He lost a terrible lot of blood, you know. I can administer a stimulant, of course, but we've already done all that is possible in that direction.'

Nevertheless, he administered a hypodermic injection, and I stayed by the bed, hoping against hope for a word – a sign – that might be of the utmost value to me in my work. But the minutes sped on and no sign came.

And suddenly a baleful idea shot across my mind. Was I not already falling into the trap? Suppose that this Chinaman had merely assumed the part of Ingles's servant, that he was in reality an agent of the Big Four? Had I not once read that certain Chinese priests were capable of simulating death? Or, to go further still, Li Chang Yen might command a little band of fanatics who would welcome death itself if it came at the command of their master. I must be on my guard.

Even as these thoughts flashed across my mind, the man in the bed stirred. His eyes opened. He murmured something incoherently. Then I saw his glance fasten upon me. He made no sign of recognition, but I was at once aware that he was trying to speak to me. Be he friend or foe, I must hear what he had to say.

I leaned over the bed, but the broken sounds conveyed no sort of meaning to me. I thought I caught the word 'hand', but in what connection it was used I could not tell. Then it came again, and this time I heard another word, the word 'Largo'. I stared in amazement, as the possible juxtaposition of the two suggested itself to me.

'Handel's Largo?' I queried.

The Chinaman's eyelids flickered rapidly, as though in assent, and he added another Italian word, the word *'carrozza'*. Two or three more words of murmured Italian came to my ears, and then he fell back abruptly.

The doctor pushed me aside. It was all over. The man was dead. I went out into the air again thoroughly bewildered.

'Handel's Largo', and a *'carrozza'*. If I remembered rightly, a *carrozza* was a carriage. What possible meaning could lie behind those simple words? The man was a Chinaman, not an Italian, why should he speak in Italian? Surely, if he were indeed Ingles's servant, he must know English? The whole thing was profoundly mystifying. I puzzled over it all the way home. Oh, if only Poirot had been there to solve the problem with his lightning ingenuity!

I let myself in with my latch-key and went slowly up to my room. A letter was lying on the table, and I tore it open carelessly enough. But in a minute I stood rooted to the ground whilst I read.

It was a communication from a firm of solicitors.

Dear Sir (it ran) – As instructed by our late client, M. Hercule Poirot, we forward you the enclosed letter. This letter was placed in our hands a week before his death, with instructions that in the event of his demise, it should be sent to you at a certain date after his death.

Yours faithfully, etc.

I turned the enclosed missive over and over. It was undoubtedly from Poirot. I knew that familiar writing only too well. With a heavy heart, yet a certain eagerness, I tore it open.

Mon Cher Ami (it began) – When you receive this I shall be no more. Do not shed tears about me, but follow my orders. Immediately upon receipt of this, return to South America. Do not be pig-headed about this. It is not for sentimental reasons that I bid you undertake the journey. *It is necessary*. It is part of the plan of Hercule Poirot! To say more is unnecessary, to anyone who has the acute intelligence of my friend Hastings.

A bas the Big Four! I salute you, my friend, from beyond the grave.

Ever thine,

Hercule Poirot

I read and re-read this astonishing communication. One thing was evident. The amazing man had so provided for every eventuality that even his own death did not upset the sequence of his plans! Mine was to be the active part – his the directing genius. Doubtless I should find full instructions awaiting me beyond the seas. In the meantime my enemies, convinced that I was obeying their warning, would cease to trouble their heads about me. I could return, unsuspected, and work havoc in their midst.

There was now nothing to hinder my immediate departure. I sent off cables, booked my passage, and one week later found me embarking in the *Ansonia*, en route for Buenos Aires.

Just as the boat left the quay, a steward brought me a note. It had been given him, so he explained, by a big gentleman in a fur coat who had left the boat last thing before the gangway planks were lifted.

I opened it. It was terse and to the point.

'You are wise,' it ran. It was signed with a big figure 4.

I could afford to smile to myself!

The sea was not too choppy. I enjoyed a passable dinner, made up my mind as to the majority of my fellow passengers, and had a rubber or two of Bridge. Then I turned in and slept like a log as I always do on board ship.

I was awakened by feeling myself persistently shaken. Dazed and bewildered, I saw that one of the ship's officers was standing over me. He gave a sigh of relief as I sat up.

'Thank the Lord I've got you awake at last. I've had no end of a job. Do you always sleep like that?'

'What's the matter?' I asked, still bewildered and not fully awake. 'Is there anything wrong with the ship?'

'I expect you know what's the matter better than I do,' he replied drily. 'Special instructions from the Admiralty. There's a destroyer waiting to take you off.'

'What?' I cried. 'In mid-ocean?'

'It seems a most mysterious affair, but that's not my business. They've sent a young fellow aboard who is to take your place, and we are all sworn to secrecy. Will you get up and dress?'

Utterly unable to conceal my amazement I did as I was told.

A boat was lowered, and I was conveyed aboard the destroyer. There I was received courteously, but got no further information. The commander's instructions were to land me at a certain spot on the Belgian coast. There his knowledge and responsibility ended.

The whole thing was like a dream. The one idea I held to firmly was that all this must be part of Poirot's plan. I must simply go forward blindly, trusting in my dead friend.

I was duly landed at the spot indicated. There a motor was waiting, and soon I was rapidly whirling across the flat Flemish plains. I slept that night at a small hotel in Brussels. The next day we went on again. The country became wooded and hilly. I realized that we were penetrating into the Ardennes, and I suddenly remembered Poirot saying that he had a brother who lived at Spa.

But we did not go to Spa itself. We left the main road and wound into the leafy fastnesses of the hills, till we reached a little hamlet, and an isolated white villa high on the hillside. Here the car stopped in front of the green door of the villa.

The door opened as I alighted. An elderly manservant stood in the doorway bowing.

'M. le Capitaine Hastings?' he said in French. 'M. le Capitaine is expected. If he will follow me.'

He led the way across the hall, and flung open a door at the back, standing aside to let me pass in.

I blinked a little, for the room faced west and the afternoon sun was pouring in. Then my vision cleared and I saw a figure waiting to welcome me with outstretched hands.

It was – oh, impossible, it couldn't be – but yes!

'Poirot!' I cried, and for once did not attempt to evade the embrace with which he overwhelmed me.

'But yes, but yes, it is indeed I! Not so easy to kill Hercule Poirot!'

'But Poirot – *why*?'

'A *ruse de guerre*, my friend, a *ruse de guerre*. All is now ready for our grand *coup*.'

'But you might have told *me*!'

'No, Hastings, I could not. Never, never, in a thousand years, could you have acted the part at the funeral. As it was, it was perfect. It could not fail to carry conviction to the Big Four.'

'But what I've been through –'

'Do not think me too unfeeling. I carried out the deception partly for your sake. I was willing to risk my own life, but I had qualms about continually risking yours. So, after the explosion, I have an idea of great brilliancy. The good Ridgeway, he enables me to carry it out. I am dead, you will return to South America. But, *mon ami*, that is just what you would not do. In the end I have to arrange a solicitor's letter, and a long rigmarole. But, at all events, here you are – that is the great thing. And now we lie here – *perdus* – till the moment comes for the last grand *coup* – the final overthrowing of the Big Four.'

CHAPTER XVII

Number Four Wins a Trick

From our quiet retreat in the Ardennes we watched the progress of affairs in the great world. We were plentifully supplied with newspapers, and every day Poirot received a bulky envelope, evidently containing some kind of report. He never showed these reports to me, but I could usually tell from his manner whether their contents had been satisfactory or otherwise. He never wavered in his belief that our present plan was the only one likely to be crowned by success.

'As a minor point, Hastings,' he remarked one day, 'I was in continual fear of your death lying at my door. And that rendered me nervous – like a cat upon the jumps, as you say. But now I am well satisfied. Even if they discover that the Captain Hastings who landed in South America is an impostor (and I do not think they will discover it, they are not likely to send an agent out there who knows you personally), they will only believe that you are trying to circumvent them in some clever manner of your own, and will pay no serious attention to discovering your whereabouts. Of the one vital fact, my supposed death, they are thoroughly convinced. They will go ahead and mature their plans.'

'And then?' I asked eagerly.

'And then, *mon ami*, grand resurrection of Hercule Poirot! At the eleventh hour I reappear, throw all into confusion, and achieve the supreme victory in my own unique manner!'

I realized that Poirot's vanity was of the case-hardened variety which could withstand all attacks. I reminded him that once or twice the honours of the game had lain with our adversaries. But I might have known that it was impossible to diminish Hercule Poirot's enthusiasm for his own methods.

'See you, Hastings, it is like the little trick that you play with the cards. You have seen it without doubt? You take the four knaves, you divide them, one on top of the pack, one underneath, and so on – you cut and you shuffle, and there they are all together again. That is my object. So far I have been contending, now against one of the Big Four, now against another. But let me get them all together, like the four knaves in the pack of cards, and then, with one *coup*, I destroy them all!'

'And how do you propose to get them all together?' I asked.

'By awaiting the supreme moment. By lying *perdu* until they are ready to strike.'

'That may mean a long wait,' I grumbled.

'Always impatient, the good Hastings! But no, it will not be so long. The one man they were afraid of – myself – is out of the way. I give them two or three months at most.'

His speaking of someone being out of the way reminded me of Ingles and his tragic death, and I remembered that I had never told Poirot about the dying Chinaman in St Giles's Hospital.

He listened with keen attention to my story.

'Ingles's servant, eh? And the few words he uttered were in Italian? Curious.'

'That's why I suspected it might have been a plant on the part of the Big Four.'

'Your reasoning is at fault, Hastings. Employ the little grey cells. If your enemies wished to deceive you they would assuredly have seen to it that the Chinaman spoke in intelligible pidgin English. No, the message was genuine. Tell me again all that you heard?'

'First of all he made a reference to Handel's Largo, and then he said something that sounded like *"carrozza"* – that's a carriage, isn't it?'

'Nothing else?'

'Well, just at the end he murmured something like *"Cara"* somebody or other – some woman's name. Zia, I think. But I don't suppose that that had any bearing on the rest of it.'

'You would not suppose so, Hastings. Cara Zia is very important, very important indeed.'

'I don't see –'

'My dear friend, you *never* see – and anyway the English know no geography.'

'Geography?' I cried. 'What has geography got to do with it?'

'I dare say M. Thomas Cook would be more to the point.'

As usual, Poirot refused to say anything more – a most irritating trick of his. But I noticed that his manner became extremely cheerful, as though he had scored some point or other.

The days went on, pleasant if a trifle monotonous. There were plenty of books in the villa, and delightful rambles all around, but I chafed sometimes at the forced inactivity of our life, and marvelled at Poirot's state of placid content. Nothing occurred to ruffle our quiet existence, and it was not until the end of June, well within the limit that Poirot had given them, that we had our news of the Big Four.

A car drove up to the villa early one morning, such an unusual event in our peaceful life that I hurried down to satisfy my curiosity. I found Poirot talking to a pleasant-faced young fellow of about my own age.

He introduced me.

'This is Captain Harvey, Hastings, one of the most famous members of your Intelligence Service.'

'Not famous at all, I'm afraid,' said the young man, laughing pleasantly.

'Not famous except to those in the know, I should have said. Most of Captain Harvey's friends and acquaintances consider him an amiable but brainless young man – devoted only to the trot of the fox or whatever the dance is called.'

We both laughed.

'Well, well, to business,' said Poirot. 'You are of opinion the time has come, then?'

'We are sure of it, sir. China was isolated politically yesterday. What is going on out there, nobody knows. No news of any kind, wireless or otherwise, has come through – just a complete break – and silence!'

'Li Chang Yen has shown his hand. And the others?'

'Abe Ryland arrived in England a week ago, and left for the Continent yesterday.'

'And Madame Olivier?'

'Madame Olivier left Paris last night.'

'For Italy?'

'For Italy, sir. As far as we can judge, they are both making for the resort you indicated – though how you knew that –'

'Ah, that is not the cap with the feather for me! That was the work of Hastings here. He conceals his intelligence, you comprehend, but it is profound for all that.'

Harvey looked at me with due appreciation, and I felt rather uncomfortable.

'All is in train, then,' said Poirot. He was pale now, and completely serious. 'The time has come. The arrangements are all made?'

'Everything you ordered has been carried out. The governments of Italy, France and England are behind you, and are all working harmoniously together.'

'It is, in fact, a new *Entente*,' observed Poirot drily. 'I am glad that Desjardeaux is convinced at last. *Eh bien*, then, we will start – or rather, I will start. You, Hastings, will remain here – yes, I pray of you. In verity, my friend, I am serious.'

I believed him, but it was not likely that I should consent to being left behind in that fashion. Our argument was short but decisive.

It was not until we were in the train, speeding towards Paris, that he admitted that he was secretly glad of my decision.

'For you have a part to play, Hastings. An important part! Without you, I might well fail. Nevertheless, I felt that it was my duty to urge you to remain behind –'

'There is danger, then?'

'*Mon ami*, where there is the Big Four there is always danger.'

On arrival in Paris, we drove across to the Gare de L'Est, and Poirot at last announced our destination. We were bound for Bolzano and the Italian Tyrol.

During Harvey's absence from our carriage I took the

opportunity of asking Poirot why he had said that the discovery of the rendezvous was my work.

'Because it was, my friend. How Ingles managed to get hold of the information I do not know, but he did, and he sent it to us by his servant. We are bound, *mon ami,* for Karersee, the new Italian name for which is Lago di Carrezza. You see now where your *"Cara Zia"* comes in and also your *"carrozza"* and "Largo" – the Handel was supplied by your own imagination. Possibly some reference to the information coming from the "hand" of Mr Ingles started the train of association.'

'Karersee?' I queried. 'I never heard of it.'

'I always tell you that the English know no geography. But as a matter of fact it is a well-known and very beautiful summer resort, four thousand feet up, in the heart of the Dolomites.'

'And it is in this out of the way spot that the Big Four have their rendezvous?'

'Say rather their headquarters. The signal has been given, and it is their intention to disappear from the world and issue orders from their mountain fastness. I have made the inquiries – a lot of quarrying of stone and mineral deposits is done there, and the company, apparently a small Italian firm, is in reality controlled by Abe Ryland. I am prepared to swear that a vast subterranean dwelling has been hollowed out in the very heart of the mountain, secret and inaccessible. From there the leaders of the organization will issue by wireless their orders to their followers who are numbered by thousands in every country. And from that crag in the Dolomites the dictators of the world will emerge. That is to say – they would emerge were it not for Hercule Poirot.'

'Do you seriously believe all this, Poirot? – What about the armies and general machinery of civilization?'

'What about it in Russia, Hastings? This will be Russia on an infinitely larger scale – and with this additional menace – that Madame Olivier's experiments have proceeded further than she has ever given out. I believe that she has, to a certain extent, succeeded in liberating atomic energy and harnessing it to her purpose. Her experiments with the nitrogen of the air have been very remarkable, and she has also experimented in the concentration of wireless energy, so that a beam of great intensity can be focused upon some given spot. Exactly how far she has progressed, nobody knows, but it is certain that it is much farther than has ever been given out. She is a genius, that woman – the Curies were as nothing to her. Add to her genius the powers of Ryland's almost unlimited wealth, and, with the brain of Li Chang Yen, the finest criminal brain ever known, to direct and plan – *eh bien*, it will not be, as you say, all jam for civilization.'

His words made me very thoughtful. Although Poirot was given at times to exaggeration of language, he was not really an alarmist. For the first time I realized what a desperate struggle it was upon which we were engaged.

Harvey soon rejoined us and the journey went on.

We arrived at Bolzano about midday. From there the journey on was by motor. Several big blue motor cars were waiting in the central square of the town, and we three got into one of them. Poirot, notwithstanding the heat of the day, was muffled to the eyes in greatcoat and scarf. His eyes and the tips of his ears were all that could be seen of him.

I did not know whether this was due to precaution or merely his exaggerated fear of catching a chill. The motor journey took a couple of hours. It was a really wonderful drive. For the first part of the way we wound in and out of huge cliffs, with a trickling waterfall on one hand. Then we emerged into a fertile valley, which continued for some miles, and then, still winding steadily upwards, the bare rock peaks began to show with dense clustering pinewoods at their base. The whole place was wild and lovely. Finally a series of abrupt curves, with the road running through the pinewoods on either side, and we came suddenly upon a big hotel and found we had arrived.

Our rooms had been reserved for us, and under Harvey's guidance we went straight up to them. They looked straight out over the rocky peaks and the long slopes of pinewoods leading up to them. Poirot made a gesture towards them.

'It is there?' he asked in a low voice.

'Yes,' replied Harvey. 'There is a place called the Felsenlaby-rinth – all big boulders piled about in a most fantastic way – a path winds through them. The quarrying is to the right of that, but we think that the entrance is probably in the Felsen-labyrinth.'

Poirot nodded.

'Come, *mon ami*,' he said to me. 'Let us go down and sit upon the terrace and enjoy the sunlight.'

'You think that wise?' I asked.

He shrugged his shoulders.

The sunlight was marvellous – in fact the glare was almost too great for me. We had some creamy coffee instead of tea, then went upstairs and unpacked our few belongings. Poirot was in his most unapproachable mood, lost in a kind of reverie. Once or twice he shook his head and sighed.

I had been rather intrigued by a man who had got out of our train at Bolzano, and had been met by a private car. He was a small man, and one thing about him that attracted my attention was that he was almost as much muffled up as Poirot had been. More so, indeed, for in addition to greatcoat and muffler, he was wearing huge blue spectacles. I was convinced that here we had an emissary of the Big Four. Poirot did not seem very impressed by my idea. But when, leaning out of my bedroom window, I reported that the man in question was stroll-ing about in the vicinity of the hotel, he admitted that there might be something in it.

I urged my friend not to go down to dinner, but he insisted on doing so. We entered the dining-room rather late, and were shown to a table by the window. As we sat down, our attention was attracted by an exclamation and a crash of falling china. A dish of haricots verts had been upset over a man who was sitting at the table next to ours.

The head waiter came up and was vociferous in apologies.

Presently, when the offending waiter was serving us with soup, Poirot spoke to him.

'An unfortunate accident, that. But it was not your fault.'

'Monsieur saw that? No, indeed it was not my fault. The

gentleman half sprang up from his chair – I thought he was going to have an attack of some kind. I could not save the catastrophe.'

I saw Poirot's eyes shining with the green light I knew so well, and as the waiter departed he said to me in a low voice:

'You see, Hastings, the effect of Hercule Poirot – alive and in the flesh?'

'You think –'

I had not time to continue. I felt Poirot's hand on my knee, as he whispered excitedly:

'Look, Hastings, look. *His trick with the bread!* Number Four!'

Sure enough, the man at the next table to ours, his face unusually pale, was dabbing a small piece of bread mechanically about the table.

I studied him carefully. His face, clean-shaven and puffily fat, was of a pasty, unhealthy sallowness, with heavy pouches under the eyes and deep lines running from his nose to the corners of his mouth. His age might have been anything from thirty-five to forty-five. In no particular did he resemble any one of the characters which Number Four had previously assumed. Indeed, had it not been for his little trick with the bread, of which he was evidently quite unaware, I would have sworn readily enough that the man sitting there was someone whom I had never seen before.

'He has recognized you,' I murmured. 'You should not have come down.'

'My excellent Hastings, I have feigned death for three months for this one purpose.'

'To startle Number Four?'

'To startle him at a moment when he must act quickly or not at all. And we have this great advantage – he does not know that we recognize him. He thinks that he is safe in his new disguise. How I bless Flossie Monro for telling us of that little habit of his.'

'What will happen now?' I asked.

'What can happen? He recognizes the only man he fears, miraculously resurrected from the dead, at the very minute when the plans of the Big Four are in the balance. Madame Olivier and Abe Ryland lunched here today, and it is thought that they went to Cortina. Only we know that they have retired to their hiding-place. How much do we know? That is what Number Four is asking himself at this minute. He dare take no risks. I must be suppressed at all costs. *Eh bien,* let him try to suppress Hercule Poirot! I shall be ready for him.'

As he finished speaking, the man at the next table got up and went out.

'He has gone to make his little arrangements,' said Poirot placidly. 'Shall we have our coffee on the terrace, my friend? It would be pleasanter, I think. I will just go up and get a coat.'

I went out on to the terrace, a little disturbed in mind. Poirot's assurance did not quite content me. However, so long as we were on guard, nothing could happen to us. I resolved to keep thoroughly on the alert.

It was quite five minutes before Poirot joined me. With his usual precautions against cold, he was muffled up to the ears. He sat down beside me and sipped his coffee appreciatively.

'Only in England is the coffee so atrocious,' he remarked. 'On the Continent they understand how important it is for the digestion that it should be properly made.'

As he finished speaking, the man from the next table suddenly appeared on the terrace. Without any hesitation, he came over and drew up a third chair to our table.

'You do not mind my joining you, I hope,' he said in English.

'Not at all, monsieur,' said Poirot.

I felt very uneasy. It is true that we were on the terrace of the hotel, with people all around us, but nevertheless I was not satisfied. I sensed the presence of danger.

Meanwhile Number Four chatted away in a perfectly natural manner. It seemed impossible to believe that he was anything but a *bona fide* tourist. He described excursions and motor trips, and posed as quite an authority on the neighbourhood.

He took a pipe from his pocket and began to light it. Poirot drew out his case of tiny cigarettes. As he placed one between his lips, the stranger leant forward with a match.

'Let me give you a light.'

As he spoke, without the least warning, all the lights went out. There was a chink of glass, and something pungent under my nose, suffocating me –

CHAPTER XVIII

In the Felsenlabyrinth

I could not have been unconscious more than a minute. I came to myself being hustled along between two men. They had me under each arm, supporting my weight, and there was a gag in my mouth. It was pitch dark, but I gathered that we were not outside, but passing through the hotel. All round I could hear people shouting and demanding in every known language what had happened to the lights. My captors swung me down some stairs. We passed along a basement passage, then through a door and out into the open again through a glass door at the back of the hotel. In another moment we had gained the shelter of the pine trees.

I had caught a glimpse of another figure in a similar plight to myself, and realized that Poirot, too, was a victim of this bold *coup*.

By sheer audacity, Number Four had won the day. He had employed, I gathered, an instant anaesthetic, probably ethyl chloride – breaking a small bulb of it under our noses. Then, in the confusion of the darkness, his accomplices, who had probably been guests sitting at the next table, had thrust gags in our mouths and hurried us away, taking us through the hotel to baffle pursuit.

I cannot describe the hour that followed. We were hurried through the woods at a break-neck pace, going uphill the whole time. As last we emerged in the open, on the mountain-side, and I saw just in front of us an extraordinary conglomeration of fantastic rocks and boulders.

This must be the Felsenlabyrinth of which Harvey had spoken. Soon we were winding in and out of its recesses. The place was like a maze devised by some evil genie.

Suddenly we stopped. An enormous rock barred our path. One of the men stopped and seemed to push on something when, without a sound, the huge mass of rock turned on itself and disclosed a small tunnel-like opening leading into the mountain-side.

Into this we were hurried. For some time the tunnel was narrow, but presently it widened, and before very long we came out into a wide rocky chamber lighted by electricity. Then the gags were removed. At a sign from Number Four, who stood facing us with mocking triumph in his face, we were searched and every article was removed from our pockets, including Poirot's little automatic pistol.

A pang smote me as it was tossed down on the table. We were defeated – hopelessly defeated and outnumbered. It was the end.

'Welcome to the headquarters of the Big Four, M. Hercule Poirot,' said Number Four in a mocking tone. 'To meet you again is an unexpected pleasure. But was it worth while returning from the grave only for this?'

Poirot did not reply. I dared not look at him.

'Come this way,' continued Number Four. 'Your arrival will be somewhat of a surprise to my colleagues.'

He indicated a narrow doorway in the wall. We passed through and found ourselves in another chamber. At the very end of it was a table behind which four chairs were placed. The end chair was empty, but it was draped with a mandarin's cape. On the second, smoking a cigar, sat Mr Abe Ryland. Leaning back on the third chair, with her burning eyes and her nun's face, was Madame Olivier. Number Four took his seat on the fourth chair.

We were in the presence of the Big Four.

Never before had I felt so fully the reality and the presence of Li Chang Yen as I did now when confronting his empty seat. Far away in China, he yet controlled and directed this malign organization.

Madame Olivier gave a faint cry on seeing us. Ryland, more self-controlled, only shifted his cigar, and raised his grizzled eyebrows.

'M. Hercule Poirot,' said Ryland slowly. 'This is a pleasant surprise. You put it over on us all right. We thought you were good and buried. No matter, the game is up now.'

There was a ring as of steel in his voice. Madame Olivier said nothing, but her eyes burned, and I disliked the slow way she smiled.

'Madame and messieurs, I wish you good evening,' said Poirot quietly.

Something unexpected, something I had not been prepared to hear in his voice made me look at him. He seemed quite composed. Yet there was something about his whole appearance that was different.

Then there was a stir of draperies behind us, and the Countess Vera Rossakoff came in.

'Ah!' said Number Four. 'Our valued and trusted lieutenant. An old friend of yours is here, my dear lady.'

The countess whirled round with her usual vehemence of movement.

'God in heaven!' she cried. 'It is the little man! Ah! but he has the nine lives of a cat! Oh, little man, little man! Why did you mix yourself up in this?'

'Madame,' said Poirot with a bow. 'Me, like the great Napoleon, I am on the side of the big battalions.'

As he spoke I saw a sudden suspicion flash into her eyes, and at the same moment I knew the truth which subconsciously I already sensed.

The man beside me was not Hercule Poirot.

He was very like him, extraordinarily like him. There was the same egg-shaped head, the same strutting figure, delicately plump. But the voice was different, and the eyes instead of being green were dark, and surely the moustaches – those famous moustaches – ?

My reflections were cut short by the countess's voice. She stepped forward, her voice ringing with excitement.

'You have been deceived. This man is not Hercule Poirot!'

Number Four uttered an incredulous exclamation, but the countess leant forward and snatched at Poirot's moustaches.

They came off in her hand, and then, indeed, the truth was plain. For this man's upper lip was disfigured by a small scar which completely altered the expression of the face.

'Not Hercule Poirot,' muttered Number Four. 'But who can he be then?'

'I know,' I cried suddenly, and then stopped dead, afraid I had ruined everything.

But the man I will still refer to as Poirot had turned to me encouragingly.

'Say it if you will. It makes no matter now. The trick has succeeded.'

'This is Achille Poirot,' I said slowly. 'Hercule Poirot's twin brother.'

'Impossible,' said Ryland sharply, but he was shaken.

'Hercule's plan has succeeded to a marvel,' said Achille placidly.

Number Four leapt forward, his voice harsh and menacing.

'Succeeded, has it?' he snarled. 'Do you realize that before many minutes have passed you will be dead – dead?'

'Yes,' said Achille Poirot gravely. 'I realize that. It is you who do not realize that a man may be willing to purchase success by his life. There were men who laid down their lives for their country in the war. I am prepared to lay down mine in the same way for the world.'

It struck me just then that although perfectly willing to lay down my life I might have been consulted in the matter. Then I remembered how Poirot had urged me to stay behind and I felt appeased.

'And in what way will your laying down your life benefit the world?' asked Ryland sardonically.

'I see that you do not perceive the true inwardness of Hercule's plan. To begin with, your place of retreat was known some months ago, and practically all the visitors, hotel assistants and others are detectives or Secret Service men. A cordon has been drawn round the mountain. You may have more than one means of egress, but even so you cannot escape. Poirot himself is directing the operations outside. My boots were smeared with a preparation of aniseed tonight, before I came down to the terrace in my brother's place. Hounds are following the trail. It will lead them infallibly to the rock in the Felsenlabyrinth where the entrance is situated. You see, do what you will to us, the net is drawn tightly round you. You cannot escape.'

Madame Olivier laughed suddenly.

'You are wrong. There is one way we can escape, and, like Samson, of old, destroy our enemies at the same time. What do you say, my friends?'

Ryland was staring at Achille Poirot.

'Suppose he's lying,' he said hoarsely.

The other shrugged his shoulders.

'In an hour it will be dawn. Then you can see for yourself the truth of my words. Already they should have traced me to the entrance in the Felsenlabyrinth.'

Even as he spoke, there was a far-off reverberation, and a man ran in shouting incoherently. Ryland sprang up and went out. Madame Olivier moved to the end of the room and opened a door that I had not noticed. Inside I caught a glimpse of a perfectly equipped laboratory which reminded me of the one in Paris. Number Four also sprang up and went out. He returned with Poirot's revolver which he gave to the countess.

'There is no danger of their escaping,' he said grimly. 'But still you had better have this.'

Then he went out again.

The countess came over to us and surveyed my companion attentively for some time. Suddenly she laughed.

'You are very clever, M. Achille Poirot,' she said mockingly.

'Madame, let us talk business. It is fortunate that they have left us alone together. What is your price?'

'I do not understand. What price?'

'Madame, you can aid us to escape. You know the secret way out of this retreat. I ask you, what is your price?'

She laughed again.

'More than you could pay, little man! Why, all the money in the world would not buy me!'

'Madame, I did not speak of money. I am a man of intelligence. Nevertheless, this is a true fact – *everyone has his price!* In exchange for life and liberty, I offer you your heart's desire.'

'So you are a magician!'

'You can call me so if you like.'

The countess suddenly dropped her jesting manner. She spoke with passionate bitterness.

'Fool! My heart's desire! Can you give me revenge upon my enemies? Can you give me back youth and beauty and a gay heart? Can you bring the dead to life again?'

Achille Poirot was watching her very curiously.

'Which of the three, Madame? Make your choice.'

She laughed sardonically.

'You will send me the Elixir of Life, perhaps? Come, I will make a bargain with you. Once, I had a child. Find my child for me – and you shall go free.'

'Madame, I agree. It is a bargain. Your child shall be restored to you. On the faith of – on the faith of Hercule Poirot himself.'

Again that strange woman laughed – this time long and unrestrainedly.

'My dear M. Poirot, I am afraid I laid a little trap for you. It is very kind of you to promise to find my child for me, but, you see, I happen to know that you would not succeed, and so that would be a very one-sided bargain, would it not?'

'Madame, I swear to you by the Holy Angels that I will restore your child to you.'

'I asked you before, M. Poirot, could you restore the dead to life?'

'Then the child is –'

'Dead? Yes.'

He stepped forward and took her wrist.

'Madame, I – I who speak to you, swear once more. *I will bring the dead back to life.*'

She stared at him as though fascinated.

'You do not believe me. I will prove my words. Get my pocketbook which they took from me.'

She went out of the room, and returned with it in her hand. Throughout all she retained her grip on the revolver. I felt that

Achille Poirot's chances of bluffing her were very slight. The Countess Vera Rossakoff was no fool.

'Open it, madame. The flap on the left-hand side. That is right. Now take out that photograph and look at it.'

Wonderingly, she took out what seemed to be a small snapshot. No sooner had she looked at it than she uttered a cry and swayed as though about to fall. Then she almost flew at my companion.

'Where? Where? You shall tell me. Where?'

'Remember your bargain, madame.'

'Yes, yes, I will trust you. Quick, before they come back.'

Catching him by the hand, she drew him quickly and silently out of the room. I followed. From the outer room she led us into the tunnel by which we had first entered, but a short way along this forked, and she turned off to the right. Again and again the passage divided, but she led us on, never faltering or seeming to doubt her way, and with increasing speed.

'If only we are in time,' she panted. 'We must be out in the open before the explosion occurs.'

Still we went on. I understood that this tunnel led right through the mountain and that we should finally emerge on the other side, facing a different valley. The sweat streamed down my face, but I raced on.

And then, far away, I saw a gleam of daylight. Nearer and nearer. I saw green bushes growing. We forced them aside, pushed our way through. We were in the open again, with the faint light of dawn making everything rosy.

Poirot's cordon was a reality. Even as we emerged, three men fell upon us, but released us again with a cry of astonishment.

'Quick,' cried my companion. 'Quick – there is no time to lose –'

But he was not destined to finish. The earth shook and trembled under our feet, there was a terrific roar and the whole mountain seemed to dissolve. We were flung headlong through the air.

I came to myself at last. I was in a strange bed and a strange room. Someone was sitting by the window. He turned and came and stood by me.

It was Achille Poirot – or, stay, was it –

The well-known ironical voice dispelled any doubts I might have had.

'But yes, my friend, it is. Brother Achille has gone home again – to the land of myths. It was I all the time. It is not only Number Four who can act a part. Belladonna in the eyes, the sacrifice of the moustaches, and a real scar the inflicting of which caused me much pain two months ago – but I could not risk a fake beneath the eagle eyes of Number Four. And the final touch, your own knowledge and belief that there was such a person as Achille Poirot! It was invaluable, the assistance you rendered me, half the success of the *coup* is due to you! The whole crux of the affair was to make them believe that Hercule Poirot was still at large directing operations. Otherwise, everything was true, the aniseed, the cordon, etc.'

'But why not really send a substitute?'

'And let you go into danger without me by your side? You have a pretty idea of me there! Besides, I always had a hope of finding a way out through the countess.'

'How on earth did you manage to convince her? It was a pretty thin story to make her swallow – all that about a dead child.'

'The countess has a great deal more perspicacity than you have, my dear Hastings. She was taken in at first by my disguise; but she soon saw through it. When she said, "You are very clever, M. Achille Poirot," I knew that she had guessed the truth. It was then or never to play my trump card.'

'All that rigmarole about bringing the dead to life?'

'Exactly – but then, you see, I had the child all along.'

'*What?*'

'But yes! You know my motto – Be prepared. As soon as I found that the Countess Rossakoff was mixed up with the Big Four, I had every possible inquiry made as to her antecedents. I learnt that she had had a child who was reported to have been killed, and I also found that there were discrepancies in the story which led me to wonder whether it might not, after all, be alive. In the end, I succeeded in tracing the boy, and by paying out a big sum I obtained possession of the child's person. The poor little fellow was nearly dead of starvation. I placed him in a safe place, with kindly people, and took a snapshot of him in his new surroundings. And so, when the time came, I had my little *coup de théâtre* all ready!'

'You are wonderful, Poirot; absolutely wonderful!'

'I was glad to do it, too. For I had admired the countess. I should have been sorry if she had perished in the explosion.'

'I've been half afraid to ask you – what of the Big Four?'

'All the bodies have now been recovered. That of Number Four was quite unrecognizable, the head blown to pieces. I wish – I rather wish it had not been so. I should have liked to be *sure* – but no more of that. Look at this.'

He handed me a newspaper in which a paragraph was marked. It reported the death, by suicide, of Li Chang Yen, who had engineered the recent revolution which had failed so disastrously.

'My great opponent,' said Poirot gravely. 'It was fated that he and I should never meet in the flesh. When he received the news of the disaster here, he took the simplest way out. A great brain, my friend, a great brain. But I wish I had seen the face of the man who was Number Four . . . Supposing that, after all – but I romance. He is dead. Yes, *mon ami*, together we have faced and routed the Big Four; and now you will return to your charming wife, and I – I shall retire. The great case of my life is over. Anything else will seem tame after this. No, I shall retire. Possibly I shall grow vegetable marrows! I might even marry and arrange myself!'

He laughed heartily at the idea, but with a touch of embarrassment. I hope . . . small men always admire big, flamboyant women –

'Marry and arrange myself,' he said again. 'Who knows?'

Postscript

The writing of The Big Four *was embarked upon at the worst time in Agatha Christie's life, in the year that followed the death of her mother, while her marriage was foundering and Archibald was urging her to divorce him so that he could marry Nancy Neele . . .*

Since the death of her mother, she had been incapable of writing a single line. But, having invested all her money in buying the Sunningdale house – called 'Styles' at Archie's instigation – she found herself in a difficult financial situation. The only way for her to earn some money was to write a new book.

Her brother-in-law Campbell Christie – 'who had always been a great friend and was a kind and lovable person' – suggested she gather together in one volume a dozen short stories which had appeared in The Sketch *magazine, in which Hercule Poirot confronted same gang of four great criminals: The Four or The Big Four, and their scheme of destruction and global conquest. (The Four is something of a double take on* The Four Just Men *(1906), Edgar Wallace's great classic criminal adventure story.)*

It was enough to write an opening chapter and a final chapter and to thread together the different episodes of this fierce battle between Poirot, Hastings and their four 'Moriartys': Number One Li Chang Yen, the American Number Two, the Frenchwoman Number Three and the man known by the nickname of the Destroyer or Number Four.

In The Big Four, *Hercule Poirot finds himself submerged in a universe of international intrigue, secret arms, underground laboratories, kidnapped physicists, perpetual ambushes with the inevitable Fu Manchu and a secret leader capable of one hundred different identities (a sort of man of a hundred masks, to imitate Edgar Wallace). In short, this is the world of the 'thriller', a departure from the three 'mystery' stories in which Poirot's detective career had started. By bringing Agatha*

Christie's first two styles together, The Big Four *is therefore something of a curiosity, as much for its background as its subject matter.*

It is also a sort of review-story, where Agatha Christie brings back a number of her characters: Inspector Japp from The Mysterious Affair of Styles, *Giraud of the Sûreté, already seen in* Murder on the Links, *Hastings summoned from a peaceful Argentinean retreat, Joseph Aarons, the Jewish theatrical agent friend of Hercule Poirot, also from* Murder on the Links, *Countess Vera Rossakoff, a very beautiful Russian aristocrat whom Poirot met for the first time in a short story in 1925,* The Double Clue, *regarding a burglary in a jeweller's shop in London. In* The Big Four, *he is so taken with the beautiful countess that he even envisages marriage!*

The Big Four *shows, on several occasions, undeniable influences of Holmes. Countess Rossakoff – who hides in Paris under the identity of Inez Veroneau – gets this description: 'Poirot, for some reason or other, had always had a sneaking fondness for the countess. She was, he was wont to declare in moments of enthusiasm, a woman in a thousand.' Here we see the terms used by Sherlock Holmes concerning Irene Adler in* The Bohemian Scandal *(even the name Inez suggests Irene). Just as, when Poirot announces to Hastings the existence of his twin brother Achille Poirot, there is a clear reference to Mycroft Holmes.*

Finally, The Big Four *contains an intriguing cinematic paradox. In Chapter XIV – entitled 'The Peroxide Blonde' – the subject is an actress called Miss Monro. However, in 1927, Marilyn Monroe – only one year old – was just Norma Jean Baker . . .*

The Big Four, *published in January 1927, was very successful with the public as more than 8,500 copies were sold. (*The Murder of Roger Ackroyd *had sold around 4,000 copies, which was considered to be a great result at that time.) The media uproar about the disappearance of Agatha Christie in December 1926 had obviously had some beneficial effect!*

THE MYSTERY OF
THE BLUE TRAIN

CHAPTER I

The Man with the White Hair

It was close on midnight when a man crossed the Place de la Concorde. In spite of the handsome fur coat which garbed his meagre form, there was something essentially weak and paltry about him.

A little man with a face like a rat. A man, one would say, who could never play a conspicuous part, or rise to prominence in any sphere. And yet, in leaping to such a conclusion, an onlooker would have been wrong. For this man, negligible and inconspicuous as he seemed, played a prominent part in the destiny of the world. In an Empire where rats ruled, he was the king of the rats.

Even now, an Embassy awaited his return. But he had business to do first – business of which the Embassy was not officially cognizant. His face gleamed white and sharp in the moonlight. There was the least hint of a curve in the thin nose. His father had been a Polish Jew, a journeyman tailor. It was business such as his father would have loved that took him abroad tonight.

He came to the Seine, crossed it, and entered one of the less reputable quarters of Paris. Here he stopped before a tall, dilapidated house and made his way up to an apartment on the fourth floor. He had barely time to knock before the door was opened by a woman who had evidently been awaiting his arrival. She gave him no greeting, but helped him off with his overcoat and then led the way into the tawdrily furnished sitting-room. The electric light was shaded with dirty pink festoons, and it softened, but could not disguise, the girl's face with its mask of crude paint. Could not disguise, either, the broad Mongolian cast of her countenance. There was no doubt of Olga Demiroff's profession, nor of her nationality.

'All is well, little one?'

'All is well, Boris Ivanovitch.'

He nodded, murmuring: 'I do not think I have been followed.'

But there was anxiety in his tone. He went to the window, drawing the curtains aside slightly, and peering carefully out. He started away violently.

'There are two men – on the opposite pavement. It looks to me –' He broke off and began gnawing at his nails – a habit he had when anxious.

The Russian girl was shaking her head with a slow, reassuring action.

'They were here before you came.'

'All the same, it looks to me as though they were watching this house.'

'Possibly,' she admitted indifferently.

'But then –'

'What of it? Even if they *know* – it will not be *you* they will follow from here.'

A thin, cruel smile came to his lips.

'No,' he admitted, 'that is true.'

He mused for a minute or two, and then observed,

'This damned American – he can look after himself as well as anybody.'

'I suppose so.'

He went again to the window.

'Tough customers,' he muttered, with a chuckle. 'Known to the police, I fear. Well, well, I wish Brother Apache good hunting.'

Olga Demiroff shook her head.

'If the American is the kind of man they say he is, it will take more than a couple of cowardly apaches to get the better of him.' She paused. 'I wonder –'

'Well?'

'Nothing. Only twice this evening a man has passed along this street – a man with white hair.'

'What of it?'

'This. As he passed those two men, he dropped his glove. One of them picked it up and returned it to him. A threadbare device.'

'You mean – that the white-haired man is – their employer?'

'Something of the kind.'

The Russian looked alarmed and uneasy.

'You are sure – the parcel is safe? It has not been tampered with? There has been too much talk ... much too much talk.'

He gnawed his nails again.

'Judge for yourself.'

She bent to the fireplace, deftly removing the coals. Underneath, from amongst the crumpled balls of newspaper, she selected from the very middle an oblong package wrapped round with grimy newspaper, and handed it to the man.

'Ingenious,' he said, with a nod of approval.

'The apartment has been searched twice. The mattress on my bed was ripped open.'

'It is as I said,' he muttered. 'There has been too much talk. This haggling over the price – it was a mistake.'

He had unwrapped the newspaper. Inside was a small brown paper parcel. This in turn he unwrapped, verified the contents, and quickly wrapped it up once more. As he did so, an electric bell rang sharply.

'The American is punctual,' said Olga, with a glance at the clock.

She left the room. In a minute she returned ushering in a stranger, a big, broad-shouldered man whose transatlantic origin was evident. His keen glance went from one to the other.

'M. Krassnine?' he inquired politely.

'I am he,' said Boris. 'I must apologize for – for the unconventionality of this meeting-place. But secrecy is urgent. I – I cannot afford to be connected with this business in any way.'

'Is that so?' said the American politely.

'I have your word, have I not, that no details of this transaction will be made public? That is one of the conditions of – sale.'

The American nodded.

'That has already been agreed upon,' he said indifferently. 'Now, perhaps, you will produce the goods.'

'You have the money – in notes?'

'Yes,' replied the other.

He did not, however, make any attempt to produce it. After a moment's hesitation, Krassnine gestured towards the small parcel on the table.

The American took it up and unrolled the wrapping paper. The contents he took over to a small electric lamp and submitted them to a very thorough examination. Satisfied, he drew from his pocket a thick leather wallet and extracted from it a wad of notes. These he handed to the Russian, who counted them carefully.

'All right?'

'I thank you, Monsieur. Everything is correct.'

'Ah!' said the other. He slipped the brown paper parcel negligently into his pocket. He bowed to Olga. 'Good evening, Mademoiselle. Good evening, M. Krassnine.'

He went out, shutting the door behind him. The eyes of the two in the room met. The man passed his tongue over his dry lips.

'I wonder – will he ever get back to his hotel?' he muttered.

By common accord, they both turned to the window. They were just in time to see the American emerge into the street below. He turned to the left and marched along at a good pace without once turning his head. Two shadows stole from a doorway and followed noiselessly. Pursuers and pursued vanished into the night. Olga Demiroff spoke.

'He will get back safely,' she said. 'You need not fear – or hope – whichever it is.'

'Why do you think he will be safe?' asked Krassnine curiously.

'A man who has made as much money as he has could not possibly be a fool,' said Olga. 'And talking of money –'

She looked significantly at Krassnine.

'Eh?'

'My share, Boris Ivanovitch.'

With some reluctance, Krassnine handed over two of the

notes. She nodded her thanks, with a complete lack of emotion, and tucked them away in her stocking.

'That is good,' she remarked, with satisfaction.

He looked at her curiously.

'You have no regrets, Olga Vassilovna?'

'Regrets? For what?'

'For what has been in your keeping. There are women – most women, I believe, who go mad over such things.'

She nodded reflectively.

'Yes, you speak truth there. Most women have that madness. I – have not. I wonder now –' She broke off.

'Well?' asked the other curiously.

'The American will be safe with them – yes, I am sure of that. But afterwards –'

'Eh? What are you thinking of?'

'He will give them, of course, to some woman,' said Olga thoughtfully. 'I wonder what will happen then . . .'

She shook herself impatiently and went over to the window. Suddenly she uttered an exclamation and called to her companion.

'See, he is going down the street now – the man I mean.'

They both gazed down together. A slim, elegant figure was progressing along at a leisurely pace. He wore an opera hat and a cloak. As he passed a street lamp, the light illuminated a thatch of thick white hair.

CHAPTER II

M. le Marquis

The man with the white hair continued on his course, unhurried, and seemingly indifferent to his surroundings. He took a side turning to the right and another one to the left. Now and then he hummed a little air to himself.

Suddenly he stopped dead and listened intently. He had heard a certain sound. It might have been the bursting of a tyre or it might have been – a shot. A curious smile played round his lips for a minute. Then he resumed his leisurely walk.

On turning a corner he came upon a scene of some activity. A representative of the law was making notes in a pocket-book, and one or two late passers-by had collected on the spot. To one of these the man with the white hair made a polite request for information.

'Something has been happening, yes?'

'*Mais oui*, Monsieur. Two apaches set upon an elderly American gentleman.'

'They did him no injury?'

'No, indeed.' The man laughed. 'The American, he had a revolver in his pocket, and before they could attack him, he fired shots so closely round them that they took alarm and fled. The police, as usual, arrived too late.'

'Ah!' said the inquirer.

He displayed no emotion of any kind.

Placidly and unconcernedly he resumed his nocturnal strolling. Presently he crossed the Seine and came into the richer areas of the city. It was some twenty minutes later that he came to a stop before a certain house in a quiet but aristocratic thoroughfare.

The shop, for shop it was, was a restrained and unpretentious one. D. Papopolous, dealer in antiques, was so known to fame that he needed no advertisement, and indeed most of his business was not done over a counter. M. Papopolous had a very handsome apartment of his own overlooking the Champs Elysées, and it might reasonably be supposed that he would have been found there and not at his place of business at such an hour, but the man with the white hair seemed confident of success as he pressed the obscurely placed bell, having first given a quick glance up and down the deserted street.

His confidence was not misplaced. The door opened and a man stood in the aperture. He wore gold rings in his ears and was of a swarthy cast of countenance.

'Good evening,' said the stranger. 'Your master is within?'

'The master is here, but he does not see chance visitors at this time of night,' growled the other.

'I think he will see me. Tell him that his friend M. le Marquis is here.'

The man opened the door a little wider and allowed the visitor to enter.

The man who gave his name as M. le Marquis had shielded his face with his hand as he spoke. When the manservant returned with the information that M. Papopolous would be pleased to receive the visitor a further change had taken place in the stranger's appearance. The manservant must have been very unobservant or very well trained, for he betrayed no surprise at the small black satin mask which hid the other's features. Leading the way to a door at the end of the hall, he opened it and announced in a respectful murmur: '*M. le Marquis.*'

The figure which rose to receive this strange guest was an imposing one. There was something venerable and patriarchal about M. Papopolous. He had a high domed forehead and a beautiful white beard. His manner had in it something ecclesiastical and benign.

'My dear friend,' said M. Papopolous.

He spoke in French and his tones were rich and unctuous.

'I must apologize,' said the visitor, 'for the lateness of the hour.'

'Not at all. Not at all,' said M. Papopolous – 'an interesting time of night. You have had, perhaps, an interesting evening?'

'Not personally,' said M. le Marquis.

'Not personally,' repeated M. Papopolous, 'no, no, of course not. And there is news, eh?'

He cast a sharp glance sideways at the other, a glance that was not ecclesiastical or benign in the least.

'There is no news. The attempt failed. I hardly expected anything else.'

'Quite so,' said M. Papopolous: 'anything crude –'

He waved his hand to express his intense distaste for crudity in any form. There was indeed nothing crude about M. Papopolous nor about the goods he handled. He was well known in most European courts, and kings called him Demetrius in a friendly manner. He had the reputation for the most exquisite discretion. That, together with the nobility of his aspect, had carried him through several very questionable transactions.

'The direct attack –' said M. Papopolous. He shook his head. 'It answers sometimes – but very seldom.'

The other shrugged his shoulders.

'It saves time,' he remarked, 'and to fail costs nothing – or next to nothing. The other plan – will not fail.'

'Ah,' said M. Papopolous, looking at him keenly.

The other nodded slowly.

'I have great confidence in your – er – reputation,' said the antique dealer.

M. le Marquis smiled gently.

'I think I may say,' he murmured, 'that your confidence will not be misplaced.'

'You have unique opportunities,' said the other, with a note of envy in his voice.

'I make them,' said M. le Marquis.

He rose and took up the cloak which he had thrown carelessly on the back of a chair.

'I will keep you informed, M. Papopolous, through the usual channels, but there must be no hitch in your arrangements.'

M. Papopolous was pained.

'There is *never* a hitch in my arrangements,' he complained.

The other smiled, and without any further word of adieu he left the room, closing the door behind him.

M. Papopolous remained in thought for a moment, stroking his venerable white beard, and then moved across to a second door which opened inwards. As he turned the handle, a young woman, who only too clearly had been leaning against it with her ear to the keyhole, stumbled headlong into the room. M. Papopolous displayed neither surprise nor concern. It was evidently all quite natural to him.

'Well, Zia?' he asked.

'I did not hear him go,' explained Zia.

She was a handsome young woman, built on Junoesque lines, with dark flashing eyes and such a general air of resemblance to M. Papopolous that it was easy to see they were father and daughter.

'It is annoying,' she continued vexedly, 'that one cannot see through a keyhole and hear through it at the same time.'

'It has often annoyed me,' said M. Papopolous, with great simplicity.

'So that is M. le Marquis,' said Zia slowly. 'Does he always wear a mask, Father?'

'Always.'

There was a pause.

'It is the rubies, I suppose?' asked Zia.

Her father nodded.

'What do you think, my little one?' he inquired, with a hint of amusement in his beady black eyes.

'Of M. le Marquis?'

'Yes.'

'I think,' said Zia slowly, 'that it is a very rare thing to find a well-bred Englishman who speaks French as well as that.'

'Ah!' said M. Papopolous, 'so that is what you think.'

As usual, he did not commit himself, but he regarded Zia with benign approval.

'I thought, too,' said Zia, 'that his head was an odd shape.'

'Massive,' said her father – 'a trifle massive. But then that effect is always created by a wig.'

They both looked at each other and smiled.

CHAPTER III

Heart of Fire

Rufus Van Aldin passed through the revolving doors of the Savoy, and walked to the reception desk. The desk clerk smiled a respectful greeting.

'Pleased to see you back again, Mr Van Aldin,' he said.

The American millionaire nodded his head in a casual greeting.

'Everything all right?' he asked.

'Yes, sir. Major Knighton is upstairs in the suite now.'

Van Aldin nodded again.

'Any mail?' he vouchsafed.

'They have all been sent up, Mr Van Aldin. Oh! wait a minute.'

He dived into a pigeon hole, and produced a letter.

'Just come this minute,' he explained.

Rufus Van Aldin took the letter from him, and as he saw the handwriting, a woman's flowing hand, his face was suddenly transformed. The harsh contours of it softened, and the hard line of his mouth relaxed. He looked a different man. He walked across to the lift with the letter in his hand and the smile still on his lips.

In the drawing-room of his suite, a young man was sitting at a desk nimbly sorting correspondence with the ease born of long practice. He sprang up as Van Aldin entered.

'Hallo, Knighton!'

'Glad to see you back, sir. Had a good time?'

'So so!' said the millionaire unemotionally. 'Paris is rather a one-horse city nowadays. Still – I got what I went over for.'

He smiled to himself rather grimly.

'You usually do, I believe,' said the secretary, laughing.

'That's so,' agreed the other.

He spoke in a matter-of-fact manner, as one stating a well-known fact. Throwing off his heavy overcoat, he advanced to the desk.

'Anything urgent?'

'I don't think so, sir. Mostly the usual stuff. I have not quite finished sorting it out.'

Van Aldin nodded briefly. He was a man who seldom expressed either blame or praise. His methods with those he employed were simple; he gave them a fair trial and dismissed promptly those who were inefficient. His selections of people were unconventional. Knighton, for instance, he had met casually at a Swiss resort two months previously. He had approved of the fellow, looked up his war record, and found in it the explanation of the limp with which he walked. Knighton had made no secret of the fact that he was looking for a job, and indeed diffidently asked the millionaire if he knew of any available post. Van Aldin remembered, with a grim smile of amusement, the young man's complete astonishment when he had been offered the post of secretary to the great man himself.

'But – but I have no experience of business,' he had stammered.

'That doesn't matter a cuss,' Van Aldin had replied. 'I have got three secretaries already to attend to that kind of thing. But I am likely to be in England for the next six months, and I want an Englishman who – well, knows the ropes – and can attend to the social side of things for me.'

So far, Van Aldin had found his judgment confirmed. Knighton had proved quick, intelligent, and resourceful, and he had a distinct charm of manner.

The secretary indicated three or four letters placed by themselves on the top of the desk.

'It might perhaps be as well, sir, if you glanced at these,' he suggested. 'The top one is about the Colton agreement –'

But Rufus Van Aldin held up a protesting hand.

'I am not going to look at a darned thing tonight,' he declared. 'They can all wait till the morning. Except this one,' he added, looking down at the letter he held in his hand. And again that strange transforming smile stole over his face.

Richard Knighton smiled sympathetically.

'Mrs Kettering?' he murmured. 'She rang up yesterday and today. She seems very anxious to see you at once, sir.'

'Does she, now!'

The smile faded from the millionaire's face. He ripped open the envelope which he held in his hand and took out the enclosed sheet. As he read it his face darkened, his mouth set grimly in the line which Wall Street knew so well, and his brows knit themselves ominously. Knighton turned tactfully away, and went on opening letters and sorting them. A muttered oath escaped the millionaire, and his clenched fist hit the table sharply.

'I'll not stand for this,' he muttered to himself. 'Poor little girl, it's a good thing she has her old father behind her.'

He walked up and down the room for some minutes, his brows drawn together in a scowl. Knighton still bent assiduously over the desk. Suddenly Van Aldin came to an abrupt halt. He took up his overcoat from the chair where he had thrown it.

'Are you going out again, sir?'

'Yes, I'm going round to see my daughter.'

'If Colton's people ring up –?'

'Tell them to go to the devil,' said Van Aldin.

'Very well,' said the secretary unemotionally.

Van Aldin had his overcoat on by now. Cramming his hat upon his head, he went towards the door. He paused with his hand upon the handle.

'You are a good fellow, Knighton,' he said. 'You don't worry me when I am rattled.'

Knighton smiled a little, but made no reply.

'Ruth is my only child,' said Van Aldin, 'and there is no one on this earth who knows quite what she means to me.'

A faint smile irradiated his face. He slipped his hand into his pocket.

'Care to see something, Knighton?'

He came back towards the secretary.

From his pocket he drew out a parcel carelessly wrapped in

brown paper. He tossed off the wrapping and disclosed a big, shabby, red velvet case. In the centre of it were some twisted initials surmounted by a crown. He snapped the case open, and the secretary drew in his breath sharply. Against the slightly dingy white of the interior, the stones glowed like blood.

'My God! sir,' said Knighton. 'Are they – are they real?'

Van Aldin laughed a quiet little cackle of amusement.

'I don't wonder at your asking that. Amongst these rubies are the three largest in the world. Catherine of Russia wore them, Knighton. That centre one there is known as "Heart of Fire". It's perfect – not a flaw in it.'

'But,' the secretary murmured, 'they must be worth a fortune.'

'Four or five hundred thousand dollars,' said Van Aldin nonchalantly, 'and that is apart from the historical interest.'

'And you carry them about – like that, loose in your pocket?'

Van Aldin laughed amusedly.

'I guess so. You see, they are my little present for Ruthie.'

The secretary smiled discreetly.

'I can understand now Mrs Kettering's anxiety over the telephone,' he murmured.

But Van Aldin shook his head. The hard look returned to his face.

'You are wrong there,' he said. 'She doesn't know about these; they are my little surprise for her.'

He shut the case, and began slowly to wrap it up again.

'It's a hard thing, Knighton,' he said, 'how little one can do for those one loves. I can buy a good portion of the earth for Ruth, if it would be any use to her, but it isn't. I can hang these things round her neck and give her a moment or two's pleasure, maybe, but –'

He shook his head.

'When a woman is not happy in her home –'

He left the sentence unfinished. The secretary nodded discreetly. He knew, none better, the reputation of the Hon. Derek Kettering. Van Aldin sighed. Slipping the parcel back in his coat pocket, he nodded to Knighton and left the room.

CHAPTER IV

In Curzon Street

The Hon. Mrs Derek Kettering lived in Curzon Street. The butler who opened the door recognized Rufus Van Aldin at once and permitted himself a discreet smile of greeting. He led the way upstairs to the big double drawing-room on the first floor.

A woman who was sitting by the window started up with a cry.

'Why, Dad, if that isn't too good for anything! I've been telephoning Major Knighton all day to try and get hold of you, but he couldn't say for sure when you were expected back.'

Ruth Kettering was twenty-eight years of age. Without being beautiful, or in the real sense of the word even pretty, she was striking looking because of her colouring. Van Aldin had been called Carrots and Ginger in his time, and Ruth's hair was almost pure auburn. With it went dark eyes and very black lashes – the effect somewhat enhanced by art. She was tall and slender, and moved well. At a careless glance it was the face of a Raphael Madonna. Only if one looked closely did one perceive the same line of jaw and chin as in Van Aldin's face, bespeaking the same hardness and determination. It suited the man, but suited the woman less well. From her childhood upward Ruth Van Aldin had been accustomed to having her own way, and anyone who had ever stood up against her soon realized that Rufus Van Aldin's daughter never gave in.

'Knighton told me you'd phoned him,' said Van Aldin. 'I only got back from Paris half an hour ago. What's all this about Derek?'

Ruth Kettering flushed angrily.

'It's unspeakable. It's beyond all limits,' she cried. 'He – he doesn't seem to listen to anything I say.'

There was bewilderment as well as anger in her voice.

'He'll listen to me,' said the millionaire grimly.

Ruth went on.

'I've hardly seen him for the last month. He goes about everywhere with that woman.'

'With what woman?'

'Mirelle. She dances at the Parthenon, you know.'

Van Aldin nodded.

'I was down at Leconbury last week. I – I spoke to Lord Leconbury. He was awfully sweet to me, sympathized entirely. He said he'd give Derek a good talking to.'

'Ah!' said Van Aldin.

'What do you mean by "Ah!", Dad?'

'Just what you think I mean, Ruthie. Poor old Leconbury is a washout. Of course he sympathized with you, of course he tried to soothe you down. Having got his son and heir married to the daughter of one of the richest men in the States, he naturally doesn't want to mess the thing up. But he's got one foot in the grave already, everyone knows that, and anything he may say will cut darned little ice with Derek.'

'Can't *you* do anything, Dad?' urged Ruth, after a minute or two.

'I might,' said the millionaire. He waited a second reflectively, and then went on. 'There are several things I might do, but there's only one that will be any real good. How much pluck have you got, Ruthie?'

She stared at him. He nodded back at her.

'I mean just what I say. Have you got the grit to admit to all the world that you've made a mistake? There's only one way out of this mess, Ruthie. Cut your losses and start afresh.'

'You mean –?'

'Divorce.'

'Divorce!'

Van Aldin smiled drily.

'You say that word, Ruth, as though you'd never heard it

before. And yet your friends are doing it all round you every day.'

'Oh! I know that. But –'

She stopped, biting her lip. Her father nodded comprehendingly.

'I know, Ruth. You're like me, you can't bear to let go. But I've learnt, and you've got to learn, that there are times when it's the only way. I might find ways of whistling Derek back to you, but it would all come to the same in the end. *He's no good*, Ruth; he's rotten through and through. And mind you, I blame myself for ever letting you marry him. But you were kind of set on having him, and he seemed in earnest about turning over a new leaf – and well, I'd crossed you once, honey . . .'

He did not look at her as he said the last words. Had he done so, he might have seen the swift colour that came up in her face.

'You did,' she said in a hard voice.

'I was too darned soft-hearted to do it a second time. I can't tell you how I wish I had, though. You've led a poor kind of life for the last few years, Ruth.'

'It has not been very – agreeable,' agreed Mrs Kettering.

'That's why I say to you that this thing has got to *stop*!' He brought his hand down with a bang on the table. 'You may have a hankering after the fellow still. *Cut it out.* Face facts. Derek Kettering married you for your money. That's all there is to it. Get rid of him, Ruth.'

Ruth Kettering looked down at the ground for some moments, then she said, without raising her head:

'Supposing he doesn't consent?'

Van Aldin looked at her in astonishment.

'He won't have a say in the matter.'

She flushed and bit her lip.

'No – no – of course not. I only meant –'

She stopped. Her father eyed her keenly.

'What did you mean?'

'I meant –' She paused, choosing her words carefully. 'He mayn't take it lying down.'

The millionaire's chin shot out grimly.

'You mean he'll fight the case? Let him! But, as a matter of fact, you're wrong. He won't fight. Any solicitor he consults will tell him he hasn't a leg to stand upon.'

'You don't think' – she hesitated – 'I mean – out of sheer spite against me – he might, well, try to make it awkward?'

Her father looked at her in some astonishment.

'Fight the case, you mean?'

He shook his head.

'Very unlikely. You see, he would have to have something to go upon.'

Mrs Kettering did not answer. Van Aldin looked at her sharply.

'Come, Ruth, out with it. There's something troubling you – what is it?'

'Nothing, nothing at all.'

But her voice was unconvincing.

'You are dreading the publicity, eh? Is that it? You leave it to me. I'll put the whole thing through so smoothly that there will be no fuss at all.'

'Very well, Dad, if you really think it's the best thing to be done.'

'Got a fancy for the fellow still, Ruth? Is that it?'

'No.'

The word came with no uncertain emphasis. Van Aldin seemed satisfied. He patted his daughter on the shoulder.

'It will be all right, little girl. Don't you worry any. Now let's forget about all this. I have brought you a present from Paris.'

'For me? Something very nice?'

'I hope you'll think so,' said Van Aldin, smiling.

He took the parcel from his coat pocket and handed it to her. She unwrapped it eagerly, and snapped open the case. A long-drawn 'Oh!' came from her lips. Ruth Kettering loved jewels – always had done so.

'Dad, how – how wonderful!'

'Rather in a class by themselves, aren't they?' said the millionaire with satisfaction. 'You like them, eh.'

'Like them? Dad, they're unique. How did you get hold of them?'

Van Aldin smiled.

'Ah! that's my secret. They had to be bought privately, of course. They are rather well known. See that big stone in the middle? You have heard of it, maybe; that's the historic "Heart of Fire".'

'Heart of Fire!' repeated Mrs Kettering.

She had taken the stones from the case and was holding them against her breast. The millionaire watched her. He was thinking of the series of women who had worn the jewels. The heartaches, the despairs, the jealousies. 'Heart of Fire', like all famous stones, had left behind it a trail of tragedy and violence. Held in Ruth Kettering's assured hand, it seemed to lose its potency of evil. With her cool, equable poise, this woman of the Western world seemed a negation to tragedy or heart-burnings. Ruth returned the stones to their case; then, jumping up, she flung her arms round her father's neck.

'Thank you, thank you, thank you, Dad. They are wonderful! You do give me the most marvellous presents always.'

'That's all right,' said Van Aldin, patting her shoulder. 'You are all I have, you know, Ruthie.'

'You will stay to dinner, won't you, Father?'

'I don't think so. You were going out, weren't you?'

'Yes, but I can easily put that off. Nothing very exciting.'

'No,' said Van Aldin. 'Keep your engagement. I have got a good deal to attend to. See you tomorrow, my dear. Perhaps if I phone you, we can meet a Galbraiths'?'

Messrs Galbraith, Galbraith, Cuthbertson & Galbraith were Van Aldin's London solicitors.

'Very well, Dad.' She hesitated. 'I suppose it – this – won't keep me from going to the Riviera?'

'When are you off?'

'On the fourteenth.'

'Oh, that will be all right. These things take a long time to mature. By the way, Ruth, I shouldn't take those rubies abroad if I were you. Leave them at the bank.'

Mrs Kettering nodded.

'We don't want to have you robbed and murdered for the sake of "Heart of Fire",' said the millionaire jocosely.

'And yet you carried it about in your pocket loose,' retorted his daughter, smiling.

'Yes –'

Something, some hesitation, caught her attention.

'What is it, Dad?'

'Nothing.' He smiled. 'Thinking of a little adventure of mine in Paris.'

'An adventure?'

'Yes, the night I bought these things.'

He made a gesture towards the jewel case.

'Oh, do tell me.'

'Nothing to tell, Ruthie. Some apache fellows got a bit fresh and I shot at them and they got off. That's all.'

She looked at him with some pride.

'You're a tough proposition, Dad.'

'You bet I am, Ruthie.'

He kissed her affectionately and departed. On arriving back at the Savoy, he gave a curt order to Knighton.

'Get hold of a man called Goby; you'll find his address in my private book. He's to be here tomorrow morning at half-past nine.'

'Yes, sir.'

'I also want to see Mr Kettering. Run him to earth for me if you can. Try his Club – at any rate, get hold of him somehow, and arrange for me to see him here tomorrow morning. Better make it latish, about twelve. His sort aren't early risers.'

The secretary nodded in comprehension of these instructions. Van Aldin gave himself into the hands of his valet. His bath was prepared, and as he lay luxuriating in the hot water, his mind went back over the conversation with his daughter. On the whole he was well satisfied. His keen mind had long since accepted the fact that divorce was the only possible way out. Ruth had agreed to the proposed solution with more readiness than he had hoped for. Yet, in spite of her acquiescence, he was left with a vague sense of uneasiness. Something about her manner, he felt, had not been quite natural. He frowned to himself.

'Maybe I'm fanciful,' he muttered, 'and yet – I bet there's something she has not told me.'

CHAPTER V

A Useful Gentleman

Rufus Van Aldin had just finished the sparse breakfast of coffee and dry toast, which was all he ever allowed himself, when Knighton entered the room.

'Mr Goby is below, sir, waiting to see you.'

The millionaire glanced at the clock. It was just half-past nine.

'All right,' he said curtly. 'He can come up.'

A minute or two later, Mr Goby entered the room. He was a small, elderly man, shabbily dressed, with eyes that looked carefully all round the room, and never at the person he was addressing.

'Good morning, Goby,' said the millionaire. 'Take a chair.'

'Thank you, Mr Van Aldin.'

Mr Goby sat down with his hands on his knees, and gazed earnestly at the radiator.

'I have got a job for you.'

'Yes, Mr Van Aldin?'

'My daughter is married to the Hon. Derek Kettering, as you may perhaps know.'

Mr Goby transferred his gaze from the radiator to the left-hand drawer of the desk, and permitted a deprecating smile to pass over his face. Mr Goby knew a great many things, but he always hated to admit the fact.

'By my advice, she is about to file a petition for divorce. That, of course, is a solicitor's business. But, for private reasons, I want the fullest and most complete information.'

Mr Goby looked at the cornice and murmured:

'About Mr Kettering?'

'About Mr Kettering.'

'Very good, sir.'

Mr Goby rose to his feet.

'When will you have it ready for me?'

'Are you in a hurry, sir?'

'I'm always in a hurry,' said the millionaire.

Mr Goby smiled understandingly at the fender.

'Shall we say two o'clock this afternoon, sir?' he asked.

'Excellent,' approved the other. 'Good morning, Goby.'

'Good morning, Mr Van Aldin.'

'That's a very useful man,' said the millionaire as Goby went out and his secretary came in. 'In his own line he's a specialist.'

'What is his line?'

'Information. Give him twenty-four hours and he would lay the private life of the Archbishop of Canterbury bare for you.'

'A useful sort of chap,' said Knighton, with a smile.

'He has been useful to me once or twice,' said Van Aldin. 'Now then, Knighton, I'm ready for work.'

The next few hours saw a vast quantity of business rapidly transacted. It was half-past twelve when the telephone bell rang, and Mr Van Aldin was informed that Mr Kettering had called. Knighton looked at Van Aldin, and interpreted his brief nod.

'Ask Mr Kettering to come up, please.'

The secretary gathered up his papers and departed. He and the visitor passed each other in the doorway, and Derek Kettering stood aside to let the other go out. Then he came in, shutting the door behind him.

'Good morning, sir. You are very anxious to see me, I hear.'

The lazy voice with its slightly ironic inflection roused memories in Van Aldin. There was charm in it – there had always been charm in it. He looked piercingly at his son-in-law. Derek Kettering was thirty-four, lean of build, with a dark, narrow face, which had even now something indescribably boyish in it.

'Come in,' said Van Aldin curtly. 'Sit down.'

Kettering flung himself lightly into an arm-chair. He looked at his father-in-law with a kind of tolerant amusement.

'Not seen you for a long time, sir,' he remarked pleasantly. 'About two years, I should say. Seen Ruth yet?'

'I saw her last night,' said Van Aldin.

'Looking very fit, isn't she?' said the other lightly.

'I didn't know you had had much opportunity of judging,' said Van Aldin drily.

Derek Kettering raised his eyebrows.

'Oh, we sometimes meet at the same night club, you know,' he said airily.

'I am not going to beat about the bush,' Van Aldin said curtly. 'I have advised Ruth to file a petition for divorce.'

Derek Kettering seemed unmoved.

'How drastic!' he murmured. 'Do you mind if I smoke, sir?'

He lit a cigarette, and puffed out a cloud of smoke as he added nonchalantly:

'And what did Ruth say?'

'Ruth proposes to take my advice,' said her father.

'Does she really?'

'Is that all you have got to say?' demanded Van Aldin sharply.

Kettering flicked his ash into the grate.

'I think, you know,' he said, with a detached air, 'that she's making a great mistake.'

'From your point of view she doubtless is,' said Van Aldin grimly.

'Oh, come now,' said the other; 'don't let's be personal. I really wasn't thinking of myself at the moment. I was thinking of Ruth. You know my poor old Governor really can't last much longer; all the doctors say so. Ruth had better give it a couple more years, then I shall be Lord Leconbury, and she can be châtelaine of Leconbury, which is what she married me for.'

'I won't have any of your darned impudence,' roared Van Aldin.

Derek Kettering smiled at him unmoved.

'I agree with you. It's an obsolete idea,' he said. 'There's nothing in a title nowadays. Still, Leconbury is a very fine old place, and, after all, we are one of the oldest families in England. It will be very annoying for Ruth if she divorces me to find me marrying again, and some other woman queening it at Leconbury instead of her.'

'I am serious, young man,' said Van Aldin.

'Oh, so am I,' said Kettering. 'I am in very low water financially; it will put me in a nasty hole if Ruth divorces me, and, after all, if she has stood it for ten years, why not stand it a little longer? I give you my word of honour that the old man can't possibly last out another eighteen months, and, as I said before, it's a pity Ruth shouldn't get what she married me for.'

'You suggest that my daughter married you for your title and position?'

Derek Kettering laughed a laugh that was not all amusement.

'You don't think it was a question of a love match?' he asked.

'I know,' said Van Aldin slowly, 'that you spoke very differently in Paris ten years ago.'

'Did I? Perhaps I did. Ruth was very beautiful, you know – rather like an angel or a saint, or something that had stepped down from a niche in a church. I had fine ideas, I remember, of turning over a new leaf, of settling down and living up to the highest traditions of English home life with a beautiful wife who loved me.'

He laughed again, rather more discordantly.

'But you don't believe that, I suppose?' he said.

'I have no doubt at all that you married Ruth for her money,' said Van Aldin unemotionally.

'And that she married me for love?' asked the other ironically.

'Certainly,' said Van Aldin.

Derek Kettering stared at him for a minute or two, then he nodded reflectively.

'I see you believe that,' he said. 'So did I at the time. I can assure you, my dear father-in-law, I was very soon undeceived.'

'I don't know what you are getting at,' said Van Aldin, 'and I don't care. You have treated Ruth darned badly.'

'Oh, I have,' agreed Kettering lightly, 'but she's tough, you know. She's your daughter. Underneath the pink-and-white softness of her she's as hard as granite. You have always been known as a hard man, so I have been told, but Ruth is harder than you are. You, at any rate, love one person better than yourself. Ruth never has and never will.'

'That is enough,' said Van Aldin. 'I asked you here so that I could tell you fair and square what I meant to do. My girl has got to have some happiness, and remember this, I am behind her.'

Derek Kettering got up and stood by the mantelpiece. He tossed away his cigarette. When he spoke, his voice was very quiet.

'What exactly do you mean by that, I wonder?' he said.

'I mean,' said Van Aldin, 'that you had better not try to defend the case.'

'Oh,' said Kettering, 'is that a threat?'

'You can take it any way you please,' said Van Aldin.

Kettering drew a chair up to the table. He sat down fronting the millionaire.

'And supposing,' he said softly, 'that, just for argument's sake, I did defend the case?'

Van Aldin shrugged his shoulders.

'You have not got a leg to stand upon, you young fool. Ask your solicitors, they will soon tell you. Your conduct has been notorious, the talk of London.'

'Ruth has been kicking up a row about Mirelle, I suppose. Very foolish of her. I don't interfere with her friends.'

'What do you mean?' said Van Aldin sharply.

Derek Kettering laughed.

'I see you don't know everything, sir,' he said. 'You are, perhaps naturally, prejudiced.'

He took up his hat and stick and moved towards the door.

'Giving advice is not much in my line.' He delivered his final thrust. 'But, in this case, I should advise most strongly perfect frankness between father and daughter.'

He passed quickly out of the room and shut the door behind him just as the millionaire sprang up.

'Now, what the hell did he mean by that?' said Van Aldin as he sank back into his chair again.

All his uneasiness returned in full force. There was something here that he had not yet got to the bottom of. The telephone was by his elbow; he seized it, and asked for the number of his daughter's house.

'Hallo! Hallo! Is that Mayfair 81907? Mrs Kettering in? Oh, she's out, is she? Yes, out to lunch. What time will she be in? You don't know? Oh, very good; no, there's no message.'

He slammed the receiver down again angrily. At two o'clock he was pacing the floor of his room waiting expectantly for Goby. The latter was ushered in at ten minutes past two.

'Well?' barked the millionaire sharply.

But little Mr Goby was not to be hurried. He sat down at the table, produced a very shabby pocket-book, and proceeded to read from it in a monotonous voice. The millionaire listened attentively, with an increasing satisfaction. Goby came to a full stop, and looked attentively at the wastepaper-basket.

'Um!' said Van Aldin. 'That seems pretty definite. The case will go through like winking. The hotel evidence is all right, I suppose?'

'Cast iron,' said Mr Goby, and looked malevolently at a gilt arm-chair.

'And financially he's in very low water. He's trying to raise a loan now, you say? Has already raised practically all he can upon his expectations from his father. Once the news of the divorce gets about, he won't be able to raise another cent, and not only that, his obligations can be bought up and pressure can be put upon him from that quarter. We have got him, Goby; we have got him in a cleft stick.'

He hit the table a bang with his fist. His face was grim and triumphant.

'The information,' said Mr Goby in a thin voice, 'seems satisfactory.'

'I have got to go round to Curzon Street now,' said the millionaire. 'I am much obliged to you, Goby. You are the goods all right.'

A pale smile of gratification showed itself on the little man's face.

'Thank you, Mr Van Aldin,' he said; 'I try to do my best.'

Van Aldin did not go direct to Curzon Street. He went first to the City, where he had two interviews which added to his satisfaction. From there he took the tube to Down Street. As he was walking along Curzon Street, a figure came out of No. 160, and turned up the street towards him, so that they passed each other on the pavement. For a moment, the millionaire had fancied it might be Derek Kettering himself; the height and build were not unlike. But as they came face to face, he saw that the man was a stranger to him. At least – no, not a stranger; his face awoke some call of recognition in the millionaire's mind, and it was associated definitely with something unpleasant. He cudgelled his brains in vain, but the thing eluded him. He went on, shaking his head irritably. He hated to be baffled.

Ruth Kettering was clearly expecting him. She ran to him and kissed him when he entered.

'Well, Dad, how are things going?'

'Very well,' said Van Aldin; 'but I have got a word or two to say to you, Ruth.'

Almost insensibly he felt the change in her; something shrewd and watchful replaced the impulsiveness of her greeting. She sat down in a big arm-chair.

'Well, Dad?' she asked. 'What is it?'

'I saw your husband this morning,' said Van Aldin.

'You saw Derek?'

'I did. He said a lot of things, most of which were darned cheek. Just as he was leaving, he said something that I didn't understand. He advised me to be sure that there was perfect frankness between father and daughter. What did he mean by that, Ruthie?'

Mrs Kettering moved a little in her chair.

'I – I don't know, Dad. How should I?'

'Of course you know,' said Van Aldin. 'He said something else, about his having his friends and not interfering with yours. What did he mean by that?'

'I don't know,' said Ruth Kettering again.

Van Aldin sat down. His mouth set itself in a grim line.

'See here, Ruth. I am not going into this with my eyes closed. I am not at all sure that that husband of yours doesn't mean to make trouble. Now, he can't do it, I am sure of that. I have got the means to silence him, to shut his mouth for good and all, but I have got to know if there's any need to use those means. What did he mean by your having your own friends?'

Mrs Kettering shrugged her shoulders.

'I have got lots of friends,' she said uncertainly. 'I don't know what he meant, I am sure.'

'You do,' said Van Aldin.

He was speaking now as he might have spoken to a business adversary.

'I will put it plainer. Who is the man?'

'What man?'

'*The man.* That's what Derek was driving at. Some special man who is a friend of yours. You needn't worry, honey, I know there is nothing in it, but we have got to look at everything as it might appear to the Court. They can twist these things about a good deal, you know. I want to know who the man is, and just how friendly you have been with him.'

Ruth didn't answer. Her hands were kneading themselves together in intense nervous absorption.

'Come, honey,' said Van Aldin in a softer voice. 'Don't be afraid of your old Dad. I was not too harsh, was I, even that time in Paris? – By gosh!'

He stopped, thunderstruck.

'That's who it was,' he murmured to himself. 'I thought I knew his face.'

'What are you talking about, Dad? I don't understand.'

The millionaire strode across to her and took her firmly by the wrist.

'See here, Ruth, have you been seeing that fellow again?'

'What fellow?'

'The one we had all that fuss about years ago. You know who I mean well enough.'

'You mean' – she hesitated – 'you mean the Comte de la Roche?'

'Comte de la Roche!' snorted Van Aldin. 'I told you at the time that the man was no better than a swindler. You had entangled yourself with him then very deeply, but I got you out of his clutches.'

'Yes, you did,' said Ruth bitterly. 'And I married Derek Kettering.'

'You wanted to,' said the millionaire sharply.

She shrugged her shoulders.

'And now,' said Van Aldin slowly, 'you have been seeing him again – after all I told you. He has been in the house today. I met him outside, and couldn't place him for the moment.'

Ruth Kettering had recovered her composure.

'I want to tell you one thing, Dad; you are wrong about Armand – the Comte de la Roche, I mean. Oh, I know there were several regrettable incidents in his youth – he has told me about them; but – well, he has cared for me always. It broke his heart when you parted us in Paris, and now –'

She was interrupted by the snort of indignation her father gave.

'So you fell for that stuff, did you? You, a daughter of mine! My God!'

He threw up his hands.

'That women can be such darned fools!'

CHAPTER VI

Mirelle

Derek Kettering emerged from Van Aldin's suite so precipitantly that he collided with a lady passing across the corridor. He apologized, and she accepted his apologies with a smiling reassurance and passed on, leaving with him a pleasant impression of a soothing personality and rather fine grey eyes.

For all his nonchalance, his interview with his father-in-law had shaken him more than he cared to show. He had a solitary lunch, and after it, frowning to himself a little, he went round to the sumptuous flat that housed the lady known as Mirelle. A trim Frenchwoman received him with smiles.

'But enter then, Monsieur. Madame reposes herself.'

He was ushered into the long room with its Eastern setting which he knew so well. Mirelle was lying on the divan, supported by an incredible number of cushions, all in varying shades of amber, to harmonize with the yellow ochre of her complexion. The dancer was a beautifully made woman, and if her face, beneath its mask of yellow, was in truth somewhat haggard, it had a bizarre charm of its own, and her orange lips smiled invitingly at Derek Kettering.

He kissed her, and flung himself into a chair.

'What have you been doing with yourself? Just got up, I suppose?'

The orange mouth widened into a long smile.

'No,' said the dancer. 'I have been at work.'

She flung out a long, pale hand towards the piano, which was littered with untidy music scores.

'Ambrose has been here. He has been playing me the new Opera.'

Kettering nodded without paying much attention. He was

profoundly uninterested in Claud Ambrose and the latter's operatic setting of Ibsen's *Peer Gynt*. So was Mirelle, for that matter, regarding it merely as a unique opportunity for her own presentation as Anitra.

'It is a marvellous dance,' she murmured. 'I shall put all the passion of the desert into it. I shall dance hung over with jewels – ah! and, by the way, *mon ami*, there is a pearl that I saw yesterday in Bond Street – a black pearl.'

She paused, looking at him invitingly.

'My dear girl,' said Kettering, 'it's no use talking of black pearls to me. At the present minute, as far as I am concerned, the fat is in the fire.'

She was quick to respond to his tone. She sat up, her big black eyes widening.

'What is that you say, Derek? What has happened?'

'My esteemed father-in-law,' said Kettering, 'is preparing to go off the deep end.'

'Eh?'

'In other words, he wants Ruth to divorce me.'

'How stupid!' said Mirelle. 'Why should she want to divorce you?'

Derek Kettering grinned.

'Mainly because of you, *chérie*!' he said.

Mirelle shrugged her shoulders.

'That is foolish,' she observed in a matter-of-fact voice.

'Very foolish,' agreed Derek.

'What are you going to do about it?' demanded Mirelle.

'My dear girl, what can I do? On the one side, the man with unlimited money; on the other side, the man with unlimited debts. There is no question as to who will come out on top.'

'They are extraordinary, these Americans,' commented Mirelle. 'It is not as though your wife were fond of you.'

'Well,' said Derek, 'what are we going to do about it?'

She looked at him inquiringly. He came over and took both her hands in his.

'Are you going to stick to me?'

'What do you mean? After –?'

'Yes,' said Kettering. 'After, when the creditors come down like wolves on the fold. I am damned fond of you, Mirelle; are you going to let me down?'

She pulled her hands away from him.

'You know I adore you, Dereek.'

He caught the note of evasion in her voice.

'So that's that, is it? The rats will leave the sinking ship.'

'Ah, Dereek!'

'Out with it,' he said violently. 'You will fling me over; is that it?'

She shrugged her shoulders.

'I am very fond of you, *mon ami* – indeed I am fond of you. You are very charming – *un beau garçon*, but *ce n'est pas practique*.'

'You are a rich man's luxury, eh? Is that it?'

'If you like to put it that way.'

She leaned back on the cushions, her head flung back.

'All the same, I am fond of you, Dereek.'

He went over to the window and stood there some time looking out, with his back to her. Presently the dancer raised herself on her elbow and stared at him curiously.

'What are you thinking of, *mon ami*?'

He grinned at her over his shoulder, a curious grin, that made her vaguely uneasy.

'As it happened, I was thinking of a woman, my dear.'

'A woman, eh?'

Mirelle pounced on something that she could understand.

'You are thinking of some other woman, is that it?'

'Oh, you needn't worry; it is purely a fancy portrait. "Portrait of a lady with grey eyes."'

Mirelle said sharply, 'When did you meet her?'

Derek Kettering laughed, and his laughter had a mocking, ironical sound.

'I ran into the lady in the corridor of the Savoy Hotel.'

'Well! What did she say?'

'As far as I can remember, I said, "I beg your pardon," and she said, "It doesn't matter," or words to that effect.'

'And then?' persisted the dancer.

Kettering shrugged his shoulders.

'And then – nothing. That was the end of the incident.'

'I don't understand a word of what you are talking about,' declared the dancer.

'Portrait of a lady with grey eyes,' murmured Derek reflectively. 'Just as well I am never likely to meet her again.'

'Why?'

'She might bring me bad luck. Women do.'

Mirelle slipped quietly from her couch, and came across to him, laying one long, snake-like arm round his neck.

'You are foolish, Dereek,' she murmured. 'You are very foolish. You are *un beau garçon*, and I adore you, but I am not made to be poor – no, decidedly I am not made to be poor. Now listen to me; everything is very simple. You must make it up with your wife.'

'I am afraid that's not going to be actually in the sphere of practical politics,' said Derek drily.

'How do you say? I do not understand.'

'Van Aldin, my dear, is not taking any. He is the kind of man who makes up his mind and sticks to it.'

'I have heard of him,' nodded the dancer. 'He is very rich, is he not? Almost the richest man in America. A few days ago, in Paris, he bought the most wonderful ruby in the world – "Heart of Fire" it is called.'

Kettering did not answer. The dancer went on musingly:

'It is a wonderful stone – a stone that should belong to a woman like me. I love jewels, Dereek; they say something to me. Ah! to wear a ruby like "Heart of Fire".'

She gave a little sigh, and then became practical once more.

'You don't understand these things, Dereek; you are only a man. Van Aldin will give these rubies to his daughter, I suppose. Is she his only child?'

'Yes.'

'Then when he dies, she will inherit all his money. She will be a rich woman.'

'She is a rich woman already,' said Kettering drily. 'He settled a couple of millions on her at her marriage.'

'A couple of million! But that is immense. And if she died suddenly, eh? That would all come to you?'

'As things stand at present,' said Kettering slowly, 'it would. As far as I know she has not made a will.'

'*Mon Dieu!*' said the dancer. 'If she were to die, what a solution that would be.'

There was a moment's pause, and then Derek Kettering laughed outright.

'I like your simple, practical mind, Mirelle, but I am afraid what you desire won't come to pass. My wife is an extremely healthy person.'

'*Eh bien!*' said Mirelle; 'there are accidents.'

He looked at her sharply but did not answer.

She went on.

'But you are right, *mon ami*, we must not dwell on possibilities. See now, my little Dereek, there must be no more talk of this divorce. Your wife must give up the idea.'

'And if she won't?'

The dancer's eyes narrowed to slits.

'I think she will, my friend. She is one of those who would not like the publicity. There are one or two pretty stories that she would not like her friends to read in the newspapers.'

'What do you mean?' asked Kettering sharply.

Mirelle laughed, her head thrown back.

'*Parbleu!* I mean the gentleman who calls himself the Comte de la Roche. I know all about him. I am Parisienne, you remember. He was her lover before she married you, was he not?'

Kettering took her sharply by the shoulders.

'That is a damned lie,' he said, 'and please remember that, after all, you are speaking of my wife.'

Mirelle was a little sobered.

'You are extraordinary, you English,' she complained. 'All the same, I dare say that you may be right. The Americans are so cold, are they not? But you will permit me to say, *mon ami*, that she was *in love with him* before she married you, and her father stepped in and sent the Comte about his business. And the little Mademoiselle, she wept many tears! But she obeyed.

Still, you must know as well as I do, Dereek, that it is a very different story now. She sees him nearly every day, and on the fourteenth she goes to Paris to meet him.'

'How do you know all this?' demanded Kettering.

'Me? I have friends in Paris, my dear Dereek, who know the Comte intimately. It is all arranged. She is going to the Riviera, so she says, but in reality the Comte meets her in Paris and – who knows! Yes, yes, you can take my word for it, it is all arranged.'

Derek Kettering stood motionless.

'You see,' purred the dancer, 'if you are clever, you have her in the hollow of your hand. You can make things very awkward for her.'

'Oh, for God's sake be quiet,' cried Kettering. 'Shut your cursed mouth!'

Mirelle flung herself down on the divan with a laugh. Kettering caught up his hat and coat and left the flat, banging the door violently. And still the dancer sat on the divan and laughed softly to herself. She was not displeased with her work.

CHAPTER VII

Letters

'Mrs Samuel Harfield presents her compliments to Miss Katherine Grey and wishes to point out that under the circumstances Miss Grey may not be aware –'

Mrs Harfield, having written so far fluently, came to a dead stop, held up by what has proved an insuperable difficulty to many other people – namely, the difficulty of expressing oneself fluently in the third person.

After a minute or two of hesitation, Mrs Harfield tore up the sheet of notepaper and started afresh.

'Dear Miss Grey, – Whilst fully appreciating the adequate way you discharged your duties to my Cousin Emma (whose recent death has indeed been a severe blow to us all), I cannot but feel –'

Again Mrs Harfield came to a stop. Once more the letter was consigned to the wastepaper-basket. It was not until four false starts had been made that Mrs Harfield at last produced an epistle that satisfied her. It was duly sealed and stamped and addressed to Miss Katherine Grey, Little Crampton, St Mary Mead, Kent, and it lay beside the lady's plate on the following morning at breakfast-time in company with a more important-looking communication in a long blue envelope.

Katherine Grey opened Mrs Harfield's letter first. The finished production ran as follows:

Dear Miss Grey, – My husband and I wish to express our thanks to you for your services to my poor cousin, Emma. Her death has been a great blow to us, though we were, of course, aware that her mind had been failing for some time past. I understand that her latter testamentary dispositions have been of a most peculiar character, and they would not hold good, of course, in any court of law. I have no doubt that, with your usual good sense, you have already realized this fact. If these matters can be arranged privately it is always so much better, my husband says. We shall be pleased to recommend you most highly for a similar post, and hope that you will also accept a small present. Believe me, dear Miss Grey, yours cordially,

Mary Anne Harfield

Katherine Grey read the letter through, smiled a little, and read it a second time. Her face as she laid the letter down after the second reading was distinctly amused. Then she took up the second letter. After one brief perusal she laid it down and stared very straight in front of her. This time she did not smile. Indeed, it would have been hard for anyone watching her to guess what emotions lay behind that quiet, reflective gaze.

Katherine Grey was thirty-three. She came of a good family, but her father had lost all his money, and Katherine had had to work for her living from an early age. She had been just twenty-three when she had come to old Mrs Harfield as companion.

It was generally recognized that old Mrs Harfield was 'difficult'. Companions came and went with startling rapidity. They arrived full of hope and they usually left in tears. But from the moment Katherine Grey set foot in Little Crampton, ten years ago, perfect peace had reigned. No one knows how these things come about. Snake-charmers, they say, are born, not made. Katherine Grey was born with the power of managing old ladies, dogs, and small boys, and she did it without any apparent sense of strain.

At twenty-three she had been a quiet girl with beautiful eyes. At thirty-three she was a quiet woman, with those same grey eyes, shining steadily out on the world with a kind of happy serenity that nothing could shake. Moreover, she had been born with, and still possessed, a sense of humour.

As she sat at the breakfast-table, staring in front of her, there was a ring at the bell, accompanied by a very energetic rat-a-tat-tat at the knocker. In another minute the little maidservant opened the door and announced rather breathlessly:

'Dr Harrison.'

The big, middle-aged doctor came bustling in with the energy and breeziness that had been foreshadowed by his onslaught on the knocker.

'Good morning, Miss Grey.'

'Good morning, Dr Harrison.'

'I dropped in early,' began the doctor, 'in case you should have heard from one of those Harfield cousins. Mrs Samuel, she calls herself – a perfectly poisonous person.'

Without a word, Katherine picked up Mrs Harfield's letter from the table and gave it to him. With a good deal of amusement she watched his perusal of it, the drawing together of the bushy eyebrows, the snorts and grunts of violent disapproval. He dashed it down again on the table.

'Perfectly monstrous,' he fumed. 'Don't you let it worry you, my dear. They're talking through their hat. Mrs Harfield's intellect was as good as yours or mine, and you won't get anyone to say the contrary. They wouldn't have a leg to stand upon, and they know it. All that talk of taking it into court is pure bluff. Hence this attempt to get round you in a hole-and-corner way. And look here, my dear, don't let them get round you with soft soap either. Don't get fancying it's your duty to hand over the cash, or any tomfoolery of conscientious scruples.'

'I'm afraid it hasn't occurred to me to have scruples,' said Katherine. 'All these people are distant relatives of Mrs Harfield's husband, and they never came near her or took any notice of her in her lifetime.'

'You're a sensible woman,' said the doctor. 'I know, none better, that you've had a hard life of it for the last ten years. You're fully entitled to enjoy the old lady's savings, such as they were.'

Katherine smiled thoughtfully.

'Such as they were,' she repeated. 'You've no idea of the amount, doctor?'

'Well – enough to bring in five hundred a year or so, I suppose.'

Katherine nodded.

'That's what I thought,' she said. 'Now read this.'

She handed him the letter she had taken from the long blue envelope. The doctor read and uttered an exclamation of utter astonishment.

'Impossible,' he muttered. 'Impossible.'

'She was one of the original shareholders in Mortaulds. Forty years ago she must have had an income of eight or ten thousand a year. She has never, I am sure, spent more than four hundred a year. She was always terribly careful about money. I always believed that she was obliged to be careful about every penny.'

'And all the time the income has accumulated at compound interest. My dear, you're going to be a very rich woman.'

Katherine Grey nodded.

'Yes,' she said, 'I am.'

She spoke in a detached, impersonal tone, as though she were looking at the situation from outside.

'Well,' said the doctor, preparing to depart, 'you have all my congratulations.' He flicked Mrs Samuel Harfield's letter with his thumb. 'Don't worry about that woman and her odious letter.'

'It really isn't an odious letter,' said Miss Grey tolerantly. 'Under the circumstances, I think it's really quite a natural thing to do.'

'I have the gravest suspicions of you sometimes,' said the doctor.

'Why?'

'The things that you find perfectly natural.'

Katherine Grey laughed.

Dr Harrison retailed the great news to his wife at lunchtime. She was very excited about it.

'Fancy old Mrs Harfield – with all that money. I'm glad she left it to Katherine Grey. That girl's a saint.'

The doctor made a wry face.

'Saints I always imagined must have been difficult people. Katherine Grey is too human for a saint.'

'She's a saint with a sense of humour,' said the doctor's wife, twinkling. 'And, though I don't suppose you've ever noticed the fact, she's extremely good looking.'

'Katherine Grey?' The doctor was honestly surprised. 'She's got very nice eyes, I know.'

'Oh, you men!' cried his wife. 'Blind as bats. Katherine's got all the makings of a beauty in her. All she wants is clothes!'

'Clothes? What's wrong with her clothes? She always looks very nice.'

Mrs Harrison gave an exasperated sigh, and the doctor rose preparatory to starting on his rounds.

'You might look in on her, Polly,' he suggested.

'I'm going to,' said Mrs Harrison, promptly.

She made her call about three o'clock.

'My dear, I'm so glad,' she said warmly, as she squeezed Katherine's hand. 'And everyone in the village will be glad too.'

'It's very nice of you to come and tell me,' said Katherine. 'I hoped you would come in because I wanted to ask about Johnnie.'

'Oh! Johnnie. Well –'

Johnnie was Mrs Harrison's youngest son. In another minute she was off, retailing a long history in which Johnnie's adenoids and tonsils bulked largely. Katherine listened sympathetically. Habits die hard. Listening had been her portion for ten years now. 'My dear, I wonder if I ever told you about the naval ball at Portsmouth? When Lord Charles admired my gown?' and composedly, kindly, Katherine would reply: 'I rather think you have, Mrs Harfield, but I've forgotten about it. Won't you tell it me again?' And then the old lady would start off full swing, with numerous corrections, and stops, and remembered details. And half of Katherine's mind would be listening, saying the right things mechanically when the old lady paused . . .

Now, with the same curious feeling of duality to which she was accustomed, she listened to Mrs Harrison.

At the end of half an hour, the latter recalled herself suddenly.

'I've been talking about myself all this time,' she exclaimed. 'And I came here to talk about you and your plans.'

'I don't know that I've got any yet.'

'My dear – you're not going to stay on *here*.'

Katherine smiled at the horror in the other's tone.

'No; I think I want to travel. I've never seen much of the world, you know.'

'I should think not. It must have been an awful life for you cooped up here all these years.'

'I don't know,' said Katherine. 'It gave me a lot of freedom.'

She caught the other's gasp, and reddened a little.

'It must sound foolish – saying that. Of course, I hadn't much freedom in the downright physical sense –'

'I should think not,' breathed Mrs Harrison, remembering that Katherine had seldom had that useful thing, a 'day off'.

'But in a way, being tied physically gives you lots of scope mentally. You're always free to think. I've had a lovely feeling always of mental freedom.'

Mrs Harrison shook her head.

'I can't understand that.'

'Oh! you would if you'd been in my place. But, all the same, I feel I want a change. I want – well, I want things to happen. Oh! not to me – I don't mean that. But to be in the midst of things – exciting things – even if I'm only the looker-on. You know, things don't happen in St Mary Mead.'

'They don't indeed,' said Mrs Harrison, with fervour.

'I shall go to London first,' said Katherine. 'I have to see the solicitors, anyway. After that, I shall go abroad, I think.'

'Very nice.'

'But of course, first of all –'

'Yes?'

'I must get some clothes.'

'Exactly what I said to Arthur this morning,' cried the doctor's wife. 'You know, Katherine, you could look possibly positively beautiful if you tried.'

Miss Grey laughed unaffectedly.

'Oh! I don't think you could ever make a beauty out of me,' she said sincerely. 'But I shall enjoy having some really good clothes. I'm afraid I'm talking about myself an awful lot.'

Mrs Harrison looked at her shrewdly.

'It must be quite a novel experience for you,' she said drily.

Katherine went to say goodbye to old Miss Viner before leaving the village. Miss Viner was two years older than Mrs Harfield, and her mind was mainly taken up with her own success in outliving her dead friend.

'You wouldn't have thought I'd have outlasted Jane Harfield, would you?' she demanded triumphantly of Katherine. 'We were at school together, she and I. And here we are, she taken, and I left. Who would have thought it?'

'You've always eaten brown bread for supper, haven't you?' murmured Katherine mechanically.

'Fancy your remembering that, my dear. Yes; if Jane Harfield had had a slice of brown bread every evening and taken a little stimulant with her meals she might be here today.'

The old lady paused, nodding her head triumphantly; then added in sudden remembrance:

'And so you've come into a lot of money, I hear? Well, well. Take care of it. And you're going up to London to have a good time? Don't think you'll get married, though, my dear, because you won't. You're not the kind to attract the men. And, besides, you're getting on. How old are you now?'

'Thirty-three,' Katherine told her.

'Well,' remarked Miss Viner doubtfully, 'that's not so very bad. You've lost your first freshness, of course.'

'I'm afraid so,' said Katherine, much entertained.

'But you're a very nice girl,' said Miss Viner kindly. 'And I'm sure there's many a man might do worse than take you for a wife instead of one of these flibbertigibbets running about nowadays showing more of their legs than the Creator ever intended them to. Goodbye, my dear, and I hope you'll enjoy yourself, but things are seldom what they seem in this life.'

Heartened by these prophecies, Katherine took her

departure. Half the village came to see her off at the station, including the little maid of all work, Alice, who brought a stiff wired nosegay and cried openly.

'There ain't a many like her,' sobbed Alice when the train had finally departed. 'I'm sure when Charlie went back on me with that girl from the Dairy, nobody could have been kinder than Miss Grey was, and though particular about the brasses and the dust, she was always one to notice when you'd give a thing an extra rub. Cut myself in little pieces for her, I would, any day. A real lady, that's what I call her.'

Such was Katherine's departure from St Mary Mead.

CHAPTER VIII

Lady Tamplin Writes a Letter

'Well,' said Lady Tamplin, 'well.'

She laid down the continental *Daily Mail* and stared out across the blue waters of the Mediterranean. A branch of golden mimosa, hanging just above her head, made an effective frame for a very charming picture. A golden-haired, blue-eyed lady in a very becoming *négligée*. That the golden hair owed something to art, as did the pink-and-white complexion, was undeniable, but the blue of the eyes was Nature's gift, and at forty-four Lady Tamplin could still rank as a beauty.

Charming as she looked, Lady Tamplin was, for once, not thinking of herself. That is to say, she was not thinking of her appearance. She was intent on graver matters.

Lady Tamplin was a well-known figure on the Riviera, and her parties at the Villa Marguerite were justly celebrated. She was a woman of considerable experience, and had had four husbands. The first had been merely an indiscretion, and so was seldom referred to by the lady. He had had the good sense to die with commendable promptitude, and his widow thereupon espoused a rich manufacturer of buttons. He too had departed for another sphere after three years of married life – it was said after a congenial evening with some boon companions. After him came Viscount Tamplin, who had placed Rosalie securely on those heights where she wished to tread. She retained her title when she married for a fourth time. This fourth venture had been undertaken for pure pleasure. Mr Charles Evans, an extremely good-looking young man of twenty-seven, with delightful manners, a keen love of sport, and an appreciation of this world's goods, had no money of his own whatsoever.

Lady Tamplin was very pleased and satisfied with life generally, but she had occasional faint preoccupations about money.
The button manufacturer had left his widow a considerable
fortune, but, as Lady Tamplin was wont to say, 'what with one
thing and another –' (one thing being the depreciation of
stocks owing to the War, and the other the extravagances of
the late Lord Tamplin). She was still comfortably off. But to be
merely comfortably off was hardly satisfactory to one of Rosalie
Tamplin's temperament.

So, on this particular January morning, she opened her blue
eyes extremely wide as she read a certain item of news and
uttered that non-committal monosyllable 'Well'. The only other
occupant of the balcony was her daughter, the Hon. Lenox
Tamplin. A daughter such as Lenox was a sad thorn in Lady
Tamplin's side, a girl with no kind of tact, who actually looked
older than her age, and whose peculiar sardonic form of
humour was, to say the least of it, uncomfortable.

'Darling,' said Lady Tamplin, 'just fancy.'

'What is it?'

Lady Tamplin picked up the *Daily Mail*, handed it to her
daughter, and indicated with an agitated forefinger the paragraph of interest.

Lenox read it without any of the signs of agitation shown by
her mother. She handed back the paper.

'What about it?' she asked. 'It is the sort of thing that is
always happening. Cheese-paring old women are always dying
in villages and leaving fortunes of millions to their humble
companions.'

'Yes, dear, I know,' said her mother, 'and I dare say the
fortune is not anything like as large as they say it is; newspapers
are so inaccurate. But even if you cut it down by half –'

'Well,' said Lenox, 'it has not been left to us.'

'Not exactly, dear,' said Lady Tamplin; 'but this girl, this
Katherine Grey, is actually a cousin of mine. One of the Wor-
cestershire Greys, the Edgeworth lot. My very own cousin!
Fancy!'

'Ah-ha,' said Lenox.

'And I was wondering –' said her mother.

'What there is in it for us,' finished Lenox, with that sideways smile that her mother always found difficult to understand.

'Oh, darling,' said Lady Tamplin, on a faint note of reproach.

It was very faint, because Rosalie Tamplin was used to her daughter's outspokenness and to what she called Lenox's uncomfortable way of putting things.

'I was wondering,' said Lady Tamplin, again drawing her artistically pencilled brows together, 'whether – oh, good morning, Chubby darling: are you going to play tennis? How nice!'

Chubby, thus addressed, smiled kindly at her, remarked perfunctorily, 'How topping you look in that peach-coloured thing,' and drifted past them and down the steps.

'The dear thing,' said Lady Tamplin, looking affectionately after her husband. 'Let me see, what was I saying? Ah!' She switched her mind back to business once more. 'I was wondering –'

'Oh, for God's sake get on with it. That is the third time you have said that.'

'Well, dear,' said Lady Tamplin, 'I was thinking that it would be very nice if I wrote to dear Katherine and suggested that she should pay us a little visit out here. Naturally, she is quite out of touch with Society. It would be nicer for her to be launched by one of her own people. An advantage for her and an advantage for us.'

'How much do you think you would get her to cough up?' asked Lenox.

Her mother looked at her reproachfully and murmured:

'We should have to come to some financial arrangement, of course. What with one thing and another – the War – your poor father –'

'And Chubby now,' said Lenox. 'He is an expensive luxury if you like.'

'She was a nice girl as I remember her,' murmured Lady Tamplin, pursuing her own line of thought – 'quiet, never wanted to shove herself forward, not a beauty, and never a man-hunter.'

'She will leave Chubby alone, then?' said Lenox.

Lady Tamplin looked at her in protest. 'Chubby would never –' she began.

'No,' said Lenox, 'I don't believe he would; he knows a jolly sight too well which way his bread is buttered.'

'Darling,' said Lady Tamplin, 'you have such a coarse way of putting things.'

'Sorry,' said Lenox.

Lady Tamplin gathered up the *Daily Mail* and her *négligée*, a vanity bag, and various odd letters.

'I shall write to dear Katherine at once,' she said, 'and remind her of the dear old days at Edgeworth.'

She went into the house, a light of purpose shining in her eyes.

Unlike Mrs Samuel Harfield, correspondence flowed easily from her pen. She covered four sheets without pause or effort, and on re-reading it found no occasion to alter a word.

Katherine received it on the morning of her arrival in London. Whether she read between the lines of it or not is another matter. She put it in her handbag and started out to keep the appointment she had made with Mrs Harfield's lawyers.

The firm was an old-established one in Lincoln's Inn Fields, and after a few minutes' delay Katherine was shown into the presence of the senior partner, a kindly, elderly man with shrewd blue eyes and a fatherly manner.

They discussed Mrs Harfield's will and various legal matters for some twenty minutes, then Katherine handed the lawyer Mrs Samuel's letter.

'I had better show you this, I suppose,' she said, 'though it is really rather ridiculous.'

He read it with a slight smile.

'Rather a crude attempt, Miss Grey. I need hardly tell you, I suppose, that these people have no claim of any kind upon the estate, and if they endeavour to contest the will no court will uphold them.'

'I thought as much.'

'Human nature is not always very wise. In Mrs Samuel Harfield's place, I should have been more inclined to make an appeal to your generosity.'

'That is one of the things I want to speak to you about. I should like a certain sum to go to these people.'

'There is no obligation.'

'I know that.'

'And they will not take it in the spirit it is meant. They will probably regard it as an attempt to pay them off, though they will not refuse it on that account.'

'I can see that, and it can't be helped.'

'I should advise you, Miss Grey, to put that idea out of your mind.'

Katherine shook her head. 'You are quite right, I know, but I should like it done all the same.'

'They will grab at the money and abuse you all the more afterwards.'

'Well,' said Katherine, 'let them if they like. We all have our own ways of enjoying ourselves. They were, after all, Mrs Harfield's only relatives, and though they despised her as a poor relation and paid no attention to her when she was alive, it seems to me unfair that they should be cut off with nothing.'

She carried her point, though the lawyer was still unwilling, and she presently went out into the streets of London with a comfortable assurance that she could spend money freely and make what plans she liked for the future. Her first action was to visit the establishment of a famous dressmaker.

A slim, elderly Frenchwoman, rather like a dreaming duchess, received her, and Katherine spoke with a certain *naïveté*.

'I want, if I may, to put myself in your hands. I have been very poor all my life and know nothing about clothes, but now I have come into some money and want to look really well dressed.'

The Frenchwoman was charmed. She had an artist's temperament, which had been soured earlier in the morning by a visit from an Argentine meat queen, who had insisted on having those models least suited to her flamboyant type of beauty. She scrutinized Katherine with keen, clever eyes. 'Yes – yes, it will be a pleasure. Mademoiselle has a very good figure; for her the simple lines will be best. She is also *très anglaise*. Some people it would offend them if I said that, but Mademoiselle no. *Une belle Anglaise*, there is no style more delightful.'

The demeanour of a dreaming duchess was suddenly put off. She screamed out directions to various mannequins. 'Clothilde, Virginie, quickly, my little ones, the little *tailleur gris clair* and the *robe de soirée "soupir d'automne"*. Marcelle, my child, the little mimosa suit of crêpe de chine.'

It was a charming morning. Marcelle, Clothilde, Virginie, bored and scornful, passed slowly round, squirming and wriggling in the time-honoured fashion of mannequins. The Duchess stood by Katherine and made entries in a small notebook.

'An excellent choice, Mademoiselle. Mademoiselle has great *goût*. Yes, indeed. Mademoiselle cannot do better than those little suits if she is going to the Riviera, as I suppose, this winter.'

'Let me see that evening dress once more,' said Katherine – 'the pinky mauve one.'

Virginie appeared, circling slowly.

'That is the prettiest of all,' said Katherine, as she surveyed the exquisite draperies of mauve and grey and blue. 'What do you call it?'

'*Soupir d'automne*; yes, yes, that is truly the dress of Mademoiselle.'

What was there in these words that came back to Katherine with a faint feeling of sadness after she had left the dressmaking establishment?

'"*Soupir d'automne*; that is truly the dress of Mademoiselle."' Autumn, yes, it was autumn for her. She who had never known spring or summer, and would never know them now. Something she had lost never could be given to her again. These years of servitude in St Mary Mead – and all the while life passing by.

'I am an idiot,' said Katherine. 'I am an idiot. What do I want? Why, I was more contented a month ago than I am now.'

She drew out from her handbag the letter she had received that morning from Lady Tamplin. Katherine was no fool. She understood the *nuances* of that letter as well as anybody and the reason for Lady Tamplin's sudden show of affection towards a long-forgotten cousin was not lost upon her. It was for profit and not for pleasure that Lady Tamplin was so anxious for the company of her dear cousin. Well, why not? There would be profit on both sides.

'I will go,' said Katherine.

She was walking down Piccadilly at the moment, and turned into Cook's to clinch the matter then and there. She had to wait for a few minutes. The man with whom the clerk was engaged was also going to the Riviera. Everyone, she felt, was going. Well, for the first time in her life, she, too, would be doing what 'everybody' did.

The man in front of her turned abruptly, and she stepped into his place. She made her demand to the clerk, but at the same time half of her mind was busy with something else. That man's face – in some vague way it was familiar to her. Where had she seen him before? Suddenly she remembered. It was in the Savoy outside her room that morning. She had collided with him in the passage. Rather an odd coincidence that she should run into him twice in a day. She glanced over her shoulder, rendered uneasy by something, she knew not what. The man was standing in the doorway looking back at her. A cold shiver passed over Katherine; she had a haunting sense of tragedy, of doom impending ...

Then she shook the impression from her with her usual good sense and turned her whole attention to what the clerk was saying.

CHAPTER IX

An Offer Refused

It was rarely that Derek Kettering allowed his temper to get the better of him. An easy-going insouciance was his chief characteristic, and it had stood him in good stead in more than one tight corner. Even now, by the time he had left Mirelle's flat, he had cooled down. He had need of coolness. The corner he was in now was a tighter one than he had ever been in before, and unforeseen factors had arisen with which, for the moment, he did not know how to deal.

He strolled along deep in thought. His brow was furrowed, and there was none of the easy, jaunty manner which sat so well upon him. Various possibilities floated through his mind. It might have been said of Derek Kettering that he was less of a fool than he looked. He saw several roads that he might take – one in particular. If he shrank from it, it was for the moment only. Desperate ills need desperate remedies. He had gauged his father-in-law correctly. A war between Derek Kettering and Rufus Van Aldin could end only one way. Derek damned money and the power of money vehemently to himself. He walked up St James's Street, across Piccadilly, and strolled along it in the direction of Piccadilly Circus. As he passed the offices of Messrs Thomas Cook & Sons his footsteps slackened. He walked on, however, still turning the matter over in his mind. Finally, he gave a brief nod of his head, turned sharply – so sharply as to collide with a couple of pedestrians who were following in his footsteps, and went back the way he had come. This time he did not pass Cook's, but went in. The office was comparatively empty, and he got attended to at once.

'I want to go to Nice next week. Will you give me particulars?'
'What date, sir?'

'The fourteenth. What is the best train?'

'Well, of course, *the* best train is what they call "The Blue Train". You avoid the tiresome Customs business at Calais.'

Derek nodded. He knew all this, none better.

'The fourteenth,' murmured the clerk; 'that is rather soon. The Blue Train is nearly always all booked up.'

'See if there is a berth left,' said Derek. 'If there is not –' He left the sentence unfinished, with a curious smile on his face.

The clerk disappeared for a few minutes, and presently returned. 'That is all right, sir; still three berths left. I will book you one of them. What name?'

'Pavett,' said Derek. He gave the address of his rooms in Jermyn Street.

The clerk nodded, finished writing it down, wished Derek good morning politely, and turned his attention to the next client.

'I want to go to Nice – on the fourteenth. Isn't there a train called the Blue Train?'

Derek looked round sharply.

Coincidence – a strange coincidence. He remembered his own half-whimsical words to Mirelle. '*Portrait of a lady with grey eyes. I don't suppose I shall ever see her again.*' But he *had* seen her again, and, what was more, she proposed to travel to the Riviera on the same day as he did.

Just for a moment a shiver passed over him; in some ways he was superstitious. He had said, half-laughingly, that this woman might bring him bad luck. Suppose – suppose that should prove to be true. From the doorway he looked back at her as she stood talking to the clerk. For once his memory had not played him false. A lady – a lady in every sense of the word. Not very young, not singularly beautiful. But with something – grey eyes that might perhaps see too much. He knew as he went out of the door that in some way he was afraid of this woman. He had a sense of fatality.

He went back to his rooms in Jermyn Street and summoned his man.

'Take this cheque, Pavett, and go round to Cook's in

Piccadilly. They will have some tickets there booked in your name, pay for them, and bring them back.'

'Very good, sir.'

Pavett withdrew.

Derek strolled over to a side-table and picked up a handful of letters. They were of a type only too familiar. Bills, small bills and large bills, one and all pressing for payment. The tone of the demands was still polite. Derek knew how soon that polite tone would change if – if certain news became public property.

He flung himself moodily into a large, leather-covered chair. A damned hole – that was what he was in. Yes, a damned hole! And ways of getting out of that damned hole were not too promising.

Pavett appeared with a discreet cough.

'A gentleman to see you – sir – Major Knighton.'

'Knighton, eh?'

Derek sat up, frowned, became suddenly alert. He said in a softer tone, almost to himself: 'Knighton – I wonder what is in the wind now?'

'Shall I – er – show him in, sir?'

His master nodded. When Knighton entered the room he found a charming and genial host awaiting him.

'Very good of you to look me up,' said Derek.

Knighton was nervous.

The other's keen eyes noticed that at once. The errand on which the secretary had come was clearly distasteful to him. He replied almost mechanically to Derek's easy flow of conversation. He declined a drink, and, if anything, his manner became stiffer than before. Derek appeared at last to notice it.

'Well,' he said cheerfully, 'what does my esteemed father-in-law want with me? You have come on his business, I take it?'

Knighton did not smile in reply.

'I have, yes,' he said carefully. 'I – I wish Mr Van Aldin had chosen someone else.'

Derek raised his eyebrows in mock dismay.

'Is it as bad as all that? I am not very thin-skinned, I can assure you, Knighton.'

'No,' said Knighton; 'but this –'

He paused.

Derek eyed him keenly.

'Go on, out with it,' he said kindly. 'I can imagine my dear father-in-law's errands might not always be pleasant ones.'

Knighton cleared his throat. He spoke formally in tones that he strove to render free of embarrassment.

'I am directed by Mr Van Aldin to make you a definite offer.'

'An offer?' For a moment Derek showed his surprise. Knighton's opening words were clearly not what he had expected. He offered a cigarette to Knighton, lit one himself, and sank back in his chair, murmuring in a slightly sardonic voice:

'An offer? That sounds rather interesting.'

'Shall I go on?'

'Please. You must forgive my surprise, but it seems to me that my dear father-in-law has rather climbed down since our chat this morning. And climbing down is not what one associates with strong men, Napoleons of finance, etc. It shows – I think it shows that he finds his position weaker than he thought it.'

Knighton listened politely to the easy, mocking voice, but no sign of any kind showed itself on his rather stolid countenance. He waited until Derek had finished, and then he said quietly:

'I will state the proposition in the fewest possible words.'

'Go on.'

Knighton did not look at the other. His voice was curt and matter-of-fact.

'The matter is simply this. Mrs Kettering, as you know, is about to file a petition for divorce. If the case goes undefended you will receive one hundred thousand on the day that the decree is made absolute.'

Derek, in the act of lighting his cigarette, suddenly stopped dead. 'A hundred thousand!' he said sharply. 'Dollars?'

'Pounds.'

There was dead silence for at least two minutes. Kettering had his brows together thinking. A hundred thousand pounds. It meant Mirelle and a continuance of his pleasant, careless life. It meant that Van Aldin knew something. Van Aldin did not pay for nothing. He got up and stood by the chimney-piece.

'And in the event of my refusing his handsome offer?' he asked, with a cold, ironical politeness.

Knighton made a deprecating gesture.

'I can assure you, Mr Kettering,' he said earnestly, 'that it is with the utmost unwillingness that I came here with this message.'

'That's all right,' said Kettering. 'Don't distress yourself; it's not your fault. Now then – I asked you a question, will you answer it?'

Knighton also rose. He spoke more reluctantly than before.

'In the event of your refusing this proposition,' he said, 'Mr Van Aldin wished me to tell you in plain words that he proposes to break you. Just that.'

Kettering raised his eyebrows, but he retained his light, amused manner.

'Well, well!' he said. 'I suppose he can do it. I certainly should not be able to put up much of a fight against America's man of many millions. A hundred thousand! If you are going to bribe a man there is nothing like doing it thoroughly. Supposing I were to tell you that for two hundred thousand I'd do what he wanted, what then?'

'I would take your message back to Mr Van Aldin,' said Knighton unemotionally. 'Is that your answer?'

'No,' said Derek; 'funnily enough it is not. You can go back to my father-in-law and tell him to take himself and his bribes to hell. Is that clear?'

'Perfectly,' said Knighton. He got up, hesitated, and then flushed. 'I – you will allow me to say, Mr Kettering, that I am glad you have answered as you have.'

Derek did not reply. When the other had left the room he remained for a minute or two lost in thought. A curious smile came to his lips.

'And that is that,' he said softly.

CHAPTER X

On the Blue Train

'Dad!'

Mrs Kettering started violently. Her nerves were not completely under control this morning. Very perfectly dressed in a long mink coat and a little hat of Chinese lacquer red, she had been walking along the crowded platform of Victoria deep in thought, and her father's sudden appearance and hearty greeting had an unlooked-for effect upon her.

'Why, Ruth, how you jumped!'

'I didn't expect to see you, I suppose, Dad. You said goodbye to me last night and said you had a conference this morning.'

'So I have,' said Van Aldin, 'but you are more to me than any number of darned conferences. I came to take a last look at you, since I am not going to see you for some time.'

'That is very sweet of you, Dad. I wish you were coming too.'

'What would you say if I did?'

The remark was merely a joking one. He was surprised to see the quick colour of flame in Ruth's cheeks. For a moment he almost thought he saw dismay flash out of her eyes. She laughed uncertainly and nervously.

'Just for a moment I really thought you meant it,' she said.

'Would you have been pleased?'

'Of course.' She spoke with exaggerated emphasis.

'Well,' said Van Aldin, 'that's good.'

'It isn't really for very long, Dad,' continued Ruth; 'you know, you are coming out next month.'

'Ah!' said Van Aldin unemotionally, 'sometimes I guess I will go to one of these big guys in Harley Street and have him tell me that I need sunshine and change of air right away.'

'Don't be so lazy,' cried Ruth; 'next month is ever so much

nicer than this month out there. You have got all sorts of things you can't possibly leave just now.'

'Well, that's so, I suppose,' said Van Aldin, with a sigh. 'You had better be getting on board this train of yours, Ruth. Where is your seat?'

Ruth Kettering looked vaguely up at the train. At the door of one of the Pullman cars a thin, tall woman dressed in black was standing – Ruth Kettering's maid. She drew aside as her mistress came up to her.

'I have put your dressing-case under your seat, Madam, in case you should need it. Shall I take the rugs, or will you require one?'

'No, no, I shan't want one. Better go and find your own seat now, Mason.'

'Yes, Madam.'

The maid departed.

Van Aldin entered the Pullman car with Ruth. She found her seat, and Van Aldin deposited various papers and magazines on the table in front of her. The seat opposite to her was already taken, and the American gave a cursory glance at its occupant. He had a fleeting impression of attractive grey eyes and a neat travelling costume. He indulged in a little more desultory conversation with Ruth, the kind of talk peculiar to those seeing other people off by train.

Presently, as whistles blew, he glanced at his watch.

'I had best be clearing out of here. Goodbye, my dear. Don't worry. I will attend to things.'

'Oh, Father!'

He turned back sharply. There had been something in Ruth's voice, something so entirely foreign to her usual manner, that he was startled. It was almost a cry of despair. She had made an impulsive movement towards him, but in another minute she was mistress of herself once more.

'Till next month,' she said carefully.

Two minutes later the train started.

Ruth sat very still, biting her underlip and trying hard to keep the unaccustomed tears from her eyes. She felt a sudden

sense of horrible desolation. There was a wild longing upon
her to jump out of the train and to go back before it was too
late. She, so calm, so self-assured, for the first time in her life
felt like a leaf swept by the wind. If her father knew – what
would he say?

Madness! Yes, just that, madness! For the first time in her life
she was swept away by emotion, swept away to the point of
doing a thing which even she knew to be incredibly foolish and
reckless. She was enough Van Aldin's daughter to realize her
own folly, and level-headed enough to condemn her own action.
But she was his daughter in another sense also. She had that
same iron determination that would have what it wanted, and
once it had made up its mind would not be balked. From her
cradle she had been self-willed; the very circumstances of her
life had developed that self-will in her. It drove her now remorselessly. Well, the die was cast. She must go through with it now.

She looked up, and her eyes met those of the woman sitting
opposite. She had a sudden fancy that in some way this other
woman had read her mind. She saw in those grey eyes understanding and – yes – compassion.

It was only a fleeting impression. The faces of both women
hardened to well-bred impassiveness. Mrs Kettering took up a
magazine, and Katherine Grey looked out of the window and
watched a seemingly endless vista of depressing streets and sub-
urban homes.

Ruth found an increasing difficulty in fixing her mind on the
printed page in front of her. In spite of herself, a thousand
apprehensions preyed on her mind. What a fool she had been!
What a fool she was! Like all cool and self-sufficient people,
when she did lose her self-control she lost it thoroughly. It was
too late . . . Was it too late? Oh, for someone to speak to, for
someone to advise her. She had never before had such a wish;
she would have scorned the idea of relying on any judgment
other than her own, but now – what was the matter with her?
Panic. Yes, that would describe it best – panic. She, Ruth Kettering, was completely and utterly panic-stricken.

She stole a covert glance at the figure opposite. If only she knew someone like that, some nice, cool, calm sympathetic creature. That was the sort of person one could talk to. But you can't, of course, confide in a stranger. And Ruth smiled to herself a little at the idea. She picked up the magazine again. Really she must control herself. After all she had thought all this out. She had decided of her own free will. What happiness had she ever had in her life up to now? She said to herself restlessly: 'Why shouldn't I be happy? No one will ever know.'

It seemed no time before Dover was reached. Ruth was a good sailor. She disliked the cold, and was glad to reach the shelter of the private cabin she had telegraphed for. Although she would not have admitted the fact, Ruth was in some ways superstitious. She was of the order of people to whom coincidence appeals. After disembarking at Calais and settling herself down with her maid in her double compartment in the Blue Train, she went along to the luncheon car. It was with a little shock of surprise that she found herself set down to small table with, opposite her, the same woman who had been her *vis-à-vis* in the Pullman. A faint smile came to the lips of both women.

'This is quite a coincidence,' said Mrs Kettering.

'I know,' said Katherine; 'it is odd the way things happen.'

A flying attendant shot up to them with the wonderful velocity always displayed by the Compagnie Internationale des Wagon-Lits and deposited two cups of soup. By the time the omelette succeeded the soup they were chatting together in friendly fashion.

'It will be heavenly to get into the sunshine,' sighed Ruth.

'I am sure it will be a wonderful feeling.'

'You know the Riviera well?'

'No; this is my first visit.'

'Fancy that.'

'You go every year, I expect?'

'Practically. January and February in London are horrible.'

'I have always lived in the country. They are not very inspiring months there either. Mostly mud.'

'What made you suddenly decide to travel?'

'Money,' said Katherine. 'For ten years I have been a paid

companion with just enough money of my own to buy myself strong country shoes; now I have been left what seems to me a fortune, though I dare say it would not seem so much to you.'

'Now I wonder why you said that – that it would not seem so to me.'

Katherine laughed. 'I don't really know. I suppose one forms impressions without thinking of it. I put you down in my own mind as one of the very rich of the earth. It was just an impression. I dare say I am wrong.'

'No,' said Ruth, 'you are not wrong.' She had suddenly become very grave. 'I wish you would tell me what other impressions you formed about me.'

'I –'

Ruth swept on, disregarding the other's embarrassment. 'Oh, please, don't be conventional. I want to know. As we left Victoria I looked across at you, and I had the sort of feeling that you – well, understood what was going on in my mind.'

'I can assure you I am not a mind reader,' said Katherine smiling.

'No, but will you tell me, please, just what you thought.' Ruth's eagerness was so intense and so sincere that she carried her point.

'I will tell you if you like, but you must not think me impertinent. I thought that for some reason you were in great distress of mind, and I was sorry for you.'

'You are right. You are quite right. I am in terrible trouble. I – I should like to tell you something about it, if I may.'

'Oh, dear,' Katherine thought to herself, 'how extraordinarily alike the world seems to be everywhere! People were always telling me things in St Mary Mead, and it is just the same thing here, and I don't really want to hear anybody's troubles!'

She replied politely:

'Do tell me.'

They were just finishing their lunch. Ruth gulped down her coffee, rose from her seat, and quite oblivious of the fact that Katherine had not begun to sip her coffee, said: 'Come to my compartment with me.'

They were two single compartments with a communicating door between them. In the second of them a thin maid, whom Katherine had noticed at Victoria, was sitting very upright on the seat, clutching a big scarlet morocco case with the initials 'R.V.K.' on it. Mrs Kettering pulled the communicating door to and sank down on the seat. Katherine sat down beside her.

'I am in trouble and I don't know what to do. There is a man whom I am fond of – very fond of indeed. We cared for each other when we were young, and we were thrust apart most brutally and unjustly. Now we have come together again.'

'Yes?'

'I – I am going to meet him now. Oh! I dare say you think it is all wrong, but you don't know the circumstances. My husband is impossible. He has treated me disgracefully.'

'Yes,' said Katherine again.

'What I feel so badly about is this. I have deceived my father – it was he who came to see me off at Victoria today. He wishes me to divorce my husband, and, of course, he has no idea – that I am going to meet this other man. He would think it extraordinarily foolish.'

'Well, don't you think it is?'

'I – I suppose it is.'

Ruth Kettering looked down at her hands; they were shaking violently.

'But I can't draw back now.'

'Why not?'

'I – it is all arranged, and it would break his heart.'

'Don't you believe it,' said Katherine robustly; 'hearts are pretty tough.'

'He will think I have no courage, no strength of purpose.'

'It seems to me an awfully silly thing that you are going to do,' said Katherine. 'I think you realize that yourself.'

Ruth Kettering buried her face in her hands. 'I don't know – I don't know. Ever since I left Victoria I have had a horrible feeling of something – something that is coming to me very soon – that I can't escape.'

She clutched convulsively at Katherine's hand.

'You must think I am mad talking to you like this, but I tell you I know something horrible is going to happen.'

'Don't think it,' said Katherine; 'try to pull yourself together. You could send your father a wire from Paris, if you like, and he would come to you at once.'

The other brightened.

'Yes, I could do that. Dear old Dad. It is queer – but I never knew until today how terribly fond of him I am.' She sat up and dried her eyes with a handkerchief. 'I have been very foolish. Thank you so much for letting me talk to you. I don't know why I got into such a queer, hysterical state.'

She got up. 'I am quite all right now. I suppose, really, I just needed someone to talk to. I can't think now why I have been making such an absolute fool of myself.'

Katherine got up too.

'I am glad you feel better,' she said, trying to make her voice sound as conventional as possible. She was only too well aware that the aftermath of confidences is embarrassment. She added tactfully:

'I must be going back to my own compartment.'

She emerged into the corridor at the same time as the maid was also coming out from the next door. The latter looked towards Katherine, over her shoulder, and an expression of intense surprise showed itself on her face. Katherine turned also, but by that time whoever it was who had aroused the maid's interest had retreated into his or her compartment, and the corridor was empty. Katherine walked down it to regain her own place, which was in the next coach. As she passed the end compartment the door opened and a woman's face looked out for a moment and then pulled the door to sharply. It was a face not easily forgotten, as Katherine was to know when she saw it again. A beautiful face, oval and dark, very heavily made up in a bizarre fashion. Katherine had a feeling that she had seen it before somewhere.

She regained her own compartment without other adventure and sat for some time thinking of the confidence which had just been made to her. She wondered idly who the woman in the mink coat might be, wondered also how the end of her story would turn out.

'If I have stopped anyone from making an idiot of themselves, I suppose I have done good work,' she thought to herself. 'But who knows? That is the kind of woman who is hard-headed and egotistical all her life, and it might be good for her to do the other sort of thing for a change. Oh, well – I don't suppose I shall ever see her again. She certainly won't want to see *me again*. That is the worst of letting people tell you things. They never do.'

She hoped that she would not be given the same place at dinner. She reflected, not without humour, that it might be awkward for both of them. Leaning back with her head against a cushion she felt tired and vaguely depressed. They had reached Paris, and the slow journey round the *ceinture*, with its interminable stops and waits, was very wearisome. When they arrived at the Gare de Lyon she was glad to get out and walk up and down the platform. The keen cold air was refreshing after the steam-heated train. She observed with a smile that her friend of the mink coat was solving the possible awkwardness of the dinner problem in her own way. A dinner basket was being handed up and received through the window by the maid.

When the train started once more, and dinner was announced by a violent ringing of bells, Katherine went along to it much relieved in her mind. Her *vis-à-vis* tonight was of an entirely different kind – a small man, distinctly foreign in appearance, with rigidly waxed moustache and an egg-shaped head which he carried rather on one side. Katherine had taken in a book to dinner with her. She found the little man's eyes fixed upon it with a kind of twinkling amusement.

'I see, Madame, that you have a "*roman policier*". You are fond of such things?'

'They amuse me,' Katherine admitted.

The little man nodded with the air of complete understanding.

'They have a good sale always, so I am told. Now why is that,

eh, Mademoiselle? I ask you as a student of human nature –
why should that be?'

Katherine felt more and more amused.

'Perhaps they give one the illusion of living an exciting life,'
she suggested.

He nodded gravely.

'Yes; there is something in that.'

'Of course, one knows that such things don't really
happen,' Katherine was continuing, but he interrupted her
sharply.

'Sometimes, Mademoiselle! Sometimes! I who speak to you
– they have happened to *me*.'

She threw him a quick, interested glance.

'Some day, who knows, *you* might be in the thick of things,'
he went on. 'It is all chance.'

'I don't think it is likely,' said Katherine. 'Nothing of that
kind ever happens to me.'

He leaned forward.

'Would you like it to?'

The question startled her, and she drew in her breath sharply.

'It is my fancy, perhaps,' said the little man, as he dexterously
polished one of the forks, 'but I think that you have a yearning
in you for interesting happenings. *Eh bien*, Mademoiselle, all
through my life I have observed one thing – "All one wants
one gets!" Who knows?' His face screwed itself up comically.
'You may get more than you bargain for.'

'Is that a prophecy?' asked Katherine, smiling as she rose
from the table.

The little man shook his head.

'I never prophesy,' he declared pompously. 'It is true that I
have the habit of being always right – but I do not boast of it.
Goodnight, Mademoiselle, and may you sleep well.'

Katherine went back along the train amused and entertained
by her little neighbour. She passed the open door of her
friend's compartment and saw the conductor making up the
bed. The lady in the mink coat was standing looking out of the
window. The second compartment, as Katherine saw through

the communicating door, was empty, with rugs and bags heaped up on the seat. The maid was not there.

Katherine found her own bed prepared, and since she was tired, she went to bed and switched off her light about half-past nine.

She woke with a sudden start; how much time had passed she did not know. Glancing at her watch, she found that it had stopped. A feeling of intense uneasiness pervaded her and grew stronger moment by moment. At last she got up, threw her dressing-gown round her shoulders, and stepped out into the corridor. The whole train seemed wrapped in slumber. Katherine let the window down and sat by it for some minutes, drinking in the cool night air and trying vainly to calm her uneasy fears. She presently decided that she would go along to the end and ask the conductor for the right time so that she could set her watch. She found, however, that his little chair was vacant. She hesitated for a moment and then walked through into the next coach. She looked down the long, dim line of the corridor and saw, to her surprise, that a man was standing with his hand on the door of the compartment occupied by the lady in the mink coat. That is to say, she thought it was the compartment. Probably, however, she was mistaken. He stood there for a moment or two with his back to her, seeming uncertain and hesitating in his attitude. Then he slowly turned, and with an odd feeling of fatality, Katherine recognized him as the same man whom she had noticed twice before – once in the corridor of the Savoy Hotel and once in Cook's offices. Then he opened the door of the compartment and passed in, drawing it to behind him.

An idea flashed across Katherine's mind. Could this be the man of whom the other woman had spoken – the man she was journeying to meet?

Then Katherine told herself that she was romancing. In all probability she had mistaken the compartment.

She went back to her own carriage. Five minutes later the train slackened speed. There was the long plaintive hiss of the Westinghouse brake, and a few minutes later the train came to a stop at Lyons.

CHAPTER XI

Murder

Katherine wakened the next morning to brilliant sunshine. She went along to breakfast early, but met none of her acquaintances of the day before. When she returned to her compartment it had just been restored to its daytime appearance by the conductor, a dark man with a drooping moustache and melancholy face.

'Madame is fortunate,' he said; 'the sun shines. It is always a great disappointment to passengers when they arrive on a grey morning.'

'I should have been disappointed, certainly,' said Katherine.

The man prepared to depart.

'We are rather late, Madame,' he said. 'I will let you know just before we get to Nice.'

Katherine nodded. She sat by the window, entranced by the sunlit panorama. The palm trees, the deep blue of the sea, the bright yellow mimosa came with all the charm of novelty to the woman who for fourteen years had known only the drab winters of England.

When they arrived at Cannes, Katherine got out and walked up and down the platform. She was curious about the lady in the mink coat, and looked up at the windows of her compartment. The blinds were still drawn down – the only ones to be so on the whole train. Katherine wondered a little, and when she re-entered the train she passed along the corridor and noticed that these two compartments were still shuttered and closed. The lady of the mink coat was clearly no early riser.

Presently the conductor came to her and told her that in a few minutes the train would arrive at Nice. Katherine handed him a tip; the man thanked her, but still lingered. There was something odd about him. Katherine, who had at first wondered whether the tip had not been big enough, was now convinced that something far more serious was amiss. His face was of a sickly pallor, he was shaking all over, and looked as if he had been frightened out of his life. He was eyeing her in a curious manner. Presently he said abruptly: 'Madame will excuse me, but is she expecting friends to meet her at Nice?'

'Probably,' said Katherine. 'Why?'

But the man merely shook his head and murmured something that Katherine could not catch and moved away, not reappearing until the train came to rest at the station, when he started handing her belongings down from the window.

Katherine stood for a moment or two on the platform rather at a loss, but a fair young man with an ingenuous face came up to her and said rather hesitatingly:

'Miss Grey, is it not?'

Katherine said that it was, and the young man beamed upon her seraphically and murmured: 'I am Chubby, you know – Lady Tamplin's husband. I expect she mentioned me, but perhaps she forgot. Have you got your *billet de bagages*? I lost mine when I came out this year, and you would not believe the fuss they made about it. Regular French red tape!'

Katherine produced it, and was just about to move off beside him when a very gentle and insidious voice murmured in her ear:

'A little moment, Madame, if you please.'

Katherine turned to behold an individual who made up for insignificance of stature by a large quantity of gold lace and uniform. The individual explained. 'There were certain formalities. Madame would perhaps be so kind as to accompany him. The regulations of the police –' he threw up his arms. 'Absurd, doubtless, but there it was.'

Mr Chubby Evans listened with a very imperfect comprehension, his French being of a limited order.

'So like the French,' murmured Mr Evans. He was one of those staunch patriotic Britons who, having made a portion of a foreign country their own, strongly resent the original inhabitants of it. 'Always up to some silly dodge or other. They've never tackled people on the station before, though. This is something quite new. I suppose you'll have to go.'

Katherine departed with her guide. Somewhat to her surprise, he led her towards a siding where a coach of the departed train had been shunted. He invited her to mount into this, and, preceding her down the corridor, held aside the door of one of the compartments. In it was a pompous-looking official personage, and with him a nondescript being who appeared to be a clerk. The pompous-looking personage rose politely, bowed to Katherine, and said:

'You will excuse me, Madame, but there are certain formalities to be complied with. Madame speaks French, I trust?'

'Sufficiently, I think, Monsieur,' replied Katherine in that language.

'That is good. Pray be seated, Madame. I am M. Caux, the Commissary of Police.' He blew out his chest importantly, and Katherine tried to look sufficiently impressed.

'You wish to see my passport?' she inquired. 'Here it is.'

The Commissary eyed her keenly and gave a little grunt.

'Thank you, Madame,' he said, taking the passport from her. He cleared his throat. 'But what I really desire is a little information.'

'Information?'

The Commissary nodded his head slowly.

'About a lady who has been a fellow passenger of yours. You lunched with her yesterday.'

'I am afraid I can't tell you anything about her. We fell into conversation over our meal, but she is a complete stranger to me. I have never seen her before.'

'And yet,' said the Commissary sharply, 'you returned to her compartment with her after lunch and sat talking for some time?'

'Yes,' said Katherine; 'that is true.'

The Commissary seemed to expect her to say something more. He looked at her encouragingly.

'Yes, Madame?'

'Well, Monsieur?' said Katherine.

'You can, perhaps, give me some kind of idea of that conversation?'

'I could,' said Katherine, 'but at the moment I see no reason to do so.'

In a somewhat British fashion she felt annoyed. This foreign official seemed to her impertinent.

'No reason?' cried the Commissary. 'Oh yes, Madame, I can assure you that there *is* a reason.'

'Then perhaps you will give it to me.'

The Commissary rubbed his chin thoughtfully for a minute or two without speaking.

'Madame,' he said at last, 'the reason is very simple. The lady in question was found dead in her compartment this morning.'

'Dead!' gasped Katherine. 'What was it – heart failure?'

'No,' said the Commissary in a reflective, dreamy voice. 'No – she was murdered.'

'Murdered!' cried Katherine.

'So you see, Madame, why we are anxious for any information we can possibly get.'

'But surely her maid –'

'The maid has disappeared.'

'Oh!' Katherine paused to assemble her thoughts.

'Since the conductor had seen you talking with her in her compartment, he quite naturally reported the fact to the police, and that is why, Madame, we have detained you, in the hope of gaining some information.'

'I am very sorry,' said Katherine; 'I don't even know her name.'

'Her name is Kettering. That we know from her passport and from the labels on her luggage. If we –'

There was a knock on the compartment door. M. Caux frowned. He opened it about six inches.

'What is the matter?' he said peremptorily. 'I cannot be disturbed.'

The egg-shaped head of Katherine's dinner acquaintance showed itself in the aperture. On his face was a beaming smile.

'My name,' he said, 'is Hercule Poirot.'

'Not,' the Commissary stammered, 'not *the* Hercule Poirot?'

'The same,' said M. Poirot. 'I remember meeting you once, M. Caux, at the Sûreté in Paris, though doubtless you have forgotten me?'

'Not at all, Monsieur, not at all,' declared the Commissary heartily. 'But enter, I pray you. You know of this – ?'

'Yes, I know,' said Hercule Poirot. 'I came to see if I might be of any assistance?'

'We should be flattered,' replied the Commissary promptly. 'Let me present you, M. Poirot, to' – he consulted the passport he still held in his hand – 'to Madame – er – Mademoiselle Grey.'

Poirot smiled across at Katherine.

'It is strange, is it not,' he murmured, 'that my words should have come true so quickly?'

'Mademoiselle, alas! can tell us very little,' said the Commissary.

'I have been explaining,' said Katherine, 'that this poor lady was a complete stranger to me.'

Poirot nodded.

'But she talked to you, did she not?' he said gently. 'You formed an impression – is it not so?'

'Yes,' said Katherine thoughtfully. 'I suppose I did.'

'And that impression was – ?'

'Yes, Mademoiselle' – the Commissary jerked himself forward – 'let us by all means have your impressions.'

Katherine sat turning the whole thing over in her mind. She felt in a way as if she were betraying a confidence, but with that ugly word 'Murder' ringing in her ears she dared not keep anything back. Too much might hang upon it. So, as nearly as she could, she repeated word for word the conversation she had had with the dead woman.

'That is interesting,' said the Commissary, glancing at the other. 'Eh, M. Poirot, that is interesting? Whether it has anything to do with the crime –' He left the sentence unfinished.

'I suppose it could not be suicide,' said Katherine, rather doubtfully.

'No,' said the Commissary, 'it could not be suicide. She was strangled with a length of black cord.'

'Oh!' Katherine shivered. M. Caux spread out his hands apologetically. 'It is not nice – no. I think that our train robbers are more brutal than they are in your country.'

'It is horrible.'

'Yes, yes' – he was soothing and apologetic – 'but you have great courage, Mademoiselle. At once, as soon as I saw you, I said to myself, "Mademoiselle has great courage." That is why I am going to ask you to do something more – something distressing, but I assure you very necessary.'

Katherine looked at him apprehensively.

He spread out his hands apologetically.

'I am going to ask you, Mademoiselle, to be so good as to accompany me to the next compartment.'

'Must I?' asked Katherine in a low voice.

'Someone must identify her,' said the Commissary, 'and since the maid has disappeared' – he coughed significantly – 'you appear to be the person who has seen most of her since she joined the train.'

'Very well,' said Katherine quietly; 'if it is necessary –'

She rose. Poirot gave her a little nod of approval.

'Mademoiselle is sensible,' he said. 'May I accompany you, M. Caux?'

'Enchanted, my dear M. Poirot.'

They went out into the corridor, and M. Caux unlocked the door of the dead woman's compartment. The blinds on the far side had been drawn half-way up to admit light. The dead woman lay on the berth to their left, in so natural a posture that one could have thought her asleep. The bedclothes were drawn up over her, and her head was turned to the wall, so that only the red auburn curls showed. Very gently M. Caux laid a hand on her shoulder and turned the body back so that the face came into view. Katherine flinched a little and dug her nails into her palms. A heavy blow had disfigured the features almost beyond recognition. Poirot gave a sharp exclamation.

'When was that done, I wonder?' he demanded. 'Before death or after?'

'The doctor says after,' said M. Caux.

'Strange,' said Poirot, drawing his brows together. He turned to Katherine. 'Be brave, Mademoiselle; look at her well. Are you sure that this is the woman you talked to in the train yesterday?'

Katherine had good nerves. She steeled herself to look long and earnestly at the recumbent figure. Then she leaned forward and took up the dead woman's hand.

'I am quite sure,' she replied at length. 'The face is too disfigured to recognize, but the build and carriage and hair are exact, and besides I noticed *this*' – she pointed to a tiny mole on the dead woman's wrist – 'while I was talking to her.'

'*Bon*,' approved Poirot. 'You are an excellent witness, Mademoiselle. There is, then, no question as to the identity, but it is strange, all the same.' He frowned down on the dead woman in perplexity.

M. Caux shrugged his shoulders.

'The murderer was carried away by rage, doubtless,' he suggested.

'If she had been struck down, it would have been comprehensible,' mused Poirot, 'but the man who strangled her slipped up behind and caught her unawares. A little choke – a little gurgle – that is all that would be heard, and then afterwards – that smashing blow on her face. Now why? Did he hope that if the face were unrecognizable she might not be identified? Or did he hate her so much that he could not resist striking that blow even after she was dead?'

Katherine shuddered, and he turned at once to her kindly.

'You must not let me distress you, Mademoiselle,' he said. 'To you this is all very new and terrible. To me, alas! it is an old story. One moment, I pray of you both.'

They stood against the door watching him as he went quickly round the compartment. He noted the dead woman's clothes neatly folded on the end of the berth, the big fur coat that hung from a hook, and the little red lacquer hat tossed on the rack. Then he passed through into the adjoining compartment, that in which Katherine had seen the maid sitting. Here the berth had not been made up. Three or four rugs were piled loosely on the seat; there was a hat-box and a couple of suit-cases. He turned suddenly to Katherine.

'You were in here yesterday,' he said. 'Do you see anything changed, anything missing?'

Katherine looked carefully round both compartments.

'Yes,' she said, 'there is something missing – a scarlet morocco case. It had the initials "R.V.K." on it. It might have been a small dressing-case or a big jewel-case. When I saw it, the maid was holding it.'

'Ah!' said Poirot.

'But, surely,' said Katherine, 'I – of course, I don't know anything about such things, but surely it is plain enough, if the maid and the jewel-case are missing?'

'You mean that it was the maid who was the thief? No, Mademoiselle, there is a very good reason against that.'

'What?'

'The maid was left behind in Paris.'

He turned to Poirot. 'I should like you to hear the conductor's story yourself,' he murmured confidentially. 'It is very suggestive.'

'Mademoiselle would doubtless like to hear it also,' said Poirot. 'You do not object, Monsieur le Commissaire?'

'No,' said the Commissary, who clearly did object very much. 'No, certainly, M. Poirot, if you say so. You have finished here?'

'I think so. One little minute.'

He had been turning over the rugs, and now he took one to the window and looked at it, picking something off it with his fingers.

'What is it?' demanded M. Caux sharply.

'Four auburn hairs.' He bent over the dead woman. 'Yes, they are from the head of Madame.'

'And what of it? Do you attach importance to them?'

Poirot let the rug drop back on the seat.

'What is important? What is not? One cannot say at this stage. But we must note each little fact carefully.'

They went back again into the first compartment, and in a minute or two the conductor of the carriage arrived to be questioned.

'Your name is Pierre Michel?' said the Commissary.

'Yes, Monsieur le Commissaire.'

'I should like you to repeat to this gentleman' – he indicated Poirot – 'the story that you told me as to what happened in Paris.'

'Very good, Monsieur le Commissaire. It was after we had left the Gare de Lyon I came along to make the beds, thinking that Madame would be at dinner, but she had a dinner-basket in her compartment. She said to me that she had been obliged to leave her maid behind in Paris, so that I only need make up one berth. She took her dinner basket into the adjoining compartment, and sat there while I made up the bed; then she told me that she did not wish to be wakened early in the morning, that she liked to sleep on. I told her I quite understood, and she wished me "goodnight".'

'You yourself did not go into the adjoining compartment?'

'No, Monsieur.'

'Then you did not happen to notice if a scarlet morocco case was amongst the luggage there?'

'No, Monsieur, I did not.'

'Would it have been possible for a man to have been concealed in the adjoining compartment?'

The conductor reflected.

'The door was half open,' he said. 'If a man had stood behind the door I should not have been able to see him, but he would, of course, have been perfectly visible to Madame when she went in there.'

'Quite so,' said Poirot. 'Is there anything more you have to tell us?'

'I think that is all, Monsieur. I can remember nothing else.'

'And now this morning?' prompted Poirot.

'As Madame had ordered, I did not disturb her. It was not until just before Cannes that I ventured to knock at the door. Getting no reply, I opened it. The lady appeared to be in her bed asleep. I took her by the shoulder to rouse her, and then –'

'And then you saw what had happened,' volunteered Poirot. '*Très bien.* I think I know all I want to know.'

'I hope, Monsieur le Commissaire, it is not that I have been guilty of any negligence,' said the man piteously. 'Such an affair to happen on the Blue Train! It is horrible.'

'Console yourself,' said the Commissary. 'Everything will be done to keep the affair as quiet as possible, if only in the interests of justice. I cannot think you have been guilty of any negligence.'

'And Monsieur le Commissaire will report as much to the Company?'

'But certainly, but certainly,' said M. Caux, impatiently. 'That will do now.'

The conductor withdrew.

'According to the medical evidence,' said the Commissary, 'the lady was probably dead before the train reached Lyons. Who then was the murderer? From Mademoiselle's story, it seems clear that somewhere on her journey she was to meet this man of whom she spoke. Her action in getting rid of the maid seems significant. Did the man join the train at Paris, and did she conceal him in the adjoining compartment? If so, they may have quarrelled, and he may have killed her in a fit of rage. That is one possibility. The other, and the more likely to my mind, is that her assailant was a train robber travelling on the train; that he stole along the corridor unseen by the conductor, killed her, and went off with the red morocco case, which doubtless contained jewels of some value. In all probability he left the train at Lyons, and we have already telegraphed to the station there for full particulars of anyone seen leaving the train.'

'Or he might have come on to Nice,' suggested Poirot.

'He might,' agreed the Commissary, 'but that would be a very bold course.'

Poirot let a minute or two go by before speaking, and then he said:

'In the latter case you think the man was an ordinary train robber?'

The Commissary shrugged his shoulders.

'It depends. We must get hold of the maid. It is possible that she has the red morocco case with her. If so, then the man of whom she spoke to Mademoiselle may be concerned in the case, and the affair is a crime of passion. I myself think the solution of a train robber is the more plausible. These bandits have become very bold of late.'

Poirot looked suddenly across at Katherine.

'And you, Mademoiselle,' he said, 'you heard and saw nothing during the night?'

'Nothing,' said Katherine.

Poirot turned to the Commissary.

'We need detain Mademoiselle no longer, I think,' he suggested.

The latter nodded.

'She will leave us her address?' he said.

Katherine gave him the name of Lady Tamplin's villa. Poirot made her a little bow.

'You permit that I see you again, Mademoiselle?' he said. 'Or have you so many friends that your time will be all taken up?'

'On the contrary,' said Katherine, 'I shall have plenty of leisure, and I shall be very pleased to see you again.'

'Excellent,' said Poirot, and gave her a little friendly nod. 'This shall be a *"roman policier" à nous*. We will investigate this affair together.'

CHAPTER XII

At the Villa Marguerite

'Then you were really in the thick of it all!' said Lady Tamplin enviously. 'My dear, how thrilling!' She opened her china blue eyes very wide and gave a little sigh.

'A real murder,' said Mr Evans gloatingly.

'Of course Chubby had no idea of anything of the kind,' went on Lady Tamplin; 'he simply could *not* imagine why the police wanted you. My dear, what an opportunity! I think, you know – yes, I certainly think something might be made out of this.'

A calculating look rather marred the ingenuousness of the blue eyes.

Katherine felt slightly uncomfortable. They were just finishing lunch, and she looked in turn at the three people sitting round the table. Lady Tamplin, full of practical schemes; Mr Evans, beaming with naïve appreciation, and Lenox with a queer crooked smile on her dark face.

'Marvellous luck,' murmured Chubby; 'I wish I could have gone along with you – and seen – all the exhibits.' His tone was wistful and childlike.

Katherine said nothing. The police had laid no injunctions of secrecy upon her, and it was clearly impossible to suppress the bare facts or try to keep them from her hostess. But she did rather wish it had been possible to do so.

'Yes,' said Lady Tamplin, coming suddenly out of her reverie, 'I do think something might be done. A little account, you know, cleverly written up. An eye-witness, a feminine touch: "*How I chatted with the dead woman, little thinking –*" that sort of thing, you know.'

'Rot!' said Lenox.

'You have no idea,' said Lady Tamplin in a soft, wistful voice, 'what newspapers will pay for a little titbit! Written, of course, by someone of really unimpeachable social position. You would not like to do it yourself, I dare say, Katherine dear, but just give me the bare bones of it, and *I* will manage the whole thing for you. Mr de Haviland is a special friend of mine. We have a little understanding together. A most delightful man – not at all reporterish. How does the idea strike you, Katherine?'

'I would much prefer to do nothing of the kind,' said Katherine bluntly.

Lady Tamplin was rather disconcerted at this uncompromising refusal. She sighed and turned to the elucidation of further details.

'A very striking-looking woman, you said? I wonder now who she could have been. You didn't hear her name?'

'It was mentioned,' Katherine admitted, 'but I can't remember it. You see, I was rather upset.'

'I should think so,' said Mr Evans; 'it must have been a beastly shock.'

It is to be doubted whether, even if Katherine had remembered the name, she would have admitted the fact. Lady Tamplin's remorseless cross-examination was making her restive. Lenox, who was observant in her own way, noticed this, and offered to take Katherine upstairs to see her room. She left her there, remarking kindly before she went: 'You mustn't mind Mother; she would make a few pennies' profit out of her dying grandmother if she could.'

Lenox went down again to find her mother and stepfather discussing the newcomer.

'Presentable,' said Lady Tamplin, 'quite presentable. Her clothes are all right. That grey thing is the same model that Gladys Cooper wore in *Palm Trees in Egypt.*'

'Have you noticed her eyes – what?' interposed Mr Evans.

'Never mind her eyes, Chubby,' said Lady Tamplin tartly; 'we are discussing things that really matter.'

'Oh, quite,' said Mr Evans, and retired into his shell.

'She doesn't seem to me very – malleable,' said Lady Tamplin, rather hesitating to choose the right word.

'She has all the instincts of a lady, as they say in books,' said Lenox, with a grin.

'Narrow-minded,' murmured Lady Tamplin. 'Inevitable under the circumstances, I suppose.'

'I expect you will do your best to broaden her,' said Lenox, with a grin, 'but you will have your work cut out. Just now, you noticed, she stuck down her fore feet and laid back her ears and refused to budge.'

'Anyway,' said Lady Tamplin hopefully, 'she doesn't look to me at all mean. Some people, when they come into money, seem to attach undue importance to it.'

'Oh, you'll easily touch her for what you want,' said Lenox; 'and, after all, that is all that matters, isn't it? That is what she is here for.'

'She is my own cousin,' said Lady Tamplin, with dignity.

'Cousin, eh?' said Mr Evans, waking up again. 'I suppose I call her Katherine, don't I?'

'It is of no importance at all what you call her, Chubby,' said Lady Tamplin.

'Good,' said Mr Evans; 'then I will. Do you suppose she plays tennis?' he added hopefully.

'Of course not,' said Lady Tamplin. 'She has been a companion, I tell you. Companions don't play tennis – or golf. They might possibly play golf-croquet, but I have always understood that they wind wool and wash dogs most of the day.'

'O God!' said Mr Evans; 'do they really?'

Lenox drifted upstairs again to Katherine's room. 'Can I help you?' she asked rather perfunctorily.

On Katherine's disclaimer, Lenox sat on the edge of the bed and stared thoughtfully at her guest.

'Why did you come?' she said at last. 'To us, I mean. We're not your sort.'

'Oh, I am anxious to get into Society.'

'Don't be an ass,' said Lenox promptly, detecting the flicker of a smile. 'You know what I mean well enough. You are not a bit what I thought you would be. I say, you *have* got some decent clothes.' She sighed. 'Clothes are no good to me. I was born awkward. It's a pity, because I love them.'

'I love them too,' said Katherine, 'but it has not been much use my loving them up to now. Do you think this is nice?'

She and Lenox discussed several models with artistic fervour.

'I like you,' said Lenox suddenly. 'I came up to warn you not to be taken in by Mother, but I think now that there is no need to do that. You are frightfully sincere and upright and all those queer things, but you are not a fool. Oh hell! what is it now?'

Lady Tamplin's voice was calling plaintively from the hall:

'Lenox, Derek has just rung up. He wants to come to dinner tonight. Will it be all right? I mean, we haven't got anything awkward, like quails, have we?'

Lenox reassured her and came back into Katherine's room. Her face looked brighter and less sullen.

'I'm glad old Derek is coming,' she said; 'you'll like him.'

'Who is Derek?'

'He is Lord Leconbury's son, married a rich American woman. Women are simply potty about him.'

'Why?'

'Oh, the usual reason – very good-looking and a regular bad lot. Everyone goes off their head about him.'

'Do you?'

'Sometimes I do,' said Lenox, 'and sometimes I think I would like to marry a nice curate and live in the country and grow things in frames.' She paused a minute, and then added, 'An Irish curate would be best, and then I should hunt.'

After a minute or two she reverted to her former theme. 'There is something queer about Derek. All that family are a bit potty – mad gamblers, you know. In the old days they used to gamble away their wives and their estates, and did most reckless things just for the love of it. Derek would have made a perfect highwayman – debonair and gay, just the right manner.' She moved to the door. 'Well, come down when you feel like it.'

Left alone, Katherine gave herself up to thought. Just at present she felt thoroughly ill at ease and jarred by her surroundings. The shock of the discovery in the train and the reception of the news by her new friends jarred upon her susceptibilities. She thought long and earnestly about the murdered woman. She had been sorry for Ruth, but she could not honestly say that she had liked her. She had divined only too well the ruthless egoism that was the keynote of her personality, and it repelled her.

She had been amused and a trifle hurt by the other's cool dismissal of her when she had served her turn. That she had come to some decision, Katherine was quite certain, but she wondered now what that decision had been. Whatever it was, death had stepped in and made all decisions meaningless. Strange that it should have been so, and that a brutal crime should have been the ending of that fateful journey. But suddenly Katherine remembered a small fact that she ought, perhaps, to have told the police – a fact that had for the moment escaped her memory. Was it of any real importance? She had certainly thought that she had seen a man going into that particular compartment, but she realized that she might easily have been mistaken. It might have been the compartment next door, and certainly the man in question could be no train robber. She recalled him very clearly as she had seen him on those two previous occasions – once at the Savoy and once at Cook's office. No, doubtless she had been mistaken. He had not gone into the dead woman's compartment, and it was perhaps as well that she had said nothing to the police. She might have done incalculable harm by doing so.

She went down to join the others on the terrace outside. Through the branches of mimosa, she looked out over the blue of the Mediterranean, and, whilst listening with half an ear to Lady Tamplin's chatter, she was glad that she had come. This was better than St Mary Mead.

That evening she put on the mauvy pink dress that went by the name of *soupir d'automne*, and after smiling at her reflection in the mirror, went downstairs with, for the first time in her life, a faint feeling of shyness.

Most of Lady Tamplin's guests had arrived, and since noise was the essential of Lady Tamplin's parties, the din was already terrific. Chubby rushed up to Katherine, pressed a cocktail upon her, and took her under his wing.

'Oh, here you are, Derek,' cried Lady Tamplin, as the door opened to admit the last comer. 'Now at last we can have something to eat. I am starving.'

Katherine looked across the room. She was startled. So this – was Derek, and she realized that she was not surprised. She had always known that she would some day meet the man whom she had seen three times by such a curious chain of coincidences. She thought, too, that he recognized her. He paused abruptly in what he was saying to Lady Tamplin, and went on again as though with an effort. They all went in to dinner, and Katherine found that he was placed beside her. He turned to her at once with a vivid smile.

'I knew I was going to meet you soon,' he remarked, 'but I never dreamt that it would be here. It had to be, you know. Once at the Savoy and once at Cook's – never twice without three times. Don't say you can't remember me or never noticed me. I insist upon your pretending that you noticed me, anyway.'

'Oh, I did,' said Katherine; 'but this is not the third time. It is the fourth time. I saw you on the Blue Train.'

'On the Blue Train!' Something undefinable came over his manner; she could not have said just what it was. It was as though he had received a check, a set-back. Then he said carelessly:

'What was the rumpus this morning? Somebody had died, hadn't they?'

'Yes,' said Katherine slowly; 'somebody had died.'

'You shouldn't die on a train,' remarked Derek flippantly. 'I believe it causes all sorts of legal and international complications, and it give the train an excuse for being even later than usual.'

'Mr Kettering?' A stout American lady, who was sitting opposite, leaned forward and spoke to him with the deliberate intonation of her race. 'Mr Kettering, I do believe you have forgotten me, and I thought you such a perfectly lovely man.'

Derek leaned forward, answering her, and Katherine sat almost dazed.

Kettering! That was the name, of course! She remembered it now – but what a strange, ironical situation! Here was this man whom she had seen go into his wife's compartment last night, who had left her alive and well, and now he was sitting at dinner, quite unconscious of the fate that had befallen her. Of that there was no doubt. He did not know.

A servant was leaning over Derek, handing him a note and murmuring in his ear. With a word of excuse to Lady Tamplin, he broke it open, and an expression of utter astonishment came over his face as he read; then he looked at his hostess.

'This is most extraordinary. I say, Rosalie, I am afraid I will have to leave you. The Prefect of Police wants to see me at once. I can't think what about.'

'Your sins have found you out,' remarked Lenox.

'They must have,' said Derek; 'probably some idiotic non-sense, but I suppose I shall have to push off to the Préfecture. How dare the old boy rout me out from dinner? It ought to be something deadly serious to justify that,' and he laughed as he pushed back his chair and rose to leave the room.

CHAPTER XIII

Van Aldin Gets a Telegram

On the afternoon of the 15th February a thick yellow fog had settled down on London. Rufus Van Aldin was in his suite at the Savoy and was making the most of the atmospheric conditions by working double time. Knighton was overjoyed. He had found it difficult of late to get his employer to concentrate on the matters in hand. When he had ventured to urge certain courses, Van Aldin had put him off with a curt word. But now Van Aldin seemed to be throwing himself into work with redoubled energy, and the secretary made the most of his opportunities. Always tactful, he plied the spur so unobtrusively that Van Aldin never suspected it.

Yet in the middle of this absorption in business matters, one little fact lay at the back of Van Aldin's mind. A chance remark of Knighton's, uttered by the secretary in all unconsciousness, had given rise to it. It now festered unseen, gradually reaching further and further forward into Van Aldin's consciousness, until at last, in spite of himself, he had to yield to its insistence.

He listened to what Knighton was saying with his usual air of keen attention, but in reality not one word of it penetrated his mind. He nodded automatically, however, and the secretary turned to some other paper. As he was sorting them out, his employer spoke:

'Do you mind telling me that over again, Knighton?'

For a moment Knighton was at a loss.

'You mean about this, sir?' He held up a closely written Company report.

'No, no,' said Van Aldin; 'what you told me about seeing Ruth's maid in Paris last night. I can't make it out. You must have been mistaken.'

'I can't have been mistaken, sir; I actually spoke to her.'

'Well, tell me the whole thing again.'

Knighton complied.

'I had fixed up the deal with Bartheimers,' he explained, 'and had gone back to the Ritz to pick up my traps preparatory to having dinner and catching the nine o'clock train from the Gare du Nord. At the reception desk I saw a woman whom I was quite sure was Mrs Kettering's maid. I went up to her and asked if Mrs Kettering was staying there.'

'Yes, yes,' said Van Aldin. 'Of course. Naturally. And she told you that Ruth had gone on to the Riviera and had sent her to the Ritz to await further orders there?'

'Exactly that, sir.'

'It is very odd,' said Van Aldin. 'Very odd, indeed, unless the woman had been impertinent or something of that kind.'

'In that case,' objected Knighton, 'surely Mrs Kettering would have paid her down a sum of money, and told her to go back to England? She would hardly have sent her to the Ritz.'

'No,' muttered the millionaire; 'that's true.'

He was about to say something further, but checked himself. He was fond of Knighton and liked and trusted him, but he could hardly discuss his daughter's private affairs with his secretary. He had already felt hurt by Ruth's lack of frankness, and this chance information which had come to him did nothing to allay his misgivings.

Why had Ruth got rid of her maid in Paris? What possible object or motive could she have had in so doing?

He reflected for a moment or two on the curious combination of chance. How should it have occurred to Ruth, except as the wildest coincidence, that the first person that the maid should run across in Paris should be her father's secretary? Ah, but that was the way things happened. That was the way things got found out.

He winced at the last phrase; it had arisen with complete naturalness to his mind. Was there then 'something to be found out'? He hated to put this question to himself; he had no doubt of the answer. The answer was – he was sure of it – Armand de la Roche.

It was bitter to Van Aldin that a daughter of his should be gulled by such a man, yet he was forced to admit that she was in good company – that other well-bred and intelligent women had succumbed just as easily to the Count's fascination. Men saw through him, women did not.

He sought now for a phrase that would allay any suspicion that his secretary might have felt.

'Ruth is always changing her mind about things at a moment's notice,' he remarked, and then he added in a would-be careless tone: 'The maid didn't give any – er – reason for this change of plan?'

Knighton was careful to make his voice as natural as possible as he replied:

'She said, sir, that Mrs Kettering had met a friend unexpectedly.'

'Is that so?'

The secretary's practised ears caught the note of strain underlying the seemingly casual tone.

'Oh, I see. Man or woman?'

'I think she said a man, sir.'

Van Aldin nodded. His worst fears were being realized. He rose from his chair, and began pacing up and down the room, a habit of his when agitated. Unable to contain his feelings any longer, he burst forth:

'There is one thing no man can do, and that is to get a woman to listen to reason. Somehow or other, they don't seem to have any kind of *sense*. Talk of woman's instinct – why, it is well known all the world over that a woman is the surest mark for any rascally swindler. Not one in ten of them knows a scoundrel when she meets one; they can be preyed on by any good-looking fellow with a soft side to his tongue. If I had my way –'

He was interrupted. A page-boy entered with a telegram. Van Aldin tore it open, and his face went a sudden chalky white. He caught hold of the back of a chair to steady himself, and waved the page-boy from the room.

'What's the matter, sir?'

Knighton had risen in concern.

'Ruth!' said Van Aldin hoarsely.

'Mrs Kettering?'

'Killed!'

'An accident to the train?'

Van Aldin shook his head.

'No. From this it seems she has been robbed as well. They don't use the word, Knighton, but my poor girl has been murdered.'

'Oh, my God, sir!'

Van Aldin tapped the telegram with his forefinger.

'This is from the police at Nice. I must go out there by the first train.'

Knighton was efficient as ever. He glanced at the clock.

'Five o'clock from Victoria, sir.'

'That's right. You will come with me, Knighton. Tell my man, Archer, and pack your own things. See to everything here. I want to go round to Curzon Street.'

The telephone rang sharply, and the secretary lifted the receiver.

'Yes; who is it?'

Then to Van Aldin:

'Mr Goby, sir.'

'Goby? I can't see him now. No – wait, we have plenty of time. Tell them to send him up.'

Van Aldin was a strong man. Already he had recovered that iron calm of his. Few people would have noticed anything amiss in his greeting to Mr Goby.

'I am pressed for time, Goby. Got anything important to tell me?'

Mr Goby coughed.

'The movements of Mr Kettering, sir. You wished them reported to you.'

'Yes – well?'

'Mr Kettering, sir, left London for the Riviera yesterday morning.'

'What?'

Something in his voice must have startled Mr Goby. That worthy gentleman departed from his usual practice of never looking at the person to whom he was talking, and stole a fleeting glance at the millionaire.

'What train did he go on?' demanded Van Aldin.

'The Blue Train, sir.'

Mr Goby coughed again and spoke to the clock on the mantelpiece.

'Mademoiselle Mirelle, the dancer from the Parthenon, went by the same train.'

CHAPTER XIV

Ada Mason's Story

'I cannot repeat to you often enough, Monsieur, our horror, our consternation, and the deep sympathy we feel for you.'

Thus M. Carrège, the Juge d'Instruction, addressed Van Aldin. M. Caux, the Commissary, made sympathetic noises in his throat. Van Aldin brushed away horror, consternation, and sympathy with an abrupt gesture. The scene was the Examining Magistrate's room at Nice. Besides M. Carrège, the Commissary, and Van Aldin, there was a further person in the room. It was that person who now spoke.

'M. Van Aldin,' he said, 'desires action – swift action.'

'Ah!' cried the Commissary, 'I have not yet presented you. M. Van Aldin, this is M. Hercule Poirot; you have doubtless heard of him. Although he has retired from his profession for some years now, his name is still a household word as one of the greatest living detectives.'

'Pleased to meet you, M. Poirot,' said Van Aldin, falling back mechanically on a formula that he had discarded some years ago. 'You have retired from your profession?'

'That is so, Monsieur. Now I enjoy the world.'

The little man made a grandiloquent gesture.

'M. Poirot happened to be travelling on the Blue Train,' explained the Commissary, 'and he has been so kind as to assist us out of his vast experience.'

The millionaire looked at Poirot keenly. Then he said unexpectedly:

'I am a very rich man, M. Poirot. It is usually said that a rich man labours under the belief that he can buy everything and everyone. That is not true. I am a big man in my way, and one big man can ask a favour from another big man.'

Poirot nodded a quick appreciation.

'That is very well said, M. Van Aldin. I place myself entirely at your service.'

'Thank you,' said Van Aldin. 'I can only say call upon me at any time, and you will not find me ungrateful. And now, gentlemen, to business.'

'I propose,' said M. Carrège, 'to interrogate the maid, Ada Mason. You have her here, I understand?'

'Yes,' said Van Aldin. 'We picked her up in Paris in passing through. She was very upset to hear of her mistress's death, but she tells her story coherently enough.'

'We will have her in, then,' said M. Carrège.

He rang the bell on his desk, and in a few minutes Ada Mason entered the room.

She was very neatly dressed in black, and the tip of her nose was red. She had exchanged her grey travelling gloves for a pair of black suède ones. She cast a look round the Examining Magistrate's office in some trepidation, and seemed relieved at the presence of her mistress's father. The Examining Magistrate prided himself on his geniality of manner, and did his best to put her at her ease. He was helped in this by Poirot, who acted as interpreter, and whose friendly manner was reassuring to the Englishwoman.

'Your name is Ada Mason; is that right?'

'Ada Beatrice I was christened, sir,' said Mason primly.

'Just so. And we can understand, Mason, that this has all been very distressing.'

'Oh, indeed it has, sir. I have been with many ladies and always given satisfaction, I hope, and I never dreamt of anything of this kind happening in any situation where I was.'

'No, no,' said M. Carrège.

'Naturally, I have read of such things, of course, in the Sunday papers. And then I always have understood that those foreign trains –' She suddenly checked her flow, remembering that the gentlemen who were speaking to her were of the same nationality as the trains.

'Now let us talk this affair over,' said M. Carrège. 'There was,

I understand, no question of your staying in Paris when you started from London?'

'Oh no, sir. We were to go straight through to Nice.'

'Have you ever been abroad with your mistress before?'

'No, sir. I had only been with her two months, you see.'

'Did she seem quite as usual when starting on this journey?'

'She was worried like and a bit upset, and she was rather irritable and difficult to please.'

M. Carrège nodded.

'Now then, Mason, what was the first you heard of your stopping in Paris?'

'It was at the place they call the Gare de Lyon, sir. My mistress was thinking of getting out and walking up and down the platform. She was just going out into the corridor when she gave a sudden exclamation, and came back into her compartment with a gentleman. She shut the door between her carriage and mine, so that I didn't see or hear anything, till she suddenly opened it again and told me that she had changed her plans. She gave me some money and told me to get out and go to the Ritz. They knew her well there, she said, and would give me a room. I was to wait there until I heard from her; she would wire me what she wanted me to do. I had just time to get my things together and jump out of the train before it started off. It was a rush.'

'While Mrs Kettering was telling you this, where was the gentleman?'

'He was standing in the other compartment, sir, looking out of the window.'

'Can you describe him to us?'

'Well, you see, sir, I hardly saw him. He had his back to me most of the time. He was a tall gentleman and dark; that's all I can say. He was dressed very like another gentleman in a dark blue overcoat and a grey hat.'

'Was he one of the passengers on the train?'

'I don't think so, sir; I took it that he had come to the station to see Mrs Kettering in passing through. Of course he might have been one of the passengers; I never thought of that.'

Mason seemed a little flurried by the suggestion.

'Ah!' M. Carrège passed lightly to another subject. 'Your mistress later requested the conductor not to rouse her early in the morning. Was that a likely thing for her to do, do you think?'

'Oh yes, sir. The mistress never ate any breakfast and she didn't sleep well at nights, so that she liked sleeping on in the morning.'

Again M. Carrège passed to another subject.

'Amongst the luggage there was a scarlet morocco case, was there not?' he asked. 'Your mistress's jewel-case?'

'Yes, sir.'

'Did you take that case to the Ritz?'

'*Me* take the mistress's jewel-case to the Ritz! Oh no, indeed, sir.' Mason's tones were horrified.

'You left it behind you in the carriage?'

'Yes, sir.'

'Had your mistress many jewels with her, do you know?'

'A fair amount, sir; made me a bit uneasy sometimes, I can tell you, with those nasty tales you hear of being robbed in foreign countries. They were insured, I know, but all the same it seemed a frightful risk. Why, the rubies alone, the mistress told me, were worth several hundred thousand pounds.'

'The rubies! What rubies?' barked Van Aldin suddenly.

Mason turned to him. 'I think it was you who gave them to her, sir, not very long ago.'

'My God!' cried Van Aldin. 'You don't say she had those rubies with her? I told her to leave them at the bank.'

Mason gave once more the discreet cough which was apparently part of her stock-in-trade as a lady's maid. This time it expressed a good deal. It expressed far more clearly than words could have done, that Mason's mistress had been a lady who took her own way.

'Ruth must have been mad,' muttered Van Aldin. 'What on earth could have possessed her?'

M. Carrège in turn gave vent to a cough, again a cough of significance. It riveted Van Aldin's attention on him.

'For the moment,' said M. Carrège, addressing Mason, 'I think that is all. If you will go into the next room, Mademoiselle, they will read over to you the questions and answers, and you will sign accordingly.'

Mason went out escorted by the clerk, and Van Aldin said immediately to the Magistrate:

'Well?'

M. Carrège opened a drawer in his desk, took out a letter, and handed it across to Van Aldin.

'This was found in Madame's handbag.'

Chere Amie (the letter ran), – I will obey you; I will be prudent, discreet – all those things that a lover most hates. Paris would perhaps have been unwise, but the Isles d'Or are far away from the world, and you may be assured that nothing will leak out. It is like you and your divine sympathy to be so interested in the work on famous jewels that I am writing. It will, indeed, be an extraordinary privilege to actually see and handle these historic rubies. I am devoting a special passage to "Heart of Fire". My wonderful one! Soon I will make up to you for all those sad years of separation and emptiness. – Your ever-adoring,

ARMAND.

CHAPTER XV

The Comte de la Roche

Van Aldin read the letter through in silence. His face turned a dull angry crimson. The men watching him saw the veins start out on his forehead, and his big hands clench themselves unconsciously. He handed back the letter without a word. M. Carrège was looking with close attention at his desk, M. Caux's eyes were fixed upon the ceiling, and M. Hercule Poirot was tenderly brushing a speck of dust from his coat sleeve. With the greatest tact they none of them looked at Van Aldin.

It was M. Carrège, mindful of his status and his duties, who tackled the unpleasant subject.

'Perhaps, Monsieur,' he murmured, 'you are aware by whom – er – this letter was written?'

'Yes, I know,' said Van Aldin heavily.

'Ah?' said the magistrate inquiringly.

'A scoundrel who calls himself the Comte de la Roche.'

There was a pause; then M. Poirot leaned forward, straightened a ruler on the judge's desk, and addressed the millionaire directly.

'M. Van Aldin, we are all sensible, deeply sensible, of the pain it must give you to speak of these matters, but believe me, Monsieur, it is not the time for concealments. If justice is to be done, we must know everything. If you will reflect a little minute you will realize the truth of that clearly for yourself.'

Van Aldin was silent for a moment or two, then almost reluctantly he nodded his head in agreement.

'You are quite right, M. Poirot,' he said. 'Painful as it is, I have no right to keep anything back.'

The Commissary gave a sigh of relief, and the Examining

Magistrate leaned back in his chair and adjusted a pince-nez on his long thin nose.

'Perhaps you will tell us in your own words, M. Van Aldin,' he said, 'all that you know of this gentleman.'

'It began eleven or twelve years ago – in Paris. My daughter was a young girl then, full of foolish, romantic notions, like all young girls are. Unknown to me, she made the acquaintance of this Comte de la Roche. You have heard of him, perhaps?'

The Commissary and Poirot nodded in assent.

'He calls himself the Comte de la Roche,' continued Van Aldin, 'but I doubt if he has any right to the title.'

'You would not have found his name in the *Almanac de Gotha*,' agreed the Commissary.

'I discovered as much,' said Van Aldin. 'The man was a good-looking, plausible scoundrel, with a fatal fascination for women. Ruth was infatuated with him, but I soon put a stop to the whole affair. The man was no better than a common swindler.'

'You are quite right,' said the Commissary. 'The Comte de la Roche is well known to us. If it were possible, we should have laid him by the heels before now, but *ma foi!* it is not easy; the fellow is cunning, his affairs are always conducted with ladies of high social position. If he obtains money from them under false pretences or as the fruit of blackmail, *eh bien!* naturally they will not prosecute. To look foolish in the eyes of the world, oh no, that would never do, and he has an extraordinary power over women.'

'That is so,' said the millionaire heavily. 'Well, as I told you, I broke the affair up pretty sharply. I told Ruth exactly what he was, and she had, perforce, to believe me. About a year afterwards, she met her present husband and married him. As far as I knew, that was the end of the matter; but only a week ago, I discovered, to my amazement, that my daughter had resumed her acquaintance with the Comte de la Roche. She had been meeting him frequently in London and Paris. I remonstrated with her on her imprudence, for I may tell you gentlemen that, on my insistence, she was preparing to bring a suit for divorce against her husband.'

'That is interesting,' murmured Poirot softly, his eyes on the ceiling.

Van Aldin looked at him sharply, and then went on.

'I pointed out to her the folly of continuing to see the Comte under the circumstances. I thought she agreed with me.'

The Examining Magistrate coughed delicately.

'But according to this letter –' he began, and then stopped.

Van Aldin's jaw set itself squarely.

'I know. It's no good mincing matters. However unpleasant, we have got to face facts. It seems clear that Ruth had arranged to go to Paris and meet de la Roche there. After my warnings to her, however, she must have written to the Count suggesting a change of rendezvous.'

'The Isles d'Or,' said the Commissary thoughtfully, 'are situated just opposite Hyères, a remote and idyllic spot.'

Van Aldin nodded.

'My God! How could Ruth be such a fool?' he exclaimed bitterly. 'All this talk about writing a book on jewels! Why, he must have been after the rubies from the first.'

'There are some very famous rubies,' said Poirot, 'originally part of the Crown jewels of Russia; they are unique in character, and their value is almost fabulous. There has been a rumour that they have lately passed into the possession of an American. Are we right in concluding, Monsieur, that you were the purchaser?'

'Yes,' said Van Aldin. 'They came into my possession in Paris about ten days ago.'

'Pardon me, Monsieur, but you have been negotiating for their purchase for some time?'

'A little over two months. Why?'

'These things became known,' said Poirot. 'There is always a pretty formidable crowd on the track of jewels such as these.'

A spasm distorted the other's face.

'I remember,' he said brokenly, 'a joke I made to Ruth when I gave them to her. I told her not to take them to the Riviera with her, as I could not afford to have her robbed and murdered for the sake of the jewels. My God! The things one says – never dreaming or knowing they will come true.'

There was a sympathetic silence, and then Poirot spoke in a detached manner.

'Let us arrange our facts with order and precision. According to our present theory, this is how they run. The Comte de la Roche knows of your purchase of these jewels. By an easy stratagem he induces Madame Kettering to bring the stones with her. He, then, is the man Mason saw in the train at Paris.'

The other three nodded in agreement.

'Madame is surprised to see him, but he deals with the situation promptly. Mason is got out of the way; a dinner basket is ordered. We know from the conductor that he made up the berth for the first compartment, but he did not go into the second compartment, and that a man could quite well have been concealed from him. So far the Comte could have been hidden to a marvel. No one knows of his presence on the train except Madame; he has been careful that the maid did not see his face. All that she could say is that he was tall and dark. It is all most conveniently vague. They are alone – and the train rushes through the night. There would be no outcry, no struggle, for the man is, so she thinks, her lover.'

He turned gently to Van Aldin.

'Death, Monsieur, must have been almost instantaneous. We will pass over that quickly. The Comte takes the jewel-case which lies ready to his hand. Shortly afterwards the train draws into Lyons.'

M. Carrège nodded his approval.

'Precisely. The conductor without descends. It would be easy for our man to leave the train unseen; it would be easy to catch a train back to Paris or anywhere he pleases. And the crime would be put down as an ordinary train robbery. But for the letter found in Madame's bag, the Comte would not have been mentioned.'

'It was an oversight on his part not to search that bag,' declared the Commissary.

'Without doubt he thought she had destroyed that letter. It

was – pardon me, Monsieur – it was an indiscretion of the first water to keep it.'

'And yet,' murmured Poirot, 'it was an indiscretion the Comte might have foreseen.'

'You mean?'

'I mean we are all agreed on one point, and that is that the Comte de la Roche knows one subject *à fond*: Women. How was it that, knowing women as he does, he did not foresee that Madame would have kept that letter?'

'Yes – yes,' said the Examining Magistrate doubtfully, 'there is something in what you say. But at such times, you understand, a man is not master of himself. He does not reason calmly. *Mon Dieu!*' he added, with feeling, 'if our criminals kept their heads and acted with intelligence, how should we capture them?'

Poirot smiled to himself.

'It seems to me a clear case,' said the other, 'but a difficult one to prove. The Comte is a slippery customer, and unless the maid can identify him –'

'Which is most unlikely,' said Poirot.

'True, true.' The Examining Magistrate rubbed his chin. 'It is going to be difficult.'

'If he did indeed commit the crime –' began Poirot. M. Caux interrupted.

'If – you say *if*?'

'Yes, Monsieur le Commissaire, I say *if*.'

The other looked at him sharply. 'You are right,' he said at last, 'we go too fast. It is possible that the Comte may have an alibi. Then we should look foolish.'

'*Ah, ça par example*,' replied Poirot, 'that is of no importance whatever. Naturally, if he committed the crime he will have an alibi. A man with the Comte's experience does not neglect to take precautions. No, I said *if* for a very definite reason.'

'And what was that?'

Poirot wagged an emphatic forefinger. 'The psychology.'

'Eh?' said the Commissary.

'The psychology is at fault. The Comte is a scoundrel – yes. The Comte is a swindler – yes. The Comte preys upon women

– yes. He proposes to steal Madame's jewels – again yes. Is he the kind of man to commit murder? I say *no*! A man of the type of the Comte is always a coward; he takes no risks. He plays the safe, the mean, what the English call the lowdown game; but murder, a hundred times no!' He shook his head in a dissatisfied manner.

The Examining Magistrate, however, did not seem disposed to agree with him.

'The day always comes when such gentry lose their heads and go too far,' he observed sagely. 'Doubtless that is the case here. Without wishing to disagree with you, M. Poirot –'

'It was only an opinion,' Poirot hastened to explain. 'The case is, of course, in your hands, and you will do what seems fit to you.'

'I am satisfied in my own mind the Comte de la Roche is the man we need to get hold of,' said M. Carrège. 'You agree with me, Monsieur le Commissaire?'

'Perfectly.'

'And you, M. Van Aldin?'

'Yes,' said the millionaire. 'Yes; the man is a thorough paced villain, no doubt about it.'

'It will be difficult to lay hands on him, I am afraid,' said the Magistrate, 'but we will do our best. Telegraphed instructions shall go out at once.'

'Permit me to assist you,' said Poirot. 'There need be no difficulty.'

'Eh?'

The others stared at him. The little man smiled beamingly back at them.

'It is my business to know things,' he explained. 'The Comte is a man of intelligence. He is at present at a villa he has leased, the Villa Marina at Antibes.'

CHAPTER XVI

Poirot Discusses the Case

Everybody looked respectfully at Poirot. Undoubtedly the little man had scored heavily. The Commissary laughed – on a rather hollow note.

'You teach us all our business,' he cried. .'M. Poirot knows more than the police.'

Poirot gazed complacently at the ceiling, adopting a mock-modest air.

'What will you; it is my little hobby,' he murmured, 'to know things. Naturally I have the time to indulge it. I am not overburdened with affairs.'

'Ah!' said the Commissary shaking his head portentously. 'As for me –'

He made an exaggerated gesture to represent the cares that lay on his shoulders.

Poirot turned suddenly to Van Aldin.

'You agree, Monsieur, with this view? You feel certain that the Comte de la Roche is the murderer?'

'Why, it would seem so – yes, certainly.'

Something guarded in the answer made the Examining Magistrate look at the American curiously. Van Aldin seemed aware of his scrutiny and made an effort as though to shake off some preoccupation.

'What about my son-in-law?' he asked. 'You have acquainted him with the news? He is in Nice, I understand.'

'Certainly, Monsieur.' The Commissary hesitated, and then murmured very discreetly: 'You are doubtless aware, M. Van Aldin, that M. Kettering was also one of the passengers on the Blue Train that night?'

The millionaire nodded.

'Heard it just before I left London,' he vouchsafed laconically.

'He tells us,' continued the Commissary, 'that he had no idea his wife was travelling on the train.'

'I bet he hadn't,' said Van Aldin grimly. 'It would have been rather a nasty shock to him if he'd come across her on it.'

The three men looked at him questioningly.

'I'm not going to mince matters,' said Van Aldin savagely. 'No one knows what my poor girl has had to put up with. Derek Kettering wasn't alone. He had a lady with him.'

'Ah?'

'Mirelle – the dancer.'

M. Carrège and the Commissary looked at each other and nodded as though confirming some previous conversation. M. Carrège leaned back in his chair, joined his hands, and fixed his eyes on the ceiling.

'Ah!' he murmured again. 'One wondered.' He coughed. 'One has heard rumours.'

'The lady,' said M. Caux, 'is very notorious.'

'And also,' murmured Poirot softly, 'very expensive.'

Van Aldin had gone very red in the face. He leant forward and hit the table a bang with his fist.

'See here,' he cried, 'my son-in-law is a damned scoundrel!'

He glared at them, looking from one face to another.

'Oh, I don't know,' he went on. 'Good looks and a charming, easy manner. It took me in once upon a time. I suppose he pretended to be broken-hearted when you broke the news to him – that is, if he didn't know it already.'

'Oh, it came as a surprise to him. He was overwhelmed.'

'Darned young hypocrite,' said Van Aldin. 'Simulated great grief, I suppose?'

'N – no,' said the Commissary cautiously. 'I would not quite say that – eh, M. Carrège?'

The Magistrate brought the tips of his fingers together, and half closed his eyes.

'Shock, bewilderment, horror – these things, yes,' he declared judicially. 'Great sorrow – no – I should not say that.'

Hercule Poirot spoke once more.

'Permit me to ask, M. Van Aldin, does M. Kettering benefit by the death of his wife?'

'He benefits to the tune of a couple of millions,' said Van Aldin.

'Dollars?'

'Pounds. I settled that sum on Ruth absolutely on her marriage. She made no will and leaves no children, so the money will go to her husband.'

'Whom she was on the point of divorcing,' murmured Poirot. 'Ah, yes – *précisément.*'

The Commissary turned and looked sharply at him.

'Do you mean –?' he began.

'I mean nothing,' said Poirot. 'I arrange the facts, that is all.'

Van Aldin stared at him with awakening interest.

The little man rose to his feet.

'I do not think I can be of any further service to you, M. le Juge,' he said politely, bowing to M. Carrège. 'You will keep me informed of the course of events? It will be a kindness.'

'But certainly – most certainly.'

Van Aldin rose also.

'You don't want me any more at present?'

'No, Monsieur; we have all the information we need for the moment.'

'Then I will walk a little way with M. Poirot. That is, if he does not object?'

'Enchanted, Monsieur,' said the little man, with a bow.

Van Aldin lighted a large cigar, having first offered one to Poirot, who declined it and lit one of his own tiny cigarettes. A man of great strength of character, Van Aldin already appeared to be his everyday, normal self once more. After strolling along for a minute or two in silence, the millionaire spoke:

'I take it, M. Poirot, that you no longer exercise your profession?'

'That is so, Monsieur. I enjoy the world.'

'Yet you are assisting the police in this affair?'

'Monsieur, if a doctor walks along the street and an accident happens, does he say, "I have retired from my profession, I will continue my walk,'' when there is someone bleeding to death at his feet? If I had been already in Nice, and the police had sent to me and asked me to assist them, I should have refused. But this affair, the good God thrust it upon me.'

'You were on the spot,' said Van Aldin thoughtfully. 'You examined the compartment, did you not?'

Poirot nodded.

'Doubtless you found things that were, shall we say, suggestive to you?'

'Perhaps,' said Poirot.

'I hope you see what I am leading up to?' said Van Aldin. 'It seems to me that the case against this Comte de la Roche is perfectly clear, but I am not a fool. I have been watching you for this last hour or so, and I realize that for some reason of your own you don't agree with that theory?'

Poirot shrugged his shoulders.

'I may be wrong.'

'So we come to the favour I want to ask you. Will you act in this matter for me?'

'For you, personally?'

'That was my meaning.'

Poirot was silent for a moment or two. Then he said:

'You realize what you are asking?'

'I guess so,' said Van Aldin.

'Very well,' said Poirot. 'I accept. But in that case, I must have frank answers to my questions.'

'Why, certainly. That is understood.'

Poirot's manner changed. He became suddenly brusque and business-like.

'This question of a divorce,' he said. 'It was you who advised your daughter to bring the suit?'

'Yes.'

'When?'

'About ten days ago. I had had a letter from her complaining of her husband's behaviour, and I put it to her very strongly that divorce was the only remedy.'

'In what way did she complain of his behaviour?'

'He was being seen about with a *very* notorious lady – the one we have been speaking of – Mirelle.'

'The dancer. Ah-ha! And Madame Kettering objected? Was she very devoted to her husband?'

'I would not say that,' said Van Aldin, hesitating a little.

'It was not her heart that suffered, it was her pride – is that what you would say?'

'Yes, I suppose you might put it like that.'

'I gather that the marriage has not been a happy one from the beginning?'

'Derek Kettering is rotten to the core,' said Van Aldin. 'He is incapable of making any woman happy.'

'He is, as you say in England, a bad lot. That is right, is it not?'

Van Aldin nodded.

'*Très bien!* You advise Madame to seek a divorce, she agrees; you consult your solicitors. When does M. Kettering get news of what is in the wind?'

'I sent for him myself, and explained the course of action I proposed to take.'

'And what did he say?' murmured Poirot softly.

Van Aldin's face darkened at the remembrance.

'He was infernally impudent.'

'Excuse the question, Monsieur, but did he refer to the Comte de la Roche?'

'Not by name,' growled the other unwillingly, 'but he showed himself cognizant of the affair.'

'What, if I may ask, was M. Kettering's financial position at the time?'

'How do you suppose I should know that?' asked Van Aldin, after a very brief hesitation.

'It seemed likely to me that you would inform yourself on that point.'

'Well – you are quite right, I did. I discovered that Kettering was on the rocks.'

'And now he has inherited two million pounds! *La vie* – it is a strange thing, is it not?'

Van Aldin looked at him sharply.

'What do you mean?'

'I moralize,' said Poirot, 'I reflect, I speak the philosophy. But to return to where we were. Surely M. Kettering did not propose to allow himself to be divorced without making a fight for it?'

Van Aldin did not answer for a minute or two, then he said:

'I don't exactly know what his intentions were.'

'Did you hold any further communications with him?'

Again a slight pause, then Van Aldin said:

'No.'

Poirot stopped dead, took off his hat, and held out his hand.

'I must wish you good day, Monsieur. I can do nothing for you.'

'What are you getting at?' demanded Van Aldin angrily.

'If you do not tell me the truth, I can do nothing.'

'I don't know what you mean.'

'I think you do. You may rest assured, M. Van Aldin, that I know how to be discreet.'

'Very well, then,' said the millionaire. 'I'll admit that I was not speaking the truth just now. I *did* have further communication with my son-in-law.'

'Yes?'

'To be exact, I sent my secretary, Major Knighton, to see him, with instructions to offer him the sum of one hundred thousand pounds in cash if the divorce went through undefended.'

'A pretty sum of money,' said Poirot appreciatively: 'and the answer of Monsieur your son-in-law?'

'He sent back word that I could go to hell,' replied the millionaire succinctly.

'Ah!' said Poirot.

He betrayed no emotion of any kind. At the moment he was engaged in methodically recording facts.

'Monsieur Kettering has told the police that he neither saw nor spoke to his wife on the journey from England. Are you inclined to believe that statement, Monsieur?'

'Yes, I am,' said Van Aldin. 'He would take particular pains to keep out of her way, I should say.'

'Why?'

'Because he had got that woman with him.'

'Mirelle?'

'Yes.'

'How did you come to know that fact?'

'A man of mine, whom I had put on to watch him, reported to me that they both left by that train.'

'I see,' said Poirot. 'In any case, as you said before, he would not be likely to attempt to hold any communication with Madame Kettering.'

The little man fell silent for some time. Van Aldin did not interrupt his meditation.

CHAPTER XVII

An Aristocratic Gentleman

'You have been to the Riviera before, Georges?' said Poirot to his valet the next morning.

George was an intensely English, rather wooden-faced individual.

'Yes, sir. I was here two years ago when I was in the service of Lord Edward Frampton.'

'And today,' murmured his master, 'you are here with Hercule Poirot. How one mounts in the world!'

The valet made no reply to this observation. After a suitable pause he asked:

'The brown lounge suit, sir? The wind is somewhat chilly today.'

'There is a grease spot on the waistcoat,' objected Poirot. 'A *morceau* of *Filet de sole à la Jeanette* alighted there when I was lunching at the Ritz last Tuesday.'

'There is no spot there now, sir,' said George reproachfully. 'I have removed it.'

'*Très bien!*' said Poirot. 'I am pleased with you, Georges.'

'Thank you, sir.'

There was a pause, and then Poirot murmured dreamily:

'Supposing, my good Georges, that you have been born in the same social sphere as your late master, Lord Edward Frampton – that, penniless yourself, you had married an extremely wealthy wife, but that wife proposed to divorce you, with excellent reasons, what would you do about it?'

'I should endeavour, sir,' replied George, 'to make her change her mind.'

'By peaceful or by forcible methods?'

George looked shocked.

'You will excuse me, sir,' he said, 'but a gentleman of the aristocracy would not behave like a Whitechapel coster. He would not do anything low.'

'Would he not, Georges? I wonder now. Well, perhaps you are right.'

There was a knock on the door. George went to it and opened it a discreet inch or two. A low murmured colloquy went on, and then the valet returned to Poirot.

'A note, sir.'

Poirot took it. It was from M. Caux, the Commissary of Police.

'We are about to interrogate the Comte de la Roche. The Juge d'Instruction begs that you will be present.'

'Quickly, my suit, Georges! I must hasten myself.'

A quarter of an hour later, spick and span in his brown suit, Poirot entered the Examining Magistrate's room. M. Caux was already there, and both he and M. Carrège greeted Poirot with polite *empressement*.

'The affair is somewhat discouraging,' murmured M. Caux. 'It appears that the Comte arrived in Nice the day before the murder.'

'If that is true, it will settle your affair nicely for you,' responded Poirot.

M. Carrège cleared his throat.

'We must not accept this alibi without very cautious inquiry,' he declared. He struck the bell upon the table with his hand.

In another minute a tall dark man, exquisitely dressed, with a somewhat haughty cast of countenance, entered the room. So very aristocratic-looking was the Count, that it would have seemed sheer heresy even to whisper that his father had been an obscure corn-chandler in Nantes – which, as a matter of fact, was the case. Looking at him, one would have been prepared to swear that innumerable ancestors of his must have perished by the guillotine in the French Revolution.

'I am here, gentlemen,' said the Count haughtily. 'May I ask why you wish to see me?'

'Pray be seated, Monsieur le Comte,' said the Examining

Magistrate politely. 'It is the affair of the death of Madame Kettering that we are investigating.'

'The death of Madame Kettering? I do not understand.'

'You were – ahem! – acquainted with the lady, I believe, Monsieur le Comte?'

'Certainly I was acquainted with her. What has that to do with the matter?'

Sticking an eyeglass in his eye, he looked coldly round the room, his glance resting longest on Poirot, who was gazing at him with a kind of simple, innocent admiration which was most pleasing to the Count's vanity. M. Carrège leaned back in his chair and cleared his throat.

'You do not perhaps know, Monsieur le Comte' – he paused – 'that Madame Kettering was murdered?'

'Murdered? *Mon Dieu*, how terrible!'

The surprise and the sorrow were excellently done – so well done, indeed, as to seem wholly natural.

'Madame Kettering was strangled between Paris and Lyons,' continued M. Carrège, 'and her jewels were stolen.'

'It is iniquitous!' cried the Count warmly; 'the police should do something about these train bandits. Nowadays no one is safe.'

'In Madame's handbag,' continued the Judge, 'we found a letter to her from you. She had, it seemed, arranged to meet you?'

The Count shrugged his shoulders, and spread out his hands.

'Of what use are concealments?' he said frankly. 'We are all men of the world. Privately and between ourselves, I admit the affair.'

'You met her in Paris and travelled down with her, I believe?' said M. Carrège.

'That was the original arrangement, but by Madame's wish it was changed. I was to meet her at Hyères.'

'You did not meet her on the train at the Gare de Lyon on the evening of the 14th?'

'On the contrary, I arrived in Nice on the morning of that day, so what you suggest is impossible.'

'Quite so, quite so,' said M. Carrège. 'As a matter of form, you would perhaps give me an account of your movements during the evening and night of the 14th.'

The Count reflected for a minute.

'I dined in Monte Carlo at the Café de Paris. Afterwards I went to the Le Sporting. I won a few thousand francs,' he shrugged his shoulders. 'I returned home at perhaps one o'clock.'

'Pardon me, Monsieur, but how did you return home?'

'In my own two-seater car.'

'No one was with you?'

'No one.'

'You could produce witnesses in support of this statement?'

'Doubtless many of my friends saw me there that evening. I dined alone.'

'Your servant admitted you on your return to your villa?'

'I let myself in with my own latch-key.'

'Ah!' murmured the Magistrate.

Again he struck the bell on the table with his hand. The door opened, and a messenger appeared.

'Bring in the maid, Mason,' said M. Carrège.

'Very good, Monsieur le Juge.'

Ada Mason was brought in.

'Will you be so good, Mademoiselle, as to look at this gentleman. To the best of your ability was it he who entered your mistress's compartment in Paris?'

The woman looked long and searchingly at the Count, who was, Poirot fancied, rather uneasy under this scrutiny.

'I could not say, sir, I am sure,' said Mason at last. 'It might be and again it might not. Seeing as how I only saw his back, it's hard to say. I rather think it *was* the gentleman.'

'But you are not sure?'

'No – o,' said Mason unwillingly; 'n – no, I am not sure.'

'You have seen this gentleman before in Curzon Street?'

Mason shook her head.

'I should not be likely to see any visitors that come to Curzon Street,' she explained, 'unless they were staying in the house.'

'Very well, that will do,' said the Examining Magistrate sharply.

Evidently he was disappointed.

'One moment,' said Poirot. 'There is a question I would like to put to Mademoiselle, if I may?'

'Certainly, M. Poirot – certainly, by all means.'

Poirot addressed himself to the maid.

'What happened to the tickets?'

'The tickets, sir?'

'Yes; the tickets from London to Nice. Did you or your mistress have them?'

'The mistress had her own Pullman ticket, sir; the others were in my charge.'

'What happened to them?'

'I gave them to the conductor on the French train, sir; he said it was usual. I hope I did right, sir?'

'Oh, quite right, quite right. A mere matter of detail.'

Both M. Caux and the Examining Magistrate looked at him curiously. Mason stood uncertainly for a minute or two, and then the Magistrate gave her a brief nod of dismissal, and she went out. Poirot scribbled something on a scrap of paper and handed it across to M. Carrège. The latter read it and his brow cleared.

'Well, gentlemen,' demanded the Count haughtily, 'am I to be detained further?'

'Assuredly not, assuredly not,' M. Carrège hastened to say, with a great deal of amiability. 'Everything is now cleared up as regards your own position in this affair. Naturally, in view of Madame's letter, we were bound to question you.'

The Count rose, picked up his handsome stick from the corner, and, with rather a curt bow, left the room.

'And that is that,' said M. Carrège. 'You were quite right, M. Poirot – much better to let him feel he is not suspected. Two of my men will shadow him night and day, and at the same time we will go into the question of the alibi. It seems to me rather – er – a fluid one.'

'Possibly,' agreed Poirot thoughtfully.

'I asked M. Kettering to come here this morning,' continued the Magistrate, 'though really I doubt if we have much to ask him, but there are one or two suspicious circumstances –' He paused, rubbing his nose.

'Such as?' asked Poirot.

'Well' – the Magistrate coughed ' 'this lady with whom he is said to be travelling – Mademoiselle Mirelle. She is staying at one hotel and he at another. That strikes me – er – as rather odd.'

'It looks,' said M. Caux, 'as though they were being careful.'

'Exactly,' said M. Carrège triumphantly; 'and what should they have to be careful about?'

'An excess of caution is suspicious, eh?' said Poirot.

'*Précisément.*'

'We might, I think,' murmured Poirot, 'ask M. Kettering one or two questions.'

The Magistrate gave instructions. A moment or two later, Derek Kettering, debonair as ever, entered the room.

'Good morning, Monsieur,' said the Judge politely.

'Good morning,' said Derek Kettering curtly. 'You sent for me. Has anything fresh turned up?'

'Pray sit down, Monsieur.'

Derek took a seat and flung his hat and stick on the table.

'Well?' he asked impatiently.

'We have, so far, no fresh data,' said M. Carrège cautiously.

'That's very interesting,' said Derek drily. 'Did you send for me here in order to tell me that?'

'We naturally thought, Monsieur, that you would like to be informed of the progress of the case,' said the Magistrate severely.

'Even if the progress is non-existent.'

'We also wished to ask you a few questions.'

'Ask away.'

'You are quite sure that you neither saw nor spoke with your wife on the train?'

'I've answered that already. I did not.'

'You had, no doubt, your reasons.'

Derek stared at him suspiciously.

'I – did – not – know – she – was – on – the – train,' he explained, spacing his words elaborately, as though to someone dull of intellect.

'That is what you say, yes,' murmured M. Carrège.

A quick frown suffused Derek's face.

'I should like to know what you are driving at. Do you know what I think, M. Carrège?'

'What do you think, Monsieur?'

'I think the French police are vastly overrated. Surely you must have some data as to these gangs of train robbers. It's outrageous that such a thing could happen on a *train de luxe* like that, and that the French police should be helpless to deal with the matter.'

'We are dealing with it, Monsieur, never fear.'

'Madame Kettering, I understand, did not leave a will,' interposed Poirot suddenly. His fingertips were joined together, and he was looking intently at the ceiling.

'I don't think she ever made one,' said Kettering. 'Why?'

'It is a very pretty little fortune that you inherit there,' said Poirot – 'a very pretty little fortune.'

Although his eyes were still on the ceiling, he managed to see the dark flush that rose to Derek Kettering's face.

'What do you mean, and who are you?'

Poirot gently uncrossed his knees, withdrew his gaze from the ceiling, and looked the young man full in the face.

'My name is Hercule Poirot,' he said quietly, 'and I am probably the greatest detective in the world. You are quite sure that you did not see or speak to your wife on that train?'

'What are you getting at? Do you – do you mean to insinuate that I – I killed her?'

He laughed suddenly.

'I mustn't lose my temper; it's too palpably absurd. Why, if I killed her I should have had no need to steal her jewels, would I?'

'That is true,' murmured Poirot, with a rather crestfallen air. 'I did not think of that.'

'If ever there were a clear case of murder and robbery this is it,' said Derek Kettering. 'Poor Ruth, it was those damned rubies did for her. It must have got about she had them with her. There has been murder done for those same stones before now, I believe.'

Poirot sat up suddenly in his chair. A very faint green light glowed in his eyes. He looked extraordinarily like a sleek, well-fed cat.

'One more question, M. Kettering,' he said. 'Will you give me the date when you last saw your wife?'

'Let me see,' Kettering reflected. 'It must have been – yes, over three weeks ago. I am afraid I can't give you the date exactly.'

'No matter,' said Poirot drily; 'that is all I wanted to know.'

'Well,' said Derek Kettering impatiently, 'anything further?'

He looked towards M. Carrège. The latter sought inspiration from Poirot, and received it in a very faint shake of the head.

'No, M. Kettering,' he said politely; 'no, I do not think we need trouble you any further. I wish you good morning.'

'Good morning,' said Kettering. He went out, banging the door behind him.

Poirot leaned forward and spoke sharply, as soon as the young man was out of the room.

'Tell me,' he said peremptorily, 'when did you speak of these rubies to M. Kettering?'

'I have not spoken of them,' said M. Carrège. 'It was only yesterday afternoon that we learnt about them from M. Van Aldin.'

'Yes; but there was a mention of them in the Comte's letter.'

M. Carrège looked pained.

'Naturally I did not speak of that letter to M. Kettering,' he said in a shocked voice. 'It would have been most indiscreet at the present juncture of affairs.'

Poirot leaned forward and tapped the table.

'*Then how did he know about them?*' he demanded softly. 'Madame could not have told him, for he has not seen her for three weeks. It seems unlikely that either M. Van Aldin or his secretary would have mentioned them; their interviews with him have been on entirely different lines, and there has not been any hint or reference to them in the newspapers.'

He got up and took his hat and stick.

'And yet,' he murmured to himself, 'our gentleman knows all about them. I wonder now, yes, I wonder!'

CHAPTER XVIII

Derek Lunches

Derek Kettering went straight to the Negresco, where he ordered a couple of cocktails and disposed of them rapidly; then he stared moodily out over the dazzling blue sea. He noted the passers-by mechanically – a damned dull crowd, badly dressed, and painfully uninteresting; one hardly ever saw anything worthwhile nowadays. Then he corrected this last impression rapidly, as a woman placed herself at a table a little distance away from him. She was wearing a marvellous confection of orange and black, with a little hat that shaded her face. He ordered a third cocktail; again he stared out to sea, and then suddenly he started. A well-known perfume assailed his nostrils, and he looked up to see the orange-and-black lady standing beside him. He saw her face now, and recognized her. It was Mirelle. She was smiling that insolent, seductive smile he knew so well.

'Dereek!' she murmured. 'You are pleased to see me, no?'

She dropped into a seat the other side of the table.

'But welcome me, then, stupid one,' she mocked.

'This is an unexpected pleasure,' said Derek. 'When did you leave London?'

She shrugged her shoulders.

'A day or two ago?'

'And the Parthenon?'

'I have, how do you say it? – given them the chuck!'

'Really?'

'You are not very amiable, Dereek.'

'Do you expect me to be?'

Mirelle lit a cigarette and puffed at it for a few minutes before saying:

'You think, perhaps, that it is not prudent so soon?'

Derek stared at her, then he shrugged his shoulders, and remarked formally:

'You are lunching here?'

'*Mais oui.* I am lunching with you.'

'I am exceedingly sorry,' said Derek. 'I have a very important engagement.'

'*Mon Dieu!* But you men are like children,' exclaimed the dancer. 'But yes, it is the spoilt child that you act to me, ever since that day in London when you flung yourself out of my flat, you sulk. Ah! *mais c'est inouï!*'

'My dear girl,' said Derek, 'I really don't know what you are talking about. We agreed in London that rats desert a sinking ship, that is all that there is to be said.'

In spite of his careless words, his face looked haggard and strained. Mirelle leaned forward suddenly.

'You cannot deceive me,' she murmured. 'I know – I know what you have done for me.'

He looked up at her sharply. Some undercurrent in her voice arrested his attention. She nodded her head at him.

'Ah! have no fear; I am discreet. You are magnificent! You have a superb courage, but, all the same, it was I who gave you the idea that day, when I said to you in London that accidents sometimes happened. And you are not in danger? The police do not suspect you?'

'What the devil –?'

'Hush!'

She held up a slim olive hand with one big emerald on the little finger.

'You are right, I should not have spoken so in a public place. We will not speak of the matter again, but our troubles are ended; our life together will be wonderful – wonderful!'

Derek laughed suddenly – a harsh, disagreeable laugh.

'So the rats come back, do they? Two million makes a difference – of course it does. I ought to have known that.' He laughed again. 'You will help me to spend that two million, won't you, Mirelle? You know how, no woman better.' He laughed again.

'Hush!' cried the dancer. 'What is the matter with you, Dereek? See – people are turning to stare at you.'

'Me? I will tell you what is the matter. I have finished with you, Mirelle. Do you hear? Finished!'

Mirelle did not take it as he expected her to do. She looked at him for a minute or two, and then she smiled softly.

'But what a child! You are angry – you are sore, and all because I am practical. Did I not always tell you that I adored you?'

She leaned forward.

'But I know you, Dereek. Look at me – see, it is Mirelle who speaks to you. You cannot live without her, you know it. I loved you before, I will love you a hundred times more now. I will make life wonderful for you – but wonderful. There is no one like Mirelle.'

Her eyes burned into his. She saw him grow pale and draw in his breath, and she smiled to herself contentedly. She knew her own magic and power over men.

'That is settled,' she said softly, and gave a little laugh. 'And now, Dereek, will you give me lunch?'

'No.'

He drew in his breath sharply and rose to his feet.

'I am sorry, but I told you – I have got an engagement.'

'You are lunching with someone else? Bah! I don't believe it.'

'I am lunching with that lady over there.'

He crossed abruptly to where a lady in white had just come up the steps. He addressed her a little breathlessly.

'Miss Grey, will you – will you have lunch with me? You met me at Lady Tamplin's, if you remember.'

Katherine looked at him for a minute or two with those thoughtful grey eyes that said so much.

'Thank you,' she said, after a moment's pause; 'I should like to very much.'

CHAPTER XIX

An Unexpected Visitor

The Comte de la Roche had just finished *déjeuner*, consisting of an *omelette fines herbes*, an *entrecôte Béarnaise*, and a *Savarin au Rhum*. Wiping his fine black moustache delicately with his table napkin, the Comte rose from the table. He passed through the salon of the villa, noting with appreciation the few *objets d'art* which were carelessly scattered about. The Louis XV snuff-box, the satin shoe worn by Marie Antoinette, and the other historic trifles that were part of the Comte's *mise en scène*. They were, he would explain to his fair visitors, heirlooms in his family. Passing through on to the terrace the Comte looked out on to the Mediterranean with an unseeing eye. He was in no mood for appreciating the beauties of scenery. A fully matured scheme had been rudely brought to naught, and his plans had to be cast afresh. Stretching himself out in a basket chair, a cigarette held between his white fingers, the Comte pondered deeply.

Presently Hipolyte, his manservant, brought out coffee and a choice of liqueurs. The Comte selected some very fine old brandy.

As the manservant was preparing to depart, the Comte arrested him with a slight gesture. Hipolyte stood respectfully to attention. His countenance was hardly a prepossessing one, but the correctitude of his demeanour went far to obliterate the fact. He was now the picture of respectful attention.

'It is possible,' said the Comte, 'that in the course of the next few days various strangers may come to the house. They will endeavour to scrape acquaintance with you and with Marie. They will probably ask you various questions concerning me.'

'Yes, Monsieur le Comte.'

'Perhaps this has already happened?'

'No, Monsieur le Comte.'

'There have been no strangers about the place? You are certain?'

'There has been no one, Monsieur le Comte.'

'That is well,' said the Comte drily; 'nevertheless they will come – I am sure of it. They will ask questions.'

Hipolyte looked at his master in intelligent anticipation.

The Comte spoke slowly, without looking at Hipolyte.

'As you know, I arrived here last Tuesday morning. If the police or any other inquirer should question you, do not forget that fact. I arrived on Tuesday, the 14th – not Wednesday, the 15th. You understand?'

'Perfectly, Monsieur le Comte.'

'In an affair where a lady is concerned, it is always necessary to be discreet. I feel certain, Hipolyte, that you can be discreet.'

'I can be discreet, Monsieur.'

'And Marie?'

'Marie also. I will answer for her.'

'That is well then,' murmured the Comte.

When Hipolyte had withdrawn, the Comte sipped his black coffee with a reflective air. Occasionally he frowned, once he shook his head slightly, twice he nodded it. Into the midst of these cogitations came Hipolyte once more.

'A lady, Monsieur.'

'A lady?'

The Comte was surprised. Not that a visit from a lady was an unusual thing at the Villa Marina, but at this particular moment the Comte could not think who the lady was likely to be.

'She is, I think, a lady not known to Monsieur,' murmured the valet helpfully.

The Comte was more and more intrigued.

'Show her out here, Hipolyte,' he commanded.

A moment later a marvellous vision in orange and black stepped out on the terrace, accompanied by a strong perfume of exotic blossoms.

'Monsieur le Comte de la Roche?'

'At your service, Mademoiselle,' said the Comte, bowing.

'My name is Mirelle. You may have heard of me.'

'Ah, indeed, Mademoiselle, but who has not been enchanted by the dancing of Mademoiselle Mirelle? Exquisite!'

The dancer acknowledged this compliment with a brief mechanical smile.

'My descent upon you is unceremonious,' she began.

'But seat yourself, I beg of you, Mademoiselle,' cried the Comte, bringing forward a chair.

Behind the gallantry of his manner he was observing her narrowly. There were very few things that the Comte did not know about women. True, his experience had not lain much in ladies of Mirelle's class, who were themselves predatory. He and the dancer were, in a sense, birds of a feather. His arts, the Comte knew, would be thrown away on Mirelle. She was a Parisienne, and a shrewd one. Nevertheless, there was one thing that the Comte could recognize infallibly when he saw it. He knew at once that he was in the presence of a very angry woman, and an angry woman, as the Comte was well aware, always says more than is prudent, and is occasionally a source of profit to a level-headed gentleman who keeps cool.

'It is most amiable of you, Mademoiselle, to honour my poor abode thus.'

'We have mutual friends in Paris,' said Mirelle. 'I have heard of you from them, but I come to see you today for another reason. I have heard of you since I came to Nice – in a different way, you understand.'

'Ah?' said the Comte softly.

'I will be brutal,' continued the dancer; 'nevertheless, believe that I have your welfare at heart. They are saying in Nice, Monsieur le Comte, that you are the murderer of the English lady, Madame Kettering.'

'I! – the murderer of Madame Kettering? Bah! But how absurd!'

He spoke more languidly than indignantly, knowing that he would thus provoke her further.

'But yes,' she insisted, 'it is as I tell you.'

'It amuses people to talk,' murmured the Comte indifferently.

'It would be beneath me to take such wild accusations seriously.'

'You do not understand.' Mirelle bent forward, her dark eyes flashing. 'It is not the idle talk of those in the street. It is the police.'

'The police – ah?'

The Comte sat up, alert once more.

Mirelle nodded her head vigorously several times.

'Yes, yes. You comprehend me – I have friends everywhere. The Prefect himself – ' She left the sentence unfinished, with an eloquent shrug of the shoulders.

'Who is not indiscreet where a beautiful woman is concerned?' murmured the Count politely.

'The police believe that you killed Madame Kettering. But they are wrong.'

'Certainly they are wrong,' agreed the Comte easily.

'You say that, but you do not know the truth. I do.'

The Comte looked at her curiously.

'You know who killed Madame Kettering? Is that what you would say, Mademoiselle?'

Mirelle nodded vehemently.

'Yes.'

'Who was it?' asked the Comte sharply.

'Her husband.' She leant across to the Comte, speaking in a low voice that vibrated with anger and excitement. 'It was her husband who killed her.'

The Comte leaned back in his chair. His face was a mask.

'Let me ask you, Mademoiselle – how do you know this?'

'How do I know it?' Mirelle sprang to her feet, with a laugh. 'He boasted of it beforehand. He was ruined, bankrupt, dishonoured. Only the death of his wife could save him. He told me so. He travelled on the same train – but she was not to know it. Why was that, I ask you? So that he might creep upon her in the night – Ah!' – she shut her eyes – 'I can see it happening . . .'

The Count coughed.

'Perhaps – perhaps,' he murmured. 'But surely, Mademoiselle, in that case he would not steal the jewels?'

'The jewels!' breathed Mirelle. 'The jewels. Ah! Those rubies . . .'

Her eyes grew misty, a far-away light in them. The Comte looked at her curiously, wondering for the hundredth time at the magical influence of precious stones on the female sex. He recalled her to practical matters.

'What do you want me to do, Mademoiselle?'

Mirelle became alert and business-like once more.

'Surely it is simple. You will go to the police. You will say to them that M. Kettering committed this crime.'

'And if they do not believe me? If they ask for proof?' He was eyeing her closely.

Mirelle laughed softly, and drew her orange-and-black wrap closer round her.

'Send them to me, Monsieur le Comte,' she said softly; 'I will give them the proof they want.'

Upon that she was gone, an impetuous whirlwind, her errand accomplished.

The Comte looked after her, his eyebrows delicately raised.

'She is in a fury,' he murmured. 'What has happened now to upset her? But she shows her hand too plainly. Does she really believe that Mr Kettering killed his wife? She would like me to believe it. She would even like the police to believe it.'

He smiled to himself. He had no intention whatsoever of going to the police. He saw various other possibilities; to judge by his smile, an agreeable vista of them.

Presently, however, his brow clouded. According to Mirelle, he was suspected by the police. That might be true or it might not. An angry woman of the type of the dancer was not likely to bother about the strict veracity of her statements. On the other hand, she might easily have obtained – inside information. In that case – his mouth set grimly – in that case he must take certain precautions.

He went into the house and questioned Hipolyte closely once more as to whether any strangers had been to the house. The valet was positive in his assurances that this was not the case. The Comte went up to his bedroom and crossed over to an old bureau that stood against the wall. He let down the lid of this, and his delicate fingers sought for a spring at the back of one of the pigeon-holes. A secret drawer flew out; in it was a small brown paper package. The Comte took this out and weighed it in his hand carefully for a minute or two. Raising his hand to his head, with a slight grimace he pulled out a single hair. This he placed on the lip of the drawer and shut it carefully. Still carrying the small parcel in his hand, he went downstairs and out of the house to the garage, where stood a scarlet two-seater car. Ten minutes later he had taken the road for Monte Carlo.

He spent a few hours at the Casino, then sauntered out into the town. Presently he re-entered the car and drove off in the direction of Mentone. Earlier in the afternoon he had noticed an inconspicuous grey car some little distance behind him. He noticed it again now. He smiled to himself. The road was climbing steadily upwards. The Comte's foot pressed hard on the accelerator. The little red car had been specially built to the Comte's design, and had a far more powerful engine than would have been suspected from its appearance. It shot ahead.

Presently he looked back and smiled; the grey car was following behind. Smothered in dust, the little red car leapt along the road. It was travelling now at a dangerous pace, but the Comte was a first-class driver. Now they were going downhill, twisting and curving unceasingly. Presently the car slackened speed, and finally came to a standstill before a Bureau de Poste. The Comte jumped out, lifted the lid of the tool chest, extracted the small brown paper parcel and hurried into the post office. Two minutes later he was driving once more in the direction of Mentone. When the grey car arrived there, the Comte was drinking English five o'clock tea on the terrace of one of the hotels.

Later, he drove back to Monte Carlo, dined there, and reached home once more at eleven o'clock. Hipolyte came out to meet him with a disturbed face.

'Ah! Monsieur le Comte has arrived. Monsieur le Comte did not telephone me, by any chance?'

The Comte shook his head.

'And yet at three o'clock I received a summons from Monsieur le Comte, to present myself to him at Nice, at the Negresco.'

'Really,' said the Comte; 'and you went?'

'Certainly, Monsieur, but at the Negresco they knew nothing of Monsieur le Comte. He had not been there.'

'Ah,' said the Comte, 'doubtless at that hour Marie was out doing her afternoon marketing?'

'That is so, Monsieur le Comte.'

'Ah, well,' said the Comte, 'it is of no importance. A mistake.' He went upstairs, smiling to himself.

Once within his own room, he bolted his door and looked sharply round. Everything seemed as usual. He opened various drawers and cupboards. Then he nodded to himself. Things had been replaced almost exactly as he had left them, but not quite. It was evident that a very thorough search had been made.

He went over to the bureau and pressed the hidden spring. The drawer flew open, but the hair was no longer where he had placed it. He nodded his head several times.

'They are excellent, our French police,' he murmured to himself – 'excellent. Nothing escapes them.'

CHAPTER XX

Katherine Makes a Friend

On the following morning Katherine and Lenox were sitting on the terrace of the Villa Marguerite. Something in the nature of a friendship was springing up between them, despite the difference in age. But for Lenox, Katherine would have found life at the Villa Marguerite quite intolerable. The Kettering case was the topic of the moment. Lady Tamplin frankly exploited her guest's connection with the affair for all it was worth. The most persistent rebuffs that Katherine could administer quite failed to pierce Lady Tamplin's self-esteem. Lenox adopted a detached attitude, seemingly amused at her mother's manoeuvres, and yet with a sympathetic understanding of Katherine's feelings. The situation was not helped by Chubby, whose naïve delight was unquenchable, and who introduced Katherine to all and sundry as:

'This is Miss Grey. You know that Blue Train business? She was in it up to the ears! Had a long talk with Ruth Kettering a few hours before the murder! Bit of luck for her, eh?'

A few remarks of this kind had provoked Katherine that morning to an unusually tart rejoinder, and when they were alone together Lenox observed in her slow drawl:

'Not used to exploitation, are you? You have a lot to learn, Katherine.'

'I am sorry I lost my temper. I don't, as a rule.'

'It is about time you learnt to blow off steam. Chubby is only an ass; there is no harm in him. Mother, of course, is trying, but you can lose your temper with her until Kingdom come, and it won't make any impression. She will open large, sad blue eyes at you and not care a bit.'

Katherine made no reply to this filial observation, and Lenox presently went on:

'I am rather like Chubby. I delight in a good murder, and besides – well, knowing Derek makes a difference.'

Katherine nodded.

'So you lunched with him yesterday,' pursued Lenox reflectively. 'Do you like him, Katherine?'

Katherine considered for a minute or two.

'I don't know,' she said very slowly.

'He is very attractive.'

'Yes, he is attractive.'

'What don't you like about him?'

Katherine did not reply to the question, or at any rate not directly. 'He spoke of his wife's death,' she said. 'He said he would not pretend that it had been anything but a bit of most marvellous luck for him.'

'And that shocked you, I suppose,' said Lenox. She paused, and then added in rather a queer tone of voice: 'He likes you, Katherine.'

'He gave me a very good lunch,' said Katherine, smiling.

Lenox refused to be side-tracked.

'I saw it the night he came here,' she said thoughtfully. 'The way he looked at you; and you are not his usual type – just the opposite. Well, I suppose it is like religion – you get it at a certain age.'

'Mademoiselle is wanted at the telephone,' said Marie, appearing at the window of the salon. 'M. Hercule Poirot desires to speak with her.'

'More blood and thunder. Go on, Katherine; go and dally with your detective.'

M. Hercule Poirot's voice came neat and precise in its intonation to Katherine's ear.

'That is Mademoiselle Grey who speaks? *Bon.* Mademoiselle, I have a word for you from M. Van Aldin, the father of Madame Kettering. He wishes very much to speak with you, either at the Villa Marguerite or at his hotel, whichever you prefer.'

Katherine reflected for a moment, but she decided that for

Van Aldin to come to the Villa Marguerite would be both painful and unnecessary. Lady Tamplin would have hailed his advent with far too much delight. She never lost a chance to cultivate millionaires. She told Poirot that she would much rather come to Nice.

'Excellent, Mademoiselle. I will call for you myself in an auto. Shall we say in about three-quarters of an hour?'

Punctually to the moment Poirot appeared. Katherine was waiting for him, and they drove off at once.

'Well, Mademoiselle, how goes it?'

She looked at his twinkling eyes, and was confirmed in her first impression that there was something very attractive about M. Hercule Poirot.

'This is our own *roman policier*, is it not?' said Poirot. 'I made you the promise that we should study it together. And me, I always keep my promises.'

'You are too kind,' murmured Katherine.

'Ah, you mock yourself at me; but do you want to hear the developments of the case, or do you not?'

Katherine admitted that she did, and Poirot proceeded to sketch for her a thumbnail portrait of the Comte de la Roche.

'You think he killed her,' said Katherine thoughtfully.

'That is the theory,' said Poirot guardedly.

'Do you yourself believe that?'

'I did not say so. And you, Mademoiselle, what do you think?'

Katherine shook her head.

'How should I know? I don't know anything about those things, but I should say that –'

'Yes,' said Poirot encouragingly.

'Well – from what you say the Count does not sound the kind of man who would actually kill anybody.'

'Ah! Very good,' cried Poirot. 'You agree with me; that is just what I have said.' He looked at her sharply. 'But tell me, you have met Mr Derek Kettering?'

'I met him at Lady Tamplin's, and I lunched with him yesterday.'

'A *mauvais sujet*,' said Poirot, shaking his head; 'but *les femmes* – they like that, eh?'

He twinkled at Katherine and she laughed.

'He is the kind of man one would notice anywhere,' continued Poirot. 'Doubtless you observed him on the Blue Train?'

'Yes, I noticed him.'

'In the restaurant car?'

'No. I didn't notice him at meals at all. I only saw him once – going into his wife's compartment.'

Poirot nodded. 'A strange business,' he murmured. 'I believe you said you were awake, Mademoiselle, and looked out of your window at Lyons? You saw no tall dark man such as the Comte de la Roche leave the train?'

Katherine shook her head. 'I don't think I saw anyone at all,' she said. 'There was a youngish lad in a cap and overcoat who got out, but I don't think he was leaving the train, only walking up and down the platform. There was a fat Frenchman with a beard, in pyjamas and an overcoat, who wanted a cup of coffee. Otherwise, I think there were only the train attendants.'

Poirot nodded his head several times. 'It is like this, you see,' he confided, 'the Comte de la Roche has an alibi. An alibi, it is a very pestilential thing, and always open to the gravest suspicion. But here we are!'

They went straight up to Van Aldin's suite, where they found Knighton. Poirot introduced him to Katherine. After a few commonplaces had been exchanged, Knighton said: 'I will tell Mr Van Aldin that Miss Grey is here.'

He went through a second door into an adjoining room. There was a low murmur of voices, and then Van Aldin came into the room and advanced towards Katherine with outstretched hand, giving her at the same time a shrewd and penetrating glance.

'I am pleased to meet you, Miss Grey,' he said simply. 'I have been wanting very badly to hear what you can tell me about Ruth.'

The quiet simplicity of the millionaire's manner appealed to Katherine strongly. She felt herself in the presence of a very genuine grief, the more real for its absence of outward sign.

He drew forward a chair.

'Sit here, will you, and just tell me all about it.'

Poirot and Knighton retired discreetly into the other room, and Katherine and Van Aldin were left alone together. She found no difficulty in her task. Quite simply and naturally she related her conversation with Ruth Kettering, word for word as nearly as she could. He listened in silence, leaning back in his chair, with one hand shading his eyes. When she had finished he said quietly:

'Thank you, my dear.'

They both sat silent for a minute or two. Katherine felt that words of sympathy would be out of place. When the millionaire spoke, it was in a different tone:

'I am very grateful to you, Miss Grey. I think you did something to ease my poor Ruth's mind in the last hours of her life. Now I want to ask you something. You know – M. Poirot will have told you – about the scoundrel that my poor girl had got herself mixed up with. He was the man of whom she spoke to you – the man she was going to meet. In your judgment, do you think she might have changed her mind after her conversation with you? Do you think she meant to go back on her word?'

'I can't honestly tell you. She had certainly come to some decision, and seemed more cheerful in consequence of it.'

'She gave you no idea where she intended to meet the skunk – whether in Paris or at Hyères?'

Katherine shook her head.

'She said nothing as to that.'

'Ah!' said Van Aldin thoughtfully, 'and that is the important point. Well, time will show.'

He got up and opened the door of the adjoining room. Poirot and Knighton came back.

Katherine declined the millionaire's invitation to lunch, and Knighton went down with her and saw her into the waiting car. He returned to find Poirot and Van Aldin deep in conversation.

'If we only knew,' said the millionaire thoughtfully, 'what

decision Ruth came to. It might have been any of half a dozen. She might have meant to leave the train at Paris and cable to me. She may have meant to have gone on to the south of France and have an explanation with the Count there. We are in the dark – absolutely in the dark. But we have the maid's word for it that she was both startled and dismayed at the Count's appearance at the station in Paris. That was clearly not part of the preconceived plan. You agree with me, Knighton?'

The secretary started. 'I beg your pardon, Mr Van Aldin. I was not listening.'

'Day-dreaming, eh?' said Van Aldin. 'That's not like you. I believe that girl has bowled you over.'

Knighton blushed.

'She is a remarkably nice girl,' said Van Aldin thoughtfully, 'very nice. Did you happen to notice her eyes?'

'Any man,' said Knighton, 'would be bound to notice her eyes.'

CHAPTER XXI

At the Tennis

Several days had elapsed. Katherine had been for a walk by herself one morning, and came back to find Lenox grinning at her expectantly.

'Your young man has been ringing you up, Katherine!'

'Who do you call my young man?'

'A new one – Rufus Van Aldin's secretary. You seem to have made rather an impression there. You are becoming a serious breaker of hearts, Katherine. First Derek Kettering, and now this young Knighton. The funny thing is that I remember him quite well. He was in Mother's War Hospital that she ran out here. I was only a kid of about eight at the time.'

'Was he badly wounded?'

'Shot in the leg, if I remember rightly – rather a nasty business. I think the doctors messed it up a bit. They said he wouldn't limp or anything, but when he left here he was still completely dot and go one.'

Lady Tamplin came out and joined them.

'Have you been telling Katherine about Major Knighton?' she asked. 'Such a dear fellow! Just at first I didn't remember him – one had so many – but now it all comes back.'

'He was a bit too unimportant to be remembered before,' said Lenox. 'Now that he is a secretary to an American millionaire, it is a very different matter.'

'Darling!' said Lady Tamplin in her vague reproachful voice.

'What did Major Knighton ring up about?' inquired Katherine.

'He asked if you would like to go to the tennis this afternoon. If so, he would call for you in a car. Mother and I accepted for you with *empressement*. Whilst you dally with a millionaire's secretary, you might give me a chance with the millionaire, Katherine. He is about sixty, I suppose, so that he will be looking about for a nice sweet young thing like me.'

'I should like to meet Mr Van Aldin,' said Lady Tamplin earnestly; 'one has heard so much of him. Those fine rugged figures of the Western world' – she broke off – 'so fascinating,' she murmured.

'Major Knighton was very particular to say it was Mr Van Aldin's invitation,' said Lenox. 'He said it so often that I began to smell a rat. You and Knighton would make a very nice pair, Katherine. Bless you, my children.'

Katherine laughed, and went upstairs to change her clothes. Knighton arrived soon after lunch and endured manfully Lady Tamplin's transports of recognition.

When they were driving together towards Cannes he remarked to Katherine: 'Lady Tamplin has changed wonderfully little.'

'In manner or appearance?'

'Both. She must be, I suppose, well over forty, but she is a remarkably beautiful woman still.'

'She is,' agreed Katherine.

'I am very glad that you could come today,' went on Knighton. 'M. Poirot is going to be there also. What an extraordinary little man he is. Do you know him well, Miss Grey?'

Katherine shook her head. 'I met him on the train on the way here. I was reading a detective novel, and I happened to say something about such things not happening in real life. Of course, I had no idea of who he was.'

'He is a very remarkable person,' said Knighton slowly, 'and has done some very remarkable things. He has a kind of genius for going to the root of the matter, and right up to the end no one has any idea of what he is really thinking. I remember I was staying at a house in Yorkshire, and Lady Clanravon's jewels were stolen. It seemed at first to be a simple robbery, but it completely baffled the local police. I wanted them to call in Hercule Poirot, and said he was the only man who could help them, but they pinned their faith to Scotland Yard.'

'And what happened?' said Katherine curiously.

'The jewels were never recovered,' said Knighton drily.

'You really do believe in him?'

'I do indeed. The Comte de la Roche is a pretty wily customer. He has wriggled out of most things. But I think he has met his match in Hercule Poirot.'

'The Comte de la Roche,' said Katherine thoughtfully; 'so you really think he did it?'

'Of course.' Knighton looked at her in astonishment. 'Don't you?'

'Oh yes,' said Katherine hastily; 'that is, I mean, if it was not just an ordinary train robbery.'

'It might be, of course,' agreed the other, 'but it seems to me that the Comte de la Roche fits into this business particularly well.'

'And yet he has an alibi.'

'Oh, alibis!' Knighton laughed, his face broke into his attractive boyish smile.

'You confess that you read detective stories, Miss Grey. You must know that anyone who has a perfect alibi is always open to grave suspicion.'

'Do you think that real life is like that?' asked Katherine, smiling.

'Why not? Fiction is founded on fact.'

'But is rather superior to it,' suggested Katherine.

'Perhaps. Anyway, if I was a criminal I should not like to have Hercule Poirot on my track.'

'No more should I,' said Katherine, and laughed.

They were met on arrival by Poirot. As the day was warm he was attired in a white duck suit, with a white camellia in his buttonhole.

'*Bonjour*, Mademoiselle,' said Poirot. 'I look very English, do I not?'

'You look wonderful,' said Katherine tactfully.

'You mock yourself at me,' said Poirot genially. 'But no matter. Papa Poirot, he always laughs the last.'

'Where is Mr Van Aldin?' asked Knighton.

'He will meet us at our seats. To tell you the truth, my friend, he is not too well pleased with me. Oh, those Americans – the repose, the calm, they know it not! Mr Van Aldin, he would that I fly myself in the pursuit of criminals through all the byways of Nice.'

'I should have thought myself that it would not have been a bad plan,' observed Knighton.

'You are wrong,' said Poirot; 'in these matters one needs not energy but finesse. At the tennis one meets everyone. That is so important. Ah, there is Mr Kettering.'

Derek came abruptly up to them. He looked reckless and angry, as though something had arisen to upset him. He and Knighton greeted each other with some frigidity. Poirot alone seemed unconscious of any sense of strain, and chatted pleasantly in a laudable attempt to put everyone at their ease. He paid little compliments.

'It is amazing, M. Kettering, how well you speak the French,' he observed – 'so well that you could be taken for a Frenchman if you choose. That is a very rare accomplishment among Englishmen.'

'I wish I did,' said Katherine. 'I am only too well aware that my French is of a painfully British order.'

They reached their seats and sat down, and almost immediately Knighton perceived his employer signalling to him from the other end of the court, and went off to speak to him.

'Me, I approve of that young man,' said Poirot, sending a beaming smile after the departing secretary; 'and you, Mademoiselle?'

'I like him very much.'

'And you, M. Kettering?'

Some quick rejoinder was springing to Derek's lips, but he checked it as though something in the little Belgian's twinkling eyes had made him suddenly alert. He spoke carefully, choosing his words.

'Knighton is a very good fellow,' he said.

Just for a moment Katherine fancied that Poirot looked disappointed.

'He is a great admirer of yours, M. Poirot,' she said, and she related some of the things that Knighton had said. It amused her to see the little man plume himself like a bird, thrusting out his chest, and assuming an air of mock modesty that would have deceived no one.

'That reminds me, Mademoiselle,' he said suddenly, 'I have a little matter of business I have to speak to you about. When you were sitting talking to that poor lady in the train, I think you must have dropped a cigarette case.'

Katherine looked rather astonished. 'I don't think so,' she said. Poirot drew from his pocket a cigarette case of soft blue leather, with the initial 'K' on it in gold.

'No, that is not mine,' Katherine said.

'Ah, a thousand apologies. It was doubtless Madame's own. "K", of course, stands for Kettering. We were doubtful, because she had another cigarette case in her bag, and it seemed odd that she should have two.' He turned to Derek suddenly. 'You do not know, I suppose, whether this was your wife's case or not?'

Derek seemed momentarily taken aback. He stammered a little in his reply: 'I – I don't know. I suppose so.'

'It is not yours by any chance?'

'Certainly not. If it were mine it would hardly have been in my wife's possession.'

Poirot looked more ingenuous and childlike than ever.

'I thought perhaps you might have dropped it when you were in your wife's compartment,' he explained guilelessly.

'I never was there. I have already told the police that a dozen times.'

'A thousand pardons,' said Poirot, with his most apologetic air. 'It was Mademoiselle here who mentioned having seen you going in.'

He stopped with an air of embarrassment.

Katherine looked at Derek. His face had gone rather white, but perhaps that was her fancy. His laugh, when it came, was natural enough.

'You made a mistake, Miss Grey,' he said easily. 'From what

the police have told me, I gather that my own compartment was only a door or two away from that of my wife's – though I never suspected the fact at the time. You must have seen me going into my own compartment.' He got up quickly as he saw Van Aldin and Knighton approaching.

'I'm going to leave you now,' he announced. 'I can't stand my father-in-law at any price.'

Van Aldin greeted Katherine very courteously, but was clearly in a bad humour.

'You seem fond of watching tennis, M. Poirot,' he growled.

'It is a pleasure to me, yes,' replied Poirot placidly.

'It is as well you are in France,' said Van Aldin. 'We are made of sterner stuff in the States. Business comes before pleasure there.'

Poirot did not take offence; indeed, he smiled gently and confidingly at the irate millionaire.

'Do not enrage yourself, I beg of you. Everyone has his own methods. Me, I have always found it a delightful and pleasing idea to combine business and pleasure together.'

He glanced at the other two. They were deep in conversation, absorbed in each other. Poirot nodded his head in satisfaction, and then leant towards the millionaire, lowering his voice as he did so.

'It is not only for pleasure that I am here, M. Van Aldin. Observe just opposite us that tall old man – the one with the yellow face and the venerable beard.'

'Well, what of him?'

'That,' Poirot said, 'is M. Papopolous.'

'A Greek, eh?'

'As you say – a Greek. He is a dealer in antiques of world-wide reputation. He has a small shop in Paris, and he is suspected by the police of being something more.'

'What?'

'A receiver of stolen goods, especially jewels. There is nothing as to the re-cutting and re-setting of gems that he does not know. He deals with the highest in Europe and with the lowest of the riff-raff of the underworld.'

Van Aldin was looking at Poirot with suddenly awakened attention.

'Well?' he demanded, a new note in his voice.

'I ask myself,' said Poirot, 'I, Hercule Poirot' – he thumped himself dramatically on the chest – 'ask myself *why is M. Papopolous suddenly come to Nice?*'

Van Aldin was impressed. For a moment he had doubted Poirot and suspected the little man of being past his job, a *poseur* only. Now, in a moment, he switched back to his original opinion. He looked straight at the little detective.

'I must apologize to you, M. Poirot.'

Poirot waved the apology aside with an extravagant gesture.

'Bah!' he cried, 'all that is of no importance. Now listen, M. Van Aldin; I have news for you.'

The millionaire looked sharply at him, all his interest aroused. Poirot nodded.

'It is as I say. You will be interested. As you know, M. Van Aldin, the Comte de la Roche has been under surveillance ever since his interview with the Juge d'Instruction. The day after that, during his absence, the Villa Marina was searched by the police.'

'Well,' said Van Aldin, 'did they find anything? I bet they didn't.'

Poirot made him a little bow.

'Your acumen is not at fault, M. Van Aldin. They found nothing of an incriminating nature. It was not to be expected that they would. The Comte de la Roche, as your expressive idiom has it, was not born on the preceding day. He is an astute gentleman with great experience.'

'Well, go on,' growled Van Aldin.

'It may be, of course, that the Comte had nothing of a compromising nature to conceal. But we must not neglect the possibility. If, then, he has something to conceal, where is it? Not in his house – the police searched thoroughly. Not on his person, for he knows that he is liable to arrest at any minute. There remains – his car. As I say, he was under surveillance. He was followed on that day to Monte Carlo. From there he went by road to Mentone, driving himself. His car is a very powerful one, it outdistanced his pursuers, and for about a quarter of an hour they completely lost sight of him.'

'And during that time you think he concealed something by the roadside?' asked Van Aldin, keenly interested.

'By the roadside, no. *Ça n'est pas pratique.* But listen now – me, I have made a little suggestion to M. Carrège. He is graciously pleased to approve of it. In each Bureau de Poste in the neighbourhood it has been seen to that there is someone who knows the Comte de la Roche by sight. Because, you see, Messieurs, the best way of hiding a thing is by sending it away by the post.'

'Well?' demanded Van Aldin; his face was keenly alight with interest and expectation.

'Well – *voilà!*' With a dramatic flourish Poirot drew out from his pocket a loosely wrapped brown paper package from which the string had been removed.

'During that quarter of an hour's interval, our good gentleman mailed this.'

'The address?' asked the other sharply.

Poirot nodded his head.

'Might have told us something, but unfortunately it does not. The package was addressed to one of these little newspaper shops in Paris where letters and parcels are kept until called for on payment of a small commission.'

'Yes, but what is inside?' demanded Van Aldin impatiently.

Poirot unwrapped the brown paper and disclosed a square cardboard box. He looked round him.

'It is a good moment,' he said quietly. 'All eyes are on the tennis. Look, Monsieur!'

He lifted the lid of the box for a fraction of a second. An exclamation of utter astonishment came from the millionaire. His face turned as white as chalk.

'My God!' he breathed, 'the rubies.'

He sat for a minute as though dazed. Poirot restored the box to his pocket and beamed placidly. Then suddenly the millionaire seemed to come out of his trance; he leaned across to Poirot and wrung his hand so heartily that the little man winced with pain.

'This is great,' said Van Aldin. 'Great! You are the goods, M. Poirot. Once and for all, you are the goods.'

'It is nothing,' said Poirot modestly. 'Order, method, being prepared for eventualities beforehand – that is all there is to it.'

'And now, I suppose, the Comte de la Roche has been arrested?' continued Van Aldin eagerly.

'No,' said Poirot.

A look of utter astonishment came over Van Aldin's face.

'But why? What more do you want?'

'The Comte's alibi is still unshaken.'

'But that is nonsense.'

'Yes,' said Poirot; 'I rather think it is nonsense, but unfortunately we have to prove it so.'

'In the meantime he will slip through your fingers.'

Poirot shook his head very energetically.

'No,' he said, 'he will not do that. The one thing the Comte cannot afford to sacrifice is his social position. At all costs he must stop and brazen it out.'

Van Aldin was still dissatisfied.

'But I don't see –'

Poirot raised a hand. 'Grant me a little moment, Monsieur. Me, I have a little idea. Many people have mocked themselves at the little ideas of Hercule Poirot – and they have been wrong.'

'Well,' said Van Aldin, 'go ahead. What is this little idea?'

Poirot paused for a moment and then he said:

'I will call upon you at your hotel at eleven o'clock tomorrow morning. Until then, say nothing to anyone.'

CHAPTER XXII

M. Papopolous Breakfasts

M. Papopolous was at breakfast. Opposite him sat his daughter, Zia.

There was a knock at the sitting-room door, and a chasseur entered with a card which he brought to M. Papopolous. The latter scrutinized it, raised his eyebrows, and passed it over to his daughter.

'Ah!' said M. Papopolous, scratching his left ear thoughtfully, 'Hercule Poirot. I wonder now.'

Father and daughter looked at each other.

'I saw him yesterday at the tennis,' said M. Papopolous. 'Zia, I hardly like this.'

'He was very useful to you once,' his daughter reminded him.

'That is true,' acknowledged M. Papopolous; 'also he has retired from active work, so I hear.'

These interchanges between father and daughter had passed in their own language. Now M. Papopolous turned to the chasseur and said in French:

'*Faîtes monter ce monsieur.*'

A few minutes later Hercule Poirot, exquisitely attired, and swinging a cane with a jaunty air, entered the room.

'My dear M. Papopolous.'

'My dear M. Poirot.'

'And Mademoiselle Zia.' Poirot swept her a low bow.

'You will excuse us going on with our breakfast,' said M. Papopolous, pouring himself out another cup of coffee. 'Your call is – ahem! – a little early.'

'It is scandalous,' said Poirot, 'but you see, I am pressed.'

'Ah!' murmured M. Papopolous, 'you are on an affair then?'

'A very serious affair,' said Poirot; 'the death of Madame Kettering.'

'Let me see,' M. Papopolous looked innocently up at the ceiling, 'that was the lady who died on the Blue Train, was it not? I saw a mention of it in the papers, but there was no suggestion of foul play.'

'In the interests of justice,' said Poirot, 'it was thought best to suppress that fact.'

There was a pause.

'And in what way can I assist you, M. Poirot?' asked the dealer politely.

'*Voilà*,' said Poirot, 'I shall come to the point.' He took from his pocket the same box that he had displayed at Cannes, and, opening it, he took out the rubies and pushed them across the table to Papopolous.

Although Poirot was watching him narrowly, not a muscle of the old man's face moved. He took up the jewels and examined them with a kind of detached interest, then he looked across at the detective inquiringly:

'Superb, are they not?' asked Poirot.

'Quite excellent,' said M. Papopolous.

'How much should you say they are worth?'

The Greek's face quivered a little.

'Is it really necessary to tell you, M. Poirot?' he asked.

'You are shrewd, M. Papopolous. No, it is not. They are not, for instance, worth five hundred thousand dollars.'

Papopolous laughed, and Poirot joined with him.

'As an imitation,' said Papopolous, handing them back to Poirot, 'they are, as I said, quite excellent. Would it be indiscreet to ask, M. Poirot, where you came across them?'

'Not at all,' said Poirot; 'I have no objection to telling an old friend like yourself. They were in the possession of the Comte de la Roche.'

M. Papopolous' eyebrows lifted themselves eloquently.

'In-deed,' he murmured.

Poirot leaned forward and assumed his most innocent and beguiling air.

'M. Papopolous,' he said, 'I am going to lay my cards upon the table. The original of these jewels was stolen from Madame Kettering on the Blue Train. Now I will say to you first this: *I am not concerned with the recovery of these jewels. That is the affair of the police.* I am working not for the police but for M. Van Aldin. I want to lay hands on the man who killed Madame Kettering. I am interested in the jewels only in so far as they may lead me to the man. You understand?'

The last two words were uttered with great significance. M. Papopolous, his face quite unmoved, said quietly:

'Go on.'

'It seems to me probable, Monsieur, that the jewels will change hands in Nice – may already have done so.'

'Ah!' said M. Papopolous.

He sipped his coffee reflectively, and looked a shade more noble and patriarchal than usual.

'I say to myself,' continued Poirot, with animation, 'what good fortune! My old friend, M. Papopolous, is in Nice. He will aid me.'

'And how do you think I can aid you?' inquired M. Papopolous coldly.

'I said to myself, without doubt M. Papopolous is in Nice on business.'

'Not at all,' said M. Papopolous, 'I am here for my health – by the doctor's orders.'

He coughed hollowly.

'I am desolated to hear it,' replied Poirot, with somewhat insincere sympathy. 'But to continue. When a Russian Grand Duke, an Austrian Archduchess, or an Italian Prince wish to dispose of their family jewels – to whom do they go? To M. Papopolous, is it not? He who is famous all over the world for the discretion with which he arranges these things.'

The other bowed.

'You flatter me.'

'It is a great thing, discretion,' mused Poirot, and was rewarded by the fleeting smile which passed across the Greek's face. 'I, too, can be discreet.'

The eyes of the two men met.

Then Poirot went on speaking very slowly, and obviously picking his words with care.

'I say to myself, this: if these jewels have changed hands in Nice, M. Papopolous would have heard of it. He has knowledge of all that passes in the jewel world.'

'Ah!' said M. Papopolous, and helped himself to a *croissant.*

'The police, you understand,' said M. Poirot, 'do not enter into the matter. It is a personal affair.'

'One hears rumours,' admitted M. Papopolous cautiously.

'Such as?' prompted Poirot.

'Is there any reason why I should pass them on?'

'Yes,' said Poirot, 'I think there is. You may remember, M. Papopolous, that seventeen years ago there was a certain article in your hands, left there as security by a very – er – Prominent Person. It was in your keeping and it unaccountably disappeared. You were, if I may use the English expression, in the soup.'

His eyes came gently round to the girl. She had pushed her cup and plate aside, and with both elbows on the table and her chin resting on her hands, was listening eagerly. Still keeping an eye on her he went on:

'I am in Paris at the time. You send for me. You place yourself in my hands. If I restore to you that – article, you say I shall earn your undying gratitude. *Eh bien!* I did restore it to you.'

A long sigh came from M. Papopolous.

'It was the most unpleasant moment of my career,' he murmured.

'Seventeen years is a long time,' said Poirot thoughtfully, 'but I believe that I am right in saying, Monsieur, that your race does not forget.'

'A Greek?' murmured Papopolous, with an ironical smile.

'It was not as a Greek I meant,' said Poirot.

There was a silence, and then the old man drew himself up proudly.

'You are right, M. Poirot,' he said quietly. 'I am a Jew. And, as you say, our race does not forget.'

'You will aid me then?'

'As regards the jewels, Monsieur, I can do nothing.'

The old man, as Poirot had done just now, picked his words carefully.

'I know nothing. I have heard nothing. But I can perhaps do you a good turn – that is, if you are interested in racing.'

'Under certain circumstances I might be,' said Poirot, eyeing him steadily.

'There is a horse running at Longchamps that would, I think, repay attention. I cannot say for certain, you understand; this news passed through so many hands.'

He stopped, fixing Poirot with his eyes, as though to make sure that the latter was comprehending him.

'Perfectly, perfectly,' said Poirot, nodding.

'The name of the horse,' said M. Papopolous, leaning back and joining the tips of his fingers together, 'is the Marquis. I think, but I am not sure, that it is an English horse, eh, Zia?'

'I think so too,' said the girl.

Poirot got up briskly.

'I thank you, Monsieur,' he said. 'It is a great thing to have what the English call a tip from the stable. Au revoir, Monsieur, and many thanks.'

He turned to the girl.

'Au revoir, Mademoiselle Zia. It seems to me but yesterday that I saw you in Paris. One would say that two years had passed at most.'

'There is a difference between sixteen and thirty-three,' said Zia ruefully.

'Not in your case,' declared Poirot gallantly. 'You and your father will perhaps dine with me one night.'

'We shall be delighted,' replied Zia.

'Then we will arrange it,' declared Poirot, 'and now – *je me sauve.*'

Poirot walked along the street humming a little tune to himself. He twirled his stick with a jaunty air, once or twice he smiled to himself quietly. He turned into the first Bureau de Poste he came to and sent off a telegram. He took some time in wording it, but it was in code and he had to call upon his memory. It purported to deal with a missing scarf-pin, and was addressed to Inspector Japp, Scotland Yard.

Decoded, it was short and to the point. '*Wire me everything known about man whose soubriquet is the Marquis.*'

CHAPTER XXIII

A New Theory

It was exactly eleven o'clock when Poirot presented himself at Van Aldin's hotel. He found the millionaire alone.

'You are punctual, M. Poirot,' he said, with a smile, as he rose to greet the detective.

'I am always punctual,' said Poirot. 'The exactitude – always do I observe it. Without order and method –'

He broke off. 'Ah, but it is possible that I have said these things to you before. Let us come at once to the object of my visit.'

'Your little idea?'

'Yes, my little idea.' Poirot smiled.

'First of all, Monsieur, I should like to interview once more the maid, Ada Mason. She is here?'

'Yes, she's here.'

'Ah!'

Van Aldin looked at him curiously. He rang the bell, and a messenger was despatched to find Mason.

Poirot greeted her with his usual politeness, which was never without effect on that particular class.

'Good afternoon, Mademoiselle,' he said cheerfully. 'Be seated, will you not, if Monsieur permits.'

'Yes, yes, sit down, my girl,' said Van Aldin.

'Thank you, sir,' said Mason primly, and she sat down on the extreme edge of a chair. She looked bonier and more acid than ever.

'I have come to ask you yet more questions,' said Poirot. 'We must get to the bottom of this affair. Always I return to the question of the man in the train. You have been shown the Comte de la Roche. You say that it is possible he was the man, but you are not sure.'

'As I told you, sir, I never saw the gentleman's face. That is what makes it so difficult.'

Poirot beamed and nodded.

'Precisely, exactly. I comprehend well the difficulty. Now, Mademoiselle, you have been in the service of Madame Kettering two months, you say. During that time, how often did you see your master?'

Mason reflected a minute or two, and then said:

'Only twice, sir.'

'And was that near to, or far away?'

'Well once, sir, he came to Curzon Street. I was upstairs, and I looked over the banisters and saw him in the hall below. I was a bit curious like, you understand, knowing the way things – er – were.' Mason finished up with her discreet cough.

'And the other time?'

'I was in the Park, sir, with Annie – one of the housemaids, sir, and she pointed out the master to me walking with a foreign lady.'

Again Poirot nodded.

'Now listen, Mason, this man whom you saw in the carriage talking to your mistress at the Gare de Lyon, how do you know it was not your master?'

'The master, sir? Oh, I don't think it could have been.'

'But you are not sure,' Poirot persisted.

'Well – I never thought of it, sir.'

Mason was clearly upset at the idea.

'You have heard that your master was also on the train. What more natural than that it should be he who came along the corridor?'

'But the gentleman who was talking to the mistress must have come from outside, sir. He was dressed for the street. In an overcoat and soft hat.'

'Just so, Mademoiselle, but reflect a minute. The train has just arrived at the Gare de Lyon. Many of the passengers promenade themselves upon the quay. Your mistress was about to do so, and for that purpose had doubtless put on her fur coat, eh?'

'Yes, sir,' agreed Mason.

'Your master, then, does the same. The train is heated, but outside in the station it is cold. He puts on his overcoat and his hat and he walks along beside the train, and looking up at the lighted windows he suddenly sees Madame Kettering. Until then he has had no idea that she was on the train. Naturally, he mounts the carriage and goes to her compartment. She gives an exclamation of surprise at seeing him and quickly shuts the door between the two compartments since it is possible that their conversation may be of a private nature.'

He leaned back in his chair and watched the suggestion slowly take effect. No one knew better than Hercule Poirot that the class to which Mason belongs cannot be hurried. He must give her time to get rid of her own preconceived ideas. At the end of three minutes she spoke:

'Well, of course, sir, it might be so. I never thought of it that way. The master is tall and dark, and just about that build. It was seeing the hat and coat that made me say it was a gentleman from outside. Yes, it might have been the master. I would not like to say either way, I'm sure.'

'Thank you very much, Mademoiselle. I shall not require you any further. Ah, just one thing more.' He took from his pocket the cigarette case he had already shown to Katherine. 'Is that your mistress's case?' he said to Mason.

'No, sir, it is not the mistress's – at least –'

She looked suddenly startled. An idea was clearly working its way to the forefront of her mind.

'Yes?' said Poirot encouragingly.

'I think, sir – I can't be sure, but I think – it is a case that the mistress bought to give to the master.'

'Ah,' said Poirot in a non-committal manner.

'But whether she ever did give it to him or not, I can't say, of course.'

'Precisely,' said Poirot, 'precisely. That is all, I think, Mademoiselle. I wish you good afternoon.'

Ada Mason retired discreetly, closing the door noiselessly behind her.

Poirot looked across at Van Aldin, a faint smile upon his face. The millionaire looked thunderstruck.

'You think – you think it was Derek?' he queried, 'but – everything points the other way. Why, the Count has actually been caught red-handed with the jewels on him.'

'No.'

'But you told me –'

'What did I tell you?'

'That story about the jewels. You showed them to me.'

'No.'

Van Aldin stared at him.

'You mean to say you didn't show them to me?'

'No.'

'Yesterday – at the tennis?'

'No.'

'Are you crazy, M. Poirot, or am I?'

'Neither of us is crazy,' said the detective. 'You ask me a question; I answer it. You say have I not shown you the jewels yesterday? I reply – no. What I showed you, M. Van Aldin, was a first-class imitation, hardly to be distinguished except by an expert from the real ones.'

CHAPTER XXIV

Poirot Gives Advice

It took the millionaire some few minutes to take the thing in. He stared at Poirot as though dumbfounded. The little Belgian nodded at him gently.

'Yes,' he said, 'it alters the position, does it not?'

'Imitation!'

He leaned forward.

'All along, M. Poirot, you have had this idea? All along this is what you have been driving at? You never believed that the Comte de la Roche was the murderer?'

'I have had doubts,' said Poirot quietly. 'I said as much to you. Robbery with violence and murder' – he shook his head energetically – 'no, it is difficult to picture. It does not harmonize with the personality of the Comte de la Roche.'

'But you believe that he meant to steal the rubies?'

'Certainly. There is no doubt as to that. See, I will recount to you the affair as I see it. The Comte knew of the rubies and he laid his plans accordingly. He made up a romantic story of a book he was writing, so as to induce your daughter to bring them with her. He provided himself with an exact duplicate. It is clear, is it not, that substitution is what he was after. Madame, your daughter, was not an expert on jewels. It would probably be a long time before she discovered what had occurred. When she did so – well – I do not think she would prosecute the Comte. Too much would come out. He would have in his possession various letters of hers. Oh yes, a very safe scheme from the Comte's point of view – one that he has probably carried out before.'

'It seems clear enough, yes,' said Van Aldin musingly.

'It accords with the personality of the Comte de la Roche,' said Poirot.

'Yes, but now –' Van Aldin looked searchingly at the other. 'What actually happened? Tell me that, M. Poirot.'

Poirot shrugged his shoulders.

'It is quite simple,' he said; 'someone stepped in ahead of the Comte.'

There was a long pause.

Van Aldin seemed to be turning things over in his mind. When he spoke it was without beating about the bush.

'How long have you suspected my son-in-law, M. Poirot?'

'From the very first. He had the motive and the opportunity. Everyone took for granted that the man in Madame's compartment in Paris was the Comte de la Roche. I thought so, too. Then you happened to mention that you had once mistaken the Comte for your son-in-law. That told me that they were of the same height and build, and alike in colouring. It put some curious ideas in my head. The maid had only been with your daughter a short time. It was unlikely that she would know Mr Kettering well by sight, since he had not been living in Curzon Street; also the man was careful to keep his face turned away.'

'You believe he – murdered her?' said Van Aldin hoarsely.

Poirot raised a hand quickly.

'No, no, I did not say that – but it is a possibility – a very strong possibility. He was in a tight corner, a very tight corner, threatened with ruin. This was the one way out.'

'But why take the jewels?'

'To make the crime appear an ordinary one committed by train robbers. Otherwise suspicion might have fallen on him straight away.'

'If that is so, what has he done with the rubies?'

'That remains to be seen. There are several possibilities. There is a man in Nice who may be able to help, the man I pointed out at the tennis.'

He rose to his feet and Van Aldin rose also and laid his hand on the little man's shoulder. His voice when he spoke was harsh with emotion.

'Find Ruth's murderer for me,' he said, 'that is all I ask.'

Poirot drew himself up.

'Leave it in the hands of Hercule Poirot,' he said superbly; 'have no fears. I will discover the truth.'

He brushed a speck of fluff from his hat, smiled reassuringly at the millionaire, and left the room. Nevertheless, as he went down the stairs some of the confidence faded from his face.

'It is all very well,' he murmured to himself, 'but there are difficulties. Yes, there are great difficulties.' As he was passing out of the hotel he came to a sudden halt. A car had drawn up in front of the door. In it was Katherine Grey, and Derek Kettering was standing beside it talking to her earnestly. A minute or two later the car drove off and Derek remained standing on the pavement looking after it. The expression on his face was an odd one. He gave a sudden impatient gesture of the shoulders, sighed deeply, and turned to find Hercule Poirot standing at his elbow. In spite of himself he started. The two men looked at each other. Poirot steadily and unwaveringly and Derek with a kind of light-hearted defiance. There was a sneer behind the easy mockery of his tone when he spoke, raising his eyebrows slightly as he did so.

'Rather a dear, isn't she?' he asked easily.

His manner was perfectly natural.

'Yes,' said Poirot thoughtfully, 'that describes Mademoiselle Katherine very well. It is very English, that phrase there, and Mademoiselle Katherine, she also is very English.'

Derek remained perfectly still without answering.

'And yet she is *sympathique*, is it not so?'

'Yes,' said Derek; 'there are not many like her.'

He spoke softly, almost as though to himself. Poirot nodded significantly. Then he leant towards the other and spoke in a different tone, a quiet, grave tone that was new to Derek Kettering.

'You will pardon an old man, Monsieur, if he says to you something that you may consider impertinent. There is one of your English proverbs that I would quote to you. It says that "it is well to be off with the old love, before being on with the new." '

Kettering turned on him angrily.

'What the devil do you mean?'

'You enrage yourself at me,' said Poirot placidly. 'I expected as much. As to what I mean – I mean, Monsieur, that there is a second car with a lady in it. If you turn your head you will see her.'

Derek spun round. His face darkened with anger.

'Mirelle, damn her!' he muttered. 'I will soon –'

Poirot arrested the movement he was about to make.

'Is it wise what you are about to do there?' he asked warningly. His eyes shone softly with a green light in them. But Derek was past noticing the warning signs. In his anger he was completely off his guard.

'I have broken with her utterly, and she knows it,' cried Derek angrily.

'You have broken with her, yes, but has *she* broken with you?'

Derek gave a sudden harsh laugh.

'She won't break with two million pounds if she can help it,' he murmured brutally; 'trust Mirelle for that.'

Poirot raised his eyebrows.

'You have the outlook cynical,' he murmured.

'Have I?' There was no mirth in his sudden wide smile. 'I have lived in the world long enough, M. Poirot, to know that all women are pretty much alike.' His face softened suddenly. 'All save one.'

He met Poirot's gaze defiantly. A look of alertness crept into his eyes, then faded again. 'That one,' he said, and jerked his head in the direction of Cap Martin.

'Ah!' said Poirot.

This quiescence was well calculated to provoke the impetuous temperament of the other.

'I know what you are going to say,' said Derek rapidly, 'the kind of life I have led, the fact that I am not worthy of her. You will say that I have no right to think even of such a thing. You will say that it is not a case of giving a dog a bad name – I know that it is not decent to be speaking like this with my wife dead only a few days, and murdered at that.'

He paused for breath, and Poirot took advantage of the pause to remark in his plaintive tone:

'But, indeed, I have not said anything at all.'

'But you will.'

'Eh?' said Poirot.

'You will say that I have no earthly chance of marrying Katherine.'

'No,' said Poirot, 'I would not say that. Your reputation is bad, yes, but with women – never does that deter them. If you were a man of excellent character, of strict morality who had done nothing that he should not do, and – possibly everything that he should do – *eh bien!* then I should have grave doubts of your success. Moral worth, you understand, it is not romantic. It is appreciated, however, by widows.'

Derek Kettering stared at him, then he swung round on his heel and went up to the waiting car.

Poirot looked after him with some interest. He saw the lovely vision lean out of the car and speak.

Derek Kettering did not stop. He lifted his hat and passed straight on.

'*Ça y est,*' said M. Hercule Poirot, 'it is time, I think, that I return *chez moi.*'

He found an imperturbable George pressing trousers.

'A pleasant day, Georges, somewhat fatiguing, but not without interest,' he said.

George received these remarks in his usual wooden fashion.

'Indeed, sir.'

'The personality of a criminal, Georges, is an interesting matter. Many murderers are men of great personal charm.'

'I always heard, sir, that Dr Crippen was a pleasant-spoken gentleman. And yet he cut up his wife like so much mince-meat.'

'Your instances are always apt, Georges.'

The valet did not reply, and at that moment the telephone rang. Poirot took up the receiver.

''Allo – 'allo – yes, yes, it is Hercule Poirot who speaks.'

'This is Knighton. Will you hold the line a minute, M. Poirot. Mr Van Aldin would like to speak to you.'

There was a moment's pause, then the millionaire's voice came through.

'Is that you, M. Poirot? I just wanted to tell you that Mason came to me now of her own accord. She has been thinking it over, and she says that she is almost certain that the man at Paris was Derek Kettering. There was something familiar about him at the time, she says, but at the minute she could not place it. She seems pretty certain now.'

'Ah,' said Poirot, 'thank you, M. Van Aldin. That advances us.'

He replaced the receiver, and stood for a minute or two with a very curious smile on his face. George had to speak to him twice before obtaining an answer.

'Eh?' said Poirot. 'What is that that you say to me?'

'Are you lunching here, sir, or are you going out?'

'Neither,' said Poirot. 'I shall go to bed and take a *tisane.* The expected has happened, and when the expected happens, it always causes me emotion.'

CHAPTER XXV

Defiance

As Derek Kettering passed the car, Mirelle leant out.

'Dereek – I must speak to you for a moment –'

But, lifting his hat, Derek passed straight on without stopping.

When he got back to his hotel, the concierge detached himself from his wooden pen and accosted him.

'A gentleman is waiting to see you, Monsieur.'

'Who is it?' asked Derek.

'He did not give his name, Monsieur, but he said his business with you was important, and that he would wait.'

'Where is he?'

'In the little salon, Monsieur. He preferred it to the lounge, he said, as being more private.'

Derek nodded, and turned his steps in that direction.

The small salon was empty except for the visitor, who rose and bowed with easy foreign grace as Derek entered. As it chanced, Derek had only seen the Comte de la Roche once, but found no difficulty in recognizing that aristocratic nobleman, and he frowned angrily. Of all the consummate impertinence!

'The Comte de la Roche, is it not?' he said. 'I am afraid you have wasted your time in coming here.'

'I hope not,' said the Comte agreeably. His white teeth glittered.

The Comte's charm of manner was usually wasted on his own sex. All men, without exception, disliked him heartily. Derek Kettering was already conscious of a distinct longing to kick the Count bodily out of the room. It was only the realization that scandal would be unfortunate just at present that restrained him. He marvelled anew that Ruth could have cared, as she certainly had, for this fellow. A bounder, and worse than a bounder. He looked with distaste at the Count's exquisitely manicured hands.

'I called,' said the Comte, 'on a little matter of business. It would be advisable, I think, for you to listen to me.'

Again Derek felt strongly tempted to kick him out, but again he refrained. The hint of a threat was not lost upon him, but he interpreted it in his own way. There were various reasons why it would be better to hear what the Comte had to say.

He sat down and drummed impatiently with his fingers on the table.

'Well,' he said sharply, 'what is it?'

It was not the Comte's way to come out into the open at once.

'Allow me, Monsieur, to offer you my condolences on your recent bereavement.'

'If I have any impertinence from you,' said Derek quietly, 'you go out by that window.'

He nodded his head towards the window beside the Comte, and the latter moved uneasily.

'I will send my friends to you, Monsieur, if that is what you desire,' he said haughtily.

Derek laughed.

'A duel, eh? My dear Count, I don't take you seriously enough for that. But I should take a good deal of pleasure in kicking you down the Promenade des Anglais.'

The Comte was not at all anxious to take offence. He merely raised his eyebrows and murmured:

'The English are barbarians.'

'Well,' said Derek, 'what is it you have to say to me?'

'I will be frank,' said the Comte, 'I will come immediately to the point. That will suit us both, will it not?'

Again he smiled in his agreeable fashion.

'Go on,' said Derek curtly.

The Comte looked at the ceiling, joined the tips of his fingers together, and murmured softly:

'You have come into a lot of money, Monsieur.'

'What the devil has that got to do with you?'

The Comte drew himself up.

'Monsieur, my name is tarnished! I am suspected – accused – of foul crime.'

'The accusation does not come from me,' said Derek coldly; 'as an interested party I have not expressed any opinion.'

'I am innocent,' said the Comte. 'I swear before heaven' – he raised his hand to heaven – 'that I am innocent.'

'M. Carrège is, I believe, the Juge d'Instruction in charge of the case,' hinted Derek politely.

The Comte took no notice.

'Not only am I unjustly suspected of a crime that I did not commit, but I am also in serious need of money.'

He coughed softly and suggestively.

Derek rose to his feet.

'I was waiting for that,' he said softly; 'you blackmailing brute! I will not give you a penny. My wife is dead, and no scandal that you can make can touch her now. She wrote you foolish letters, I dare say. If I were to buy them from you for a round sum at this minute, I am pretty certain that you would manage to keep one or two back; and I will tell you this, M. de la Roche, blackmailing is an ugly word both in England and France. That is my answer to you. Good afternoon.'

'One moment' – the Comte stretched out a hand as Derek was turning to leave the room. 'You are mistaken, Monsieur. You are completely mistaken. I am, I hope, a "gentleman".' Derek laughed. 'Any letters that a lady might write to me I should hold sacred.' He flung back his head with a beautiful air of nobility. 'The proposition that I was putting before you was of quite a different nature. I am, as I said, extremely short of money, and my conscience might impel me to go to the police with certain information.'

Derek came slowly back into the room.

'What do you mean?'

The Comte's agreeable smile flashed forth once more.

'Surely it is not necessary to go into details,' he purred. 'Seek whom the crime benefits, they say, don't they? As I said just now, you have come into a lot of money lately.'

Derek laughed.

'If that is all –' he said contemptuously.

But the Comte was shaking his head.

'But it is not all, my dear sir. I should not come to you unless I had much more precise and detailed information than that. It is not agreeable, Monsieur, to be arrested and tried for murder.'

Derek came close up to him. His face expressed such furious anger that involuntarily the Comte drew back a pace or two.

'Are you threatening *me*?' the young man demanded angrily.

'You shall hear nothing more of the matter,' the Comte assured him.

'Of all the colossal bluffs that I have ever struck –'

The Comte raised a white hand.

'You are wrong. It is not a bluff. To convince you I will tell you this. My information was obtained from a certain lady. It is she who holds the irrefutable proof that you committed the murder.'

'She? Who?'

'Mademoiselle Mirelle.'

Derek drew back as though struck.

'Mirelle,' he muttered.

The Comte was quick to press what he took to be his advantage.

'A bagatelle of one hundred thousand francs,' he said. 'I ask no more.'

'Eh?' said Derek absently.

'I was saying, Monsieur, that a bagatelle of one hundred thousand francs would satisfy my – conscience.'

Derek seemed to recollect himself. He looked earnestly at the Comte.

'You would like my answer now?'

'If you please, Monsieur.'

'Then here it is. You can go to the devil. See?'

Leaving the Comte too astonished to speak, Derek turned on his heel and swung out of the room.

Once out of the hotel he hailed a taxi and drove to Mirelle's hotel. On inquiring, he learned that the dancer had just come in. Derek gave the concierge his card.

'Take this up to Mademoiselle and ask if she will see me.'

A very brief interval elapsed, and then Derek was bidden to follow a chasseur.

A wave of exotic perfume assailed Derek's nostrils as he stepped over the threshold of the dancer's apartments. The room was filled with carnations, orchids, and mimosa. Mirelle was standing by the window in a *peignoir* of foamy lace.

She came towards him, her hands outstretched.

'Dereek – you have come to me. I knew you would.'

He put aside the clinging arms and looked down on her sternly.

'Why did you send the Comte de la Roche to me?'

She looked at him in astonishment, which he took to be genuine.

'I? Send the Comte de la Roche to you? But for what?'

'Apparently – for blackmail,' said Derek grimly.

Again she stared. Then suddenly she smiled and nodded her head.

'Of course. It was to be expected. It is what he would do, *ce type là*. I might have known it. No, indeed, Dereek, I did not send him.'

He looked at her piercingly, as though seeking to read her mind.

'I will tell you,' said Mirelle. 'I am ashamed, but I will tell you. The other day, you comprehend, I was mad with rage, quite mad' – she made an eloquent gesture. 'My temperament, it is not a patient one. I want to be revenged on you, and so I go to the Comte de la Roche, and I tell him to go to the police and say so and so, and so and so. But have no fear, Dereek. Not completely did I lose my head; the proof rests with me alone. The police can do nothing without my word, you understand? And now – now?'

She nestled up close to him, looking at him with melting eyes.

He thrust her roughly away from him. She stood there, her breast heaving, her eyes narrowing to a cat-like slit.

'Be careful, Dereek, be very careful. You have come back to me, have you not?'

'I shall never come back to you,' said Derek steadily.

'Ah!'

More than ever the dancer looked like a cat. Her eyelids flickered.

'So there is another woman? The one with whom you lunched that day. Eh! am I right?'

'I intend to ask that lady to marry me. You might as well know.'

'That prim Englishwoman! Do you think that I will support that for one moment? Ah, no.' Her beautiful lithe body quivered. 'Listen, Dereek, do you remember that conversation we had in London? You said the only thing that could save you was the death of your wife. You regretted that she was so healthy. Then the idea of an accident came to your brain. And more than an accident.'

'I suppose,' said Derek contemptuously, 'that it was this conversation that you repeated to the Comte de la Roche.'

Mirelle laughed.

'Am I a fool? Could the police do anything with a vague story like that? See – I will give you a last chance. You shall give up this Englishwoman. You shall return to me. And then, *chéri*, never, never will I breathe –'

'Breathe what?'

She laughed softly. 'You thought no one saw you –'

'What do you mean?'

'As I say, you thought no one saw you – but *I* saw you, Dereek, *mon ami; I saw you coming out of the compartment of Madame your wife just before the train got into Lyons that night.* And I know more than that. I know that when you came out of her compartment she was dead.'

He stared at her. Then, like a man in a dream, he turned very slowly and went out of the room, swaying slightly as he walked.

CHAPTER XXVI

A Warning

'And so it is,' said Poirot, 'that we are the good friends and have no secrets from each other.'

Katherine turned her head to look at him. There was something in his voice, some undercurrent of seriousness, which she had not heard before.

They were sitting in the gardens of Monte Carlo. Katherine had come over with her friends, and they had run into Knighton and Poirot almost immediately on arrival. Lady Tamplin had seized upon Knighton and had overwhelmed him with reminiscences, most of which Katherine had a faint suspicion were invented. They had moved away together, Lady Tamplin with her hand on the young man's arm. Knighton had thrown a couple of glances back over his shoulder, and Poirot's eyes twinkled a little as he saw them.

'Of course we are friends,' said Katherine.

'From the beginning we have been sympathetic to each other,' mused Poirot.

'When you told me that a "*roman policier*" occurs in real life.'

'And I was right, was I not?' he challenged her, with an emphatic forefinger. 'Here we are, plunged in the middle of one. That is natural for me – it is my *métier* – but for you it is different. Yes,' he added in a reflective tone, 'for you it is different.'

She looked sharply at him. It was as though he were warning her, pointing out to her some menace that she had not seen.

'Why do you say that I am in the middle of it? It is true that I had that conversation with Mrs Kettering just before she died, but now – now all that is over. I am not connected with the case any more.'

'Ah, Mademoiselle, Mademoiselle, can we ever say, "I have finished with this or that"?'

Katherine turned defiantly round to face him.

'What is it?' she asked. 'You are trying to tell me something – to convey it to me rather. But I am not clever at taking hints. I would much rather that you said anything you have to say straight out.'

Poirot looked at her sadly. '*Ah, mais c'est anglais ça,*' he murmured, 'everything in black and white, everything clear cut and well defined. But life, it is not like that, Mademoiselle. There are the things that are not yet, but which cast their shadow before.'

He dabbed his brow with a very large silk pocket-handkerchief and murmured:

'Ah, but it is that I become poetical. Let us, as you say, speak only of facts. And, speaking of facts, tell me what you think of Major Knighton.'

'I like him very much indeed,' said Katherine warmly; 'he is quite delightful.'

Poirot sighed.

'What is the matter?' asked Katherine.

'You reply so heartily,' said Poirot. 'If you had said in an indifferent voice, "Oh, quite nice," *eh bien*, do you know I should have been better pleased.'

Katherine did not answer. She felt slightly uncomfortable. Poirot went on dreamily:

'And yet, who knows? With *les femmes*, they have so many ways of concealing what they feel – and heartiness is perhaps as good a way as any other.'

He sighed.

'I don't see –' began Katherine.

He interrupted her.

'You do not see why I am being so impertinent, Mademoiselle? I am an old man, and now and then – not very often – I come across someone whose welfare is dear to me. We are friends, Mademoiselle. You have said so yourself. And it is just this – I should like to see you happy.'

Katherine stared very straight in front of her. She had a cretonne sunshade with her, and with its point she traced little designs in the gravel at her feet.

'I have asked you a question about Major Knighton, now I will ask you another. Do you like Mr Derek Kettering?'

'I hardly know him,' said Katherine.

'That is not an answer, that.'

'I think it is.'

He looked at her, struck by something in her tone. Then he nodded his head gravely and slowly.

'Perhaps you are right, Mademoiselle. See you, I who speak to you have seen much of the world, and I know that there are two things which are true. A good man may be ruined by his love for a bad woman – but the other way holds good also. A bad man may equally be ruined by his love for a good woman.'

Katherine looked up sharply.

'When you say ruined –'

'I mean from his point of view. One must be whole-hearted in crime as in everything else.'

'You are trying to warn me,' said Katherine in a low voice. 'Against whom?'

'I cannot look into your heart, Mademoiselle; I do not think you would let me if I could. I will just say this. There are men who have a strange fascination for women.'

'The Comte de la Roche,' said Katherine, with a smile.

'There are others – more dangerous than the Comte de la Roche. They have qualities that appeal – recklessness, daring, audacity. You are fascinated, Mademoiselle; I see that, but I think that it is no more than that. I hope so. This man of whom I speak, the emotion he feels is genuine enough, but all the same –'

'Yes?'

He got up and stood looking down at her. Then he spoke in a low, distinct voice:

'You could, perhaps, love a thief, Mademoiselle, *but not a murderer.*'

He wheeled sharply away on that and left her sitting there.

He heard the little gasp she gave and paid no attention. He had said what he meant to say. He left her there to digest that last unmistakable phrase.

Derek Kettering, coming out of the Casino into the sunshine, saw her sitting alone on the bench and joined her.

'I have been gambling,' he said, with a light laugh, 'gambling unsuccessfully. I have lost everything – everything, that is, that I have with me.'

Katherine looked at him with a troubled face. She was aware at once of something new in his manner, some hidden excitement that betrayed itself in a hundred different infinitesimal signs.

'I should think you were always a gambler. The spirit of gambling appeals to you.'

'Every day and in every way a gambler? You are about right. Don't *you* find something stimulating in it? To risk all on one throw – there is nothing like it.'

Calm and stolid as she believed herself to be, Katherine felt a faint answering thrill.

'I want to talk to you,' went on Derek, 'and who knows when I may have another opportunity? There is an idea going about that I murdered my wife – no, please don't interrupt. It is absurd, of course.' He paused for a minute or two, then went on, speaking more deliberately. 'In dealing with the police and Local Authorities here I have had to pretend to – well – a certain decency. I prefer not to pretend with you. I meant to marry money. I was on the lookout for money when I first met Ruth Van Aldin. She had the look of a slim Madonna about her, and – I – well – I made all sorts of good resolutions – and was bitterly disillusioned. My wife was in love with another man when she married me. She never cared for me in the least. Oh, I am not complaining; the thing was a perfectly respectable bargain. She wanted Leconbury and I wanted money. The trouble arose simply through Ruth's American blood. Without caring a pin for me, she would have liked me to be continually dancing attendance. Time and again she as good as told me that she had bought me and that I belonged to her. The result was that

I behaved abominably to her. My father-in-law will tell you that, and he is quite right. At the time of Ruth's death, I was faced with absolute disaster.' He laughed suddenly. 'One *is* faced with absolute disaster when one is up against a man like Rufus Van Aldin.'

'And then?' asked Katherine in a low voice.

'And then,' Derek shrugged his shoulders, 'Ruth was murdered – very providentially.'

He laughed, and the sound of his laugh hurt Katherine. She winced.

'Yes,' said Derek, 'that wasn't in very good taste. But it is quite true. Now I am going to tell you something more. From the very first moment I saw you I knew you were the only woman in the world for me. I was – afraid of you. I thought you might bring me bad luck.'

'Bad luck?' said Katherine sharply.

He stared at her. 'Why do you repeat it like that? What have you got in your mind?'

'I was thinking of things that people have said to me.'

Derek grinned suddenly. 'They will say a lot to you about me, my dear, and most of it will be true. Yes, and worse things too – things that I shall never tell you. I have been a gambler always – and I have taken some long odds, I shan't confess to you now or at any other time. The past is done with. There is one thing I do wish you to believe. I swear to you solemnly that I did not kill my wife.'

He said the words earnestly enough, yet there was somehow a theatrical touch about them. He met her troubled gaze and went on:

'I know. I lied the other day. It *was* my wife's compartment I went into.'

'Ah,' said Katherine.

'It's difficult to explain just why I went in, but I'll try. I did it on an impulse. You see, I was more or less spying on my wife. I kept out of sight on the train. Mirelle had told me that my wife was meeting the Comte de la Roche in Paris. Well, as far as I had seen, that was not so. I felt ashamed, and I thought suddenly that it would be a good thing to have it out with her once and for all, so I pushed open the door and went in.'

He paused.

'Yes,' said Katherine gently.

'Ruth was lying on the bunk asleep – her face was turned away from me – I could only see the back of her head. I could have woken her up, of course. But suddenly I felt a reaction. What, after all, was there to say that we hadn't both of us said a hundred times before? She looked so peaceful lying there. I left the compartment as quietly as I could.'

'Why lie about it to the police?' asked Katherine.

'Because I'm not a complete fool. I've realized from the beginning that, from the point of view of motive, I'm the ideal murderer. If I once admitted that I had been in her compartment just before she was murdered, I'd do for myself once and for all.'

'I see.'

Did she see? She could not have told herself. She was feeling the magnetic attraction of Derek's personality, but there was something in her that resisted, that held back . . .

'Katherine –'

'I –'

'You know that I care for you. Do – do you care for me?'

'I – I don't know.'

Weakness there. Either she knew or she did not know. If – if only –

She cast a look round desperately as though seeking something that would help her. A soft colour rose in her cheeks as a tall fair man with a limp came hurrying along the path towards them – Major Knighton.

There was relief and an unexpected warmth in her voice as she greeted him.

Derek stood up, scowling, his face black as a thunder-cloud.

'Lady Tamplin having a flutter?' he said easily. 'I must join her and give her the benefit of my system.'

He swung round on his heel and left them together. Katherine sat down again. Her heart was beating rapidly and unevenly, but as she sat there, talking commonplaces to the quiet, rather shy man beside her, her self-command came back.

Then she realized with a shock that Knighton also was laying bare his heart, much as Derek had done, but in a very different manner.

He was shy and stammering. The words came haltingly with no eloquence to back them.

'From the first moment I saw you – I – I ought not to have spoken so soon – but Mr Van Aldin may leave here any day, and I might not have another chance. I know you can't care for me so soon – that is impossible. I dare say it is presumption anyway on my part. I have private means, but not very much – no, please don't answer now. I know what your answer would be. But in case I went away suddenly I just wanted you to know – that I care.'

She was shaken – touched. His manner was so gentle and appealing.

'There's one thing more. I just wanted to say that if – if you are ever in trouble, anything that I can do –'

He took her hand in his, held it tightly for a minute, then dropped it and walked rapidly away towards the Casino without looking back.

Katherine sat perfectly still, looking after him. Derek Kettering – Richard Knighton – two men so different – so very different. There was something kind about Knighton, kind and trustworthy. As to Derek –

Then suddenly Katherine had a very curious sensation. She felt that she was no longer sitting alone on the seat in the Casino gardens, but that someone was standing beside her, and that that someone was the dead woman, Ruth Kettering. She had a further impression that Ruth wanted – badly – to tell her something. The impression was so curious, so vivid, that it could not be driven away. She felt absolutely certain that the spirit of Ruth Kettering was trying to convey something of vital importance to her. The impression faded. Katherine got up, trembling a little. What was it that Ruth Kettering had wanted so badly to say?

CHAPTER XXVII

Interview with Mirelle

When Knighton left Katherine he went in search of Hercule Poirot, whom he found in the Rooms, jauntily placing the minimum stake on the even numbers. As Knighton joined him, the number thirty-three turned up, and Poirot's stake was swept away.

'Bad luck!' said Knighton; 'are you going to stake again?'

Poirot shook his head.

'Not at present.'

'Do you feel the fascination of gambling?' asked Knighton curiously.

'Not at roulette.'

Knighton shot a swift glance at him. His own face became troubled. He spoke haltingly, with a touch of deference.

'I wonder, are you busy, M. Poirot? There is something I would like to ask you about.'

'I am at your disposal. Shall we go outside? It is pleasant in the sunshine.'

They strolled out together, and Knighton drew a deep breath.

'I love the Riviera,' he said. 'I came here first twelve years ago, during the War, when I was sent to Lady Tamplin's Hospital. It was like Paradise, coming from Flanders to this.'

'It must have been,' said Poirot.

'How long ago the War seems now!' mused Knighton.

They walked on in silence for some little way.

'You have something on your mind?' said Poirot.

Knighton looked at him in some surprise.

'You are quite right,' he confessed. 'I don't know how you knew it, though.'

'It showed itself only too plainly,' said Poirot drily.

'I did not know that I was so transparent.'

'It is my business to observe the physiognomy,' the little man explained, with dignity.

'I will tell you, M. Poirot. You have heard of this dancer woman – Mirelle?'

'She who is the *chère amie* of M. Derek Kettering?'

'Yes, that is the one; and, knowing this, you will understand that Mr Van Aldin is naturally prejudiced against her. She wrote to him, asking for an interview. He told me to dictate a curt refusal, which of course I did. This morning she came to the hotel and sent up her card, saying that it was urgent and vital that she should see Mr Van Aldin at once.'

'You interest me,' said Poirot.

'Mr Van Aldin was furious. He told me what message to send down to her. I ventured to disagree with him. It seemed to me both likely and probable that this woman Mirelle might give us valuable information. We know that she was on the Blue Train, and she may have seen or heard something that it might be vital for us to know. Don't you agree with me, M. Poirot?'

'I do,' said Poirot drily. 'M. Van Aldin, if I may say so, behaved exceedingly foolishly.'

'I am glad you take that view of the matter,' said the secretary. 'Now I am going to tell you something, M. Poirot. So strongly did I feel the unwisdom of Mr Van Aldin's attitude that I went down privately and had an interview with the lady.'

'*Eh bien?*'

'The difficulty was that she insisted on seeing Mr Van Aldin himself. I softened his message as much as I possibly could. In fact – to be candid – I gave it in a very different form. I said that Mr Van Aldin was too busy to see her at present, but that she might make any communication she wished to me. That, however, she could not bring herself to do, and she left without saying anything further. But I have a strong impression, M. Poirot, that that woman knows something.'

'This is serious,' said Poirot quietly. 'You know where she is staying?'

'Yes.' Knighton mentioned the name of the hotel.

'Good,' said Poirot; 'we will go there immediately.'

The secretary looked doubtful.

'And Mr Van Aldin?' he queried doubtfully.

'M. Van Aldin is an obstinate man,' said Poirot drily. 'I do not argue with obstinate men. I act in spite of them. We will go and see the lady immediately. I will tell her that you are empowered by M. Van Aldin to act for him, and you will guard yourself well from contradicting me.'

Knighton still looked doubtful, but Poirot took no notice of his hesitation.

At the hotel, they were told that Mademoiselle was in, and Poirot sent up both his and Knighton's cards, with 'From Mr Van Aldin' pencilled upon them.

Word came down that Mademoiselle Mirelle would receive them.

When they were ushered into the dancer's apartments, Poirot immediately took the lead.

'Mademoiselle,' he murmured, bowing very low, 'we are here on behalf of M. Van Aldin.'

'Ah! And why did he not come himself?'

'He is indisposed,' said Poirot mendaciously; 'the Riviera throat, it has him in its grip, but me, I am empowered to act for him, as is Major Knighton, his secretary. Unless, of course, Mademoiselle would prefer to wait a fortnight or so.'

If there was one thing of which Poirot was tolerably certain, it was that to a temperament such as Mirelle's the mere word 'wait' was anathema.

'*Eh bien*, I will speak, Messieurs,' she cried. 'I have been patient. I have held my hand. And for what? That I should be insulted! Yes, insulted! Ah! Does he think to treat Mirelle like that? To throw her off like an old glove. I tell you never has a man tired of me. Always it is I who tire of them.'

She paced up and down the room, her slender body trembling with rage. A small table impeded her free passage, and she flung it from her into a corner, where it splintered against the wall.

'That is what I will do to him,' she cried, 'and that!'

Picking up a glass bowl filled with lilies she flung it into the grate, where it smashed into a hundred pieces.

Knighton was looking at her with cold British disapproval. He felt embarrassed and ill at ease. Poirot, on the other hand, with twinkling eyes was thoroughly enjoying the scene.

'Ah, it is magnificent!' he cried. 'It can be seen – Madame has a temperament.'

'I am an artist,' said Mirelle; 'every artist has a temperament. I told Dereek to beware, and he would not listen.' She whirled round on Poirot suddenly. 'It is true, is it not, that he wants to marry that English miss?'

Poirot coughed.

'*On m'a dit*,' he murmured, 'that he adores her passionately.'

Mirelle came towards them.

'He murdered his wife,' she screamed. 'There – now you have it! He told me beforehand that he meant to do it. He had got to an *impasse* – zut! he took the easiest way out.'

'You say that M. Kettering murdered his wife.'

'Yes, yes, yes. Have I not told you so?'

'The police,' murmured Poirot, 'will need proof of that – er – statement.'

'I tell you I saw him come out of her compartment that night on the train.'

'When?' asked Poirot sharply.

'Just before the train reached Lyons.'

'You will swear to that, Mademoiselle?'

It was a different Poirot who spoke now, sharp and decisive. 'Yes.'

There was a moment's silence. Mirelle was panting, and her eyes, half defiant, half frightened, went from the face of one man to the other.

'This is a serious matter, Mademoiselle,' said the detective. 'You realize how serious?'

'Certainly I do.'

'That is well,' said Poirot. 'Then you understand, Mademoiselle, that no time must be lost. You will, perhaps, accompany us immediately to the office of the Examining Magistrate.'

Mirelle was taken aback. She hesitated, but, as Poirot had foreseen, she had no loophole for escape.

'Very well,' she muttered, 'I will fetch a coat.'

Left alone together, Poirot and Knighton exchanged glances.

'It is necessary to act while – how do you say it? – the iron is hot,' murmured Poirot. 'She is temperamental; in an hour's time, maybe, she will repent, and she will wish to draw back. We must prevent that at all costs.'

Mirelle reappeared, wrapped in a sand-coloured velvet wrap trimmed with leopard skin. She looked not altogether unlike a leopardess, tawny and dangerous. Her eyes still flashed with anger and determination.

They found M. Caux and the Examining Magistrate together. A few brief introductory words from Poirot, and Mademoiselle Mirelle was courteously entreated to tell her tale. This she did in much the same words as she had done to Knighton and Poirot, though with far more soberness of manner.

'This is an extraordinary story, Mademoiselle,' said M. Carrège slowly. He leant back in his chair, adjusted his pince-nez, and looked keenly and searchingly at the dancer through them.

'You wish us to believe M. Kettering actually boasted of the crime to you beforehand?'

'Yes, yes. She was too healthy, he said. If she were to die it must be an accident – he would arrange it all.'

'You are aware, Mademoiselle,' said M. Carrège sternly, 'that you are making yourself out to be an accessory before the fact?'

'Me? But not the least in the world, Monsieur. Not for a moment did I take that statement seriously. Ah no indeed! I know men, Monsieur; they say many wild things. It would be an odd state of affairs if one were to take all they said *au pied de la lettre.*'

The Examining Magistrate raised his eyebrows.

'We are to take it, then, that you regarded M. Kettering's threats as mere idle words? May I ask, Mademoiselle, what made you throw up your engagements in London and come out to the Riviera?'

Mirelle looked at him with melting black eyes.

'I wished to be with the man I loved,' she said simply. 'Was it so unnatural?'

Poirot interpolated a question gently.

'Was it, then, at M. Kettering's wish that you accompanied him to Nice?'

Mirelle seemed to find a little difficulty in answering this. She hesitated perceptibly before she spoke. When she did, it was with a haughty indifference of manner.

'In such matters I please myself, Monsieur,' she said.

That the answer was not an answer at all was noted by all three men. They said nothing.

'When were you first convinced that M. Kettering had murdered his wife?'

'As I tell you, Monsieur, I saw M. Kettering come out of his wife's compartment just before the train drew in to Lyons. There was a look on his face – ah! at the moment I could not understand it – a look haunted and terrible. I shall never forget it.'

Her voice rose shrilly, and she flung out her arms in an extravagant gesture.

'Quite so,' said M. Carrège.

'Afterwards, when I found that Madame Kettering was dead when the train left Lyons, then – then I knew!'

'And still – you did not go to the police, Mademoiselle,' said the Commissary mildly.

Mirelle glanced at him superbly; she was clearly enjoying herself in the rôle she was playing.

'Shall I betray my lover?' she asked. 'Ah no; do not ask a woman to do that.'

'Yet now –' hinted M. Caux.

'Now it is different. He has betrayed me! Shall I suffer that in silence? . . .'

The Examining Magistrate checked her.

'Quite so, quite so,' he murmured soothingly. 'And now, Mademoiselle, perhaps you will read over the statement of what you have told us, see that it is correct, and sign it.'

Mirelle wasted no time on the document.

'Yes, yes,' she said, 'it is correct.' She rose to her feet. 'You require me no longer, Messieurs?'

'At present, no, Mademoiselle.'

'And Dereek will be arrested?'

'At once, Mademoiselle.'

Mirelle laughed cruelly and drew her fur draperies closer about her.

'He should have thought of this before he insulted me,' she cried.

'There is one little matter' – Poirot coughed apologetically – 'just a matter of detail.'

'Yes?'

'What makes you think that Madame Kettering was dead when the train left Lyons?'

Mirelle stared.

'But she *was* dead.'

'Was she?'

'Yes, of course. I –'

She came to an abrupt stop. Poirot was regarding her intently, and he saw the wary look that came into her eyes.

'I have been told so. Everybody says so.'

'Oh,' said Poirot, 'I was not aware that the fact had been mentioned outside the Examining Magistrate's office.'

Mirelle appeared somewhat discomposed.

'One hears those things,' she said vaguely; 'they get about. Somebody told me. I can't remember who it was.'

She moved to the door. M. Caux sprang forward to open it for her, and as he did so, Poirot's voice rose gently once more.

'And the jewels? Pardon, Mademoiselle. Can you tell me anything about those?'

'The jewels? What jewels?'

'The rubies of Catherine the Great. Since you hear so much, you must have heard of them.'

'I know nothing about any jewels,' said Mirelle sharply.

She went out, closing the door behind her. M. Caux came back to his chair; the Examining Magistrate sighed.

'What a fury!' he said, 'but *diablement chic*. I wonder if she is telling the truth? I think so.'

'There is *some* truth in her story, certainly,' said Poirot. 'We have confirmation of it from Miss Grey. She was looking down the corridor a short time before the train reached Lyons, and she saw M. Kettering go into his wife's compartment.'

'The case against him seems quite clear,' said the Commissary, sighing: 'it is a thousand pities,' he murmured.

'How do you mean?' asked Poirot.

'It has been the ambition of my life to lay the Comte de la Roche by the heels. This time, *ma foi*, I thought we had got him. This other – it is not nearly so satisfactory.'

M. Carrège rubbed his nose.

'If anything goes wrong,' he observed cautiously, 'it will be most awkward. M. Kettering is of the aristocracy. It will get into the newspapers. If we have made a mistake –' He shrugged his shoulders forebodingly.

'The jewels now,' said the Commissary, 'what do you think he has done with them?'

'He took them for a plant, of course,' said M. Carrège; 'they must have been a great inconvenience to him and very awkward to dispose of.'

Poirot smiled.

'I have an idea of my own about the jewels. Tell me, Messieurs, what do you know of a man called the Marquis?'

The Commissary leant forward excitedly.

'The Marquis,' he said, 'the Marquis? Do you think he is mixed up in this affair, M. Poirot?'

'I ask you what you know of him.'

The Commissary made an expressive grimace.

'Not as much as we should like to,' he observed ruefully. 'He works behind the scenes, you understand. He has underlings who do his dirty work for him. But he is someone high up. That we are sure of. He does not come from the criminal classes.'

'A Frenchman?'

'Y – es. At least we believe so. But we are not sure. He has worked in France, in England, in America. There was a series of robberies in Switzerland last autumn which were laid at his door. By all accounts he is a *grand seigneur*, speaking French and English with equal perfection, and his origin is a mystery.'

Poirot nodded and rose to take his departure.

'Can you tell us nothing more, M. Poirot?' urged the Commissary.

'At present, no,' said Poirot, 'but I may have news awaiting me at my hotel.'

M. Carrège looked uncomfortable. 'If the Marquis is concerned in this –' he began, and then stopped.

'It upsets our ideas,' complained M. Caux.

'It does not upset mine,' said Poirot. 'On the contrary, I think it agrees with them very well. Au revoir, Messieurs; if news of any importance comes to me I will communicate it to you immediately.'

He walked back to his hotel with a grave face. In his absence, a telegram had come for him. Taking a paper-cutter from his pocket, he slit it open. It was a long telegram, and he read it over twice before slowly putting it in his pocket. Upstairs, George was awaiting his master.

'I am fatigued, Georges, much fatigued. Will you order for me a small pot of chocolate?'

The chocolate was duly ordered and brought, and George set it at the little table at his master's elbow. As he was preparing to retire, Poirot spoke:

'I believe, Georges, that you have a good knowledge of the English aristocracy?' murmured Poirot.

George smiled apologetically.

'I think that I might say that I have, sir,' he replied.

'I suppose that it is your opinion, Georges, that criminals are invariably drawn from the lower orders?'

'Not always, sir. There was great trouble with one of the Duke of Devizes' younger sons. He left Eton under a cloud, and after that he caused great anxiety on several occasions. The police would not accept the view that it was kleptomania. A very clever young gentleman, sir, but vicious through and through, if you take my meaning. His Grace shipped him to Australia, and I hear he was convicted out there under another name. Very odd, sir, but there it is. The young gentleman, I need hardly say, was not in want financially.'

Poirot nodded his head slowly.

'Love of excitement,' he murmured, 'and a little kink in the brain somewhere. I wonder now –'

He drew out the telegram from his pocket and read it again.

'Then there was Lady Mary Fox's daughter,' continued the valet in a mood of reminiscence. 'Swindled tradespeople something shocking, she did. Very worrying to the best families, if I may say so, and there are many other queer cases I could mention.'

'You have a wide experience, Georges,' murmured Poirot. 'I often wonder having lived so exclusively with titled families that you demean yourself by coming as a valet to me. I put it down to love of excitement on your part.'

'Not exactly, sir,' said George. 'I happened to see in *Society Snippets* that you had been received at Buckingham Palace. That was just when I was looking for a new situation. His Majesty, so it said, had been most gracious and friendly and thought very highly of your abilities.'

'Ah,' said Poirot, 'one always likes to know the reason for things.'

He remained in thought for a few moments and then said:

'You rang up Mademoiselle Papopolous?'

'Yes, sir; she and her father will be pleased to dine with you tonight.'

'Ah,' said Poirot thoughtfully. He drank off his chocolate, set the cup and saucer neatly in the middle of the tray, and spoke gently, more to himself than to the valet.

'The squirrel, my good Georges, collects nuts. He stores them up in the autumn so that they may be of advantage to him later. To make a success of humanity, Georges, we must profit by the lessons of those below us in the animal kingdom. I have always done so. I have been the cat, watching the mouse hole. I have been the good dog following up the scent, and not taking my nose from the trail. And also, my good Georges, I have been the squirrel. I have stored away the little fact here, the little fact there. I go now to my store and I take out one particular nut, a nut that I stored away – let me see, seventeen years ago. You follow me, Georges?'

'I should hardly have thought, sir,' said George, 'that nuts would have kept so long as that, though I know one can do wonders with preserving bottles.'

Poirot looked at him and smiled.

CHAPTER XXVIII

Poirot Plays the Squirrel

Poirot started to keep his dinner appointment with a margin of three-quarters of an hour to spare. He had an object in this. The car took him, not straight to Monte Carlo, but to Lady Tamplin's house at Cap Martin, where he asked for Miss Grey. The ladies were dressing and Poirot was shown into a small salon to wait, and here, after a lapse of three or four minutes, Lenox Tamplin came to him.

'Katherine is not quite ready yet,' she said. 'Can I give her a message, or would you rather wait until she comes down?'

Poirot looked at her thoughtfully. He was a minute or two in replying, as though something of great weight hung upon his decision. Apparently the answer to such a simple question mattered.

'No,' he said at last. 'No, I do not think it is necessary that I should wait to see Mademoiselle Katherine. I think perhaps, that it is better that I should not. These things are sometimes difficult.'

Lenox waited politely, her eyebrows slightly raised.

'I have a piece of news,' continued Poirot. 'You will, perhaps, tell your friend. M. Kettering was arrested tonight for the murder of his wife.'

'You want me to tell Katherine that?' asked Lenox. She breathed rather hard, as though she had been running; her face, Poirot thought, looked white and strained – rather noticeably so.

'If you please, Mademoiselle.'

'Why?' said Lenox. 'Do you think Katherine will be upset? Do you think she cares?'

'I don't know, Mademoiselle,' said Poirot. 'See, I admit it

frankly. As a rule I know everything, but in this case, I – well, I do not. You, perhaps, know better than I do.'

'Yes,' said Lenox, 'I know – but I am not going to tell you all the same.'

She paused for a minute or two, her dark brows drawn together in a frown.

'You believe he did it?' she said abruptly.

Poirot shrugged his shoulders.

'The police say so.'

'Ah,' said Lenox, 'hedging, are you? So there is something to hedge about.'

Again she was silent, frowning. Poirot said gently:

'You have known Derek Kettering a long time, have you not?'

'Off and on ever since I was a kid,' said Lenox gruffly. Poirot nodded his head several times without speaking.

With one of her brusque movements Lenox drew forward a chair and sat down on it, her elbows on the table and her face supported by her hands. Sitting thus, she looked directly across the table at Poirot.

'What have they got to go on?' she demanded. 'Motive, I suppose. Probably came into money at her death.'

'He came into two million.'

'And if she had not died he would have been ruined?'

'Yes.'

'But there must have been more than that,' persisted Lenox. 'He travelled by the same train, I know, but – that would not be enough to go on by itself.'

'A cigarette case with the letter "K" on it which did not belong to Mrs Kettering was found in her carriage, and he was seen by two people entering and leaving the compartment just before the train got into Lyons.'

'What two people?'

'Your friend Miss Grey was one of them. The other was Mademoiselle Mirelle, the dancer.'

'And he, Derek, what has he got to say about it?' demanded Lenox sharply.

'He denies having entered his wife's compartment at all,' said Poirot.

'Fool!' said Lenox crisply, frowning. 'Just before Lyons, you say? Does nobody know when – when she died?'

'The doctors' evidence necessarily cannot be very definite,' said Poirot; 'they are inclined to think that death was unlikely to have occurred after leaving Lyons. And we know this much, that a few moments after leaving Lyons Mrs Kettering was dead.'

'How do you know that?'

Poirot was smiling rather oddly to himself.

'Someone else went into her compartment and found her dead.'

'And they did not rouse the train?'

'No.'

'Why was that?'

'Doubtless they had their reasons.'

Lenox looked at him sharply.

'Do you know the reason?'

'I think so – yes.'

Lenox sat still turning things over in her mind. Poirot watched her in silence. At last she looked up. A soft colour had come into her cheeks and her eyes were shining.

'You think someone on the train must have killed her, but that need not be so at all. What is to stop anyone swinging themselves on to the train when it stopped at Lyons? They could go straight to her compartment, strangle her, and take the rubies and drop off the train again without anyone being the wiser. She may have been actually killed while the train was in Lyons station. Then she would have been alive when Derek went in, and dead when the other person found her.'

Poirot leant back in his chair. He drew a deep breath. He looked across at the girl and nodded his head three times, then he heaved a sigh.

'Mademoiselle,' he said, 'what you have said there is very just – very true. I was struggling in the darkness, and you have shown me a light. There was a point that puzzled me and you have made it plain.'

He got up.

'And Derek?' said Lenox.

'Who knows?' said Poirot, with a shrug of his shoulders. 'But I will tell you this, Mademoiselle. I am not satisfied; no, I, Hercule Poirot, am not yet satisfied. It may be that this very night I shall learn something more. At least, I go to try.'

'You are meeting someone?'

'Yes.'

'Someone who knows something?'

'Someone who might know something. In these matters one must leave no stone unturned. Au revoir, Mademoiselle.'

Lenox accompanied him to the door.

'Have I – helped?' she asked.

Poirot's face softened as he looked up at her standing on the doorstep above him.

'Yes, Mademoiselle, you have helped. If things are very dark, always remember that.'

When the car had driven off he relapsed into a frowning absorption, but in his eyes was that faint green light which was always the precursor of the triumph to be.

He was a few minutes late at the rendezvous, and found that M. Papopolous and his daughter had arrived before him. His apologies were abject, and he outdid himself in politeness and small attentions. The Greek was looking particularly benign and noble this evening, a sorrowful patriarch of blameless life. Zia was looking handsome and good-humoured. The dinner was a pleasant one. Poirot was his best and most sparkling self. He told anecdotes, he made jokes, he paid graceful compliments to Zia Papopolous, and he told many interesting incidents of his career. The menu was a carefully selected one, and the wine was excellent.

At the close of dinner M. Papopolous inquired politely:

'And the tip I gave you? You have had your little flutter on the horse?'

'I am in communication with – er – my bookmaker,' replied Poirot.

The eyes of the two men met.

'A well-known horse, eh?'

'No,' said Poirot; 'it is what our friends, the English, call a dark horse.'

'Ah!' said M. Papopolous thoughtfully.

'Now we must step across to the Casino and have our little flutter at the roulette table,' cried Poirot gaily.

At the Casino the party separated, Poirot devoting himself solely to Zia, whilst Papopolous himself drifted away.

Poirot was not fortunate, but Zia had a run of good luck, and had soon won a few thousand francs.

'It would be as well,' she observed drily to Poirot, 'if I stopped now.'

Poirot's eyes twinkled.

'Superb!' he exclaimed. 'You are the daughter of your father, Mademoiselle Zia. To know when to stop. Ah! that is the art.'

He looked round the rooms.

'I cannot see your father anywhere about,' he remarked carelessly. 'I will fetch your cloak for you, Mademoiselle, and we will go out in the gardens.'

He did not, however, go straight to the cloakroom. His sharp eyes had seen but a little while before the departure of M. Papopolous. He was anxious to know what had become of the wily Greek. He ran him to earth unexpectedly in the big entrance hall. He was standing by one of the pillars, talking to a lady who had just arrived. The lady was Mirelle.

Poirot sidled unostentatiously round the room. He arrived at the other side of the pillar, and unnoticed by the two who were talking together in an animated fashion – or rather, that is to say, the dancer was talking, Papopolous contributing an occasional monosyllable and a good many expressive gestures.

'I tell you I must have time,' the dancer was saying. 'If you give me time I will get the money.'

'To wait' – the Greek shrugged his shoulders – 'it is awkward.'

'Only a very little while,' pleaded the other. 'Ah! but you must! A week – ten days – that is all I ask. You can be sure of your affair. The money will be forthcoming.'

Papopolous shifted a little and looked round him uneasily –

to find Poirot almost at his elbow with a beaming innocent face.

'*Ah! vous voilà*, M. Papopolous. I have been looking for you. It is permitted that I take Mademoiselle Zia for a little turn in the gardens? Good evening, Mademoiselle.' He bowed very low to Mirelle. 'A thousand pardons that I did not see you immediately.'

The dancer accepted his greetings rather impatiently. She was clearly annoyed at the interruption of her *tête-à-tête*. Poirot was quick to take the hint. Papopolous had already murmured: 'Certainly – but certainly,' and Poirot withdrew forthwith.

He fetched Zia's cloak, and together they strolled out into the gardens.

'This is where the suicides take place,' said Zia.

Poirot shrugged his shoulders. 'So it is said. Men are foolish, are they not, Mademoiselle? To eat, to drink, to breathe the good air, it is a very pleasant thing, Mademoiselle. One is foolish to leave all that simply because one has no money – or because the heart aches. *L'amour*, it causes many fatalities, does it not?'

Zia laughed.

'You should not laugh at love, Mademoiselle,' said Poirot, shaking an energetic forefinger at her. 'You who are young and beautiful.'

'Hardly that,' said Zia; 'you forget that I am thirty-three, M. Poirot. I am frank with you, because it is no good being otherwise. As you told my father it is exactly seventeen years since you aided us in Paris that time.'

'When I look at you, it seems much less,' said Poirot gallantly. 'You were then very much as you are now, Mademoiselle, a little thinner, a little paler, a little more serious. Sixteen years old and fresh from your *pension*. Not quite the *petite pensionnaire*, not quite a woman. You were very delicious, very charming, Mademoiselle Zia; others thought so too, without doubt.'

'At sixteen,' said Zia, 'one is simple and a little fool.'

'That may be,' said Poirot; 'yes, that well may be. At sixteen one is credulous, is one not? One believes what one is told.'

If he saw the quick sideways glance that the girl shot at him, he pretended not to have done so. He continued dreamily: 'It was a curious affair that, altogether. Your father, Mademoiselle, has never understood the true inwardness of it.'

'No?'

'When he asked me for details, for explanations, I said to him thus: "Without scandal, I have got back for you that which was lost. You must ask no questions." Do you know, Mademoiselle, why I said these things?'

'I have no idea,' said the girl coldly.

'It was because I had a soft spot in my heart for a little *pensionnaire*, so pale, so thin, so serious.'

'I don't understand what you are talking about,' cried Zia angrily.

'Do you not, Mademoiselle? Have you forgotten Antonio Pirezzio?' He heard the quick intake of her breath – almost a gasp.

'He came to work as an assistant in the shop, but not thus could he have got hold of what he wanted. An assistant can lift his eyes to his master's daughter, can he not? If he is young and handsome with a glib tongue. And since they cannot make love all the time, they must occasionally talk of things that interest them both – such as that very interesting thing which was temporarily in M. Papopolous' possession. And since, as you say, Mademoiselle, the young are foolish and credulous, it was easy to believe him and to give him a sight of that particular thing, to show him where it was kept. And afterwards when it is gone – when the unbelievable catastrophe has happened – Alas! the poor little *pensionnaire*. What a terrible position she is in. She is frightened, the poor little one. To speak or not to speak? And then there comes along that excellent fellow, Hercule Poirot. Almost a miracle it must have been, the way things arranged themselves. The priceless heirlooms are restored and there are no awkward questions.'

Zia turned on him fiercely.

'You have known all the time? Who told you? Was it – was it Antonio?'

Poirot shook his head.

'No one told me,' he said quietly. 'I guessed. It was a good guess, was it not, Mademoiselle? You see, unless you are good at guessing, it is not much use being a detective.'

The girl walked along beside him for some minutes in silence. Then she said in a hard voice:

'Well, what are you going to do about it; are you going to tell my father?'

'No,' said Poirot sharply. 'Certainly not.'

She looked at him curiously.

'You want something from me?'

'I want your help, Mademoiselle.'

'What makes you think that I can help you?'

'I do not think so. I only hope so.'

'And if I do not help you, then – you will tell my father?'

'But no, but no! Debarrass yourself of that idea, Mademoiselle. I am not a blackmailer. I do not hold your secret over your head and threaten you with it.'

'If I refuse to help you –?' began the girl slowly.

'Then you refuse, and that is that.'

'Then why –?' she stopped.

'Listen, and I will tell you why. Women, Mademoiselle, are generous. If they can render a service to one who has rendered a service to them, they will do it. I was generous once to you, Mademoiselle. When I might have spoken, I held my tongue.'

There was another silence; then the girl said, 'My father gave you a hint the other day.'

'It was very kind of him.'

'I do not think,' said Zia slowly, 'that there is anything that I can add to that.'

If Poirot was disappointed he did not show it. Not a muscle of his face changed.

'*Eh bien!*' he said cheerfully, 'then we must talk of other things.'

And he proceeded to chat gaily. The girl was *distraite*, however, and her answers were mechanical and not always to the point. It was when they were approaching the Casino once more that she seemed to come to a decision.

'M. Poirot?'

'Yes, Mademoiselle?'

'I – I should like to help you if I could.'

'You are very amiable, Mademoiselle – very amiable.'

Again there was a pause. Poirot did not press her. He was quite content to wait and let her take her own time.

'Ah bah,' said Zia, 'after all, why should I not tell you? My father is cautious – always cautious in everything he says. But I know that with you it is not necessary. You have told us it is only the murderer you seek, and that you are not concerned over the jewels. I believe you. You were quite right when you guessed that we were in Nice because of the rubies. They have been handed over here according to plan. My father has them now. He gave you a hint the other day as to who our mysterious client was.'

'The Marquis?' murmured Poirot softly.

'Yes, the Marquis.'

'Have you ever seen the Marquis, Mademoiselle Zia?'

'Once,' said the girl. 'But not very well,' she added. 'It was through a keyhole.'

'That always presents difficulties,' said Poirot sympathetically, 'but all the same you saw him. You would know him again?'

Zia shook her head.

'He wore a mask,' she explained.

'Young or old?'

'He had white hair. It may have been a wig, it may not. It fitted very well. But I do not think he was old. His walk was young, and so was his voice.'

'His voice?' said Poirot thoughtfully. 'Ah, his voice! Would you know it again, Mademoiselle Zia?'

'I might,' said the girl.

'You were interested in him, eh? It was that that took you to the keyhole?'

Zia nodded.

'Yes, yes, I was curious. One had heard so much – he is not the ordinary thief – he is more like a figure of history or romance.'

'Yes,' said Poirot thoughtfully; 'yes, perhaps so.'

'But it is not this that I meant to tell you,' said Zia. 'It was just one other little fact that I thought might be – well – useful to you.'

'Yes?' said Poirot encouragingly.

'The rubies, as I say, were handed over to my father here at Nice. I did not see the person who handed them over, but –'

'Yes?'

'I know one thing. *It was a woman.*'

CHAPTER XXIX

A Letter from Home

Dear Katherine, – Living among grand friends as you are doing now, I don't suppose you will care to hear any of our news; but as I always thought you were a sensible girl, perhaps you are a trifle less swollen-headed than I suppose. Everything goes on much the same here. There was great trouble about the new curate, who is scandalously high. In my view, he is neither more nor less than a Roman. Everybody has spoken to the Vicar about it, but you know what the Vicar is – all Christian charity and no proper spirit. I have had a lot of trouble with maids lately. That girl Annie was no good – skirts up to her knees and wouldn't wear sensible woollen stockings. Not one of them can bear being spoken to. I have had a lot of pain with my rheumatism one way and another, and Dr Harris persuaded me to go and see a London specialist – a waste of three guineas and a railway fare, as I told him; but by waiting until Wednesday I managed to get a cheap return. The London doctor pulled a long face and talked all round about and never straight out, until I said to him, "I'm a plain woman, Doctor, and I like things to be plainly stated. Is it cancer, or is it not?" And then, of course, he had to say it was. They say a year with care, and not too much pain, though I'm sure I can bear pain as well as any other Christian woman. Life seems rather lonely at times, with most of my friends dead or gone before. I wish you were in St Mary Mead, my dear, and that is a fact. If you hadn't come into this money and gone off into grand society, I would have offered you double the salary poor Jane gave you to come and look after me; but there – there's no good wanting what we can't get. However, if things should go ill with you – and that is always possible. I have heard no end of tales of bogus noblemen marrying girls and getting hold of their money and then leaving them at the church door. I dare say you are too sensible for anything of the kind to happen to you, but one never knows; and never having had much attention of any kind it might easily go to your head now. So just in case, my dear, remember there is always a home for you here; and though a plain-spoken woman I am a warm-hearted one too. – Your affectionate old friend,

AMELIA VINER.

PS. – I saw a mention of you in the paper with your cousin, Viscountess Tamplin, and I cut it out and put it with my cuttings. I prayed for you on Sunday night that you might be kept from pride and vainglory.

Katherine read this characteristic epistle through twice, then she laid it down and stared out of her bedroom window across the blue waters of the Mediterranean. She felt a curious lump in her throat. A sudden wave of longing for St Mary Mead swept over her. So full of familiar, everyday, stupid little things – and yet – home. She felt very inclined to lay her head down on her arms and indulge in a real good cry.

Lenox, coming in at the moment, saved her.

'Hello, Katherine,' said Lenox. 'I say – what is the matter?'

'Nothing,' said Katherine, grabbing up Miss Viner's letter and thrusting it into her handbag.

'You looked rather queer,' said Lenox. 'I say – I hope you don't mind – I rang up your detective friend, M. Poirot, and asked him to lunch with us in Nice. I said you wanted to see him, as I thought he might not come for me.'

'Did you want to see him then?' asked Katherine.

'Yes,' said Lenox. 'I have rather lost my heart to him. I never met a man before whose eyes were really green like a cat's.'

'All right,' said Katherine. She spoke listlessly. The last few days had been trying. Derek Kettering's arrest had been the topic of the hour, and the Blue Train Mystery had been thrashed out from every conceivable standpoint.

'I have ordered the car,' said Lenox, 'and I have told Mother some lie or other – unfortunately I can't remember exactly what; but it won't matter, as she never remembers. If she knew where we were going, she would want to come too, to pump M. Poirot.'

The two girls arrived at the Negresco to find Poirot waiting.

He was full of Gallic politeness, and showered so many compliments upon the two girls that they were soon helpless with laughter; yet for all that the meal was not a gay one. Katherine was dreamy and distracted, and Lenox made bursts of conversation, interspersed by silences. As they were sitting on the terrace sipping their coffee she suddenly attacked Poirot bluntly.

'How are things going? You know what I mean?'

Poirot shrugged his shoulders. 'They take their course,' he said.

'And you are just letting them take their course?'

He looked at Lenox a little sadly.

'You are young, Mademoiselle, but there are three things that cannot be hurried – *le bon Dieu*, Nature, and old people.'

'Nonsense!' said Lenox. 'You are not old.'

'Ah, it is pretty, what you say there.'

'Here is Major Knighton,' said Lenox.

Katherine looked round quickly and then turned back again.

'He is with Mr Van Aldin,' continued Lenox. 'There is something I want to ask Major Knighton about. I won't be a minute.'

Left alone together, Poirot bent forward and murmured to Katherine:

'You are *distraite*, Mademoiselle; your thoughts, they are far away, are they not?'

'Just as far as England, no farther.'

Guided by a sudden impulse, she took the letter she had received that morning and handed it across to him to read.

'That is the first word that has come to me from my old life; somehow or other – it hurts.'

He read it through and then handed it back to her.

'So you are going back to St Mary Mead?' he said.

'No, I am not,' said Katherine; 'why should I?'

'Ah,' said Poirot, 'it is my mistake. You will excuse me one little minute.'

He strolled across to where Lenox Tamplin was talking to Van Aldin and Knighton. The American looked old and haggard. He greeted Poirot with a curt nod but without any other sign of animation.

As he turned to reply to some observation made by Lenox, Poirot drew Knighton aside.

'M. Van Aldin looks ill,' he said.

'Do you wonder?' asked Knighton. 'The scandal of Derek Kettering's arrest has about put the lid on things, as far as he is concerned. He is even regretting that he asked you to find out the truth.'

'He should go back to England,' said Poirot.

'We are going the day after tomorrow.'

'That is good news,' said Poirot.

He hesitated, and looked across the terrace to where Katherine was sitting.

'I wish,' he murmured, 'that you could tell Miss Grey that.'

'Tell her what?'

'That you – I mean that M. Van Aldin is returning to England.'

Knighton looked a little puzzled, but he readily crossed the terrace and joined Katherine.

Poirot saw him go with a satisfied nod of the head, and then joined Lenox and the American. After a minute or two they joined the others. Conversation was general for a few minutes, then the millionaire and his secretary departed. Poirot also prepared to take his departure.

'A thousand thanks for your hospitality, Mesdemoiselles,' he cried; 'it has been a most charming luncheon. *Ma foi*, I needed it!' He swelled out his chest and thumped it. 'I am now a lion – a giant. Ah, Mademoiselle Katherine, you have not seen me as I can be. You have seen the gentle, the calm Hercule Poirot; but there is another Hercule Poirot. I go now to bully, to threaten, to strike terror into the hearts of those who listen to me.'

He looked at them in a self-satisfied way, and they both appeared to be duly impressed, though Lenox was biting her underlip, and the corners of Katherine's mouth had a suspicious twitch.

'And I shall do it,' he said gravely. 'Oh yes, I shall succeed.'

He had gone but a few steps when Katherine's voice made him turn.

'M. Poirot, I – I want to tell you. I think you were quite right in what you said. I am going back to England almost immediately.'

Poirot stared at her very hard, and under the directness of his scrutiny she blushed.

'I see,' he said gravely.

'I don't believe you do,' said Katherine.

'I know more than you think, Mademoiselle,' he said quietly.

He left her, with an odd little smile upon his lips. Entering a waiting car, he drove to Antibes.

Hipolyte, the Comte de la Roche's wooden-faced manservant, was busy at the Villa Marina polishing his master's beautiful cut glass table. The Comte de la Roche himself had gone to Monte Carlo for the day. Chancing to look out of the window, Hipolyte espied a visitor walking briskly up to the hall door, a visitor of so uncommon a type that Hipolyte, experienced as he was, had some difficulty in placing him. Calling to his wife, Marie, who was busy in the kitchen, he drew her attention to what he called *ce type là*.

'It is not the police again?' said Maria anxiously.

'Look for yourself,' said Hipolyte.

Marie looked.

'Certainly not the police,' she declared. 'I am glad.'

'They have not really worried us much,' said Hipolyte. 'In fact, but for Monsieur le Comte's warning, I should never have guessed that stranger at the wine-shop to be what he was.'

The hall bell pealed and Hipolyte, in a grave and decorous manner, went to open the door.

'M. le Comte, I regret to say, is not at home.'

The little man with the large moustaches beamed placidly.

'I know that,' he replied. 'You are Hipolyte Flavelle, are you not?'

'Yes, Monsieur, that is my name.'

'And you have a wife, Marie Flavelle?'

'Yes, Monsieur, but –'

'I desire to see you both,' said the stranger, and he stepped nimbly past Hipolyte into the hall.

'Your wife is doubtless in the kitchen,' he said. 'I will go there.'

Before Hipolyte could recover his breath, the other had selected the right door at the back of the hall and passed along the passage and into the kitchen, where Marie paused open-mouthed to stare at him.

'*Voilà*,' said the stranger, and sank into a wooden arm-chair; 'I am Hercule Poirot.'

'Yes, Monsieur?'

'You do not know the name?'

'I have never heard it,' said Hipolyte.

'Permit me to say that you have been badly educated. It is the name of one of the great ones of this world.'

He sighed and folded his hands across his chest.

Hipolyte and Marie were staring at him uneasily. They were at a loss what to make of this unexpected and extremely strange visitor. 'Monsieur desires –?' murmured Hipolyte mechanically.

'I desire to know why you have lied to the police.'

'Monsieur!' cried Hipolyte; 'I – lied to the police? Never have I done such a thing.'

M. Poirot shook his head.

'You are wrong,' he said; 'you have done it on several occasions. Let me see.' He took a small notebook from his pocket and consulted it. 'Ah, yes; on seven occasions at least. I will recite them to you.'

In a gentle unemotional voice he proceeded to outline the seven occasions.

Hipolyte was taken aback.

'But it is not of these past lapses that I wish to speak,' continued Poirot, 'only, my dear friend, do not get into the habit of thinking yourself too clever. I come now to the particular lie in which I am concerned – your statement that the Comte de la Roche arrived at this villa on the morning of 14th January.'

'But that was no lie, Monsieur; that was the truth. Monsieur le Comte arrived here on the morning of Tuesday, the 14th. That is so, Marie, is it not?'

Marie assented eagerly.

'Ah, yes, that is quite right. I remember it perfectly.'

'Oh,' said Poirot, 'and what did you give your good master for *déjeuner* that day?'

'I –' Marie paused, trying to collect herself.

'Odd,' said Poirot, 'how one remembers some things – and forgets others.'

He leant forward and struck the table a blow with his fist; his eyes flashed with anger.

'Yes, yes, it is as I say. You tell your lies and you think nobody knows. But there are two people who know. Yes – two people. One is *le bon Dieu* –'

He raised a hand to heaven, and then settling himself back in his chair and shutting his eyelids, he murmured comfortably:

'And the other is Hercule Poirot.'

'I assure you, Monsieur, you are completely mistaken. Monsieur le Comte left Paris on Monday night –'

'True,' said Poirot – 'by the Rapide. I do not know where he broke his journey. Perhaps you do not know that. What I do know is that he arrived here on Wednesday morning, and not on Tuesday morning.'

'Monsieur is mistaken,' said Marie stolidly.

Poirot rose to his feet.

'Then the law must take its course,' he murmured. 'A pity.'

'What do you mean, Monsieur?' asked Marie, with a shade of uneasiness.

'You will be arrested and held as accomplices concerned in the murder of Mrs Kettering, the English lady who was killed.'

'Murder!'

The man's face had gone chalk white, his knees knocked together. Marie dropped the rolling-pin and began to weep.

'But it is impossible – impossible. I thought –'

'Since you stick to your story, there is nothing to be said. I think you are both foolish.'

He was turning towards the door when an agitated voice arrested him.

'Monsieur, Monsieur, just a little moment. I – I had no idea that it was anything of this kind. I – I thought it was just a matter concerning a lady. There have been little awkwardnesses with the police over ladies before. But murder – that is very different.'

'I have no patience with you,' cried Poirot. He turned round on them and angrily shook his fist in Hipolyte's face. 'Am I to stop here all day, arguing with a couple of imbeciles thus? It is the truth I want. If you will not give it to me, that is your lookout. *For the last time, when did Monsieur le Comte arrive at the Villa Marina – Tuesday morning or Wednesday morning?*'

'Wednesday,' gasped the man, and behind him Marie nodded confirmation.

Poirot regarded them for a minute or two, then inclined his head gravely.

'You are wise, my children,' he said quietly. 'Very nearly you were in serious trouble.'

He left the Villa Marina, smiling to himself.

'One guess confirmed,' he murmured to himself. 'Shall I take a chance on the other?'

It was six o'clock when the card of Monsieur Hercule Poirot was brought up to Mirelle. She stared at it for a moment or two, and then nodded. When Poirot entered, he found her walking up and down the room feverishly. She turned on him furiously.

'Well?' she cried. 'Well? What is it now? Have you not tortured me enough, all of you? Have you not made me betray my poor Dereek? What more do you want?'

'Just one little question, Mademoiselle. After the train left Lyons, when you entered Mrs Kettering's compartment –'

'What is that?'

Poirot looked at her with an air of mild reproach and began again.

'I say when you entered Mrs Kettering's compartment –'

'I never did.'

'And found her –'

'I never did.'

'*Ah, sacré!*'

He turned on her in a rage and shouted at her, so that she cowered back before him.

'Will you lie to me? I tell you I know what happened as well as though I had been there. You went into her compartment and you found her dead. I tell you I know it. To lie to me is dangerous. Be careful, Mademoiselle Mirelle.'

Her eyes wavered beneath his gaze and fell.

'I – I didn't –' she began uncertainly, and stopped.

'There is only one thing about which I wonder,' said Poirot – 'I wonder, Mademoiselle, if you found what you were looking for or whether –'

'Whether what?'

'Or whether someone else had been before you.'

'I will answer no more questions,' screamed the dancer. She tore herself away from Poirot's restraining hand, and flinging herself down on the floor in a frenzy, she screamed and sobbed. A frightened maid came rushing in.

Hercule Poirot shrugged his shoulders, raised his eyebrows, and quietly left the room.

But he seemed satisfied.

Miss Viner
Gives Judgment

Katherine looked out of Miss Viner's bedroom window. It was raining, not violently, but with a quiet, well-bred persistence. The window looked out on a strip of front garden with a path down to the gate and neat little flower-beds on either side, where later roses and pinks and blue hyacinths would bloom.

Miss Viner was lying in a large Victorian bedstead. A tray with the remains of breakfast had been pushed to one side and she was busy opening her correspondence and making various caustic comments upon it.

Katherine had an open letter in her hand and was reading it through for the second time. It was dated from the Ritz Hotel, Paris.

> Chere Mademoiselle Katherine (It began) – 'I trust that you are in good health and that the return to the English winter has not proved too depressing. Me, I prosecute my inquiries with the utmost diligence. Do not think that it is the holiday that I take here. Very shortly I shall be in England, and I hope then to have the pleasure of meeting you once more. It shall be so, shall it not? On arrival in London I shall write to you. You remember that we are the colleagues in this affair? But indeed I think you know that very well. Be assured, Mademoiselle, of my most respectful and devoted sentiments.
>
> HERCULE POIROT.

Katherine frowned slightly. It was as though something in the letter puzzled and intrigued her.

'A choirboys' picnic indeed,' came from Miss Viner, 'Tommy Saunders and Albert Dykes ought to be left behind, and I shan't subscribe to it unless they are. What those two boys think they are doing in church on Sundays I don't know. Tommy sang, "O God, make speed to save us," and never opened his lips again, and if Albert Dykes wasn't sucking a mint humbug, my nose is not what it is and always has been.'

'I know, they are awful,' agreed Katherine.

She opened her second letter, and a sudden flush came to her cheeks. Miss Viner's voice in the room seemed to recede into the far distance.

When she came back to a sense of her surroundings Miss Viner was bringing a long speech to a triumphant termination.

'And I said to her, "Not at all. As it happens, Miss Grey is Lady Tamplin's own cousin." What do you think of that?'

'Were you fighting my battles for me? That was very sweet of you.'

'You can put it that way if you like. There is nothing to me in a title. Vicar's wife or no vicar's wife, that woman is a cat. Hinting you had bought your way into Society.'

'Perhaps she was not so very far wrong.'

'And look at you,' continued Miss Viner. 'Have you come back a stuck-up fine lady, as well you might have done? No, there you are, as sensible as ever you were, with a pair of good Balbriggan stockings on and your sensible shoes. I spoke to Ellen about it only yesterday. "Ellen," I said, "you look at Miss Grey. She has been hobnobbing with some of the greatest in the land, and does she go about as you do with skirts up to her knees and silk stockings that ladder when you look at them, and the most ridiculous shoes that ever I set eyes on?"'

Katherine smiled a little to herself. It had apparently been worth while to conform to Miss Viner's prejudices. The old lady went on with increasing gusto.

'It has been a great relief to me that you have not had your head turned. Only the other day I was looking for my cuttings. I have several about Lady Tamplin and her War Hospital and what not, but I cannot lay my hand upon them. I wish you would look, my dear; your eyesight is better than mine. They are all in a box in the bureau drawer.'

Katherine glanced down at the letter in her hand and was about to speak, but checked herself, and going over to the bureau found the box of cuttings and began to look over them. Since her return to St Mary Mead, her heart had gone out to Miss Viner in admiration of the old woman's stoicism and pluck. She felt that there was little she could do for her old friend, but she knew from experience how much those seemingly small trifles meant to old people.

'Here is one,' she said presently. ' "Viscountess Tamplin, who is running her villa at Nice as an Officers' Hospital, has just been the victim of a sensational robbery, her jewels having been stolen. Amongst them were some very famous emeralds, heirlooms of the Tamplin family." '

'Probably paste,' said Miss Viner; 'a lot of these Society women's jewels are.'

'Here is another,' said Katherine. 'A picture of her. "A charming camera study of Viscountess Tamplin with her little daughter Lenox." '

'Let me look,' said Miss Viner. 'You can't see much of the child's face, can you? But I dare say that is just as well. Things go by contraries in this world and beautiful mothers have hideous children. I dare say the photographer realized that to take the back of the child's head was the best thing he could do for her.'

Katherine laughed.

' "One of the smartest hostesses on the Riviera this season is Viscountess Tamplin, who has a villa at Cap Martin. Her cousin, Miss Grey, who recently inherited a vast fortune in a most romantic manner, is staying with her there." '

'That is the one I wanted,' said Miss Viner. 'I expect there has been a picture of you in one of the papers that I have missed; you know the kind of thing. Mrs Somebody or other Jones-Williams, at the something or other Point-to-Point, usually carrying a shooting-stick and having one foot lifted up in the air. It must be a trial to some of them to see what they look like.'

Katherine did not answer. She was smoothing out the cutting with her finger, and her face had a puzzled, worried look. Then she drew the second letter out of its envelope and mastered its contents once more. She turned to her friend.

'Miss Viner? I wonder – there is a friend of mine, someone I met on the Riviera, who wants very much to come down and see me here.'

'A man?' said Miss Viner.

'Yes.'

'Who is he?'

'He is secretary to Mr Van Aldin, the American millionaire.'

'What is his name?'

'Knighton. Major Knighton.'

'H'm – secretary to a millionaire. And wants to come down here. Now, Katherine, I am going to say something to you for your own good. You are a nice girl and a sensible girl, and though you have your head screwed on the right way about most things, every woman makes a fool of herself once in her life. Ten to one what this man is after is your money.'

With a gesture she arrested Katherine's reply. 'I have been waiting for something of this kind. What is a secretary to a millionaire? Nine times out of ten it is a young man who likes living soft. A young man with nice manners and a taste for luxury and no brains and no enterprise, and if there is anything that is a softer job than being secretary to a millionaire it is marrying a rich woman for her money. I am not saying that you might not be some man's fancy. But you are not young, and though you have a very good complexion you are not a beauty, and what I say to you is, don't make a fool of yourself; but if you are determined to do so, do see that your money is properly tied up on yourself. There, now I have finished. What have you got to say?'

'Nothing,' said Katherine, 'but would you mind if he did come down to see me?'

'I wash my hands of it,' said Miss Viner. 'I have done my duty, and whatever happens now is on your own head. Would you like him to lunch or to dinner? I dare say Ellen could manage dinner – that is, if she didn't lose her head.'

'Lunch would be very nice,' said Katherine. 'It is awfully kind of you, Miss Viner. He asked me to ring him up, so I will do so and say that we shall be pleased if he will lunch with us. He will motor down from town.'

'Ellen does a steak with grilled tomatoes pretty fairly,' said Miss Viner. 'She doesn't do it well, but she does it better than anything else. It is no good having a tart because she is heavy-handed with pastry; but her little castle puddings are not bad, and I dare say you could find a nice piece of Stilton at Abbot's. I have always heard that gentlemen like a nice piece of Stilton, and there is a good deal of Father's wine left, a bottle of sparkling Moselle, perhaps.'

'Oh no, Miss Viner; that is really not necessary.'

'Nonsense, my child. No gentleman is happy unless he drinks something with his meal. There is some good pre-war whisky if you think he would prefer that. Now do as I say and don't argue. The key of the wine-cellar is in the third drawer down in the dressing-table, in the second pair of stockings on the left-hand side.'

Katherine went obediently to the spot indicated.

'The second pair, now mind,' said Miss Viner. 'The first pair has my diamond earrings and my filigree brooch in it.'

'Oh,' said Katherine, rather taken aback, 'wouldn't you like them put in your jewel-case?'

Miss Viner gave vent to a terrific and prolonged snort.

'No, indeed! I have much too much sense for that sort of thing, thank you. Dear, dear, I well remember how my poor father had a safe built in downstairs. Pleased as Punch he was with it, and he said to my mother, "Now, Mary, you bring me your jewels in their case every night and I will lock them away for you." My mother was a very tactful woman, and she knew that gentlemen like having their own way, and she brought him the jewel-case to be locked up just as he said.

'And one night burglars broke in, and of course – naturally

– the first thing they went for was the safe! It would be, with my father talking up and down the village and bragging about it until you might have thought he kept all King Solomon's diamonds there. They made a clean sweep, got the tankards, the silver cups, and the presentation gold plate that my father had had presented to him, *and* the jewel-case.'

She sighed reminiscently. 'My father was in a great state over my mother's jewels. There was the Venetian set and some very fine cameos, and some pale pink corals, and two diamond rings with quite large stones in them. And then, of course, she had to tell him that, being a sensible woman, she had kept her jewellery rolled up in a pair of corsets, and there it was still as safe as anything.'

'And the jewel-case had been quite empty?'

'Oh no, dear,' said Miss Viner, 'it would have been too light a weight then. My mother was a very intelligent woman; she saw to that. She kept her buttons in the jewel-case, and a very handy place it was. Boot buttons in the top tray, trouser buttons in the second tray, and assorted buttons below. Curiously enough, my father was quite annoyed with her. He said he didn't like deceit. But I mustn't go chattering on; you want to go and ring up your friend, and mind you choose a nice piece of steak, and tell Ellen she is not to have holes in her stockings when she waits at lunch.'

'Is her name Ellen or Helen, Miss Viner? I thought –'

Miss Viner closed her eyes.

'I can sound my 'h's, dear, as well as anyone, but Helen is *not* a suitable name for a servant. I don't know what the mothers in the lower classes are coming to nowadays.'

The rain had cleared away when Knighton arrived at the cottage. The pale fitful sunshine shone down on it and burnished Katherine's head as she stood in the doorway to welcome him. He came up to her quickly, almost boyishly.

'I say, I hope you don't mind. I simply had to see you again soon. I hope the friend you are staying with does not mind.'

'Come in and make friends with her,' said Katherine. 'She

can be most alarming, but you will soon find that she has the softest heart in the world.'

Miss Viner was enthroned majestically in the drawing-room, wearing a complete set of the cameos which had been so providentially preserved in the family. She greeted Knighton with dignity and an austere politeness which would have damped many men. Knighton, however, had a charm of manner which was not easily set aside, and after about ten minutes Miss Viner thawed perceptibly. Luncheon was a merry meal, and Ellen, or Helen, in a new pair of silk stockings devoid of ladders, performed prodigies of waiting. Afterwards, Katherine and Knighton went for a walk, and they came back to have tea *tête-à-tête*, since Miss Viner had gone to lie down.

When the car had finally driven off Katherine went slowly upstairs. A voice called her and she went in to Miss Viner's bedroom.

'Friend gone?'

'Yes. Thank you so much for letting me ask him down.'

'No need to thank me. Do you think I am the sort of old curmudgeon who never will do anything for anybody?'

'I think you are a dear,' said Katherine affectionately.

'Humph,' said Miss Viner, mollified.

As Katherine was leaving the room she called her back.

'Katherine?'

'Yes.'

'I was wrong about that young man of yours. A man when he is making up to anybody can be cordial and gallant and full of little attentions and altogether charming. But when a man is really in love he can't help looking like a sheep. Now, whenever that young man looked at you he looked like a sheep. I take back all I said this morning. It is genuine.'

CHAPTER XXXI

Mr Aarons Lunches

'Ah!' said Mr Joseph Aarons appreciatively.

He took a long draught from his tankard, set it down with a sigh, wiped the froth from his lips, and beamed across the table at his host, Monsieur Hercule Poirot.

'Give me,' said Mr Aarons, 'a good Porterhouse steak and a tankard of something worth drinking, and anyone can have your French fallals and whatnots, your ordoovres and your omelettes and your little bits of quail. Give me,' he reiterated, 'a Porterhouse steak.'

Poirot, who had just complied with this request, smiled sympathetically.

'Not that there is much wrong with a steak and kidney pudding,' continued Mr Aarons. 'Apple tart? Yes, I will take apple tart, thank you, Miss, and a jug of cream.'

The meal proceeded. Finally, with a long sigh, Mr Aarons laid down his spoon and fork preparatory to toying with some cheese before turning his mind to other matters.

'There was a little matter of business I think you said, Monsieur Poirot,' he remarked. 'Anything I can do to help you I am sure I shall be most happy.'

'That is very kind of you,' said Poirot. 'I said to myself, "If you want to know anything about the dramatic profession there is one person who knows all that is to be known and that is my old friend, Mr Joseph Aarons."'

'And you don't say far wrong,' said Mr Aarons complacently; 'whether it is past, present, or future, Joe Aarons is the man to come to.'

'*Précisément.* Now I want to ask you, Monsieur Aarons, what you know about a young woman called Kidd.'

'Kidd? Kitty Kidd?'

'Kitty Kidd.'

'Pretty smart, she was. Male impersonator, song and a dance – That one?'

'That is the one.'

'*Very* smart, she was. Made a good income. Never out of an engagement. Male impersonation mostly, but, as a matter of fact, you could not touch her as a character actress.'

'So I have heard,' said Poirot; 'but she has not been appearing lately, has she?'

'No. Dropped right out of things. Went over to France and took up with some swell nobleman there. She quitted the stage then for good and all, I guess.'

'How long ago was that?'

'Let me see. Three years ago. And she has been a loss – let me tell you that.'

'She was clever?'

'Clever as a cartload of monkeys.'

'You don't know the name of the man she became friends with in Paris?'

'He was a swell, I know that. A Count – or was it a Marquis? Now I come to think of it, I believe it was a Marquis.'

'And you know nothing about her since?'

'Nothing. Never even run across her accidentally like. I bet she is tooling it round some of these foreign resorts. Being a Marquise to the life. You couldn't put one over on Kitty. She would give as good as she got any day.'

'I see,' said Poirot thoughtfully.

'I am sorry I can't tell you more, Monsieur Poirot,' said the other. 'I would like to be of use to you if I could. You did me a good turn once.'

'Ah, but we are quits on that; you, too, did me a good turn.'

'One good turn deserves another. Ha, ha!' said Mr Aarons.

'Your profession must be a very interesting one,' said Poirot.

'So-so,' said Mr Aarons non-committally. 'Taking the rough with the smooth, it is all right. I don't do so badly at it, all things considered, but you have to keep your eyes skinned. Never know what the public will jump for next.'

'Dancing has come very much to the fore in the last few years,' murmured Poirot reflectively.

'*I* never saw anything in this Russian ballet, but people like it. Too highbrow for me.'

'I met one dancer out on the Riviera – Mademoiselle Mirelle.'

'Mirelle? She is hot stuff, by all accounts. There is always money going to back her – though, so far as that goes, the girl can dance; I have seen her, and I know what I am talking about. I never had much to do with her myself, but I hear she is a terror to deal with. Tempers and tantrums all the time.'

'Yes,' said Poirot thoughtfully; 'yes, so I should imagine.'

'Temperament!' said Mr Aarons, 'temperament! That is what they call it themselves. My missus was a dancer before she married me, but I am thankful to say she never had any temperament. You don't want temperament in the home, Monsieur Poirot.'

'I agree with you, my friend; it is out of place there.'

'A woman should be calm and sympathetic, and a good cook,' said Mr Aarons.

'Mirelle has not been long before the public, has she?' asked Poirot.

'About two and half years, that is all,' said Mr Aarons. 'Some French duke started her. I hear now that she has taken up with the ex-Prime Minister of Greece. These are the chaps who manage to put money away quietly.'

'That is news to me,' said Poirot.

'Oh, she's not one to let the grass grow under her feet. They say that young Kettering murdered his wife on her account. I don't know, I am sure. Anyway, he is in prison, and she had to look round for herself, and pretty smart she has been about it. They say she is wearing a ruby the size of a pigeon's egg – not that I have ever seen a pigeon's egg myself, but that is what they always call it in works of fiction.'

'A ruby the size of a pigeon's egg!' said Poirot. His eyes were green and catlike. 'How interesting!'

'I had it from a friend of mine,' said Mr Aarons. 'But for all I know, it may be coloured glass. They are all the same, these women – they never stop telling tall stories about their jewels. Mirelle goes about bragging that it has got a curse on it. "Heart of Fire", I think she calls it.'

'But if I remember rightly,' said Poirot, 'the ruby that is named "Heart of Fire" is the centre stone in a necklace.'

'There you are! Didn't I tell you there is no end to the lies women will tell about their jewellery? This is a single stone, hung on a platinum chain round her neck; but, as I said before, ten to one it is a bit of coloured glass.'

'No,' said Poirot gently; 'no – somehow I do not think it is coloured glass.'

CHAPTER XXXII

Katherine and Poirot
Compare Notes

'You have changed, Mademoiselle,' said Poirot suddenly. He and Katherine were seated opposite each other at a small table at the Savoy.

'Yes, you have changed,' he continued.

'In what way?'

'Mademoiselle, these *nuances* are difficult to express.'

'I am older.'

'Yes, you are older. And by that I do not mean that the wrinkles and the crows' feet are coming. When I first saw you, Mademoiselle, you were a looker-on at life. You had the quiet, amused look of one who sits back in the stalls and watches the play.'

'And now?'

'Now you no longer watch. It is an absurd thing, perhaps, that I say here, but you have the wary look of a fighter who is playing a difficult game.'

'My old lady is difficult sometimes,' said Katherine, with a smile; 'but I can assure you that I don't engage in deadly contests with her. You must go down and see her some day, Monsieur Poirot. I think you are one of the people who would appreciate her pluck and her spirit.'

There was a silence while the waiter deftly served them with chicken *en casserole*. When he had departed, Poirot said: 'You have heard me speak of my friend Hastings? – he who said that I was a human oyster. *Eh bien*, Mademoiselle, I have met my match in you. You, far more than I, play a lone hand.'

'Nonsense,' said Katherine lightly.

'Never does Hercule Poirot talk nonsense. It is as I say.'

Again there was a silence. Poirot broke it by inquiring:

'Have you seen any of our Riviera friends since you have been back, Mademoiselle?'

'I have seen something of Major Knighton.'

'A-ha. Is that so?'

Something in Poirot's twinkling eyes made Katherine lower hers.

'So Mr Van Aldin remains in London?'

'Yes.'

'I must try to see him tomorrow or the next day.'

'You have news for him?'

'What makes you think that?'

'I – wondered, that is all.'

Poirot looked across at her with twinkling eyes.

'And now, Mademoiselle, there is much that you wish to ask me, I can see that. And why not? Is not the affair of the Blue Train our own "*roman policier*"?'

'Yes, there are things I should like to ask you.'

'*Eh bien?*'

Katherine looked up with a sudden air of resolution.

'What were you doing in Paris, Monsieur Poirot?'

Poirot smiled slightly.

'I made a call at the Russian Embassy.'

'Oh.'

'I see that that tells you nothing. But I will not be a human oyster. No, I will lay my cards on the table, which is assuredly a thing that oysters never do. You suspect, do you not, that I am not satisfied with the case against Derek Kettering?'

'That is what I have been wondering. I thought, in Nice, that you had finished with the case.'

'You do not say all that you mean, Mademoiselle. But I admit everything. It was I – my researches – which placed Derek Kettering where he now is. But for me the Examining Magistrate would still be vainly trying to fasten the crime on the Comte de la Roche. *Eh bien*, Mademoiselle, what I have done I do not regret. I have only one duty – to discover the truth, and that way led straight to Mr Kettering. But did it end there? The police say yes, but I, Hercule Poirot, am not satisfied.'

He broke off suddenly. 'Tell me, Mademoiselle, have you heard from Mademoiselle Lenox lately?'

'One very short, scrappy letter. She is, I think, annoyed with me for coming back to England.'

Poirot nodded.

'I had an interview with her the night that Monsieur Kettering was arrested. It was an interesting interview in more ways than one.'

Again he fell silent, and Katherine did not interrupt his train of thought. 'Mademoiselle,' he said at last, 'I am now on delicate ground, yet I will say this to you. There is, I think, someone who loves Monsieur Kettering – correct me if I am wrong – and for her sake – well – for her sake I hope that I am right and the police are wrong. You know who that someone is?'

There was a pause, then Katherine said:

'Yes – I think I know.'

Poirot leant across the table towards her.

'I am not satisfied, Mademoiselle; no, I am not satisfied. The facts, the main facts, led straight to Monsieur Kettering. But there is one thing that has been left out of account.'

'And what is that?'

'The disfigured face of the victim. I have asked myself, Mademoiselle, a hundred times, "Was Derek Kettering the kind of man who would deal that smashing blow after having committed the murder?" What end would it serve? What purpose would it accomplish? Was it a likely action for one of Monsieur Kettering's temperament? And, Mademoiselle, the answer to these questions is profoundly unsatisfactory. Again and again I go back to that one point – "why?" And the only things I have to help me to a solution of the problem are these.'

He whipped out his pocket-book and extracted something from it which he held between his finger and thumb.

'Do you remember, Mademoiselle? You saw me take these hairs from the rug in the railway carriage.'

Katherine leant forward, scrutinizing the hairs keenly.

Poirot nodded his head slowly several times.

'They suggest nothing to you, I see that, Mademoiselle. And yet – I think somehow that you see a good deal.'

'I have had ideas,' said Katherine slowly, 'curious ideas. That is why I ask you what you were doing in Paris, Monsieur Poirot.'

'When I wrote to you –'

'From the Ritz?'

A curious smile came over Poirot's face.

'Yes, as you say, from the Ritz. I am a luxurious person sometimes – when a millionaire pays.'

'The Russian Embassy,' said Katherine, frowning. 'No, I don't see where that comes in.'

'It does not come in directly, Mademoiselle. I went there to get certain information. I saw a particular personage and I threatened him – yes, Mademoiselle, I, Hercule Poirot, threatened him.'

'With the police?'

'No,' said Poirot drily, 'with the Press – a much more deadly weapon.'

He looked at Katherine and she smiled at him, just shaking her head.

'Are you not just turning back into an oyster again, Monsieur Poirot?'

'No, no; I do not wish to make mysteries. See, I will tell you everything. I suspect this man of being the active party in the sale of the jewels of Monsieur Van Aldin. I tax him with it, and in the end I get the whole story out of him. I learn where the jewels were handed over, and I learn, too, of the man who paced up and down outside in the street – a man with a venerable head of white hair, but who walked with the light, springy step of a young man – and I give that man a name in my own mind – the name of "Monsieur le Marquis".'

'And now you have come to London to see Mr Van Aldin?'

'Not entirely for that reason. I had other work to do. Since I have been in London I have seen two more people – a theatrical agent and a Harley Street doctor. From each of them I have got certain information. Put these things together, Mademoiselle, and see if you can make of them the same as I do.'

'I?'

'Yes, you. I will tell you one thing, Mademoiselle. There has been a doubt all along in my mind as to whether the robbery and the murder were done by the same person. For a long time I was not sure –'

'And now?'

'And now I *know*.'

There was a silence. Then Katherine lifted her head. Her eyes were shining.

'I am not clever like you, Monsieur Poirot. Half the things that you have been telling me don't seem to me to point anywhere at all. The ideas that came to me came from such an entirely different angle –'

'Ah, but that is always so,' said Poirot quietly. 'A mirror shows the truth, but everyone stands in a different place for looking into the mirror.'

'My ideas may be absurd – they may be entirely different from yours, but –'

'Yes?'

'Tell me, does this help you at all?'

He took a newspaper cutting from her outstretched hand. He read it and, looking up, he nodded gravely.

'As I told you, Mademoiselle, one stands at a different angle for looking into the mirror, but it is the same mirror and the same things are reflected there.'

Katherine got up. 'I must rush,' she said. 'I have only just time to catch my train. Monsieur Poirot –'

'Yes, Mademoiselle.'

'It – it mustn't be much longer, you understand. I – I can't go on much longer.'

There was a break in her voice.

He patted her hand reassuringly.

'Courage, Mademoiselle, you must not fail now; the end is very near.'

CHAPTER XXXIII

A New Theory

'Monsieur Poirot wants to see you, sir.'

'Damn the fellow!' said Van Aldin.

Knighton remained sympathetically silent.

Van Aldin got up from his chair and paced up and down.

'I suppose you have seen the cursed newspapers this morning?'

'I have glanced at them, sir.'

'Still at it hammer and tongs?'

'I am afraid so, sir.'

The millionaire sat down again and pressed his hand to his forehead.

'If I had had an idea of this,' he groaned. 'I wish to God I had never got that little Belgian to ferret out the truth. Find Ruth's murderer – that was all I thought about.'

'You wouldn't have liked your son-in-law to go scot free?'

Van Aldin sighed.

'I would have preferred to take the law into my own hands.'

'I don't think that would have been a very wise proceeding, sir.'

'All the same – are you sure the fellow wants to see me?'

'Yes, Mr Van Aldin. He is very urgent about it.'

'Then I suppose he will have to. He can come along this morning if he likes.'

It was a very fresh and debonair Poirot who was ushered in. He did not seem to see any lack of cordiality in the millionaire's manner, and chatted pleasantly about various trifles. He was in London, he explained, to see his doctor. He mentioned the name of an eminent surgeon.

'No, no, *pas la guerre* – a memory of my days in the police force, a bullet of a rascally apache.'

He touched his left shoulder and winced realistically.

'I always consider you a lucky man, Monsieur Van Aldin; you are not like our popular idea of American millionaires, martyrs to dyspepsia.'

'I am pretty tough,' said Van Aldin. 'I lead a very simple life, you know; plain fare and not too much of it.'

'You have seen something of Miss Grey, have you not?' inquired Poirot, innocently turning to the secretary.

'I – yes; once or twice,' said Knighton.

He blushed slightly and Van Aldin exclaimed in surprise:

'Funny you never mentioned to me that you had seen her, Knighton.'

'I didn't think you would be interested, sir.'

'I like that girl very much,' said Van Aldin.

'It is a thousand pities that she should have buried herself once more in St Mary Mead,' said Poirot.

'It is very fine of her,' said Knighton hotly. 'There are very few people who would bury themselves down there to look after a cantankerous old woman who has no earthly claim on her.'

'I am silent,' said Poirot, his eyes twinkling a little; 'but all the same I say it is a pity. And now, Messieurs, let us come to business.'

Both the other men looked at him in some surprise.

'You must not be shocked or alarmed at what I am about to say. Supposing, Monsieur Van Aldin, that, after all, Monsieur Derek Kettering did not murder his wife?'

'What?'

Both men stared at him in blank surprise.

'Supposing, I say, that Monsieur Kettering did not murder his wife?'

'Are you mad, Monsieur Poirot?'

It was Van Aldin who spoke.

'No,' said Poirot, 'I am not mad. I am eccentric, perhaps – at least certain people say so; but as regards my profession, I am very much, as one says, "all there". I ask you, Monsieur Van

Aldin, whether you would be glad or sorry if what I tell you should be the case?'

Van Aldin stared at him.

'Naturally I should be glad,' he said at last. 'Is this an exercise in suppositions, Monsieur Poirot, or are there any facts behind it?'

Poirot looked at the ceiling.

'There is an off-chance,' he said quietly, 'that it might be the Comte de la Roche after all. At least I have succeeded in upsetting his alibi.'

'How did you manage that?'

Poirot shrugged his shoulders modestly.

'I have my own methods. The exercise of a little tact, a little cleverness – and the thing is done.'

'But the rubies,' said Van Aldin, 'these rubies that the Count had in his possession were false.'

'And clearly he would not have committed the crime except for the rubies. But you are overlooking one point, Monsieur Van Aldin. Where the rubies were concerned, someone might have been before him.'

'But this is an entirely new theory,' cried Knighton.

'Do you really believe all this rigmarole, Monsieur Poirot?' demanded the millionaire.

'The thing is not proved,' said Poirot quietly. 'It is as yet only a theory, but I tell you this, Monsieur Van Aldin, the facts are worth investigating. You must come out with me to the south of France and go into the case on the spot.'

'You really think this is necessary – that I should go, I mean?'

'I thought it would be what you yourself would wish,' said Poirot.

There was a hint of reproach in his tone which was not lost upon the other.

'Yes, yes, of course,' he said. 'When do you wish to start, Monsieur Poirot?'

'You are very busy at present, sir,' murmured Knighton.

But the millionaire had now made up his mind, and he waved the other's objections aside.

'I guess this business comes first,' he said. 'All right, Monsieur Poirot, tomorrow. What train?'

'We will go, I think, by the Blue Train,' said Poirot, and he smiled.

CHAPTER XXXIV

The Blue Train Again

'The Millionaires' Train', as it is sometimes called, swung round a curve of line at what seemed a dangerous speed. Van Aldin, Knighton, and Poirot sat together in silence. Knighton and Van Aldin had two compartments connecting with each other, as Ruth Kettering and her maid had had on the fateful journey. Poirot's own compartment was farther along the coach.

The journey was a painful one for Van Aldin, recalling as it did the most agonizing memories. Poirot and Knighton conversed occasionally in low tones without disturbing him.

When, however, the train had completed its slow journey round the *ceinture* and reached the Gare de Lyon, Poirot became suddenly galvanized into activity. Van Aldin realized that part of his object in travelling by the train had been to attempt to reconstruct the crime. Poirot himself acted every part. He was in turn the maid, hurriedly shut into her own compartment, Mrs Kettering, recognizing her husband with surprise and a trace of anxiety, and Derek Kettering discovering that his wife was travelling on the train. He tested various possibilities, such as the best way for a person to conceal himself in the second compartment.

Then suddenly an idea seemed to strike him. He clutched at Van Aldin's arm.

'*Mon Dieu*, but that is something I have not thought of! We must break our journey in Paris. Quick, quick, let us alight at once.'

Seizing suit-cases he hurried from the train. Van Aldin and Knighton, bewildered but obedient, followed him. Van Aldin having once more formed his opinion of Poirot's ability was slow to depart from it. At the barrier they were held up. Their

634 *Agatha Christie 1920s – Volume Three*

tickets were in the charge of the conductor of the train, a fact which all three of them had forgotten.

Poirot's explanations were rapid, fluent, and impassioned, but they produced no effect upon the stolid-faced official.

'Let us get quit of this,' said Van Aldin abruptly. 'I gather you are in a hurry, Monsieur Poirot. For God's sake pay the fares from Calais and let us get right on with whatever you have got on your mind.'

But Poirot's flood of language had suddenly stopped dead, and he had the appearance of a man turned to stone. His arm, still outflung in an impassioned gesture, remained there as though stricken with paralysis.

'I have been an imbecile,' he said simply. '*Ma foi*, I lose my head nowadays. Let us return and continue our journey quietly. With reasonable luck the train will not have gone.'

They were only just in time, the train moving off as Knighton, the last of the three, swung himself and his suit-case on board.

The conductor remonstrated with them feelingly, and assisted them to carry their luggage back to their compartments. Van Aldin said nothing, but he was clearly disgusted at Poirot's extraordinary conduct. Alone with Knighton for a moment or two, he remarked:

'This is a wild goose chase. The man has lost his grip on things. He has got brains up to a point, but any man who loses his head and scuttles round like a frightened rabbit is no earthly darned good.'

Poirot came to them in a moment or two, full of abject apologies and clearly so crestfallen that harsh words would have been superfluous. Van Aldin received his apologies gravely, but managed to restrain himself from making acid comments.

They had dinner on the train, and afterwards, somewhat to the surprise of the other two, Poirot suggested that they should all three sit up in Van Aldin's compartment.

The millionaire looked at him curiously.

'Is there anything that you are keeping back from us, Monsieur Poirot?'

'I?' Poirot opened his eyes in innocent surprise. 'But what an idea.'

Van Aldin did not answer, but he was not satisfied. The conductor was told that he need not make up the beds. Any surprise he might have felt was obliterated by the largeness of the tip which Van Aldin handed to him. The three men sat in silence. Poirot fidgeted and seemed restless. Presently he turned to the secretary.

'Major Knighton, is the door of your compartment bolted? The door into the corridor, I mean.'

'Yes; I bolted it myself just now.'

'Are you sure?' said Poirot.

'I will go and make sure, if you like,' said Knighton, smiling.

'No, no, do not derange yourself. I will see for myself.'

He passed through the connecting door and returned in a second or two, nodding his head.

'Yes, yes, it is as you said. You pardon an old man's fussy ways.' He closed the connecting door and resumed his place in the right-hand corner.

The hours passed. The three men dozed fitfully, waking with uncomfortable starts. Probably never before had three people booked berths on the most luxurious train available, then declined to avail themselves of the accommodation they had paid for. Every now and then Poirot glanced at his watch, and then nodded his head and composed himself to slumber once more. On one occasion he rose from his seat and opened the connecting door, peered sharply into the adjoining compartment, and then returned to his seat, shaking his head.

'What is the matter?' whispered Knighton. 'You are expecting something to happen, aren't you?'

'I have the nerves,' confessed Poirot. 'I am like the cat upon the hot tiles. Every little noise it makes me jump.'

Knighton yawned.

'Of all the darned uncomfortable journeys,' he murmured. 'I suppose you know what you are playing at, Monsieur Poirot.'

He composed himself to sleep as best he could. Both he and Van Aldin had succumbed to slumber, when Poirot, glancing for the fourteenth time at his watch, leant across and tapped the millionaire on the shoulder.

'Eh? What is it?'

'In five or ten minutes, Monsieur, we shall arrive at Lyons.'

'My God!' Van Aldin's face looked white and haggard in the dim light. 'Then it must have been about this time that poor Ruth was killed.'

He sat staring straight in front of him. His lips twitched a little, his mind reverting back to the terrible tragedy that had saddened his life.

There was the usual long screaming sigh of the brake, and the train slackened speed and drew into Lyons. Van Aldin let down the window and leant out.

'If it wasn't Derek – if your new theory is correct, it is here that the man left the train?' he asked over his shoulder.

Rather to his surprise Poirot shook his head.

'No,' he said thoughtfully, 'no *man* left the train, but I think – yes, I think, a *woman* may have done so.'

Knighton gave a gasp.

'A woman?' demanded Van Aldin sharply.

'Yes, a woman,' said Poirot, nodding his head. 'You may not remember, Monsieur Van Aldin, but Miss Grey in her evidence mentioned that a youth in a cap and overcoat descended on to the platform ostensibly to stretch his legs. Me, I think that that youth was most probably a woman.'

'But who was she?'

Van Aldin's face expressed incredulity, but Poirot replied seriously and categorically:

'Her name – or the name under which she was known, for many years – is Kitty Kidd, but you, Monsieur Van Aldin, knew her by another name – *that of Ada Mason.*'

Knighton sprang to his feet.

'What?' he cried.

Poirot swung round to him.

'Ah! – before I forget it.' He whipped something from a pocket and held it out.

'Permit me to offer you a cigarette – out of your own cigarette-case. It was careless of you to drop it when you boarded the train on the *ceinture* at Paris.'

Knighton stood staring at him as though stupefied. Then he made a movement, but Poirot flung up his hand in a warning gesture.

'No, don't move,' he said in a silky voice; 'the door into the next compartment is open, and you are being covered from there this minute. I unbolted the door into the corridor when we left Paris, and our friends the police were told to take their places there. As I expect you know, the French police want you rather urgently, Major Knighton – or shall we say – Monsieur le Marquis?'

CHAPTER XXXV

Explanations

'Explanations?'

Poirot smiled. He was sitting opposite the millionaire at a luncheon table in the latter's private suite at the Negresco. Facing him was a relieved but very puzzled man. Poirot leant back in his chair, lit one of his tiny cigarettes, and stared reflectively at the ceiling.

'Yes, I will give you explanations. It began with the one point that puzzled me. You know what that point was? *The disfigured face.* It is not an uncommon thing to find when investigating a crime and it rouses an immediate question, the question of identity. That naturally was the first thing that occurred to me. Was the dead woman really Mrs Kettering? But that line led me nowhere, for Miss Grey's evidence was positive and very reliable, so I put that idea aside. The dead woman *was* Ruth Kettering.'

'When did you first begin to suspect the maid?'

'Not for some time, but one peculiar little point drew my attention to her. The cigarette-case found in the railway carriage and which she told us was one which Mrs Kettering had given to her husband. Now that was, on the face of it, most improbable, seeing the terms they were on. It awakened a doubt in my mind as to the general veracity of Ada Mason's statements. There was the rather suspicious fact to be taken into consideration, that she had only been with her mistress for two months. Certainly it did not seem as if she could have had anything to do with the crime since she had been left behind in Paris and Mrs Kettering had been seen alive by several people afterwards, but –'

Poirot leant forward. He raised an emphatic forefinger and wagged it with intense emphasis at Van Aldin.

'But I am a good detective. I suspect. There is nobody and
nothing that I do not suspect. I believe nothing that I am told.
I say to myself: how do we know that Ada Mason was left behind
in Paris? And at first the answer to that question seemed completely satisfactory. There was the evidence of your secretary,
Major Knighton, a complete outsider, whose testimony might
be supposed to be entirely impartial, and there were the dead
woman's own words to the conductor of the train. But I put
the latter point aside for the moment, because a very curious
idea – an idea perhaps fantastic and impossible – was growing
up in my mind. If by any outside chance it happened to be
true, that particular piece of testimony was worthless.

'I concentrated on the chief stumbling-block to my theory,
Major Knighton's statement that he saw Ada Mason at the Ritz
after the Blue Train had left Paris. That seemed conclusive
enough, but yet, on examining the facts carefully, I noted two
things. First, that by a curious coincidence he, too, had been
exactly two months in your service. Secondly, his initial letter
was the same – 'K.'. Supposing – just supposing – that it was *his*
cigarette-case which had been found in the carriage. Then, if
Ada Mason and he were working together, and she recognized
it when we showed it to her, would she not act precisely as she
had done? At first, taken aback, she quickly evolved a plausible
theory that would agree with Mr Kettering's guilt. *Bien entendu*,
that was not the original idea. The Comte de la Roche was
to be the scapegoat, though Ada Mason would not make her
recognition of him too certain, in case he should be able to
prove an alibi. Now, if you will cast your mind back to that
time, you will remember a significant thing that happened. I
suggested to Ada Mason that the man she had seen was not the
Comte de la Roche, but Derek Kettering. She seemed uncertain
at the time, but after I had got back to my hotel you rang me
up and told me that she had come to you and said that, on
thinking it over, she was now quite convinced that the man in
question *was* Mr Kettering. I had been expecting something of
the kind. There could be but one explanation of this sudden
certainty on her part. After leaving your hotel, she had had

time to consult with somebody, and had received instructions which she acted upon. Who had given her these instructions? Major Knighton. And there was another very small point, which might mean nothing or might mean a great deal. In casual conversation Knighton had talked of a jewel robbery in Yorkshire in a house where he was staying. Perhaps a mere coincidence – perhaps another small link in the chain.'

'But there is one thing I do not understand, Monsieur Poirot. I guess I must be dense or I would have seen it before now. Who was the man in the train at Paris? Derek Kettering or the Comte de la Roche?'

'That is the simplicity of the whole thing. *There was no man.* Ah – *mille tonnerres!* – do you not see the cleverness of it all? Whose word have we for it that there ever was a man there? Only Ada Mason's. And we believe in Ada Mason because of Knighton's evidence that she was left behind in Paris.'

'But Ruth herself told the conductor that she had left her maid behind there,' demurred Van Aldin.

'Ah! I am coming to that. We have Mrs Kettering's own evidence there, but, on the other hand, we have not really got her evidence, because, Monsieur Van Aldin, a dead woman cannot give evidence. It is not *her* evidence, but the evidence of the conductor of the train – a very different affair altogether.'

'So you think the man was lying?'

'No, no, not at all. He spoke what he thought to be the truth. But the woman who told him that she had left her maid in Paris was not Mrs Kettering.'

Van Aldin stared at him.

'Monsieur Van Aldin, Ruth Kettering was dead before the train arrived at the Gare de Lyon. It was Ada Mason, dressed in her mistress's very distinctive clothing, who purchased a dinner basket and who made that very necessary statement to the conductor.'

'Impossible!'

'No, no, Monsieur Van Aldin; not impossible. *Les femmes*, they look so much alike nowadays that one identifies them more by their clothing than by their faces. Ada Mason was the same height as your daughter. Dressed in that very sumptuous fur coat and the little red lacquer hat jammed down over her eyes, with just a bunch of auburn curls showing over each ear, it was no wonder that the conductor was deceived. He had not previously spoken to Mrs Kettering, you remember. True, he had seen the maid just for a moment when she handed him the tickets, but his impression had been merely that of a gaunt, black-clad female. If he had been an unusually intelligent man, he might have gone so far as to say that mistress and maid were not unlike, but it is extremely unlikely that he would even think that. And remember, Ada Mason, or Kitty Kidd, was an actress, able to change her appearance and tone of voice at a moment's notice. No, no; there was no danger of his recognizing the maid in the mistress's clothing, but there *was* the danger that when he came to discover the body he might realize it was not the woman he had talked to the night before. And now we see the reason for the disfigured face. The chief danger that Ada Mason ran was that Katherine Grey might visit her compartment after the train left Paris, and she provided against that difficulty by ordering a dinner basket and by locking herself in her compartment.'

'But who killed Ruth – and when?'

'First, bear it in mind that the crime was planned and undertaken by the two of them – Knighton and Ada Mason, working together. Knighton was in Paris that day on your business. He boarded the train somewhere on its way round the *ceinture*. Mrs Kettering would be surprised, but she would be quite unsuspicious. Perhaps he draws her attention to something out of the window, and as she turns to look he slips the cord round her neck – and the whole thing is over in a second or two. The door of the compartment is locked, and he and Ada Mason set to work. They strip off the dead woman's outer clothes. Mason and Knighton roll the body up in a rug and put it on the seat in the adjoining compartment amongst the bags and suit-cases. Knighton drops off the train, taking the jewel case containing the rubies with him. Since the crime is not supposed to have been committed until nearly twelve hours later he is perfectly safe, and his evidence and the supposed Mrs Kettering's words to the conductor will provide a perfect alibi for his accomplice.

'At the Gare de Lyon Ada Mason gets a dinner basket and, shutting herself into the toilet compartment, she quickly changes into her mistress's clothes, adjusts two false bunches of auburn curls, and generally makes up to resemble her as closely as possible. When the conductor comes to make up the bed, she tells him the prepared story about having left her maid behind in Paris; and whilst he is making up the berth, she stands looking out of the window, so that her back is towards the corridor and people passing along there. That was a wise precaution, because, as we know, Miss Grey was one of those passing, and she, among others, was willing to swear that Mrs Kettering was still alive at that hour.'

'Go on,' said Van Aldin.

'Before getting to Lyons, Ada Mason arranged her mistress's body in the bunk, folded up the dead woman's clothes neatly on the end of it, and herself changed into a man's clothes and prepared to leave the train. When Derek Kettering entered his wife's compartment, and, as he thought, saw her asleep in her berth, the scene had been set, and Ada Mason was hidden in the next compartment waiting for the moment to leave the train unobserved. As soon as the conductor had swung himself down on to the platform at Lyons, she follows, slouching along as though just taking a breath of air. At a moment when she is unobserved, she hurriedly crosses to the other platform, and takes the first train back to Paris and the Ritz Hotel. Her name has been registered there as taking a room the night before by one of Knighton's female accomplices. She has nothing to do but wait there placidly for your arrival. The jewels are not, and never have been, in her possession. No suspicion attaches to him, and, as your secretary, he brings them to Nice without the least fear of discovery. Their delivery there to Monsieur Papopolous is already arranged for, and they are entrusted to Mason at the last moment to hand over to the Greek. Altogether a very neatly planned *coup*, as one would expect from a master of the game such as the Marquis.'

'And you honestly mean that Richard Knighton is a well-known criminal, who has been at this business for years?'

Poirot nodded.

'One of the chief assets of the gentleman called the Marquis was his plausible, ingratiating manner. You fell a victim to his charm, Monsieur Van Aldin, when you engaged him as a secretary on such a slight acquaintanceship.'

'I could have sworn that he never angled for the post,' cried the millionaire.

'It was very astutely done – so astutely done that it deceived a man whose knowledge of other men is as great as yours is.'

'I looked up his antecedents too. The fellow's record was excellent.'

'Yes, yes; that was part of the game. As Richard Knighton his life was quite free from reproach. He was well born, well connected, did honourable service in the War, and seemed altogether above suspicion; but when I came to glean information about the mysterious Marquis, I found many points of similarity. Knighton spoke French like a Frenchman, he had been in America, France, and England at much the same time as the Marquis was operating. The Marquis was last heard of as engineering various jewel robberies in Switzerland, and it was in Switzerland that you had come across Major Knighton; and it was at precisely that time that the first rumours were going round of your being in treaty for the famous rubies.'

'But why murder?' murmured Van Aldin brokenly. 'Surely a clever thief could have stolen the jewels without running his head into a noose.'

Poirot shook his head. 'This is not the first murder that lies to the Marquis's charge. He is a killer by instinct; he believes, too, in leaving no evidence behind him. Dead men and women tell no tales.

'The Marquis had an intense passion for famous and historical jewels. He laid his plans far beforehand by installing himself as your secretary and getting his accomplice to obtain the situation of maid with your daughter, for whom he guessed the jewels were destined. And, though this was his matured and carefully thought-out plan, he did not scruple to attempt a short-cut by hiring a couple of apaches to waylay you in Paris on the night you bought the jewels. The plan failed, which hardly surprised him, I think. This plan was, so he thought, completely safe. No possible suspicion could attach to Richard Knighton. But like all great men – and the Marquis was a great man – he had his weaknesses. He fell genuinely in love with Miss Grey, and, suspecting her liking for Derek Kettering, he could not resist the temptation to saddle him with the crime when the opportunity presented itself. And now, Monsieur Van Aldin, I am going to tell you something very curious. Miss Grey is not a fanciful woman by any means, yet she firmly believes that she felt your daughter's presence beside her one day in the Casino Gardens at Monte Carlo, just after she had been having a long talk with Knighton. She was convinced, she says, that the dead woman was urgently trying to tell her something, and it suddenly came to her that what the dead woman was trying to say was that Knighton was her murderer! The idea seemed so fantastic at the time that Miss Grey spoke of it to no one. But she was so convinced of its truth that she acted on it – wild as it seemed. She did not discourage Knighton's advances, and she pretended to him that she was convinced of Derek Kettering's guilt.'

'Extraordinary,' said Van Aldin.

'Yes, it is very strange. One cannot explain these things. Oh, by the way, there is one little point that baffled me considerably. Your secretary has a decided limp – the result of a wound that he received in the War. Now the Marquis most decidedly did not limp. That was a stumbling block. But Miss Lenox Tamplin happened to mention one day that Knighton's limp had been a surprise to the surgeon who had been in charge of the case in her mother's hospital. That suggested camouflage. When I was in London I went to the surgeon in question, and I got several technical details from him which confirmed me in that belief. I mentioned the name of that surgeon in Knighton's hearing the day before yesterday. The natural thing would have been for Knighton to mention that he had been attended by him during the War, but he said nothing – and that little point, if nothing else, gave me the last final assurance that my theory of the crime was correct. Miss Grey, too, provided me with a cutting, showing that there had been a robbery at Lady Tamplin's Hospital during the time that Knighton had been there. She realized that I was on the same track as herself when I wrote to her from the Ritz in Paris.

'I had some trouble in my inquiries there, but I got what I wanted – evidence that Ada Mason arrived on the morning after the crime and not on the evening of the day before.'

There was a long silence, then the millionaire stretched out a hand to Poirot across the table.

'I guess you know what this means to me, Monsieur Poirot,' he said huskily. 'I am sending you round a cheque in the morning, but no cheque in the world will express what I feel about what you have done for me. You are the goods, Monsieur Poirot. Every time, you are the goods.'

Poirot rose to his feet; his chest swelled.

'I am only Hercule Poirot,' he said modestly, 'yet, as you say, in my own way I am a big man, even as you also are a big man. I am glad and happy to have been of service to you. Now I go to repair the damages caused by travel. Alas! My excellent Georges is not with me.'

In the lounge of the hotel he encountered a friend – the venerable Monsieur Papopolous, his daughter Zia beside him.

'I thought you had left Nice, Monsieur Poirot,' murmured the Greek as he took the detective's affectionately proffered hand.

'Business compelled me to return, my dear Monsieur Papopolous.'

'Business?'

'Yes, business. And talking of business, I hope your health is better, my dear friend?'

'Much better. In fact, we are returning to Paris tomorrow.'

'I am enchanted to hear such good news. You have not completely ruined the Greek ex-Minister, I hope.'

'I?'

'I understand you sold him a very wonderful ruby which – strictly *entre nous* – is being worn by Mademoiselle Mirelle, the dancer?'

'Yes,' murmured Monsieur Papopolous; 'yes, that is so.'

'A ruby not unlike the famous "Heart of Fire".'

'It has points of resemblance, certainly,' said the Greek casually.

'You have a wonderful hand with jewels, Monsieur Papopolous. I congratulate you. Mademoiselle Zia, I am desolate that you are returning to Paris so speedily. I had hoped to see some more of you now that my business is accomplished.'

'Would one be indiscreet if one asked what that business was?' asked Monsieur Papopolous.

'Not at all, not at all. I have just succeeded in laying the Marquis by the heels.'

A far-away look came over Monsieur Papopolous' noble countenance.

'The Marquis?' he murmured; 'now why does that seem familiar to me? No – I cannot recall it.'

'You would not, I am sure,' said Poirot. 'I refer to a very notable criminal and jewel robber. He has just been arrested for the murder of the English lady, Madame Kettering.'

'Indeed? How interesting these things are!'

A polite exchange of farewells followed, and when Poirot was out of earshot, Monsieur Papopolous turned to his daughter.

'Zia,' he said, with feeling, 'that man is the devil!'

'I like him.'

'I like him myself,' admitted Monsieur Papopolous. 'But he is the devil, all the same.'

CHAPTER XXXVI

By the Sea

The mimosa was nearly over. The scent of it in the air was faintly unpleasant. There were pink geraniums twining along the balustrade of Lady Tamplin's villa, and masses of carnations below sent up a sweet, heavy perfume. The Mediterranean was at its bluest. Poirot sat on the terrace with Lenox Tamplin. He had just finished telling her the same story that he had told to Van Aldin two days before. Lenox had listened to him with absorbed attention, her brows knitted and her eyes sombre.

When he had finished she said simply:

'And Derek?'

'He was released yesterday.'

'And he has gone – where?'

'He left Nice last night.'

'For St Mary Mead?'

'Yes, for St Mary Mead.'

There was a pause.

'I was wrong about Katherine,' said Lenox. 'I thought she did not care.'

'She is very reserved. She trusts no one.'

'She might have trusted me,' said Lenox, with a shade of bitterness.

'Yes,' said Poirot gravely, 'she might have trusted you. But Mademoiselle Katherine has spent a great deal of her life listening, and those who have listened do not find it easy to talk; they keep their sorrows and joys to themselves and tell no one.'

'I was a fool,' said Lenox; 'I thought she really cared for Knighton. I ought to have known better. I suppose I thought so because – well, I hoped so.'

Poirot took her hand and gave it a little friendly squeeze. 'Courage, Mademoiselle,' he said gently.

Lenox looked very straight out across the sea, and her face, in its ugly rigidity, had for the moment a tragic beauty.

'Oh, well,' she said at last, 'it would not have done. I am too young for Derek; he is like a kid that has never grown up. He wants the Madonna touch.'

There was a long silence, then Lenox turned to him quickly and impulsively. 'But I *did* help, Monsieur Poirot – at any rate I did help.'

'Yes, Mademoiselle. It was you who gave me the first inkling of the truth when you said that the person who committed the crime need not have been on the train at all. Before that, I could not see how the thing had been done.'

Lenox drew a deep breath.

'I am glad,' she said; 'at any rate – that is something.'

From far behind them there came a long-drawn-out scream of an engine's whistle.

'That is that damned Blue Train,' said Lenox. 'Trains are relentless things, aren't they, Monsieur Poirot? People are murdered and die, but they go on just the same. I am talking nonsense, but you know what I mean.'

'Yes, yes, I know. Life is like a train, Mademoiselle. It goes on. And it is a good thing that that is so.'

'Why?'

'Because the train gets to its journey's end at last, and there is a proverb about that in your language, Mademoiselle.'

'"Journeys end in lovers meeting."' Lenox laughed. 'That is not going to be true for me.'

'Yes – yes, it is true. You are young, younger than you yourself know. Trust the train, Mademoiselle, for it is *le bon Dieu* who drives it.'

The whistle of the engine came again.

'Trust the train, Mademoiselle,' murmured Poirot again. 'And trust Hercule Poirot – *He knows.*'

Postscript

In an interview published in 1966, Agatha Christie declared that The Mystery of the Blue Train *was certainly the worst book that she had ever written. 'Each time I read it again, I think it commonplace, full of clichés, with an uninteresting plot. Many people, I am sorry to say, like it.'*

The memory of the difficult conditions in which it was written is without doubt a contributing factor to this harsh judgment on a story which does not merit such an excess of indignity. The Mystery of the Blue Train *had in fact been conceived during the long, depressing period between Agatha Christie's temporary disappearance and her divorce in 1928.*

As Agatha Christie tells us in An Autobiography, *most of the story was written in February 1928, when she was with her secretary Carlo and her daughter Rosalind in the Canaries, first at Oratava, then in Las Palmas. She had resolved for some time to move away from England to try to find peace again after what she called her 'wrecked life'. She also admits that she did not feel any pleasure in writing it – a new experience for her – and that she was not driven by any desire other than 'the necessity to write another book and make some money'.*

To crown it all, the completely unoccupied Rosalind did not stop disrupting her when she was unenthusiastically dictating the story to her faithful Carlo in the gardens of the hotel. Rosalind's constant gaze stalled her, the dictated text left her with an unpleasant feeling of mediocrity, the plot seemed to slip away from her, and the characters were inconsistent.

Nevertheless, the day came when she could write the word 'End', and from the ordeal that the writing of The Mystery of the Blue Train *had been, Agatha Christie gained the certitude of having become a professional writer, one who was capable of writing even without having the least desire to do so.*

The plot of The Mystery of the Blue Train *takes up that of one of her short stories,* The Plymouth Express, *which was published in volume form in the USA in* The Underdog *(1951) and in the UK in* Poirot's Early Cases *(1974).*

The blue train in question had been created in December 1883 by the famous Georges Nagelmackers to allow rich people to travel in the greatest comfort down to the Côte d'Azur or the Riviera, traditional places for winter breaks. Known under the official name of 'Calais–Paris–Nice', its nickname became 'The Blue Train' in 1922 because of the colour of its luxurious sleeping carriages. According to Gwen Robyns, one of Agatha Christie's first biographers, Archie and his wife would have taken the Blue Train in 1926, and it was after this journey that the idea of the novel would have been born.

In their Agatha Christie Companion, *Dennis Sanders and Len Lovello underline a small contradiction:* The Mystery of the Blue Train *appeared in England in March 1928, and it seemed impossible to them that the story had been written in the month prior to its publication – they are inclined to suggest February/March 1927. But in her biography, Janet Morgan confirms the date of February 1928 for the journey to the Canaries. Mystery indeed . . . (Be that as it may, it would seem, as Gwen Robyns suggests, that the draft of the story was being mapped out as early as 1926.)*

A small but significant detail: reference is made on several occasions in The Mystery of the Blue Train *to the village of St Mary Mead, where we later meet the famous Miss Jane Marple. The first book in which she appears –* Murder at the Vicarage *– was not published until 1930, although she first turned up in a short story published in* The Sketch *magazine in 1928.*

'I have always hated The Mystery of the Blue Train,*' declared Agatha Christie in her autobiography. Do you share this opinion?*